CHAINFIRE

A Sword of Truth novel

Voyager

CHAINFIRE

TERRY GOODKIND

HarperCollins*Publishers*

Voyager
An Imprint of HarperCollins*Publishers*
77–85 Fulham Palace Road,
Hammersmith, London W6 8JB

www.voyager-books.co.uk

Published by *Voyager* 2005
1

Copyright © Terry Goodkind 2005

The Author asserts the moral right to
be identified as the author of this work

A catalogue record for this book
is available from the British Library

ISBN 0 00 714561 6

Typeset in Times

Printed and bound in Great Britain by
Clays Ltd, St Ives plc

To Vincent Cascella
a man of inspirational intellect, wit, strength, and courage...
and a friend who is always there for me

CHAINFIRE

How much of this blood is his?" a woman asked.

"Most of it, I'm afraid," a second woman said as they both rushed along beside him.

As Richard fought to focus his mind on his need to remain conscious, the breathless voices sounded to him as if they were coming from some great dim distance. He wasn't sure who they were. He knew that he knew them, but right then it just didn't seem to matter.

The crushing pain in the left side of his chest and his need for air had him at the ragged edge of panic. It was all he could do to try to draw each crucial breath.

Even so, he had a bigger worry.

Richard struggled to put voice to his burning concern, but he couldn't form the words, couldn't get out any more than a gasping moan. He clutched the arm of the woman beside him, desperate to get them to stop, to get them to listen. She misunderstood and instead urged the men carrying him to hurry, even though they were already panting with the effort of bearing him over the rocky ground in the deep shade among the towering pines. They tried to be as gentle as possible, but they never dared to slow.

Not far off, a rooster crowed into the still air, as if this were an ordinary morning like any other.

Richard observed the storm of activity swirling around him with an odd sense of detachment. Only the pain seemed real. He remembered hearing it once said that when you died, no matter how many people were there with you, you died all alone. That's how he felt now—alone.

As they broke from the timber into a thinly wooded, rough field of clumped grass, Richard saw above the leafy limbs a leaden sky threatening to unleash torrents of rain. Rain was the last thing he needed. If only it would hold off.

As they raced along, the unpainted wooden walls of a small building came into view, followed by a twisting livestock fence weathered to a silver gray. Startled chickens squawked in fright as they scattered out of the way. Men shouted orders. Richard hardly noticed the ashen faces watching him being carried past as he stiffened himself against the dizzying pain of the rough journey. It felt as if he were being ripped apart.

The whole mob around him funneled through a narrow doorway and shuffled into the darkness beyond.

"Here," the first woman said. Richard was surprised to realize, then, that it was Nicci's voice. "Put him here, on the table. Hurry."

Richard heard tin cups clatter as someone swept them aside. Small items thunked to the ground and bounced across a dirt floor. The shutters banged back as they were flung open to let some of the flat light into the musty room.

It appeared to be a deserted farmhouse. The walls tilted at an odd angle as if the place were having difficulty standing, as if it might collapse at any moment. Without the people who had once made it home, given it life, it had the aura of a place waiting for death to settle in.

Men holding his legs and arms lifted him and then carefully set him down on the crudely hewn plank table. Richard wanted to hold his breath against the crushing agony radiating from the left side of his chest, but he desperately needed the breath that he couldn't seem to get.

He needed the breath in order to speak.

Lightning flashed. A moment later thunder rumbled heavily.

"Lucky we made it into shelter before the rain," one of the men said.

Nicci nodded absently as she leaned close, groping purposefully across Richard's chest. He cried out, arching his back against the heavy wooden tabletop, trying to twist away from her probing fingers. The other woman immediately pressed his shoulders down to keep him in place.

He tried to speak. He almost got the words out, but then he coughed up a mouthful of thick blood. He started choking as he tried to breathe.

The woman holding his shoulders turned his head aside. "Spit," she told him as she bent close.

The feeling of not being able to get any air brought a flash of hot fear. Richard did as she said. She swept her fingers through his mouth, working to clear an airway. With her help he finally managed to cough and spit out enough blood to be able to pull in some of the air he so desperately needed.

As Nicci's fingers probed the area around the arrow jutting from the left side of his chest, she cursed under her breath.

"Dear spirits," she murmured in soft prayer as she tore open his blood-soaked shirt, "let me be in time."

"I was afraid to pull out the arrow," the other woman said. "I didn't know what would happen—didn't know if I should—so I decided I'd better leave it and hope I could find you."

"Be thankful you didn't try," Nicci said, her hand slipping under Richard's back as he writhed in pain. "If you'd pulled it out he'd be dead by now."

"But you can heal him." It sounded more a plea than a question.

Nicci didn't answer.

"You can heal him." That time the words hissed out through gritted teeth.

At the tone of command born of frayed patience, Richard realized that it was Cara. He hadn't had time to tell her before the attack. Surely she would have to know. But if she knew, then why didn't she say? Why didn't she put him at ease?

"If it hadn't been for him, we'd have been taken by surprise," said a man standing off to the side. "He saved us all when he waylaid those soldiers sneaking up on us."

"You have to help him," another man insisted.

Nicci impatiently waved her arm. "All of you, get out. This place is small enough as it is. I can't afford the distraction right now. I need some quiet."

Lightning flashed again, as if the good spirits intended to deny her what she needed. Thunder boomed with a deep, resonant threat of the storm closing around them.

"You'll send Cara out when you know something?" one of the men asked.

"Yes, yes. Go."

"And make sure there aren't any more soldiers around to surprise us," Cara added. "Keep out of sight in case there are. We can't afford to be discovered here—not right now."

Men swore to do her bidding. Hazy light spilled across a dingy plastered wall when the door opened. As the men departed, their shadows ghosted through the patch of light, like the good spirits themselves abandoning him.

On his way by, one of the men briefly touched Richard's shoulder—an offer of comfort and courage. Richard vaguely recognized the face. He hadn't seen these men for quite a while. The thought occurred to him that this was no way to have a reunion. The light vanished as the men pulled the door closed behind themselves, leaving the room in the gloom of light coming from the single window.

"Nicci," Cara pressed in a low voice, "you can heal him?"

Richard had been on his way to meet up with Nicci when troops sent to put down the uprising against the brutal rule of the Imperial Order had accidentally come upon his secluded camp. His first thought, just before the soldiers had blundered upon him, had been that he had to find Nicci. A spark of hope flared down into the darkness of his frantic worry; Nicci could help him.

Now Richard needed to get her to listen.

As she leaned close, her hand sliding around under him, apparently trying to see how close the arrow came to penetrating all the way through his back, Richard managed to clutch her black dress at the shoulder. He saw that his hand glistened with blood. He felt more running back across his face when he coughed.

Her blue eyes turned to him. "Everything will be all right, Richard. Lie still." A skein of blond hair slipped forward over her other shoulder as he tried to pull her closer. "I'm here. Calm down. I won't leave you. Lie still. It's all right. I'm going to help you."

Despite how smoothly she covered it, panic lurked in her voice. Despite her reassuring smile, her eyes glistened with tears. He knew then that his wound might very well be beyond her ability to heal.

That only made it all the more important that he get her to listen.

Richard opened his mouth, trying to speak. He couldn't seem to get enough air. He shivered with cold, each breath a struggle that produced little more than a wet rattle. He couldn't die, not here, not now. Tears stung his eyes.

Nicci gently pressed him back down.

"Lord Rahl," Cara said, "lie still. Please." She took his hand from its hold on Nicci's dress and held it against herself in a tight grip. "Nicci will take care of you. You'll be fine. Just lie still and let her do what she needs to do to heal you."

Where Nicci's blond hair was loose and flowing, Cara's was woven into a single braid. Despite how concerned he knew her to be, Richard could see in Cara's posture only her powerful presence, and in her features and her iron blue eyes her strength of will. Right then, that strength, that self-assurance, was solid ground for him in the quicksand of terror.

"The arrow doesn't go all the way through," Nicci told Cara as she pulled her hand out from under his back.

"I told you so. He managed to at least deflect it with his sword. That's good, isn't it? It's better that it didn't pierce his back as well, isn't it?"

"No," Nicci said under her breath.

"No?" Cara leaned closer to Nicci. "But how can it be worse that it didn't rip through his back as well?"

Nicci glanced up at Cara. "It's a crossbow bolt. If it were sticking out his back, or close enough to need only to be pushed just a little more, we could break off the barbed head and pull the shaft back out."

She left unsaid what they would now have to do.

"His bleeding isn't as bad," Cara offered. "We've stopped that, at least."

"Maybe on the outside," Nicci said in a confidential tone. "But he is bleeding into his chest—blood is filling his left lung."

This time it was Cara who snatched a fistful of Nicci's dress. "But you're going to do something. You're going to—"

"Of course," Nicci growled as she pulled her shoulder free of Cara's grip.

Richard gasped in pain. The rising waters of panic threatened to overwhelm him.

Nicci laid her other hand on his chest to hold him still as well as to offer comfort.

"Cara," Nicci said, "why don't you wait outside with the others."

"That isn't going to happen. You'd best just get on with it."

Nicci appraised Cara's eyes briefly, then leaned in and again grasped the shaft jutting from Richard's chest. He felt the probing tingle of magic follow the course of the arrow down deep inside him. Richard recognized the unique feel of Nicci's power, much as he could recognize her singular silken voice.

He knew that there was no time to delay in what he had to do. Once she started, there was no telling how long it would be until he woke . . . if he woke.

With all his effort, Richard lunged, seizing her dress at the collar. He pulled himself close to her face, pulled her down toward him so she could hear him.

He had to ask if they knew where Kahlan was. If they didn't, then he had to ask Nicci to help him find her.

The only thing he could get out was the single word.

"Kahlan," he whispered with all his strength.

"All right, Richard. All right." Nicci gripped his wrists and pulled his hands off her dress. "Listen to me." She pressed him back down against the table. "Listen. There's no time. You have to calm down. Be still. Just relax and let me do the work."

She brushed back his hair and laid a gentle, caring hand to his forehead as her other hand again grasped the cursed arrow.

Richard desperately struggled to say no, struggled to tell them that they needed to find Kahlan, but already the tingle of magic was intensifying into paralyzing pain.

Richard went rigid with the agony of the power lancing into his chest.

He could see Nicci and Cara's faces above him.

And then a deadly darkness ignited within the room.

He had been healed by Nicci before. Richard knew the feel of her power. This time, something was different. Dangerously different.

Cara gasped. "What are you doing!"

"What I must if I'm to save him. It's the only way."

"But you can't—"

"If you'd rather I let him slip into the arms of death, then say so. Otherwise, let me do as I must to keep him among us."

Cara studied Nicci's heated expression for only a moment before letting out a noisy breath and nodding.

Richard reached for Nicci's wrist, but Cara caught his first and pressed it back to the table. His fingers came to rest on the woven gold wire spelling out the word TRUTH on the hilt of his sword. He spoke Kahlan's name again, but this time no sound would cross his lips.

Cara frowned as she leaned toward Nicci. "Did you hear what it was he said?"

"I don't know. Some name. Kahlan, I think."

Richard tried to cry "Yes," but it came out as little more than a hoarse moan.

"Kahlan?" Cara asked. "Who's Kahlan?"

"I have no idea," Nicci murmured as her concentration returned to the task at hand. "He's obviously in delirium from loss of blood."

Richard truly couldn't draw a breath against the pain that suddenly screamed through him.

Lightning flashed and thunder pealed again, this time unleashing a torrent of rain that began to drum against the roof.

Against his will, hazy darkness drew in around the faces.

Richard managed only to whisper Kahlan's name one last time before Nicci opened into him the full flood of magic.

The world dissolved into nothingness.

The distant howl of a wolf woke Richard from a dead sleep. The forlorn cry echoed through the mountains, but went unanswered. Richard lay on his side, in the surreal light of false dawn, idly listening, waiting, for a return cry that never came.

Try as he might, he couldn't seem to open his eyes for longer than the span of a single, slow heartbeat, much less gather the energy to lift his head. Shadowy tree limbs appeared to move about in the murky darkness. It was odd that such an ordinary sound as the distant howl of a wolf should wake him.

He remembered that Cara had third watch. She would no doubt come to wake them soon enough. With great effort, he summoned the strength to roll over. He needed to touch Kahlan, to embrace her, to go back to sleep with her in his protective arms for a few more delicious minutes. His hand found only an expanse of empty ground.

Kahlan wasn't there.

Where was she? Where had she gone off to? Perhaps she'd awakened early and gone to talk to Cara.

Richard sat up. He instinctively checked to make sure that his sword was at hand. The reassuring feel of the polished scabbard and wire-wound hilt greeted his fingers. The sword lay on the ground beside him.

Richard heard the soft whisper of a slow, steady rain. He remembered that for some reason he needed it not to rain.

But if it was raining, then why didn't he feel it? Why was his face dry? Why was the ground dry?

He sat up rubbing his eyes, trying to get his bearings, trying to clear his foggy mind as he fought to herd together scattered thoughts. He peered into the darkness and realized that he wasn't outside. In the faint gray light of dawn coming in through a single small window he saw that he was in a derelict room. The place smelled of wet wood and damp decay. Dying embers glowed deep within the ash in a hearth set into a plastered wall rising up before him. A blackened wooden spoon hung to one side of the hearth, a mostly bald broom leaned against the other side, but other than that he saw no personal items to distinguish the people who lived there.

Daybreak looked to be still some time off. The incessant patter of the rain against the roof promised that there would be no sun this chilly and damp day. Besides dripping through several holes in the tattered roof, rain leaked in around the chimney, adding yet another layer of stain to the dingy plaster.

Seeing the plastered wall, the hearth, and the heavy plank table brought back spectral fragments of memories.

Driven by his need to know where Kahlan was, Richard staggered to his feet, clutching at the lingering pain in the left side of his chest with one hand and the edge of the table with his other.

At hearing him stand in the dimly lit room, Cara, leaning back in a chair not far away, shot to her feet. "Lord Rahl!"

He saw his sword lying on the table. But he had thought—

"Lord Rahl, you're awake!" In the somber light Richard could see that Cara looked exuberant. He also saw that she was wearing her red leather.

"A wolf howled and woke me."

Cara shook her head. "I've been sitting right there, awake, watching over you. No wolf howled. You must have dreamed it." Her smile returned. "You look better!"

He recalled not being able to breathe, not being able to get enough air. He took an experimental deep breath and found that it came easily. While the ghost of terrible pain still haunted him, the reality of it had nearly faded away.

"Yes, I think I'm all right."

Short, disjointed memories flashed in fits before his mind's eye. He remembered standing alone and still in the eerie early light as the dark tide of Imperial Order soldiers flooded through the trees. He remembered bits of their wild charge, their raised weapons. He remembered releasing himself into the fluid dance with death. He remembered, too, the hail of arrows and bolts from crossbows, and, finally, other men joining the battle.

Richard lifted the front of his shirt out away from himself, looking down at it, not understanding why it was whole.

"Your shirt was ruined," Cara offered, noticing his puzzlement. "We washed and shaved you, then we put a clean shirt on you."

We. That one word rose up above all others in his mind. *We.* Cara and Kahlan. That had to be what Cara meant.

"Where is she?"

"Who?"

"Kahlan," he said as he took a stride away from the support of the table. "Where is she?"

"Kahlan?" Cara's features meandered into a provocative smile. "Who's Kahlan?"

Richard sighed with relief. Cara would not be needling him in such a way if Kahlan were hurt or in any kind of trouble—that much he knew for certain. An overwhelming sense of relief purged his dread and with it some of his weariness. Kahlan was safe.

He couldn't help being cheered, too, by Cara's impish expression. He loved to see her with a lighthearted smile, in part because it was such a rare sight. Usually when a Mord-Sith smiled it was a menacing prelude to something wholly unpleasant. The same was true when they wore their red leather.

"Kahlan," Richard said, playing along, "you know, my wife. Where is she?"

Cara's nose wrinkled with seldom-seen feminine mirth. Such an extraordinary look was so uncommon on Cara that it not only surprised him, but spurred him into a grin.

"A wife," she drawled, turning coy. "Now, there's a novel concept—the Lord Rahl taking a wife."

That he found himself to be the Lord Rahl, the leader of D'Hara, at times still seemed unreal to him. It was not the kind of thing a woods guide growing up in far-off Westland would ever have dreamed up in his wildest imaginings.

"Yes, well, one of us had to be the first." He wiped a hand across his face, still trying to clear the web of sleep from his mind. "Where is she?"

Cara's smile widened. "Kahlan." She tilted her head toward him, arching one brow. "Your wife."

"Yes, Kahlan, my wife," Richard said offhandedly. He had long ago learned that it was best not to give Cara the satisfaction of seeing her mischievous antics get to him. "You remember her—intelligent, green eyes, tall, long hair, and of course the most beautiful woman I've ever laid eyes on."

The leather of Cara's outfit creaked as she straightened her back and folded her arms. "You mean the most beautiful besides me, of course." Her eyes were luminous when she smiled. He didn't rise to the bait.

"Well," Cara finally said with a sigh, "the Lord Rahl certainly seems to have had an interesting dream during his long sleep."

"Long sleep?"

"You've been asleep for two days—after Nicci healed you."

Richard raked his fingers back through his dirty, matted hair. "Two days . . ." he said as he tried to reconcile his fragmented memories. He was becoming annoyed with Cara's game. "So where is she?"

"Your wife?"

"Yes, my wife." Richard planted his fists on his hips as he leaned toward the irksome woman. "You know, the Mother Confessor."

"Mother Confessor! My, my, Lord Rahl, but when you dream you certainly do dream big. Smart, beautiful, and the Mother Confessor as well." Cara leaned in with a taunting look. "And no doubt she's also madly in love with you?"

"Cara—"

"Oh, wait." She held up a hand to stop him as she abruptly turned serious. "Nicci said that she wanted me to go get her if you woke. She was really insistent about it—said that if you woke she needed to have a look at you." Cara started toward the single closed door at the back of the room. "She's only been asleep for a couple of hours, but she'll want to know that you're awake."

Cara was in the back room for no more than a moment when Nicci burst out of the darkness, pausing briefly to grasp the doorframe. "Richard!"

Before Richard could say anything, Nicci, her eyes wide with relief at seeing him alive, dashed to him and seized his shoulders as if she thought he were a good spirit come to the world of the living and only her firm grip would keep him there.

"I was so worried. How are you feeling?"

She looked as drained as he felt. Her mane of blond hair hadn't been brushed out and it looked like she'd been sleeping in her black dress. Even so, the contrast of her disheveled appearance only served to highlight her exquisite beauty.

"Well, all right for the most part, except that I feel exhausted and light-headed despite having had what Cara tells me was quite a long sleep."

Nicci dismissively waved a slender hand. "That's to be expected. With rest you will have your full strength back soon enough. You lost a lot of blood. It will take time for your body to recover."

"Nicci, I need—"

"Hush," she said as she put one hand behind his back and pressed the flat of her other to his chest. Her smooth brow drew together in concentration.

Though she appeared to be about his age, or at most only a year or two older, she had lived a very long time as a Sister of the Light at the Palace of the Prophets, where those within the walls aged differently. Nicci's graceful manner, the keen appraisal of her blue eyes, and her singular sub-dued smile—always delivered with her knowing gaze locked on his—had been at first distracting and then unsettling, but was now merely familiar.

Richard winced as he felt Nicci's power tingling deep into his chest, be-tween her hands. It was a disconcerting penetration. It made his heart flut-ter. A mild wave of nausea coursed through him.

"It's holding," Nicci murmured to herself. She looked up into his eyes then. "The vessels are whole and strong." The look of wonder in her eyes betrayed how uncertain she had been of success. Some of her reassuring smile returned. "You still need to rest, but you're doing well, Richard, you really are."

He nodded, relieved to hear that he was healthy, even if she sounded a little surprised by it. But his other concerns needed to be put to rest, as well.

"Nicci, where's Kahlan? Cara's in one of her moods this morning and won't say."

Nicci looked to be at a loss. "Who?"

Richard took hold of her wrist and removed her hand from his chest. "What's wrong? Is she hurt? Where is she?"

Cara tilted her head toward Nicci. "While he slept, Lord Rahl dreamed himself up a wife."

Nicci turned an astonished frown on Cara. "A wife!"

"Remember the name he called out when he was delirious?" Cara flashed a conspiratorial smile. "That's the one he married in his dream. She's beautiful—and smart, of course."

"Beautiful." Nicci blinked at the woman. "And smart."

Cara cocked an eyebrow. "And she's the Mother Confessor."

Nicci looked incredulous. "The Mother Confessor."

"Enough," Richard said as he released Nicci's wrist. "I mean it, now. Where is she?"

It was immediately apparent to both women that his indulgent sense of humor had evaporated. The intensity in his voice, to say nothing of his glare, gave them pause.

"Richard," Nicci said in a cautious tone, "you were hurt pretty bad. For a time I didn't think . . ." She hooked a stray strand of hair behind her ear and started over. "Look, when a person is hurt as seriously as you were, it can play tricks with their mind. It's only natural. I've seen it before. When you were shot with that arrow you couldn't breathe. Not getting air, like when you're drowning, causes—"

"What's the matter with you two? What's going on?" Richard couldn't understand why they were stalling. His heart felt as if it were galloping out of control. "Is she hurt? Tell me!"

"Richard," Nicci said in a calm voice obviously meant to settle him down, "the bolt from that crossbow came perilously close to going right through your heart. If it had, there wouldn't have been anything I could have done. I can't raise the dead.

"Even though it missed your heart, the arrow still did serious damage. People just don't survive a wound as grave as you had. I wouldn't have been able to heal you in the conventional manner because it couldn't be done. There was no time to even try to get the arrow out in any other way. You were bleeding inside. I had to . . ."

She faltered as she stared up into his eyes. Richard bent down a little toward her. "You had to what?"

Nicci shrugged one shoulder self-consciously. "I had to use Subtractive Magic."

Nicci was a powerful sorceress in her own right, but she was infinitely more exceptional in that she was able to wield underworld forces as well. She had once been committed to those forces. She had once been known as Death's Mistress. Healing was not exactly her specialty.

Richard's caution flared. "Why?"

"To get the arrow out of you."

"You eliminated the arrow with Subtractive Magic?"

"There was no time and no other way." She again clasped his shoulders, although more compassionately this time. "If I hadn't done something you would have been dead in mere moments. I had to."

Richard glanced to Cara's grim expression and then back to Nicci. "Well, I guess that makes sense."

At least, it sounded like it made sense. He didn't really know if it did or not. Having been raised in the vast woods of Westland, Richard didn't know a great deal about magic.

"And some of your blood," Nicci added in a low voice.

He didn't like the sound of that. "What?"

"You were bleeding into your chest. One lung had already failed. I was able to perceive that your heart was being forced out of place. The major arteries were in danger of being ripped apart from the pressure. I needed the blood out of the way in order to heal you—so that your lungs and heart could work properly. They were failing. You were in a state of shock and delirium. You were near death."

Nicci's blue eyes brimmed with tears. "I was so afraid, Richard. There was no one but me to help you and I was so afraid that I would fail. Even after I did everything I could to heal you, I still wasn't sure you would ever wake again."

Richard could see the toll of that fear in her expression and feel it in the way her fingers trembled on his arms. It spoke to how far she had come since she had given up her belief in the cause of the Sisters of the Dark and then the Imperial Order.

The haunted look on Cara's face confirmed for him the truth of how desperate the situation had been. For all the sleep he'd apparently gotten, neither of them appeared to have had much more than brief naps. It must have been a frightening vigil.

The rain drummed without letup against the roof. Other than that, the dank husk of a house was dead quiet. Life seemed all the more fleeting in the abandoned home. The forsaken place gave Richard the chills.

"You saved my life, Nicci. I remember being afraid I was going to die. But you saved my life." He touched his fingertips to her cheek. "Thank you. I wish there was a better way to say it, a better way to tell you how much I appreciate what you did, but I can't think of any."

Nicci's small smile and simple nod told him that she grasped the depth of his sincerity.

Another thought struck him. "Do you mean to say that using Subtractive Magic caused some kind of . . . problem?"

"No, no, Richard." Nicci squeezed his arms as if to allay his fears. "No, I don't think that it caused any harm."

"What do you mean, you don't think it did?"

She hesitated a moment before explaining. "I've never done anything like that before. I've never even heard of it being done. Dear spirits, I didn't even know that it could be done. As I'm sure you can imagine, using Subtractive Magic in such a way is risky, to put it mildly. Anything living touched by it would also be destroyed. I had to use the core of the arrow itself as a pathway into you. I was as careful as I could possibly be that I only eliminated the arrow . . . and the spent blood."

Richard wondered what happened to things when Subtractive Magic was used—what would have happened to his blood—but his head was already spinning with the story and he most wanted her to get to the point.

"But between all that," Nicci added, "between the massive loss of blood, the injury, the dire condition of not being able to get enough air, the stress you underwent while I used regular Additive Magic to heal you—to say nothing of the unknown element that Subtractive Magic added into the mix—you were going through an experience that can only be described as unpredictable. Such a terrible crisis can cause unexpected things to happen."

Richard didn't know what she was getting at. "What unexpected things?"

"There's no telling. I had no choice but to use extreme methods. You were beyond what I thought were all limits. You have to try to understand that you were not yourself there for a while."

Cara hooked a thumb behind her red leather belt. "Nicci is right, Lord Rahl. You weren't yourself. You were fighting us. I had to hold you down just so she could help you.

"I've stood over men at the cusp of death. Strange things happen when they're in that place. Believe me, you were there a long time into that first night."

Richard knew very well what she meant when she said that she had stood over men on the cusp of death. The profession of Mord-Sith had been torture—at least it had been until he changed all that. He carried the Agiel of Denna, the Mord-Sith who had once stood over him in that capacity. She had given him her Agiel as a solemn gift in gratitude for freeing her from the madness of her terrible duty . . . even though she had known that the price of that freedom was to be his sword through her heart.

Right then Richard felt a very long way from the peaceful woods where he'd grown up.

Nicci spread her hands as if imploring him to try harder to understand. "You were unconscious and then asleep for quite a time. I had to revive you enough to get you to drink water and a broth, but I needed you to stay in a deep sleep so that you could begin to recover your strength. I had to use a spell to keep you in that state. You'd lost a lot of blood; had I allowed you to awake too soon it would have sapped your tenuous strength and you still could have slipped away from us."

Died, that was what she meant. He could have died. Richard took a deep breath. He'd had no idea of everything that had gone on over the last three days. He basically recalled the battle and then waking when he heard the wolf howl.

"Nicci," he said, trying to show her that he could be calm and understanding even though he felt neither, "what does this have to do with Kahlan?"

Her features were set in an uneasy mix of empathy and disquiet. "Richard, this woman, Kahlan, is just a product of your mind when you were in that confused state of shock and delirium before I could heal you."

"Nicci, I wasn't imagining—"

"You were at the brink of death," she said as she held up a hand, commanding silence and for him to listen. "In your mind you were grasping for someone to help you—someone like this person, Kahlan. Please believe me when I say that it's understandable. But you're awake now and must face the truth. She was figment born of your dire condition."

Richard was dumbfounded to hear her even suggesting such a thing. He turned to Cara, imploring her to come to her senses, if not his rescue. "How could you possibly think such a thing? How could you believe it?"

"Haven't you ever had a dream where you were terrified and then your long-dead mother was there, alive, and she was going to help you?" Cara's unblinking blue eyes seemed focused elsewhere. "Don't you remember waking after such dreams and feeling sure that it had been real, that your mother was alive again, really alive, and that she was going to help you?

Don't you remember how much you wanted to cling to that feeling? Don't you remember how desperately you wanted it to be real?"

Nicci lightly touched the place where the arrow had been, where his flesh was now whole. "After I'd healed you to the point that you were past the worst of the crisis, you went into a long dreaming state of sleep. You carried these desperate illusions forward with you. You dreamed about them, added to them, lived with them longer than any ordinary sleep. This prolonged dream, this comforting illusion, this divine longing, had time to seep into every corner of your thoughts, saturate every part of your mind, and became real to you, just as Cara says, but, because of the length of time you were asleep, it gained even more power. Now that you've only just come awake from that protracted sleep you are merely having a little trouble filtering out what part of your ordeal was a dream and what was real."

"Nicci is right, Lord Rahl." Richard couldn't remember Cara ever looking so dead serious. "You just dreamed it—like you dreamed that you heard a wolf howl. It sounds like a nice dream—this woman you dreamed you married—but that's all it is: a dream."

Richard's mind reeled. The concept of Kahlan being nothing more than a dream, a figment of his imagination born in his delirium, was, at its core, terrifying. That terror stormed unchecked through him. If what they were saying was true, then he didn't want to be awake. If it was true, then he wished that Nicci had never healed him. He didn't want to live in a world where Kahlan wasn't real.

He groped for solid ground in a sea of dark disorder, too stunned to think of a way to fight such a shapeless threat. He felt confused by his ordeal and that he didn't remember much of it. His certainty in what he regarded as truth began to crumble.

He caught himself. He knew better than to believe a fear and thus give it life. While he could not fathom how they'd latched on to such a monstrous idea, he knew that Kahlan wasn't a dream.

"After all that you've both shared with her, how can you two possibly say that Kahlan is just a dream?"

"How indeed," Nicci asked, "if what you're saying were true?"

"Lord Rahl, we would never be so cruel as to try to deceive you about something so important to you."

Richard blinked at them. Could it be? He frantically tried to imagine if there was any possibility that what they were saying could be true.

His fists tightened. "Stop it—both of you!"

It was a plea for a return of sanity. He hadn't meant for it to come out as threatening, but it did. Nicci took half a step back. Cara's face lost a little of its color.

Richard couldn't slow his breathing, his racing heart.

"I don't remember my dreams." He looked at each of them in turn. "Not since I was little. I don't remember any dreams while I was hurt, or while I slept. None. Dreams are meaningless. Kahlan is not. Don't do this to me—please. This isn't helping anything, it's only making it worse. Please, if something has happened to Kahlan, I need to know."

That had to be it. Something had happened to her and they just didn't think he was strong enough yet to handle the news.

A worse fear by far welled up when he recalled Nicci saying that she couldn't raise the dead. Could they be trying to shield him from that?

He gritted his teeth with the effort not to scream at them, to keep his voice level and in control. "Where is Kahlan?"

Nicci cautiously dipped her head, as if beseeching his forgiveness. "Richard, she is just in your mind. I know that such things can seem very real, but it's not. You dreamed her up while you were hurt . . . nothing more."

"I did not dream up Kahlan." He again turned his plea to the Mord-Sith. "Cara, you've been with us for more than two years. You've fought with us, fought for us. Back when Nicci was a Sister of the Dark and she brought me down here to the Old World, you stood in for me and protected Kahlan. She has protected you. You've shared and endured things that most people could never even imagine. You've become friends."

He gestured to her Agiel, the weapon that looked like nothing more than a short, thin red leather rod hanging by a thin gold chain from her right wrist.

"You even named Kahlan a sister of the Agiel."

Cara stood stiff and mute.

Cara's conferring on Kahlan the title of sister of the Agiel had been an informal but deeply solemn accolade from a former mortal enemy to a woman she had come to respect and trust.

"Cara, you may have started out as a protector to the Lord Rahl, but you've become more than that to Kahlan and me. You've become like family."

Cara would willingly and without hesitation sacrifice her life to protect Richard. She was not only ruthless but fearless in her defense of him.

The one thing Cara did fear was disappointing him.

That fear was clearly evident in her eyes.

"Thank you, Lord Rahl," she finally said in a meek voice, "for including me in your wonderful dream."

Richard's flesh prickled as a wave of cold dread washed up through him. Overwhelmed, he pressed his hand to his forehead, pushing back his hair. These two women were not inventing some story for fear of telling him bad news. They were telling him the truth.

The truth as they saw it, anyway. The truth somehow twisted into a nightmare.

He couldn't make any of it work in his mind, couldn't make any sense of it. After all they had shared with Kahlan, all they had been through with her, all their time together, it was impossible for him to understand how these two women could be saying this to him.

And yet, they were.

Although he couldn't conceive of the cause, something was obviously and dreadfully wrong. A suffocating sense of foreboding settled over him. It felt as if the whole world had been turned upside down and now he couldn't make the pieces fit back together.

He had to do something—what he had been about to do just before the soldiers had attacked them. Maybe it wasn't too late.

Richard knelt beside his bedroll and started jamming clothes into his pack. The cold drizzle he could see through the small window didn't look like it would be ending anytime soon, so he left his cloak out.

"What do you think you're doing?" Nicci asked.

He spotted a cake of soap lying nearby and snatched it up. "What does it look like I'm doing?"

He had already lost far too much time; he'd lost days. There was no time to waste. He shoved the cake of soap, packets of dried herbs and spices, and a pouch of dried apricots down into the pack before quickly furling his bedroll. Cara abandoned questioning or objecting and instead set about packing her own things.

"That's not what I mean and you know it." Nicci squatted down beside him and took hold of his arm, pulling him around to look at her. "Richard, you can't leave. You need to rest. I told you, you lost a lot of blood. You aren't strong enough yet to go running off chasing phantoms."

He stifled an indignant reply and yanked tight a leather thong around his bedroll. "I feel fine." He didn't, of course, but he felt good enough.

Nicci had just spent days of intense effort saving his life. Besides being worried for him, she was exhausted and probably wasn't thinking clearly. All of those things likely contributed to her believing he was acting irresponsibly.

Still, he bristled that she didn't give him more credit.

Nicci insistently gripped a fistful of his shirt as he cinched the second thong tight. "You don't yet realize how weak you really are, Richard. You're jeopardizing your life. You need to rest in order for your body to be able to recover. You haven't had nearly enough time to build your strength."

"And how much time does Kahlan have?" He seized Nicci's upper arm and in heated frustration pulled her close. "She's out there, somewhere, in trouble. You don't realize it, Cara doesn't realize it, but I do. Do you think

I can just lie around here when the person I love more than anything in the world is in peril?

"If it were you in trouble, Nicci, would you wish me to so easily give up on you? Wouldn't you want me to try? I don't know what's gone wrong, but something has. If I'm right—and I am—then I can't even begin to guess at the implications or imagine the consequences."

"What do you mean?"

"Well, if you're right then I'm just imagining things out of my dreams. But if I'm right—and since it's pretty obvious that you and Cara can't both be sharing the same mental disorder—that would have to mean that whatever is happening has a cause that isn't benevolent. I can't afford to delay and risk everything while I try to convince you of the seriousness of the situation. Too much time has already been lost. Too much is at stake."

Nicci looked too startled by the notion to speak. Richard released her and turned back to fasten down the flap on his pack. He didn't have the time to try to solve the puzzle of whatever was going on with Nicci and Cara.

Nicci finally found her voice. "Richard, don't you see what you're doing? You're beginning to invent absurd notions in order to justify what you want to believe. You said it yourself—Cara and I can't both be sharing the same disorder of the mind. Stay and rest. We can try to discover the nature of this dream that has taken such strong root in your mind and hopefully set it right. I probably caused it with something I did when I was trying to heal you. If so, I'm sorry. Please, Richard, stay for now."

She was focused only on what she saw as the problem. Zedd, his grandfather, the man who had helped raise him, had often said as Richard was growing up, *Don't think of the problem, think of the solution.* The solution he needed to concentrate on, now, was how to find Kahlan before it was too late. He wished he had Zedd's help to find the solution to where she was.

"You aren't out of serious danger yet," Nicci insisted as she dodged drips of rainwater trickling through holes in the roof. "Pushing yourself too hard could be fatal."

"I understand—I really do." Richard checked the knife he wore at his belt and then slipped it back into its sheath. "I don't intend to ignore your advice. I'll take it as easy as I can."

"Richard, listen to me," Nicci said, rubbing her fingers against her temple as if her head was aching, "it's more than that alone."

She paused to run her hand back over her hair as she searched for the words. "You aren't invincible. You may carry that sword, but it can't always protect you. Your ancestors, every Lord Rahl before you, despite their mastery of the gift, still kept bodyguards close at hand. You may have been born with the gift but even if you were competent in its use such power is no assurance of protection—*especially* not now.

"That arrow only served to show how vulnerable you really are. You may be an important man, Richard, but you are just a man. We all need you. We all so desperately need you."

Richard looked away from the anguish in Nicci's blue eyes. He knew very well how vulnerable he was. Life was his highest value; he didn't take it for granted. He almost never objected to Cara being close at hand. She and the rest of the Mord-Sith as well as other bodyguards he seemed to have inherited had proven their worth more than once. But that didn't mean that he was helpless or that he could allow caution to prevent him from doing what was necessary.

More than that, though, he grasped Nicci's larger meaning. He had learned while at the Palace of the Prophets that the Sisters of the Light believed that he was deeply enmeshed in ancient prophecy—that he was a central figure around whom events revolved.

According to the Sisters, if their side was to prevail over the dark forces arrayed against them, it would only be if Richard led them to victory. Prophecy said that without him all would be lost. Their prelate, Annalina, had spent a great deal of her life manipulating events to make sure that he survived to grow up and lead them in this war. Ann's hopes for everything they held dear, to hear her tell it, rested on his shoulders. At least Kahlan had thankfully taken the fire out of Ann in that regard. He knew, though, that many others still held the same view. He knew, too, that his leadership had galvanized a great many people who longed to simply live free.

Richard had been down in the vaults at the Palace of the Prophets and had seen some of the most important and well-guarded books of prophecy in existence. He had to admit that some of it was pretty uncanny. Nevertheless, his experience had been that prophecy seemed to say whatever it was people wanted it to say.

He had personal experience with prophecy involving Kahlan and himself, especially those prophecies of Shota, the witch woman. As far as he was concerned, prophecy had proven itself to be of little value and great trouble.

Richard forced a smile. "Nicci, you're sounding like a Sister of the Light." She didn't look to be amused. "Cara will be with me," he said, trying to ease her mind.

He realized, after he'd said it, that having Cara with him hadn't stopped the arrow that had taken him down. Come to think of it, where had she been during the battle? He didn't remember her being there with him. Cara didn't fear a fight; a team of horses couldn't drag her away from protecting him. Surely, she must have been close beside him, but he just didn't recall seeing her.

He picked up his big leather over-belt and fastened it around his waist. He had gotten the belt and other parts of the outfit, which had once belonged to a great wizard, from the Wizard's Keep, where Zedd now stood guard, protecting the Keep from Emperor Jagang and his horde from the Old World.

Nicci heaved an impatient sigh—a glimpse of a stern and implacable side of her that Richard knew all too well. He knew, though, that this time it was powered by sincere concern for his well-being.

"Richard, we simply can't afford this distraction. There are important things we need to talk about. That's why I was coming to you in the first place. Didn't you get the letter I sent?"

Richard paused. Letter . . . letter . . . "Yes," he said, at last remembering. "I did get your letter. I sent word to you—with a soldier Kahlan had touched with her power."

Richard caught Cara's brief glance up at Nicci—a surprised look that said that she didn't recall any such thing.

Nicci appraised him with an unreadable look. "The word you sent never found me."

Somewhat surprised, Richard gestured toward the New World. "His primary mission was to go north and assassinate Emperor Jagang. He was touched by a Confessor's power; he would die before ever abandoning her command. If he couldn't find you, he would have gone after Jagang. I suppose it's also possible that something happened to him first. There are perils enough in the Old World."

The look on Nicci's face made him feel like he had just offered her further evidence that he was losing his mind. "Do you honestly think, even in your wildest imaginings, that the dream walker can be so easily eliminated?"

"No, of course not." He pushed the bulge of a cooking pot in his pack back into place. "We expected that the soldier would probably be killed in the attempt. We sent him after Jagang because he was a murdering thug and deserved to die. But I also thought that there was a possibility that he might succeed. Even if he didn't, I wanted Jagang to at least lose some sleep knowing that any of his men could be assassins."

He could see by Nicci's too-calm expression that she thought that this, too, was no more than part of his elaborate delusion about a woman he had dreamed.

Richard recalled, then, what else had happened. "Nicci, I'm afraid that shortly after Sabar delivered your letter we were attacked. He died in that fight."

A furtive glance to Cara brought a nod in confirmation.

"Dear spirits," Nicci said in sorrow at hearing the news about young Sabar. Richard shared her sentiment.

He remembered Nicci's urgent warning in the letter about how Jagang had started to create weapons out of gifted people, as had been done three thousand years before in the great war. It was a frightening development that had been thought impossible, but Jagang had discovered a way to accomplish the task by using the Sisters of the Dark he held captive.

During the attack on their camp, Nicci's letter had been knocked into the fire. Richard hadn't had the chance to read the whole letter before it had been destroyed. He'd read enough, though, to understand the danger.

When he made for the table, where his sword lay, Nicci stepped in front of him. "Richard, I know it's hard, but you have to put this dream business behind you. We don't have time for it. We need to talk. If you got my letter, then at least you know that you can't—"

"Nicci," Richard said, silencing her, "I must do this." He laid a hand on her shoulder and spoke as patiently as he could, considering his sense of urgency, but by his tone let her know that he was not going to discuss it further. "If you come with us then we can talk later, when there is time and it doesn't interfere with what I need to do, but right now I don't have the time and neither does Kahlan."

Pressing the back of his hand against the side of her shoulder, Richard moved her aside and strode to the table.

As he lifted his sword by its polished scabbard, he briefly wondered why, when he had heard the wolf howl and he woke up, he'd thought the sword had been lying on the ground beside him. Maybe he had remembered a fragment of a dream. Impatient to get going, he dismissed it.

He slipped the ancient tooled-leather baldric over his head and quickly adjusted the scabbard at his left hip, making sure it was securely fastened. With two fingers he lifted the sword by the downswept crossguard, not only to be sure that it was clear in its sheath, but to check that the blade was sound. He couldn't remember everything that had happened in the fight and he didn't recall putting the sword away himself.

The polished steel gleamed through a film of dried blood.

Fragmented memories of the battle flashed through his mind. It had been sudden and unexpected, but once he had pulled the sword free in anger, unexpected no longer mattered. Being so heavily outnumbered, though, had mattered. He understood all too well that Nicci was right about him not being invincible.

Not long after he'd met Kahlan, Zedd, in his capacity as First Wizard, had named Richard to the post of Seeker and had given him the sword. Richard had hated the weapon because of what he mistakenly thought it represented. Zedd told him that the Sword of Truth—as it was named—was but a tool and that it was the intent of the individual wielding a sword that gave it meaning. That had never been so true as it was with this particular weapon.

The sword was now bonded to Richard, bonded to his intent, driven by his purpose. From the beginning, his intent and purpose had been to protect those he loved and cared about. To do that, he had come to realize that he had to help shape a world in which they could live in safety and peace.

It was that intent that gave the sword meaning for him.

The steel hissed as he slid it back into its scabbard.

His intent now was to find Kahlan. If the sword could help him accomplish that goal then he would not hesitate to put it to use.

He hoisted his pack and swung it around, settling it onto its familiar place on his back as he scanned the nearly barren room for any of his things he might have missed. On the floor beside the hearth he saw dried meat and travel biscuits. Beside them lay other bundled foodstuffs. Richard's and Cara's simple wooden bowls were there as well, one with broth and the other holding the remnants of porridge.

"Cara," he said as he swept up three waterskins and hung their straps around his neck, "be sure to get all the food that can travel and bring it along. Don't forget the bowls."

Cara nodded. She packed methodically, now that she realized he had no intention of leaving her behind.

Nicci caught his sleeve. "Richard, I mean it, we have to talk. It's important."

"Then do as I asked; get your things and come with me." He snatched up his bow and quiver. "You can talk all you want as long as you don't hold me up."

With a nod of resignation, Nicci finally abandoned her arguments and rushed to the back room to gather her own things. Far from minding having Nicci along, Richard wanted her help; her gift might be useful in finding Kahlan. In fact, finding Nicci so she could help him had been his intention when he first awoke before the attack and realized that Kahlan was missing.

Richard threw his hooded forest cloak around his shoulders and headed for the door. Cara looked up from beside the hearth, where she hurried to finish collecting her gear, and gave him a nod to let him know she'd be right behind him. He could see Nicci in the back room rushing to get her things before he got far.

In his urgent need to find Kahlan, Richard's imagination was beginning to get the better of him. He could see her hurt, see her in pain. The thought of Kahlan somewhere alone and in trouble made his heart quicken with dread.

Against his will, the crushing memory of the time she had been beaten nearly to death flooded forth. He had given up everything else and had taken her far away back into the mountains where no one could find them so that she would be safe and could have time to heal. That summer, after she had started to recover her strength, and before Nicci had shown up to capture him and take him away, had been one of the best summers of his life. How Cara could forget that special time was incomprehensible to him.

From force of habit, he lifted his sword to make sure it was clear in its scabbard before he threw open the simple plank door.

Damp air and iron gray morning light greeted him. Water collected by the roof dripped from the eaves, splashing back against his boots. Cold drizzle prickled against his face. At least it was no longer pouring rain. Clouds hung low and thick, hiding the tops of oaks walling off the far side of the small pasture, where trailers of mist drifted like phantoms above the glistening grass. Massive gnarled trunks sheltered dark shadows.

Richard was angry and frustrated that it had to rain now, of all times. If it hadn't rained, his chances would have been far better. Still, it would not be impossible. There were always signs.

There would still be tracks.

The rain would make it harder to read them, but even this much rain would not erase all trace of the tracks. Richard had grown up tracking animals and people through the woods. He could follow tracks in the rain. It was more difficult and more time-consuming, and it required intense concentration, but he could certainly do it.

And then it hit him.

When he found Kahlan's tracks, then he would have proof that she was real. Nicci and Cara would at last have no choice but to believe him.

Everyone left unique tracks. He knew Kahlan's. He also knew the route they'd come in by. Along with his and Cara's tracks, Kahlan's tracks would also be there for all to see. A sense of hope, if not relief, surged up through him. Once he found a set of readable prints and showed them to Nicci and Cara, there would be no more arguing. They would realize that it wasn't a dream and that there really was something seriously wrong.

Then he could start following Kahlan's tracks out of their camp and find her. The rain would slow that effort but it wouldn't stop him, and there might be a way for Nicci's ability to help speed that search.

Men milling about outside saw him stepping out of the small house and rushed in from all around. These men were not soldiers, in the strict sense. They were wagon drivers, millers, carpenters, stonemasons, farmers, and merchants who had struggled their whole life under the repressive rule of the Order, trying to eke out a living and support their families.

For most of these working people, life in the Old World meant living in constant fear. Anyone who dared to speak out against the ways of the Order was swiftly arrested, charged with sedition, and executed. There was a steady stream of charges and arrests, whether true or not. Such swift "justice" kept people in fear and in line.

Continual indoctrination, especially of the young, produced a significant segment of the population who fanatically believed in the ways of the Order. From birth, children were taught that thinking for themselves was wrong and that fervent faith in selfless sacrifice for the greater good was the only means to an afterlife of glory in the Creator's light, and the only way to avoid an eternity in the dark depths of the underworld in the merciless hands of the Keeper. Any other way of thinking was evil.

The properly devout were only too eager to see things remain as they were. The promise of riches to be shared with the common people kept the ever-pious supporters of the Order perpetually waiting for their quota of the blood of others, waiting to share in the loot of the wicked, who, they were taught, were their selfish oppressors and therefore sinners who deserved their fate.

From the ranks of the righteous came a flood of young men volunteering into the army, eager to be part of the noble struggle to crush the nonbelievers, to punish the wicked, to confiscate ill-gotten gains. The sanction of the plunder, the free rein of brutality, and the widespread rape of the unconverted bred a particularly vicious, and virulent, kind of zealotry. It had spawned an army of savages.

Such was the nature of the Imperial Order soldiers who had poured into the New World and now rampaged nearly unchecked across Richard and Kahlan's homeland.

The world stood at the brink of a very dark age.

It was this very threat that Ann believed Richard had been born to fight. She and many others believed it was foretold that if free people were to have a chance to survive this great battle, have a chance to triumph, it would only be if Richard led them.

These men before him saw through the empty ideas and corrupt promises of the Order, saw it for what it was: tyranny. They had decided to take back their lives. That made them warriors in the struggle for freedom.

A surprised upwelling of shouted greetings and cries of delight broke the early-morning stillness. As they gathered in close, the men all talked at once, asking if he was well and how he felt. Their sincere concern touched him. Despite his sense of urgency, Richard forced himself to smile and clasp arms with men he knew from the city of Altur'Rang. This was more the kind of reunion they had been hoping for.

Besides having worked beside many of these men and having become acquainted with others, Richard knew that he was also a symbol of liberty to them—the Lord Rahl from the New World, the Lord Rahl from a land where men were free. He had shown them that such things were possible for them, too, and given them a vision of the way their lives could be.

To his own mind, Richard saw himself as the same woods guide he had always been—even if he had been named the Seeker and now led the D'Haran Empire. While he had gone through many trying times since leaving home, he was really the same person with the same beliefs. Where he had once stood up to bullies, he now had to face armies. While the scale was different, the principles were the same.

But right then, all he cared about was finding Kahlan. Without her, the rest of the world—life itself—didn't seem very important to him.

Not far off, leaning against a post, stood a brawny man wearing not a smile but a menacing glare that had set permanent creases in his brow. The man folded his powerful arms across his chest as he watched the rest of the men greeting Richard.

Richard hurried through the crowd of men, clasping hands as he went, toward the scowling blacksmith. "Victor!"

The scowl gave way to a helpless grin. The man gripped arms with Richard. "Nicci and Cara would only let me go in to see you twice. If they didn't let me see you this morning, I was going to wrap iron bars around their necks."

"Was that you—the first morning? You passed me on your way out and touched my shoulder?"

Victor grinned as he nodded. "It was. I helped carry you back here." He put a powerful hand on Richard's shoulder and gave him an experimental shake. "You look well mended even if a little pale. I have lardo—it will give you strength."

"I'm fine. Maybe later. Thanks for helping bring me in here. Listen, Victor, have you seen Kahlan?"

Victor's brow bunched back up with deep creases. "Kahlan?"

"My wife."

Victor stared without reaction. His hair was cropped so close that his head almost appeared shaved. The rain beaded on his scalp. One brow arched.

"Richard, since you have been gone you took a wife?"

Richard anxiously looked over his shoulder to the other men watching him. "Have any of you seen Kahlan?"

He was greeted with blank expressions from many. Others shared a puzzled look with one another. The gray morning had fallen silent. They didn't know who he was talking about. Many of these men knew Kahlan and should have remembered her. Now they were shaking their heads or shrugging their regrets.

Richard's mood sank; the problem was worse than he thought. He had thought that maybe it was only something that had happened to Nicci and Cara's memory.

He turned back to the master blacksmith's frown. "Victor, I have trouble and I don't have time to explain. I don't even know how I would explain. I need help."

"What can I do?"

"Take me to the place where we had the fight."

Victor nodded. "Easy enough."

The man turned and started out toward the dark woods.

With two fingers, Nicci pushed a wet balsam bough out of her way as she followed several of the men through the dense woods. At the edge of a thickly forested ridge they headed down a trail that switched back and forth in order to negotiate the steep descent. Slippery rocks made the climb down treacherous. It was a shorter route than the one they had used to carry Richard back to the deserted farmhouse after he'd been hurt. At the bottom they picked their way over exposed fractured rock and boulders, skirting the fringe of a boggy area guarded by a towering cluster of silvered skeletons of cedars standing vigil in the stagnant water.

Runnels pouring down mossy banks carved deep cuts through the forest loam to expose speckled granite beneath. Several days of steady rain had left standing ponds in a number of low places. For the most part the rain filled the woods with the pleasing fragrance of damp soil, but in low places and crannies the damp, decomposing vegetation smelled of rot.

Even though she was warm from the short, arduous trek, the damp, cool air still left Nicci's fingers and ears numb with cold. She knew that this far south in the Old World the heat and humidity would soon return with such vengeance that it would make her long for the unusual spell of cool weather.

Having grown up in a city, Nicci had spent little time outdoors. At the Palace of the Prophets, where she had lived most of her life, outdoors meant the manicured lawns and gardens of the grounds covering Halsband Island. The countryside had always seemed vaguely hostile to her, an obstacle between one city and another, something to be avoided. Cities and buildings were a refuge from the inscrutable dangers of the wilderness.

More than that, though, cities had been where she toiled for the betterment of mankind. That work had had no end. Forests and fields had not been any of her concern.

Nicci had never appreciated the beauty of hills, trees, streams, lakes, and mountains until she had come to know Richard. Even cities were new to her eyes after Richard. Richard made all of life a wonder.

Carefully making her way up the slippery, dark rock of a brief rise, she finally spotted the rest of the men quietly waiting under the outstretched limbs of an ancient maple. Farther away, Richard crouched, studying a patch of ground. He finally rose to stare off into the dark expanse of woods beyond. Cara, his ever-present shadow, waited near him. Under the dense vault of soothing green, the Mord-Sith's red leather outfit stood out like a clot of blood on a tablecloth at tea.

Nicci understood Cara's fierce and passionate protection of Richard. Cara, too, had once been his enemy. Richard had not simply gained Cara's blind allegiance by virtue of becoming the Lord Rahl; he had, far more importantly, earned her respect, trust, and loyalty. Her red leather outfit was intimidating by design, a promise of violence should anyone even think of causing him harm. It was not an empty promise. Mord-Sith had been trained since they were young to be absolutely ruthless. While their primary purpose had been to capture the gifted and use their power against them, they were perfectly capable of using their ability against any opposition. Men who knew and trusted Cara, without realizing they were doing it, kept more distance from her when she wore her red leather.

Nicci knew how it felt for Cara to be brought back from the numb madness of mindless duty, to come to again value life.

Off in the distance, through the gloom and shadows and dripping leaves, the hoarse croak of ravens echoed through the forest. Nicci caught the sickening stench of rotting carrion. Looking around for landmarks as Richard had taught her, she spotted, at the base of a rocky outcropping, a pine that she remembered because it had a secondary trunk that curved out low to the ground almost like a seat. She recognized the spot; beyond the screen of vines and brush lay the scene of the battle.

Before Nicci could get to Richard, he ducked under low-hanging branches and started into the underbrush. Rising up on the far side, he waved his arms over his head and yelled like a lunatic. The deep shade among towering spruce erupted with the flapping of wings as, all at once, hundreds of the huge black birds bounded into the air, shrieking with indignation at having their feast interrupted. At first it looked as if the birds might contest the field of battle, but when the air sang with the unique sound of Richard's sword being drawn, they fled into the darkness back among the trees almost as if they knew what a weapon was and feared this one in particular. Their deep, angry croaking receded into the hazy mist. Richard, the triumphant scarecrow, glowered after them for a time before sliding his sword back into its scabbard.

He finally turned to the men. "All of you, please stay out of this area for now." His voice echoed off through the tall pines. "Just wait back there."

Considering herself sovereign in matters of Richard's safety, Cara paid no heed to his request. Instead, she followed him as he made his way into the small clearing beyond, staying close but out of his way. Nicci wove her way among the saplings and wet ferns, moving past silent men, until she reached a thin patch of white birch topping a hillock that edged one side of the clearing. Hundreds of black eyes set in the white bark watched as she made her way among them to finally halt at the brow of the bank. When she rested her hand on the peeling papery bark of one, she noticed the bolt from a crossbow stuck in the tree. Arrows jutted from other trees as well.

Beyond, dead soldiers lay sprawled everywhere. The stench staggered her. The ravens had been driven off, but the flies, fearing no sword, remained to feast and breed. The first hatch of blowfly maggots were already hard at work.

A good number of men were headless or were missing limbs. Some lay partly submerged in the stagnant pools of water. The ravens, along with other animals, had been at many of them, taking advantage of the opportunity afforded by gaping wounds. The thick leather armor, heavy hides, studded belts, chain mail, and wicked assortment of weapons no longer did these men any good. Here and there the clothes around bloated bodies strained to remain buttoned, as if trying to maintain dignity where there could be none.

Everything—from the men's flesh and bone to their fanatical beliefs— would lie here and rot in this forgotten patch of forest.

Waiting in the trees, Nicci watched as Richard briefly inspected the corpses. That first morning he'd already killed a great many of the soldiers before Victor and his men arrived and charged in to help him. She didn't know how long Richard had been fighting with that arrow in his chest, but it wasn't the kind of injury that anyone could endure for long.

Huddled back under the partial shelter of the huge maple, the nearly two dozen men pulled cloaks tight against the chill and settled in to wait.

Everywhere in the hushed forest, boughs of pine and spruce hung heavy and wet, quietly dripping water to the sodden ground. Here and there the drooping branches of maple, oak, and elm lifted whenever a breath of breeze relieved them of their heavy load of water, making it appear as if the trees were gently waving. The humid air dampened what the drizzle didn't reach, making everyone miserable.

Beyond the standing water, Richard crouched again, studying the ground. Nicci couldn't imagine what he was looking for.

None of the men waiting back under the tree appeared at all interested in revisiting the site of the pitched battle or seeing the dead. They were content to wait back where they were. Killing was unnatural and difficult for these men. They fought for what was right and they did what they had to do, but they didn't relish it. That in itself spoke to their values. They had buried three of their own dead, but they had not buried the bodies of close to a hundred soldiers who would have eagerly killed them had Richard not intervened.

Nicci remembered her surprise, the morning of the battle, coming upon Richard among all the dead and not at first understanding what had felled so many of them. Then she'd seen Richard slipping among those brutes, his sword moving with the fluid grace of a dance. It had been spellbinding to watch. With every thrust or slice, a man died. There had been a thick swarm of the soldiers—many bewildered by seeing so many of their fellows crashing to the ground. Most had been burly young men who always dominated because of their muscle—the type who enjoyed intimidating people. The soldiers moved in jerks and fits, chopping and lurching at Richard, but they always seemed to strike just after he had already gone. His flowing movement didn't fit the blundering attack they were looking for. They began to fear that the spirits themselves had set upon them. In a way, perhaps they had.

Still, their numbers were too great for one man, even if that one man was Richard and he wielded the Sword of Truth. Just one of those ignorant, lumbering, brawny men connecting with a lucky swing of his axe would be all it took. Or one arrow finding its mark. Richard was neither invincible nor immortal.

Victor and the rest of his men had arrived just in time—a few moments before Nicci, too, made it to the scene. Victor's men had flown into the fray, drawing the attention away from Richard. Once Nicci arrived, she had ended it in a blinding flash as she unleashed her power against the soldiers still standing.

Fearful of being exposed not only to the impending storm but, far more troubling, to potentially untold numbers of enemy soldiers who could appear on the scene at any moment, Nicci had instructed the men to carry Richard back through the woods to the secluded farmhouse. The most she had been able to do for him on that terrible race to cover had been to trickle a thread of her Han into him, hoping it would help keep him alive until she was able to do more. Nicci swallowed back the anguish of the ghastly memory.

From a distance, she watched as Richard continued his meticulous inspection of the scene of the battle, ignoring the fallen soldiers, for the most part, and paying particular attention to the surrounding area. She couldn't imagine what he hoped to discover. As he searched, he had begun moving in a back-and-forth pattern, progressing steadily outward from the small clearing, circling the scene in ever-widening arcs. At times he inched along the ground on all fours.

By late in the morning Richard had vanished into the woods.

Victor finally tired of the silent vigil and marched through a bed of ferns nodding under the gentle fall of rain to where Nicci waited.

"What's going on?" he asked her in a low voice.

"He's looking for something."

"I can see that. I mean what's going on with this business about a wife?"

Nicci let out a tired sigh. "I don't know."

"But you have an idea."

Nicci spotted Richard, briefly, moving among the trees some distance away. "He was seriously wounded. People in that state sometimes suffer delirium."

"But he's healed, now. He doesn't look or act feverish. He sounds normal enough in everything else, not like a person suffering visions and such. I've never seen Richard behave like this."

"Nor have I," Nicci admitted. She knew that Victor would never voice to her such concerns about Richard unless he was deeply worried. "I would suggest we try to be as understanding as possible of what he's gone through and see if he doesn't soon start to get his thoughts sorted out. He was unconscious for days. He's only been awake for a few hours. Let's give him some time to clear his head."

Victor considered her words before finally sighing and giving his nod of agreement. She was relieved that he didn't ask what they would do if Richard didn't soon get over his delirium.

She saw Richard, then, returning through the shadows and drizzle. Nicci and Victor crossed the field of battle to meet him. On the surface his face seemed to show only stony intensity, but, as well as she knew him, Nicci could read in his expression that something was seriously wrong.

Richard brushed leaves, moss, and twigs from the knees of his trousers as he finally reached them. "Victor, these soldiers weren't coming to take back Altur'Rang."

Victor's eyebrows went up. "They weren't?"

"No. They would need thousands of men for such a task—maybe tens of thousands. This many soldiers certainly weren't going to accomplish any such thing. And besides, if that was their intent, then what would be the point to slogging through the bush this far away from Altur'Rang?"

Victor made a sour face in admission that it had to be that Richard was right. "Then what do you think they were doing?"

"It wasn't yet dawn when they were out here moving through the woods. That suggests to me that they might have been reconnoitering." Richard gestured off through the woods. "There's a road in that direction. We'd been using it to travel up from the south. I had thought we would be camped far enough off it for the night to avoid trouble. Obviously, I was wrong."

"We last heard that you were to the south," Victor said. "The road makes for quicker traveling, so we were using the trails to cut cross-country so we could catch the road and take it south."

"It's an important road," Nicci added. "It's one of the main arteries— one of the first—that Jagang built. It allowed him to move soldiers swiftly. The roads he built enabled him to subdue all of the Old World under the rule of the Imperial Order."

Richard gazed off in the direction of the road, almost as if he could see through the wall of trees and vines. "Such a well-made road also allows him to move supplies. I think that's what was happening here. Being this close to Altur'Rang, and being well aware of the revolt that had taken place there, they were probably concerned about the possibility of an attack as they passed through the area. Since these soldiers weren't massing for an attack on Altur'Rang, I'd guess they had something more important going on: watching over supplies moving north for Jagang's army. He needs to crush the last of the resistance in the New World before the revolution at home burns his tail."

Richard's gaze returned to Victor. "I think these soldiers were reconnoitering—clearing the countryside in advance of a supply convoy. They were most likely scouting in the predawn in the hopes of catching any insurgents asleep."

"As we were." Victor folded his muscular arms in obvious discontent. "We never expected there would be any soldiers out here in these woods. We were sleeping like babies. If you hadn't been here and intercepted them, they would have soon snuck up on us where we slept. Then we'd likely be the ones feeding the flies and ravens, instead of them."

Everyone fell silent as they considered the might-have-been.

"Have you been hearing any news of supplies moving north?" Richard asked.

"Sure," Victor said. "There's a lot of talk about large quantities of goods going north. Some convoys are accompanied by new troops being sent to the war. What you say about these men scouting for such a convoy makes sense."

Richard squatted down and pointed. "See these tracks? These are a little more recent than the battle. It was a large contingent—most likely more soldiers who came looking for these dead men. This was as far as they came. These side ridges in the prints show where they turned around, here. It looks like they came in, spotted the dead soldiers, and left. You can see by their tracks as they left that they were in a hurry."

Richard stood and rested his left hand on the pommel of his sword. "Had you not taken me away right after the battle, these soldiers would have been on us. Fortunately they went back rather than search the woods."

"Why do you suppose that they would do that?" Victor asked. "Why would they see these men freshly killed and then leave?"

"They probably feared that a large force was lying in wait, so they rushed back to raise an alarm and insure that the supply column was well protected. Since they didn't even take the time to bury their fellow soldiers, I'd guess that their most urgent concern was getting their convoy out of the area."

Victor scowled at the tracks and then back in the direction of the dead soldiers. "Well," he said as he ran his hand back over his head, wiping away beads of water, "at least we can take advantage of the situation. While Jagang is preoccupied with the war that gives us time down here to work to knock support for the Order's rule right out from under them."

Richard shook his head. "Jagang may be preoccupied with the war, but that won't stop him from moving to restore his authority back here. If there's one thing we've learned about the dream walker, it's that he's methodical about annihilating any and all opposition."

"Richard is right," Nicci said. "It's a dangerous error to dismiss Jagang as a mere brute. While he is indeed brutal, he is also a highly intelligent individual and a brilliant tactician. He's had a lot of experience over the years. It's nearly impossible to goad him into acting impulsively. He can be bold—when he has good reason to believe boldness will win the day—but he's more given to calculated campaigns. He acts out of firm convictions, not bruised pride. He's content to let you think you've won—to let you think whatever you want, for that matter—while he methodically plans how he will gut you. His patience is his most deadly quality.

"When he attacks, he is indifferent to how many casualties his army takes, as long as he knows he will have more than enough men left to win. But over the course of his career—until his campaign to take the New World, anyway—he's tended to experience far fewer casualties than his enemies. That's because he holds no favor with naive notions of classic battle, of troops clashing on a field of honor. His way is usually to attack with such overwhelming numbers as to grind to dust the bones of his opposition.

"What his horde does to the vanquished is legend. For those in their path, the terror of the wait is unbearable. No sane person would want to be left alive to be captured by Jagang's men.

"For that reason, many welcome him with open arms, with blessings for their liberation, with supplications to be allowed to convert and join the Order."

The only sound under the embracing shelter of the trees was the gentle patter of the light rain. Victor did not doubt her word; she had been witness to such events.

At times, the knowledge that she had been a part of that perverted cause, that she had been a party to irrational beliefs that reduced men to nothing more than savages, made Nicci long for death. Certainly she deserved no less. But she was now in the unique position of having the opportunity and ability to help reverse the success of the Order. Setting matters right had become the cause that now drove her, sustained her, gave her purpose.

"It's only a matter of time before Jagang moves to retake Altur'Rang," Richard said into the silence.

Victor nodded. "Yes, if Jagang thought the revolution was confined to Altur'Rang then he would logically put all his efforts into taking back the city and being as ruthless about it as Nicci says, but we're making sure that doesn't happen." He showed Richard a grim smile. "We're lighting fires in cities and towns wherever we can, wherever people are ready to cast off their chains. We're pumping the bellows and spreading the flames of rebellion and freedom far and wide so that Jagang can't confine and crush it."

"Don't fool yourself," Richard said. "Altur'Rang is his home city. It's where the revolt against the Order began. A popular uprising in the very city where Jagang was building his grand palace undermines everything the Imperial Order teaches. It was to be the city, the palace, from where Jagang and the high priests of the Fellowship of Order were for all time to rule over mankind in the name of the Creator. The people destroyed that palace and instead embraced freedom.

"Jagang will not allow such subversion of his authority to stand. He must crush the rebellion there if the Order is to survive to rule the Old World—and the New. It will be a matter of principled belief for him; he considers opposition to the ways of the Fellowship of Order to be blasphemy against the Creator. He will not be shy about throwing his most brutal and experienced soldiers into the task. He will want to make a bloody example of you. I'd expect such an attack sooner rather than later."

Victor looked unsettled but not entirely surprised.

"And don't forget," Nicci added, "the Brothers of the Fellowship of Order who escaped will be among those working to help to reestablish the Order's authority. Such gifted men are no ordinary foe. We've hardly begun to root them out."

"All true enough, but you can' t work iron to your will until you get it good and hot." Victor tightened a defiant fist before them. "At least we've begun to do what must be done."

Nicci conceded that much with a nod and a small smile to soften the dark picture she had helped paint. She knew that Victor was right, that the task had to begin somewhere and at some point. He had already helped ring the hammer of freedom for a people who had all but given up hope. She just didn't want him to lose sight of the reality of the difficulty that lay ahead.

Nicci would have been relieved to hear Richard dealing logically with the important matters at hand, but she knew better. When Richard locked on to something vital to him, he might address peripheral issues when necessary but it would be a grave mistake to think that it diminished in the least his focus on his objective. In fact, he had delivered his warnings to Victor in swift summary—a mere matter to be gotten out of the way. She could see in his eyes that he was preoccupied with matters of far more importance to him.

Richard finally turned his riveting gray eyes on Nicci.

"You weren't with Victor and his men?"

In a sudden flash of comprehension, Nicci realized why the matter of the soldiers and their supply convoy was important to him: It was a mere element of a greater equation. He was trying to unravel how and if the convoy figured into the illusion he still clung to. It was that calculation he was working to resolve.

"No," Nicci said. "We'd had no word and didn't know what had happened to you. In my absence, Victor left to begin searching for you. Not long after, I returned to Altur'Rang. I found out where Victor had gone and set out to join him. I was still some distance behind at the end of my second day of travel, so the third day I started out before dawn, hoping to catch up with him. I'd been traveling for almost two hours when I arrived nearby and heard the battle. I reached the fighting right at the end."

Richard nodded thoughtfully. "I woke and Kahlan was gone. Since we were close to Altur'Rang, my first thought was that if I could find you, then maybe you could help me find Kahlan. That's when I heard the soldiers coming through the woods."

Richard gestured up a rise. "I heard them coming through those trees, there. I had darkness on my side. They hadn't seen me yet, so I was able to surprise them."

"Why didn't you hide?" Victor asked.

"More were coming down from that way, and others were coming in from that direction. I didn't know how many there were, but the way they were fanned out suggested to me that they were searching the woods. That made hiding risky. As long as there was any possibility that Kahlan might be close and maybe hurt, I couldn't run. If I hid and waited until the soldiers had a chance to find me then I would lose the element of surprise. Worse yet, dawn was approaching. Darkness and surprise worked to my advantage. With Kahlan missing I didn't have a moment to lose. If they had her, I had to stop them."

No one commented.

Richard turned to Cara, next. "And where were you?"

Cara blinked in surprise. She had to think a moment before she could answer. "I . . . I'm not exactly sure."

Richard frowned. "You're not sure? What do you remember?"

"I was on watch. I was checking some distance out from our camp. I guess something must have aroused my concern and so I was making sure the area was clear. I caught a whiff of smoke and was starting to investigate that when I heard battle cries."

"So you rushed back?"

Cara idly pulled her braid forward over her shoulder. She looked to be having difficulty remembering clearly. "No . . ." She frowned in recollection. "No, I knew what was happening—that you were being attacked—because I heard the clash of steel and men dying. I had only just realized that it was Victor and his men camped off in that direction, that it was the smoke from their campfire I smelled. I knew that I was much closer to them than you, so I thought that the smartest thing to do would be to rouse them and bring their help with me."

"That makes sense," Richard said. He wearily wiped beads of rain from his face.

"That's right," Victor said. "Cara was right there close when I heard the clash of steel as well. I remember because I was lying awake in the quiet."

Richard's brow drew together. He looked up. "You were awake?"

"Yes. The howl of a wolf woke me."

With sudden intensity Richard leaned in a little toward the black-smith. "You heard wolves howl?"

"No," Victor said as he frowned in recollection, "there was just one."

The three of them waited in silence as Richard stared off into the dis-tance, as if he were mentally trying to fit together the pieces of some great puzzle. Nicci glanced over her shoulder at the men back near the maple tree. Some yawned as they waited. Some had found seats on a fallen log. A few were engaged in hushed conversation. Others, arms folded, leaned against the trunks of trees and watched the surrounding woods as they waited.

"It didn't happen this morning," Richard whispered to himself. "When I was waking up this morning, when I was still half asleep, I was really re-membering what had happened the morning Kahlan disappeared."

"The morning of the battle," Nicci said softly in correction.

Lost in thought, Richard didn't appear to hear her correction. "I must have been remembering, for some reason, what happened back when I woke that morning." He turned suddenly and seized her arm. "A rooster crowed when I was being carried back to the farmhouse."

Surprised by his abrupt change of subject, and not knowing what he was getting at, Nicci shrugged. "I suppose it could have. I don't remem-ber. Why?"

"There was no wind. I remember hearing the rooster crow and looking up and seeing motionless tree limbs above me. There was no wind at all. I remember how dead still it was."

"You're right, Lord Rahl," Cara said. "I remember when I ran into Vic-tor's camp seeing the smoke from the fire going straight up because the air was dead calm. I think that was why we could hear the clash of steel and the cries from so far away—because there wasn't even a breath of breeze to cut the sound from carrying."

"If it helps," the blacksmith said, "there were a few chickens roaming around when we brought you to the farm. And you're right, there was a rooster and it did crow. Matter of fact, we were trying not to be found so that Nicci could have the time to heal you, and I was afraid that the rooster might attract unwanted attention, so I told the men to cut its throat."

After hearing Victor's account, Richard drifted back into thought. He tapped a finger against his lower lip as he considered yet another piece of his puzzle. Nicci thought he might have forgotten they were standing there.

She leaned a little closer to him. "So?"

He blinked and finally looked at her. "It had to be that when I woke today I was really remembering that morning—remembering for a reason. Sometimes you do that—remember because there was some part of it that doesn't make sense, remember for some reason."

"What reason?" Nicci asked.

"The wind. There was no wind that morning. But I remember that when I woke that morning, in the faint light of false dawn, I saw tree limbs moving, like in a breeze."

Nicci was not just confused by his concern for wind, but worried for his state of mind. "Richard, you were asleep and just waking up. It was dark. You probably just thought you saw the tree branches moving."

"Maybe" was all he said.

"Maybe it was the soldiers coming," Cara offered.

"No," he said, dismissing her suggestion with an irritable wave of his hand, "that was a little later, after I'd discovered that Kahlan was missing."

Seeing that neither Victor nor Cara was going to argue the point, Nicci decided to hold her tongue as well. Richard seemed to put the puzzle from his mind. He turned a deadly serious expression on the three of them.

"Look, I have to show you all something. But you need to realize, despite how little you may be able to make out, that I know what I'm talking about. I don't expect you to take my word, but you need to understand that I have a lifetime of experience in this and routinely used such ability. I trust each of you in your area of expertise. This is mine. Don't close your minds to what I have to show you."

Nicci, Cara, and Victor shared a look.

With a nod to Richard, Victor set his reservations aside and turned to the men. "You boys keep your eyes open, now." He circled a finger in the air. "There could be soldiers about, so let's keep it quiet and stay alert. Ferran, double-check the area."

The men nodded. Some came to their feet, apparently glad to have something to do other than just sit there wet and cold. Four men set out through the trees to set up guard.

Ferran handed his pack and bedroll to one of the other men for safe-keeping before nocking an arrow and slipping quietly into the brush. The young man was learning the trade of blacksmithing from Victor. Raised on a farm, he also had a natural talent for scouting unseen in the woods. He idolized Victor. Nicci knew that Victor was fond of the young man as well, but because he was fond of him he was probably harder on him than on the other men. Victor had told her once, referring to his tough demands of his apprentice, that you had to pound the imperfections out of iron and work it hard if you wanted to shape it into something truly worthwhile.

Since the battle, Victor had had sentries and lookouts on constant watch while Ferran and several of the others scouted the surrounding forest. None of them had wanted to take any chance that enemy soldiers would unexpectedly come upon them while Nicci was trying to save Richard's life. After she had done all she could for Richard, Nicci had healed a nasty gash to one man's leg and taken care of a few other less serious wounds suffered by a half-dozen other men.

Since the morning of the battle and Richard being hurt, she had gotten little sleep. She was exhausted.

After watching the men set about the tasks assigned them, Victor clapped Richard on the shoulder. "Show us, then."

Richard lead Cara, Victor, and Nicci past the clearing with the dead men and then off through the woods. He took a route between trees where the ground was more open. At the crest of a gentle rise, he stopped and crouched down.

Seeing Richard on bended knee, his cloak draped over his back, his sword in a gleaming scabbard at his hip, his hood pushed back to expose strands of wet hair lying against his muscular neck, his bow and quiver strapped over his left shoulder, he looked at once regal—a warrior king—and at the same time like nothing so much as the wilderness guide from a distant land that he had once been. With intimate familiarity, his fingers brushed the pine needles, twigs, crumbles of leaves, bark, and loam. Nicci could sense, just by that touch, his breadth of understanding of the seemingly simple things spread out before them, yet to him those things revealed another world.

Richard remembered, then, his purpose and gestured, urging them to squat down close beside him.

"Here," he said, pointing. "See this?" His fingers carefully traced a vague depression in the dense tangle of forest litter. "This is Cara's footprint."

"Well, that's no surprise," Cara said. "This is the way we came in from the road on our way to where we set up camp back there."

"That's right." Richard leaned out a little, pointing as he went on. "See here, and then off there? Those are more of your tracks, Cara. See how they come in here in a line showing where you were walking?"

Cara shrugged suspiciously. "Sure."

Richard moved to his right. They all followed. He again carefully traced a depression so they could make it out. Nicci couldn't see anything at all in the forest floor until he carefully drew the outline with a finger just above the ground. In doing so, he seemed to make the footprint magically appear for them. After he pointed it out, Nicci could tell what it was.

"This is my track," he said, watching it as if fearing that were he to look away it might vanish. "The rain works to wear them down—some places more than others—but it hasn't made all of them disappear." With a finger and thumb, he carefully lifted a wet, brown oak leaf from the center of the print. "Look, you can see under here how the pressure of my weight under the ball of my foot broke these small twigs. See? Rain can't obliterate things like that."

He looked up at them to make sure they were all paying attention and then pointed off into the shadowy mist. "You can see my tracks coming in this direction, toward us, just like Cara's." He stretched out and quickly traced two more vague depressions in the matted forest floor to show them what he meant. "See? You can still make them out."

"What's the point?" Victor asked.

Richard glanced back over his shoulder again before gesturing between the sets of tracks. "See the distance between Cara's tracks and mine? When we walked in here I was on the left and Cara was to my right. See how far apart our tracks are?"

"What of it?" Nicci asked as she pulled the hood of her cloak forward, trying to shield her face from the frigid drizzle. She pulled her hands back under the cloak and snugged them in her armpits for warmth.

"They're that far apart," Richard said, "because when we walked through here Kahlan was in the middle, between us."

Nicci stared again at the ground. She was no expert, so she wasn't especially surprised that she couldn't see any other tracks. But this time, she didn't think that Richard could, either.

"And can you show us Kahlan's tracks?" she asked.

Richard turned a look on her of such intensity that it momentarily halted the breath she was about to take.

"That's the point." He held up a finger with the same deliberate care with which he lifted his blade. "Her tracks are gone. Not washed away by the rain, but gone . . . gone as if they were never there."

Victor let out a very quiet and very troubled-sounding sigh. If she was shocked, Cara hid it well. Nicci knew that he hadn't told them all of what he had to say, so she remained guarded in her question.

"You're showing us that there are no tracks from this woman?"

"That's right. I've searched. I found my tracks and Cara's tracks in various places, but where Kahlan's tracks should be there are none."

In the uncomfortable silence no one wanted to say anything. Nicci finally took it upon herself to do so.

"Richard, you have to know why that is. Don't you see, now? It's just your dream. There are no tracks because this woman doesn't exist."

With him there on his knees before her, looking up at her, it seemed she could see his soul laid bare in his gray eyes. She would have given nearly anything at that moment to be able to simply comfort him. But she couldn't do that. Nicci had to force herself to go on.

"You said yourself that you know about tracking and yet even you can't find any tracks left by this woman. This should put the matter to rest. This should finally convince you that she just doesn't exist—that she never did exist." She took a hand from under her cloak, from its warm resting place, and gently laid it on his shoulder in an effort to soften her words. "You need to let it go, Richard."

He looked away from her eyes as he drew his lower lip through his teeth. "It's not as simple a picture as you're painting it," he said in a calm voice. "I'm asking you all to look—just look—and try to understand the significance of what it is I'm showing you. Look at how far apart Cara and my tracks are. Can't you see that there was a third person there, between us, as we walked?"

Nicci wearily rubbed her eyes. "Richard, people don't always walk close together. Maybe you and Cara were both looking around for any sign of threat as you walked through here, or maybe you were both just tired and not paying attention. There could be any number of simple explanations as to why you two weren't walking closer together."

"When only two people walk together they don't habitually walk this far apart." He pointed behind them. "Look at the tracks we made coming over her. Cara again walked to my right. Look at how much closer together the tracks are. That's typical of two people walking side by side. You and Victor were behind us. Look at how close together your tracks are.

"These tracks are different. Can't you see by their nature that they're this far apart because there was another person walking between us?"

"Richard . . ."

Nicci paused. She didn't want to argue. She was tempted to keep quiet and let him have his way, let him believe what he wanted to believe. And yet, silence would be feeding a lie, lending life to an illusion. While she ached for his difficulty and wanted to be on his side, she couldn't let him delude himself or she would be causing him greater harm. He could never get better, never fully recover, until he faced the truth of the real world. Helping him see reality was the only way she could really help him.

"Richard," she said softly, trying to get that truth through to him without sounding harsh or condescending, "your tracks are there, and Cara's tracks are there. We can see that—you showed us. There are no others. You showed us that, too. If she was there, between you and Cara, then why are her tracks not?"

They all hunched their shoulders in the wet and cold as they waited. Richard finally gathered his composure and spoke in a clear, firm voice.

"I think Kahlan's tracks were erased with magic."

"Magic?" Cara asked, suddenly alert and ill-tempered.

"Yes. I think that whoever took Kahlan erased her tracks with magic." Nicci was dumbfounded and made no attempt to conceal it.

Victor's gaze shifted back and forth between Nicci and Richard. "Can that be done?"

"Yes," Richard insisted. "When I first met Kahlan, Darken Rahl was after us. He was close on our trail. Zedd, Kahlan, and I had to run. If Darken Rahl had caught us we would have been finished. Zedd's a wizard but he isn't as powerful as Darken Rahl was, so Zedd cast some magic dust back down the trail to hide our tracks. That has to be what happened here. Whoever took Kahlan covered their tracks with the use of magic."

Victor and Cara glanced at Nicci for confirmation. As a blacksmith, Victor was not familiar with magic. Mord-Sith didn't like magic and pointedly avoided the details of its workings; their well-honed instinct was simply to violently eliminate anyone with magic if they posed even a potential threat to the Lord Rahl. Both Victor and Cara waited to hear what Nicci had to say about the possibility of using magic to cover tracks.

Nicci hesitated. Her being a sorceress didn't mean that she knew everything there was to know about magic. But still . . .

"I suppose that such a use of magic is in theory possible, but I've never heard of it being done." Nicci made herself look into Richard's expectant gaze. "I think the explanation of why there are no tracks is quite a bit simpler and I think you know it, Richard."

Richard couldn't mask his disappointment. "Looking at this by itself, and not being familiar with the nature of tracks and what they reveal, I'll grant that maybe it's hard to see what I'm saying. But this isn't all. I have something else to show you that may help you see the whole picture. Come on."

"Lord Rahl," Cara said as she tucked a wet wisp of hair back under the hood of her dark cloak and avoided looking at him, "shouldn't we be getting on to other important matters?"

"I have something important to show the three of you. Are you saying that you wish to wait here while I show Victor and Nicci?"

Her blue eyes turned up to him. "Of course not."

"Fine. Let's go."

Without further protest, they followed him at a quick pace as he headed in a northerly direction, deeper into the woods. They tiptoed from rock to rock to cross a broad ravine with dark eddies of murky water flowing through it. When Nicci nearly slipped and fell, Richard took her hand and helped her across. His big hand was warm, but not feverish, at least. She wished he would slow down and not stress his fragile health.

The gentle slope on the far side revealed itself only by degree as they they climbed higher through the drizzle and trailers of low clouds. To the left loomed the dark shadow of a rocky rise. Nicci could hear the burbling rush of water tumbling down that rise.

As they went deeper into the swirling gray mist and dense green vegetation, huge birds lifted from their perches. Wings spread wide, the wary creatures silently glided away beyond sight. Harsh screeches of unseen animals echoed through the somber woods. With the mass of overlapping spruce and balsam boughs and the tangled dead limbs of ancient oaks draped with gossamer moss curtains, to say nothing of the gloomy drizzle, vines, and dense tangle of saplings struggling to reach up for the elusive light, it was not easy to see very far. Only lower to the forest floor, where the sunlight rarely reached, was it more open.

Farther into the sodden forest, dark trunks of trees stood clear of the brush and thick foliage like sentinels watching the three people move among their gathered army. The ground where Richard took them was easier traveling since it was more open and covered with soft, sprawling mats of pine needles. Nicci imagined that even on the sunniest of days, only thin streamers of sunlight ever penetrated all the way down to the forest floor. Off to the sides here and there she saw nearly impenetrable tangles of brush and tightly knitted walls of young conifers. The expanse under the towering pines made a natural but unmarked pathway.

At last Richard halted, lifting his arms out to his sides so that they wouldn't step out past him. Spread out before them was more of the same—sparse growth sprouting among the thick bed of brown needles. Following his direction, they squatted down beside him.

Richard gestured over his right shoulder. "Back that way is where Cara, Kahlan, and I came in on the night we camped—by where the battle took place. In various places around our camp are my tracks from when I stood second watch, and Cara's tracks from third watch. Kahlan had first watch that night. There are no tracks from her watch."

His glance to each of them in turn was a silent request to hear him out before they started arguing.

"Back that way," he said, pointing as he went on, "was where the soldiers were coming up through the woods. From over in that direction, Victor, you and your men came to join the battle. In nearly the same place are your tracks from when you carried me back to the farmhouse. Off that way, where I already showed you, are the tracks of other soldiers who came in and found their fellow soldiers dead.

"None of us or any of the soldiers has been up this way.

"Here, where we are now, there are no tracks. Look around. You'll see only my fresh tracks from this morning when I was searching. Other than that, there are no footprints from anyone else coming through here—in fact, there's no sign that anyone has ever been here. At least, it would appear that no one has ever been here before."

Victor idly rubbed his thumb on the steel shaft of the mace hanging from his belt. "But you think otherwise?"

"Yes. Even though there are no tracks, someone did come this way. And, they left evidence." Richard leaned out and with one finger touched a smooth rock about the size of a loaf of bread. "As they hurried past, they stumbled on this rock."

Victor seemed caught up in the story. "How can you tell?"

"Look carefully at the markings on the rock." As Victor leaned in a bit, Richard pointed. "See here, the way the top of the rock, where it was exposed to the air and weather, has the pale tannish yellow discoloration of lichen and such? And here—like the hull of a boat below the waterline—you can see the dark brown rime that shows where the belly of the rock had been lying beneath the ground.

"But it's not lying that way now. It's not settled into its socket in the ground, its recent resting place. It's now lifted a little out of that socket and turned partway over. See how a section of the dark bottom is now exposed? Were it out of the ground for longer, the dark color would be worn away and the lichen would begin to grow there, too. But it hasn't had that much time yet. This is recent."

Richard waggled his finger back and forth. "Look at the ground, here, on this side of the rock. You can see the socket where the rock originally rested, but now the rock has been shoved back a little, leaving a void between this side of the rock and the wall of the cavity. On the back side, away from us, because the rock was recently disturbed, you can still see a ridge of dirt and debris that has been pushed up.

"The open socket on this side and the ridge on the far side shows that whoever stumbled on this rock and disturbed it was moving away from our camp, going north."

"But then where's their trail?" Victor asked. "Their footprints?"

Richard raked back his wet hair. "The trail has been erased with magic. I searched; there is no trail.

"Look at the rock. It's been disturbed, kicked partway out of its resting place in the ground. But there is no scuff mark on it. While the rock wasn't moved much, it was moved. A boot grazing this rock enough to move it like this would have to leave a mark. Yet there is no mark, just as there are no other footprints."

Nicci pushed her hood back. "You're twisting everything you find around to fit what you want to believe, Richard. You can't have it both ways. If magic was used to erase their trail, then why is it that are you able to detect their trail by this rock?"

"Probably because the magic they used erases footprints. The person who used that magic must not know a great deal about tracks or tracking. I don't think they're very familiar with the outdoors. When they used magic to erase their footprints, they probably never gave any thought to putting disturbed stones back in place."

"Richard, surely—"

"Look around," he said as he swept his arm out. "Look at how perfect the forest floor is."

"What do you mean?" Victor asked.

"It's too perfect. Twigs, leaves, bark are too evenly distributed. Nature is more erratic."

Nicci, Victor, and Cara peered at the ground. Nicci saw only a normal-looking forest floor. Here and there small things—pine seedlings, spindly weeds, an oak sapling with only three big leaves—sprouted up through the litter of twigs, moss, bark, and fallen leaves sprinkled over the bed of pine needles. She didn't know all that much about tracks or tracking, or forests, for that matter—Richard always left blazes on trees when he wanted her to be able to find and follow his trail—but it didn't look like anyone had been through the place, nor did it look overly perfect, as Richard suggested. As she looked around, it appeared the same as other places she eyed for comparison. Victor and Cara seemed equally confounded.

"Richard," Nicci said with strained patience, "I'm sure there could be any number of explanations as to why a rock looks disturbed to you. For all I know, it could be disturbed, as you suggest. But maybe an elk or a deer kicked it as they went by and over time their tracks have been worn away."

Richard was shaking his head. "No. Look at the socket. It's still well formed. You can read by how much the edges have degraded that it happened only a few days ago. Time—especially in the rain—erodes such edges and works to fill in the gap. Any deer or elk kicking this rock would have left tracks that would be just as recent. Not only that, but a hoof would have scuffed it, the same as a boot. I'm telling you, three days ago someone stumbled on this rock."

Nicci gestured. "Well, that dead branch over there could have fallen on it and disturbed it."

"If it did, then the lichen growing on the rock would show the scar of the impact and the branch would show evidence that it had hit something hard. It doesn't—I already looked."

Cara threw up her hands. "Maybe a squirrel jumped from a tree and landed on it."

"Not nearly heavy enough to have moved this rock," Richard said.

Nicci drew a weary breath. "So what you're saying is that the fact that there are no tracks from this woman, Kahlan, proves that she exists."

"No, that's not what I'm saying, not the way you're putting it, anyway. But it does confirm it if you look at everything together—if you put it all into context."

Nicci's hands fisted at her sides. There were important matters that had to be addressed. They were running out of time. Instead of dealing with urgent matters in need of their attention, they were out in the middle of the woods looking at a rock. She could feel the blood going to her face.

"That's ridiculous. All you've shown us, Richard, is proof that this woman you imagined is just that—imagined. She doesn't exist. She left no tracks—because you only dreamed her! There's nothing mysterious about it! It's not magic! It's simply a dream!"

Richard abruptly rose up before her. He changed in a heartbeat from a man of calm intensity to a figure of heart-stopping presence, power, and awakening anger.

But rather than confront her, he took a step past her, back toward the way they'd come from, and stopped. Still and tense, Richard stared back through the woods.

"Something's wrong," he said in low warning.

Cara's Agiel spun up into her fist. Victor's brow tightened as his fingers found the mace hanging from his belt.

In the distance back through the dripping forest, Nicci heard the sudden, wild alarm cries of ravens.

The cries that came next reminded her of nothing so much as the sounds of bloody murder.

Richard bounded back through the woods, back toward the waiting men, back toward the screams. He raced headlong through a blur of trees, branches, brush, ferns, and vines. He leaped over rotting logs and used a well-planted boot to bound over a boulder. He dodged his way through stands of young pines and a cluster of flowering dogwood. Without slowing, he batted aside tamarack limbs and ducked under balsam boughs. Nets of dead branches on the lower trunks of young spruce trees snatched at his clothes as he charged past. More than once, dead limbs jutting out, spearlike, from larger trees nearly impaled him before he sidestepped at the last instant.

Running at such a reckless speed through dense woods, let alone in the rain, was treacherous. It was hard to recognize hazards in time to avoid them. Any one of a number of protruding branches could easily gouge out an eye. One slip on wet leaves or moss or rocks could cause a skull-splitting tumble. Driving a foot down into a crevice or fissure at a dead run would likely shatter a leg. Richard had once known a young man who had done just that. His broken leg and ankle had never mended right, leaving him partially crippled for life.

Richard focused his concentration on his intended path, taking as much care as possible without slowing.

He dared not slow.

The whole way as he ran, he heard the terrible screams and cries, the shrieks, and the sickening snapping sounds. He could also hear Cara, Victor, and Nicci crashing through the brush behind him. He didn't wait for them to catch up. Every long stride, every leap, took him farther out ahead of them.

Running as fast as he could, gasping for air, Richard was surprised to find himself winded before he should have been. At first disconcerted, he then remembered the reason. Nicci had said that he wasn't yet recovered and because he had lost a lot of blood he would need rest to gain back his strength. He kept running. He would have to make do with what strength he had. It wasn't that much farther.

More than that, though, he kept running because the men needed help. These were men who had come to his aid when he had been in trouble. He didn't know what was happening, but it was clear to Richard that they were in some kind of peril.

On the morning of the attack, if he'd known more about how to call upon his gift, he might have been able to use that ability to stop the soldiers before Victor and his men had arrived. Had he been able to do that, three of those men would not have died in the fighting. Of course, had Richard not been where he was and taken action to stop the soldiers, then Victor and his men might well have all ended up murdered at their camp, most while they slept.

Richard couldn't help feeling that he might have done more. He didn't want to see any of these men hurt; he kept running with all his strength, holding back nothing. He would use whatever strength he had. He could gain back his strength. Lives could not be gotten back.

There were times like this when he wished that he knew more about how to call upon his gift, but his ability regrettably worked differently than in others. Instead of functioning through cognizant direction, as Nicci's power did, Richard's ability worked through anger and need. The morning that the Imperial Order soldiers had poured in all around him he had drawn his sword for the purpose of his survival and in so doing had given his anger over to the weapon. Unlike his own gift, he knew that he could count on the power of his sword.

Others with the gift learned to use their ability from a young age. Richard never had. It had been an upbringing of peace and security that had given him a chance at life, at growing up to profoundly value life. The drawback was that such an upbringing had also left him unaware of and ignorant of his own talent.

Now that Richard was grown, though, learning to use his latent ability was proving more than difficult, not only because of his upbringing, but because his particular form of the gift was so extraordinarily rare. Neither Zedd nor the Sisters of the Light had had any success at all in teaching him how to consciously direct his power.

He knew little more than what Nathan Rahl, the prophet, had told him, that his power was most often sparked through anger and a particular, specific kind of desperate need, which Richard had not been able to identify or isolate. As far as he had been able to determine, the character of the need required to ignite his power was unique to each circumstance.

Richard also knew that using magic did not involve whim. No amount of wishing or straining could ever produce results. The initiation and use of magic required specific conditions; he just didn't understand how to produce or provide those conditions.

Even wizards of great ability sometimes had to use books to insure that they got the details right if the specific magic they wanted was to work. At a young age, Richard had memorized one of those books, *The Book of Counted Shadows.* That was the book which Darken Rahl had been hunting for after he had put the boxes of Orden in play.

On the morning Kahlan had vanished, to meet the threat of the seemingly endless ranks of soldiers charging in upon him, Richard had had to depend on his sword and not his own innate powers. The frenzied fighting had taken him to the brink of exhaustion. At the same time, his worry for Kahlan left him distracted to the point where his mind wasn't fully on the fight. He knew that allowing such a diversion to beguile his attention was dangerous and foolish . . . but it was Kahlan. He had been helplessly worried for her.

Had his need not summoned his gift when it did, the hail of arrows suddenly showering in at him would have been fatal a few dozen times over.

He hadn't seen the bolt fired from a crossbow. As it shot for his heart, he only recognized the threat at the last possible instant and, because of the crucial need to also stop the three soldiers lunging for him at the same time, he'd only been able to deflect the path of the arrow's flight, not stop it.

It seemed like he'd already gone over the memory a thousand times and come up with any number of could-haves and should-haves that, in his mind's harsh judgment, would have prevented what had happened. As Nicci had said, though, he was not invincible.

As he plunged through the woods, the forest unexpectedly fell silent. The echoing screams died away. The misty green wilderness was again left to the muted whisper of the light rain falling though the leafy canopy. In the outwardly peaceful and once again quiet world around him, it almost seemed as if he had only imagined the terrible sounds he'd heard.

Despite his fatigue, Richard didn't slow. As he ran, he listened for any sign of the men, but he could hear little more than his own labored breathing, his heartbeat pounding in his ears, and his swift footfalls. Occasionally he also heard branches behind him breaking as the other three tried to catch up with him, but they were still falling farther behind.

For some reason, the eerie calm was somehow more frightening than the screams had been. What had started out sounding like the ravens—hoarse croaks rising into the kinds of terrified cries an animal makes only when it's being killed—had, somewhere along the line, begun to sound human. And now there was only the menacing silence.

Richard tried to convince himself that he had only imagined that the screams had turned human. As chilling as such cries had been, it was the haunting, unnatural stillness after they'd ended that made gooseflesh prickle the hair at the back of his neck.

Just before he reached the brink of the clearing, Richard finally drew his sword. The singular sound of freeing the blade sent the cutting ring of steel through the damp woodland, ending the silence.

Instantly, the heat of the sword's anger flooded through every fiber of his being, to be answered in kind by his own anger. Once again, Richard committed himself to the magic he knew, and upon which he could depend.

Filled with the sword's power, he ached for the source of the threat, and lusted to end it.

There had been a time when fear and uncertainty made him reluctant to surrender to the rising storm brought forth from the ancient, wizard-wrought blade, hesitant to answer the call with his own anger, but he had long since learned to let himself go into the rapture of the rage. It was that righteous wrath that he had learned to bend to his will. It was that power he directed to his purpose.

There had been those in the past who'd coveted the sword's power, but in their blind lust for that which belonged to others, had ignored the darker perils they stirred by using such a weapon. Instead of being masters of the magic, they had become servants to the blade, to its anger, and to their own rapacious greed. There had been those who had used the power of the weapon for evil ends. Such was not the fault of the blade. The use of the sword, for good or for evil, was the conscious choice made by the person wielding it and all responsibility fell to them.

Racing through the wall of tree limbs, shrubs, and vines, Richard came to a halt at the edge of the clearing where the soldiers had fallen in the battle several days before. Sword in hand, he gasped for air—despite how putrid the air smelled—struggling to catch his breath.

At first, as he scanned the bizarre scene spread out before him, he had trouble comprehending what it was he was seeing.

Dead ravens lay everywhere. Not just dead, but ripped apart. Wings, heads, and parts of carcasses littered the clearing. Feathers by the thousands had settled like black snow over the rotting corpses of the soldiers.

Frozen in shock for only an instant, and still breathless, Richard knew that this was not what he sought. Tearing across the battle site, he bounded up the short bank, through the gaps in the trees, and over trampled vegetation, toward where the men had been waiting.

The rage of the sword spiraled up through him as he ran, making him forget that he was tired, that he was winded, that he wasn't yet fully recovered, preparing him for the fight to come. In that moment, the only thing that mattered to Richard was getting to the men, or, more precisely, getting at the threat to the men.

There was a matchless rapture in killing those who served evil. Evil unchallenged was evil sanctioned. Destroying evil was really a celebration of the value of life, made real by destroying those who existed to deny others their life.

Therein lay the fundamental purpose behind the sword's essential, indispensable requirement for rage. Rage blunted the horror of killing, stripped away the natural reluctance to kill, leaving only its naked necessity if there was to be true justice.

As Richard raced out of the stand of birch, the first thing that caught his attention was the maple tree where the men had been waiting. The lower limbs had been stripped bare of leaves. It looked like a storm had swooped down to rip through the woods. Where only a short time ago small trees grew, now all that was left was shattered stumps. Branches thick with shimmering, wet leaves or pine needles lay scattered about. Huge jagged splinters of tree trunks stuck up from the ground like spent spears after a battle.

Beneath the maple, scattered across the forest floor, was a scene that, at first, Richard could make no sense of. Nearly everything that before had been some shade of green, whether dusty sage, yellowish, or rich emerald, was now tainted with the stain of red.

Richard stood panting, his heart pounding, fighting to focus the rage on a threat he could not identify. He scanned the shadows and darkness back among the trees, looking for any movement. At the same time he struggled to sort out the confusion of what he was seeing on the ground before him.

Cara skidded to a halt to his left, ready for a fight. An instant later, Victor stumbled to a stop on his right, his mace held in a tight fist. Nicci raced in right behind, no weapon evident, but Richard could sense the air around her virtually crackling with her power ready to be unleashed.

"Dear spirits," the blacksmith whispered. His six-bladed mace, a deadly weapon the man had made himself, rose in his fist as he cautiously started forward.

Richard lifted his sword in front of Victor to bar him from going any farther. His chest against the blade, the blacksmith reluctantly heeded the silent command and stopped.

What, at first, had been a bewildering sight became at last all too clear. A man's forearm, missing the hand but still covered with a brown flannel shirtsleeve, lay in a bed of ferns at Richard's feet. Not far away stood a heavy, laced boot with a jagged white shinbone stripped of sinew and muscle jutting out from the top. In a thicket of roughleaf dogwood just to the side lay a section of a torso, its flesh torn away to lay bare a section of the spine and blanched rib bones. Squiggles of pink viscera lay strewn over the log where the men had been sitting. Ragged pieces of scalp and skin lay atop bare rock and scattered everywhere through the grass and bushes.

Richard could not imagine what power could have caused such a shocking scene.

A thought struck him. He glanced back over his shoulder at Nicci. "Sisters of the Dark?"

Nicci slowly shook her head as she studied the carnage. "There are a few similar characteristics, but on balance this is nothing like the way they kill."

Richard didn't know if that was comforting news or not.

Slowly, carefully, he stepped forward among the still-bleeding remains. It didn't look to him like it had been a battle; there were no cuts from swords or axes, no arrows or spears to mark the battlefield. None of the limbs or mangled ribbons of muscle appeared to have been cut. Every piece looked as if it had been torn away from where it belonged.

It was so horrific a sight, so incomprehensible, that it was beyond sickening. Richard found it disorienting trying to conceive of what could have created such devastation—not just of the men, but of the landscape where they had been. From somewhere beyond the boiling rage of the sword's magic, he felt an agony of sorrow for what he had not been able to stop, and he knew that that sorrow would only grow. But right then, he wanted nothing so much as to get his hands on whoever—or whatever—had done this.

"Richard," Nicci whispered from close behind, "I think it best if we get out of here."

The direct, calm tone of her voice could not have been any more compelling a warning.

Filled with the rage from the sword in his fist, and his own impassioned anger at what he was seeing, he ignored her. If there was anyone left alive, he had to find them.

"There's no one left," Nicci murmured, as if in answer to his thoughts.

If the threat still lurked nearby, he needed to know.

"Who could have done this?" Victor whispered, clearly not interested in leaving until he had the guilty party in his grip.

"It doesn't look like anything human," Cara answered in quiet indictment.

As Richard stepped carefully through the remains, the silence of the shrouding woods pressed in on him like a great weight. No birds called, no bugs buzzed, no squirrels chattered. The muting effect of the heavy overcast and drizzle only served to thicken the hush.

Blood dripped from leaves, branches, and the tips of bent grasses. The trunks of trees were splattered with it. The coarse bark of an ash was smeared with oozing tissue. A hand, fingers open and slack, empty of any weapon, lay palm-up on a gravel slope beneath the large leaves of a mountain maple.

Richard spotted the footprints of where they all had entered the area and some of his own footprints where he had left only a short time ago with Nicci, Cara, and Victor. Many of the remains lay in virgin forest where none of them had walked. There were no peculiar footprints among the carnage, although there were unexplained places where the ground had been ripped open. Some of those gouges cut right through thick roots.

Taking a better look, Richard realized that the plowed gashes were places where men had been smashed to the ground with such violence that it had torn open the forest floor. In some spots, flesh still clung to the exposed ends of splintered roots.

Cara gripped his shirt at the shoulder, trying to urge him back. "Lord Rahl, I want you away from here."

Richard pulled his shoulder free of her grip. "Quiet."

As he stepped silently among the remains, the countless voices of those who had used the sword in the past whispered in the back of his mind.

Don't focus on what you're seeing, on what is done. Watch for what caused it and might yet come. Now is the time for vigilance.

Richard hardly needed such a warning. He was gripping the wirewound hilt of the sword so tightly that he could feel the raised lettering of the word TRUTH formed by gold wire woven through the sliver. That golden word bit into the flesh of his palm on one side and his fingertips on the other.

At his feet a man's head stared up at him from among scrub sumac. A mute cry twisted the expression fixed on the face. Richard knew him. His name had been Nuri. All that this young man had learned, all that he had experienced, all that he had planned for, the world he had begun to make for himself, was ended. For all these men, the world was finished; the one life they had had was gone forever.

The agony of that terrible loss, that ghastly finality, threatened to extinguish the rage from the sword and swamp him in sorrow. All these men were loved and cherished by those waiting for them to return. Each one of these individuals would be grieved over with heartache that would indelibly mark the living.

Richard made himself move on. Now was not the time to grieve. Now was the time to find the guilty and visit upon them retribution and justice before they had the chance to do this to others. Only then could the living mourn for these precious souls lost.

Despite how widely he searched, Richard didn't see a single body—not a body in the sense of a whole, recognizable person—yet the entire area where the men had been waiting was littered with their remains. The surrounding woods, also, revealed parts of those remains, as if some of the men had tried to run. If that was the case, none had gotten far. As Richard moved through the trees, looking for any tracks that might help him identify who had killed these men, he kept one eye on the shadows off in the mist. He saw tracks of men who had run, but he saw no tracks chasing after them.

As he came around an ancient pine, he was confronted by the top half of a man's chest hanging upside down from a splintered limb. The remains hung well above Richard's head. What was left of the armless torso had been impaled on the stump of a broken limb as if it were a meat hook. The face was fixed with unbridled terror. Being upside down, the hair, dripping blood, stood out straight from the scalp as if frozen in fright.

"Dear spirits," Victor whispered. Rage twisted his face. "That's Ferran."

Richard scanned the area, but saw nothing moving in the shadows. "Whatever happened here, I don't think anyone escaped." He noticed that on the ground where Ferran's blood dripped there were no tracks.

Kahlan's tracks were gone as well.

The pain, the horror, of wondering if this might be the same thing that had happened to Kahlan nearly buckled his knees. Not even the sword's rage was enough to shield him from the agony of that pain.

Nicci, right behind him, leaned close. "Richard," she said in a near whisper, "we need to get out of here."

Cara leaned in beside Nicci. "I agree."

Victor lifted his mace. "I want those who did this." His knuckles were white around the steel grip. "Can you track them?" he asked Richard.

"I don't think that would be a good idea," Nicci said.

"Good idea or not," Richard told them, "I don't see any tracks." He looked into Nicci's blue eyes. "Perhaps you would like to try to convince me that I am imagining this, as well?"

She didn't break eye contact with him, but she didn't answer his challenge, either.

Victor gazed up at Ferran. "I told his mother that I'd watch over him. What am I going to say to his family now?" Tears of rage and hurt glistened in his eyes as he pointed with the mace back to the rest of the remains. "What am I going to say to their mothers and wives and children?"

"That evil murdered them," Richard said. "That you will not rest until you know justice is done. That vengeance will be had."

Victor nodded, his anger flagging, misery now filling his voice. "We have to bury them."

"No," Nicci said with grim authority. "As much as I understand your want to care for them, your friends are no longer here, among these pieces of wrecked bodies. Your friends are now with the good spirits. It is up to us not to join them."

Victor's anger resurfaced. "But we must—"

"No," Nicci snapped. "Look around. This was a blood frenzy. We don't want to get caught in it. We can't help these men. We need to get out of here."

Before Victor could argue, Richard leaned close to the sorceress. "What do you know about this?"

"I told you before, Richard, that we needed to talk. But this is not the time or place to do it."

"I agree," Cara growled. "We need to get away from here."

Looking from the remains of Ferran back to the bloody mess beneath the maple, Richard suddenly felt a sense of overwhelming loneliness. He wanted Kahlan so bad it hurt. He wanted her comfort. He wanted her safe. The agony of not knowing if she was alive and well was unbearable.

"Cara is right." Nicci urgently gripped Richard's arm. "We don't know enough about what we're up against, but whatever did all this, I fear that as weak as you are your sword can't protect us from it—and right now, neither can I. If it's still in these woods, now is not the time to confront it. Justice and vengeance need us to see them done. To do that, we must be alive."

With the back of a hand, Victor wiped tears of grief and anger from his cheek. "I hate to admit it, but I think Nicci's right."

"Whatever was looking for you, Lord Rahl," Cara said. "I don't want you here if it should happen to return."

Richard noted the way Cara, in her red leather, no longer seemed out of place in the woods. She blended right in with all the blood.

Still not ready to abandon the search for whatever had killed these men, and with a dark sense of alarm rising within him, Richard frowned at the Mord-Sith. "What makes you think it was after me?"

"I told you," Nicci said through gritted teeth, answering in Cara's stead, "now is not the time and this is not the place to talk about it. There is nothing we can hope to accomplish here. These men are beyond our help."

Beyond help. Was Kahlan beyond help as well? He couldn't allow himself to believe that.

He looked north. Richard didn't know where to search for her. Just because the rock that had been kicked out of its resting place had been found to the north of their camp didn't mean that whoever took Kahlan went that way. They might have simply gone north, trying to avoid contact with Victor and his men and with the soldiers guarding the supply convoy. They might have only been trying to avoid being spotted until they got out of the immediate area. After that, they could have gone anywhere.

But where?

Richard knew that he needed help.

He tried to think of who could help him with something like this. Who would believe him? Zedd *might* believe him, but Richard didn't think his grandfather could offer the specific kind of help he needed in this circumstance. It was awfully far to go if it ended up that Zedd's abilities didn't fit this particular kind of problem.

Who would be willing to help him, and might know something?

Richard turned suddenly to Victor. "Where can I get horses? I need horses. Where's the closest place?"

Victor was taken off guard by the question. He let the heavy mace hang and with his other hand wiped rainwater back off his forehead as he considered the question. His brow bunched back up.

"Altur'Rang would probably be the closest place," he said after a moment's thought.

Richard slid his sword back into its sheath. "Let's go. We need to hurry."

Pleased with the decision to leave, Cara gave him a helpful shove in the direction of Altur'Rang. Suspicion lurked in Nicci's eyes, but she was so relieved to have him start away from the site of so much death that she didn't ask why he wanted horses.

Weariness forgotten, the four of them hurried away from men beyond any help. As heartsick as they felt about leaving, each of them understood that it would be too dangerous to stay to try to bury these men. A burial of the dead was not worth the risk to their lives.

With his sword put away, the anger extinguished. In its place welled up the crushing pain of grief for the dead. The forest seemed to weep with them.

Worse yet was the dread of wondering what could have happened to Kahlan. If she was in the hands of this evil . . .

Think of the solution, Richard reminded himself.

If he was to find her, he would need help. To get help, he needed horses. That was the immediate problem at hand. They still had half a day of daylight. He intended not to waste a moment of it.

Richard led them away through the tangled woods at an exhausting pace. No one complained.

In the deepening gloom of approaching nightfall, Richard and Cara used thin, wiry pine tree roots they'd pulled up from the spongy ground to lash together the trunks of small trees. Victor and Nicci foraged the understory along the base of the heavily forested slope, cutting and collecting balsam boughs. As Richard held the logs together, Cara tied off the ropelike root. Richard cut the excess for use elsewhere and slipped the knife back into its sheath at his belt. Once he had the log framework securely in place against an overhang of rock, he started stacking the balsam boughs along the bottom. Cara tied random branches on from inside to keep them all in place for the night as Richard continued layering more up the poles. Victor and Nicci dragged armfuls of boughs close to keep him supplied as he worked.

The area under the overhanging roof of rock was dry enough, it just wasn't large enough. The lean-to would expand the shelter so as to provide a snug place to sleep. Without a fire it wouldn't be especially warm, but at least it would be dry.

Throughout the day, the drizzle had turned to a slow, steady rain. While they had been on the move they had been warm enough because of their exertion, but now that they had to stop for the night, the inexorable embrace of the cold had begun. Even in chilly weather that wasn't truly cold, being wet sapped a person of their necessary warmth and thus their strength. Richard knew that, over time, constant exposure to even mildly chilly wet weather could steal enough vital heat from the body to severely debilitate and sometimes even kill a person.

With as little sleep as he knew Nicci and Cara had gotten over the previous three days, and in his own weakened condition, Richard recognized that they needed a dry, warm place to get some rest or they would all be in trouble. He couldn't allow anything to slow him down.

For the whole of the afternoon and evening they had set a steady, rapid pace on their march toward Altur'Rang. After the brutal slaughter of the men, the four of them hadn't been particularly hungry, but they knew that they had to eat if they were to have the strength for the journey, so they nibbled on dried meats and travel biscuits as they made their way through the trackless wilderness.

Richard was so exhausted he could hardly stand. Both to cut the distance and to avoid being spotted by anyone, he had guided the others through dense forest, most of it tough going and all of it well off any trails. It had been a grueling day's travel. His head ached. His back ached. His legs ached. If they started early and kept up the strenuous pace, though, they might be able to reach Altur'Rang in one more day's travel. After they got horses, the going would be easier as well as swifter.

He wished he didn't need to go so far, but he didn't know what else to do. He couldn't spend forever searching the vast forests all around, on the off chance he would find another rock that had been disturbed so that he then might have an idea of which direction Kahlan had gone. He might never find another such rock, and even if he did, there was no reason to believe that if he kept going in that direction he would find Kahlan. Whoever took her might change direction without ever again disturbing a rock in a way that he would find it.

Their regular tracks were gone. Richard knew no way to track someone when magic had made their tracks vanish. Nicci's gift wasn't able to help. Wandering around aimlessly wasn't going to solve anything. As reluctant as he was to leave the area where he had last seen Kahlan, Richard didn't think that he had any other choice but to go for help.

He went through the motions of building the shelter without giving the work much thought. In the failing light, Cara, concerned for his well-being, kept watching him out of the corner of her eye. She looked like she expected him to fall over at any moment and if he did she intended to catch him.

As he worked, Richard mulled over the remote but real possibility that Imperial Order soldiers might be searching the woods for them. At the same time he fretted about what could have killed all of Victor's men— and might now be chasing them. He considered what other precautions he might take, and he deliberated over how he would fight whatever could have done such violence.

Through it all, he kept trying to think of where Kahlan might be. He went over everything he could remember. He brooded over whether or not she was hurt. He agonized over what he might have done wrong. He imagined that she must be filled with fear and doubt, wondering why he wasn't coming to help her escape, why he hadn't yet found her, and if he ever would before her captors killed her.

He struggled to banish from his mind the gnawing fear that she might already be dead.

He tried not to think about what might be done to her as a captive that could be infinitely more gruesome than a simple execution. Jagang had ample reason to want her to live a good long time; only the living could feel pain.

From the beginning, Kahlan had been there to frustrate Jagang's ambitions and sometimes even reverse his success. The Imperial Order's very first expeditionary force in the New World, among other things, slaughtered all the inhabitants of the great Galean city of Ebinissia. Kahlan came upon the grisly sight shortly after a troop of young Galean recruits had discovered it. In their blind rage, despite being outnumbered ten to one, those young men had been bent on the glory of vengeance and victory, on meeting upon the battlefield the soldiers who had tortured, raped, and murdered all of their loved ones.

Kahlan came across those recruits, led by Captain Bradley Ryan, just before they were about to march into a textbook battle that she realized would be their death. In their bold inexperience, they were convinced that they could make such tactics work and snatch victory, despite being overwhelmingly outnumbered.

Kahlan knew how the experienced Imperial Order soldiers fought. She knew that if she allowed those young recruits to do as they planned, they would be marching into a merciless meat grinder and all of them would die. The results of their shortsighted notions of the righteous glory of combat would be that those Imperial Order soldiers would then go on, unopposed, to other cities and continue to murder and plunder innocent people.

Kahlan took command of the young recruits and set about dissuading them of their ignorant notions of a fair fight. She brought them to fully understand that their only goal was killing the invaders. It didn't matter how the Galeans came to stand over the corpses of those brutes, it only mattered that they did. In that undertaking of killing, there was no glory, there was simply survival. They were killing so that there could be life. Kahlan taught those recruits what they needed to know about fighting a force that greatly outnumbered them, and she shaped them into men who could accomplish the grim task.

The night before leading those young men into combat, Kahlan went alone into the enemy camp and killed their wizard along with some of the officers. The next day, those five thousand young men fought at her side, followed her instructions, learned from her, and along the way took terrible casualties, but they eventually killed every last one of the Imperial Order's fifty-thousand-man advance force. It had been an accomplishment rarely equaled in history.

That had been the first of many blows Kahlan struck against Jagang. In answer, he sent assassins after her. They failed.

In Richard's absence, after Nicci had taken him away to the heart of the Old World, Kahlan had gone to join Zedd and the D'Haran Empire forces. She found them dispirited and on the run after having lost a three-day battle. In Richard's place, carrying the Sword of Truth, the Mother Confessor pulled the army back onto its feet and immediately counterattacked, surprising the enemy and bloodying them. She brought backbone and fire to the D'Haran forces. She inspired them to the challenge. Captain Ryan's men arrived to join with her in the fight against Jagang's invading horde. For nearly a year, Kahlan led the D'Haran Empire forces as they frustrated Jagang's efforts to swiftly subdue the New World. She harried and harassed him without pause. She helped direct plans that resulted in Jagang's army losing hundreds of thousands of men.

Kahlan had bled the Imperial Order army, and helped grind them to a halt outside Aydindril. In winter, she had evacuated the people of Aydindril, and had the army take them over the passes into D'Hara. The D'Haran forces then sealed off those passes and, for the time being, held the Imperial Order at bay short of their final objective of conquering D'Hara and finally bringing the New World under the brutal rule of the Fellowship of Order.

Jagang's hatred for Kahlan was exceeded only by his hatred for Richard. Most recently, the dream walker had sent an extremely dangerous wizard named Nicholas after them. Richard and Kahlan had only narrowly escaped capture.

Richard knew that the Order relished seeing to it that captured foes suffered monstrous abuse, and there was no one, other than Richard, whom Emperor Jagang wanted to put to torture more than the Mother Confessor.

There were no lengths to which he would not go to get his hands on her. Emperor Jagang would reserve for Kahlan the most unspeakable torture.

Richard realized that he was standing frozen, trembling, his fingers gripping a fistful of balsam boughs. Cara silently watched him. He knelt and again started laying the branches in place while struggling to put terrible thoughts from his mind. Cara went back to her work. He put all his effort into concentrating on the task of completing their shelter. The sooner they got to sleep, the more rested they would be when they woke, and the faster they could travel.

Even though they were nowhere near any roads and a great distance from the trails, Richard still didn't want to have a fire for fear that scouting soldiers might spot it. Although they wouldn't be able see the fire's smoke through all the drizzle and fog, such weather tended to keep smoke low to the ground, drifting this way and that through the woods, so any Imperial Order patrols would be able to smell it. It was a real enough possibility that none of the others argued for a fire. Being cold was a lot better than having to fight for their lives.

Nicci dragged an armful of balsam boughs close as Richard continued to weave them up the lean-to. None of the others spoke, apparently absorbed in worry that whatever had killed the men might be out there, among the deepening shadows, hunting the four of them as they prepared to go to sleep in a fortress made of nothing more than balsam boughs.

Their first day's journey toward Altur'Rang had felt less like traveling and more like running for their lives. But whatever had killed Victor's men had not chased them. At least, Richard didn't think it had. He couldn't really imagine that whatever had the power to kill that many men in such a brutal fashion couldn't manage to catch up with them if it had their trail. Especially not something filled with a blood frenzy, as Nicci had described it.

Besides, when he was in the woods Richard usually knew when there were animals about and where they likely were, and, as a rule, he knew when people were close. Had Victor and his men not been camped quite so far from Richard, Kahlan, and Cara's camp, he would have known they were there. He also had a keen sense of when he was being pursued and if someone was following his trail. As a guide, he sometimes tracked people lost in the woods. He and other guides sometimes had contests to track one another. Richard knew how to watch for someone tracking him.

This, however, was less a matter of suspecting that someone was following them and more a feeling of icy dread, as if they were being chased by a murderous phantom in a blood frenzy. That fear constantly urged them to run. He knew, too, that running was often the trigger that made a predator pounce.

Richard realized, though, that it was only his imagination making him feel the hot breath of pursuers. Zedd had taught him that it was always important to understand why you had specific feelings so that you could decide if those feelings were caused by something that warranted attention, or something that didn't. Other than the palpable fear caused by the brutality of the slaughter, Richard had no evidence that they were being chased, so he tried to keep the emotion in proper perspective.

Fear itself often proved to be the greatest threat. Fear made people do thoughtless things that often got them into trouble. Fear made people stop thinking. When they stopped thinking, they often made foolish choices.

Several times when he was growing up, Richard had tracked people who had gotten lost in the vast forests around Hartland. One boy Richard had tracked for two days kept running in the dark until he eventually fell from a cliff. Luckily it wasn't a long fall. Richard found him at the bottom of the steep bank with a twisted ankle that was swollen but not broken. The boy was only cold, tired, and frightened. It could have been far worse and he knew it. He had been very glad to see Richard appear and held him tightly around the neck all the way home.

There were any number of ways to die out in the woods. Richard had heard of people attacked by a bear, or a cougar, or bitten by a snake. But he couldn't imagine what had killed Victor's men. He'd never seen anything like it. He knew it hadn't been soldiers. He supposed that it could have been the gifted using some kind of terrible power to slaughter the men, but he just didn't think that was the explanation.

He realized, then, that he was already thinking of it as a beast.

Whatever killed the men, Richard had taken precautions as they had set out. He followed shallow streams until they were a good distance from the sight of the slaughter. He was careful to lead them up out of the rushing water and away from the stream across ground where it would be much more difficult to track them. More than once throughout the day he had led them over bare rock or through water to make it extremely time-consuming for someone good at tracking to follow them. The shelter, too, was designed to blend into the surrounding woods. It would be hard to spot, unless someone passed very near to it.

Victor dragged a heavy load of balsam boughs close and laid them at Richard's feet. "Need more?"

With the toe of his boot, Richard nudged the pile, judging by its density how much and how well it would cover the remaining poles. "No, I think these and the ones Nicci is bringing should be enough."

Nicci dropped her load beside Victor's. It seemed odd to him seeing Nicci doing such work. Even dragging balsam boughs she had a regal look about her. While Cara was a strikingly beautiful woman as well, her audacious bearing made it seem rather natural for her to be building a shelter—or a spiked flail cocked to kill intruders. Nicci, though, looked unnatural working in the woods—as if she would complain about getting her hands dirty, although she never once did. It wasn't that she was at all unwilling to do whatever Richard needed her to do, it was just that she looked completely out of place doing it. She simply had a noble bearing that seemed too stately for the task of hauling branches for a shelter in the woods.

Now that she had brought all the balsam boughs that Richard needed, Nicci stood quietly under the dripping trees, hugging herself as she shivered. Richard's fingers were numb with cold as he quickly wove on the remaining boughs. He saw Cara, as she worked to secure the limbs, occasionally putting her hands under her armpits. Only Victor showed no outward appearance of being cold. Richard imagined that the blacksmith's glower was enough to warm him most of the time.

"Why don't you three get some sleep," Victor said as Richard placed the last of the boughs over the shelter. "I'll take watch for now if no one objects. I'm not much sleepy."

From the undercurrent of anger in the man's voice, Richard imagined that Victor might not be sleepy for quite a long while. He could certainly understand Victor's bitter sorrow. The man would no doubt spend his watch trying to think of what he would say to Ferran's mother and the relatives of the other men.

Richard laid an understanding hand on Victor's shoulder. "We don't know what we're up against. Don't hesitate to wake us if you hear or see anything at all unusual. And don't forget to come inside and have your share of sleep; tomorrow will be a long day of traveling. We all need to be strong."

Victor nodded. Richard watched as the blacksmith picked up his cloak and threw it around his shoulders before seizing roots and clinging vines to help him scale the rock above the shelter to where he would watch over them. Richard wondered if perhaps the outcome might have been different had Victor been with the men. Then he thought about the aftermath of splintered trees, deep gouges in the ground carved with such force that it had overturned rocks and torn thick roots apart. He remembered the ripped leather armor, the shattered bones, the rent bodies, and was glad that Victor had not been with the men when the attack had come. Even a heavy mace wielded in anger by the powerful arms of the master blacksmith would not have stopped whatever had come into that clearing.

Nicci pressed a hand to Richard's forehead, testing for fever. "You need rest. No watch for you tonight. The three of us will each take a turn."

Richard wanted to argue, but he knew that she was right. This was not a battle he should take up, so he didn't and instead nodded his agreement. Cara, obviously prepared to take Nicci's side if he argued, turned back from watching them from out of the small opening between the boughs.

From the gathering darkness all around a grating sound had begun to build into a shrill chirr. Now that they were finished with the effort of building the shelter, the noise was hard to ignore. It made the whole forest seem alive with raucous activity. Nicci finally took notice of it and paused to look around.

She frowned. "What is that sound, anyway?"

Richard plucked an empty skin from a tree trunk. Everywhere throughout the forest the trees were covered with the pale, tannish, thumb-sized husks.

"Cicadas." Richard smiled to himself as he let the gossamer ghost of the creature that had once lived inside roll into his palm. "This is what's left after they molt."

Nicci glanced at the empty skin in his hand and briefly looked at some of the others clinging to the trees. "While I spent most of my life in towns and cities, and indoors, I've spent a great deal of time outdoors since leaving the Palace of the Prophets. These insects must be unique to these woods; I don't recall ever seeing them before—or hearing them."

"You wouldn't have. I was a boy the last time I saw them. This kind of cicada emerges from underground every seventeen years. Today is the first day they all have begun to emerge. They will only be around for a few weeks while they mate and lay their eggs. Then we won't see them again for another seventeen years."

"Really?" Cara asked as she poked her head back out. "Every seventeen years?" She thought it over for a moment and then scowled up at Richard. "They better not keep us awake."

"Because of their numbers they create quite an unforgettable sound. With countless of the cicadas all trilling together, you can sometimes hear the harmonic rise and fall of their song moving through the forest in a wave. In the quiet of night, their stridulation may seem deafening at first, but, believe it or not, it will actually lull you to sleep."

Satisfied to know that the noisy insects would not keep her charge awake, Cara disappeared back inside.

Richard recalled his wonder when Zedd had walked with him through the woods, showing him the newly emerged creatures, telling him all about their seventeen-year life cycle. To Richard, as a boy, it was a memorable wonder. Zedd told him how he would be grown up when they came again, that he had first seen them as a boy, and the next time he would see them as a grown man. Richard remembered marveling at the event and promising himself that when they came again, he would be sure to spend more time watching the rare creatures when they appeared from the ground.

Richard felt a wave of profound sadness for the loss of that innocent time in life. As a boy, the emergence of the cicadas had seemed like just about the most amazing phenomenon he could imagine, and waiting seventeen years until they returned seemed like the hardest thing he would ever have to do. And now they were back.

And now he was a man. He cast the empty husk aside.

After Richard removed his wet cloak and crawled in behind Nicci, he pulled branches together to cover over the opening to the snug shelter. The thick branches toned down the high-pitched song of the cicadas. The ceaseless buzzing was making him sleepy.

He was pleased to see that the balsam boughs worked to shed the rain, leaving the cavelike refuge dry, if not warm. They had laid down a bed of boughs over the exposed ground so they would have a relatively soft and dry platform upon which to sleep. Even without rain dripping on them, though, the humidity and fog still dampened everything. Their breath came out in ephemeral clouds.

Richard was weary of being wet. Handling trees had left him covered with bark and needles and dirt. His hands were sticky from tree sap. He couldn't remember ever being so miserable with grime and grit clinging to his wet skin and wet clothes. At least the pine and balsam pitch left the shelter smelling pleasant.

He wished he could have a hot bath. He hoped that Kahlan was warm and dry and unharmed.

Tired as he was, and as sleepy as the sound of the cicadas was making him, there were things Richard needed to know. There were matters far more important to him than sleep, or his simple boyhood wonder.

He needed to find out what Nicci knew about what had killed Victor's men. There were too many connections to ignore. The attack had come right near where Richard, Kahlan, and Cara had been camped a few days before. More importantly, whatever had killed the men didn't seem to have left any tracks, at least none that he been able to find in his brief search, and, other than that displaced rock, Richard couldn't find any tracks from either Kahlan or her abductor.

Richard intended, before he slept, to find out what Nicci knew about what had killed the men.

Richard untied the leather thongs beneath his pack and opened his bedroll, spreading it out in the narrow space left between the other two.

"Nicci, back at the place where the men were killed you said that it had been a blood frenzy." He leaned back against the rock wall underneath the overhang. "What did you mean?"

Nicci folded herself into a sitting position to his right, atop her own bedroll. "What we saw back there wasn't simply killing. Isn't that obvious?"

He supposed she had a point. He had never witnessed a scene so shaped by rage. He was well aware, though, that she knew far more about it.

Cara curled up to his left. "I'm telling you," she said to Nicci, "I don't think he knows."

Richard cast a leery gaze at the Mord-Sith and then at the sorceress. "Knows what?"

Nicci ran her fingers back through her wet hair, pulling strands off her face. She looked a little puzzled. "You said that you got the letter I sent."

"I did." It had been quite a while back. He tried to remember through the daze of weariness and worry everything Nicci's letter had said— something about Jagang creating weapons out of people. "Your letter was valuable in helping figure out what was happening at the time. And I did appreciate your warning about Jagang's darker pursuits of creating weapons out of the gifted; Nicholas the Slide was as nasty a piece of work."

"Nicholas." Nicci spat the name before wrapping a blanket around her shoulders. "He is but a flea on the rump of the wolf."

If Nicholas was the flea, Richard hoped never to run into the wolf. Nicholas the Slide had been a wizard whom the Sisters of the Dark had altered to have abilities that were well beyond any human traits. It had been thought that accomplishing such conjuring with people was not only a lost art but impossible because, among other things, such nefarious work required the use of not only Additive but Subtractive Magic. While a rare few had learned to manipulate it, until Richard's birth there hadn't been anyone born with the actual gift for Subtractive Magic in thousands of years.

But there had been those who, even though they had not been born with that side of the gift, still had managed to gain the use of Subtractive Magic. Darken Rahl had been one such person. It was said that he had traded the pure souls of children to the Keeper of the underworld in exchange for dark indulgences, including the ability to use Subtractive Magic.

Richard supposed that it could also have been through morbid promises to the Keeper that the first Sisters of the Dark had contrived to obtain the knowledge of how to use Subtractive Magic, thereafter passing it on in secret to their covert disciples.

When the Palace of the Prophets had fallen, Jagang had captured many of the Sisters, both Sisters of the Light and Sisters of the Dark, but their numbers were dwindling. From what Richard had learned, the dream walker's ability enabled him to enter every part of a person's mind and thereby control them. There was no private thought he did not know or intimate deed he could not witness. It was an inner violation so complete that no hidden corner of the mind was safe from the dream walker's direct scrutiny. What was worse, the victim could not always tell if Jagang was lurking there, in their mind, witness to their most secret thoughts.

Nicci had said that the haunting possession by the dream walker had driven a few of the Sisters mad. Richard also knew that through that link Jagang could measure out excruciating pain and, if he wished it, death. With such control, the dream walker could make the Sisters do anything he wished.

Through an ancient magic created by one of Richard's ancestors to protect his people from the dream walkers of that time, those who swore fidelity to the Lord Rahl were protected. Along with the rest of his gift, Richard had inherited that bond and, with a dream walker again born into the world, it now safeguarded those loyal to him from Jagang stealing into their minds and enslaving them. While a formal devotion was spoken by the people of D'Hara to their Lord Rahl, the protection that the bond provided was actually invoked through the conviction of the person bonded— through their doing what they thought was called for by their fidelity.

Both Ann, the Prelate of the Sisters of the Light, and Verna, the woman

Ann had named as her successor, had stolen into the Imperial Order's camp and tried to rescue their Sisters. The captive Sisters had been offered the protection of the bond—all they had to do was accept in their hearts their loyalty to Richard—but most were so terrified of Jagang that more than once they had refused their chance at freedom. Not everyone was willing to embrace liberty; liberty required not just effort, but risk. Some people chose to delude themselves and see their chains as protective armor.

Nicci had once been in servitude to the Fellowship of Order, the Sisters of the Light, and then the Sisters of the Dark, and finally to Jagang. She no longer was; she had instead embraced Richard's love of life. Her steadfast loyalty to him and what he believed in had freed her from the clutches of the dream walker, but far more than that, it had freed her from the yoke of servitude she had worn her whole life. Her life was now hers alone. He thought that maybe that might have something to do with the resolute nobility of her bearing.

"I didn't read the whole letter," Richard admitted. "Before I was able to finish it, we were attacked by men that Nicholas had sent to capture us. I told you about it before—that was when Sabar was killed. During that fight the letter fell into the fire."

Nicci slouched back. "Dear spirits," she murmured. "I thought you knew."

Richard was tired and at the end of his patience. "Knew what?"

Nicci let her arms slip to her sides. She looked up at him in the dim light and let out a frazzled sigh.

"Jagang found a way for the Sisters of the Dark he holds captive to use their ability to begin creating weapons out of people, as had been done during the great war. In many ways, he is a brilliant man. He makes it his business to learn. He collects books from the places he sacks. I've seen some of those books. Among all sorts of tomes, he has ancient handbooks of magic from around the time of the great war.

"The problem is, while he may be a dream walker and brilliant in certain areas, he does not have the gift and so his understanding of it, of exactly what Han is and how this force of life functions, is crude at best. It's not easy for one without magic to comprehend such things. You have the gift and yet even you don't really understand it or know very much about how it works. But because Jagang doesn't know how to work magic, he blunders around demanding that things be done simply because he has dreamed them up, because he is the great emperor and he wishes his visions to be brought to life."

Richard rubbed his fingers back and forth on his brow, rolling off the dirt. "Don't sell him short in that regard. It's possible that he knows more about what he's doing than you realize."

"What do you mean?"

"I may not know a lot about the subject of magic, but one of the things I have learned is that magic can also be thought of much like an art form. Through artistic expression—for lack of a better term—magic that has never been before can be created."

Nicci stared in astonished disbelief. "Richard, I don't know where you could have heard such a thing, but it just doesn't work that way."

"I know, I know. Kahlan thinks I'm out on a limb with this, too. Having been raised around wizards, she knows a lot about magic and in the past she has flatly insisted that I'm wrong. But I'm not. I've done it before. Using the gift in such a way, in new and original ways, got me out of what would otherwise have been unbreakable traps."

Nicci was peering at him in that analytical way of hers. He suddenly realized why. It wasn't only what he'd said about magic. He was talking about Kahlan again. The woman who did not exist, the woman he had dreamed. Cara's expression betrayed her mute concern.

"Anyway," Richard said, getting back to the crux of the matter, "just because Jagang doesn't have the gift, doesn't mean he can't still dream up things—dream up nightmares—like Nicholas. It is through such original conceptualization that the most deadly things, for which there may be no conventional counter, are created. I suspect that this may have been the method those wizards in ancient times used for creating weapons out of people in the first place."

Nicci was beside herself with bottled agitation.

"Richard, magic just doesn't work like that. You can't dream up whatever you'd like to have, wish for what you want. Magic functions by the laws of its nature, just like all other things in the world. Whim will not make boards out of trees; you must cut the tree to the desired form. If you want a house, you can't wish up bricks and boards to stack themselves into a dwelling; you must use your hands to craft the structure."

Richard leaned toward the sorceress. "Yes, but it's the human imagination that makes those concrete actions not just possible, but effective. Most builders think in terms of houses or barns; they do what's been done before simply because that was what was done before. Much of the time they don't want to think, so they never envision anything more. They limit themselves to repetition and as an excuse they insist that it must be done that way because it has always been done that way. Most magic is like that—the gifted simply repeating what has already been done before, believing that it must be done that way with no more justification than that it has always been done that way.

"Before a grand palace can be built, it first has to be imagined by someone bold enough to have a vision of what could be. A palace will not spontaneously spring forth to the surprise of all while men are attempting to build a barn. Only the conscious act of conceptualization can bring about the reality.

"For that act of creative imagination to bring about the existence of a palace, it cannot violate any of the laws of the nature of the things that are used. On the contrary, the person who imagines a grand palace with the goal of seeing it built must be intimately aware of the nature of all the things he will use in the construction. If he isn't, the palace will fall down. He must know the nature of the materials better than the man who uses them to build a simple barn. It's not a matter of wishing for something that transcends the laws of nature, but a matter of original thinking based on those laws of nature.

"I grew up in the woods around Hartland, never having seen a palace." Richard spread his arms, as if to show her the things he had seen since leaving his homeland. "Until I saw the castle at Tamarang, the Wizard's Keep and the Confessors' Palace in Aydindril, or the People's Palace in D'Hara, I never imagined that such places existed—or even that they could exist. They were beyond the scope of my thinking at the time.

"And yet, even though I never imagined that such places could be built, other men thought them up, and they were built. I think that one of the important functions of grand creations is that they inspire people."

Nicci appeared not only to be swept up in his explanation, but to be considering his words with serious interest. "Do you mean to say, then, that you think an art form can also shape such important things as the function of magic?"

Richard smiled. "Nicci, you could not grasp the importance of life until I carved the statue back in Altur'Rang. When you saw the concept in tangible form you were able at last to put together all the things you had learned throughout your life and finally grasp its meaning. An artistic creation touched your soul. That's what I mean about an important function of great works is that they inspire people.

"Because it inspired you with the beauty of life, with the nobility of man, you acted to become free—something you had never thought was possible. Because the people of Altur'Rang as well could see in that statue what could and should be, they were stirred to stand up to the tyranny crushing their lives. It was not accomplished by copying other statues, by doing what was the accepted norm for statues in the Old World of showing man as weak and ineffective, but by an idea of beauty, a vision of nobility, that shaped what I carved.

"I didn't violate the nature of the marble I used, but rather I used the nature of the stone to accomplish something different than what others routinely did with it. I studied the properties of stone, I learned how to work it, and I sought to understand what more I could do with it in order to bring about my objective. I had Victor make me the finest tools that would enable me to do the work in the way it needed to be done. In that way I brought to reality what I wanted to create, what had never been before.

"I think that magic can work this way as well. I believe that such original ideas played a part in how weapons were once created out of people. After all, when such weapons were made, they were effective in large part because they were original, because they had never been thought of or seen before. In many instances, the other side in the war then had to work to create entirely new things out of magic that were able to counter those weapons. In many cases they were able to render the weapon obsolete by creating a countermagic, and then someone on the other side immediately went to work thinking up some new horror. If using magic creatively was not possible, then how did the wizards of old create weapons with it? You can't say they simply got the knowledge from a book, or from past experience; where and how would the first such weapons have originated if not with an original idea? Someone had to have used magic creatively in the first place.

"I think that Jagang is again doing this very thing with magic. He has studied some of what was done in the great war, what weapons were created, and learned from that. He sometimes may direct that what was once created to be created again, such as with Nicholas, but in other instances I think he imagines what has never been, what goes beyond what has been done before, and has it brought to reality by those who know how to use magic to build what he wants.

"In these acts of creation it isn't the work that is the most remarkable aspect, but the idea and vision that makes the labor effective, just as carpenters and bricklayers who built houses and barns can be employed to construct a palace. It wasn't so much their labor that was remarkable in the creation of palaces, but the act of insight and creation that gave it direction."

Nicci nodded ever so slightly in concentration as she weighed his words. "I can see that your notion isn't at all the wild idea I thought it was at first. This is a line of reasoning that I've never encountered. I'll have to think about the possibilities. You may be the first to really understand the mechanism behind Jagang's scheme—or, for that matter, behind the creations of wizards in ancient times. This would explain a great many things that have nagged at me over the years."

Nicci's words were spoken with intellectual respect for a concept new to her, but a concept she fully grasped. No one who had ever spoken to Richard about magic had ever treated his ideas with such an insightful understanding. He felt as if this was the first time anyone had truly understood what he saw.

"Well," he said, "I've had to deal with Jagang's creations. Like I said, Nicholas was a great deal of trouble."

In the dim light, Nicci studied his face for a moment.

"Richard, from what I was able to find out," she said in a soft voice, "Nicholas was not Jagang's actual goal. Nicholas was merely practice."

"Practice!" Richard thumped his head back against the wall. "I don't know, Nicci. I'm not so sure about that. Nicholas the Slide was a formidable creation and one nasty piece of work. You don't know the trouble he caused us."

Nicci shrugged. "You defeated him."

Richard blinked in astonishment. "You make it sound like he was just a bump in the road. He wasn't. I'm telling you, he was a frightening creation who nearly killed us."

Nicci slowly shook her head. "And I'm telling you, as formidable as he may have been, Nicholas was not what Jagang was after. You told me not to sell the dream walker short—don't you now do that same thing. He never thought Nicholas was fully your match.

"What you say about the process of imagination in creating new things actually makes sense, especially in this instance. It may even explain a few things. From the little I was able to learn, I believe that from the beginning Nicholas was only meant to expand the skills of the Sisters that Jagang had assigned to the task of creating weapons. Nicholas was not Jagang's objective, but simply practice on the way to that objective.

"With his dwindling number of Sisters that practice has gained a new urgency. Even so, he apparently has enough Sisters for the work of creating his weapons."

Richard felt goose bumps tingling up his arms as he began to realize the full implications of what Nicci was telling him.

"You mean to say that in creating Nicholas, it was like Jagang was just having his carpenters build a house as practice before he sends them on to build something vastly more complicated, like a palace?"

Nicci looked up at him and smiled. "Yes, that's it exactly."

"But he sent Nicholas with troops to govern a land as well as to capture us."

"A mere matter of convenience. Jagang had instilled in Nicholas a need to hunt you, but only as part of the testing for his greater goals. He didn't really expect the Slide to be able to accomplish his transcendent ambitions. The emperor may hate you for impeding his progress in conquering the New World, he may consider you unworthy as an opponent, and he may deem you an immoral heathen worthy only of death, but he's smart enough to give you credit for your ability. It's like when you said that you sent that captured soldier to assassinate Jagang. You didn't really expect that lone soldier to succeed at the difficult task of assassinating a well-guarded emperor, but the soldier was of no other value to you and since you thought that there was at least a chance that he might accomplish something, you might as well send him on the mission while you worked on far better ideas that you expected to have a more reasonable chance of success. And if the soldier was killed, then that was fine by you because he only got what was coming to him anyway.

"Nicholas was like that. He was a conjured creation, practice along the path to something altogether superior. In the scheme of things, Nicholas wasn't all that valuable to Jagang, so Jagang, instead of having him killed, used him. If Nicholas succeeded, then Jagang would be ahead of the game, and if you killed him, then you did him a service."

Richard ran his hand back over his hair. He felt overwhelmed at the implications. He had criticized Nicci for not being open to seeing the larger picture, and here he had just been guilty of doing the same thing.

"Well then," he asked her, "what do you think Jagang might conjure up that's worse than Nicholas the Slide?"

The drone of the cicadas seemed oppressive, invasive, at that moment, as if they were the enemy surrounding him.

"I believe he has forged ahead and already created such a masterwork," Nicci said with quiet finality. She pulled her blanket up around her shoulders and held it closed at her throat. "I think that's what those men back there in the woods faced."

Richard watched her expression in the near darkness. "What do you know about what Jagang has done?"

"Not a great deal," Nicci admitted. "Only a few words whispered as one of my former fellow Sisters was leaving on a journey."

"A journey?"

"To the world of the dead."

By her tone of voice and the way she stared off, Richard didn't want to ask what had brought about the woman's travel plans. "So, what did she tell you?"

Nicci let out a weary sigh. "That Jagang had been making things from the lives of captives and volunteers both. Some of those young wizards actually think they are sacrificing themselves for a greater good." Nicci shook her head at such a sad delusion. "The Sister was the one who told me that Nicholas was but a stepping-stone to His Excellency's true and noble ends." Nicci looked up again to make sure that Richard was paying attention. "She said that Jagang was on the brink of creating a creature similar to one he had found in ancient writings, but far better, far more deadly, and invincible."

The hair at the back of Richard's neck lifted. "A creature? What kind of creature?"

"A beast. An invincible beast."

Richard swallowed at the baleful sound of the word. "What's this creature do? Were you able to find out? What's its nature?"

For some reason, he just couldn't seem to bring himself to use the same word aloud right then, as if speaking it might summon it from out of the surrounding night.

Nicci's troubled eyes turned away. "As the Sister slipped into the arms of death, she smiled like the Keeper himself with a booty of souls, and said, 'Once he uses his power, the beast will at last know Richard Rahl. Then it will find him, and kill him. His life, like mine, is finally at its end.' "

Richard made himself blink. "Did she say anything else?"

Nicci shook her head. "At that point, she convulsed in the agony of death. The room went black as the Keeper snatched her soul in payment for bargains she had once struck.

"The one thing that's been troubling me is how this creature found us. Still, I don't think the situation is as desperate as it may seem. There is really no conclusive evidence to make us believe that it really was this beast that attacked the men back there. After all, you haven't used your power, so there wouldn't have been any way for Jagang's beast to find you."

Richard looked down at his boots. "When the soldiers attacked," he said in a low voice as he rubbed a finger along the edge of the leather sole, "I used my gift to deflect the arrows. I didn't do so well with the last one."

"Lord Rahl," Cara said, "I don't think that's true. I think you used your sword to deflect the arrows."

"You weren't there right then so you didn't see what was happening," Richard said as he grimly shook his head. "I was using my sword on the soldiers; I couldn't use it to deflect the dozens of arrows as well. I deflected the arrows with my gift."

Nicci was now sitting up straight. "You used your gift? How did you summon it?"

Richard shrugged self-consciously. He wished he knew more about what he'd done. "Through need, I guess. I didn't know I would end up being responsible . . ."

She gently touched his arm. "Don't foolishly blame yourself. You had no way to know. Had you not done as you did you would have been killed. You were acting to save your life. You didn't know anything about the beast. More than that, though, you may not be entirely responsible."

Richard frowned at her. "What do you mean?"

Nicci sank back against the rock wall. "I fear that I may have contributed to its finding us."

"You? But how?"

"I used Subtractive Magic to get rid of your blood so I could heal you. While the Sister didn't say anything specific that I could point to, I still got the uneasy feeling that this creature may somehow be tied to the underworld. If that's true, then when I got rid of your blood with the use of Subtractive Magic I may have inadvertently given it a taste of your blood, so to speak."

"You did the right thing," Cara said. "You did the only thing you could do. To let Lord Rahl die instead would have been handing Jagang what he sought."

Nicci nodded her appreciation of Cara's words.

Richard let out the breath he had been holding. "What else can you tell me about this thing?"

"Nothing of any consequence, I'm afraid. The Sister told me that the Sisters who were experimenting with creating weapons out of people had only created Nicholas to work out some of the preliminary details before moving on to their important work. Even so, some of them died in the task of conjuring the Slide—and, with as many as have already died, Jagang is getting to the point where he has few to spare. He has used those he still has, while he still has enough, to accomplish his goal. Apparently, creating the beast was vastly more complex and difficult than creating a Slide, but the results were said to have been worth it. I suspect that along the way he may have directed that shortcuts be taken, shortcuts that involve the underworld.

"If we're going to fight this thing, we need to find out everything we can about this beast. And we need to find out before it catches us. With what happened to the men, I don't think we have much time."

Richard knew that what she meant, but hadn't said, was that she wanted him to forget what she thought were his meaningless dreams about Kahlan and to put his full concentration and effort toward this dangerous creation of Jagang's.

"I have to find Kahlan," he said in a quiet tone meant to convey his conviction and his resolve.

"You can't do anything if you're dead," Nicci said.

Richard lifted the baldric over his head. He leaned the polished scabbard holding the Sword of Truth against the rock.

"Look, we're not even sure that whatever killed those men back there really is this beast you're talking about."

"What do you mean?" Nicci asked.

"Well, if it can find me when I use my gift, then why did it attack the men? Sure, it was the place where I'd used my ability, but the attack was three days after the fact. If it was supposed to know me after I used my power then why attack the men?"

"Maybe it just thought you were among them," Cara offered.

Nicci nodded. "Cara might be right."

"Maybe," Richard said. "But if it recognized me by me using my gift and in addition you gave it a taste of my blood, then wouldn't it know that I wasn't among the men?"

Nicci shrugged. "I don't know. It very well could be that by using your gift you only summoned it to the general area, but when you stopped using your ability then the beast was blind to you, so to speak. Maybe it was so angry that it just missed you it went into a frenzy of killing whoever was there. If that's true, then I would suspect that it needs you to again use your gift, now that it's close, to finally be able to catch you."

"But she said that once I used my gift it would know me. That doesn't sound to me like I need to use it again for it to find me."

"Maybe it does now know you," Nicci said. "But maybe it still needs to find you. Since it knows you, now, maybe all the beast needs is for you to again use your gift so that it can pounce."

That had a frightening kind of logic to it. "I guess it's good that I don't depend on my gift."

"You'd better make sure you let us protect you," Cara said. "I don't think you had better do anything that might even inadvertently cause you to use your magic."

"I'm afraid that I agree with Cara," Nicci said. "I'm not sure about it having a taste of your blood, but the one thing we do know for sure is what the Sister told me—that if you use your gift it will find you. As long as the beast is hunting you, and until we can learn more about it and nullify the threat, you must not use your gift for any reason."

Richard conceded with a nod. He didn't know if that was possible. While he didn't know how to call upon his gift, he wasn't sure that he knew how to prevent it coming forth, either. It was awakened by anger and answered a certain kind of need. He wasn't aware of the specific conditions that invoked his ability; it just happened. While their theory of not using his gift made sense, he wasn't sure he could actually control it enough to prevent it if conditions caused it to spring to life.

Another frightening thought occurred to him. It was possible that the beast had found him, and knew precisely where he was, and it had only killed the men out of blood lust. For all he knew, the beast could be out in the woods watching, using the noise of the cicadas to cover its footsteps as it approached their shelter.

In the dim light Nicci watched him. As he pondered the grim possibilities, she reached out again and felt his forehead.

Drawing back, she said, "We'd better get some rest. You're shivering with the cold. I'm afraid that in your condition you may lapse into a fever. Lie down. We'll all have to keep each other warm. But first, you need to be dry or you'll never get warm."

Cara leaned past Richard, toward Nicci. "How do you think you can get him dry without a fire?"

Nicci gestured. "Both of you, lie back."

Richard lay back; Cara hesitantly complied. Nicci leaned over them, placing a hand just above their heads. Richard felt the warm tingle of magic, but not an uncomfortable sensation like the last time. He could see the soft glow above Cara as well. It struck him how remarkable it was for Nicci to trust Cara enough to use magic on her. Using magic on a Mord-Sith gave them the opportunity to seize that magic in order to control the gifted person. Richard found it even more remarkable that Cara would trust Nicci enough to allow her to use magic on her. Mord-Sith did not like magic one bit.

Nicci's hands moved slowly downward, just above their bodies. By the time she reached Richard's boots, he realized that he felt dry. He ran a hand over his shirt, then his pants, and found that both were dry.

"How is that?" Nicci asked.

Cara was scowling. "I'd rather be wet."

Nicci arched an eyebrow. "I can arrange that, if you like."

Cara put her hands under her arms to warm them and remained silent. Satisfied that Richard was pleased, Nicci did the same for herself, moving both hands down her dress as if slowly pressing away the water.

When she finished, she was shivering and her teeth were chattering, but she and her black dress were dry.

Concerned by the way she wavered that she might pass out, Richard sat up and gently gripped her arm. "Are you all right?"

"I'm just exhausted," she admitted. "I've not had much sleep for days, on top of the effort of healing you and then the exertion of the traveling we did after the attack today. I'm afraid that it's all caught up with me. This bit of magic took what strength and warmth I had left. I just need to get some sleep, that's all. But even if you don't realize it, Richard, you need it even more. Lie back and sleep, now. Please. If we all lie close we can keep each other warm."

Dry, but weary and still cold, Richard wriggled into his bedroll. She was right; he did need rest. He couldn't get help for Kahlan if he wasn't rested.

Without hesitation, Cara pressed up close on his left to help get him warm. Nicci pushed in on his other side. The warmth was a relief. He hadn't realized how cold he was until the three of them crowded in tight together. He knew by how he felt that Nicci was right, that he wasn't fully well yet. At least he only needed rest and not magic.

"Do you think this beast could have taken Kahlan in order to get to me? he asked into the dark and quiet shelter.

Nicci was a moment in answering. "Such a creature needs no perverse method to get to you, Richard. From what the Sister said, and from what I fear I may have done, to say nothing of you having used your gift, the beast will be able to find you. From all those dead men back there, I fear it already has."

Richard felt the weight of guilt crush down upon him. If not for him, those men would be alive.

He had difficulty swallowing past the lump in his throat. He wished there were some way to undo what was done, some way to give them their lives and their futures back.

"Lord Rahl?" Cara whispered. "I would like to make a confession, if you will swear never to repeat it."

Richard had never heard her say such an odd thing. "All right. What is it that you wish to confess?"

Her answer was a while in coming, and then it was so soft he would not have been able to hear it were she not so close. "I'm afraid."

Almost against his better judgment, Richard lifted his arm around her shoulders and held her close. "Don't be. It's coming after me, not you."

She lifted her head and scowled at him. "That is the reason I'm afraid. After seeing what it did to those men, I'm afraid that it's coming for you and there is nothing I can do to protect you."

"Oh," Richard said. "Well, if it makes you feel any better, I'm afraid of that, too."

Cara laid her head back down on his shoulder, content to stay under the protective comfort of his arm. The surrounding strum of the cicadas somehow made him feel more vulnerable. The seventeen-year cycle of the insects was inescapable, inexorable, unstoppable.

So was Jagang's beast. How could he hide from such a thing?

"So," Nicci asked, apparently trying to lighten the somber mood in the shelter, "where did you meet this woman of your dreams?"

Richard didn't know if she was trying to soften the question with a little humor, or if she was being sarcastic. If he didn't know better he would have thought it sounded like jealously.

He stared up in the darkness as he thought back to that day. "I was out in the woods, looking for evidence of who had killed my father—the man I grew up thinking was my father, George Cypher, the man who'd raised me. That was when I spotted Kahlan moving along a trail around Trunt Lake.

"Four men were following her. They were assassins sent by Darken Rahl to kill her. He had already killed all the other Confessors. She is the last."

"So you rescued her?" Cara asked.

"I helped her. Together we were able to kill the assassins.

"She'd come to Westland looking for a long-lost wizard. It turned out that Zedd was the great wizard she had been sent to find—he still held the position of First Wizard, even though he had given up the Midlands and fled to Westland before I was born. The whole time I grew up I never knew that Zedd was a wizard, or my grandfather. I only knew him as my best friend in the world."

He could sense Nicci looking at him, and feel her warm, soft breath against the side of his face. "Why did she want this great wizard?"

"Darken Rahl had put the boxes of Orden in play. It was everyone's worst nightmare." Richard clearly recalled his dread at hearing that news. "He had to be stopped before he opened the correct box. Kahlan had been sent to ask this long-vanished First Wizard to appoint a Seeker. After that first day when I saw her by Trunt Lake, my life was never again the same."

Into the silence, Cara asked, "So, was it love at first sight?"

They were humoring him, trying to take his thoughts off the men who had been slaughtered by a beast sent by Jagang to kill him, trying to take his mind off the monster now coming for him.

The thought struck him that maybe somewhere back in the woods around where they had camped, somewhere in an undiscovered place where he hadn't looked, lay Kahlan's torn remains.

Such a thought was so painful to contemplate that it felt like it was crushing his heart.

Richard didn't reach up and wipe away the tear that ran down his cheek. But with a gentle touch, Nicci did. Her hand briefly, tenderly, caressed his cheek.

"I think we'd better try to get some sleep," he said.

Nicci drew back her hand and laid her head against his arm.

In the darkness, Richard couldn't seem to make his burning eyes close. Before long he could hear Cara's even breathing as she surrendered to sleep. Nicci softly pressed her cheek against his shoulder as she snugged up close in their shared warmth.

"Nicci?" he whispered.

"Yes?"

"What kind of torture does Jagang use on captives?"

He could feel Nicci take a deep breath and let it out slowly. "Richard, I'm not going to answer that question. I'm sure you have to know that Jagang is a man who needs killing."

Richard had had to ask the question. He was relieved that Nicci was kind enough not to answer it.

"When Zedd first gave me the sword, I told him that I would not be an assassin. I have since come to understand the principled value of preserving life through the task of killing evil men. I wish that driving the Imperial Order out of the New World was as simple as killing Jagang."

"I can't tell you how many times I wished I had killed him when I had the chance, even though you are right about it not ending the war. I wish I could stop thinking about all the opportunities I missed. I wish I could stop thinking about all the things I should have done."

Richard reached around her and held her trembling shoulders.

He felt her muscles slowly relax. Her breathing finally slowed as she slipped into sleep.

If he was to find Kahlan, Richard had to get the rest he needed. He closed his eyes as another tear leaked out. He missed her so much.

His thoughts lingered on that first day he saw Kahlan in the white, satiny smooth dress that he only much later found out distinguished her as the Mother Confessor. He remembered the way it hugged her shape, the way it made her look so noble. He remembered the way her long hair cascaded down around her shoulders, framing her in the dappled forest light. He remembered looking into her beautiful green eyes and seeing the gleam of intelligence looking back at him. He remembered feeling, from that first instant, from that first shared gaze, as if he had always known her.

He told her that there were four men following her. She asked, "Do you choose to help me?"

Before his mind could form a thought, he heard himself say, "Yes."

He had never for an instant been sorry that he said yes.

She needed help now.

His last thoughts as he drifted into tormented sleep were of Kahlan.

Ann hurriedly hung the simple tin lantern on the hook outside the door. She focused her Han into a bud of heat and it bloomed into a small flame in the air above her upturned palm. As she stepped into the small room, she gently sent the little flame flitting onto the wick of a candle on the table. As the candle came to life she closed the door.

It had been quite a while since she had a received a message in her journey book. She was impatient to get to it.

The room was sparse. The plain plastered walls had no windows. A small table and a straight-backed, wooden chair that she had asked to have brought in almost filled the space not used by the bed. Besides its use as a bedroom, the room also made a suitable sanctuary, a place where Ann could be alone, where she could think, reflect, and pray. It also provided privacy for when she used the journey book.

A small plate of cheese and sliced fruit sat waiting for her on the table. Jennsen had probably left the plate before going off with Tom to stare at the moon.

No matter how old Ann got, it invariably brought her a sense of warm inner satisfaction when she saw that look of love in a couple's eyes. They always seemed to think they did a fine job of hiding their feelings from others, but, as obvious as it usually was, they might as well be painted purple.

At times, Ann privately regretted that she had never had a time like that with Nathan, a time to indulge in complete, simple, extravagant attraction. Expressions of feelings, though, were deemed unbecoming for the Prelate.

Ann paused. She wondered exactly where she had come to have such a belief. When she had been a novice they didn't exactly hold classes in which they said, "Should you ever be appointed Prelate, you must always mask your feelings." Except disapproval, of course. A good prelate, with no more than a look, was supposed to be capable of making people's knees tremble uncontrollably. She didn't know where she had learned that, either, but she had always seemed to have had the knack.

Maybe all along it had been the Creator's plan for her to be the Prelate and He had given her the appropriate disposition for the job. How she sometimes missed it.

More than that, though, she had never allowed herself to consciously consider her feelings for Nathan. He was a prophet. When she was Prelate of the Sisters of the Light and sovereign authority at the Palace of the Prophets, he had been her prisoner—although they dressed it up in less harsh terms, trying to put a more humane face on it, but it had been no more complicated than that. It had always been believed that prophets were too dangerous to be allowed to run free in the world, among normal people.

In confining him from a young age they had denied the existence of free will, preordaining that he would cause harm even though he would never been given the chance to make a conscious choice in his own actions. They had pronounced him guilty without benefit of a crime. It had been an archaic and irrational belief that Ann had unthinkingly adhered to for most of her life. At times, she didn't like considering what that said about her.

Now that she and Nathan were both old and found themselves together—however improbable that might have seemed at one time—their relationship could not be described as extravagant attraction. Indeed, she had spent the vast majority of her life enduring her displeasure with the man's antics and seeing to it that he never escaped either his collar or his confinement in the palace, thereby insuring his intractable behavior, thereby incurring the ire of the Sisters, which made him more unruly yet, round and round in a circle.

No matter the uproar he had been able to ignite, seemingly at will, there had always been something about the man that made Ann smile, inwardly. At times he was like child. A child who was nearly a thousand years old. A child who was a wizard. A child who carried the gift for prophecy. A prophet had but to open his mouth, but to utter prophecy to the uneducated masses, and it would ignite riots at the least, war at the worst. At least, that had always been the fear.

Although she was hungry, Ann pushed the plate of cheese and fruit aside. It could wait. Her heart fluttered with the anticipation of what news the message from Verna might bring.

Ann sat and scooted her chair close to the simple wooden table. She pulled out the little leather-covered journey book and thumbed through the pages until she again spotted the writing. The room was small and dark. She squinted to help her better make out the words. She finally had to pull the fat candle a little closer.

My dearest Ann, began the message from Verna written in the book, *I hope this finds you and the prophet well. I know you said that Nathan was proving to be a valuable contribution to our cause, but I still worry about you being with that man. I hope his cooperation hasn't soured since last I heard from you. I admit to having difficulty imagining him being coopera-tive without a collar around his neck. I hope you are being cautious. I've never known the prophet to be entirely sincere—especially when he smiles!*

Ann had to smile herself. She understood all too well, but Verna didn't know Nathan the way Ann did. He could sometimes get them into trouble faster than ten boys bringing frogs to dinner, and yet, after all was said and done, after so many centuries knowing the prophet, there really wasn't anyone with whom she had more in common.

Ann sighed and turned her attention back to the message in the jour-ney book.

We have been kept quite busy warding off Jagang's siege of the passes into D'Hara, Verna wrote, *but at least we have been successful. Perhaps too successful. If you are there, Prelate, please answer.*

Ann frowned. How could one be too successful in keeping marauding hordes from overrunning your defenses, slaughtering your defenders, and enslaving a free people? She impatiently pulled the candle closer still. In truth she was quite jumpy over what Jagang was up to, now that winter had ended and the spring mud was past.

The dream walker was a patient foe. His men were from far to the south, in the Old World, and weren't used to the winters up north in the New World. While many had fallen victim to the harsh conditions, vast numbers died of the diseases that swept through his winter encampment. Despite losing men in battles, to sickness, and by a variety of other causes, more of the invaders poured north all the time so that, despite everything, Jagang's army inexorably continued to grow. Even so, the man did not waste any of his vast numbers in pointless and futile winter campaigns. He didn't care about the lives of his soldiers, but he did care about conquering the New World, so he only moved when the weather was not a factor. Jagang did not take risks he didn't need to. He simply, steadily, resolutely ground his enemies to dust. Bringing the world to heel was all that mattered to him, not how long it took. He viewed the world of life through the prism of the beliefs of the Fellowship of Order. Individual life, including his, was of no importance; only the contribution that a person's life could make to the Order was meaningful.

With such a vast army in the New World, the forces of the D'Haran Empire were now at the mercy of what the dream walker did next. To be sure, the D'Haran forces were formidable, but they certainly weren't enough to withstand, much less turn back, the full weight of the seemingly endless numbers of Imperial Order troops. At least, not until Richard did whatever he could to effect some change in the tide of war.

Prophecy said that Richard was the "pebble in the pond," meaning that he caused ripples that spread through everything, affected everything. Prophecy also said, in many different ways and in many different texts, that only if Richard led them in the final battle did they have a chance to triumph.

If he didn't guide them in that final battle, prophecy was clear and unambiguous; it said that all would be lost.

Ann pressed her fist against the queazy pain in the pit of her stomach and then pulled the stylus from the spine of the book that was the twin to the one Verna had.

I am here, Verna, she wrote, *but you are the Prelate now. The prophet and I are long dead and buried.*

It was a deception that had enabled the two of them to save a great many lives. There were times when Ann missed being Prelate and missed her flock of Sisters. She had dearly loved many of them, at least the ones who hadn't ended up being in truth Sisters of the Dark. The burning pain of that betrayal, not just of her but of the Creator, never eased.

Still, being free of such towering responsibility left her better able to put her mind to other, more important work. While she hated having lost her old way of life, of being Prelate and running the Palace of the Prophets, her calling was to a higher purpose, not to stone walls and the administration of an entire palace of Sisters, novices, and young wizards in training. Her true calling was helping to preserve the world of life. In order for her to do that, it was better that the Sisters of the Light and everyone else believed her and Nathan dead.

Ann sat up straighter when Verna's writing began appearing across the page.

Ann, I am comforted to have you back with me, if only in the journey book. There are so few of us left. I confess that sometimes I long for the days of peace back at the palace, the times when everything seemed to be so much easier and to make so much more sense and I only thought it was all so difficult. The world certainly has changed since Richard was born.

Ann couldn't argue with that. She popped a piece of cheese in her mouth and then leaned in and began writing.

I pray every day that such order and peace can again settle over the world and we can go back to complaining about the weather.

Verna, I am confused. What did you mean when you said that perhaps you were too successful in defending the passes? Please explain. I await your reply.

Ann leaned back in her straight-backed chair and chewed a slice of pear as she waited. Since her journey book was twinned with the one Verna had, anything written in one appeared at the same time in the other. It was one of the few ancient items of magic left from the Palace of the Prophets.

Verna's words again began moving across the blank page. *Our scouts and trackers report that Jagang has begun his move. Because he has not been able to break through the passes, the emperor has split his forces and is taking an army south. General Meiffert had been fearing that he would do something like this.*

It's not hard to guess his strategy. Jagang undoubtedly plans to take a large force of his troops down through the Kern Valley and then south around the mountains. Once he finally is clear of all the barriers he will swing around into the southern reaches of D'Hara and then head north.

This is the worst possible news for us. We can't abandon the protection of the passes, not while part of his army lies in wait on the other side. And yet, we cannot allow Jagang's forces to sweep up on us from the south. General Meiffert says we will have to leave sufficient forces here to guard the passes while the bulk of our army heads south to meet the invaders.

We have no choice. With half of Jagang's force to the north, on the other side of the passes, and half heading down to go around the mountains and come up from the south, that leaves the People's Palace right in the middle. Jagang is no doubt licking his chops over such a prospect.

Ann, I'm afraid I don't have much time. The entire camp is in an uproar.

We only just learned the news that Jagang has split his army and we are rushing to strike camp and start south.

I must also divide up the Sisters. So many have been lost that there are not many left to divide. At times I feel as if we are in a contest with Jagang to see who will be the last one with a Sister left. I fear what will happen to all these good people if none of us survive. If not for that, I would be satisfied to leave this world behind and join Warren in the spirit world.

General Meiffert says that we can't spare a moment and must be on our way at first light. I will be up the entire night with the arrangements, seeing to it that we have sufficient men and Sisters here to defend each of the passes, and inspecting the shields to make sure they are sound. If the Order's northern army were to break through up here, it would be a much quicker death for us.

Unless you have something important that must be discussed right now, I'm afraid that I must go.

Ann covered her mouth with a hand as she read. The news certainly was disheartening. She wrote an immediate reply, so as not to inconvenience Verna.

No, my dear, nothing important just now. You know that you are in my heart always.

A message came back almost immediately.

The passes are narrow so we have been successful at defending them. The Imperial Order can't use their overwhelming power in such narrow places. I feel confident the passes will hold. Since Jagang is stymied by not having been able to cross the mountains, this buys us time while he is forced to take an army all the way south and then back up into D'Hara, now that he has the weather to his advantage. Since this is the greatest danger and threat, I will be heading south with the army.

Pray for us. We will eventually be forced to meet Jagang's horde in the open plains where he has the room to throw the full weight of his forces against us. I am afraid that, unless something changes, we will have no chance to survive such a battle.

I can only hope that Richard fulfills prophecy before we are all dead.

Ann swallowed before answering. *Verna, you have my word that I will do what I must to see to it. Know that Nathan and I will be dedicated to the task of seeing prophecy fulfilled. Perhaps no one but you would truly un-*

derstand that this is what I have devoted myself to for over half a millen-nium. I will not abandon my cause; I will do whatever I can to see that Richard does what only he can. May the Creator be with you and all our brave defenders. You will all be in my prayers every day. Have faith in the Creator, Verna. You are prelate, now. Give that faith to all of those with you.

In a moment, a message began appearing. *Thank you, Ann. I will check my journey book every night as we travel to see if you have any news of Richard. I miss you. I hope we can be together again in this life.*

Ann carefully wrote her last reply.

Me too, child. Fair journey.

Ann leaned on her elbows and rubbed her temples. This was not good news, but it was not all bad. Jagang had wanted to break through the passes and end it swiftly, but the passes held and he had finally been forced to split his army and begin a long, grueling march. She tried to look at the bright side. They still had time. There were any number of things they could still try. They would think of something. Richard would think of something. Prophecy had promised that he held within him the chance for their salvation.

She couldn't allow herself to believe that evil would darken the world.

A knock on the door made her jump. She pressed her hand over her rac-ing heart. Her Han hadn't warned her that someone was about.

"Yes?"

"Ann, it's me, Jennsen," came the muffled voice from the other side of the door.

Ann replaced the stylus and tucked the journey book in her belt as she slid her chair back. She smoothed her skirts and took a deep breath to try to slow her heart back to normal.

"Come in, dear," she said as she opened the door, smiling at Richard's sister. "Thank you for the plate of food." She held an arm back toward the table. "Would you like to share it with me?"

Jennsen shook her head. "No, thank you." Her face, framed by red ringlets, was a picture of concern. "Ann, Nathan sent me. He wants you. He was quite urgent about it. You know how Nathan gets. You know how his eyes get all big and round when he's excited about something."

"Yes," Ann drawled, "he does tend to get that way when he's digging up mischief."

Jennsen blinked, looking a little startled. "I fear you may be right. He told me in no uncertain terms to come get you and bring you there straight-away."

"Nathan always expects people to squeak when he pinches." Ann gestured for the young woman to lead the way. "I guess I'd best see to it. Where is the prophet, then?"

Jennsen held her lantern up to light her way as she started out of the little room. "He's at a graveyard."

Ann caught the sleeve of Jennsen's dress. "A graveyard? And he wants me to come to this graveyard?" Jennsen looked back over her shoulder and nodded. "What is he doing in a graveyard?"

Jennsen swallowed. "When I asked him that, he said he was digging up the dead."

In a broad weeping willow growing on the grassy slope leading down to the graveyard, a mockingbird was spending its night repeating a variety of strident calls meant to defend its territory against interlopers. Ordinarily, a mockingbird's calls, although intended as threats to others of its kind, to Ann's ear could be quite lovely, but in the dead-still quiet of night, such piercing whistles, chatters, and whoops were jarring to her nerves. She could hear another mockingbird in the distance making similar threats. Even the birds couldn't achieve peace.

Plowing through the long, wild grasses, Jennsen pointed as she held the lantern up with her other hand so that Ann could see her way. "Tom said that we would find him down there."

Sweating from the long hike, Ann peered down into the darkness. She couldn't imagine what the prophet was up to. In all the time that she had known the man he had never done such a strange thing. He had done any number of strange things, to be sure, but this just wasn't one of them. As old as he was, one would think that he would want to avoid spending time in a graveyard any sooner than he had to.

Ann followed Richard's younger sister as she started down the hill, trying to keep up without running. It seemed like they had already walked half the night and she was winded. Ann hadn't known of this graveyard, all but forgotten out in a distant, uninhabited expanse of wilderness. She wished that she had thought to bring along some of the food sitting on the plate back in her room.

"Are you sure Tom is still down here?"

Jennsen looked back over her shoulder. "He should be. Nathan wanted him to stand guard."

"For what? To fight off the other body snatchers?"

"I don't know, maybe," Jennsen said without so much as a hint of a giggle.

Ann wasn't very good at making people laugh. She was good at making their knees tremble, but she just wasn't all that good at jokes. She guessed that a graveyard on a dark night wasn't a good place for jokes. It certainly was a good place to make the knees tremble.

"Maybe Nathan just wanted company," Ann suggested.

"I don't think that was it." Jennsen found a fallen section in the split-rail fence that surrounded the place of the dead and stepped over it. "Nathan asked me to bring you out here and he wanted Tom to stay and stand guard over the graveyard, I think to make sure there was no one around that he didn't know about."

Nathan liked being in charge; Ann guessed that being a gifted Rahl he could do no less. It was always possible that the whole thing was a pretense just to get Jennsen, Tom, and Ann to run around doing his bidding. The prophet was given to a sense of drama and a graveyard did tend to set a mood.

Actually, right then, Ann would have been happy were it nothing more than some idiosyncratic diversion of Nathan's. Unfortunately, she had the queazy feeling that it was something not at all so simple, or so innocuous as a bit of theatrics.

In all the centuries she had known him, Nathan had at times been secretive, deceptive, and occasionally dangerous, but never to evil ends— although that hadn't always been apparent at the time. During most of his captivity at the Palace of the Prophets he had tried the Sisters' patience until they were ready to scream and tear out their hair, yet he wasn't maliciously willful or contemptuous of good people. He had an abiding hatred of tyranny and an almost childlike glee about life. No matter how exasperating the man could be at times, and he could be exasperating in the extreme, Nathan had a good heart.

Almost since the beginning, despite the circumstances, he had been Ann's confidant and ally against the Keeper getting a foothold in the world of life and against evil people having their way over the innocent. He had worked hard to help stop Jagang. He had, after all, been the one to first show her a prophecy about Richard, five hundred years before he would be born.

Ann found herself wishing that it wasn't dark, and that they weren't in a graveyard. And that Jennsen didn't have such long legs.

It suddenly occurred to Ann why Nathan would need Tom to stand guard and "make sure no one was around that they didn't know about," as

Jennsen had put it. Just like Jennsen, the people in Bandakar were pristinely ungifted. They were devoid of that infinitesimal spark of the Creator's gift carried by everyone else in the world. That essential connection made everyone else subject to the reality and nature of magic. But for these people magic did not exist.

The absence of such an inherent, elemental nucleus of the gift not only made the pristinely ungifted immune to magic, but since they could not interact with what to them did not exist, it also made them invisible to the power of the gift.

If even one parent possessed the pristinely ungifted trait, then it was always passed on to the offspring. These people had originally been banished to preserve the gift in mankind's nature. It had been a terrible solution, to be sure, but as a result the gift had survived in the human race. Had such a solution not been undertaken, magic would long ago have ceased to exist.

Because prophecy was magic, it too was blind to these people. No book of prophecy had ever had anything at all to say about the pristinely ungifted, or about the future of mankind and magic now that Richard had discovered these people and ended the banishment. What would happen now was completely unknown.

Ann supposed that Richard would have it no other way. He did not exactly enthusiastically embrace prophecy. Despite what prophecy had to say about him, Richard by and large discounted it. He believed in free will. He took a dim view of the notion that there were things about himself that were predestined.

In all things in life, and in magic especially, there had to be balance. In a way, Richard's acts of free will were the balance to prophecy. He was the center of a vortex of forces. With Richard, prophecy was attempting to predict the unpredictable. And yet, it had to.

Most troubling was that Richard's free will made him a wild card in prophecy, even those prophecies in which he was the subject. He was chaos among patterns, disorder among organization, and as capricious as lightning. And yet, he was guided by truth and driven by reason, not whim or chance, nor was he arbitrary. That he could be chaos among prophecy and at the same time be completely rational was an enigma to her.

Ann worried greatly about Richard because such contradictory aspects of the gifted were occasionally a prelude to delusional behavior. The last thing they would want was a leader who was delusional.

But all of that was academic. The central problem was that while there was still time they had to find some way to make sure he took up the cause fated to him in the prophecies and to fulfil his destiny. If they failed, if he failed, then all was lost.

Verna's message sat like the shadow of death in the back of Ann's mind.

Having spotted their light, Tom appeared out of the darkness, sprinting through the long grass to meet them. "There you are," he said to Ann. "Nathan will be happy that you're finally here. Come on and I'll show you the way."

By the brief glimpse she got in the weak yellow light from the lantern, Tom's face looked troubled.

The big D'Haran led them deeper into the graveyard, where in areas there were rows of gently mounded graves outlined in stones. These had to be newer, because most of what Ann could see was nothing but tall grass that over time covered over stones and the graves they marked. In one area there were a few small granite gravestones. They were so weathered it could only be that they were ancient. Some of the graves were marked with simple boards with names carved in them. Most such markers had long ago turned to dust, leaving much of the graveyard looking like nothing more than a grassy field.

"Do you know what the fat bugs are that are making all the noise?" Jennsen asked Tom.

"I'm not sure," Tom said. "I've never seen them before. They suddenly seem to be all over the place."

Ann smiled to herself. "They're cicadas."

Jennsen frowned back over her shoulder. "They're what?"

"Cicadas. You wouldn't know what they are. At the last molt you would have probably still been a toddler, too young to remember. The life cycle of these cicadas with the red eyes is seventeen years."

"Seventeen years!" Jennsen said in astonishment. "You mean they only come out every seventeen years?"

"Without fail. After the females mate with these noisy fellows, they will lay their eggs in twigs. When they hatch, the nymphs will drop from the trees and burrow into the ground, not to emerge for another seventeen years where their life as adults will be brief."

Jennsen and Tom murmured their amazement as they moved on into the graveyard. Ann couldn't see much of anything else by the light coming from Jennsen's lantern, except the dark shapes of trees moving in the occasional muggy breeze. As the three of them quietly slipped through the graveyard, cicadas chirped incessantly from the darkness all around. Ann used her Han to try to sense if anyone else was about, but she didn't feel anyone other than Tom and somewhere in the distance one other person, no doubt Nathan. Since Jennsen was one of the pristinely ungifted, she was intangible to Ann's Han.

Like Richard, Jennsen had been fathered by Darken Rahl. Births of the pristinely ungifted, such as Jennsen's, had been an unexpected and random side effect of the magic of the bond carried by every gifted Lord Rahl. In ancient times, when that trait began to spread, the solution had been to banish the pristinely ungifted, sealing them away in the forgotten land of Bandakar. After that, all ungifted offspring of the Lord Rahl were put to death.

Unlike any past Lord Rahl, Richard had been jubilant to discover that he had a sister. He would never allow her to be put to death for the nature of her birth, nor would he allow her and those like her to be forced into banishment.

Even though Ann had been around these people for some time now, she was still not used to how disorienting it could be. Even when one of them was standing right in front of her, Ann's ability said that there was no one there. It was a haunting sort of blindness, a loss of one of her senses that she had always taken for granted.

Jennsen had to take long strides to keep pace with Tom. To keep up with the two of them, Ann had to trot.

And then, as they came around a small knoll, a stone monument loomed up into view. The light from the lantern lit one side of a rectangular stone base that was a little taller than Ann, but not as tall as Jennsen. The coarse stone was heavily weathered and pitted, with stone molding carved around recessed squares on the sides. If it had ever been polished, the stone no longer showed any evidence of it. As the lantern light swept across the surface, it revealed layers of dirty discoloration from great age as well as the mottled growth of mustard-colored lichen. Atop the imposing base sat a large carved urn with stone grapes hanging out over one side. Grapes were a favorite of Nathan's.

As Tom led them around the front of the stone monument, Ann was astonished to see that the rectangle of stone sat off kilter.

On the far side, faint light oozed up from beneath it.

It appeared that the entire monument had been pivoted aside, revealing steep stone steps that led down into the ground, down into the soft glow of light.

Tom gave them both a meaningful look. "He's down in there."

Jennsen leaned over a little and peered into the steep cavity. "Nathan is down there? Down those steps?"

"I'm afraid so," Tom told her.

"What is this place?" Ann asked.

Tom shrugged apologetically. "I'm afraid I have no idea. I didn't even know this was here until just a little while ago when Nathan showed me where I could find him. He told me to send you down just as soon as you got here. He was pretty insistent about it. He doesn't want anyone knowing this place is here. He wanted me to stand lookout and keep any people away from the graveyard, although I really don't think anyone ever comes out here anymore, especially at night. The Bandakaran people aren't the kind to go looking for an adventure."

"Unlike Nathan," Ann muttered. She patted Tom's muscled arm. "Thank you, my boy. Best do as Nathan said and stand watch. I'll go down and see what this is all about."

"We'll both go," Jennsen said.

Driven by worried curiosity, Ann immediately started down the dusty steps. Jennsen followed close on her heels. A landing turned them to the right and down another flight. At a third landing, a long run of stairs turned to the left. The dusty stone walls were uncomfortably close together. The ceiling hunkered low, even for Ann; Jennsen had to crouch. It felt to Ann like she was being swallowed down though a moldering gullet into the graveyard's belly.

At the bottom of the steps she halted to stare in disbelief. Jennsen let out a low whistle. Beyond was not a dungeon, but a strange, twisting room unlike any Ann had ever seen. The stone walls zigged and zagged at odd angles, each of its own design and independently of the others. Plastering covered some of the stone walls. In a series of the convoluted angles, the whole room snaked off into the distance, disappearing around projections and pointed corners.

The place had a strange orderly disorder about it that Ann found somewhat unsettling. Dark niches here and there in the plastered walls were surrounded with faded blue symbols and decorations that had flaked off in places. There were words as well, but they were too old and dull to be legible without careful study. Bookshelves as well as ancient wooden tables, all layered in dirt, sat in several places up against the angled walls.

Dead-still cobwebs, heavy with dust, hung everywhere like drapes meant to decorate the room beneath the graves. Dozens of candles sat on tables and in some of the empty niches, giving the whole place a soft, otherworldly glow, as if all the dead above Ann's head must periodically descend to this place to discuss matters important only to the deceased, and to welcome new members into their eternal order.

Beyond the diaphanous curtains of dust-choked cobwebs, amongst four massive tables that had been dragged together, stood Nathan. Disorderly stacks of books were piled high all around him on the tables.

"Ah, there you are," Nathan called from his book fort.

Ann cast a sidelong glance at Jennsen.

"I had no idea that this place was down here," the young woman said in answer to the question that remained unasked on Ann's tongue. Points of candlelight danced in her blue eyes. "I didn't even know this place existed."

Ann looked around again. "I doubt anyone in the last few thousand years knew this place existed. I wonder how *he* found it."

Nathan snapped a book shut and placed it on a pile behind him. His straight white hair brushed his broad shoulders as he turned back. His hooded, dark azure eyes fixed on Ann.

Ann caught the unspoken meaning in Nathan's gaze. She turned to Jennsen. "Why don't you go up and wait with Tom, my dear. It can be a lonely job standing watch in a graveyard."

Jennsen looked disappointed, but seemed to understand their need to be left to their business. She flashed a smile. "Sure. I'll be right up top if you need anything."

As the sound of Jennsen's footsteps on the stone stairs dwindled away into a distant, echoing whisper, Ann struck a weaving course through the vails of cobwebs.

"Nathan, what in the world is this place?"

"No need to whisper," he said. "See how the walls turn at all those odd angles? It cuts the echo."

Ann was a little surprised to hear that he was right. Usually, the echo in stone rooms was annoying, but this odd twisting room had the hush of the dead.

"There's something strangely familiar about the shape of this place."

"Concealment spell," the prophet said, offhandedly.

Ann frowned. "What?"

"The configuration of the whole thing is in the form of a concealment spell." He gestured to each side when he saw the puzzled look she gave him. "It's not the layout of the entire place, the placement of rooms and the course of the various halls and passageways—like at the People's Palace—that is the spell-form, but rather it's the precise line of the walls themselves that make up the spell-form, as if someone drew the spell large on the ground and then simply built the walls touching right against that line before hollowing out the middle. Because the walls are a uniform thickness, that means that the outside of the walls are also the shape of the spell-form, so that tends to reinforce the whole thing. Quite clever, actually."

For such a spell to work, it had probably been drawn in blood and with the aid of human bones. There would have been an ample supply of those at hand.

"Someone certainly went to a lot of trouble," Ann said as she appraised the space again. This time she began to recognize some of the shapes and angles in opposition. "What exactly is this place used for?"

"I'm not entirely sure," he admitted with a sigh. "I don't know if these books were meant to be buried with the dead for all time, or they were being hidden, or there was some other purpose." Nathan beckoned with his hand. "This way. Let me show you something."

Ann followed him through several of the zigzags, around turns, and past yet more shelves lined with dusty books, until they reached an area of niches three high to each side.

Nathan leaned an elbow against the wall. "Look there," he said as he pointed a long finger downward, indicating one of the low, arched openings in the stone wall.

Ann stooped and peered inside. It contained a body.

All that was left were bones clothed in dusty tatters of robes. A leather belt circled the waist while a strap crossed over one shoulder. Skeletal arms were folded over the chest. Gold chains hung around the neck. Ann could see by the glint of light off the medallion on one of the chains that Nathan must have lifted it for a look, and in so doing his fingers had cleaned off the dust.

"Any idea who he is?" she asked as she straightened and folded her hands before herself.

Nathan leaned down close to her.

"I believe he was a prophet."

"I thought there was no need to whisper."

He arched an eyebrow as he straightened his frame to its considerable height. "There are a number of other people interred here." He flicked a hand off toward the darkness. "Back that way."

Ann wondered if they could all be prophets as well. "And the books?"

Nathan leaned down again, and whispered again. "Prophecy."

She frowned and looked back the way they had come. "Prophecy? You mean all of them? Those are all books of prophecy?"

"Most of them."

Excitement bubbled up through her. Books of prophecy were invaluable. They were the rarest of jewels. Such books could offer guidance, provide answers they needed, spare them futile endeavors, fill in gaps in their knowledge. Perhaps more than at any other time in history, they needed those answers. They needed to know more about the final battle in which Richard was supposed to lead them.

As of yet they had not discovered when this battle was to take place. With the frustrating vagary of prophecy, it could yet be many years off. For that matter, it was even possible that it was not to take place until Richard was an old man. With all the difficulties they had faced in the past several years, they could only hope that it was still many years off and they would have time to prepare. Prophecy could help with that.

The vaults at the Palace of the Prophets had been filled with thousands of volumes of prophecy, but they had all been destroyed along with the palace to prevent it from falling into the hands of Emperor Jagang. Better to lose such works for all time than allow evil to look upon their pages.

But no one knew of this place. This place was hidden beneath a concealment spell. The dizzying possibilities spun through Ann's mind.

"Nathan . . . this is wonderful."

She turned and looked up at the man. He was watching her in a way that made her fidgety. She reached out and placed a hand on his arm.

"Nathan, this is more than we could ever have hoped."

"This is something more than that," he said cryptically as he started back. "There are books here that make me doubt my sanity," he said with a sullen flourish of an arm.

"Ah," Ann quipped as she followed along in his wake, "verification at last."

He halted and turned a glare on her. "This is nothing to joke about."

Ann felt goose flesh ripple up her arms. "Show me then," she said in a serious tone. "What is it you've found?"

He shook his head, seeming to lose his momentary flash of ill humor. "I'm not even sure." His usual flamboyance was nowhere in evidence as he moved in among the tables he'd dragged together. His dark mood turned guarded. "I've been sorting the books."

Ann wanted to hurry him along and get to the meat of his discovery, but she knew that when he was troubled it was best to let Nathan explain things in his own way, especially when there was arcane speculation involved.

"Sorting them?"

He nodded. "These here in this pile don't appear to be of any real use to us. Most are prophecy long since outdated, contain only irrelevant records, or are in unknown languages—things like that."

He turned and slapped a hand to the top of another stack. Dust boiled up. "These here are all books that we had back at the palace." He swept his hand back and forth in front of the stacks of books piled high on the table behind him. "All of them. This whole tableful."

Her eyes wide, Ann glanced at the shelves and niches going back along the strange room. "There are a great many more books other than these you have here on the tables. This is only a fraction of them."

"Indeed. I haven't had a chance to even begin to look at them all yet. I finally decided that I'd better send Tom off to find you. I wanted you to see what I've discovered. That, and there is a lot of reading to do. I've been pulling out one book at a time, checking through it, and placing it in one one of the piles on these tables."

Ann wondered how many books could still be viable, could still be usable, after thousands of years underground. She had found books before that had been ruined by the effects of time and the elements, especially mildew and water. She peered around, inspecting the walls and ceiling, but she saw no evidence of water leaking through.

"At first glance, none of these books look to be damaged by water. How can this place underground be so dry? It would seem that water would seep in through the joints in the stone and make everything down here wet and moldy. I can hardly believe that the books appear to be in such good condition."

"*Appear* being the operative word," Nathan said under his breath.

She turned back to scowl at him. "What do you mean?"

He waved a hand irritably. "In a moment. In a moment. The interesting thing is, the ceiling and walls are sheathed in lead to help keep out the water. The place also has a shield of magic around it for even more protection. The entrance, too, was shielded."

"But the Bandakar people have no magic and their land was sealed off. There was no one with magic to shield against."

"That seal to their banished land finally failed, though," Nathan reminded her.

"Yes, that's right, it did." Ann tapped a finger against her chin. "I wonder how that happened."

Nathan shrugged. "How isn't so important for now, although I am concerned about it."

He flipped a hand, as if setting aside the issue. "For the moment, that it did is what's meaningful. Whoever put these books here wanted them hidden and protected—and they went to a great deal of trouble to insure that they remained that way. The ungifted people here wouldn't be hindered by shields, the weight of the stone monument would be an obstacle in and of itself, but they would have no reason to want to move it in the first place unless they had a good reason to believe something was under it. What would cause them to suspect such a thing? The fact that this place has remained undisturbed for thousands of years proves that they never realized that this place was down here. I believe that the shields were placed to ward any invaders who might eventually make it into Bandakar, like Jagang's men did."

"That makes sense, I suppose," she murmured as she considered it. "Not really expecting that the seal to Bandakar would ever be breached, the shields were a simple act of precaution."

"Or prophecy," Nathan added.

Ann look up. "There is that." It would take a wizard of Nathan's ability to breach such shields. Even Ann didn't have the ability necessary for some shields. She knew, too, that there were shields placed in ancient times that could only be passed with the aid of Subtractive Magic.

"It's also possible that these books were simply placed here as a way of safekeeping such valuable works—in case anything happened to others of their kind."

"You really think they would go to this much trouble to do such a thing?" she asked.

"Well, all the books at the Palace of the Prophets were lost, now, weren't they? Books of prophecy are always at risk. Some have been destroyed, some have fallen into enemy hands, and some have simply disappeared. Places like this provide a backup for those other works—especially if prophecy foretells the need of such a contingency."

"I guess you could be right. I have heard about rare finds of prophecy that had been secreted away to preserve them, or to keep innocent eyes from viewing them." She shook her head as her gaze scanned the room. "Still, I've never heard of any find to approach the likes of this one."

Nathan handed her a book. Its ancient red leather cover was faded nearly to brown. Even so, there was something familiar-looking about it, about the faded gilded ribs on the spine. She lifted the cover and the first blank page.

"My, my, my," Ann softly mused as she saw the title. "The *Glendhill Book of Deviation Theory*. How very wonderful to hold this in my hands again." She closed the cover and clasped the book to her breast. "It's like an old friend come back from the dead."

The book had been one of her favorite volumes on forked prophecy. Because it was a pivotal volume that held valuable information about Richard, she had studied it and referred to it so often over the centuries as she waited for him to be born that she practically knew it by memory. She had been heartbroken that it had to be destroyed along with all the rest of the books in the vaults at the Palace of the Prophets. There was still a great deal of information in it about the possibilities of what was yet to come.

Nathan plucked another volume from a stack and waggled it before her as he arched an eyebrow. "*Precession and Binary Inversions*."

"No!" She snatched it from his hands. "It can't be."

None of the accounts could ever say for sure that the elusive volume had in fact ever really existed. Ann herself had hunted for it, at Nathan's request, whenever she traveled. She'd also had trusted Sisters look for it whenever they went on a journey. There had been leads, but none of the clues ever resulted in anything but dead ends.

She looked up at the tall prophet. "Is this real? Many accounts deny that it ever really existed."

"Missing, according to some. A mere myth, according to others. I read a little of it and by the branches of prophecy it fills in, it can only be genuine—or a brilliant fake. I'd have to study it further to tell which, but from what I've seen, so far, I tend to believe it's genuine. Besides, what purpose would there be in hiding a fake? Fakes are generally created in order to exchange them for gold."

That was true enough. "And here it was all the time. Buried beneath the bones."

"Along with what I suspect may be a great many other volumes that are just as valuable."

Ann clicked her tongue as she again gazed about at all the books, her sense of awe growing by the moment. "Nathan, you've uncovered a treasure. A treasure of incalculable value."

"Perhaps," he said. When she shot him a puzzled frown, he lifted a hefty tome off the top of another stack. "You won't even believe what this is. Here. Open it and read the title yourself."

Ann reluctantly set down *Precession and Binary Inversions* in order to take the heavy book from Nathan. She set it on the table, too, and bent close. With great care, she lifted open the cover. She blinked, then straightened.

"*Selleron's Seventh Task!*" She gapped at the prophet. "But I thought there was only one copy and it was destroyed."

One side of Nathan's mouth cocked with a quirky smile. He held up another book "*Twelve Words Left for Reason.* I found *Destiny's Twin* as well." He waggled a finger at a pile. "It's in there somewhere."

Ann's jaw worked for a moment until the words finally came. "I thought we had lost those prophecies for all time." The odd smile still on his lips, he only watched her. She reached out and gripped his arm. "Could we be so fortunate that there really were copies made?"

Nathan nodded, confirming her guess. The smile ghosted away.

"Ann," he said as he handed her *Twelve Words Left for Reason*, "take a look through here and tell me what you think."

Puzzled by the grim expression that had settled on his face, she placed the book in a clear spot and began carefully turning pages. The writing was a little faded, but no more so than any book its age. For as old as it was, it was still in good condition and quite legible.

Twelve Words Left for Reason was a book containing twelve core prophecies and a number of ancillary branches. Those ancillary branches, when carefully cross-referenced, connected actual events to a number of other books of prophecy that were otherwise impossible to place chronologically. The twelve core prophecies actually weren't all that important. It was the ancillary branches that served to link other trunks and branches in the tree of prophecy that made *Twelve Words Left for Reason* so invaluable.

Chronology was often the most trying problem facing those working with prophecy. It was often impossible to tell if a prophecy was going to unfold the next day, or the next century. Events were in a constant state of flux. The setting of prophecy in the context of time was essential, not just to know when a particular prophecy was to become viable, but because what was of overriding importance next year might be nothing more than an unimportant minor event if set in the environment of the year after. Unless they knew which year the prophecy took place, they didn't know if it foretold danger or simply a matter of note.

Most prophets, when they set down their prophecy, left it up to those who would come later to fit it into its proper place in real-world events. There was no clear consensus on whether this had been done deliberately, through carelessness, or because the prophet, in the throes of having his visions, had never realized how important, and difficult, it would later be to chronologically place his vision. She had often observed with Nathan that a prophecy was so crystal-clear to the prophet himself that he simply failed to comprehend how formidable a task it would be for others to read and fit into the puzzle of life.

"Wait," Nathan said as she turned the pages. "Go back a page."

Ann glanced up at him and then flipped the vellum back.

"There," Nathan said as he tapped a finger to the page. "Look here. There are several lines missing."

Ann peered at the small gap in the writing, but didn't see what was so meaningful about it. Books often had spaces left blank for a wide variety of reasons.

"So?"

Rather than answer, he rolled his hand, motioning for her to go on. She started flipping over the pages. Nathan thrust his hand in to stop her and tapped another blank spot so she would note it. He then urged her to continue.

Ann noticed that the blank places became more frequent. Finally, she came to entire pages that were blank. Even that, though, was not unheard of. There were any number of books that simply ended in the middle. It was thought that the prophet who had been working on such books had most likely died and those coming after didn't want to interfere with what a predecessor had done, or perhaps they wanted to work on branches of prophecy which were more interesting or relevant to them.

"*Twelve Words Left for Reason* is one of the few books of prophecy that is chronological," he reminded her in a soft voice.

She knew that, of course. That was what made the book such a valuable tool. She couldn't imagine, though, why he had felt it important to point it out.

"Well," Ann said with a sigh as she reached the end, "it is odd, I suppose. What do you make of the blank places?"

Rather than answer her directly, he handed her another book. "*Subdivision of Burkett's Root.* Take a look."

Ann turned the pages of yet another priceless find, looking for something out of the ordinary. She came across three blank pages followed by more prophecy.

She was growing impatient with Nathan's game. "What am I supposed to see?"

Nathan was a moment in answering. When he finally did, his voice had that quality about it that tended to run shivers up her spine.

"Ann, we had that book down in the vaults."

She was still not following what was obviously of critical importance to him. "Yes, we did. I remember it quite well."

"The copy we had didn't have those blank pages."

She frowned and then turned back to the book. She leafed through the pages again until she found the empty spot.

"Well," she said as she studied the place where the prophecy ended and then where an entirely new branch of prophecy resumed after the empty pages, "maybe whoever made this copy, for some reason, decided not to include some of it. Perhaps they had sound reason to believe that the particular branch had been a dead end and, rather than include dead wood in the tree of prophecy, they simply left it out. Such pruning is not uncommon. Then, because they didn't want to make it appear they were trying to deceive anyone, they went ahead and left the appropriate space blank to denote the deletion."

She looked up. The prophet's azure eyes were fixed on her. Ann felt sweat trickle down between her shoulder blades.

"Take a look at *The Glendhill Book of Deviation Theory*," he said in a quiet voice without taking his penetrating gaze from her.

Ann broke contact with that gaze and pulled the copy of *The Glendhill Book of Deviation Theory* close. She flipped through the pages as she had done with the previous book, if a little faster.

There were blank pages, only more of them.

She shrugged. "Not a very accurate copy, I'd say."

Nathan impatiently reached in with a long arm and turned the stack of pages back to the front.

There, on a page at the beginning, all alone, was the author's mark.

"Dear Creator," Ann whispered when she saw the little symbol. It still glimmered with the magic the author had invested in his mark. She felt goose bumps tingle up from her toes. "This is isn't a copy. It's the original."

"That's right. If you recall, the one we had in the vaults was a copy."

"Yes, I remember that ours was a copy."

She had assumed this one as well had been one of a number of copies. Many of the books of prophecy were copies, but that didn't diminish their value. They were checked and marked by respected scholars who then left their own mark to vouch for the copy's accuracy. A book of prophecy was valued for the precision and veracity of its content, not because it was the original. It was the prophecy itself that was valuable, not the hand that had set it down.

Still, to see the original of a book she loved as much as she loved this particular volume was a memorable experience. This was the actual book, written in the hand of the prophet who had given these precious prophecies.

"Nathan . . . what can I say. This is a personal delight for me. You know how much this book means to me."

Nathan took a patient breath. "And the blank pages?"

Ann shrugged with one shoulder. "I don't know. I'm not really prepared to venture a guess. What are you getting at?"

"Look at the place where the blanks fit into the text."

Ann turned her attention back to the book. She read a little of the text before one of the blank areas, then read some of what followed. It was a prophecy about Richard. She randomly picked another blank place, reading before the blank area and after. It was another section about Richard.

"It would seem," she said as she studied a third place, "that the blanks appear in places where it talks about Richard."

Nathan was getting more edgy looking by the moment. "That's only because most of *The Glendhill Book of Deviation Theory* is about Richard. That pattern of blank pages associated with him doesn't hold true when you start looking at the other books."

Ann lifted her arms and let them fall to her sides. "Then I give up. I don't see what you see."

"It's what we're not seeing. It's the blank places that are the problem."

"What makes you say that?"

"Because," he said with a little more force in his voice, "there is something quite odd about those blank sections."

Ann pushed a stray wisp of gray hair back into the bun she always wore at the back of her head. She was becoming frazzled.

"Like what?"

"You tell me," he said. "I would bet that you could practically quote *The Glendhill Book of Deviation Theory.*"

Ann shrugged. "Perhaps."

"Well, I *can* quote it. The copy we had back in the vaults, anyway. I went through this book, testing it against my memory."

For some reason, Ann's stomach was churning with anxiety. She began to dread that the copy they had back in the vaults at the palace might have had fraudulent prophecy filling in what the original author had left blank. That was almost too overwhelming a deception to contemplate.

"And what did you discover?" she asked.

"That I can quote this original exactly. No more, no less."

Ann sighed in relief. "Nathan, that's wonderful. That means that our copy wasn't filled with fabricated prophecy. Why would you be troubled because you can't remember blank places? They are blank, there is nothing there. There is nothing *to* remember."

"The copy we had back at the palace didn't have any blank places."

Ann blinked as she thought back. "No, it didn't. I remember it well." She offered the prophet a warm smile. "But don't you see? If you can quote this one, no more or no less, and you learned it from our copy, then that means that whoever made the copy simply pulled the text together rather than include the meaningless blank places left by the original prophet. The prophet probably left blank places as a provision in case he had any further visions about the prophecies and he needed to add to what he had already written. Apparently, he never had that need, so the blanks remain."

"I know that there were more pages in our copy."

"I'm not following you, then."

This time it was Nathan who threw up his hands. "Ann, don't you see? Here, look at the book." He turned it toward her. "Look at this next-to-last branch of prophecy. It's one page and then six blank pages. Do you remember *any* branch of prophecy in our copy of *The Glendhill Book of Deviation Theory* that was only one page? No. None were this short. They were too complex. You know that there is more to the prophecy, I know there is more to the prophecy, but my mind is as blank as these pages. What was there is not only missing from the book, but it's missing from my mind as well. Unless you can quote me the rest of the prophecy that you know should be there, then it's missing from your mind as well."

"Nathan, that's just not—I mean, I don't see how . . ." Ann sputtered in confusion.

"Here," he said as he snatched a book from behind him. "*Collected Origins*. You must remember this."

Ann reverently lifted the book from his hands. "Oh, Nathan, of course I remember it. How could one forget such a short but beautiful book."

Collected Origins was an exceedingly rare prophecy in that it was written entirely in story form. Ann loved the story. She had a soft spot for romance, although she never admitted it to anyone. Since this tale of romance was actually a prophecy, that made it an official requirement that she be familiar with it.

She smiled as she lifted open the cover of the small book.

The pages were blank.

All of them.

"Tell me," Nathan said in that quietly commanding, deep Rahl voice, "what is *Collected Origins* about?"

Ann opened her mouth, but no words would come forth.

"Tell me, then," Nathan went on in that quietly powerful voice of his that seemed as if it could crack stone, "a single line of this beloved volume. Tell me who it is about. Tell me how it started, how it ended, or anything in the middle."

Her mind was stark naked blank.

As she stared up into Nathan's cutting gaze, he leaned a little closer. "Tell me one single thing you remember from this book."

"Nathan," she finally managed to whisper, her own eyes wide, "you often used to keep this book in your rooms. You know it better than I do. What do you remember about *Collected Origins*?"

"Not . . . one . . . thing."

Ann swallowed. "Nathan, how can we both not remember a book we love as much as we do this one? And why is it that the specific parts we both don't remember correspond to the blank spots?"

"Now, *that* is a very good question."

An idea suddenly hit her. She gasped in a breath. "A spell. It has to be that these books were spelled."

Nathan made a face. "What?"

"Many books are spelled to protect the information. I've not encountered it with a book of prophecy but it's common enough in books of instruction on magic. This place was designed with the intent of concealment. Perhaps that's what is happening with the information protected here."

Such a spell would be activated when anyone but the right person with the required power opened it. Spells of that nature were sometimes even keyed to specific individuals. The usual method of protection if the wrong person saw the book was to erase from their memory everything they'd seen in it. They would see it and at the same time forget it. The effect in one's mind was to blank out the text.

Nathan didn't answer, but his scowl softened as he considered her idea. She could tell by his expression that he doubted her theory was the answer but he apparently didn't want to argue the point just then, probably because he had something more important that he wanted to go on to.

Sure enough, he tapped a finger on top of a small stack of books standing all by themselves. "These books," he said with a weighty undertone, "are predominantly about Richard. I've never seen most of them before. I find that alarming, that such books would be hidden away in a place like this. Most have extensive stretches of blank pages."

For that many books of prophecy, especially about Richard, not to have been at the Palace of the Prophets was indeed alarming. For five centuries she had scoured the world for copies of any book she could find that contained anything at all about Richard.

Ann scratched an eyebrow as she considered the implications. "Were you able to learn anything?"

Nathan picked up the volume on the top and flipped the book open. "Well, for one thing, this symbol, here, troubles me greatly. It's an exceedingly rare form of prophecy, undertaken while the prophet was under siege by a storm of revelation. Such graphic prophecies are drawn in the heat of a powerful vision, when writing would take too long and interrupt the rush of what is rampaging through his mind."

Ann was only vaguely aware of such representational prophecy. She recalled a few from the vaults at the palace. Nathan had never before mentioned to her what they had been, and no one else had known. Yet another of Nathan's little thousand year old secrets.

She bent close and studied the intricate drawing that took for itself most of a page. There were no straight lines in it at all, only curved swirls and arcs that eddied all around in a circular design that somehow seemed almost alive. Here and there the pen had dug violently into the surface of the vellum, ploughing up parallel rows of fibers where the two halves of the pen's point had spread under the pressure. Ann lifted the book closer to a candle and carefully examined a curious place that was particularly rough. She saw in the ancient dried bed of an inky pool a fine, pointed sliver of metal: one side of the pen's point had broken off where it had been stabbed into the page. It was still embedded there. Right after, the cleaner marks of a fresh pen began anew, although they were no less forceful.

Nothing in the ink drawing represented any identifiable subject—it appeared to be completely nonobjective—and yet it was for some reason so gravely disturbing that it made her hackles lift. It seemed as if the drawing was almost recognizable but its meaning was just outside of her conscious awareness.

"What is it?" She laid the book on the table, open to the drawing. "What does it mean?"

Nathan stroked a finger along his strong jaw. "It's rather hard to explain. There are no precise words to describe what comes as a picture in my mind when I view it."

"Do you think," Ann asked with exaggerated patience as she clasped her hands, "that you could make an effort to describe to me as best you can the picture in your mind?"

Nathan viewed her askance. "The only words I can think of that fit are 'the beast comes.' "

"The beast?"

"Yes. I don't know what the impression means. The prophecy is partially cloaked, either deliberately or perhaps because it's meant to represent something I've never encountered before, or maybe even because it's linked to the blank pages and without their associated text the drawing won't fully come to life for me."

"What is it that this beast is coming to do?"

Nathan flipped the cover closed so that she could see the title: *A Pebble in the Pond*.

Cold sweat broke out across her brow.

"The symbol is a graphic warning," he said.

Prophecy often referred to Richard as the "pebble in the pond." The text of such a volume would probably be of incalculable value. If only it weren't missing.

"You mean, it's a warning for Richard that some kind of beast is coming?"

Nathan nodded. "That's about as much as I can get from this—that and a vague impression of the ghastly aura around the thing."

"Around the beast."

"Yes. The supporting text preceding the drawing would have been critical to understanding it better, to being able to comprehend the nature of this beast, but that text is missing. The branches after are blank as well so there is no way to place the warning contextually or chronologically. For all I know, it could be something he has already faced and defeated, or something that in his old age might defeat him. Without at least some of the supporting prophecy or a context there simply isn't any way to tell."

Chronology was vital to understanding prophecy, but just from the dread that she felt when viewing the drawing, Ann didn't believe it was anything Richard had yet faced.

"Perhaps it's meant as a metaphor. Jagang's army behaves like a beast and they could certainly be described as ghastly. They slaughter everything in their path. For free people, and for Richard especially, the Imperial Order is a beast coming to destroy them and everything they hold dear."

Nathan shrugged. "That very well could be the explanation. I just don't know."

He paused a moment before he went on. "There is one more disturbing bit of oblique counsel to be found not only in this book but in several of the other books"—he cast a meaningful look her way—"books that I've never seen before."

For a whole variety of reasons, Ann, too, found it disturbing to learn that there were all these books hidden in such a strange, underground, graveyard room.

Nathan gestured again to the books stacked all over the four large tables. "While there certainly are copies of a number of books we've seen, and I've showed those to you, most of these books are new to me. For any library to deviate to this degree from the classic masterworks is unprecedented. Each library has its own unique volumes, to be sure, but this place is like another world altogether. Nearly every volume in here is an astonishing discovery."

Ann's caution awakened. She had the uncanny feeling that Nathan had at last arrived at the core of the labyrinth through which his mind traveled. One thing he had just said loomed in the back of her mind.

"Counsel?" She frowned suspiciously. "What sort of counsel?"

"It advises the reader that if their interest is not of a general nature but they instead have cause to seek more extensive and specific knowledge on the subjects therein, then they should consult the pertinent volumes kept with the bones."

Ann's brow drew even tighter. "Kept with the bones?"

"Yes. It referred to these caches as 'central sites.' " Nathan leaned close again, like a washwoman with a load of dirty gossip. "The 'central sites' are mentioned in a number of places, but I've so far only been able to find where one of these sites was named: the catacombs beneath the vaults at the Palace of the Prophets."

Ann's jaw fell open. "Catacombs . . . That's preposterous. There was no such place beneath the Palace of the Prophets."

"None we knew of," Nathan said in a grave tone. "That doesn't mean it didn't exist."

"But, but," Ann stammered, "that's just not possible. It's just not. Such a thing could not have gone unnoticed. In all that time Sisters lived there we would have known."

Nathan shrugged. "In all this time no one knew of this place, here, beneath the bones."

"But no one lived right above here."

"What if the presence of catacombs beneath the palace was not common knowledge? After all, we know little of the wizards of that time, and not a great deal about the specific people involved in the construction of the Palace of the Prophets. It could be that they had reason to conceal such a place, just as this place was concealed."

Nathan arched an eyebrow. "What if part of the purpose of the palace—the training of young wizards—was part of an elaborate ruse to hide the existence of such a secret site?"

Ann could feel her face going red. "Are you suggesting that our calling was meaningless? How dare you even suggest that all our lives have been devoted to nothing more than a deception, and that the lives of those with the gift would not have been spared had we not—"

"I'm not suggesting anything of the kind. I'm not saying the Sisters were being duped or that what they did didn't spare the lives of boys with the gift and help preserve it. I'm only saying that these books suggest that there may have been more to it. What if there was not only the intent to have a place for the Sisters to practice their useful calling, but there was in part a grander purpose behind the place where they practiced that calling? After all, think of the graveyard above us; it has a valid reason to exist, but it also conveniently provides a shroud to hide this place.

"Perhaps such catacombs were deliberately covered over thousands of years ago with the intent of hiding them? If so, then by design we would never be aware of their existence. If it was a secret cache there wouldn't have been any records of it.

"From the impression I got from the references in these books, I have reason to believe that there were at one time books that were considered so disturbing and in some cases containing spells so dangerous that it was decided that they had to be confined to a few hidden 'central sites' as a precaution, so that they didn't end up in circulation, where they would be copied, as is the practice with most prophecy. What better way to restrict access? Since these references speak of 'the books kept with the bones,' I suspect that these other 'central sites' may be catacombs like the one said to be beneath the Palace of the Prophets."

Ann slowly shook her head as she tried to take it all in, as she tried to imagine if there was any possibility that it could be true. She looked again at the table with the stacks of books that were mostly about Richard, and which they had never seen before.

Ann gestured. "And these, here?"

"What is there I almost wish I'd not read."

Ann clutched his sleeve. "Why? What did you read?"

His seemed to catch himself. He waved a dismissal, smiled briefly, and changed the subject.

"What I find the most troubling about the blank places in the books is their common thread. While not all of the missing text is in prophecy about Richard, I have determined that they all do have one thing in common."

"And what would that be?"

Nathan held up a finger to emphasize his point. "Every one of the missing portions are in prophecies that pertain to a time after Richard was born. None of the prophecies that belong to a time before Richard's birth, or thereabouts, have copy missing."

Ann carefully clasped her hands together as she considered the mystery and how to solve the puzzle.

"Well," she said at last, "There is one thing we could check. I could have Verna send a messenger to the Wizard's Keep in Aydindril. Zedd is there protecting the place so that it can't fall into Jagang's hands. We could have Verna send a messenger and ask that Zedd check specific places in his copies of books we have here and see if they are missing the same text."

"That's a good idea," Nathan said.

"With the extent of the libraries at the Keep, he's bound to have a number of the classic books on prophecy that we recognize and have here."

Nathan's face brightened. "As a matter of fact, it would be even better if we could have Verna send someone to the People's Palace in D'Hara. While I was there I spent a lot of time in the palace libraries. I clearly remember seeing copies of a number of these books. If we had someone check them, that would tell us if the books here are spelled, as you suggested, and the problem is confined to these editions, or if it's some kind of wider phenomenon. We need to have Verna send someone to the People's Palace at once."

"That should be easy enough. Verna is just about to depart for the south. On their way they will no doubt be traveling near the People's Palace."

Nathan frowned down at her. "You heard from Verna? And she said she is heading south? Why?"

Ann's mood sank. "I received a message from her earlier tonight—just before I came here."

"And what did our young prelate have to say? Why is she traveling south?"

In resignation, Ann let out a deep sigh. "I'm afraid the news is not the best. She said that Jagang has split his army. He is taking part of his horde down around the mountains in order to sweep up into D'Hara from the south. Verna is leaving with a large contingent of the D'Haran forces to eventually stand and face the Order's army."

The blood drained from Nathan's face.

"What did you say?" he whispered.

Ann puzzled at his wide-eyed look. "You mean, that Jagang split his army?"

She didn't think it was possible, but the prophet's face went even more ashen.

"Dear spirits preserve us," he whispered. "It's too soon. We're not ready."

Ann felt a tingling dread start at her toes and begin working its way up her legs. Her thighs prickled with gooseflesh. "Nathan, what are you talking about? What's wrong?"

He turned and frantically searched the spines of the books stacked all over the tables. He finally found what he wanted in the middle of a pile and yanked it out, letting the rest of the stack topple over. He hurriedly leafed through the book, muttering to himself as he searched.

"Here it is," he said as he pressed a finger to a page. "There are any number of prophecies down here that I've found in books I've never seen before. These prophecies surrounding the final battle are veiled to me—I cannot see them in visions—but the words are frightening enough. This one sums them up as clearly as any."

He bent close and in the candlelight read to her from the book. " 'In the year of the cicadas, when the champion of sacrifice and suffering, under the banner of both mankind and the Light, finally splits his swarm, thus shall be the sign that prophecy has been awakened and the final and deciding battle is upon us. Be cautioned, for all true forks and their derivatives are tangled in this mantic root. Only one trunk branches from this conjoined primal origin. If *fuer grissa ost drauka* does not lead this final battle, then the world, already standing at the brink of darkness, will fall under that terrible shadow.' "

Fuer grissa ost drauka was one of the prophetic names for Richard. It was from a well-known prophecy in the ancient language of High D'Haran. Its translation was *the bringer of death*. To here call him by that name in this prophecy was a means of linking the two prophecies in a conjugate fork.

"If the cicadas should come this year," Nathan said, "then that will verify that this prophecy is not just authentic but active."

Ann's knees felt weak. "The cicadas began to emerge today."

Nathan stared down at her like the Creator Himself pronouncing judgment. "Then the chronology is fixed. The prophecies have all tumbled into place. Events are marked. The end is upon us."

"Dear Creator protect us," Ann whispered.

Nathan slipped the book into his pocket. "We must get to Richard."

She was already nodding. "Yes, you're right. There is no time to lose."

Nathan glanced about. "We certainly can't take all these books with us and there is no time to read them. We must seal this place back up, like it was, and leave immediately."

Before Ann could add her agreement, Nathan swept out an arm. The candles all extinguished. Only the lantern on the corner of one of the tables remained lit. On his way past, he swept it up in his big hand.

"Come on," he said.

Ann scurried to catch up with him, trying to stay in the small circle of light now that the odd room had been plunged into darkness. "Are you sure that we shouldn't take any of these books?"

The prophet rushed into the narrow stairwell, the light funneling in with him. "We can't be slowed down to carry them. Besides, which would we take?" He paused momentarily to look back over his shoulder. His face was all angles and sharp lines in the harsh lanternlight. "We already know what prophecy says and now, for the first time, we know the chronology. We must get to Richard. He has to be there at the battle when the armies clash or all will be lost."

"Yes, and we will have to make sure that he is there to complete the word of prophecy."

"We are in agreement, then," he said as he turned and rushed onward up the stairs. The tunneled stairwell was so narrow and low that he had trouble making his way up.

At the top, they burst out into the night, to the shrill, buzzing song of the cicadas. Nathan called out for Tom and Jennsen. The trees gently swayed in the humid breeze as they waited for an answer. It seemed an eternity, but it was really only a moment before both Tom and Jennsen came running out of the darkness.

"What is it?" Jennsen asked, breathlessly.

The dark shadow of Tom towered at her side. "Is there trouble?"

"Grave trouble," Nathan confirmed.

Ann thought that he might be a little more discreet about it, but as serious as the situation was, discretion probably was pointless. He pulled the book he had taken from the library out of his pocket. He opened it to a blank page where prophecy was missing.

"Tell me what this says." he commanded, holding it out to Jennsen.

She frowned at him. "What it says? Nathan, it's blank."

He grumbled his discontent. "That means Subtractive was somehow involved. Subtractive is underworld magic, the power of death, so it affects her the same as us."

Nathan turned back to Jennsen. "We have found prophecy that pertains to Richard. We must find him or Jagang will win the war."

Jennsen gasped. Tom let out a low whistle.

"Do you know where he is?" Nathan asked.

Without hesitation, Tom turned a little and lifted an arm to point off into the night. His bond told him what their gift could not. "He is that way. Not a great distance, but not close, either."

Ann peered into the darkness. "We'll have to get our things together and be on our way at first light."

"He's on the move," Tom said. "I doubt you will find him there in that spot by the time you get there."

Nathan cursed under his breath. "There's no telling where that boy is heading."

"I'd guess that he is headed back to Altur'Rang," Ann said.

"Yes, but what if he doesn't stay there?" He laid a hand on Tom's shoulder. "We will need you to come with us. You are one of the covert protectors to the Lord Rahl. This is important."

Ann saw Tom's hand gripped tightly around the knife at his belt. The silver hilt of that knife was emblazoned with the ornate letter "R," standing for the House of Rahl. It was a rare knife carried by rare individuals who worked unseen to protect the life of the Lord Rahl.

"Of course," Tom said.

"I'll come as well," Jennsen added in a rush. "I only have to get—"

"No," Nathan said, silencing her. "We need you to stay here."

"Why?"

"Because," Ann said in a more sympathetic tone than Nathan had used, "you are Richard's link with these people. They are in need of help in understanding the wider world only just opened to them. They are vulnerable to the Imperial Order and vulnerable to being used against us. They have only just made the choice to be part of our cause and part of the D'Haran Empire. Richard needs you to be here for now, and right now Tom's place is with us and his duty to Richard."

With panic in her eyes, she looked to Tom. "But I—"

"Jennsen," Nathan said, his arm encircling her shoulders, "look there." He pointed down the stairwell. "You know what's down there. If anything happens to us, Richard may need to know as well. You must be here to guard this place for him. This is important—just as important as Tom coming with us. We're not trying to spare you danger; this may in fact be more dangerous than going with us."

Jennsen looked from Nathan's eyes to Ann's and reluctantly recognized how serious the situation was. "If you think Richard might need me here, then I must stay."

Ann touched her fingertips to the underside of the young woman's chin. "Thank you, child, for understanding the importance of this."

"We must close this place up, like it was when I found it," Nathan said, swirling his arms with his urgency. "I'll show you the mechanism and how to make it function. Then we must get back to town and gather our things. We will only be able to snatch a few hours' sleep before sunrise, but it can't be helped."

"It's a long walk out of Bandakar," Tom said. "After we're over the mountain pass we'll have to find some horses if we're to catch Lord Rahl."

"It's decided then," the prophet said. "Let's get this tomb closed back up and be on our way."

Ann frowned. "Nathan, this cache of books has been hidden under this gravestone for thousands of years. In all that time no one has ever discovered it was there. Just how did you manage to find it?"

Nathan lifted an eyebrow. "Actually, I didn't think it was all that difficult."

He stepped around to the front of the huge stone monument and waited for Ann to come closer. Once she had, he held up his lantern.

There, carved into the face of the ancient stone were but two words: NATHAN RAHL.

It was late afternoon by the time Victor, Nicci, Cara, and Richard passed through the long shadows among the olive groves covering the southern hills outside of Altur'Rang. Richard had never eased the pace and they were all tired from the arduous, if relatively short, journey. The chill rain had moved on, pushed away by the oppressive weight of heat and humidity. With as much as they were all sweating, it might as well have still been raining.

Even though he was bone-weary, Richard felt better than he had only a couple of days before. Despite the exertion, his strength was gradually returning.

He was also relieved that they had seen no sign of the beast. Several times he had let the others go on while he checked their backtrail to see if they were being followed. He had never seen any sign of anyone or anything following behind them and so he was starting to breathe a little easier. He also had to consider the possibility that Nicci's information about Jagang creating such a monster was not the explanation for what had killed Victor's men. Even if, as Nicci said, Jagang had succeeded in creating such a beast, that didn't mean that it was the explanation for the violent and deadly attack or even that this beast had yet begun to hunt Richard. But if that wasn't it, then he couldn't even begin to imagine what it could have been.

Carts, wagons, and people moved at a brisk pace along the crowded roads around the city. Commerce seemed to be flourishing even more than the last time Richard had been in Altur'Rang. Some of the people recognized Victor, and some Nicci. Since the revolt, both of them had played important roles in Altur'Rang. A good number of the people recognized Richard, either because they had been there the night the revolution for their liberty had begun, or because they recognized his sword. It was a unique weapon and the polished silver and gold scabbard was hard to miss, especially in the Old World under the drab rule of the Order.

People smiled at the four of them as they passed, or tipped a hat, or gave them a friendly nod. Cara eyed every passing smile with suspicion.

Richard would have been pleased to see the emerging vitality in Altur'Rang had his mind not been on things far more important to him. And to deal with those important matters, he needed horses. Since it was so late in the day, it would be dark before he could hope to have horses and supplies collected and ready for a journey. He was reluctantly reconciled to spending the night in Altur'Rang.

Many of the people on the bustling country lanes and roads around the city seemed to be traveling to and from nearby towns, or possibly even places much farther. Whereas people once came to the city in the desperate hope of finding work at building the emperor's palace, they now arrived filled with optimism that they would be able to find a new life, a free life.

Every one of the people traveling away from the city, besides carrying goods for trade, also carried word of the profound changes since the revolt. They were an army carrying the bright shining weapon of an idea. In Altur'Rang they no longer had to mold their lives around their fear of the Order; they could now shape their lives to their own needs and aspirations made possible by personal liberty and their own enterprise. They owed their lives to no one. Swords could enforce tyranny, but only if it relentlessly crushed such ideas.

Ultimately, only brutality could enforce the irrationality and dead end of self-sacrifice.

That was why the Order would have to send its most savage troops to crush the very idea of liberty. If they didn't, then liberty would spread and people would prosper. If that came to be, then liberty would triumph.

Richard noticed that new market stands seemed to have sprung up at junctions of what had once been little more than rutted paths and lanes but were now active byways. The stands sold goods of every sort, from a variety of vegetables to stacks of firewood to rows of jewelry. Merchants at the outskirts of the city eagerly offered travelers a variety of cheeses, sausages, and breads. Closer to the city, people milled about, scrutinizing bolts of cloth or inspecting the quality of an array of leather goods.

Richard remembered how when Nicci had first brought him to Altur'Rang they'd had to stand in lines all day for a loaf of bread and often the store would run out before they ever got anywhere near the front of the line. So that everyone could afford bread, bakeries had been strictly regulated and prices had been fixed by a whole variety of committees, boards, and layers of ordinances. No consideration was given to the cost of ingredients or labor, only to what was judged to be the price people could afford to pay. The price of bread had seemed cheap, but there was never enough bread, nor any other foodstuff. Richard considered it a perversion of logic to call something unavailable inexpensive. Laws that the hungry be fed had only resulted in widespread hunger haunting the streets and dark homes of the city. The true cost of the altruistic ideas that spawned such laws was starvation and death. Those who championed the lofty notions of the Order were indignantly blind to the endless misery and death they caused.

Now, at stands on almost every corner, bread was plentiful and starvation looked to have receded into nothing more than a horrific memory. It was amazing to see how freedom had made everything so plentiful. It was amazing to see so many people in Altur'Rang smiling.

The revolt had been opposed by a good number of people who supported the Imperial Order, who wanted things to continue the way they were. There were many who believed that people were wicked and deserved no more out of their lives than misery. Such people believed that happiness and accomplishment were sinful, that individuals, on their own, could not make their own lives better without causing harm to others. Such people scorned the very idea of individual liberty.

For the most part, those people had been defeated—either killed in the fighting or driven away. Those who had fought for and won their liberty had fierce reasons to value it. Richard hoped that they would have the will to hang on to what they had won.

As they passed into the older sections of the city, he noticed that many of the dingy brick buildings had been cleaned so that they almost looked new. Shutters were painted bright colors that actually looked cheerful in the hazy, late-afternoon sun. A number of the buildings that had been burned down in the revolt were already being rebuilt. Richard thought it a wonder, after the way it used to be, that Altur'Rang could look cheerful. It gave him a flutter of excitement to see a place so alive.

He knew, too, that it was the simple, sincere happiness of people pursuing their own interests and living their lives for the sake of themselves that would draw the hate and wrath of some. The followers of the Order believed that mankind was inherently evil. Such people would stop at nothing to suffocate the blasphemy of happiness.

As they turned onto a broader street that led deeper into the city, Victor came to a stop at a corner of major thoroughfares.

"I need to go see Ferran's family and the families of some of the other men. If it's all right with you, Richard, I think I should speak with them alone, for now at least. The grief of sudden loss and important visitors are a confusing mix."

Richard felt awkward being viewed as an important visitor, especially to people who had just lost loved ones, but in the midst of such bad news it was not the time for him to try to soften that view.

"I understand, Victor."

"But I was hoping that maybe later you could say some words to them. It would be a comfort if you told them how brave their men had been. Your words would honor their loved ones."

"I'll do my best."

"There are others who will need to know that I've returned. They will be eager to see you."

Richard gestured to Cara and Nicci. "I want to show them something"—he pointed toward the center of the city—"down this way."

"You mean Liberty Square?"

Richard nodded.

"Then I will meet you there as soon as I can manage it."

Richard briefly watched as Victor vanished down a narrow cobbled street to the right.

"What do you want to show us?" Cara asked.

"Something that I'm hoping may help jog your memory."

The first sight of the majestic statue carved from the finest white Cavatura marble, glowing in the amber light of the late-day sun, nearly buckled Richard's knees.

He knew every intimate curve of the figure, every fold of the flowing robes. He knew because he had carved the original.

"Richard?" Nicci said as she clasped his arm. "Are you all right?"

He could manage hardly more than a whisper as he stared at the statue off across the green sweep of lawns. "I'm fine."

The vast open expanse had been the site of the construction of the former palace that was to be the seat of rule for the Imperial Order. It had been where Nicci had brought Richard to toil for the greater glory of the cause of the Order in the hope that he would learn the importance of self-sacrifice and the corrupt nature of mankind. Instead, in the process, she had learned the value of life.

But while he'd still been Nicci's captive, he had worked for months in the construction of the emperor's palace. That palace was gone, now, erased from the face of the ground. Only a semicircle of columns from the main entrance remained to stand watch around the proud statue in white marble that marked the place where the flame of freedom had first ignited in the heart of darkness.

After the revolt against the rule of the Order, the statue had been carved and dedicated to the free people of Altur'Rang and the memory of those who had given their lives for that freedom. This place, where people had first spilled blood to gain their liberty, was now hallowed ground. Victor had named the place Liberty Square.

Lit by the warm light of the low sun, the statue shone like a beacon.

"What do you two see?" Richard asked.

Cara, too, had a hand on his arm. "Lord Rahl, it's the same statue we saw the last time we were here."

Nicci nodded her agreement. "The statue that the carvers created after the revolt."

The sight of the statue made Richard ache. The feminity of its exquisite shape, the curves, the bone and muscle, were clearly evident beneath the flowing robes of stone. The woman in marble almost looked alive.

"And where did the carvers get the model for this statue?" Richard asked the two women.

Both gave him a blank look.

With a hooked finger, Nicci pulled back a strand of hair that the humid breeze had lifted across her face. "What do you mean?"

"To carve such a statue, expert carvers typically scale it up from a model. What do you recall about that model?"

"Yes," Cara said as her face brightened in recollection, "it was some-thing you carved."

"That's right," he said to Cara. "You and I searched together for the wood for the small statue. You were the one who found the walnut tree I used. It had been growing on a slope just above a broad valley. The tree had been knocked over by a windblown spruce. You were there when I cut the wood from that fallen, weathered walnut tree. You were there when I carved that small statue. We sat together on the banks of the stream and talked the hours away as I worked on it."

"Yes, I remember you carving while we sat in the countryside." A hint of a smile ghosted across Cara's face. "What of it?"

"We were at the home I built in the mountains. Why were we there?"

Cara looked up at him, puzzled by the question, as if it seemed too obvious to warrant the effort of retelling. "After the people of Anderith voted to side with the Imperial Order, rather than with you and D'Hara, you gave up on trying to lead people against the Order. You said that you couldn't force people to want to be free, but that they must choose it for themselves before you could lead them."

It was difficult for Richard to calmly tell things to a woman who should know them as well as he did, but he knew that reproach wouldn't help to spark her memory. Besides, whatever was going on, he knew it wasn't a willful deception on the part of Nicci and Cara.

"That was part of it," he said. "But there was a much more important reason why we were there in those trackless mountains."

"A more important reason?"

"Kahlan had been beaten nearly to death. I took her there so that she would be safe while she recovered. You and I spent months caring for her, trying to nurse her back to health.

"But she wasn't getting better. She sank into a deep despondency. She had despaired of ever recovering, of ever being whole again."

He couldn't bring himself to say that part of the reason Kahlan had nearly given up was because when those men had beaten her nearly to death, it had caused her to lose her child.

"And so you carved this statue of her?" Cara asked.

"Not exactly."

He stared off at the proud figure in white stone rising up against the deep blue sky. He had not intended the little statue he'd carved to look like Kahlan. Through this figure, her robes flowing as she faced into a wind, as she stood with her head thrown back, her chest out, her hands fisted at her sides, her back arched and strong as if in opposition to an invisible power trying to subdue her, Richard had conveyed not what Kahlan looked like, but rather a sense of her inner nature.

This was not a statue of Kahlan, but of her living force, her soul. The magnificent statue before them was her spirit encased in stone.

"It's Kahlan's courage, her heart, her valor, her determination. That's why I named this statue *Spirit*.

"When she saw it, she understood what she was seeing. It made her hunger to be well again, to be strong and independent again. It made her want to be fully alive again. That was when she started to get well."

Both women looked more than simply dubious, but they didn't dispute his story.

"The thing is," Richard said as he started out across the broad stretch of grass, "if you were to ask the men who carved this statue where that small statue is, that statue I carved and which they used as a model to scale up this one, they would not be able to find it or tell you what happened to it."

Nicci hurried to keep up with him. "So where is it, then?"

"That little statue I carved for her out of walnut wood that summer in the mountains meant a great deal to Kahlan. She was eager to have it back after the men were finished using it. Kahlan has it."

Nicci let out a sigh as she returned her gaze to where she was walking. "Of course she does."

He frowned over at the sorceress. "And what does that mean?"

"Richard, when a person is suffering delirium, their mind works to come up with things to fill in the blank places, to knit together the tattered fabric of that delirium. It's a way for them to try to make sense out of their confusion."

"Then where is the statue?" he asked both women.

Cara shrugged. "I don't know. I don't remember what happened to it. There is this big one now, in marble. That's the one that seems important."

"I don't know, either, Richard," Nicci said when he looked her way. "Maybe if the carvers look around they will be able to come up with it."

It seemed like she was missing the purpose of his story and that they only thought that he was interested in finding his carving.

"No, they won't be able to come up with it. That's the whole point. That's what I'm trying to make you understand. Kahlan has it. I remember her pleasure the day she got it back. Don't you see? No one will be able to find it or remember what happened to it. Don't you see how things don't fit? Don't you see that something strange is going on? Don't you see that something is wrong?"

They paused at the base of the broad expanse of steps.

"The truth? Not really." Nicci gestured up at the statue standing before the semicircle of pillars. "After this statue was finally finished and the model was no longer needed it was probably lost or destroyed. As Cara said, we now have the statue here in stone."

"But don't you see the importance of the small carving? Don't you see the importance of what I'm telling you? I remember what happened to it, but no one else will. I'm tying to prove a point—to show you something, to show you that I'm not dreaming up Kahlan, to show you that things just don't add up and you need to believe me."

Nicci slipped a thumb under the strap of her pack in an effort to ease the ache caused by the burden of its weight.

"Richard, your subconscious mind in all likelihood recalls what happened to the carving—that it was lost or destroyed after this statue was finished—and so it uses that small detail to try to patch in one of the holes in the insubstantial story you dreamed up in your delirium. It's just your inner mind trying to make things seem like it all makes sense for you."

So that was it. It wasn't that they didn't get his point, it was that they got it all too well and simply didn't belive it. Richard took a deep breath. He still hoped to be able to convince them that they were the ones who were mistaken, who weren't taking everything into account.

"But why would I invent such a story?"

"Richard," Nicci said as she gently gripped his arm, "please, let's just drop it. I've said enough. I'm only making you angry."

"I asked you a question. What possible reason would I have for creating such a story?"

Nicci cast a sidelong glance at Cara before finally giving in. "If you want to know the truth, Richard, I think you recalled this statue here—partly because it was only recently carved after the revolt and it was fresh in your memory—and when you were hurt, when you were at the brink of death, because this was fresh in your mind you wove it into your dream. It became part of this woman you dreamed up—part of the story. You linked it all together and used it to help create something meaningful for yourself, something you could hang on to. Your mind used this statue because it serves to connect your dream to something in the real world. In that way, it serves to help make your dream more real for you."

"What?" Richard was stunned. "Why would—"

"Because," Nicci said, fists at her sides, "it makes it look as if you can point to something solid in the real world and say 'this is her.' "

Richard blinked, unable to speak.

Nicci glanced away. Her voice lost its heat and dropped to a near whisper. "Forgive me, Richard."

He withdrew his glare from her. How could he forgive her for what she sincerely believed? How could he forgive himself for not being able to make her understand?

Fearing to test his voice just then, he started up the expanse of steps. He couldn't look into her eyes, couldn't look into the eyes of someone who thought he was mad. He was hardly aware of the effort of climbing the hill of steps.

At the top, as he crossed the expansive marble platform he could hear Nicci and Cara rushing up the steps after him. For the first time, he noticed that there seemed to be quite a few people on the grounds of the former palace. From the height of the platform he could see the river that cut through the city. Flocks of birds wheeled above the swirling water. Beyond the towering columns behind the statue, green hills and trees wavered in the heat.

The proud figure of *Spirit* rose up before him, glorious in the golden late-day sunlight. He laid a hand against the cool, smooth stone for support. He could hardly endure the pain of what he felt at that moment.

When Cara came close he looked up into her blue eyes. "Is that what you believe, too? That I'm just inventing in my head that Kahlan was hurt and you and I cared for her? This statue doesn't spark any memory? It doesn't help you recall anything?"

Cara gazed up at the mute statue. "Now that you brought it up, Lord Rahl, I remember when I found the tree. I remember you smiling at me when I showed it to you. I remember that you were pleased with me. I also remember some of the stories you told me when you carved, and I remember you listening to some of my stories. But you carved a lot of things that summer."

"That summer before Nicci came and took me away," he added.

"Yes."

"And if I'm only dreaming, and Kahlan doesn't exist, then how did Nicci manage to capture me and take me away if you were there to protect me?"

Cara paused, taken aback by the cutting tone of the question. "She used magic."

"Magic. Mord-Sith are the counter to magic, remember? That's their whole reason for their existence—to protect the Lord Rahl from those with magic who would do him harm. The day Nicci showed up she intended to do me harm. You were there. Why didn't you stop her?"

Terror crept incrementally into Cara's blue eyes. "Because I failed you. I should have stopped her, but I failed. A day does not go by that I don't wish you would punish me for failing in my duty to protect you." Her face stood out crimson against her blond hair as her sudden confession burst forth. "Because I failed you, you were captured by Nicci and taken away for nearly a year—all because of me. If it had been your father I failed in such a fashion he would have executed me, but only after making me beg for death until I was hoarse. And he would have been right to do so; I deserve no less. I failed you."

Richard stared in shock. "Cara . . . it wasn't your fault. That's the whole point of my question. You should remember that you could have done nothing to stop Nicci."

Cara's hands fisted. "I should have, but I didn't. I failed you."

"Cara, that's not true. Nicci used a spell on Kahlan. Had either of us done anything to stop her, Nicci would have killed Kahlan."

"What!" Nicci objected. "What in the world are you talking about?"

"You captured Kahlan with a spell. That spell connected you to Kahlan and was directly controlled by your intent. If I hadn't gone with you, you could have killed Kahlan at any time with no more than a thought. That, for the most part, was why Cara and I could do nothing."

Nicci planted her hands on her hips. "And just what kind of a spell do you think could accomplish such a thing?"

"A maternity spell."

Nicci regarded him with a blank look. "A what?"

"A maternity spell. It created a connection that made anything that happened to you happen to her. If Cara or I had harmed or killed you, the same fate would have befallen Kahlan. We were helpless. I had to do what you wanted. I had to go with you or Kahlan would have died. I had to do as you wished or you could have taken her life through the link of that spell. I had to make sure nothing happened to you or the same fate would befall Kahlan."

Nicci shook her head with incredulity and then, without comment, turned to stare off at the hills beyond the statue.

"It wasn't your fault, Cara." He lifted her chin to make her wet eyes look up at him. "Neither of us could have done anything. You didn't fail me."

"Don't you think that I would like to believe you? Don't you think that I would, if it were true?"

"If you don't remember what I'm telling you really happened," Richard said, "then just how do you think Nicci managed to capture me?"

"She used magic."

"What kind of magic?"

"I don't know what kind of magic it was—I'm no expert on how magic works. She just used magic, that's all."

He turned to Nicci. "What magic? How did you capture me? What spell did you use? Why didn't I stop you? Why didn't Cara stop you?"

"Richard, that was . . . what, a year and a half ago? I don't remember exactly what spell I used that day to capture you. It wasn't all that hard. You don't have the ability to control your gift or mount a defense against someone experienced with it. I could have tied you up in knots of magic and had you over the back of a horse without working up a sweat."

"And why didn't Cara try to stop you?"

"Because," Nicci said, gesturing in exasperation at having to try to recall the irksome details, "I had you hobbled under my ability and she knew that if she made a move I would have killed you first. It's no more complicated than that."

"That's right," Cara said. "Nicci spelled you, just as she says. I couldn't do anything because it was you she attacked. If she would have used her power against me I could have turned her gift against her, but she used it instead on you, so I could do nothing."

With a finger, Richard wiped sweat from his brow. "You're trained to kill with your bare hands. If nothing else why wouldn't you have hit her over the head with a rock?"

"I would have hurt you," Nicci said, answering for Cara, "or possibly even killed you, had she even looked like she was going to try anything."

"And then Cara would have had you," Richard reminded the sorceress.

"Back then I was willing to forfeit my life—I just didn't care. You know that."

Richard did indeed know that that much of it was true. At the time,

Nicci did not value life, not even her own. That had made her dangerous in the extreme.

"My mistake was in not attacking Nicci before she could get to you," Cara said. "If I had made her strike out at me with magic, I would have had her. That is what a Mord-Sith is supposed to do. But I failed you."

"You couldn't," Nicci said. "I surprised you both. You didn't fail, Cara. Sometimes there simply isn't any chance to succeed. Sometimes there is no solution. For the two of you, that was one of those situations. I was in control."

It was hopeless. Every time he backed them into a corner they seemed to be able to effortlessly slither out.

Richard laid a hand against the smooth marble as his mind raced, trying to think of how this could be happening—what could be causing them to forget. He reasoned that maybe he could remedy the problem if he only knew what was causing it.

And then, something about that story he had told them in the shelter a couple of nights back suddenly sprang to mind.

$\mathbf{R}$ichard snapped his fingers.

"Magic," he said. "That's it. Remember how I told you that Kahlan showed up in the Hartland woods near where I lived, and that she had come because she was looking for the long-lost great wizard?"

"What of it?" Nicci asked.

"Kahlan was looking for the great wizard because Zedd had fled the Midlands before I was born. Darken Rahl had raped my mother and Zedd wanted to take her away to safety."

Cara's brow twitched with suspicion. "Much like you say you took this woman, your wife, to those remote mountains so she would be safe after she had been attacked?"

"Well, kind of, but—"

"Do you see what you're doing, Richard?" Nicci asked. "You're taking things you heard about and putting them into your dream. Do you see the thread that runs through both stories? That's a common phenomenon when people dream. The mind falls back on what it knows or has heard about."

"No, that's not it. Just hear me out."

Nicci conceded with a single nod but she clasped her hands behind her back and lifted her chin in the manner of an uncompromising teacher dealing with an obstinate student.

"I guess there were similarities," Richard finally admitted, uncomfortable at the way Nicci had him locked in her knowing gaze, "but in a way that's the point. You see, Zedd had become fed up with the council of the Midlands, much like I gave up trying to help people who believed in the Order's lies. The difference is that Zedd wanted to leave them to suffer the consequences of their actions. He didn't want them to be able to come asking for his help in getting them out of trouble of their own making. When he left the Midlands and went to Westland he cast a wizard's web to make everyone forget him."

He thought they should understand, but they only stared at him. "Zedd used a specific magic spell to make everyone forget his name, forget who he was, so that they couldn't come looking for him. That must be what happened with Kahlan. Someone took her and used magic not only to erase her tracks, but to erase everyone's memory of her. That's why you can't remember her. That's why no one remembers her."

Cara looked surprised by the notion. She glanced at Nicci. Nicci wet her lips and sighed heavily.

"That has to be it," Richard pressed. "That has to be the answer."

"Richard," Nicci said in a quiet voice, "that's not what is going on here. It doesn't even remotely make sense."

Richard couldn't understand how Nicci, being a sorceress, couldn't see it. "Yes it does. Magic made everyone forget Zedd. After Kahlan met me in the woods that day, she told me how she was looking for the great wizard, but that no one could recall the old one's name because he had cast a web of magic to make them forget it. Magic must have been used to make everyone forget Kahlan in the same way."

"Except you?" Nicci said as she arched an eyebrow. "This magic seems to have failed where you're concerned, since you have no trouble remembering her."

Richard had been expecting just such an argument. "It's possible that since I alone have a different form of the gift, the spell didn't work on me."

Nicci again drew a deep, patient breath. "You say that this woman, Kahlan, came looking for the missing wizard, the 'old one,' right?"

"Right."

"Don't you see the problem, Richard? She knew that she was looking for this old one, the missing wizard."

Richard was nodding. "That's right."

Nicci leaned toward him. "That kind of spell is quite troublesome to create, and it has a number of complications that must be taken into account, but other than that it's not altogether remarkable. Difficult, yes, remarkable, no."

"Then that must be what was done with Kahlan. Someone—maybe one of the Order's wizards traveling with the supply convoy—took her and cast a spell to try to make us all forget her so that we wouldn't come after them."

"Why would someone go to the trouble to do such a thing?" Cara asked. "Why not simply kill her? What's the purpose in capturing her and then making everyone forget her?"

"I'm not sure. Maybe they simply wanted to have a way to escape without being followed. Maybe they intend to spirit her away and then, at a time of their choosing, parade their prisoner before their subjects to show their power, to show that they can capture anyone who opposes them. The fact remains that she's gone and no one but me remembers her. It makes sense to me that a spell must have been used, like the spell Zedd used to make people forget him."

Nicci pinched the bridge of her nose in a way that somehow made Richard feel just a little stupid, as if his idea was so foolish it was giving her a headache. "Everyone was looking for this old one, this great wizard. They remembered that he was the great wizard, that he was an important, accomplished man, even that he was from the Midlands. They merely couldn't remember his name and probably what he looked like. So, without his name or a description of him they were having a great deal of difficulty finding him."

Richard nodded. "That's right."

"Don't you see, Richard? They knew that he existed, knew that he was the old wizard, and probably had a great many memories of things he had done, but they simply couldn't recall his name—because of the spell. That's all—his name. They couldn't remember his name even though they remembered that the man existed.

"But this wife of yours is remembered by no one except you. We don't know her name or anything else about her. We have no memory of her or of anything she supposedly did with us. We have no knowledge of anything at all about her. Not one thing. She exists in no one's mind but yours."

Richard saw the distinction but wasn't ready to concede the point. "But maybe this was just a stronger spell, or something. It must have been much the same, but just more powerful so that everyone not only forgets her name, but forgets her altogether."

Nicci gently gripped his shoulders in an almost painfully sympathetic manner.

"Richard, I admit that to someone like you, who grew up without understanding magic, that might seem like it makes sense—and it's very inventive, it really is—but it simply doesn't work that way in the real world.

To someone without an understanding of how such power works it must seem entirely logical, at least on the surface. But when you look deeper the difference between a spell to make everyone forget a person's name and a spell making everyone forget that the person ever existed, it's the difference between lighting a fire at camp and igniting a second sun in the sky."

Richard threw up his hands in frustration. "But why?"

"Because the first alters only one thing, the memory of a person's name—and I must add that such a thing, as simple as it might seem on the face of it, is profoundly difficult and beyond the ability of all but a handful of the most gifted individuals and even then they must have extensive knowledge. Still, everyone knows that they have forgotten the great wizard's name so even as it does the work of making people forget that name, the spell only has to accomplish this one clearly defined and limited task. The difficulty with spells of this nature is in how broadly the task is applied, but for the purpose of this example that is beside the point.

"Where the first example alters one thing, the name of the vanished wizard, the second alters nearly everything. That is what makes it beyond difficult; it makes it impossible."

"I still don't understand." Richard paced from the statue partway out across the platform and back, gesturing as he spoke. "It seems to me like it does roughly the same thing."

"Think of all the ways a person, especially an important person such as the Mother Confessor, touches the lives of nearly everyone. Dear spirits, Richard, she oversaw the Central Council of the Midlands. She made decisions that affected every land."

Richard closed the distance to the sorceress. "What difference does that make? Zedd was First Wizard. He was important, too, and he touched a lot of lives."

"And people only forgot his name; they did not forget the man himself. Try, for a moment, to imagine what would be the result if a spell could make everyone forget a simple man." Nicci walked off a few paces and then abruptly turned back. "Say, Faval, the charcoal maker. Not just forget his name, but forget the man entirely. Forget that he exists or ever did, just like you suggest happened to this woman, Kahlan.

"What would happen? What would Faval's family do? Who would his children think fathered them? Who would his wife think made her pregnant and gave her children, if she couldn't remember Faval? Where was

this mystery man who sired a family? Would her mind invent another man
to soothe her panic and fill the void? What would her friends believe and
how would all of their thoughts mesh with hers? What would everyone believe without the truth to support their thinking? What would happen
when people's mind's fabricated patches filling the gaps in their memories, and those patches didn't match? With the charcoal ovens all around
his home, how would his wife and children think they got there and how
had all the charcoal been made? What would happen at the foundry where
Faval sold his charcoal? What would Priska think—that somehow baskets
of charcoal had magically appeared in the bins in the storage room of his
foundry?

"I'm not even beginning to scratch the surface of the ever expanding
complications such a fanciful forget-me spell cast on Faval would cause—
the accounting of money, the allocation of work, the agreements with
lumbermen and other workers, the documents, the promises he'd made
and all the rest. Think of all the confusion and disarray such a thing would
cause, and that's with one little-known man living in a tiny house down a
lonely lane."

Nicci lifted an arm as if in grand introduction, "But with a woman like
the Mother Confessor herself?" She let the arm drop. "I can't even begin
to imagine the tangle of consequences left snarled in the wake of such an
incomprehensible event."

Nicci's mane of blond hair stood out against the dark background of
trees on the hills beyond the broad, level grassy expanse. Her hair's length
and its sweeping curves looked casual, even comfortably intimate, and
complemented her shapely form in her black dress, but the power of her
presence was not to be taken lightly. At that moment, as she stood illuminated by a ray of light from the setting sun, she was a breathtaking figure
of astute perception and knowledgeable authority, a force that seemed beyond reproach. Richard stood mute and motionless as she went on in an
instructional tone.

"It's the cascade of connections to all those specific incidents that
would make such a spell impossible. Every little thing that the Mother
Confessor had ever done would snowball together with connected circumstances in which she may not even have been personally involved,
compounding the number of events that would become tainted by such a

spell. The power, the complexity, the sheer magnitude of it is beyond comprehension.

"Those complications must draw power from the spell in order to counteract the disruptive potential of such complications. Those exigencies feed off the power of the spell that seeks to command the nature of the event. At some point, a spell without the power to compensate for a growing vortex of such dissipative events would simply sputter and die like a candle in a downpour."

Nicci stepped close and jabbed a finger at his chest. "And that's not even taking into account the most glaring inconsistency of your dream. In your delirium you dreamed up an even more complex predicament. You dreamed up not only this woman, this wife, who is remembered by no one else, but in your irrational dreaming state you went further, much further, without realizing the fateful consequences. You see, it wasn't merely some country girl, who no one knew, that you dreamed up for yourself. No, you made her a known person. In the context of a dream that might seem a simple thing, but in the real world a known person creates a congruency dilemma.

"And yet, you went further still! Even a known person would not be as complicated as what you did.

"In your state of delirium you picked the Mother Confessor herself, a near mythic individual, a person of great importance, but at the same time a person far away, a person that neither Cara nor I nor Victor would know. None of us is from the distant Midlands, so we would have no way to easily offer up facts that are inconsistent with your dream. That distance might have made sense in your dream because it seemed to also solve the untidy problem of contradictory facts, but in the real world it still creates for you a problem of insurmountable magnitude: Such a woman is widely known. It's only a matter of time until your carefully constructed world clashes with the real world and begins to fall apart. By picking a known person, you have doomed your idyllic dream to destruction."

Nicci lifted his chin and made him look into her eyes. "In your troubled state of mind, Richard, you dreamed up someone comforting. You were facing the abyss of death; you desperately wanted someone to love you, someone who made you feel less afraid, less terrified, less alone. That's completely understandable, it really is. I don't think any less of you—I couldn't—because you created such a solution for yourself when you were so afraid and so alone, but it's over and you have to come to grips with it.

"If it had been an unknown woman you imagined, then the dream would have been nothing more than an ethereal abstraction. But you inadvertently linked it to reality because the Mother Confessor is known by a great many people. If you ever get back to the Midlands, or run into people from the Midlands, your dream will come face-to-face with the indisputable reality. For you, each one of those people is a lurking shadow ready to shoot an arrow, but this time an arrow that will not fail to pierce your heart.

"It could even be worse. What if the real Mother Confessor is dead?"

Richard drew back. "But she's not."

"Lord Rahl," Cara said, "I remember several years ago when Darken Rahl sent the quads to kill all the Confessors. The quads don't fail at their task of assassination."

Richard stared at the Mord-Sith. "But they failed to get her."

"Richard," Nicci said in a gentle tone, drawing his gaze back to her, "what if you someday get to the Midlands and you discover that the real Mother Confessor was not what you imagined, but was in fact an old woman? After all, the Confessors didn't name women as young as this love of yours would have been to be the Mother Confessor. What if you find out that the real woman was old, and worse, that she is long dead? The truth, now. What would you do then, if you were confronted by that and it was real?"

Richard's mouth was so dry that he had to work his tongue in order to be able to wet his lips enough to speak. "I don't know."

Nicci smiled wistfully. "An honest answer, at last." Even that smile was more than she could manage, and it vanished. "I'm afraid for you, Richard, afraid for what will become of your state of mind if you continue to cling to this, let it take over your whole life, and then it finally comes to something like that, which it will. Sooner or later you are going to come face to face with the stone cold reality of the situation."

"Nicci, just because you can't envision—"

"Richard," she said, quietly cutting him off, "I'm a sorceress. I've been a Sister of the Light and a Sister of the Dark. I know a thing or two about magic. I'm telling you that such a thing as you suggest is simply beyond the power of any magic I know of. It is not beyond the power of a desperate man to dream up, but it is unworkable in the real world. You can't even begin to imagine the dire consequences were such a thing to even be attempted, much less possible."

"Nicci, I grant you your great knowledge on the subject, but you don't know everything. Just because you don't know how to do something, that does not mean it's impossible. It only means that you don't know how it can be done. You just don't want to admit that you might be wrong."

Her hands fisted at her sides as she blinked. "Do you think that I *want* to oppose you in this? Is that what you think? Do you think I enjoy trying to make you see the truth? Do you think that I like being against you in *anything*?"

"What I know is that somehow, in some way, someone has made all of you forget that Kahlan exists. I know that she's real, and I intend on finding her. Even if you don't like it."

Nicci, her blue eyes brimming with tears, turned her back on him and gazed up briefly at the statue towering over her. "Richard, I would eagerly grant you your dream were it within my power to make it real. You cannot imagine what I would give to have you have what you want . . . to make you happy."

Richard watched the violet clouds at the horizon turning dark. It somehow seemed too peaceful to be real. Nicci stood with her arms folded, staring off in the opposite direction, staring into the gathering darkness. Cara stood nearby, keeping an eye on all the people roaming the former palace grounds.

"Nicci," Richard finally said into the uncomfortable silence atop the vast marble circle, "do you have any explanations other than this being a dream? Is there anything within your knowledge that has any chance at all of being the cause of this? Is there anything at all, any kind of magic, that you can think of that would help solve this puzzle?"

He watched her back, wondering if she would answer. A long shadow lay across the curved, bronze dial plane encircling the proud figure, telling him what he knew, that the day was dying, that valuable time was slipping away. Finally, Nicci turned to him. The fire seemed to gave gone out of her.

"Richard, I'm sorry that I can't make it real for you." She brushed away a tear as it ran down her cheek. "I'm sorry to let you down."

With a grim expression, Cara meet Nicci's gaze. "I guess we have something in common."

Richard gently touched his fingertips to the statue of *Spirit*. The up-lifted face, its proud gaze set in white marble, lost its glow as the last rays of the setting sun sank behind the hills.

"Neither one of you let me down," he said. "You both are telling me what you believe. But Kahlan is not a dream. She's as real as her spirit carved in this stone."

Richard turned to a distant commotion and spotted a group of people heading toward the monument. From atop the prominence he could see yet more people strung out behind, perhaps drawn by the activity, or perhaps by the purposeful look of the cluster of men as they made their way across the open expanse of ground. At the head of the small crowd was just the man Richard wanted to see.

Still some distance off, the man waved an arm. "Richard!"

Despite everything, Richard couldn't help but smile at the familiar stocky fellow wearing his customary, curious red hat with a narrow brim. When the man saw that Richard had seen him, he picked up his pace, trotting across the grass.

"Richard," he called again. "You've come back—just as you promised!"

As the group of people swarmed up the hill of steps, Richard started down to meet them. It was then that Richard also saw that Victor was making his way steadily through the gathering throng. At a wide marble landing, Ishaq rushed up and seized Richard's hand, pumping it with great glee.

"Richard, I'm so happy to see you back in Altur'Rang. You come to drive a wagon for my transport company, yes? I have orders stacked up. How do I get myself into these messes? I need you back. You can start tomorrow?"

"Glad to see you, too, Ishaq."

Ishaq was still pumping Richard's hand. "Then you will come back? I will make you a full partner. We share everything equal, you and I."

"Ishaq, with as much money as you owe me—"

"Money," Ishaq scoffed. "What is this talk of money? I have so much work now and more all the time that there is no time to worry about money. Forget money. We can earn all the money you want. I need a man with a good head. I will make you a partner. If you want, you can make me your partner—we will get more work that way. Everyone asks after you. 'Where is Richard?' they all say. I tell you, Richard, if you—"

"Ishaq, I can't. I'm trying to find Kahlan."

Ishaq blinked. "Kahlan?"

"His wife," a scowling Victor said as he stepped through the men behind Ishaq.

Ishaq turned to gawk at Victor. He turned back to Richard.

"Wife?" He swept his red hat off his head. "Wife? But this is wonderful!" He spread his arms. "Wonderful!" He threw his arms around Richard and hugged him as he laughed and danced back and forth on the balls of his feet. "You took a wife! This is wonderful news. We will have a banquet and—"

"She's missing," Richard said, easing Ishaq back to arm's length. "I'm looking for her. We don't know what happened."

"Missing?" Ishaq swiped back his dark hair and replaced his red hat. "I will help. I will go with you." His dark eyes turned serious. "Tell me what I can do."

It was no empty offer Ishaq made for the sake of courtesy. He was sincere. It was heartwarming to know that this man would drop everything to help.

Richard didn't think, though, that this was the time or place to explain. "It's not that simple."

"Richard," Victor said as he leaned closer, "we've got trouble."

Ishaq frowned at Victor, gesturing irritably. "Richard's wife is missing. Why you bring him more worries on top of that?"

"It's all right, Ishaq. Victor already knows about Kahlan." Richard rested his left hand on the pommel of his sword. "What sort of trouble?" he asked Victor.

"Scouts have just returned to report Imperial Order troops coming this way."

Ishaq swept his hat from his head again. "Troops?"

"Another supply convoy?" Richard asked.

"No," Victor said with a firm shake of his head. "These men are combat troops and they're coming this way."

Ishaq's eyes grew round. "Soldiers are coming? How soon?"

Voices carried the worrisome news back through the growing crowd.

"At the rate they're marching, they're still a few days out. We have some time to get our defenses organized. But not a lot of time."

Nicci stepped up close to Richard's side. With her back straight, her head held high, and her cutting gaze, she drew all eyes. Voices quieted as they watched her. Even people who didn't know who Nicci was tended to fall silent in her presence. Some because of her stunning looks, some because there was just something dangerous about her commanding presence, on top of her physical attraction, that made them tend to lose their nerve along with their voice.

"And the scouts are sure they're headed this way?" she asked. "Couldn't they just be passing near on their way north?"

"They're not heading north." Victor arched an eyebrow. "They're coming *from* the north."

Richard's fingers tightened around the hilt of his sword. "They're coming down from the north—are you sure?"

Victor nodded. "They're seasoned combat troops. Worse still, they've picked up one of those priests somewhere along the way."

The gathered men gasped. Whispers of the news spread back through the crowd. Some of the men started asking questions, each trying to be heard over the others.

Nicci lifted a hand, commanding silence. With no more effort than that, the darkening hillside of marble steps fell quiet. In the tense hush, she leaned toward the grim blacksmith. Nicci's brow drew down like a hawk that had just spotted dinner.

"They have a wizard with them?" she hissed.

Victor didn't back up—one of the few who didn't. "He's said to be a high priest of the Fellowship of Order."

"All the Brothers in the Fellowship are wizards," Ishaq pointed out. "This is not good news. Not good at all."

"Can't argue with that," Victor said. "From the reports brought back by the men, there is no doubt that this one is a wizard."

Worried conversation again swept through the crowd. Some swore that such a development would make no difference, that they would fight any attempt by the Order to take back Altur'Rang. Others weren't so sure as to what should be done.

Nicci, staring off as she considered what she'd heard, finally returned her gaze to Victor. "Do the scouts know his name or anything about him that might help identify him?"

Victor hooked his thumbs behind his belt as he gave her a single nod. "The high priest's name is Kronos."

"Kronos . . ." she murmured in thought.

"The scouts who spotted the troops used their heads," Victor told her. "They hadn't been seen, so they got out ahead of the soldiers and mingled into a town along the legion's path and waited for them to arrive. The soldiers camped just outside the town for a few nights to rest up and to resupply. Apparently they stripped the town bare in the process. When they got drunk they talked enough for my men to get the gist of what they're up to, and what they are up to is not just putting an end to the insurrection in Altur'Rang. Their orders are to crush the revolt and not to be gentle about it. They said they were to make examples of the people there. They don't seem to think it will be a big task, and they're looking forward to the fun they'll be having after the victory."

A pall of silence fell over the crowd.

"What about the wizard?" Ishaq asked.

"The men say that this fellow Kronos is a pious sort. He's average height with blue eyes. He didn't do any drinking with the soldiers. Instead, he lectured the town's folks long and often on the need to follow the Creator's true ways by sacrificing what they had for the good of their fellow man, the Imperial Order, and their beloved emperor.

"But, as it turns out, when he's not lecturing he's a letch, and apparently it doesn't matter much to him who the woman is or if she's at all willing. After one man angrily raised a ruckus about his daughter being taken right off the street by Kronos's orders, the good Brother came out and with a flash of his power burned the hide right off the father. The pious wizard left the man screaming and twitching as a lesson and he went back inside to finish his business with the daughter. The poor fellow was several hours dying. My men said it was as horrifying as anything they'd ever seen. After that, no one else had much to say when any woman caught Kronos's eye."

Murmuring broke out in the crowd. Many of the people were shocked and angered by the story. A number were frightened that this man was not only coming for them but was under orders to make examples of them.

Nicci didn't look at all surprised by the report of such brutality. After lengthy consideration, she finally shook her head.

"I don't know this Brother of the Order, but there are a number of them that I don't know."

Ishaq's dark eyes shifted between Richard and Nicci. "What are we going to do? Troops and a wizard. This is not good. But you have ideas, yes?"

Some in the crowd voiced their agreement with Ishaq, wanting to know what Richard thought. He didn't really see what there was to discuss.

"You've all fought for and won your freedom," Richard said. "I would suggest that you don't give it up."

A number of men nodded. They knew all too well what it was like to live under the heel of the Order. They had learned, too, what it meant to be free to live their own lives. Nonetheless, fear seemed to be stealing into the mood of the crowd.

"But now you're here to lead us, Lord Rahl," one of the men said. "You've faced worse than this, I'm sure. With your help we can fight off these soldiers."

In the gathering gloom Richard appraised the expectant faces watching him.

"I'm afraid that I can't stay. I have something of critical importance I must do. I will have to leave in the morning at first light."

Shocked silence greeted him.

"But the soldiers are only a few days away," one of the men finally said. "Surely, Lord Rahl, you can wait that long."

"If I could, I would stand here with you against these soldiers, just as I've stood with you before, but right now I can't afford to delay that long. I must carry the fight elsewhere. It's the same fight, so I will be with you in spirit."

The man looked stunned. "But it's just a few days. . . ."

"Don't you see that it's much more than that? If I stay, and we defeat these men who are coming to kill you, then, eventually, more will come. You have to be able to stand on your own. You can't depend on me to stay here indefinitely and help you uphold your freedom every time Jagang sends soldiers to take back Altur'Rang. The world is full of places like Altur'Rang, all facing the same ordeal. Sooner or later you'll have to accept the responsibility of standing on your own. Now is as good a time as any."

"So you're deserting us when we need you most?" A voice farther back called out.

The crowd didn't speak up to agree with the sentiment, but it was clear that more than one person had the same thought. Cara inched forward. Before she could step in front of him, Richard surreptitiously lifted his hand, touching her leg in warning for her to stay where she was.

"Now, look here," Victor growled, "Richard isn't deserting anything, and I'll hear none of that kind of talk." Men backed away at the measured menace in his voice. Victor's glare alone was enough to turn men twice his size pale. "He has already done more for us than anyone ever before. He showed us that we can each run our own lives for ourselves and that's what changed everything. You've all lived here your whole life under the Order. Richard showed us what we're really made of, showed us that we're proud men and we can handle ourselves with courage. We're the ones who took responsibility for our own lives and gained our own freedom. He didn't come here and give us anything. We earned it."

Most of the men standing on the steps and spread out across the lawns fell silent. Some, feeling shamed, stole looks around at the others. A number of the men finally spoke up that they agreed with Victor.

As the men fell to debating among themselves what it was they ought to do, Nicci seized Richard's arm from behind and drew him back to where she could speak in confidence. "Richard, this fight here is more important."

"I can't stay."

Her blue eyes flashed with bottled fury. "This is where you should be, leading these men. You're the Lord Rahl. They're counting on you."

"I am not responsible for their lives. They already made their choice as to how they will live when they started the revolt. They did that on their own and they won that battle. We all are fighting for what we believe in. We all are fighting for the same thing—the right to live the life we want for ourselves. I'm doing what I believe I must."

"You're running away from the fight to chase phantoms."

The sting of her words hung in the air, unanswered. Richard instead stepped away from the sorceress and addressed the men.

"The Old World and the New World are at war." The crowd slowly fell silent as people craned their necks in order to see Richard and hear his words. "The troops on their way here are battle-tested men from that war.

As they've rampaged across the land, they've used their swords, axes, and flails against both the armed and the unarmed people to the north, the people of the New World. Those troops are experienced at overrunning cities and slaughtering the inhabitants. When they get here, they will torture, rape, and murder the people of this city, just as they've done to the people in cities to the north . . . unless you stop them first.

"But even if you do stop them, that will not be the end of it. The Order will send more soldiers. If you defeat them, they will eventually send even more the next time."

"Richard, what are you saying?" Ishaq asked into the still evening air. "Are you saying that it is hopeless—that we should give up?"

"No. I'm saying that you need to face the true dimension of what it means to fight the Imperial Order—the true nature of the task. If you wish to be free, then you need to do more than stand here in this place and defend your city.

"No war was ever won defensively.

"If you are to be truly free, then you must fight to put a stop to those who seek to extinguish freedom. If you are to be truly free, then you must be part of the cause to rid the world of the Imperial Order. The D'Haran Empire, the land I rule, is all that now stands against the Order." Richard slowly shook his head. "But alone, they have no chance to win. Once the D'Haran Empire falls, Emperor Jagang will be freed up from the effort of that war and he will then bring his full force to bear on any pockets of resistance to the Order's beliefs.

"At the head of his list will be Altur'Rang. This is his home city. He will not allow the black mark of freedom to stand against his devout beliefs. He will turn loose on you his most vicious fighters—the sons of the Old World. You will be isolated and gutted by Jagang's army of your fellow countrymen. You will die to a man, your male children will be murdered, and your wives and sisters and daughters will be used as rewards for the brutes who enforce the Order's authority."

The crowd stood in rapt silence. They were now in the grip of fear. This was not the brave and boastful talk they had expected to hear on the eve of battle.

Victor cleared his throat. "You are trying to tell us something, Richard?"

Richard nodded as he gazed out over the mute throng watching him from below the landing where he stood. "Yes. I'm trying to tell you that you must do more than stand and defend yourselves when these men come. You can't win that kind of war. You must strike out at the Imperial Order and help bring them down."

Ishaq lifted a hand. "Bring them down? In what way?"

"As you all well know, life under the Order offers nothing but decay and ruin. There is little work, little food, little to look forward to . . . except the promise of glory in some afterworld life—but only in exchange for your selfless service in this one. The priests of the Fellowship of Order have nothing to offer you but misery, so they proclaim suffering a virtue and in exchange generously grant you extravagant, eternal rewards in some other world. Rewards that cannot be examined beforehand, rewards in a world that is unknowable, except, they claim, to them. Not one of you would be gullible enough to trade a dog for such hollow promises, and yet legions have been swindled into eagerly offering up their own lives, the only life they will ever have, in the unfair exchange.

"Jagang invokes the cause of the Creator, the fight for mankind's future, and the elimination of those with the gift as the noble reasons for the Old World to invade the New World. He tells his subjects that the people far away to the north are immoral heathens and, as a duty to the Creator, they must be struck down.

"In reality, Jagang is doing nothing more than producing a diversion to cover the widespread poverty and unemployment created by the Imperial Order's doctrines. A failed Old World of crushing poverty and widespread death is thus blamed on traitors among the people—that would be you— and on their supposedly wicked brethren to the north. Jagang gives hopeless young men an object of hatred upon which to extract revenge for their misery.

"In so doing, out of the ranks of the young men of the Old World, Jagang has created an army of zealots. You know yourselves the throngs of such young men who have departed from Altur'Rang to join the 'noble' cause. These men have little in life to look forward to and have grasped eagerly at the Order's teachings. Jagang has given them someone to blame for all their woes: those who don't submit to the teachings of the Order. These men have been indoctrinated in a culture of death and turned loose on those who have liberty, prosperity, and the most hateful thing of all, happiness. Most are well beyond reason or redemption.

"Fighting far from home, Jagang allows these savages to pillage and loot their way across the land, hoping they will forget the miserable future awaiting them back home. In the name of the Creator and the Order they slaughter all opposition and take vast territory as their own. With their great numbers they vanquish all who go up against them. They terrorize everyone in their path. The panic of waiting for the murdering horde to arrive is too much for many, and in the hopes of being spared the worst of what Jagang's men would do, some places surrender and petition to join the cause of the Imperial Order."

"You are saying it is hopeless to fight them?" someone asked into the tense evening silence.

"I am telling you the true nature of what we all face," Richard said. "But it does not have to be hopeless if you understand the essence of the fight.

"For one thing, the Imperial Order has not fully grasped the corrosive effect of distance from their homeland. No matter how much they loot, they still need vast quantities of every kind of supply, from flour to make bread to feathers to make arrows. They can't scavenge enough food to feed their numbers. They need craftsmen and workers to support their fighting men and they need a steady stream of new soldiers to replace the vast numbers lost in the battles of the campaign. It is difficult to fight in a strange and distant land. Their losses from sickness alone have been staggering. Yet with reinforcements always arriving they have been able to more than replace all they lose. Their army grows constantly, becoming more formidable with each passing day. But that means it also has more needs every day.

"Those convoys of supplies that are constantly streaming north are vital to the efforts of the Imperial Order in conquering the New World. The New World may seem a faraway problem to you, but it is your problem as much as those troops headed this way in a few days. Once those brutes up north are finished murdering my people, they will be coming back here to murder you. If the Order wins, all of us lose. It doesn't matter where we are. There will be no place to hide.

"If you want to live, not just tomorrow, or the day after you defeat those troops headed this way, but to live next season, next year, and the year after; if you want to raise a family, keep what you earn, and better yourselves and the lives of your children; then you need to help to destroy the Order's ability to survive.

"Victor and his men have already been doing this, but they are only able to whisper when they need to howl in fury. They need far more people to join them in the effort. You need to help in a determined effort to hit the Order's supply convoys and destroy them. Kill their men going to fight. Cripple their ability to carry on. You need to deprive the Order of flour and feathers and reinforcements. Every man who dies of starvation in the trackless mountains to the north is a man the Order can't send back to the Old World to shove his knife in your belly.

"In addition, there are other means to prevail." Richard gestured to Cara and Nicci. "These two who now stand with me once stood against me. They were enemies of what I believe in—of what you have come to believe in—but when I helped them to understand that I fight for life, for the values of life, they came to realize the truth and became warriors in that same cause."

Richard lifted a hand out at the crowd spread down the steps and across the lawns. "Look at all of you. Not all that long ago you were the enemies of the New World. Many of you for much of your lives might have believed the lies of the Order. But when given a glimpse of the bright flame of what life can and should be, you had the presence of mind to choose life. I now stand with former enemies, in the heart of enemy territory, among a people once my enemy. Yet now we are all believers in the same cause: that life is worth living for its own sake. Many of us have become fast friends. We are now all on the same side in the greatest struggle of our lives.

"It is possible to make some people who are working for the success of the Order see the wonder and beauty in this life. If you can do that, then you will have one less person who wants to kill you. It would be my choice to win them all over to the truth and to have a world of people living in peace.

"But there are those who are lost to the truth, lost to reason. They hate that you embrace what is good in life. If you can't win these followers of the Order to our side, then you must kill them, for surely, given the chance, they will kill you and destroy everything you hold dear. You must spread the fight everywhere—leave no place safe for those who preach death. Yes, you will need to kill the wild-eyed fanatics eagerly fighting in the cause of the Order, but far more important than that, you must strike at the root and kill those who preach the doctrines of the Imperial Order.

"They are the ones who corrupt and poison unthinking minds and, if not stopped, they will breed an endless supply of newly minted brutes to come after you and your families. Men with such hate in their hearts recognize no boundaries. They will never allow you to exist because your prosperity and happiness puts the lie to what they teach.

"If you wish to live free, then you must see to it that these disciples of hatred know that there is no safe place for them, that their ways will not be tolerated by civilized men, and that you will not rest until they are all hunted down and killed because you understand that they want nothing less than to end civilization. You must not let them have what they lust after.

"You've all bravely taken the first step and thrown off your shackles. None of you need prove yourselves to me. But this is not about a single battle won. This is about the future of how you will live your lives from now on—how your children and your grandchildren will live their lives. You've fought bravely. Many have already lost their lives pursuing our common goal and many more yet will. But victory over evil is possible and within your power. You won a battle for something profound: your own lives to live as you see fit. But don't now fail to see that the war for that ideal is a long way from being finished.

"You have won your right to live free today. Now you must have the fire to fight to live free always."

"Freedom is never easy to keep and can easily be lost. All it takes is willful indifference.

Richard lifted an arm back toward the statue standing proudly in the afterglow of sunset. "That will to hold life dear, to be free, is the spirit of this statue we all so admire."

"But Lord Rahl," someone complained, "that is too big a task for us. We are simple people, not warriors. Maybe if you were to lead us it would be different."

Richard laid a hand on his chest. "I was a simple woods guide when I realized that I had to rise to the challenges facing me. I, too, didn't want to face the seemingly invincible evil that loomed over me. But a wise woman—the woman that statue is modeled after—made me see that I had to do so. I am no better than you, no stronger than you. I am simply a man who has come to understand the need to stand without compromise against tyranny. I have taken up that cause because I no longer wanted to live in fear, but to live my own life.

"Those people in the New World to the north are fighting and dying every day. They are simple people like you. None of them wishes to fight, but they must or they will surely die. Their fate today is your fate tomorrow. They can't continue to stand alone and hope to win. When your time comes, neither will you. They need you to be a part of a free world, to attack those who bring the shadow of a dark age over all the world."

A man near the front spoke up. "But aren't you saying the same thing as the Order, that we must sacrifice for the greater good of mankind?"

Richard smiled at the very idea. "Those who wish to impose an idea of a greater good are simply haters of the good. It's enlightened self-interest that causes me to lift a sword against the Imperial Order. It's purely for your own self-interest, and your self-interest in those you love, that I think you should fight—in whatever way you think you can best help our common goal. I'm not forcing you to fight for the greater good of mankind, but trying to make you see that it's a fight for your own life.

"Don't ever make the mistake of thinking that such self-interest is wrong. Self-interest is survival. Self-interest is the substance of life.

"In your own reasoned self-interest, I suggest that you rise up and strike down the Order. Only then can you truly have freedom.

"The eyes of the Old World are upon you."

The dark figures of all the people in fading light stretched back as far as Richard could see. He was relieved to see a lot of nodding heads.

Victor's gaze swept over the men before he turned back to Richard. "I think we are of a mind, Lord Rahl. I will do what I can to see it through."

Richard clasped arms with Victor as the crowd broke into cheering. Finally, as men all across Liberty Square began talking among themselves as to how best to meet the challenge, Richard turned away and took Nicci aside. Cara followed close on his heels.

"Richard, I know the value of what you have just done, but these people still need you to—"

"Nicci," he said, cutting her off, "I have to leave in the morning. Cara is going with me. I'm not going to tell you what to do, but I think it would be a good idea if you were to choose to stay and help these people. They're facing a terrible enough challenge just with the soldiers, but they additionally must face a wizard. You know a lot better than I how to counter that kind of threat. You could be a tremendous help to these people."

She looked for a long time into his eyes before she glanced to the crowd not far off behind him and down the steps.

"I need to be with you," she said in a measured tone, but it still sounded to him like a plea.

"Like I said, it's your life and I'm not going to tell you what to do, just like I'd not like you trying to tell me what I must do."

"You should stay and help," she said. She broke eye contact and looked away. "But it's your life and you must do what you think best. I guess, after all, you are the Seeker." She again glanced at the men gathering around close to Victor, making plans. "These people may not right now voice objections to what you had to say, but they will be thinking about it and they may very well decide later, after they face the soldiers, after a terrible and bloody fight, that they don't wish to do more."

"I was kind of hoping that if you stayed and help them defeat this wizard and the troops coming this way, that you could then add your weight to my words and help convince them of what they need to do. Many of them are well aware of how much you know about the nature of the Order. They will put stock in what you say to them, especially if you've just helped them save their city and keep their families safe." Richard waited until she looked up at him before he went on. "After that, you could then come to join Cara and me."

She appraised his eyes as she folded her arms across her breasts. "You are saying that if I help stop the Order's force coming to kill all these people, then you would allow me to join you?"

"I'm just telling you what I think would be the most beneficial thing for you to do in our struggle to eliminate the Order. I'm not telling you what to do."

She looked away again. "But it would please you if I did as you suggest and stay to help these people."

Richard shrugged. "I admit to that."

Nicci sighed irritably. "Then I will stay, as you suggest, and help them defeat the threat looming a few days away. But if I do that—defeat the troops and eliminate the wizard—then you would allow me to join you?"

"I said I would."

She finally, reluctantly, nodded. "I agree."

Richard turned. "Ishaq?"

The man hurried close. "Yes?"

"I need six horses."

"Six? You will be taking others with you?"

"No, just Cara and me. We'll be needing fresh mounts along the way so we can rotate the horses we ride to keep them strong enough for the journey. We need fast horses, not the draft horses from your wagons. And tack," Richard added.

"Fast horses . . ." Ishaq lifted his hat and with the same hand scratched his scalp. He looked up. "When?"

"I need to leave as soon as it's light enough."

Ishaq eyed Richard suspiciously. "I suppose this is to be in partial payment for what I owe you?"

"I wanted to ease your conscience about when you could begin to repay me."

Ishaq succumbed to a brief laugh. "You will have what you need. I will see to it that you have supplies as well."

Richard laid a hand on Ishaq's shoulder. "Thank you, my friend. I appreciate it. I hope someday I can get back here and haul a load or two for you, just for old times' sake."

That brightened Ishaq's expression. "After we are all free for good?"

Richard nodded. "Free for good." He glanced at the stars beginning to dot the sky. "Do you know a handy place where we can get some food and a place to sleep for the night?"

Ishaq gestured off across the broad expanse of the old palace grounds to the hill where the work shacks used to be. "We have inns, now, since you were here last. People come to see Liberty Square and so they need rooms. I have built a place up there where I rent rooms. They are among the finest available." He lifted a finger. "I have a reputation to uphold of offering the best of everything, whether it be wagons to haul goods, or rooms for weary travelers."

"I have a feeling that what you owe me is going to be dwindling rapidly."

Ishaq smiled as he shrugged. "Many people come to see this remarkable statue. Rooms are hard to come by, so they are not cheap."

"I wouldn't have expected them to be."

"But they are reasonable," Ishaq insisted. "A good value for the price. And I have a stable right next door, so I can bring your horses once I collect them. I will do it now."

"All right." Richard lifted his pack and swung it onto a shoulder. "At least it's not far, even if it is expensive."

Ishaq spread his hands expansively. "And the view at sunrise is worth the price." He grinned. "But for you, Richard, Mistress Cara, and Mistress Nicci, no charge."

"No, no." Lifting a hand, Richard forestalled any argument. "It's only fair that you should be able to earn a return on your investment. Deduct it from what you owe me. What with the interest, I'm sure the amount has grown handsomely."

"Interest?"

"Of course," Richard said as he started toward the distant buildings. "You have had the use of my money. It's only fair that I be compensated for that use. The interest is not cheap, but it's fair and a good value."

As he walked into his room, Richard was pleased to see the washbasin. It wasn't a bath, but at least he would be able to clean up before bed.
He threw closed the bolt on the door, locking himself in, even though he
felt perfectly safe in the small inn. Cara was in the room beside his. Nicci
was in a room downstairs on the first floor close to the entrance and right
beside the only stairs up to the second floor. Men stood guard both inside
and outside the inn while yet more men patrolled the streets in the area
around the building. Richard hadn't thought so many men were necessary,
but Victor and the men were insistent about providing the protection since
enemy troops were in the area. In the end, appreciating the opportunity for
a safe and peaceful night's sleep, Richard hadn't objected.

He was so weary that he could hardly stand any longer. His hip sockets
ached from the long day of walking over rough terrain. On top of the journey, the emotional talk with the people at Liberty Square had taken what
energy he had left.

Richard sloughed off his pack, letting it clunk down on the floor at the
foot of the small bed, before stepping to the washstand and splashing water on his face. He didn't know that water could feel so good.

Nicci, Cara, and Richard had had a quick meal of lamb stew down in
the small dining room. Jamila, the woman who ran the place for Ishaq—
another partner—had been instructed by Ishaq to treat them as royalty.
The round-faced woman had offered to cook them anything they desired.
Richard hadn't wanted to make a fuss, and besides, the leftover lamb stew
had meant there would be no waiting and they could get to sleep all that
much sooner. Jamila had seemed a little disappointed not to have the
chance to cook them up something special. With the kind of meals they'd
had over recent days, though, the bowl of lamb stew and fresh, crusty
bread with loads of butter had been about the best food Richard could recall having. Had it not been for so many troubling things on his mind he
would have savored it more.

He knew that Cara and Nicci needed the rest as much as he did so he'd insisted that each take a room of their own. Both women had wanted to stay in the same room as Richard so that they could be close at hand and watch over him. He'd had visions of them both standing with their arms folded at the foot of his bed as he slept. He'd maintained that nothing was going to get to him on the second floor, and besides, there were plenty of men to stand guard. They had relented, but reluctantly and only after he reminded them that the two of them would be more help to him if they were well rested and alert. It was a luxury for all of them not to have to stand watch, for once, and be able to get the rest they needed.

Victor had promised to come see Richard and Cara off in the morning. Ishaq had promised to have the horses in the stable and waiting long before then. Both Victor and Ishaq were sorry that he was leaving, but they understood that he had his reasons. None of them had asked where he was going, probably because they felt ill-at-ease talking about the woman none of them believed existed. He had begun to sense the distance it created in people when he mentioned Kahlan.

From the tall window in his top floor room, Richard had a breathtaking view of *Spirit* off across the grounds below the rise where the inn stood. With the wick on the lamp in his room turned down low, he had no trouble seeing the statue in white marble lit by a ring of torches in tall iron stanchions. He idly recalled the many times he had been up on this same hillside looking down at Emperor Jagang's palace under construction. It hardly seemed like the same world. He felt as if he'd been dropped into some other life he didn't know and all the rules were different. Sometimes he wondered if he really was losing his mind.

Nicci, in a room on the bottom floor close to the front door, probably couldn't see the statue, but Cara had the room next to his so she undoubtedly had the same view. He wondered if she was taking advantage of it, and, if she was, what she thought of the statue she saw. Richard couldn't imagine how she could not clearly remember everything it meant to him—to Kahlan. He wondered if she, too, felt as if she were living someone else's life . . . or if she thought he was losing his mind.

Richard couldn't imagine what could possibly have happened to make everyone forget that Kahlan existed. He had held out some slim hope that the people in Altur'Rang would remember her, that it had only been those immediately nearby when she had disappeared who were affected. That hope was now dashed. Whatever the cause, the problem was widespread.

Richard leaned against the cabinet with the washbasin and tilted his head back as he closed his eyes for a moment. His neck and shoulders were sore from days of carrying his heavy pack as they had trudged through dense and seemingly endless woods. Throughout the swift and difficult journey even conversation had, for the most part, required too much effort. It felt good not to have to walk for a while, even if when he closed his eyes it seemed that all he could see was a parade of endless forests. With his eyes closed, it felt as if his legs were still moving.

Richard yawned as he lifted the baldric over his head and stood the Sword of Truth against a chair beside the washstand. He pulled off his shirt and tossed it on the bed. It occurred to him that this would be a good time to wash some of his clothes, but he was too worn-out. He just wanted to clean up and then fall into bed and sleep.

He stepped over to the window again as he went about washing with a soapy cloth. The night was dead quiet but for the ceaseless drone of the ci-cadas. He couldn't resist staring at the statue. There was so much of Kahlan in it that it made him heartsick. He had to force himself not to think about what horrors she might be facing, what pain she might be enduring. Anxi-ety constricted his breathing. In an effort to set his worry aside for a while, he did his best to recall Kahlan's smile, her green eyes, her arms around him, the soft moan she sometimes made as she kissed him.

He had to find her.

He dipped the cloth in the water and wrung it out, watching dirty water run back into the basin, and saw that his hands were trembling.

He had to find her.

In another attempt to force his mind onto other things, he rested his gaze on the washbasin, deliberately taking in the vines painted all around the edge. The vines were blue, not green, probably so as to match the blue flowers stenciled on the walls and the blue flowers on the simple curtains and the decorative cover on the bed. Ishaq had done an admirable job of building a warm and inviting inn.

The water in the basin, still as a woodland pool, suddenly trembled for no apparent reason.

Richard stood stock-still, staring at it.

The slack surface abruptly bunched into perfectly symmetrical harmonic waves, almost like the hair on a cat's back standing on end.

And then the whole building shuddered with a hard thump, as if struck by something huge. One of the panes of glass in the window cracked with a brittle pop. Almost instantly, from the far end of the building, came the muffled sound of splintering wood.

Richard crouched, frozen, eyes wide, unable to tell what had caused the incomprehensible sound.

His first thought was that a big tree had fallen on the place, but then he remembered that there were no large trees anywhere nearby.

A heartbeat after the first jolt, came a second thump—louder this time. Closer. The building swayed under the crash of splintering wood. He glanced up, fearing that the ceiling might collapse.

Half a heartbeat later came another thump that shook the building. Shattering, splintering wood let out a high-pitched screech as if crying out in agony as it was being ripped apart.

THUMP. Crash. Louder, closer.

Richard touched the fingers of one hand to the floor to keep his balance as the building quaked under the jolt of the heavy impact. What had started at the far end of the building was rapidly coming closer.

THUMP, CRASH. Closer yet.

Splintering shrieks howled through the night air as wood was rent violently apart. The building swayed. Water sloshed in the basin, slopping over the rolled metal edge with the painted blue vines. The sounds of ripping walls and splintering boards melted together into one continuous roar.

Suddenly, the wall to his left, the wall between his and Cara's room, exploded toward him. Clouds of dust billowed up. The noise was deafening.

Something huge and black, nearly the size of the room itself, drove through the wall, splintering lath, sending plaster and debris showering through the air.

The force of the concussion blew the door off its hinges and violently blasted the glass and the mullions out of the window.

Long ragged fragments of boards spun through the room. One smashed the chair that held his sword, another piercing the far wall. His sword tumbled out of reach. One piece whacked Richard's leg hard enough to drop him to one knee.

Animate darkness drove debris before it, sending everything flying, enveloping the light and plunging the flying wreckage into a surreal, swirling gloom.

Icy fright shimmered through Richard's veins.

He saw a cold cloud of his breath as he grunted with the effort of scrambling to his feet.

Darkness, like death itself, plunged toward him. Richard gasped a breath. Frigid air stabbed like icy needles into his lungs. Shock at the pain of the cutting cold clenched his throat shut.

Richard knew that life and death balanced on a razor's edge only an instant wide.

With every ounce of his strength driving him, he dove through the window as if he were diving into a swimming hole. The side of his body brushed past the descending inky darkness. His flesh sizzled with a sharp sensation so cold that it burned.

In midair, plummeting through the window out into the night, fearing the long drop, Richard snatched for the window's frame and only just managed to seize it with his left hand. He held on for dear life. His falling weight whipped him around so hard that his body slammed into the side of the building with enough force to knock the wind from him. He hung by his one hand, dazed by the wallop against the outside wall, trying to gasp in a breath.

The humid night air on top of the blow against the wall, coming right after the frigid gasp in the room just before he'd jumped out the window, seemed to conspire to do its best to suffocate him. From the corner of his eye he saw the statue in the fluttering torchlight. With her head thrown back, fists at her sides, and her back arched, the figure stood proud against the invisible power trying to subdue her. The sight of it, the strength of it, made Richard at last draw in an urgent breath. He coughed and drew another, gasping for air as his feet searched for any purchase. They found none. He glanced down and saw that the ground was awfully far below him.

It felt as if he might have ripped his shoulder from its socket. Hanging by one hand, he dared not let go. He feared that such a fall would at the least break his legs.

Above, from the window, came a wail so shrill that it made every hair on his body stand on end and every nerve scream in sharp pain. It was a sound so black, so poisonous, so horrific that Richard thought that, surely, the veil to underworld had ripped apart and the Keeper of the Dead had been loosed among the living.

The savage wail in the room above him drew out into a twisting, seething shriek. It was a sound of pure hate brought to life.

Richard glanced up and almost let go. The fall, he thought, might be preferable to the thing in the room now suddenly streaming out through the window.

A dark, incorporeal stain poured out of the shattered window like the exhalation of utter evil.

Although it had no shape, no form, it was somehow crystal clear to Richard that this was something beyond mere wickedness. This was a scourge, like death itself, on the hunt.

As the inky shadow slipped through the window and out into the night, it suddenly began to disintegrate into a thousand fluttering shapes that darted off in every direction, the cold darkness decomposing, melting into the night, dissolving into the heart of the blackest shadows.

Richard hung by one arm, panting, unable to move, watching, waiting for the thing to coalesce suddenly before his face and rip him apart.

The hillside fell under the spell of a still hush. Death's shadow had seemingly become part of the night. The cicadas, until then silent, started in again. As they began their shrill songs, the rising sound moved in a wave across the vast expanse of grounds off toward the distant statue.

"Lord Rahl!" a man below shouted. "Hold on!"

The man, wearing a small-brimmed hat similar to Ishaq's, scrambled around the building, heading for the door. Richard didn't think that he could hang on by his one arm until someone came to help him. He groaned in pain but managed to twist himself around enough to lunge and with his other hand grasp the windowsill, his legs swinging to and fro over a frightening drop. He was relieved to find that just taking some of the weight off his one arm helped ease the pain.

He had just pulled his upper body in through the shattered window when he heard people spilling into his room. The lantern was gone, probably buried, so it was hard to see. Men scrambled over the rubble littering the floor, their boots crunching shattered bits of the wall, snapping fragments of broken wooden furniture. Powerful hands seized him under his arms while others grabbed his belt to help lift him back inside. In the nearly pitch black room it was difficult to get his bearings.

"Did you see it?" Richard asked the men as he still struggled to get his breath. "Did you see the thing that came out of the window?"

Some of the men coughed on the dust while others spoke up that they hadn't seen anything.

"We heard the noise, the crashing, and the window breaking," one of them said. "I thought the whole building was coming down."

Someone appeared with a candle and lit a lantern. The orange glow illuminated a startling sight. A second man, and then a third, held a lantern out to be set alight. Amid the swirling dust, the room was a confusing jumble, what with the bed overturned, the washstand embedded halfway through the far wall, and a hill of rubble across the floor.

In the flickering light, Richard was able to better see the roughly round hole that had been blown through the wall. Broken lumber around the edges all jutted into his room, indicating the direction of intrusion. That was hardly a surprise. The size of the hole, though, was surprising: It spanned nearly the entire distance from floor to ceiling. Most of what had once been the wall now lay shattered all over the floor. Long splintered boards knitted together sections of lath and chunks of plaster. He couldn't imagine how something that had made such a large rupture could have then made it out a window.

Richard spotted his sword and worked it out from under broken boards. He propped it up against the windowsill where it would be handy if he needed it, although he wasn't sure what his sword could have done against whatever it was that had come through the wall only to dissolve into the night.

Men coughed from the thick dust still swirling through the air. Richard saw in the lanternlight that they were all covered with the white dust, making them look like a gathering of ghosts. He saw that he, too, was covered in the white plaster. The only difference was that he was also bleeding from dozens of small cuts. The blood looked all the more stark against the white powder. He briefly brushed some of the plaster dust from his hair, face, and arms.

Worried about others who might have been buried or hurt, Richard took one of the lanterns from a man standing nearby and then scrambled to the top of the rubble. He held up the light, peering into the darkness beyond the hole. The sight was astounding, although not unexpected because he had heard and felt each one of those walls being violently breached.

Each wall, in a straight line all the way back through the building, had a hole smashed through it. All the holes were similar to the one in the wall to his room. At the end, Richard could see stars through the round opening in the far, outside wall.

He stepped carefully over long, jagged fragments of wood. Some of the pile caved in under his weight and it was a struggle to get his foot back out. Other than sporadic coughing, the men were mostly silent as they looked around in awe at the damage wrought by something unknown, something powerful that had vanished into the night.

Through the swirling dust, Richard saw, then, Cara standing in the middle of her room looking off in the same direction as he, off toward the hole to the outside. Her back was to him, her feet spread in a defensive stance. Her Agiel was gripped tightly in her right fist.

Nicci, a flame dancing above her upturned palm, rushed into Richard's room through the broken doorway.

"Richard! Are you all right?"

From atop the wreckage, Richard rubbed his left shoulder as he moved the arm. "I guess so."

Nicci murmured angrily under her breath as she stepped carefully over debris.

"Any idea what's going on?" one of the men asked.

"I'm not sure," Richard said. "Was anyone hurt?"

The men all peered around at each other. A few offered that they didn't think so, that everyone they knew was accounted for and safe. Another man said that the other rooms on the top floor had been unoccupied.

"Cara?" Richard called as he leaned into the dark hole. "Cara, are you all right?"

Cara didn't answer, nor did she move. She stood fixed in the same stance.

His anxiety growing, Richard scrambled the rest of the way over the tangled boards and crumbled plaster. Using one hand against the ceiling to help him balance atop the unstable debris, he stepped through the hole into Cara's room. The destruction was much the same as it had been in his room. Two walls, rather than just one, were holed, but the impact had thrown the material from the second wall into Richard's room. The glass in her window, too, was blown out, but the door still hung, if crookedly, in place.

Cara stood directly in the centerline between the two holes, but she was backed closer to the void in the wall into Richard's room. Wreckage lay all around her. Her leather outfit appeared to have kept her from being shredded by the flying debris.

"Cara?" Richard called again as he made his way down the shifting pile of rubble.

Cara stood unmoving in the dark room, still staring off into the distance. Nicci scrambled over the broken boards and plaster and through the hole in the wall. She seized Richard's arm briefly for support as she caught up with him.

"Cara?" Nicci said as she brought her hand holding the flame around in front of Cara's face.

Richard held up the lantern. Cara's eyes were opened wide, staring, yet unseeing. Tears had left damp trails through the dust on her face. She still hadn't moved from her defensive stance, but now that he was close, Richard could see that her entire body trembled.

He gripped her arm but, startled, drew back.

She was as cold as ice.

"Cara? Can you hear us?" Nicci touched Cara's shoulder and with the same surprise as Richard drew back.

Cara didn't react. It was as if she really were frozen in place. Nicci held the flame up close to the Mord-Sith's face. Her skin looked almost pale blue, but with the way she was covered in a layer of white dust, he wasn't sure if that was really true or not.

Richard slipped an arm around Cara's waist. It was like putting his arm around a block of ice. His instinct was to draw back, but he refused to allow himself to do so. He realized by how his shoulder hurt that he wasn't going to easily be able to lift her by himself.

He looked back at the faces framed in the ragged round hole in the wall, "Could some of you help me with her?"

Men scrambled over the wreckage, spilling into Cara's room, causing yet more dust to billow up. With others bringing light close, Nicci let the small flame extinguish as she stepped close to the Mord-Sith. The men gathered into a knot as they silently watched the sorceress.

Frowning in concentration, she pressed the flats of her hands to Cara's temples.

With a cry Nicci staggered back. Richard reached out with his free hand and caught her elbow to prevent her from tumbling backwards over the tangled rubble.

"Dear spirits," Nicci whispered, panting to catch her breath as if from unexpected pain.

"What?" Richard asked. "What is it?"

The sorceress placed her hands over her heart, still gulping air as she recovered from the unexpected. "She's barely alive."

With his chin, Richard pointed to the door. "Let's get her out of here."

Nicci nodded. "Downstairs—my room."

Richard, without thinking, swept Cara up in his arms. Fortunately, the men were right there to help when they saw him wince in pain.

"Dear Creator," one of the men exclaimed as he lifted her leg, "she's as cold as the Keeper's heart."

"Come on," Richard said, "help me get her downstairs."

Once they lifted her, Cara's limbs were easily moved, although they wouldn't go limp. The men helping Richard carry Cara shuffled through the rubble. One of the men kicked the broken door out of the way. They carried her down the narrow stairs feet first. Richard held her shoulders.

At the bottom of the stairs, Nicci directed them into her room and to the bed. They gently laid Cara down as Nicci first yanked the covers out from under the stricken woman. Once Cara was settled into the bed, Nicci immediately covered her with the blankets.

Cara's blue eyes were still opened wide, staring, it seemed, into some distant nothingness. Occasionally, a tear set out from the corner of her eye on a slow journey across her cheek. Her chin, her shoulders, her arms trembled.

Richard pried Cara's fingers open, making her release the Agiel she still had in a death grip. Her eyes showed no reaction. He endured the excruciating pain of touching her Agiel until he got it out of her grip and was able to release it to hang by the chain around her wrist.

"Why don't you all wait outside?" Nicci said in a quiet voice. "Give me some time to see what I can do?"

The men made their way out, saying that they were going back on patrol, or to stand guard, in case they were needed.

"If that thing comes back," Richard told them, "don't try to stop it. Come get me."

One of the men cocked his head in puzzlement. "What thing, Lord Rahl? What is it we're supposed to be looking for?"

"I'm not sure. All I was able to see was a huge shadow as it came through the wall and then went out the window."

The man looked upward. "If it broke that hole through the wall to get through, then how did it get out a small window?"

"I don't know," Richard admitted. "I guess I didn't really get a good look at it."

The man glanced up again, as if he could see the wreckage above. "We'll keep our eyes wide open. You can be sure of that."

It was then that Richard remembered that he'd left his sword up in his room. It made him uneasy to be without it. He wanted to go get it, but he didn't want to leave Cara's side.

After the last man had left, Nicci sat on the side of the bed as she held a hand over Cara's forehead. Richard knelt close.

"What do you think is wrong?" he asked.

Nicci let the hand settle on Cara's forehead. "I have no idea."

"But you can do something to make her better?"

Nicci's answer was a long moment in coming. "I'm not sure. Whatever I can do, though, I will."

Richard took hold of Cara's still trembling, frigid hand. "Do you think we should shut her eyes? She hasn't even blinked."

Nicci nodded. "Probably not a bad idea. I think it's the dust making her tears run."

One at a time, Nicci carefully shut Cara's eyes. It somehow made Richard feel better that Cara wasn't staring at nothing.

Nicci returned her hand to Cara's forehead as she placed her other hand high on her chest. While Nicci held a wrist, an ankle, and slipped a hand under the back of Cara's neck, Richard went to the washbasin and returned with a wet cloth. He carefully washed Cara's face and brushed some of the dust and bits of plaster out of her hair. Through the wet cloth, he could feel the icy cold of her flesh.

With as warm and humid as it was, Richard couldn't understand how she could be this cold. He remembered, then, how when the black thing had come crashing into his room the air had suddenly gone icy cold. He remembered the painfully cold touch as he brushed past it as he leaped out the window.

"Don't you have any idea what's wrong with her?" Richard asked.

Nicci absently shook her head as she concentrated on pressing the palms of both hands against Cara's temples.

"Any idea what that thing was that came through the walls?"

Nicci turned to look up at him. "What?"

"I asked if you had any idea what could have done this? What crashed through the walls?"

Nicci looked exasperated by the question. "Richard, go wait outside. Please."

"But I want to be in here, with her."

Nicci gently took his wrist and lifted his hand off of Cara's. "You are interfering. Please, Richard, let me do this alone? It's easier without you watching over my shoulder."

Richard felt awkward being in the way. "If it will help Cara."

"It will," she said as she turned back to the woman in her bed.

He stood and watched briefly. Nicci was already absorbed in slipping a hand under Cara's back.

"Go," the sorceress murmured.

"The thing that came through our rooms was cold."

Nicci looked back over her shoulder. "Cold?"

Richard nodded. "It was so cold that I could see my breath. If felt painfully cold to be near it."

Nicci considered his words briefly before turning back to Cara. "Thank you for the information. When I can, I will come out and let you know how she is doing. I promise."

Richard felt helpless. He stood in the doorway for a moment watching the almost imperceptible movement of Cara's shallow breathing. The lamplight lit Nicci's fall of blond hair as she leaned over the Mord-Sith, working to find out what was wrong.

Richard had the awful feeling that he knew what was wrong with Cara. He feared that she had been touched by death itself.

After pulling his pack from the rubble, Richard briefly cleaned himself up and put on a shirt. He also put on his sword.

He didn't know what had crashed into the building, but it seemed pretty likely that it had been coming for him. He had no idea if his sword would help him fight such a thing, but it did make him feel a little better having it at hand.

Outside the night air was still and warm. One of the men saw him emerge from the door and stepped closer.

"How is Mistress Cara?"

"We don't know, yet. She's alive—that's encouraging, at least."

The man nodded.

Richard recognized the man's hat. "You were the one who saw me hanging from the window?"

"That's right."

"Did you get a look at the thing that attacked us?"

"I'm afraid not. I heard all the commotion, looked up, and there you were hanging by one arm. I thought you might fall. That's all I saw."

"No dark thing coming out of the window?"

The man clasped his hands behind his back as he thought about it a moment. "No . . . except maybe I might have just caught the shadow of something. At the most, that's all I might have seen, a glimpse of a shadow. I was more concerned with getting up there before you fell."

After thanking the man, Richard walked for a time without really thinking about where he was going. He felt as if he were in a daze, his thoughts as heavy and dark as the muggy night. Everything he knew and cared about seemed to be disintegrating. He felt helpless.

The murky humidity obscured the stars and the moon hadn't come up yet, but the lights burning in the city all around reflecting off the haze provided enough light for him to make his way to the edge of the hill. He felt useless, not being able to help Cara. She had so many times been there to help him. This time she had faced something that was more than she could handle.

At the brink of the drop, Richard stood for a time gazing off at the statue of *Spirit* in the distance. Victor had made the ring of iron stanchions that held the torches. Kahlan, fascinated by the process, had stood for most of a day in the blacksmith's sweltering shop watching him shape the white hot iron. Victor had not frowned once that day, but had smiled at her genuine interest as he showed her how he worked the metal to achieve what he wanted.

Richard also remembered Kahlan's awe at seeing that carving of hers being reproduced in towering white marble. He remembered when that small statue in buttery smooth, rich, aromatic walnut was finally returned to her and she had clutched it to her breast. He had watched the way her fingers had glided lovingly over the flowing robes. Richard remembered, too, the way her green eyes had then looked up into his eyes.

Having no one believe him about Kahlan made him feel completely alone and isolated. He'd never been in a situation like this before, where people—people who sincerely cared about him—thought that he was only imagining the things he told them. It was a frightening, helpless feeling to have people think he was out of touch with reality.

But even that was not nearly as frightening as his worry about what might have become of Kahlan.

He didn't know what to do to find her. All he knew for sure was that he had to get help. He didn't know if that help would be forthcoming, but he fully intended to do whatever was necessary to make sure he got it.

After a time, he made his way back to the inn. Jamila was at the bottom of the stairs sweeping up dust and bits of plaster.

She eyed him as he walked in. "You must pay for this."

"What do you mean?"

With the handle of her broom, she pointed up the stairs. "The damage. I have seen the place up there. You must pay for fixing it."

Richard was taken aback. "But I didn't do it."

"It is your fault."

"My fault? I was in my room. I didn't cause the damage and I don't know what did."

"You and the woman were the only two in rooms up there. The rooms were fine when you took them. Now they are a mess. It will cost a lot to fix them. I didn't cause the damage—why should I have to pay? The damage is your fault so you must pay—including for the loss of rent while they are being repaired."

She had demanded he pay for fixing the rooms without first asking how Cara was, or even expressing concern for her.

"I will give Ishaq my permission to deduct the cost from what he owes me." Richard glared at the woman. "Now, if you will excuse me."

With the back of his hand he pushed her aside as he stepped past her into the dark hall. She huffed at him before turning back to her sweeping. Not knowing where else to go, he paced slowly up and down the hall. Jamila finally finished collecting the debris from the first floor and trundled off to other business as he continued to pace. He finally sat with his back against the wall opposite the door to Nicci's room. He didn't know what else to do, where else to go. He wanted to see Cara.

Richard drew his knees up and locked his fingers over them. He rested his chin on the back of his hands as he thought about what Jamila had said.

In a way, she was right. The thing had been coming for him. Had he not been there it wouldn't have happened. If anyone else had been hurt or killed he would really be to blame for bringing danger near them. If not for him, Cara wouldn't be hurt.

He cautioned himself to put the blame on the guilty. That was Jagang and those working toward his goals. It was Jagang who had ordered the creation of the beast that was coming after Richard. Cara had simply been in the way. Cara had been trying to protect him from what Jagang and the Sisters of the Dark had created.

As Richard thought about Victor's men who had been killed a few days back, probably by that same beast, he couldn't help but to feel the awful weight of guilt.

And yet, the thing that had come into the inn had not harmed him. Richard had no doubt that it would have, but then it had simply vanished before its sinister work was finished. He couldn't imagine why it would do such a thing. Or why it had come through the walls the way it had. After all, if it went out the window, why didn't it just break in through the window in the first place? Whatever it was had demonstrated awareness by heading right for his room. Had it come in the window it would likely have had him before he knew what was happening. The thing that had killed Victor's men had behaved differently. Cara had not been ripped to shreds in the way they had, although it was clear that she had been seriously hurt.

He began to question that it really had been the same creature that had killed Victor's men. What if Jagang had created more than one beast, more than one weapon to come after him? What if the Sisters of the Dark had spawned an army of creatures to hunt him? All the questions seemed to swirl around in his mind, unable to form into answers.

Richard jumped when Nicci shook his shoulder. He realized that he must have fallen asleep.

"What?" he asked, rubbing his eyes. "What time is it? How long has it been . . ."

"It's been a few hours," Nicci said in a quiet, tired voice. "It's the middle of the night."

Richard rose expectantly to his feet. "Cara's all right, then? You healed her?"

Nicci stared at him for what seemed an eternity. It felt to Richard, as he looked into Nicci's timeless eyes, as if his heart were coming up in his throat.

"Richard," she finally said in a voice so soft and compassionate that it made his breathing stop, "Cara isn't going to make it."

Richard blinked at the words, trying to be certain that he understood what Nicci was really saying.

"I don't understand." He cleared his throat. "What do you mean?"

Nicci gently laid a hand on his arm. "I think you should come in and see her while she is still with us."

Richard seized her shoulders. "What are you talking about?"

"Richard . . ." Nicci's gaze sank to the floor. "Cara isn't going to make it. She is dying. She won't live the night."

Richard tried to retreat from the sorceress, but his back met the wall. "From what? What's wrong with her?"

"I don't know, exactly. She's been touched by something that has . . . has brought death into her. I don't know how to explain it because I don't really know exactly what she is dying from. All I know is that it has overwhelmed her body's defenses and moment by moment she is slipping away."

"But Cara is strong. She'll fight it. She'll make it."

Nicci was shaking her head. "No, Richard, she won't. I don't want to give you false hope. She is dying. I think she may even want to die."

Richard came forward off the wall. "What? That's crazy. She has no reason to want to die."

"You can't say that, Richard. You don't know what she is going through. You don't know her reasons. Maybe the suffering is too much for her. Maybe she can't endure the pain and she only wants it to end."

"If not for herself, Cara would do anything to stay alive in order to protect me."

Nicci licked her lips as she gave his arm a reassuring squeeze. "Maybe you're right, Richard."

Richard didn't like being humored. He looked from the door back to the sorceress. "Nicci, you can save her. You know how to do such things."

"Look, you had better come see her before—"

"You have to do something. You have to."

Nicci hugged her arms around herself. She looked away, her eyes brimming with tears.

"I swear, Richard, I tried everything I knew or could think of. Nothing was of any help. Death already has her spirit and I can no longer reach that far. She is breathing, but barely. Her heart is weak and nearly gone. Her whole body is shutting down as she slips away. I'm not even sure that she is really even still alive in the sense we think of as a person being alive. She is only here by a thread, and that thread will not hold for long."

"But, can't . . ." He could think of no words to hold back the weight of grief beginning to slide in on him.

"Please, Richard," Nicci whispered, "come see her before she is gone. Say what you would to her while you have the chance. You will forever hate yourself if you don't."

Richard felt numb as Nicci led him into the room. This couldn't be happening. It just couldn't. This was Cara. Cara was like the sun; she couldn't die. She was . . . she was his friend. She couldn't die.

C H A P T E R   1 8

The feeble glow of two lanterns failed to do much to brighten the murky room. The smaller one sat on a table in the corner, as if cowering in the presence of death itself. The other stood on a bedside table beside a glass of water and a damp cloth, struggling to hold the gathered shadows at bay. A brocade bedcover with luxuriant gold fringe was draped over Cara, her arms limp atop it, one of its corners hanging down over the side of the bed to puddle on the floor.

Cara didn't look like Cara. She looked cadaverous. Even in the golden light of the lamp, her face looked ashen. Richard didn't see her breathing.

He could hardly draw a breath himself. He could feel his knees trembling. The lump in his throat seemed as if it might choke him. He wanted to fall on her and beg her to wake.

Nicci leaned close, gently touching Cara's face. Her fingers slid down to the side of her neck. Richard noticed that Cara's terrible shuddering had finally ceased. He didn't think that was the good news it might appear to be.

"Is she . . . is she . . ."

Nicci looked back over her shoulder. "She's still breathing, but I'm afraid it's coming slower."

Richard worked his tongue, wetting the roof of his mouth so that he could form words. "You know, Cara has a man she cares about."

"She does? Really?"

Richard nodded. "Most people don't think that Mord-Sith can ever really care about anyone, but they can. Cara cares about a soldier. General Meiffert. Benjamin cares for her, too."

"You know him?"

"Yes. He's a good man." Richard stared at the blond braid lying over Cara's shoulder and out over the brocade bedcover. "I haven't seen him for ages. He's with the D'Haran army."

Nicci looked skeptical. "And Cara admitted to you that she cares about this man?"

Richard shook his head as he stared at Cara's familiar face. Her beautiful face was now sunken and pale and only looked like a ghost of her former self.

"No. Kahlan told me. The two of them became pretty close over the course of the year they were with the D'Haran army while you had me down here in Altur'Rang."

Nicci looked away and fussed with the covers over Cara. As Richard stepped closer, Nicci moved over to a chair beside the table to be out of his way. He felt as if he were outside of his own body, watching from somewhere above, watching himself go to one knee, watching himself take up Cara's cold hand, watching himself hold it to his cheek.

"Dear spirits, don't do this to her," he whispered. "Please," he added with a choking sob, "don't take her."

He looked over at Nicci. "She wanted to die as a Mord-Sith, fighting for our cause, not in bed."

Nicci offered the smallest of smiles. "She had her wish."

The words, making it sound as if Cara was already dead, hit him like a blow. He couldn't allow this to happen. He just couldn't. Kahlan was gone, and now this. He just couldn't let it happen.

He cupped a hand to Cara's icy face. It felt like touching the dead. Richard swallowed back the tears.

"Nicci, you're a sorceress. You saved me when I was near death. No one else but you would have ever been able to come up with a solution. No one but you could have saved me. Isn't there anything at all that you can think of to do for Cara?"

Nicci slipped forward off the chair to kneel beside him. She took up his hand and held it to her lips. He felt a tear fall onto the back of the hand she so tenderly held, as if she were a humble subject beseeching her king's forgiveness.

"I'm so sorry, Richard, but there isn't. I hope you know that I would do anything it took if I could save her, but I can't. This is beyond my ability. A time comes when we all have to die. Her time has come and I can't change it."

Richard blinked at the watery sight of the death scene, the room barely lit by the weak light of two small flames. The bed holding Cara seemed to float by itself in that light, with darkness waiting all around her.

He nodded. "Nicci, please, could you leave me alone with her? I want to be alone with her when the times comes that . . . It's nothing against you. It's just that I think I should be alone with her."

"I understand, Richard." Nicci's fingers touched his back as she stood and then, as if reluctant to break that contact with the living, trailed along his shoulder as she moved past. "I'll be close by if you need me," she said as her living touch ended.

The door softly shut behind her, leaving the room in silence. Even though the heavy drapes were closed over the window, Richard could hear the ceaseless chorus of the cicadas outside.

He could no longer hold back the tears. He laid his head on Cara's middle as he sobbed, clutching her limp hand.

"Cara, I'm so sorry. It's my fault. It was after me, not you. I'm so sorry. Please, Cara, don't leave me. I need you so much."

Cara was the only one who followed him because she believed in him. She might have agreed with Nicci that he was dreaming up Kahlan, but she still believed in him. With Cara, that wasn't a contradiction. More and more lately, it seemed that her faith in him was all that was holding him together and keeping him focused on what he had to do. There were frightening moments when he no longer knew if he believed in himself. It was so hard to face an entire world that thought he was delusional. It was so hard to do what he believed in when almost no one believed in him. But Cara believed in him even if she didn't believe in Kahlan's existence. There was something unique about that sentiment, something unlike even Nicci or Victor's respect for him.

He held Cara's face in both hands as he kissed her forehead.

He hoped she wasn't suffering. He hoped it was a peaceful end to a life that had been anything but peaceful.

She was so pale, her breathing so shallow.

Her flesh felt as cold as death.

Hating that she was so cold, Richard pulled the bedcover aside as he leaned over and slipped his arms around her, hoping that his warmth would help her.

"Take my warmth," he whispered in her ear. "Take all you need. Please, Cara, take warmth from me."

Lying there holding her, Richard descended into a fog of agony. He knew how much this woman had suffered. He knew what her life had been like. He knew how much she had been hurt. He had endured some of the things she had endured under the mad rule of his father, Darken Rahl. He had suffered some of the same pain and hopelessness. Perhaps more than anyone else, he could truly empathize with her. He knew how strangers had taken her into a world of pain and madness. Richard knew because he had been there, too. He had so wanted to bring her back from that dark and terrible place.

"Take my warmth, Cara. I'm here for you."

He opened himself to her, opened his need to her, opened himself to her need.

He clutched her tightly in his arms as he wept against her shoulder. He almost felt that if he were to hold her tight enough, she couldn't slip away into death.

Richard could feel as he held her in his arms that she was still alive and he couldn't bear for that to end. He wished so much that Nicci could have done something. If anyone deserved to be healed, it was Cara. At that moment, more than anything, he wanted her to be healed.

Richard opened himself, his very soul, to that purpose.

He released himself into his empathy for this woman who had given him so much. More than once she had risked her life to follow his orders. She had often risked her life for him in open defiance of his orders. She had followed him across the world. Countless times she had placed herself between danger and his and Kahlan's lives. Cara deserved life, deserved all the goodness in life. He wanted nothing but to make her whole again. He gave all of himself over to that desire. He held back nothing in his focused need to have Cara stay among the living.

To that end, to that desperate desire, he consciously sought the life within her as he descended into the swirling current of her agony. As fast as that thought, he found his mind with hers, with her agonizing pain. He held her tight in his arms as he wept with her desolate suffering.

He gritted his teeth, held his breath, and pulled her pain into himself. He wanted nothing more than to draw that pain away from her. He spared nothing to protect himself from the onslaught that suddenly inundated him. He felt everything she felt. He suffered everything she suffered. He pressed his open mouth against her shoulder, muffling his scream as the pain lanced through him.

They were in an empty, dark, and hopeless place . . . a lifeless place.

He shook with her suffering as he lifted some of her burden. She held tight to the pain, loath to release it, especially to him. But as weak as she was, he was able to draw it anyway, and then he drew yet more.

Lifting and uncovering the layers of suffering, he felt the icy touch of death within her.

The raw fear at such an encounter was as arresting as anything he had ever confronted. Cara was saturated in that dark and icy sensation. He shook with the suffering he shared with her, with the dread they together felt. His mind twisted with the wrenching pain until it was a terrible and seemingly insurmountable struggle just to maintain his own will to go on.

Richard was swept into a coursing, cold current of hopeless misery that consumed him. It seemed more than he could bear, and yet he endured it and took on more. He wanted her to take on his strength, his living warmth. But to do that, he would first have to survive pulling that dark poison into himself while at the same time giving over to her his strength.

Time lost all meaning. The pain itself was the embodiment of forever.

"Death will come often, offering to take you . . . wanting to take you," he whispered against her ear. "Don't accept the offer, Cara. Stay. Don't accept death."

I want to die.

That single thought came spiraling up through the agonizing desolation. It shocked and terrified him. What if trying to hold on to life was more than she could endure? What if it was more than he could endure? What if he was asking more of her than she could abide? . . . more than he had had a right to ask?

"Cara," he whispered into her ear, "I need you to live. Please, I need you to live."

I can't.

"Cara, you are not alone. I'm here with you. Hold on. For me, hold on and let me help you."

Please, let me go. Let me die. I'm begging you, if you care for me, then leave me . . . let me die.

She began to slip away. He clutched her tighter. He pulled more of her suffering into himself. Her inner self wailed in agony as she fought him.

"Cara, please"—he gasped against the torrent of pain flooding through him—"let me help you. Please don't leave me."

I don't want to live. I have failed you. I should have saved you when Nicci came to capture you. I know that now—you made me see it. I would die for you, but I failed in my duty, in my promises to myself. There is no reason for me to live. I am not worthy to be your protector. Please, let me go.

Richard was stunned to grasp the despair in her longing, but more than that, he was horrified by it.

He gathered that pain, too, and lifted it from her. He took it even as she tried to hold on to it, to slip away from him.

"Cara, I love you. Please don't leave me. I need you."

He fought to draw more of her agony into himself. He overpowered her resistance and took more yet. She was unable to stop him. He lifted the ashen robes of death dragging her down. Richard held her tight in his arms as he opened his heart, his need, his soul.

She wailed in heartbreak. He understood the crushing loneliness.

"I'm with you, Cara. You aren't alone."

Richard soothed her even as he struggled to endure the stunning agony of the evil that had touched her. It was not simply the pain of it, but the bleak horror of it that was killing her, and now that same cold desolation was slowly crushing him—and at the same time her blinding suffering blocked his healing power from flowing into her.

He suddenly felt as if he had swum out to save a drowning person and now they were both caught up in the same savage torrent and they were both drowning together in the black waters of death.

If he was to have a chance—if she was—he first had to lift enough of her suffering. He had to hold the weight of it for her. He pulled the pain onward, heedless of it, welcoming it, drawing it with all his might.

When he felt that full weight of misery and anguish gathered into the core of himself, he had to struggle mightily to hold on to his own life at the same time as he let flow his power, his healing strength, his healing heart. Richard had never been taught how to heal, how to direct his power, he could only let the warmth of it flow into her.

I don't want to live. I have failed you. Please, let me die.

"Why do you want to leave me? Why?

Because only in that way can I serve you, because then you can have another who will not fail you.

"Cara, that isn't true. Something is wrong. Something neither of us understands." Through the pain, Richard fought to get the words out. "You didn't fail me. You have to believe me. You must believe in me. That is what I need more than anything—for you to be with me and believe in me. It is you I need, not your service. Please, I need you. I need you to live. That is the service—your life makes mine better."

He fought with all his might to hold on—to hold Cara with him—but the weight of the darkness within seemed bottomless. As the barriers of his restraint collapsed, he felt as if he were plunging into a molten void, spiraling ever downward into that dark shadow that had come through the wall for him. He saw flashes of it as she had seen it, saw the heart-stopping terror of it crashing in on her.

That was the core of her dread, that vile thing, that death incarnate, coming for him, right through her. This was not the gentle dissolution of consciousness into the void of nonexistence. This was every nightmare come to life, come to rip the life out of the living. This was dark death descending upon her, all alone and defenseless, that merciless reaper of souls come to rip hers out while she screamed her life away.

As she'd stood before it, blocking its way, she had taken its deadly touch.

He understood, then, that Cara felt she had failed him before, with Nicci, and this time she had been determined to die to prove her oath. Madness still dwelt within her.

She believed that death falling in upon her would be her redemption in his eyes and so she refused to shrink before it.

She wanted to die for him to prove herself to him.

As it had come through the wall and through her room, Cara had tried to steal the power from death itself.

Richard felt that torturous touch envelope him in its all-consuming agony. It was a touch so cold it began to freeze his heart.

The world began slipping away from him, as it had begun to slip away from her.

He was lost in the crushing pain of that deadly touch.

It felt to Richard as if he were trapped beneath the ice in the swift, raven waters of a frozen river. The shadow of panic swirled ever closer around him.

He was exhausted and didn't have any reserve of strength left.

As the specter of failure loomed, and the full realization of what such a failure would mean came to him, he rallied his will and exerted greater effort to fight his way toward the remote light of consciousness. Even though he was aware that he had managed to come partially awake, he was still in some distant, deep place and having difficulty completing the journey. He struggled to rise up, struggled for the life above, but couldn't break through.

Even as Richard tried to press himself harder, it seemed too difficult, too far. For the first time, he considered the peace of surrender . . . truly considered it, as had she before it had dragged her under.

The deadly fangs of failure hovered closer.

Driven by the fright of the full realization of everything that such a defeat would mean, he drew together his strength, focused his will, and with desperate passion reached toward the world of life.

With a gasp, his eyes opened.

The pain had been crushing. He felt dizzy and sick from the encounter with such malevolence. He still trembled with the power of it. After such raw inner violence, he feared that every hammer beat of his heart might be the last. The slick touch of depravity had bequeathed him a repugnant memory of the gagging stench of rotting corpses, making it nearly impossible to draw the full breath he needed.

He had reached into Cara's soul and he had felt an alien evil lurking there, within her, sucking the life from her, pulling her into the dark eternity of death. It had been a debilitating dread beyond anything he had ever felt before, beyond the mere fear of the black abyss of eternity.

It had been the grinning, naked vow of unimaginable terrors that were coming for him.

At first it had seemed that he had touched the icy face of death itself, but he now knew that he hadn't. Despite his revulsion, he knew that it was something other than simply death.

Death was merely a part of its poisonous architecture.

Death was inanimate. This was not.

He hurt so much that he was unsure at that moment if he would have the strength to ever stand again, the strength required to live. His bones ached. The marrow of his bones ached. He couldn't seem to stop trembling. Yet the pain was more than mere physical agony; it was an abhorrent misery that had seeped through his soul and touched every aspect of his existence.

The quiet room at last began to float into focus around him. The lamps still held back the veil of darkness. Beyond the heavy drapes the cicadas still sang their song of life.

Lying on the bed, still embracing Cara protectively in his arms, Richard was at last able to draw the full breath he so desperately needed. As he did, he relished the fragrance of her hair, savored the scent of the warm, moist skin along the curve of her neck, and in so doing the agony began to recede.

He felt Cara's arms tightly embracing him. Downy soft hair behind her ear caressed the side of his face.

"Cara?" he whispered.

She reached up and ran a hand tenderly down the back of his head as she unashamedly held him against her. "Shh," she soothed in his ear. "It's all right."

He was having trouble making sense of things.

He was somewhat disoriented to find himself holding Cara in his arms, to find her holding him so tenderly in hers, to realize they were locked in such an intimate embrace. He could feel the entire length of her pressed against him. But then, nothing could be more intimate than what they had shared in that dark place as they together faced the evil that had taken her.

He ran his tongue across his cracked lips and tasted salty tears.

"Cara . . ."

She nodded against the side of his face. "Shh," she soothed again. "It's all right. I'm with you. I won't leave you."

He drew away just enough to look into her eyes. They were blue and clear, revealing a depth he had never seen before. She studied his face with a kind of caring, knowing sympathy.

At that moment, he clearly saw in her eyes that this was Cara and no more. In that moment, he saw that the appellation of Mord-Sith had been stripped away down to her soul. In that moment, it was Cara, the woman, the individual, and nothing else.

It was as revealing and profound a view of her as he had ever had. It was startlingly beautiful.

"You are a very rare person, Richard Rahl."

The soft breath of her words against his face soothed some of the lingering pain as seductively as did her arms, as did her eyes, as did her words, as did the living, breathing warmth of her.

Even so, the agony he had lifted from her still coursed through him, seeking to pull him back toward darkness and death. Somewhere in the back of his mind, he fought it with his love of life, and with his joy that Cara was alive.

"I am a wizard," he whispered back.

She stared up into his eyes as she slowly shook her head in wonder.

"There has never been a Lord Rahl like you before. I swear, there never has."

With her arms around his neck, she pulled his head closer and kissed him on the cheek. "Thank you, Lord Rahl, for bringing me back. Thank you for saving me. You made me see again that I want to live. It is I who is supposed to be protecting your life, and you are the one to risk yours to save me."

She again searched his eyes with leisurely satisfaction. It was completely unlike the way a Mord-Sith had of gazing through a person, of seeing all the way into their soul. This was an emotion of regard born of her appreciation for his value to her. In the purest sense, it was love. She showed absolutely no reticence in him seeing her feelings laid bare.

He supposed that, after what they had just shared, any such modesty would be pointless. He knew, though, that this was more, that this was Cara; sincere, unafraid, and unashamed.

"There has never been a Lord Rahl like you."

"Cara, you don't know how glad I am to have you back with me."

She held his head in both her hands and kissed his forehead. "Oh, but I do know. I know what you suffered for me this night. I know very well how much you wanted me back. I know very well what you did for me." She slipped her arms around his neck again and hugged him tight. "I have never been afraid like that, not even when I was first—"

He touched his fingers to her lips to silence what she had been about to say for fear that it would break the spell, that it would too soon bring the armor of Mord-Sith back into her beautiful blue eyes. He knew what she had been about to say. He knew that madness.

"Thank you, Lord Rahl," she whispered in wonder when he took his fingers away. "Thank you for everything, and for not letting me say what I had been about to say." With a twitch of her brow, pain ghosted across her face. "That is why there has never been a Lord Rahl like you before. They all created Mord-Sith. They all brought the pain. You ended it."

Richard couldn't force any words past the lump in his throat, so he simply brushed her blond hair from her forehead and smiled at her. He was so happy to have her back that he couldn't put it into words.

He gazed around the room, then, trying to judge how late it was.

"I don't know how long it took you to heal me," she said as she watched him surveying the curtains for any sign of the approach of dawn. "But after you did, you were so exhausted that you seemed to collapse into sleep. I couldn't wake you. . . . I didn't want to wake you." Her arms still loosely around his neck, she gazed up at him with a blissful smile, looking as if she never wanted to move. "I was so weak that I fell asleep as well."

"Cara, we have to get out of here."

"What do you mean?"

Richard pushed himself up, the urgency of the situation becoming all too clear. His head spun sickeningly. "I used magic to heal you."

She nodded, looking uncharacteristically content at the mention of magic and her in the same breath. This had been magic that had shown her the wonder of life.

What he was getting at abruptly became clear to her. She sat up in a rush, but had to put a hand back to steady herself.

Richard stood on trembling legs. He realized then that he was still wearing his sword. He was glad to have it at hand. "If Jagang's beast is around, then it might have sensed that I used my gift. I don't know where it might be, but I'd not like to be lying here when it returns."

"Nor would I. Once was enough for a lifetime."

He held out an arm and helped her stand. She balanced in a stiff posture for a moment before gathering her senses and loosening her pose. It somehow seemed startling to him to see that she was dressed in her red leather. After having been so close to her, after having been within her, in a sense, clothes seemed somehow alien.

In some inexplicable manner, Cara drew the aura of Mord-Sith around herself.

She smiled. The composed confidence in that smile lifting his heart. "I'm all right," she said as if to tell him to stop worrying. "I'm back with you."

The steel was back in her eyes. Cara was indeed back.

Richard nodded. "Me too. I'm feeling better now that I'm waking up." He gestured to her pack. "Let's get our things and get moving."

Nicci stood at the edge of the hill, hands clasped, gazing across the grounds at the white marble statue lit by torches. The people of Altur'Rang had thought that such a noble figure, a symbol of liberty for them, should never go dark and so it was always lit.

Nicci had slowly paced the gloomy hall in the inn for much of the night, dispirited about the life slipping away on the other side of the door. She had tried everything she knew to save Cara, but it had been hopeless.

Nicci didn't know Cara all that well, but she certainly knew Richard. She probably knew him better than anyone alive, except, perhaps, his grandfather Zedd. She didn't know his past so well, the stories about his childhood or that sort of thing; she knew Richard the man. She knew him down to the core of his soul. There was no one alive she knew better.

She understood the depth of his grief at losing Cara. Throughout the vigil, Nicci's gift, unbidden, had brought her the sounds of some of that open misery. It broke Nicci's heart to have Richard suffer such a loss. She would have done anything to have spared him that.

At one point she had thought to go in and comfort Richard's grief, to ease some of it by sparing him at least a bit of the loneliness of it. The door would not open.

While it was puzzling, what she could sense told her that there were only two people inside and what she could hear told her that there was nothing more than simple sorrow on the other side, so she hadn't tried to force open the stuck door. Unable to bear the pain of listening to Richard's supplications to Cara as she lay dying, Nicci had eventually gone outside, finally ending up staring out across the black chasm of night to the statue he had created.

Other than being with Richard himself, there were few things Nicci would rather do than gaze at the majestic things he had created.

Sometimes the death of someone close had a way of making people see the world in a new light, a way of making them come back to those things that were most important in life. She wondered what Richard would do once Cara passed away, if it would jolt him back to reality and he would finally abandon the search for phantoms and stand with the people who wanted to be free of the Imperial Order.

Hearing footsteps, and then her name called, Nicci turned.

It was Richard, with someone else, approaching through the shadows. Nicci's heart sank. That could only mean that Cara's ordeal had finally ended.

As Richard came close, Nicci saw who was with him.

"Dear spirits, Richard," she whispered, her eyes going wide, "what have you done?"

In the dim light of the distant torches Cara looked perfectly alive and well.

"Lord Rahl healed me," she said, offhandedly, as if such an accomplishment had been a minor task of no more note than if he had helped her to fetch water.

Nicci stared in shock. "How?" was all she could say.

Richard looked as weary as if he had been through a battle. She half expected to see him covered in blood.

"I couldn't stand the thought of not doing something to try to help her," he said. "I suppose that the need was strong enough so that I was able to somehow do what I needed to do in order to heal her."

The meaning of why that door wouldn't open suddenly became all too clear. He had indeed been through a battle, and he was, in a sense, covered in blood, just not the kind one could see.

Nicci leaned toward him. "You used your gift." It was a charge, not a question. Nonetheless he answered it.

"I guess so."

"You guess so." Nicci wished she could make herself not sound like she was mocking him. "I tried everything I knew. Nothing I did was able to reach her. I couldn't heal her. What did you do? And how did you manage to touch your Han?"

Richard shrugged self-consciously. "I'm not exactly sure of it all. I held her and I could feel that she was dying. I could feel her slipping farther and farther away. I kind of let myself—my mind—sink down into her, down into the core of who she is, down to where she needed the help. Once I reached that place of union with her, I collected her pain into my-

self so that she would have enough strength to take the warmth of life I offered her."

Nicci understood very well the elaborate phenomenon he was describing,
but she was astounded to hear it explained in such incidental terms. It was as
if she had asked him how he carved such a lifelike statue in marble and he
had said of his masterwork that he just cut off all the stone that didn't belong.
While accurate, such an explanation was casual to the point of absurdity.

"You took upon yourself what was killing her?"

"I had to."

Nicci pressed her fingertips to her temples. Even she, with all the powers she had at her disposal, and she had considerable power, to say nothing of her training, experience, and knowledge, could not undertake such
a deed. She had to make an effort to slow her hammering heart.

"Do you have any idea at all of the danger involved in such an endeavor?"

Richard looked a little ill at ease by the heated tone of her questions. "It
was the only way, Nicci," he said in simple summary.

"It was the only way," she repeated in astonishment. She could not believe what she was hearing. "Do you have any idea how much power it
takes to embark on such a voyage of the soul, much less to ever come
back from such a place? Or the peril in going there?"

He stuck his hands in his pockets as if he were a child being upbraided
for misbehaving. "All I know is that it was the only way to get Cara back."

"And he did," Cara said, pointing a finger at Nicci not only for empha-
sis but to stress her defense of him. "Lord Rahl came for me."

Nicci stared at the Mord-Sith. "Richard went to the brink of the world
of the dead for you . . . and perhaps beyond."

Cara stole a glance at Richard. "He did?"

Nicci slowly nodded. "Your spirit had already slipped into a twilight
realm. You were beyond my reach. That was why I could not heal you."

"Well, Lord Rahl did it."

"Yes, he did." Nicci reached out and with a finger lifted Cara's chin. "I
hope that as long as you live you never forget what this man has just done
for you. I doubt there is anyone living who could have—who would
have—attempted such a thing."

"He had to." Cara gave Nicci a brazen smile. "Lord Rahl can't get
along without me and he knows it."

Richard turned aside as he smiled to himself.

Nicci could hardly believe such a casual attitude after such a monumental event. She took a breath in an attempt to control her voice and not give the wrong impression, an impression that she was displeased that he had healed Cara.

"You used your gift, Richard. The beast is already about and you used your gift."

"I had to or we would have lost her."

To Richard, it all seemed so simple and straightforward. At least he had the sense not to look as self-satisfied as Cara. Nicci planted her fists on her hips as she leaned closer to him.

"Don't you comprehend what you've done? You used your gift again. I warned you before that you must not do so. The beast is already somewhere close and by using your gift you just told it right where you are."

"What did you expect me to do, let Cara die?"

"Yes! She is sworn to protect you with her life. That is her job—her sworn duty. Not helping you to bring the beast closer to you. We could easily have lost you in such an attempt, to say nothing of the profound menace you have just awakened. You risked all you mean to the people of D'Hara and your value to our cause just to save one person. You should have let her go. In saving her you have only allowed her to bring death to both of you because the beast will now be able to find you. What just happened will now happen again, only this time there will be no escape. You have just saved Cara's life at the price of your own, and no doubt hers in the bargain."

Even as she spoke Nicci knew by the smoldering anger in his eyes that she was not doing a good job of making him see what she meant. Cara's eyes, on the other hand, revealed sudden alarm verging on panic. Richard placed a hand on the back of her neck and gave it a reassuring squeeze, as if to tell her to ignore such a supposition.

"That's not certain, Nicci." The muscles in his jaw flexed as he gritted his teeth. "It may be a possibility, but it's not certain—and besides, I wasn't going to let someone I care about die just because it might make me a little safer. I'm already hunted. Letting Cara die wouldn't have changed that."

Nicci let her hands flop down against her thighs. He was in no mood to hear anyone speak against saving the life of a woman he cared deeply for.

Nicci had no idea how she could explain it to him in a way that could make him understand the magnitude of the forces he had invoked or the grave danger he had unleashed. How could she say anything and not have him misunderstand her meaning? In the end, she knew she couldn't.

Nicci placed a hand on his shoulder. "I guess I can't blame you, Richard. I guess that in your place, I would have done the same. Someday, when we have the luxury of time we will have to talk about this. When we are able, I would like you to tell me everything you did. Maybe I can help you learn to better control what you alone were able to harness. If nothing else maybe I can at least make things you do spontaneously a little more focused and a little less dangerous."

Richard nodded his appreciation, whether of her offer or her softer tone she wasn't sure.

Nicci could see in Richard and Cara's eyes that the experience had brought the two of them closer. When she realized that he would soon be leaving, Nicci's brief bout of joy at seeing Cara alive and well faded.

"Besides," Richard said as he scanned the darkness, "we don't even know if this had anything to do with the thing back in the woods."

"Well of course it did," Nicci said.

His gaze returned to her. "How do you know? That thing tore all those men apart. This was a different kind of attack. For that matter, we don't even know for certain that either attack was the beast that Jagang ordered to be created."

"What are you talking about? What else could it be? It has to be the weapon that Jagang directed the Sisters to conjure."

"I'm not saying that it isn't—it very well could be—but a lot of it doesn't make any sense to me."

"Like what?"

Richard raked his fingers back through his hair. "The thing in the forest attacked the men—it didn't attack me even though I wasn't far away. Here, it didn't bother to tear Cara apart like it did the men. If it was the same thing, then we know it could have easily killed me. So when it was right here and had the chance, why didn't it use the opportunity?"

"Maybe because I tried to capture its power," Cara offered. "Maybe it just passed me by because I was a threat or maybe I distracted it enough that it decided to flee."

Richard shook his head. "You were no threat. It went right through you, and besides, its touch was enough to eliminate your interference. Then, it came through the wall for me, but as it reached my room it didn't flee, it simply disappeared."

Nicci abruptly turned suspicious. She never had heard the whole story.

"You were in the room and it just vanished?"

"Not exactly. I jumped out the window to escape it as it came through the wall into my room. As I hung there some kind of dark thing, like a moving shadow, came out the window and as it did it seemed to evaporate into the night."

Nicci idly drew the end of the cord of her bodice through her fingers as she considered what he'd said. She tried to fit the pieces into everything else she knew, but none of it would match. Nothing that the beast did seemed to make sense—if it really was the same beast. Richard was right in that it all seemed to defy logic.

"Maybe it didn't see you," she murmured half to herself as she considered the puzzle.

Richard flashed her a skeptical expression. "So you're saying that it could find me, at night, inside the inn, and it then crashed right through a succession of walls as it was coming for me, but then when I just barely managed to jump through the only window, it became confused and so it wandered off?"

Nicci appraised his eyes a moment. "Both attacks have something important in common. They both displayed incredible power—shattering trees like they were twigs and going through walls as if they were no more than paper."

Richard sighed unhappily. "I suppose that's true."

"What I'd like to know," Nicci added as she folded her arms, "is why it didn't kill Cara."

She caught the slight flicker in his eyes and she knew then that he knew something more than he had said. Nicci cocked her head as she watched him while she waited.

"When I was there in Cara's mind, taking up the pain of the touch of that vile thing, there was something more that it left behind," he admitted in a quiet voice. "I think it wanted to leave a message for me to find, a message that it's coming for me, that it will find me, and that for all eternity it will make my death a luxury beyond reach."

Nicci's gaze slid to Cara.

"I didn't choose for him to come after me to that twilight place, as you called it. I didn't ask him to and I didn't want him to." The Mord-Sith's hands fisted at her sides. "But I can't lie and say that I'd rather be dead."

Nicci couldn't help but to smile at such simple honesty.

"Cara, I'm joyful that you're not dead—I truly am. What kind of man would we be following if he easily let a friend die without trying his best to save her?"

Cara's expression cooled as Nicci looked again at Richard.

"I'm still perplexed as to why it didn't kill Cara. After all, a message like that could have just as easily been given directly to you once it had you in its clutches. If the threat is credible—and I certainly don't doubt that it is—then the beast would have all the time it wished to make you suffer if it would have snatched you right then. Such a message serves no real purpose. What's more, it makes no sense for the beast to be right there and then vanish."

Richard drummed his fingers on the cross guard of his sword as he thought it over. "All good questions, Nicci, but I just don't have good answers."

With the palm of his left hand resting on the hilt of his sword, he scanned the darkness again, checking for any threat. "I think Cara and I had better be on our way. Considering what happened to Victor's men, I'm concerned about what will happen if that thing comes back here after me. I'd not like that kind of beast rampaging through the city in a blood frenzy. I don't want any more people to be needlessly hurt or killed. Whatever that thing is—the beast Jagang had his Sisters conjure, or something we don't even know about—it seems to me that I'll have a better chance to stay alive if I keep moving. Sitting in one place feels too much like waiting for the executioner to arrive."

"I don't think that you are necessarily making logical assumptions," Nicci said.

"Nonetheless I need to be going anyway and I'd feel better if it was sooner rather than later—for a variety of reasons." He hoisted his pack higher on his back. "I have to find Victor and Ishaq."

Resigned, Nicci gestured behind her. "After the attack I went and got them. They are both over at the stables, back there. Ishaq has the horses you requested. Some of the men helped him gather supplies for you." She put a hand on his arm. "Some of the relatives of Victor's men, the ones who were killed, are there, too. They want to hear from you."

Richard nodded as he let out a deep breath. "I hope I can offer them some comfort. Grief is fresh in my mind." He gave Cara a quick squeeze on her shoulder. "But mine has been lifted."

Richard hitched his bow higher up onto his shoulder as he started away. In little more than a blink he dissolved into the darkness.

As Cara went past, following in Richard's wake, Nicci caught the Mord-Sith's arm, holding her back until she could speak without Richard hearing.

"How are you, Cara? Really?"

Cara met Nicci's direct gaze with a steady look of her own. "I'm tired, but I'm fine, now. Lord Rahl made it right."

Nicci nodded her satisfaction. "Cara, may I ask you a personal question?"

"As long as I don't have to promise I'll answer it."

"Do you have a man for whom you care greatly named Benjamin Meiffert?"

Even in the dim light, Nicci could see Cara's face go as scarlet as her red leather outfit. "Who told you such a thing?"

"Do you mean to say, then, that it's a secret and no one knows?"

"Well, that's not what I'm saying, exactly," Cara stammered. "I mean . . . you're trying to trip me into saying something I don't intend."

"I'm not trying to trip you into saying anything, especially something that isn't true. I only asked about Benjamin Meiffert."

Cara's brow drew tight. "Who told you such a thing?"

"Richard." Nicci arched an eyebrow. "Is it true?"

Cara pressed her lips tight. At last she looked away from Nicci to glare off into the night. "Yes."

"So you told Richard all about how you care a great deal for this soldier?"

"Are you crazy? I would never have told such a thing to Lord Rahl. Where could he have heard it?"

For a moment, Nicci listened to the cicadas singing their incessant mating songs as she considered the Mord-Sith.

"Richard said that Kahlan told him all about it."

Cara stood with her mouth agape. She at last touched her fingers to her forehead as she worked to gather her senses.

"Well that's just crazy. . . . I, I must have told him myself. I guess I just forgot. We talk about so much. It's hard to recall everything I told him—but now that you bring it up, I think I do recall mentioning it one night when we were both talking about such sentimental things. I think that must have been when I told him about Benjamin Meiffert. I guess I pushed such a personal discussions to the back of my mind. I guess he didn't. I ought to learn to keep my mouth shut."

"You have no need to fear anything you tell Richard. You have no better friend in the world. And you have no need to fear me knowing such things, either. He told me about it in the depth of his grief for you because he wanted me to know that you are more than just Mord-Sith, that you're a person with a life and desires of your own and you had come to value a good man. He was honoring you by telling me. But I will keep it to myself. Your feelings are safe with me, Cara."

Cara idly tugged at strands of hair at the end of her single braid. "I guess I never looked at it quite that way—I mean about him honoring me by telling you. That's kind of . . . nice."

"Love is a passion for life shared with another person. You fall in love with a person who you think is wonderful. It's your deepest appreciation of the value of that individual, and that individual is a reflection of what you value most in life. Love, for sound reasons, can be one of life's greatest rewards. You shouldn't be ashamed or embarrassed about being in love. I mean, if you really do love Benjamin, that is."

Cara thought it over a moment. "I'm not ashamed of it; I am Mord-Sith." Some of the tension went out of her shoulders. "But I don't know if I'm in love with him, either. I don't know for certain what I think about it. I know I care greatly for him. I'm not sure it's love, though. Maybe it's only the first step along the path to love. It's kind of hard for me to tell about such things. I'm not used to it mattering what I think or how I feel."

Nicci nodded as she began walking slowly through the shadows. "For a lot of my life I didn't understand what love was either. Jagang used to sometimes think that he was in love with me."

"Jagang? Seriously? He's in love with you?"

"No, he's not really in love with me; he just thinks he is. Even back then I knew that it wasn't love, even if I didn't understand why. Jagang's measure of worth runs from hate to lust. He scorns and defiles anything that's good about life, so he couldn't possibly experience true love. He can only discern it as the faint fragrance of something tantalizing and mysterious beyond his reach and he longs to possess it.

"He imagined that he could experience love by grabbing me by my hair and forcing me down on him. He interpreted his enjoyment as he watched as feelings of love. He thought that I should be grateful that he had such powerful feelings for me that he would be overcome with desire for me to the exclusion of everything else. Since he believed that forcing himself on me was an expression of his love, he thought I should accept it as an honor."

"He would have liked Darken Rahl," Cara muttered. "They would have gotten along splendidly." She looked over, suddenly puzzled. "You're a sorceress. Why didn't you use your power to incinerate the bastard?"

Nicci let out a deep breath. How could she simply explain a lifetime of indoctrination?

"I don't think that a day goes by that I don't wish I would have killed that vile man. But, brought up as I was under the teachings of the Fellowship of Order, the same as he, I believed that moral virtue was only realized through self-sacrifice. Under their tenets, your duty is to those in need. Such dictates are imposed under the banner of the common good, or the betterment of mankind, or dutiful obedience to the Creator.

"By the ideology of the Order we were to devote ourselves not to those we regarded as the best among mankind, but to those who we ourselves regarded as the worst among men—not because they had earned it, but precisely because they hadn't. This, the Order claims, is the heart of morality and the only means by which we earn our entry into the everlasting light of the Creator in the afterlife. It's the sacrifice of the virtuous into servitude to the vile. It is never done under the banner of what it really is: naked greed for the unearned.

"Jagang's worldly needs revolved around his crotch. I had what he believed he needed, so I was morally required to sacrifice myself to his need. Especially since he is the leader bringing the Order's moral teachings to the heathens of the world.

"When Jagang would beat me until I was only half conscious and then throw me on his bed to have his way with me, I was doing what I had been taught was not only right, but my selfless moral duty. I thought I was evil for hating it.

"Since I believed that I was evil for such self-interest, I felt that I deserved all the pain I got in this world and eternal punishment in the next. I couldn't kill a man who was, under the creed taught to me by the Fellowship of Order, morally superior to me by virtue of his need. How could I possibly harm someone who I had been taught to serve? How could I possibly object to the harm done to me when I so deserved all I got and more? What could I object to? Justice? That's the endless, miserable trap of teachings about your duty to the greater good."

They strolled in silence as Nicci endured an array of ghastly memories.

"What changed?" Cara finally asked.

"Richard," Nicci said softly. Right then, she was glad for the darkness. Despite her tears, she lifted her head with pride. "The Imperial Order's teachings can only endure through brutality. Richard showed me that no one has a right to my life, not the whole of it, nor pieces of it. He showed me that my life is mine to live for myself, for my own purpose, and does not belong to others."

Cara watched with a kind of knowing sympathy. "I guess that you had a great deal in common with Mord-Sith under the rule of Darken Rahl. D'Hara was once a place of darkness, as life is now under the Imperial Order. Richard didn't just kill Darken Rahl, he ended that kind of sick doctrine for D'Hara. He gave us the same thing he gave you; he gave us back our lives.

"I guess Lord Rahl could understand us because he was treated much the same."

Nicci wasn't sure what Cara meant. "The same?"

"He was once a captive of a Mord-Sith named Denna. At the time it was our duty to torture Darken Rahl's enemies to death. Denna was the best of the best. Darken Rahl had personally selected her to capture Richard and be in charge of his training. Darken Rahl had been hunting Richard for quite a while because he knew something important about the boxes of Orden. Darken Rahl wanted that information. It was Denna's job to torture Richard into being eager to answer any question Darken Rahl asked."

Nicci glanced over and saw tears glistening in Cara's eyes as she slowed to a halt. She lifted her Agiel, staring at it as she rolled it in her fingers. Nicci knew all about Denna and what she had done to Richard, but she decided that right then it might be best to remain silent and simply listen. Sometimes people needed to say things for themselves more than they needed to say them for others. Nicci thought that perhaps after coming so close to dying, this was one of those times for Cara.

"I was there," Cara said in a near whisper as she stared at her Agiel. "He doesn't remember because Denna had tortured him until he was delirious and only partially conscious, but I saw him there, at the People's Palace, and I saw some of what she did to him. . . . of what we all did."

Nicci's breath paused. She cautiously glanced over at Cara. "Of what you all did? What do you mean?"

"It was standard practice for Mord-Sith to pass their captives around. It made it more difficult for them to learn to endure any particular pattern of torture from one individual. It helped to keep them confused and afraid. Fear is an integral part of torture. That's something a Mord-Sith learns from the first moment she is taken to be trained to become Mord-Sith— that fear and the unknown makes any pain infinitely worse. Most of the time Denna let a Mord-Sith named Constance share in training Richard. But sometimes Denna wanted to use others, besides Constance."

Cara stood stock-still as she stared at her Agiel. "It was not long after he arrived at the People's Palace. Richard doesn't remember—I don't think he even knew his own name at the time because Denna had him in a fog of delirium, in a state of madness from the things she had done to him . . . but he spent a day with me."

This, Nicci hadn't known. She stood frozen, afraid to say anything. She had no idea what she could say.

"Denna took Richard as her mate," Cara said. "I don't think she understood love any better than Jagang or Darken Rahl. At the end, though, she came to have a deep and genuine love for Richard. I saw the change coming over her. As you described it, she came to value him as an individual. She came to have sincere passion for him. She loved him so much that in the end she let him kill her so that he could escape.

"But before then, when Denna was still torturing him, I saw him there more than once, hanging helpless, covered in blood and begging for the release of death." A tear ran down Cara's cheek. "Dear spirits, I too made him beg for death as I stood over him."

Cara seemed to suddenly realize what she had just said aloud. Panic flooded her eyes. "Please don't say anything to him. It was so long ago—it's over and everything has changed, now. I don't want him to know . . . about me there with him like that." Tears ran down her face. "Please . . ."

Nicci took up one of Cara's hands in both of hers. "Of course I wouldn't say anything about it. I, of all people, understand the way you feel; I too, once did terrible things to him, only for a great deal longer than anyone else. As you say, that's over." Nicci let out a deep sigh. "I guess we all three know a little about what love is, and what it isn't."

Cara nodded not just her relief, but her sincere appreciation that Nicci understood. "We'd better catch up with Lord Rahl."

Nicci gestured casually toward the stables. "Richard is talking to the relatives of Victor's men who were killed." She tapped the side of her forehead. "I can just barely hear him with my gift." She reached out and gently wiped a tear from Cara's cheek. "We have the time to gather our senses before we get there."

As they started slowly walking toward the stable, Cara said, "Nicci, could I tell you something, then . . . something personal?"

On a night of such surprises, this was yet another. "Of course."

"Well . . ." Cara began as she frowned, trying to find the words, "when Lord Rahl came to me—to heal me—he was close to me."

"What do you mean?"

"I mean he was lying there with me, in the bed with me, with his arms around me—you know, protecting me and keeping me warm." She rubbed her arms as if the memory had brought the chill back. "I was so cold." Cara stole a quick glance over at Nicci. "I guess that, well, I guess that in my condition, and all, I was kind of holding on to him, too."

Nicci lifted an eyebrow. "I see."

"And the thing is, I felt things when he came into me—and if you tell him this I'll kill you, I swear I will."

Nicci smiled as she nodded her assurance. "We both care a great deal about him. I assume that what you're telling me is only because you are concerned for him."

"That's right." She rubbed her arms again as she went on. "When he came to . . . to pull me back, or whatever it is he did, it was like he was inside me, inside my head, I mean. It was a kind of intimacy unlike any other.

"Lord Rahl healed me once before when I was seriously hurt, but this was different. Parts were the same, some of the feelings were the same, the sincere caring and such that I felt from him, but this was different, somehow—really different. That time he was healing my physical injury." Cara leaned closer in an effort to try to get her point across. "This time it was more; this time the touch of that evil thing was inside me, like it was poisoning me, poisoning my existence, my will to live."

She straightened, then, seemingly frustrated and unable to think of how to explain it better.

"I know the difference you're trying to define," Nicci offered. "This time it was a more personal connection between the two of you."

Cara nodded as if relieved that Nicci seemed to understand.

"Yes, that's right, it was more personal. A lot more personal," she added under her breath. "It was like my soul was laid bare to him. It was kind of like . . . well, never mind."

Cara went silent. Nicci wondered if the woman had said all she had really wanted to say and would decide to stop there, but then she went on.

"The point is that he felt so much of me, of my inner thoughts and all. No one has ever . . ."

Cara again went silent, but this time in apparent frustration at trying to find the words to explain what she meant.

"I understand, Cara," Nicci assured her. "I really do. I've healed people so I know the sensations you experienced, if not as deeply. I've never been able to succeed to the extent that Richard did with you, but I've experienced more or less the same kinds of conditions when I heal people, especially when I healed Richard."

"That's good to hear—that you know what I'm talking about." Cara casually kicked a rock as she walked along. "Well, I don't think Lord Rahl is aware of it, but when we were together like that he didn't just . . . experience me, experience my inner feelings and thoughts, so to speak; I experienced him as well." She growled to herself. "I shouldn't be saying this." She waved a hand. "Forget I said anything."

Nicci wasn't sure what the woman was getting at. "Cara, if you aren't comfortable telling me, then don't. You know how much I care for Richard, but still, if you don't think you shouldn't say anything, or that you are stepping out of bounds in your relationship with him, then perhaps you should trust that instinct."

Cara sighed. "Maybe you're right."

Nicci couldn't ever recall Cara appearing so flustered. If there was one thing enduring about the woman it was her resolute confidence. She was always decisive about precisely what she should do in any given circumstance. Nicci didn't always think that Cara was right, and she knew that Richard didn't either, but they could always count on Cara being determined to do the best thing for Richard no matter how it might endanger Cara herself—or anger them. If she felt her actions were necessary to protect him, she simply went ahead, dismissing the consequences to herself, including his disapproval.

As they walked in silence through the dark alleyway, Nicci, with the help of her gift, could hear people in the distance speaking in low voices. She didn't try to pick out the words; she did no more than note the general nature of the conversation. It was men and women gathered at the stables, some speaking in turn. Nicci could distinguish Richard speaking gently to them, answering questions. She could hear people weeping.

At the corner of the inn where the road to the right lead down a few doors to the stables, Cara abruptly caught Nicci's arm and brought her to a halt while they were still in the deep shadows.

"Look, you and I, well, we both started out in all this determined to kill Lord Rahl."

Somewhat taken aback, Nicci didn't think that this was the time to split hairs. "I guess you're right."

"Maybe more than anyone else, you and I have a unique perspective on Lord Rahl. I think that when you start out wanting to do someone harm and they make you see how wrong you've been and how your own life means more than that, well, it kind of makes you care all that much more for them."

"I think I would have to agree with you."

Cara gestured back the way they had come, toward the grounds of the palace that was now Liberty Square. "Back there, when the revolt started, when Lord Rahl was wounded and near death, people didn't want to let you try to heal him. They were afraid that you would instead do him harm. I'm the one who told them to trust you. I understood the awakening you had gone through because I had gone through much the same thing. I was the only one who knew what you had come to feel about him. I told them to let you do it. They feared you might use the opportunity to take his life. I knew you wouldn't. I knew you would save him."

"You're right, Cara. We both care deeply for him. We both have a special bond with him."

"Yes, that's it. A special bond. Different, I think, than other people."

Mystified by what Cara could be getting at, Nicci spread her hands. "So you wish to tell me something?"

Cara looked down at her boots as she nodded. "When Lord Rahl and I shared that togetherness, I felt some of his inner emotions. Inside him he has a terrible, burning loneliness. I think that maybe all the business about this woman—this Kahlan—is because of his lonesomeness."

Nicci took a deep breath and let it out slowly as she wondered at the precise nature of what Cara had sensed in him. "I suppose that may be a part of it."

Cara cleared her throat. "Nicci, when you hold a man in your arms like that, and you have been . . . well, together in such a personal way, you come to truly feel what's inside him."

Nicci pushed her feelings farther back into the shadows. "I don't doubt that you're right, Cara."

"I mean, I just wanted to hold him forever, to comfort him, to keep him from feeling so alone."

Nicci stole a sidelong glance at the Mord-Sith. She was twisting her mouth as she studiously watched the ground. Nicci didn't say anything, waiting instead for Cara to go on.

"But I just don't think I'm the one to do such a thing for Lord Rahl."

Nicci cautiously framed her question. "You mean, you don't think that you're the woman who can satisfy . . . his loneliness?"

"I guess not."

"Benjamin?"

The woman shrugged. "That's part of it." She looked up and met Nicci's gaze. "I love Lord Rahl. I'd give my life for him. And I have to admit that lying there and having him in my arms like that made me feel . . . feel like maybe I could be more than just his bodyguard and friend. As I lay there in that bed, holding him close to me, I imagined what it would be like to be his . . ." Her voice trailed off.

Nicci swallowed. "I see."

"But I just don't think that I'm the one. I don't know why. I'm not exactly an expert in matters of the heart, but I don't feel like I'm the one he needs. I just don't think I could be. If he were to ask it of me, I would do it in a heartbeat . . . but not because I wanted it, exactly. Do you understand what I mean?"

"You mean you would do it out of your deep respect and caring for him, not out of your personal wish to be his lover."

"That's it," Cara said with a sigh of relief, apparently at having someone else say it aloud. "Besides, I just don't think that Lord Rahl feels that way about me. When I was sensing his feelings, when we were in each other's arms, I think I would have known if he felt that way about me, but he doesn't. He loves me, I know that much, but not in that way."

Nicci carefully eased out her own breath. "So . . . that's what you wanted me to know? That you think his loneliness is the source of his fantasy woman?"

Cara nodded. "Yes . . . but one more thing, too."

Nicci glanced down the street, watching men making their way to the stable. "And what would that be?"

"I think that maybe you could be the one."

Nicci's heart came up in her throat as she turned to see Cara staring right at her. "What?"

"I think you could be the one for Lord Rahl." She held up her hands to forestall any argument. "Don't say anything. I don't want you to be saying that I'm crazy. Don't say anything for now. Just think about it. We'll be leaving shortly and it will be a while until you can come to meet up with us, so you have time and you could think about it. I'm not asking you to sacrifice yourself for him or anything foolish like that.

"I'm just saying that I think Lord Rahl needs someone and you could be that woman—I mean if you felt right about it.

"I'm not the one he needs. I'm Mord-Sith, and Lord Rahl is a wizard. Dear spirits, I hate magic and he is magic. We just aren't right for each other in all kinds of little ways. But you have so much in common with him. You're a sorceress. Who could understand him better than you? Who could help him with every aspect of his life better than you?

"I remember back that night at camp, in the shelter, when the two of you were talking about the creative dimension of magic. I didn't understand half of it, but it struck me then how the two of you could talk so easily to each other and understand each other's thoughts, ideas, and meaning like no one else could. I remember being taken by how the two of you, well, seemed so right together.

"And I remember thinking, too, when we lay down close to him to keep warm, how good you looked close to him like that. Like a woman would be close to a man she cared about. I remember, for some reason, half expecting him to kiss you. It would have seemed natural."

Nicci couldn't make her heart slow down. "Cara, I . . ." Words failed her.

Cara picked at a strip of pealing paint on the corner board of the building. "Besides, you're about the most beautiful woman I've ever seen. Lord Rahl should have a wife who is his match and I can't think of a better match than you."

"Wife . . . ?"

"Don't you see how much sense it makes? It would fill the emptiness I felt inside him. It would bring him joy and happiness to replace his misery. He would have someone to share his gift and his connection to magic. He wouldn't be lonely. Just think about it."

"But, Cara, Richard doesn't love me."

Cara appraised her for a long, uncomfortable moment. Nicci recalled then Richard once telling her how paralyzing it felt to be under the scrutiny of a Mord-Sith when she looked into your eyes, really looked into them. Nicci now understood what he meant.

"Maybe he doesn't feel that way now, but maybe when you come back to join us you could do a little more to let him know you were open to such a notion about the two of you—I mean, if you wanted to, if you were open to the idea. Sometimes people just have to be made aware of something so that they will consider it seriously. That's why I felt I needed to say something to you. Maybe if he thought you might be open to such a thing then he'd get interested and start looking at you in that light.

"You know, people who are in love had to fall in love at some point. They weren't born in love with their mate. Maybe you just have to help him get to that point where he will start to think about you in that light. It could even be he thinks that a beautiful, intelligent woman like you could never care for him seriously. Sometimes men are shy that way about a woman they think is extraordinarily beautiful."

"Cara, I just don't think he—"

Cara leaned in confidentially. "It could even be that he thinks you would never be interested in him and so he dreamed up this other woman to fill the void."

Nicci wet her lips. "I think we had better get over to the stable or he may leave without you. He seems pretty set on leaving."

Cara offered a smile. "You're right. Look, Nicci, if you'd rather, you could just forget I said anything. I can see that I'm making you uncomfortable. I don't exactly feel right about saying anything, anyway."

"Then why did you?"

Cara gazed off wistfully. "I guess because as I was holding him, and I felt the depth of his loneliness, it just broke my heart." Her gaze drifted back to Nicci's. "And Mord-Sith don't get broken hearts all that often."

Nicci almost said that neither did sorceresses.

Lanterns hanging from stout posts lent a cozy glow to the stable. The dusty smell of fresh straw hung thick in the wide passageway running in front of the stalls and pens. Men and women, some with their children along, had filled the walkway and in a few places spilled over into the empty pens, but now, after Richard had talked to the relatives of the men who had been killed, many had bid him a safe journey and started for their homes.

Dawn was still a couple of hours off. Despite the hour, there had been a number of people other than grieving relatives who had come to ask questions about the impending battle for their city. More people, sitting on hay bales, had watched from the loft but now many had started down the ladders. Richard supposed that they would be going back to bed to catch a little more sleep. He knew that their sleep would be troubled by worries about the soldiers marching toward their city.

Victor, standing nearby, looked grim after speaking about the bravery of his men and how much he would miss each of them.

Many people wept openly as they'd listened. Richard had known that nothing he could have said would have lifted their grief. He had done his best to make them understand what good men he thought they had been, and how much he cared for them. In the end, all he could really do was sympathize with their loss. He had felt helpless and useless, even though they had seemed to appreciate the things he'd said.

From the corner of his eye, Richard caught sight of Nicci and Cara as they came in the big doorway at the end of the stable. They had to ease their way among people who were leaving. He had been wondering where the two of them had gone to, but, surrounded by people all wanting to speak with him, he hadn't had a chance to go check. He'd figured that either they had wanted to let him have the time to talk to people, or else Cara had wanted to look around outside to make sure that all was well. Either way, he was glad to see their faces.

"So that's what you think, then, that this thing, this beast, that crashed through the walls of Ishaq's inn was after you?" an older man named Henden asked as he paused beside Richard. He held a pipe with a long curved stem in one hand, his elbow propped on a rail as he spoke.

The skin on his thin, leathery face sagged with the weight of years. Because he was older, and possessed a quiet, prudent manner, many in the crowd had deferred to his earlier questioning of Richard. Henden drew air in through his pipe and released aromatic clouds of smoke from the opposite side of his mouth as he waited for Richard's answer.

"Like I said, the evidence seems to point to it so I think it probably was. But whatever it was, it's likely that it was coming after me, so you can see why I think it's best if I leave now and not risk that thing coming after me again in the city and maybe causing harm to a lot of people here."

The man removed the pipe from his mouth and gestured toward Richard with the stem. "You mean like those men with Victor were harmed as a result of you being near?"

Victor stepped forward. "Now look here, Henden, it's not Lord Rahl's fault that evil people are trying to kill him. Those same evil people want to come here and kill us as well—beast or no beast. Would you be to blame if Jagang's soldiers coming to kill you happened to harm Lord Rahl on their way to get you?

"My men were fighting against the Imperial Order when they were cut down by something evil. That evil was spawned by the Order. They were fighting for a world for themselves and their families in which they could live their lives free and safe. They made the choice to do that rather than live in subjugation."

Henden chewed on the pipe's stem a moment as his placid eyes considered Victor. "Just asking. Only think it's reasonable to know what the situation is and what we're up against."

Richard saw heads among the men and women nodding.

"You're right, it is reasonable," he told the man before Victor could get any hotter. "I don't begrudge a man asking questions, especially where lives are concerned. But Victor is right as well. Jagang is intent on killing us all and, as I've told you, the Order needs to be stopped or none of us, no matter where we are, will ever be able to rest easy."

Richard saw Nicci slipping effortlessly through the press of people departing. Her flowing blond hair cascaded over the shoulders of a black dress. The dress, cut low with a laced bodice, showed off her shapely form to advantage. But it was her commanding presence that made her stand out like a queen in the throng. Cara, in her red leather, could have been the royal escort.

Richard felt a little uncomfortable at the way they both stared at him as if they hadn't seen him for a month.

Henden unexpectedly clapped Richard on the back of his shoulder, bringing him out of his thoughts. The man spoke with the pipe clenched in his teeth.

"Safe journey, Lord Rahl. Thank you for everything you've done for us. We look forward to your return to the free city of Altur'Rang."

"Thanks," Richard said with a smile to the man.

Henden moved in with the flow of the others who were engaged in conversation as they made their way along the aisle and out the door. Richard had been relieved to see that these people understood what their freedom meant, and meant to keep it.

Ishaq, standing near Richard, waved his red hat at Nicci and Cara when he spotted them. "There you are," he called out. "Are you all right, mistress Cara? Richard told me you were safe, but I'm thankful to see it so with my own eyes."

Richard followed Ishaq as he rushed to meet the two women, beaming his pleasure at seeing them both.

"We're fine." Cara said. "I'm sorry about the damage to your inn."

Ishaq waved a hand, as if the matter were trivial. "It is nothing. Boards and plaster. Nothing at all. People can't so easily be fixed."

"You're right about that," Cara said as she met Richard's gaze.

Richard saw Jamila, standing on the other side of the passageway, scowl at Ishaq's dismissal of the importance of the damage to the inn, but she didn't say anything. She held the hand of a little girl as she leaned back against the wall near the big door, watching. By the girls round face, Richard thought that it had to be Jamila's daughter. The girl beamed an infectious smile at him and he couldn't help smiling back.

"Ishaq, I said that you should deduct the damage from what you owe me, and I meant it."

Ishaq replaced his hat. "Why you worry so? I told you, I fix."

Before Richard could answer, he heard a commotion just outside. Some of the men who had been patrolling the neighborhood came in the door dragging two big men with them. The two men, one with tangled, grimy strands of dark hair and the second with his hair cropped short, were both dressed in brown tunics similar to those worn by many of the people of the city.

Victor leaned closer to Richard and spoke under his breath. "Spies."

Richard didn't doubt it. He could see broad belts underneath the tunics that would probably have held weapons. With the Imperial Order soldiers getting close, they would have sent scouts ahead to gauge what they were going to be up against. Now that they were captives, it was possible that they might be prevailed upon to provide valuable information on the nature of the impending attack.

Despite their attempt to dress the part, the two looked out of place among the people of the city. The plain clothes they wore weren't quite large enough to fit their bulk. Neither was huge, nor were they massively muscular, but they had a well-honed, cool, resourceful demeanor. Both men kept silent, but their eyes were always on the move, surveying everything around them. They looked as dangerous as wolves among sheep.

As the guards pulled the two men into the passageway inside the stable, Richard instinctively lifted his sword a few inches, making sure that it was clear in its scabbard, before letting it drop back.

As one of the guards turned to look at something, the prisoner with the long hair suddenly and savagely kicked the shin of the man holding him from behind. The guard cried out in pain and shock as he crumpled to the ground. The man violently broke the grip of the men holding his arms by twisting and flinging them away. Some of the nearby people were toppled to the ground. Guards pounced on the free man. In the scramble, several crashed to the ground bloodied and another tumbled back over a rail.

In an instant, the subdued mood in the stable changed as the entire place erupted in panic. Women screamed. Children, when their mothers screamed, shrieked. Older children started wailing. Men yelled. The guards cried out orders. Confusion and fear swept through the crowd.

The free enemy spy, a powerful man who knew how to handle adversaries and how to create a break for himself in a relatively confined space where they couldn't employ the numbers necessary to apply overwhelming force, sprang up with a roar.

He had Jamila's little girl by the hair.

Somehow, in the scramble, the man had managed to snatch a knife from someone and now had it pressed to the girl's throat. The child squealed in terror. Jamila dove for the girl, only to be side-kicked in the head. The powerful blow knocked her aside. Another guard on the ground at the other side also received a wicked kick to his head as he tried to use the opportunity to get close.

Richard was already methodically advancing, his attention focused on the threat.

"Everyone back!" the man growled at all the people close in all around him.

He tossed his head to flip his greasy hair back off his face. His eyes darted around at the people trying to back up out of the away. He still panted from the effort of the brief struggle. Sweat ran down his pock-marked face.

"Everyone get back or I'll slit her throat!"

The girl, a meaty fist holding her aloft by the hair, again shrieked in terror. He held her fast against his stomach. Her feet kicked in the air as she struggled in vain to escape.

"Let him go!" the man ordered the guards holding his partner. "Now! Or she dies!"

Richard was already lost in a rage unleashed. There would be no compromise, no negotiations, no quarter given.

He stood sideways, in a slight crouch, his right side to the man holding the girl, preventing him from seeing his sword. The man kept glancing at the guards to his left who were holding the other man. He wasn't paying any particular attention to Richard.

The burly man holding the wailing girl didn't know it, but in Richard's mind the deed had already been completed. In Richard's mind the man was already dead.

The fury of the magic from Richard's sword had been freed before his hand even found the hilt. When it did, the storm thundered unrestrained up through him, powering his muscles, joining his overwhelming lust to consummate the deadly thought.

In an instant, calm had been swept away by a terrible avalanche of need for action.

In that instant, there was nothing Richard wanted more than the man's blood. Nothing less would stop him. Conviction burned away all uncertainty. The Sword of Truth was a tool of the Seeker's intent, and that intent was now simple and clear. Now that Richard's hand was on the hilt of his sword, nothing else existed but his purpose, and his singular purpose was to bring death raining down on the man before him.

His vision tunneled toward his target. His entire life narrowed down to that singular lethal commitment.

The man with the knife had only to pull it across the tender veil of flesh and the girl would die. But that would take time, brief time to be sure, but time nonetheless because he would first have to decide to do it. At that moment, the man's life was tied to the life of the girl; if she died, his shield would lose its value. He would have to weigh that choice and decide on killing her before he resolved to it. That decision would take a fleeting glimmer of time.

Richard had already made his decision and had fully charged himself to the task. He now had a sliver of time that gave him an opportunity to alter the nature of the situation, to be the one to control the outcome. He would not let that small slip of time escape him.

But even that no longer mattered to him.

Now, powered by lethal rage, both the sword's and his own, he wanted the man's blood. Nothing else would satisfy him, nothing else would stop him, he would accept nothing less.

Richard twisted away from the threat, putting the back of his shoulders to the man with the girl, feigning that he was turning away, that he was backing off as the man had commanded. In so doing, Richard knew that, with so many things pulling for his attention, the man would discount Richard and direct his concern to the more obvious threat of the men to his sides and back.

With his fist tightly gripping the wire wound hilt of his sword, Richard pulled a breath. The world around him seemed to go silent and still.

As he reached the apex of his backward twist, he paused.

Richard felt his heart begin a beat.

With all his power, as people stood frozen, as the man with the knife stood at the brink of murder, as the girl's shrill scream drew out into a wire-thin sound filling the empty void in time, Richard unleashed himself in an explosive movement.

With all his strength he uncoiled. His blade erupted from its sheath fully charged not only with a wrath of its own but with Richard's deadly resolve.

At the same time as the Sword of Truth rang with the unique sound of its liberation, Richard released a cry of fury. As he spun, he emptied all his rage into that roar. With every ounce of effort he had, he drove the blade around with as much speed and power as he could put behind it.

In a crystal-clear instant in time, Richard's vision focused on the man with the knife standing rigid with surprise. Into that void in time Richard poured all his effort, all his muscle, all his wrath, all his need. That instant belonged to him alone and he used it to his singular purpose.

He could see the drops of sweat leave the man's face as his head snapped toward Richard. Yellow-orange light from the lanterns reflected in tiny points on those drops as they floated weightless in midair. Richard could count each point of light from each lantern in each individual droplet of sweat as his sword ever so slowly swept around. He could count each greasy strand of the man's hair as it whipped around, floating up into the air with the droplets.

Richard knew that eyes all around the stable were watching, that the eyes of the girl, too, were watching, but that made no difference. The only eyes that mattered to him were the dark eyes that at last met his glare.

In those black eyes Richard could see the initiation of thought. The tip of Richard's sword whistled through the dusty air. Lantern-light glinted off the razor sharp steel. He could see the blade mirrored in the man's dark eyes. Those eyes reflected the recognition of the full dimension of the threat.

Onward came the sword, sweeping like the crack of a whip toward those eyes, sweeping around toward the target Richard held in his own sight.

In that instant, the man completed his thought and made the decision to act. But even in the infinitesimal fragment of time that it took to come to the conclusion of that thought, the lightning arc of the blade closed most of the distance. Even as the man's decision was being made, flinching fear from Richard's battle cry caused the man to tense.

For that instant in time, the muscles of the man's arms paused as fear fought intent.

It became a race to see which blade would first bite flesh.

Losing that race would be irrevocable.

With his gaze riveted on the man's eyes, Richard at last saw his sword, flying at frightening speed, entering his line of sight. Seeing that blade again filled him with exhilaration.

Driven by thundering rage, the blade caught the side of the man's head level with his dark eyes, exactly where Richard intended it.

In that instant, the crystal-clear moment in time that had been stretched to the breaking point shattered in sound and fury. The world went red in Richard's vision as the man's head came apart around the blade crashing through his skull. The hammer-hard sound of it thundered through the stables.

Bone fragmented. Crimson droplets sprayed up and away. The entire top of the skull lifted as the blade crashed through living tissue. In a long trail across the wall, bone, tissue, and blood traced the route of the sword's sweep.

In that instant of shattering violence, the man's life was gone. Richard's remorseless rage shielded him from feeling the pain of any pity.

The force of the sword's impact caused the arm with the knife to fall away from the girl even before the swing of Richard's sword was complete. The man's body, like nothing more than boneless meat, began collapsing.

The man had decided to kill the girl, but after he had made that choice, he had not had enough time to make his blade do his bidding.

Richard had.

He felt his heart finish the beat it had begun when he had leaped into the narrow window of time.

The man's body gathered speed as it descended until it hit the ground heavily, lifting a small cloud of dust. The top portion of his head, most of his scalp still attached, landed with a heavy thud just outside the open stable doors, bouncing and tumbling away into the night, leaving a trail of gore to trace its crooked route.

Richard heard people gasp in shock. Others screamed.

The little girl, shrieking in terror, scrambled away into her mother's outstretched arms.

As he held the blade cocked, ready for any other threat, Richard met the gaze of the wide eyes of the second man, still standing in place, held fast by Victor's guards. The man made no attempt to escape or to fight.

Victor charged in through a gap in the bystanders, his heavy mace raised and ready. From somewhere Cara had appeared behind Richard, her Agiel in her fist.

Richard spotted Nicci for the first time. She raced across the passageway, her arms held up.

"No!" she screamed. "Stop!"

Victor straightened in surprise. Nicci seized his raised wrist as if she believed he was about to slaughter the other prisoner.

"Stand down, blacksmith!"

Startled, Victor paused and let his arm drop.

Nicci turned a furious glare on Richard. "You too, carpenter! You will do as I say and stand down. Do you hear me!" she screamed in fury.

Richard blinked. Carpenter?

Through the haze of the sword's anger storming through him, Richard realized that Nicci had to be up to something. He didn't know her intent, but by calling both Victor and him by a trade rather than by their real names she was sending them a signal that was too obvious to miss. She was making an emphatic bid for them to catch on to her effort and to follow her lead.

Probably because people often did call him "blacksmith," Victor didn't seem to get the hint. He started to open his mouth to say something. Nicci smacked him across the face.

"Silence! I will hear none of your excuses."

Shocked, Victor took a step back. The shock quickly curdled into a dark scowl but he didn't say anything.

Seeing that Victor got the message to keep quiet, Nicci turned her ire on Richard. She shook her finger at him. "You will have to answer for this, carpenter."

Richard didn't have any idea what she was up to, but when their eyes met he gave her a slight nod. He feared to do anything else lest he spoil whatever it was she was doing.

Nicci appeared to be worked up into a fit. "What's the matter with you?" she yelled at him. "Where would you ever get the unacceptable idea that you can act of your own accord in such a manner?"

Richard didn't know what she wanted him to to say so he offered only a humble shrug, as if he were too ashamed to speak up for himself.

"He was saving my child!" cried Jamila. "That man was going to cut her throat."

Nicci wheeled indignantly to the woman. "How dare you show such little regard for our fellow man! How dare you judge what is in another man's heart! That is the Creator's exclusive right, not yours. Are you a witch woman who can see the future? If not, then you can't say what he would have done. Do you think he should be murdered for what you think he might do? Even if he would have acted, none of us alone has the authority to judge the right or wrong of whatever he did."

Nicci turned again to Richard. "What would you expect the poor man to do? The two of them are dragged in here by a mob, without any charges, trial, or even being allowed to explain themselves. You treat a man like an animal and then are surprised when he acts out of confusion and fear?

"How do you expect Jagang the Just to ever decide to give our people another chance to do what is right and proper when we act like this? The man had a right to fear for his life when among such a mindless rabble as he saw all around him.

"As the mayor's wife, I will not allow such behavior! Do you hear me! The mayor will not like to hear how shamefully some of our fellow citizens have acted tonight. In the mayor's absence, I will see that our ways are upheld. Now, put away your sword."

Beginning to understand what she was doing, Richard made no attempt to answer and instead sheathed his sword, as instructed.

As he took his hand from the hilt, the weapon's rage extinguished. Richard's knees nearly buckled. No matter the justification, the need, the number of times he righteously used the sword, killing remained a hideous deed.

Not wanting to spoil Nicci's act, Richard duly hung his head.

She turned a fierce look on the crowd. They all took a step back. "We are a peaceful people. Have you all forgotten our duty to our fellow man? To the Creator's ways? How can we ever expect the emperor to someday accept us back into the fold of the Imperial Order if we behave like subhuman animals?"

The crowd stood mute. Richard certainly hoped that they, too, grasped that Nicci had a purpose and they should not spoil what she was trying to accomplish.

"As the mayor's wife, I will not allow senseless violence to poison our people and our future."

A younger woman in the crowd put her hands on her hips and took a step forward. "But they were—"

"We must at all times keep in mind our duty to our fellow man," Nicci said in a threatening tone, cutting her off, "not our selfish desires."

With a surreptitious glance to Victor, he understood her meaning and pulled the woman back to make sure she kept her mouth shut.

Nicci glanced around at the guards. "It is our responsibility to guide our fellow man, not to butcher him. One man has been murdered this night. The people's authorities will have to hear this case and decide what will become of this carpenter. Some of you will have to see to it that he is confined until then.

"In the meantime, as the mayor's wife, I will not allow this other man to meet a similar unjust fate. I know my husband would want to set matters right but I also know that he would not want it to have to wait until tomorrow just for him to say as much. He would want it rectified immediately, so you will take this other citizen outside of the city and release him. Let him go on his way in peace. We will cause him no harm. The carpenter, as I said, will have to be held until he can be brought before the proper authorities to answer for his heinous deed."

Victor bowed. "Very wise, madam. I'm sure your husband, the mayor, would be pleased that you intervened on his behalf."

Nicci glared at the top of his head for a moment while he was bowed before her. She then turned to stand before the second captive spy. She bowed to him.

Richard noticed that somewhere along the line the cord of Nicci's bodice had come unlaced. It wasn't lost on the man, either. Her deep bow provided him a good long look at her cleavage. Once she straightened, it was a moment before he finally looked up into her eyes.

"I hope that you will accept our apology for your inhumane treatment. It is not the way we were taught to respect all people as our brothers and equals."

The man made a face, as if to say he might be able to forgive his mistreatment. "I can understand why you people are so touchy, what with your insurrection against the Imperial Order, and all."

"Insurrection?" Nicci waved a hand dismissively. "Nonsense. It was little more than a misunderstanding. Some of the workers"—she gestured toward Richard without looking—"like these ignorant, selfish men, here, wanted more say for themselves and higher wages. It was nothing more than that. As my husband has often told me, it was misconstrued and blown all out of proportion. Selfish men caused an unfortunate panic that got out of control. It was much like this terrible tragedy here tonight—a misunderstanding resulting in needless harm to one of the Creator's innocent children."

The man regarded her with a long, unreadable look before he spoke. "And all of Altur'Rang feels this way?"

Nicci sighed. "Well, along with the vast majority of the people of Altur'Rang, my husband, the mayor, certainly does. He's been working to bring to task the hotheads and troublemakers. Along with representatives of the people he has worked to make these few reactionary types see what a mistake they made and what great harm they do us all. They acted without considering the greater good. My husband has brought the leaders of the trouble before the people's council and they have decreed the proper punishment. Most have repented. At the same time, he works to reform and reeducate the less intelligent of the lot."

The man tipped his head to her in a slight bow. "Please tell your husband that he is a wise man and has a wise wife who knows that her place is properly in service to the greater good."

Nicci nodded in return. "Yes, exactly, the greater good. My husband has often said that, despite our own personal wishes or feelings, we must always consider the greater good above all else; that despite any personal sacrifice we must think only of the betterment of all people and not cling to the sinful ways of individual wishes and greed. No one has a right to place themselves above the well-being of others."

Nicci's words seemed to have struck a cord with the man; such notions were the fundamental teachings and beliefs of the Imperial Order. She knew precisely how to strum those cords.

"How true," he said as he watched her, taking another long look down the gaping neckline of her dress. "I guess I'd better be on my way."

"And where are you headed?" Nicci asked. Her hand came up to modestly contain the sagging front of her dress.

He looked back up to her face. "Oh, we were just traveling through, heading farther to the south to where we have family. We were hoping to take up some work, there. I didn't know this fellow all that well. We've simply been traveling together for the last few days."

"Well," Nicci said, "considering what happened here tonight, I'm sure that my husband would suggest that for your own safety you continue with your journey and, considering the few reactionary types still about, it would be best if you were to do so at once. There has already been one tragedy tonight; we would not like to chance another."

The man passed a murderous glare across the assembled crowd. His gaze settled on Richard, but Richard kept his eyes turned to the ground.

"Yes, of course, madam. Please thank the mayor for trying to bring the filthy troublemakers back to the ways of the Creator."

Nicci flicked her hand toward a few of the guards. "You men, show this citizen safely out of the city. Take enough men to ensure that there will be no trouble. And I need not remind you of how displeased the mayor and the people's council would be should they discover that any harm whatsoever came to this man. He is to be allowed to go on his way."

The men bowed and mumbled that they would see to it. By the way they acted, Richard could tell that they knew how to fall back into the role of what life had been like under the Imperial Order. All the people in the stable watched in silence as the men disappeared into the night with their charge. Long after they were gone, everyone stood still in tense silence, watching the empty doorway, fearful to speak until the man was far enough away, lest he hear anything.

"Well," Nicci said at last with a sigh, "I hope that he makes it back to his fellow soldiers. If he does, then we have gone a long way toward spreading a little confusion before the battle."

"Oh, he will," Victor said. "He will be eager to report such news as you have given him tonight. Hopefully, they will be so confident that we can give them a real surprise."

"Let's hope so," Nicci said.

Some of the people still remaining in the stable broke into chatter, pleased with Nicci's apparent stratagem of confusing the enemy. Some bid a good night and went on their way. Some stood around the corpse, staring.

Nicci offered Victor a brief smile. "Sorry to have to strike you."

Victor shrugged. "Well, it was to a good purpose."

When Nicci turned to Richard, she looked uneasy, as if she feared a lecture or a reprimand.

"I want the troops coming this way to think they will have no trouble crushing us," she explained. "Overconfidence leads to mistakes."

"There was more to it," Richard said.

Nicci cast a quick glance at the people still in the stables and then eased closer to him so that others couldn't hear. "You said that I could come and join up with you once the troops coming to crush the people of Altur' Rang are destroyed."

"And?"

Her blue eyes turned as hard as iron. "And I intend to see to it."

Richard considered her for a time, finally deciding to let her do what she could to help the people of Altur'Rang and not interfere with how she planned to accomplish it. Besides, he was more than a little worried about what her plan might be. Right then, he didn't really want to know what she was up to; he already had enough to worry about.

Richard took the loose ends of the cords lacing her bodice, drew them tight, and retied them.

She stood with her hands at her side, watching his eyes the whole time he did it. "Thank you," she said when he finished. "I guess that must have come undone in all the excitement."

Richard ignored her lie and checked to the side to see Jamila there, behind some of the other people. The woman, her cheek swollen and red, was kneeling, hugging the frightened little girl.

Richard stepped closer. "How is she?"

Jamila looked up at him. "Safe. Thank you, Lord Rahl. You saved her precious life. Thank you."

As the little girl sobbed and clutched her mother, she eyed Richard with a look of terror, as if she feared he might slay her next. She had witnessed something terrible at Richard's hand.

"I'm relieved that she's safe and unharmed," he said to Jamila.

Richard smiled at the girl, but received only a hateful glare in return.

Nicci clasped his arm in empathy, but said nothing.

The people still left in the stable finally spoke up to congratulate him on saving the child. They all seemed to have guessed that Nicci's words to the man were a ruse of some sort. Many spoke up, then, to tell her that they thought her deception was clever.

"That should throw them off," one of the men said.

Richard knew that she had more planned than to simply "throw them off." He was concerned about what she intended to do.

He watched briefly as some of the men dragged away the dead spy. At Ishaq's direction, others began quickly cleaning up the gore. The smell of blood made horses nervous and the sooner they were rid of it the better.

The rest of the people bid Richard a safe journey and then departed for their homes. It wasn't long before they had all gone. The men cleaning up the remains finished and left. Only Nicci, Cara, Ishaq, and Victor remained behind. The stables became a quiet and empty place.

Richard carefully surveyed the shadows before going to see to the horses that Ishaq had collected for him. The stables felt too quiet. He remembered the hush in the room in the inn before the thing came crashing through the wall. It was hard not to find the sudden quiet menacing. He wished he had a way to know if the beast was near, or if it was about to pounce. He wished he knew how to fight such a thing. His fingers touched the pommel of his sword. If nothing else, at least he had his sword and its attendant power.

He remembered all too well the inhuman promises of suffering and torment left lurking within Cara for him to find. It made him nauseated and light-headed just recalling the wordless whisper of those covenants. He had to pause and put a hand on the rail to steady himself for a moment.

As he glanced over to see Cara, he still felt the wordless joy of her being alive and well. It lifted his heart just to see her looking back at him. He felt a profound connection to her as a result of the experience of healing her. He felt as if he knew the woman beneath the armor of Mord-Sith a little better.

Now he needed to help Kahlan, to see her alive and well.

Two of the horses were already saddled and waiting, with the supplies loaded on the others. Ishaq had always been as good as his word. Richard ran his hand along the flanks of the bigger bay mare as he entered her stall, feeling her muscles and letting her know he was behind her so she wouldn't be spooked. One ear swiveled toward him.

With all that had happened, to say nothing of the scent of blood in the air, the horses were all jumpy. The mare tossed her head and stomped nervously at having a stranger near. Before he went about hooking his bow to the saddle, he first stroked the mare's neck and spoke softly to her. He reached up and gently caressed her ear. He was pleased that she settled down after a little assurance.

When he stepped back out from the stall, Nicci was watching him, waiting for him. She looked lost and lonely.

"You will be careful?" she asked.

"Don't worry," Cara said as she walked past carrying some of her things. On her way into the stall holding the smaller of the two saddled mares she said, "I will be giving him a very long lecture on the foolishness of his unthinking actions tonight."

"What unthinking actions?" Victor asked.

Cara laid an arm over the shoulder of her horse, idly running her fingers through its mane as she turned back to the blacksmith.

"We have a saying in D'Hara. We are the steel against steel so that the Lord Rahl can be the magic against magic. What it means is that it's foolish for the Lord Rahl to needlessly risk his life in things like battles with blades. We can do that. But we cannot battle the magic. He alone is the one who must do that. To do so, he must be alive. Our job is keeping the Lord Rahl safe from weapons of steel so that he can protect us against magic. That is the Lord Rahl's duty. That is his part of the bond."

Victor gestured toward Richard's sword. "I'd say he seems to do all right with a blade."

Cara arched an eyebrow. "Sometimes he is lucky. Need I remind you that he almost died from getting himself shot with a simple arrow? Without a Mord-Sith, he would be helpless," she added for good measure.

Richard silently rolled his eyes when Victor cast a worried look his way. Ishaq, too, seemed concerned as he peered at Richard as if he were a stranger he was seeing for the first time. Both men had known him for nearly a year as simply Richard, a man who loaded wagons for Ishaq's transport company and hauling iron to Victor's blacksmith shop. They had thought that he was married to Nicci. They didn't know that he had really been Nicci's captive at the time.

Discovering that he was in fact the Lord Rahl, the nearly mythical freedom fighter from far to the north, was still somewhat disorienting for both men. They tended to view him as one of their own who had risen up to fight tyranny with them. That was how they knew him. Whenever the Lord Rahl issue came up, they got nervous, as if they suddenly didn't know how they should behave around him.

As Cara went about loading the rest of her things into saddlebags, Nicci laid a hand on Ishaq's shoulder.

"If you don't mind, I need to see Richard alone for a moment before he leaves."

Ishaq nodded. "Victor and I will be outside. We have matters to discuss."

As the two men made for the door, Nicci cast Cara a brief glance. Cara gave her horse a quick pat on the side and then followed the two men out of the stable, pulling the big door closed behind herself. Richard was amazed, and just a little concerned, to see Cara leave without an argument.

Nicci stood before him in the soft lamplight twining her fingers together and looking rather uneasy, he thought.

"Richard, I'm worried about you. I should be with you."

"You've started something tonight that I think you will have to be the one to finish."

She sighed. "You're right about that."

Richard wondered just what it was she had started, what it was she had in mind, but he was in a hurry to leave. While he was concerned for Nicci's safety, he was vastly more worried about Kahlan. He wanted to get going.

"But I still—"

"When you're done helping these people end the immediate threat from the soldiers who are on their way here, you can catch up with me," Richard told her. "With this wizard, Kronos, leading them, the people here are certainly going to need your help."

"I know." She was nodding, having already been over all of this ground already. "Believe me, I intend to eliminate the threat descending upon Al-tur'Rang. I don't intend to allow it to waste a lot of my time and then I can leave to catch up with you."

A wave of cold dread washed through him as he suddenly grasped the core of her plan. He wanted to tell her to forget what she was thinking, but he made himself keep silent. He had important and perilous work of his own that he needed to get to. He wouldn't want her telling him that he couldn't do what he had planned.

Besides, she was a sorceress who knew very well what she was doing. She had been a Sister of the Dark—one of six such women who had managed to become his teachers at the Palace of the Prophets. When one of them had tried to kill him to steal his gift, Richard had killed her instead. That had been the beginning of the battle that had brought down the palace. Jagang eventually captured the rest, including Sister Ulicia, their leader. In order to save Kahlan's life, Richard had once allowed five of them to swear a bond to him so that they could escape the dream walker's hold on them. Nicci hadn't been with them at the time. Another later died in the sliph, leaving only those four Sisters of the Dark, besides Nicci, not in Jagang's clutches.

Nicci was certainly a formidable threat to any who opposed her. He just hoped she wasn't taking a foolish chance just to be able to more quickly get back to protect him.

Richard hooked his thumbs behind his belt, not quite knowing what it was she wanted. "You will be welcomed to join me whenever you can manage it. I told you that."

"I know."

"A piece of advice." He waited until her gaze turned up to his. "No matter how powerful you think you are, something as simple as an arrow can still kill you."

A brief smile visited her face. "That advice goes both ways, wizard."

A thought occurred to him. "How will you find me?"

She reached up and gripped his shirt at the collar as she leaned against him. "That's why I wanted to be alone with you. I will need to touch you with magic so that I can find you."

Richard's suspicion flared. "What kind of magic?"

"I guess you could say that it's a little like your bond to the D'Haran people which allows them to find you. Now is not the time to go into an explanation of it."

Richard began to worry about why she would need to be alone with him to do such a thing. Still gripping his shirt, she pressed against him, her eyes sliding half closed.

"Just stay still," she whispered.

She looked rather hesitant and reluctant about whatever it was she had planned. She looked and sounded as if she were slipping into a trance.

Richard could have sworn that the lamps had been brighter, before. Now the stable was dimly lit in a mellow orange glow. The hay smelled sweeter. The air felt warmer.

Richard thought that perhaps he shouldn't be allowing her to do whatever it was that she intended to do. In the end, though, he decided that he trusted her.

Nicci's left hand released its grip on his shirt and slipped up and over his shoulder to the back of his neck. Her fingers glided around his neck. Her hand fisted, holding his hair at the back of his head to keep him still.

Richard's level of alarm rose. He suddenly wasn't so sure that he wanted her to touch him with her power. He'd felt her magic several times before and it wasn't something he was exactly eager to experience again.

He wanted to back away, but, somehow, he didn't.

Nicci leaned in even more and gently kissed his cheek.

It was more than a kiss.

The world around him dissolved. The stables, the humid air, the sweet aroma of hay, all seemed to cease to exist. The only thing that existed was his connection to Nicci, as if she were all that held him from evaporating as well.

He was swept into a rising realm of breathless pleasure with all of life itself. It was an overpowering, disorienting, magnificent sensation. Everything, from the feel of the connection to her, the warmth and life of her, to all the beauty of the world, felt as if it flooded through him, filling him until it saturated his mind, making him dizzy with the staggering exhilaration of it.

Every kind of pleasure he had ever known swept through him with overwhelming force, amplified beyond anything he had ever experienced, engulfing him in bliss so intense that the satisfaction of it brought a gasp and tears.

When Nicci broke the kiss on his cheek the world inside the stables swirled back in around him, and yet it seemed more intense than it had before, the sights and smells more vibrant than he remembered. It was quiet but for the hiss of a nearby lamp and the soft neigh of one of the horses. Richard's hands trembled with the lingering sensation of her kiss.

He didn't know if what Nicci had done had lasted for a second or an hour. It was magic completely unlike any Richard had ever felt before. It left him so breathless that he had to remind himself to breath again.

He blinked at her. "What . . . what did you do?"

The slightest smile blossomed in the curve of her lips and in her blindingly blue eyes. "I touched you with a small trace of my magic so that I can find you. I recognize my power. I will be able to follow it to you. Fear not, the effect will last long enough for me to be able to find you."

"I think you did more, Nicci."

Her smile ghosted away. Her brow tightened with her concern. It took her a moment to find the words. At last she peered at him with an intensity that told him that it was important to her that he understand.

"Always before, Richard, I have hurt you with magic—when I took you away; when I held you prisoner; even when I healed you. It was always hurtful or painful. Forgive me, but I wanted, just once, to give you a touch of magic that would not leave you being hurt by me, or hating me."

Her gaze sank away from his. "I wanted you to have a better memory of me than of those times before when I touched you with the pain of magic. I wanted, just once, to give you a small trace of something pleasant, instead."

He could not begin to imagine what any more than a "small trace" would have been like.

He lifted her chin, making her look up into his eyes. "I don't hate you, Nicci. You know that. And I know that the times when you healed me you were giving me my life. That was what counted."

Finally, he was the one who had to look away from her blue eyes. It occurred to him that Nicci was probably the most beautiful woman he had ever met.

Other than Kahlan.

"Thank you, though," he managed, still feeling the lingering affects of the sensation.

She gently clutched his arm. "You did a good thing, tonight, Richard. I thought some pleasant magic would give you back some of your strength."

"I've seen a lot of people suffer and die. I couldn't stand the thought of the little girl dying, too."

"I meant in saving Cara's life."

"Oh. Well, I couldn't stand the thought of the big girl dying, either."

Nicci smiled at that.

He gestured to the horses. "I need to get going."

She nodded and he moved off to collect the horses and check their gear. Nicci went to open the stable door. After she did, Cara came back in to get her horse.

Dawn was still a couple of hours off. Richard realized that he was terribly tired, especially after the emotional strain of having used his sword, but he did feel better after what Nicci had just done. He knew, though, that they wouldn't be getting much sleep for a quite a while. They had a very long way to travel and he fully intended to do it as swiftly as possible. By taking fresh horses with them they would be able to ride hard, change mounts, and then continue to ride just as hard in order to make good time. He intended to ride more than hard.

Nicci held his horse's bit as he stuffed his boot into the stirrup and swung up into the saddle. The horse flicked her tail and danced about, eager to be out of the stable even if it was still night. Richard patted her shoulder to settle her down; she would have plenty of time to show him her spirit.

Cara, once in her saddle, turned to frown at him. "By the way, Lord Rahl, where is it we're traveling to in such a hurry?"

"I need to go see Shota."

"Shota!" Cara's jaw dropped. "We're going to see the witch woman? Are you out of your mind?"

Nicci, suddenly mortified, rushed to his side. "Going to the witch woman is madness—to say nothing of the Imperial Order troops all along the way back up through the New World. You can't do this."

"I have to. I think that Shota may be able to help me find Kahlan."

"Richard, she's a witch woman!" Nicci was beside herself. "She's not going to help you!"

"She's helped me before. She gave Kahlan and me a wedding gift. I think she may remember it."

"A wedding gift?" Cara asked. "Are you crazy? Shota would just as soon kill you as not."

There was more truth in that than Cara knew. His relation with Shota had always been an uneasy one.

Nicci put a hand on his leg. "What wedding gift? What are you talking about?"

"Shota wanted Kahlan to die because she feared that together we would conceive what Shota believed would be a monster child: a gifted Confessor. At our wedding, as a truce, she gave Kahlan a necklace with a small dark stone. It's magic of some sort that prevents Kahlan from getting pregnant. Kahlan and I decided that for the time being, with all that's going on and all that we have to worry about, we would accept Shota's truce."

There had been a time, when the chimes had been loosed, that magic of every sort had failed. For a while they hadn't known about the chimes, and that the necklace's magic had failed. It was then that Kahlan had conceived a child. The men who beat her that terrible night had ended that.

It was also possible that because of that brief failure of magic, the nature of the world had undergone a fundamental, irrevocable change that would eventually lead to the end of all magic. Kahlan certainly believed that it was happening. There had been a number of strange events that were otherwise inexplicable. Zedd had called it the cascade effect. He said that once begun such a thing could not be stopped. Richard didn't know if it was true that magic was failing or not.

"Shota will remember the necklace she gave Kahlan. She will remember her magic, just as you will remember yours so that you will be able to find me. If anyone will remember Kahlan, Shota will. I've had my disagreements with the witch woman, but in the past I've also inadvertently helped her as well. She owes me. She will help me. She has to."

Nicci threw her hands up. "Of course such a thing has to be a necklace that Kahlan would wear, and not something that you would have. Don't you see what you're doing? Once again your mind has invented something that conveniently can't be proven. Everything you come up with is somewhere else or something we can't see. This necklace is just more of your dream." Nicci pressed a hand to her forehead. "Richard, this witch woman is not going to remember Kahlan because Kahlan doesn't exist."

"Shota can help me. I know she can. I know she will. I can't think of any better opportunity to get answers. Time is slipping away. The longer Kahlan is with whoever has her, the greater the danger to her life and the less my chance of helping get her back. I have to go to Shota."

"And what if you're wrong?" Nicci demanded. "What if this witch woman refuses to help you?"

"I will do whatever it takes to make her help me."

"Richard, please, put this off for at least a day or two. We can talk it through. Let me help you properly consider your options."

Richard pulled the reins around, letting his horse and the ones tethered to it start toward the door. "Going to Shota is my best chance of getting answers. I'm going."

Richard ducked under the big doorway as they rode out into the night. Out across the expanse of grounds the cicadas droned on.

He pulled his horse around to see Nicci standing in the doorway, lit from behind by the lanternlight. "You be careful," he told her. "If not for yourself, then for me."

That, at least, made her smile. She shook her head in resignation. "By your command, Lord Rahl."

He waved his farewell to Victor and Ishaq.

"Safe journey," Ishaq said as he removed his hat.

Victor saluted with a fist over his heart. "Come back to us when you can, Richard."

Richard promised them he would.

As they started down the road, Cara shook her head. "I don't know why you bothered going to all the trouble to save my life. We're going to die, you know."

"I thought you were coming with me to prevent that from happening."

"Lord Rahl, I don't know if I can protect you against a witch woman. I've never faced their power, nor have I heard of any Mord-Sith who has. A Confessor's power used to be deadly to Mord-Sith; it could be that witch woman's power is just as fatal. I will do my best, but I just think you should know that I might not be able to protect you from a witch woman."

"Oh, I'd not worry about it, Cara." Richard said as he squeezed his legs and shifted his weight, urging his horse into a canter. "If I know Shota, she won't let you get anywhere near her, anyway."

As she marched down the side of a wide thoroughfare leading a small knot of men, Nicci thought that in a way it seemed like the sun had gone out since Richard had left. She missed just being able to look into his eyes, at the spark of life in them. For two days she had tirelessly gone about the urgent preparations for the imminent attack, but, without Richard around, life seemed empty, less bright, less . . . less of everything.

At the same time, when he had been around, his single-minded determination to find his imagined love had been draining. In fact, she had sometimes wanted to strangle him. She had tried everything from patience to anger in an attempt to get him to come around to seeing the truth, but it had been like trying to push against a mountain. In the end, nothing she'd done or said had made any difference.

For his own sake she earnestly wanted to help him to come to grips with reality. To do so she had to challenge him in an effort to try to get him to come to his senses before something terrible happened, but at the same time trying to make him see the truth somehow always seemed to cast her as a villain working against him. She hated being in that position.

Nicci hoped that by the time she finished helping to rid Altur'Rang of the threat of the approaching Imperial Order troops and their wizard, Kronos, she could quickly catch up with Richard and Cara. With spare horses and as fast as she knew he would ride, Nicci realized that she would not be able to catch up with him until after he reached the witch woman. If he even made it that far. If Shota didn't kill him once he did.

From what Nicci knew of witches, Richard's chances of coming out of her lair alive were pretty slim. He would have to face the witch woman without Nicci's help and protection. Still, he knew the woman, and she was a woman in every sense, from what Nicci had heard of her, so maybe Richard would at least be civil. It was not at all wise to be impolite to witches.

But even surviving an encounter with a witch woman he would still be devastated if she didn't help him and Nicci knew she couldn't because there was no missing woman for Richard to find. At times it infuriated her that he was so obstinate about something so obviously nothing more than an illusion. At other times she worried that he really was losing his mind. That was too chilling a thought to contemplate.

Nicci paused at the side of the road with a sudden, terrible realization.

The men following her lurched to a halt when she did, bringing her out of her thoughts. They were all with her either to see to her instructions in regard to some of the defenses of the city or else to carry messages as needed. Now they stood silent and uneasy, not knowing why she had stopped.

"Up there," she said to the men, pointing at a three story brick building on the corner across the street. "Make sure that we can use that place to good advantage and put at least a couple dozen archers in the windows. See that they have a large supply of arrows."

"I will go take a look," one of the men said before running off across the road, dodging wagons, horses, and hand-drawn carts.

People rushed along the side of the street passing around Nicci and the men with her as if they were a rock in a swiftly moving river. Passersby spoke in hushed tones among themselves as they coursed between clusters of hawkers calling out trying to sell their goods, or people gathered to urgently discuss the impending battle for the city and what they would do to protect themselves. Wagons of every sort, from big freight wagons pulled by teams of six horses to small wagons pulled by a single horse, sped past in a hurry to complete the stockpiling of provisions or other necessary work while they still could.

Despite the din of horses, wagons, and people, Nicci didn't really hear any of it; she was thinking about the witch woman.

Nicci had suddenly realized that Shota might not simply be unwilling to help Richard, but she might not tell him so. Witch women had their own way of doing things, and their own ends.

If this woman thought Richard was being too insistent or assertive, she very well might decide to get rid of him by sending him on a useless quest to the ends of the world. She very well might do such a thing simply to amuse herself, or to doom him to die a slow death on an endless march across some distant desert. A witch woman might do such a thing just because she could. Richard, in his urgency to find his fantasy woman, wouldn't consider those possibilities. He would promptly head off to where she pointed.

Nicci was furious with herself for letting him leave to go to such a dangerous woman. But what could she do? She couldn't very well forbid him from going.

Her only chance was to get rid of Brother Kronos and his troops as swiftly as possible and then go after Richard and do what she could to protect him.

She spotted the man she had sent to check the brick building sidestepping his way between the wagons and horses as he ran back across the road. Nicci noticed that even with all the people out traveling the roads of the city, it was still much less busy than an ordinary day. People everywhere were making preparations; some had already holed up in places where they thought they might be safe. Nicci had been with the Order when they swept into a city; there was no safe place.

The man dodged his way around an empty wagon bouncing past and at last reached Nicci's side. He stood silently waiting. He was afraid to speak until she requested his report. He was afraid of her. Everyone was afraid of her. She wasn't just a sorceress; she was a sorceress in a bad mood and they all knew it.

No one understood why she seemed so ill-tempered, but for two days everyone had walked on egg shells when they were around her. It had nothing to do with them, and not even anything to do with Richard racing off on his mad search for a woman who didn't exist, but none of them knew that. Nicci was mentally immersed in preparing herself for the ferocity of the violence to come, rehearsing in her mind the various things she might need to do, and hardening herself to it all.

When on the brink of unleashing almost inconceivable savagery, one did not hum a merry tune and remark on the lovely day. One nursed dark thoughts.

Nicci never bothered to try to explain her mood; going through the effort of doing so would drain some of her store of energy. Preparing in her mind to gather every bit of skill, knowledge, wisdom, and power she had at her disposal required a certain kind of withdrawal. There were violent and deadly forces these people could never begin to comprehend that she had to be ready to unleash in an instant. She couldn't explain all of that to everyone. They would just have to deal with it.

"Well?" she calmly asked the man as he stood silently catching his breath.

"It will work," he said. "They do knitting and make cloth there. All three floors are pretty open so archers will be able to quickly and easily move from window to window to get the best shot."

Nicci nodded. She put a hand to her brow to shield her eyes from the low sun as she looked back to the west along the wide boulevard. She studied the layout of the roads and the angles at which they crossed. She finally decided that the crossroads where they stood, with the brick building across the way, was the best spot. With as wide as both thoroughfares were, these roads would likely be the choice of enemy cavalry in the eastern part of the city. She knew the way the Order ran their attacks. They liked width so as to present the strongest front, the most powerful blow in order to break the enemy apart. She was pretty sure that they would send cavalry in this way if they came in from the east, as she expected.

"Good," she told the man. "See to getting archers here along with a heavy supply of arrows. Be quick about it—I don't think we have much time."

As he ran to see to it, Nicci spotted Ishaq in the distance racing up the road in a wagon pulled by two of his big draft horses. He looked to be in a hurry. She had a good idea why he was coming for her, but she tried not to think about it. She turned to another of the men with her.

"Back there, just after the brick building where we will station the archers, I want spikes placed. The span of the road is hemmed in by buildings on both sides." She gestured to the road that crossed the main thoroughfare before the brick building. "Down the street to each side as well, so that if the remaining men charging in try to take either route to escape they will get the same."

Once the enemy charged up the main route into Altur'Rang, they would abruptly pull up the spikes to impale them. The archers would then pick off all the those caught in the bottleneck between the spikes and the men still rushing up from the rear.

The man nodded and ran off to see to her orders. She had already instructed everyone on the spikes. Victor had his blacksmith shop and a number of others working feverishly to manufacture the simple but deadly traps. They were little more than sharpened iron bar stock that was all connected together, almost like a picket fence, but with different length chain between the top crossbar and the upper portion of the spikes.

Sections of these linked spikes were laid in the roads all over the city. Lying down flat they didn't prevent travel on the road, but when cavalry charged in the pointed ends of the entire section were lifted and an iron brace was jammed in place. The different length of chains attaching the spikes to the crossbar allowed the deadly spikes to hang at varying distances from the crossbar, thus making them stick up at different angles. Making them stick up at uneven angles allowed them to be far more treacherous than a simple straight line of spikes. If it was done properly, the enemy cavalry would unexpectedly run their horses right onto the sharp iron tips. Even if they tried to jump them the horses would more likely than not be ripped open. It was simple but highly effective.

There were traps made of the iron sections all over the city, usually at intersections. Once the sections were lifted they couldn't easily be lowered. The panicked horses would be gored on the spikes or at the least wouldn't be able to escape the confinement created by the obstacle. As the cavalry charged up onto the spikes, the soldiers would either be thrown off their horses and likely injured or killed, or they would have to dismount in order to try to deal with the obstruction. Either way, the archers would then have a much better chance of picking them off than if they were just charging past.

The men manning the sections of spikes were instructed to judge the situation and not to necessarily pull the spikes up just as the cavalry ran up to them. In some cases it would be better to wait until some of the men had already charged past. If there was a large number of cavalry this would allow the defenders to split the enemy force, not only spreading confusion among the attack, but breaking it apart, severing the lines of command, making it lose its advantage of unity, and making it easier to deal with the fragmented force. Decisively eliminating the cavalry was essential to stopping the invasion.

Nicci knew, though, that in the panic of facing a frightening wall of charging enemy soldiers screaming for blood, such careful plans tended to be forgotten. She knew that at the sight of such fearsome soldiers with weapons raised, some of the men would flee, failing to raise the spikes before they did. Nicci had seen such terror before. That was why she had placed redundant sections of spikes.

Nearly everyone in the city was committed to its defense. Some would be more effective than others. Even women at home with children had supplies of things, from rocks to boiling oil, that they intended to throw down on any invading soldiers. There had not been a lot of time to make extravagant weapons, but there were men everywhere with stacks of spears. A sharpened pole wasn't fancy, but if it took down a cavalry horse or impaled a man, it was fancy enough. It didn't matter if it was cavalry or foot soldiers, they all had to be defeated, so there were men of the city by the thousands with bows. With a bow, even an old man could kill a vigorous, muscular, hulking young soldier.

An arrow could even take down a wizard.

It would be futile to have the men of the city trying to fight experienced soldiers in a traditional battle. They had to deny the Order's soldiers everything they were used to using.

Nicci's object had been to make the city one big trap. Now, she had to draw the Order into that trap.

To that end, she saw Ishaq's wagon rumbling toward her. People scattered out of the way. Ishaq pulled back on the reins and drew the big horses to a halt. A cloud of dust boiled up.

He set the brake and leaped down off the wagon, something she wouldn't have expected he could do with such agility. He held his hat on with one hand as he ran. He was holding something else up in his other hand.

"Nicci! Nicci!"

She turned to the men with her. "You'd all best see to the things we've discussed. I don't think we have more than a few hours."

The men looked surprised and alarmed.

"You don't think they will wait until morning?" one asked.

"No. I believe they will attack this evening." She didn't tell them why she thought so.

The men nodded and rushed off to their assignments.

Ishaq came to a panting halt. His face was nearly as red as his hat.

"Nicci, a message." He waved the paper before her. "A message for the mayor."

Nicci's insides tightened.

"A group of men rode in," he said. "They were carrying a white flag, just as you said they would. They brought a message for 'the mayor.' How did you know?"

She ignored the question. "Have you read it, yet?"

His face went red. "Yes. So did Victor. He is very angry. It is not a good thing to make the blacksmith angry."

"Do you have a horse, as I requested?"

"Yes, yes, I have a horse." He handed her the paper. "But I think that you had better read this."

Nicci unfolded the paper and read it silently to herself.

Citizen mayor,

I received word that the people of Altur' Rang, under your direction, wish to renounce their sinful ways and bow again to the wise, merciful, and sovereign authority of the Imperial Order.

If it is true that you wish to spare the people of Altur'Rang the total destruction we reserve for insurrectionists and heathens, then as a token of your good intent and willing submission to the jurisdiction of the Imperial Order, you will bind your lovely and loyal wife's hands and send her to me as your humble gift.

Fail to turn over your wife as instructed and everyone in Altur'Rang will die.

In the service of the merciful Creator,
Brother Kronos,
Commander of His Excellency's reunification force.

Nicci crushed the message in her fist. "Let's go."

Ishaq replaced his hat and scrambled to catch up with her as she marched toward the wagon. "You don't seriously intend to do as this brute demands, do you?"

Nicci put a foot on the iron step and climbed up onto the wagon's wooden seat. "Let's go, Ishaq."

He muttered to himself as he climbed into the wagon beside her. He threw off the brake and flicked the reins, yelling for people to get out of the way as he swung the wagon around. Dirt and dust spiraled up off the wheels as he turned the wagon around in the road. He cracked his whip above the horses' flanks, crying out to urge them away. The wagon slid around and finally straightened as the horses threw their weight against the hames.

Nicci held on to the side rail with one hand as the wagon lurched ahead, letting her other hand, with the message crumpled in her fist, rest in the lap of her red dress. She watched without seeing as they raced through the streets of Altur'Rang, past buildings and storefronts, other wagons, horses, and people on foot. Low sunlight flickered through rows of trees to the left as they raced north along the wide boulevard. At vegetable, cheese, bread, and butcher stands under awnings, some drab and some striped, a press of people were buying up all the food they could before the impending storm.

The road narrowed as it passed into ancient sections of the city, becoming clogged with wagons, horses, and people. Without slowing much at all, Ishaq swung his two big draft horses off the main road and took shortcuts through alleyways behind tightly packed rows of buildings where entire families lived in a single room. Laundry stretched on lines that crisscrossed small yards and in a number of places, strung between opposing second-story apartments, stretched across the alleyway over their heads. Nearly each tiny plot in the back of the crowded buildings was used for growing food or keeping chickens. Wings flapped and feathers flew as the birds panicked at the sight of the wagon thundering past their yard.

Ishaq deftly handled the team as it raced at a frightening speed, guiding them around obstacles of shacks, fences, walls, and random trees. He called out warnings as he charged across busy roads. Startled people drew back, letting him pass.

The wagon turned up a street Nicci remembered all too well, following beside a short wall that eventually curved it along the entrance road to the warehouse doors of Ishaq's transport company. The wagon bounced into the rutted yard outside the building and came to a crooked halt in the shade of huge oaks rising above the wall.

Nicci climbed down as she saw one of the double doors opening. Apparently having heard the noise Victor emerged from the building, glowering like he intended to murder the next person he could get his hands on.

"Have you seen the message?" He demanded.

"Yes, I have. Where's the horse I asked for?"

He pointed a thumb back over his shoulder toward the open door. "Well, what are we going to do now? The attack will probably come at dawn. We can't allow those soldiers to take you back with them to the army. We can't let them leave and report that we won't do as Kronos demands. What are we going to tell them?"

Nicci tilted her head toward the building. "Ishaq, would you go get the horse, please?"

He made a sour face. "You ought to marry Richard. You make a good pair. You are both crazy."

Startled, Nicci could only stare at the man.

She finally found her voice. "Ishaq, please, we don't have a lot of time. We don't want those fellows to go back empty-handed."

"Yes, Your Highness," he mocked, "allow me to get your royal mount for you."

"I've never seen Ishaq act like that," she said to Victor as she watched the man stalking toward the door, muttering curses under his breath.

"He thinks you're crazy. So do I." Victor planted his fists on his hips. "Has that ruse back at the stables with the spy gone bad? Or is this what you planned all along?"

In no mood to discuss it with the man, Nicci returned the glare in kind. "My plan," she said through gritted teeth, "is to get this over with as soon as possible and to keep the people of Altur'Rang from being slaughtered."

"What's that got to do with turning you over to Brother Kronos as a gift?"

"If we allow them to attack at dawn, they will have the advantage. We need them to attack today."

"Today!" Victor glanced west, toward the low sun. "But it will be dark soon."

"Exactly," she said as she leaned in the back of the wagon and retrieved a length of rope.

Victor stared off at the heart of the city as he thought about it. "Well, all things considered, I guess it would be better not to face them in the day, on their terms. If we could somehow get them to attack today, they would soon run out of daylight. That would work to our advantage."

"I will bring them to you," she said. "You just be ready."

The creases across Victor's forehead deepened. "I don't know how you're going to get them to attack today, but we'll be ready if they do."

Ishaq came out of the warehouse leading a white stallion covered with mottled black spots. The mane, tail, and legs below the hocks were black. The horse looked not only elegant, but had a tough demeanor about him, as if it would have boundless endurance. Still, it wasn't what she had been expecting.

"He doesn't look all that big," she said to Ishaq.

Ishaq gave the horse an affectionate rub on its white face. "You did not say big, you said that you wanted a steady horse that would not spook easily, one that had a fearless spirit."

Nicci took another look at the horse. "I just assumed that such a horse would be big."

"She's a crazy woman," Ishaq muttered to Victor.

"She's going to be a dead crazy woman," Victor said.

Nicci handed Victor the rope. "This will be easier if you stand on the wall, after I'm mounted."

She stroked the horse under his jaw and then his silky ears. The animal nickered his appreciation and nudged his head against her. Nicci held his head and trickled a thin thread of her Han into the creature, giving him a bit of calming introduction. She ran a hand over his shoulder and then along the side of his belly as she inspected him.

Without comment, Victor climbed up the wall and waited until she boosted herself up and was seated in the saddle. Nicci arranged the skirts of her red dress and then unbuttoned it to the waist. She pulled her arms out of the sleeves one at a time, holding the front of the dress against her chest and then holding it up with her elbows as she lifted her hands toward Victor, her wrists pressed together.

Victor's face went as red as her dress. "Now what are you doing?"

"These men are experienced Imperial Order troops. Some will be officers. I spent a lot of time in the Order's camp. I was widely known—to some as the Slave Queen, and to others as Death's Mistress. It's possible that certain of these men may have served in Jagang's army during that time and so they very well may recognize me, especially if I were to wear a black dress. Just in case, I'm wearing a red dress.

"I also need to give these men something to stare at to keep them off guard and hopefully from recognizing me. It will disrupt the usual calculating judgment of soldiers such as these. It will also get Kronos's attention and make him think that the 'mayor' is desperate to appease him. Nothing rouses the blood lust in these kind of men more than weakness."

"It's going to get you in trouble before you even get to Kronos."

"I'm a sorceress. I can take care of myself."

"Seems to me that Richard is a wizard and carries a sword charged with ancient magic and even he got into trouble when he was greatly outnumbered. He was overpowered and nearly killed."

Nicci again lifted her hands out toward Victor, wrists together.

"Tie them."

Victor glared at her a moment before finally giving in. With a growl he set about binding her wrists. Ishaq held the reins just under the horse's bit as he waited.

"Is this horse fast?" she asked as she watched Victor wrapping rope around her wrists.

"Sa'din is fast," Ishaq told her.

"Sa'din? Doesn't that mean 'the wind' in the old tongue?"

Ishaq nodded. "You know the old tongue?"

"A little," she said. "Today, Sa'din will need to be as swift as the wind. Now listen to me, both of you. I don't intend on getting myself killed."

"Few people do," Victor griped.

"You don't understand; this will be my best chance to get near Kronos. Once the attack begins it would be difficult not only to find him, but, even if we did know where he was, it would be next to impossible to get close to him. He would be dealing death against the innocent in ways you cannot even imagine, spreading fear, panic, and death. That makes him valuable to them. In battle their soldiers will be looking for anyone trying to take out their wizard. I have to do it now. I intend to end it tonight."

Victor and Ishaq shared a look.

"I want everyone to be ready," she said. "When I come back I expect there will be some very angry people behind me."

Victor looked up after yanking the knot tight. "How many angry people?"

"I intend to have their entire force right on my heels."

Ishaq gently rubbed Sa'din's face. "What are they going to be angry about? If I may ask."

"Besides trying to take out their wizard, I intend to give the hornets' nest a good stiff whack."

Victor sighed irritably. "We'll be ready for them when they attack, but once you go in there I'm not so sure you will be able to get away."

Nicci wasn't either. She remembered a time when she went about her plans not caring if she lived or died carrying them out. Now she cared.

"If I don't come back, then you will just have to do your best. Hopefully, even if they kill me, I will be able to take Kronos out with me. Either way, we've laid a lot of surprises for them."

"Does Richard know what you had planned?" Ishaq asked as he squinted up at her.

"I expect he knew. He had the good grace, though, not to make me feel any more afraid by arguing with me about what I know I must do. This is not a game. We are all fighting for our very lives. If we fail, then innocent, decent people are going to be slaughtered in numbers that stagger the imagination. I've been on the other end of attacks like this. I know what's coming. I'm trying to prevent it. If you don't want to help, then just stay out of my way."

Nicci looked at each man in turn. Chagrined, they both kept silent.

Victor went back to his work and quickly finished up with binding her wrists. He pulled a knife from his boot and sliced off the excess length of rope.

"Who do you want to take you to the soldiers who are waiting?" Ishaq asked.

"I think you'd better take me, Ishaq. While Victor alerts everyone and sees to the preparations, you will be a representative of the mayor."

"All right," he said as he scratched the hollow of his cheek.

"Good," she said as she picked up the reins.

Before she could say anything else, Victor cleared his throat. "There is one other matter I've been meaning to talk to you about. But we've both been busy . . ."

Victor uncharacteristically looked away from her.

"What is is?" she asked him.

"Well, ordinarily I wouldn't say anything, but I think maybe you ought to know."

"Know what?"

"People are beginning to question Richard."

Nicci frowned. "Question him? What do you mean? Question him in what way?"

"Word has gotten around about why he left. People are worried that he is abandoning them and their cause to chase phantoms. They question if they should be following such a man. There is talk that he's . . . that he's, you know, deranged or something. What should I tell them?"

Nicci took a deep breath as she collected her thoughts. This was what she had feared. This was one of the reasons she had thought it important that he not leave—especially the way he did, right before the attack.

"Remind them," she said as she leaned toward him, "that Lord Rahl is a wizard, and a wizard can see things—such as hidden, distant threats—that they cannot. A wizard does not go around explaining his actions to people.

"The Lord Rahl has many responsibilities other than just this one place. If the people here wish to live free, to live their own lives as they wish, then they must choose to do so for their own sake. They must trust that Richard, as the Lord Rahl and as a wizard, is off doing what is best for our cause."

"And do you believe that?" the blacksmith asked.

"No. But there is a difference. I can follow the ideals he has shown me while at the same time working to bring Richard back to his senses. The two are not incompatible. But the people must trust in their leader. If they think he is a madman they may fall back on fear and give up. Right now we can't afford that risk.

"Whether Richard is sane or not it doesn't change the validity of the cause. The truth is the truth—Richard or no Richard.

"Those troops coming to murder us are real. If they win, then those who are not killed will be enslaved once more under the yoke of the Imperial Order. If Richard is alive, dead, sane, or mad, it does not change that fact."

Victor, his arms folded, nodded.

Nicci moved her leg back and pressed her heel into Sa'din's side, moving his rump closer to the wall. She turned the back of her shoulders to the blacksmith standing on that wall beside her. "Pull my dress down to my waist, and be quick about it—the sun will be setting soon."

Ishaq turned away, shaking his head.

Victor hesitated a moment, then sighed in resignation and did as she had instructed.

"All right, Ishaq, let's go. Lead the way." She looked back over her shoulder at Victor. "I will bring you the enemy, chasing the setting sun."

"What should I tell the men?" Victor asked.

Nicci shrouded herself in the cold exterior she had used so often throughout her life, the cold calm of Death's Mistress.

"Tell them to think dark and violent thoughts."

For the first time, Victor's glower twisted into a grim smile.

The soldiers atop huge warhorses peered down at Nicci as Ishaq led her horse to a stop beside the community well in the small square at the eastern edge of the city. Her stallion, Sa'din, felt small in the presence of such huge beasts. Armored plate down the front of their heads lent them a threatening appearance. These were cavalry horses and the armor helped protect them from arrows as they charged enemy lines. They pawed the ground and snorted their disdain for the smaller horse come among them. Sa'din backed a step, just out of range of one of the warhorse's teeth when it snapped, but he didn't shy away.

If the horses looked to be frightening animals, the men were clearly their masters. Dressed in dark leather armor plates and shirts of chain mail and carrying an array of sinister weapons, these men were not merely brutish-looking but larger than any of the men defending the city. Nicci knew that they would have been selected for the mission because of the way they looked. The Order liked sending such intimidating messages to strike fear into the hearts of their enemies.

From dark windows, recessed doorways, narrow streets, and the shadows in alleyways people who had retreated out of the open watched the woman stripped to her waist, her wrists bound, being handed over to the soldiers. Nicci had endured the ride through the city by not thinking about it and instead focusing on her need to get this over with so she could catch up with Richard. That was what mattered. So people looked at her—what difference did it make? She had had to endure far worse at the hands of the men of the Order.

"I am an aide to the mayor," Ishaq said in a subservient tone to the powerfully built man atop a towering, brown, bull neck gelding. The butt of the pole with the white flag rested on the man's saddle between his legs, his meaty fist gripping it halfway up the length of the stout shaft. The man sat mute, waiting. Ishaq licked his lips as he bowed before going on. "He sent me in his place with his woman, his wife . . . as a gift to the great Kronos to show our sincerity in agreeing with his wishes."

The soldier, a midlevel officer of some sort, smirked at Nicci after taking a long and deliberate look at her breasts. Broad leather belts held several knives, a flail, a short sword, and a crescent-bladed axe. The mail and metal rings along studded straps crossing his broad chest jangled when his horse stomped its hooves. She was relieved not to recognize the man and kept her head turned down to hide her face from the men with him.

Still, the officer said nothing.

With one hand Ishaq swept his hat off his head. "Please relay our message of peace to—"

The officer tossed the pole with the white flag down to Ishaq. Ishaq swiftly replaced his hat in order to catch the pole with one hand, his other still tightly gripping the reins just below Sa'din's bit. The pole looked heavy, but Ishaq had been loading wagons for most of his life and had no trouble with it.

"Kronos will let you know if the offering is satisfactory," the officer growled.

Ishaq cleared his throat, rather than say anything else, and again bowed politely. The soldiers all snickered at him before taking another knowing look at Nicci's exposed condition. They obviously greatly enjoyed exerting their dominance over others.

Most of them had metal rings or pointed metal rivets pierced through their noses, ears, and cheeks in an attempt to make them look more fierce. Nicci thought that it simply made them look silly. Several of the dozen men had wild, dark, tattooed designs sweeping across their faces, also intended to intimidate. These were men who had risen to their highest ideal in life: to be savages.

It was somewhat common for many of the women in the cities surrendering to advancing Imperial Order troops to come out stripped to the waist as a petition for leniency. Because it was such a common form of submission, the soldiers were not at all surprised by the manner in which the wife of the mayor was being surrendered. That, of course, was one of the reasons why Nicci had done it. Such bids for mercy and gentle treatment were never honored, but the women who offered themselves in such a manner didn't know that.

Nicci knew because she had often been with the Order troops when they took such women captive. Such obliging people imagined that surrender in such a subservient manner would be ingratiating and elicit reasonable treatment. They had no idea that they had willingly given themselves over to incomprehensible horrors. The soldiers' treatment of women captives was dismissed by the intellectuals of the Order as a trivial matter compared to the greater good the Order was bringing to the nonbelievers.

Nicci sometimes longed for death rather than continue to live with such memories and the knowledge that she had once been a party to such horrors. What she wanted now, though, was to set things right as only she could do. She wanted to participate in wiping the scourge of the Order from existence.

The grim officer who had carried the white flag into Altur'Rang bent down and now took the reins to her horse from Ishaq. He stepped his mount close to her. As he leaned toward her he casually seized her left nipple, twisting it as he spoke intimately to her.

"Brother Kronos tires quickly of a woman, no matter how beautiful she is. I expect it will be no different with you. When he moves on to the next he gives us the one he is finished with. Know that I will be first."

The men with him chuckled. He flashed her a grin. His dark eyes gleamed with menace. He twisted harder until she gasped in pain and tears stung her eyes. Satisfied with himself and her timid reaction, he released her. Nicci squeezed her eyes shut as she pressed the back of her bound wrists to herself trying to ease the throbbing pain.

When he batted her arms away from her breast, she jumped in surprise, then lowered her gaze in submission. How many times had she seen women do similar things trying to appease such men, praying silently for deliverance as they did so? For those women, deliverance never came. Nicci recalled thinking at the time that the Order's teachings had to be right, that the Creator really was on their side, for he easily tolerated such behavior from his champions.

Nicci did not bother to pray for deliverance; she intended to create her own.

As the man turned his horse and led her away, Nicci cast one last look over her shoulder at Ishaq, standing with his red hat in both hands, turning the brim around and around in his fingers. His eyes glistened with tears. She hoped that this wasn't the last time she would ever see him or the others, but she knew that such a possibility was all too real.

The officer kept ahold of the reins, so she rode gripping the horn of the saddle. As they rode east, the company of men closely surrounded her—more to get a good look at her, she thought, than from any worry that she might escape. By the way they swayed easily in their saddles and deftly handled their mounts, these were experienced horsemen who spent the majority of their waking hours in the saddle. They had no fear of her getting away from them.

As they rode east on a dusty road, the men all grinned their silent promises whenever they looked her over. She knew, though, that none of them had enough rank or stature to dare to drag her off her horse for a little sport along the way. Men like Kronos did not appreciate their conquests freshly raped and these men knew it. Besides, they were surely figuring that they would soon enough have their turn at her—and if not her, then their pick once they stormed into Altur'Rang.

Nicci tried to ignore the leering men by concentrating on what she had to do. She knew that such behavior was part of their routine. They could think of nothing more clever than simple innuendo and intimidation, so they used it like a worry stone turned over and over in the fingers. As she rode, her resolve became her refuge.

It would still be a while before the low sun at her back set, but already the cicadas had started in with their endless droning song. They reminded her of Richard and the night he had explained about the creatures that emerged from the ground every seventeen years. It seemed remarkable that the cicadas had come ten times in her life and Nicci had never even realized it. Life under the spell at the Palace of the Prophets had not simply been very long, but had been insulating in ways she had never even realized. While the world went on around her, she had been devoting her time to other worlds. Others, like the Sisters of the Dark who had been Richard's teachers there, had succumbed to seductive promises from those other worlds. Nicci had, as well, but not because of those promises. She had simply believed that this world held nothing of value to her.

Until, one day, when Richard had shown up.

The air was warm and humid so at least Nicci wasn't cold as she rode, but the mosquitoes were starting to come out and they were becoming obnoxious. She was glad that her hands weren't tied behind her back so she could at least keep the biting bugs off her face. The wheat-covered hills they passed through to the east of the city shimmered a greenish gold in the late light, almost like burnished bronze. She didn't see any people working in the countryside and the roads remained empty. Everyone had fled before the impending arrival of the army, like animals before a wildfire.

Cresting a hill, Nicci finally saw them, men and horses from the Imperial Order spread out across the broad valley below her like a dark flood. It appeared they hadn't been there long as it looked like they were only starting to set up camp. Apparently, they wanted to be close to the city so that when they began their attack in the morning they wouldn't have far to go.

The ground was only just beginning to be churned up by all the men, horses, mules, and wagons. Individual territory had been staked out and small tents erected. Rings of sentries and outposts guarded the sea of men. Every hilltop had lookouts watching all the approaches.

The tents cast long shadows across the trampled wheat. Already a haze of smoke hung over the valley from all the cook fires. Nicci could see that one of the nearby olive groves had been stripped of its valuable fruit trees to be used for firewood. Men cooked for themselves or in small groups—simple things, camp stew, rice and beans, bannock, and fritters. The aroma of the burning wood and cooking mingled uneasily with the smell of all the animals, men, and manure.

Her escort kept a tight formation around her as they trotted into the camp along what was quickly becoming a temporary road among the seething throng. Nicci had expected to see them in a raucous state, drinking and celebrating on the eve of a great battle. They were not. They were going about the business of preparing in earnest for the job ahead; sharpening weapons, working on saddles and other gear, tending to horses. Lances and spears were already sharpened and neatly stacked all over the camp. Blacksmiths at a traveling forge worked with tongs and hammers as helpers feverishly pumped bellows. Farriers shod horses while other men mended leather equipment. Cavalry horses were being fed, cared for, and groomed.

This was not a typical Imperial Order camp where chaos ruled. The army to the north was almost unimaginably vast. Many parts of it were little more than an unruly mob that was periodically unleashed on helpless civilians and allowed to plunder at will. This force, on the other hand, was much smaller, consisting of less than twenty thousand men. This was the camp of a well-honed war machine.

In the main army camp of the Imperial Order, a woman with her breasts exposed as Nicci's were would already have been dragged from her horse by a rabble and raped. These men were no less lecherous, but they were far better disciplined. These were not just any soldiers sent to do some dirty work; these were experienced, dedicated, handpicked troops sent to vent the emperor's rage at the insult of his home city rejecting everything for which he stood.

Nicci felt a shiver of dread at again being among such men. These were the cream of the Order's crop. These were men who gleefully killed all those who opposed them. These were brutes who reveled in violence to further their beliefs. These were the embodiment of the term "bloodthirsty." These men were the enforcers of the Order's doctrines.

As Nicci and her escort rode through the camp, the soldiers all ogled her. Every step of the way, hoots, calls, and cheering followed her. Obscene promises were laughingly given as she passed. Nothing was left to the imagination of anyone in earshot. She heard herself described in every lewd term she had ever heard before, and among Jagang's men she had heard them all. Now they were all directed at her.

She kept her eyes ahead as she rode, thinking of the way Richard treated her and just how much such respect meant.

Near a grove of cottonwood trees along the bank of a creek running through the valley, Nicci spotted lambskin tents that were a little larger than the rest. While by no means elaborate accommodations like the tents of Emperor Jagang's entourage, these were still luxurious by army standards. The small group of command tents sat atop a hillock that afforded the officers the opportunity to look down on the rest of the camp. Unlike the main army encampment, here there was no ring of guards protecting the elite forces and officers from the common soldiers. Outside the main tent, slabs of meat were being rotated on spits by slaves that always attended the higher ranking officers . . . or high priests of the Fellowship of Order. For a force such as this, only the most loyal slaves would have been brought along.

As they slowed to a halt, the man who held the reins to Nicci's horse tilted his head, ordering one of his men to go announce them. The man threw his leg over his horse's neck and jumped to the ground. With each step, dust lifted from his pants as he strode toward the main tent.

Nicci noticed that all around curious men began wandering closer, coming to see the woman being brought as a gift for their leader. She could hear them laughing and wisecracking among themselves as they leered at her. Their eyes were as cold and frightening as any she had ever seen.

What worried her the most, however, was that many of the men held spears or had arrows nocked in their bows. These were not men who took anything casually. Even as they drooled at her they were prepared for any kind of threat her appearance might present.

The man sent to announce her was ushered into the main tent by an attendant. A moment later he reappeared, followed by a tall man in flowing henna-dyed robes. His manner of dress stood out on the drab scene like clotted blood. Despite the heat and humidity the hood of his robe was draped regally over his head, a sign of pious authority.

He stalked to the edge of the rise, closer to her, and struck an arrogant pose. He took his time looking her over—inspecting the goods.

The man holding the reins to her horse bowed in his saddle.

"A humble gift from the people of Altur'Rang," he explained with mock courtliness.

Men far and wide laughed quietly to themselves at that, commenting to one another on the specific pleasures Kronos was going to enjoy from his gift. Officers came out of nearby tents to see what was going on.

A lustful grin spread across Kronos's face. "Bring her in. I will have to unwrap the gift and have a closer look."

The men laughed all the louder. Kronos's smile widened, pleased that they found his wit entertaining.

Nicci found the circumstances of her dress to be distracting, but that was the risk. She had judged the risk necessary. These men were brutes and they found her situation to their liking.

Brother Kronos took her in as he waited for her to be conveyed inside. His unflinching gaze was riveting. She found herself staring into his dark eyes.

Men closed in around her.

Nicci knew that she couldn't allow them to get her off her horse. It had to be now.

There were a thousand things she wanted to say to Brother Kronos. She wanted to tell him what she thought of him, what she was going to do to him, what Richard was going to do to all the Imperial Order.

A simple death seemed too easy for Kronos. She wanted him to suffer before he died. She wanted him to know full well what she had in store for him. She wanted him to feel it, to twist in pain and agony, to beg for mercy, to taste the bitter bile of defeat. She wanted him to suffer for the misery he spread in his wake. She wanted him to pay the price for everything he had ever done to innocent people.

She wanted him to know that his entire life had been a waste and that it was about to end.

But she knew that that was not her task. She would risk failure should she even attempt to accomplish any tiny part of it.

Instead, Nicci unceremoniously lifted her fists just a little toward the man as she willed forth her Han. Fearing to tip Kronos as to what was coming, she refrained from taking even an extra split second to conjure anything elaborate. She opened the floodgates, using nothing more complex than a blast of air directed at the man—but it was concentrated beyond anything he would expect even if he suspected she might be a sorceress.

In a blinding instant the late-afternoon camp was lit with a flash of crackling light—discharges created by the intense heat generated by a focused compression of air. Threads of light lashed around the convergent release of force.

Since even a slight slip could conceivably give him an opportunity to strike out before he died, Nicci didn't even risk the satisfaction of smiling as the iron-hard spike of air shot for his head.

Before Brother Kronos ever realized that something was happening, Nicci's sudden release of power blew a fist-sized hole through the center of his forehead. Blood and brain matter sprayed the lambskin wall of the tent behind him. He dropped like a sack of sand, his life already long gone. He never had a chance to respond in kind.

Nicci used a shard of power to at last sever the ropes binding her wrists. They hissed from the sting of heat as they were cut and then dropped away.

Without pause she fed a flow of her Han into a focused line of power that she swept around her like a blade wielded by a master swordsman. The officer who had led her horse and leered at her the whole way grunted as that hot edge ripped through him, cutting him in two below the rib cage. His mouth opened but no scream escaped as his upper half tumbled toward the ground, landing with a hard thud.

With a wet thump the second man could do no more than gasp as he was hit by the same power and torn in two. Coiled ropes of his intestines disgorged across his horse's neck. Nicci twisted in her saddle as she whipped the conjured blade around in an arc. With frightening speed and a flash that lit the shimmering leaves of the nearby cottonwood trees, the edge of deadly power sizzled as it ripped through the air. Before anyone could begin to react, it cut down all the men on horses around her as they still sat in their saddles.

The air filled with the stench of burned flesh, blood, and the contents of ruptured viscera. Horses reared up or bucked, trying to rid themselves of the disembodied legs. Ordinarily, warhorses were used to the confusion of intense battle—but that was in large part because they had familiar riders to control and direct them. Now they were on their own and they were spooked. A number of men rushing in were knocked down and trampled by the panicked horses, further adding to the disorder.

As pandemonium began to erupt all around her, as men charged in toward her, Nicci gathered her inner will, preparing to unleash an onslaught of withering destruction.

Just as she was initiating the launch of that deadly assault, she pitched forward unexpectedly. At the same time she felt the stunning pain of something heavy clouting her across her back. It was propelled by such staggering force that it drove her breath out with a cry. She saw flying past her the shattered pieces of a heavy lance that had been swung like a club.

Dazed, Nicci realized that she had just hit the ground face-first. She tried desperately to gather her senses. Her face felt oddly numb. She tasted warm blood. She saw strings of it dripping from her chin as she pushed herself up on wobbly arms.

She realized then, when she couldn't pull in a breath, that the wind had been violently knocked out of her. She frantically tried again, but, despite her desperate efforts, she couldn't draw a breath.

The world swam in dizzy disarray around her. Sa'din was above her, dancing about but unable to move away. Even though Nicci feared that the horse might accidentally step on her, she couldn't make herself move out of the way. Men all around finally muscled the horse aside. Other men dropped to their knees beside her. A knee in her back flattened her to the ground again. Powerful hands gripped her arms, her legs, her hair, holding her down—as if she could get up on her own.

These men apparently feared that if she got up she might conjure her power, as if the gifted needed to be standing and they had but to keep her on the ground to be safe. But the gifted did need to have their wits about them if they were to call upon their power, and she didn't.

Some of the men pulled her over on her back. A boot at her throat kept her her pinned to the ground. Weapons all around pointed down at her.

And then a terrible thought came to her . . . dark eyes.

The wizard she had just killed had dark eyes.

Kronos didn't have dark eyes.

Kronos was supposed to have blue eyes.

She was having difficulty sorting it all out in her mind. She had killed the high priest. It didn't make sense.

Unless there had been more than one Brother.

The men holding her down backed away.

Grim blue eyes glared down at her. It was a man wearing long robes. The hood was pulled up. A high priest.

"Well, sorceress, you have just managed to kill Brother Byron, a loyal servant to the Fellowship of Order."

She could tell by his tone that he had not yet begun to voice his building anger.

Through the shock, Nicci still couldn't draw a breath. The pain in her back radiated out in paralyzing waves. She wondered if the man who had clubbed her had broken her ribs. She wondered if her back was broken. She supposed it didn't matter, now.

"Allow me to introduce myself," the red-faced man above her said. He pushed the hood of his robes back. "I am Brother Kronos. You belong to me, now. I intend to make you pay a long and painful price for the murder of a good man who was only doing the Creator's noble work."

Nicci couldn't, simply couldn't, pull in a breath to save her life, much less to say anything. The pain of not being able to breathe cloaked her in a tight shroud of panic that prevented her from thinking. The distress of needing air and not being able to get it grew more terrifying with every passing second.

She didn't know what to do.

She remembered when Richard had been shot with the arrow and he couldn't breathe. She remembered how his skin had turned ashen, and then had begun turning blue. She had been so afraid seeing him not being able to breathe. Now she couldn't.

Kronos's smile was as humorless and wicked as any she had ever seen, but it seemed not to matter to her.

"Quite an accomplishment—for a sorceress—killing a wizard. But then, you only accomplished such a feat by treachery, so it was no real accomplishment after all. It was nothing more than simple, underhanded deceit."

He didn't know. Nicci realized that he still didn't know who she was . . . or what she was. She was no mere sorceress.

But she needed a breath to be anything.

Her vision was narrowing to a black tunnel with the face of the wizard Kronos twisting into rage at the far end. She tried with all her might to pull a breath. It felt like her body had forgotten how to breathe.

It surprised her that the lack of air made her ribs throb and ache. She wouldn't have expected that. Despite her fading, frantic effort to get air into her lungs, the life-giving breath simply would not come into her. She could only assume that whoever had clubbed her had done some kind of serious damage, and she would never again draw a life-giving breath.

And then Kronos gritted his teeth and seized her breast in a vicious, viselike grip spiked with thorns of magic intended to inflict excruciating torment.

The sudden sharp shock of pain made her gasp a breath before she realized she was doing it.

The air felt hot with life as it flooded into her lungs. Without conscious thought, she instinctively struck out with her Han at the cause of the piercing pain.

Kronos cried out and staggered back, cradling the hand that had been on her and dealing out his revenge. Blood ran down his wrist and under the sleeve of his robe.

Although she had been able to get him to release her, and even to injure him, she was still too disoriented to muster the force necessary to get past the formidable defenses of a wizard in order to kill him. She panted, gulping air, even though each breath hurt. She knew, though, that it hurt far more not to be able to get a breath.

"You filthy bitch!" he yelled. "How dare you use your power against me! You cannot hope to match me with the gift. You will soon enough learn your place."

His face flushed red with anger. With a thin thread of her Han Nicci could sense the powerful shields the man had erected before himself. Before he had, though, she had seared the flesh off his fingers. He held the trembling hand to his breast. She knew full well that his intent was to extract prolonged and gruesome retribution.

He ranted at her, cursing and calling her names, telling her what he intended to do with her and what would become of her once he was finished with her. The grins of the men watching widened at hearing the nature of those plans.

He thought she was a sorceress and that he could overpower her gift with his. He did not know that she was far more; she had become a Sister of the Dark. Even if he knew that much, Kronos might not have understood, as few people did, the full and terrible meaning behind that appellation. A Sister of the Dark wielded not only her own gift, but the Han of a wizard as well; his gift was taken before he passed through the veil into death.

As if the combined gift of a sorceress and wizard was not formidable enough, added into that powerful mix was Subtractive Magic gained while the veil was parted at the instant of the donor wizard's death. His own Han acted as the conduit, and she held within herself that power as the Subtractive essence slipped through the veil.

There were few people who could command Subtractive Magic: Richard by birth, and the Sisters of the Dark by contrivance. All of the Sisters of the Dark were now captives of Jagang except for Nicci and four others— three of Richard's former teachers from the Palace of the Prophets and their leader, Sister Ulicia.

Kronos shook his bloody fist at Nicci. "The people of Altur'Rang are traitors! They have defiled a holy place! In turning away from the ways of the Order they have turned away from the Creator Himself. Through our hands, the Creator will have His revenge and smite these sinful people. We will cleanse Altur'Rang not just of their flesh and bone but of their un-enlightened ways! The Imperial Order will once again rule Altur'Rang and from there Jagang the Just will rule the world under the rightful ways of the Creator!"

Nicci almost laughed. Kronos had no idea that he was speaking to the person who had given Jagang the title of "Jagang the Just." She had told the emperor that such pronouncements of justice under his rule would win over a great number of people without having to fight them. He had been willing to battle them all; she alone had been able to make him see that it was to his benefit to have them rally to his side of their own free will. She told Jagang that the name she had given him would bring the people to him.

She had been all too right. Many people equated intentions with the ac-tual deed. The title she had given Jagang was now widely believed by peo-ple who didn't know much at all about him or the Order. It never failed to amaze her how simply saying something, no matter how untrue, was all it took to convince a large number of people of what you wanted them to be-lieve. She supposed that it was easier for them to let someone else do their thinking for them.

Kronos's tirade had bought her time to recover. With her strength re-turning, Nicci couldn't afford to wait another instant.

She straightened her arm, pointing her fist up toward him. She wanted to draw her force out the length of her arm to let it build and converge at a point just beyond her fist. While it wasn't at all necessary, she wanted to do it that way simply because it pleased her to let Kronos see her overt threat.

Confident in his ability, and the shields of his power, her hostile posture only served to further enrage him. "How dare you threaten—"

She released a tight bolt of Additive and Subtractive Magic laced together in a fearsome cord of destruction that arced through the wizard's shields like lightning through paper and blew a mellon-sized hole right through the center of his chest.

Kronos's eyes snapped wide. His mouth hung open in mute shock as his mind registered the irredeemable.

Through that hole, Nicci could see the sky. Almost instantly the internal pressure forced what remained of his surrounding organs into the void and then out the opening as Kronos's mortally wounded body toppled back.

The man hadn't known that his power was no match for hers. He could only conjure shields of Additive Magic. Such shields were of limited use against Subtractive Magic.

All around her weapons were already being lifted. Powerful muscles drew bowstrings to cheeks. Arms with spears cocked back, the iron tips all pointing at her along with swords, axes, and pikes.

Without pause Nicci unleased a blast of opposing magic twined together in a shattering ignition that in ruinous fury leveled the officers' tents and blasted through the men on the knoll. The devastating concussion radiated outward in a circle at breathtaking speed, stripping flesh from bone. The ground was made muddy by the sudden deluge of blood.

The heat that had been focused into the blast was so intense that nearby trees erupted in flame. The clothes of men in the surrounding camp who had been rushing to meet the threat also caught fire. The flesh of those a little closer ignited. Men closer yet were ripped apart by the thunderous discharge of Nicci's power. The force of what she had unleashed dissipated with distance and men farther away were only sent sprawling.

Such an extreme effort was risky because it was so draining, but it had the desired effect. In an instant the situation had changed from arrogant brutes gloating over a captive woman to confusion and panic.

Fearing to lose the initiative, she focused intense heat into the trunks of trees along the creek bank behind the men. It was a method of getting a large return for a small investment of power. Superheated sap instantly boiled into steam and the massive cottonwood trunks exploded in thunderous blasts, sending heavy sections of splintered wood spiraling though the crowds of men, cutting them down by the dozens.

Nicci swiftly conjured a liquid fire and sent the inferno spilling out across the field and into the confusion, igniting men, horses, and equipment in the terrible fury of roaring flames. The screams of man and beast melted together into one, long, terrible cry. The air smelled of oily smoke as well as burning hair and flesh.

At last, men were no longer charging in at her. In the brief break, Nicci struggled to get up from the blood-soaked ground. She stumbled through the carnage. Sa'din raced forward through the thick haze and nudged her with his head, helping her to find her balance. She threw an arm over his neck, relieved that she had succeeded in directing her power around him and that he was all right.

She finally seized the reins and, grunting with effort, managed to pull herself up on the horse before men could spear him, or slash her, or send arrows at them. She spun Sa'din around, all the time casting boiling gouts of fire out among the men as they again began rushing in at her. As they caught on fire, they stumbled blindly, shrieking, flailing, crashing into other men or into tents, spreading the deadly conflagration.

A man on one of the big warhorses suddenly galloped out of the smoke. The soldier raised his sword as he screamed a battle cry. Before Nicci could do anything, Sa'din bellowed in rage and snapped, ripping the war-horse's ear off. The wounded horse screamed in terror and pain as it spun and bucked. The soldier was sent flying into the burning bodies.

Nicci directed a web of power at men rushing in at her, each in turn— just for an instant, but long enough to stop their hearts. They stumbled, clutching their chests. In a way, it was more frightening for men to see their comrades gasp and drop from a mysterious cause than it was to see them rent by violence. From Nicci's point of view it was just as effective and it didn't take as much of her strength; even though it required specific targeting, stopping a heart was easier than conjuring flames or lightning. With so many men all around her and all rushing in at her, she knew she was going to need all her strength if she hoped to get out of the camp alive.

While the men in the immediate area knew what was happening, as of yet those in the outlying areas of the camp weren't fully aware of what was specifically going on, although they now knew they were under some sort of attack. Being well trained, they all rallied.

From all directions, arrows zipped through the air. Spears began fly-ing past. An arrow flicked through Nicci's hair. Another clipped her shoulder just enough to cut her. Nicci drummed her heels against Sa'din's

ribs and lay forward over his whithers. She was astonished at the power
with which the horse leaped away. He fearlessly galloped right through
men rushing in at them. The stallion's hooves made a sickening sound
as they struck bone. Men tumbled away. Sa'din jumped over tents and
fires. The air was alive with terrible screams. As she raced through the
camp Nicci took every opportunity to inflict yet more death and destruction.

But from behind her, a swelling, angry roar began to lift from thousands upon thousands of men all the way across the valley. The power of
it, the ferocity, was frightening.

Nicci vividly recalled Richard's warning that all it would take was one
lucky arrow. Now there were thousands. Nicci diverted her power from attacking to shielding her and her horse.

As Sa'din carried her back through the men, horses, wagons, and tents,
Nicci let go of her defenses and again focused a scythe of her gift to slice
through anything living that was close enough. The intensely concentrated
and compacted edge of air sliced through men as they ran in to intercept
her. As her horse leaped some obstacles and dodged others, that deadly
edge of her power cut some men off at the knees and decapitated others.
Horses screamed as their legs were cleaved from under them and they
crashed to the ground. Shrieks of horror and pain from wounded men followed in her wake. But there were growing cries of rage.

As she charged through the camp, Nicci could see men all around
swiftly saddling their horses and mounting up. Spears and lances were
snatched from those stacked everywhere throughout the encampment.
Nicci wished she could destroy the weapons, but she had to concentrate
just to hold on to Sa'din as he bounded over anything in his way, including
an occasional wagon. The horse seemed possessed to get her out of the
danger as swiftly as possible. Even so, men in gathering numbers were
taking up the chase, whether on horse or foot.

As she cleared the last of the tents, Nicci looked back over her shoulder. The place was in an uproar. Flames still shot skyward. Billowing
clouds of oily black smoke rose in several places. She didn't have any
idea how many men she had killed, but there were thousands of them
coming after her. The pounding she was taking atop a galloping horse was
making her back hurt something fierce.

At least she had eliminated Kronos. They had tried to trick her, but in the end it had cost them a second wizard that she hadn't even known they had with them and would have been terrible trouble for the defenders back at Altur'Rang. It had turned out to be a bit of good fortune.

As long as they didn't have three wizards.

As Nicci crested a hill, the first glimpse of the vast city in the distance was a beautiful sight. A quick glance over her shoulder revealed the thundering cavalry right on her heels. Nicci was able to see the raised swords, axes, spears, and lances glinting in the light of the setting sun like steel quills of an immense porcupine. The cloud of dust boiling up behind them blotted out the darkening eastern sky. The bloodthirsty battle cries were terrifying.

And that was only the cavalry. She knew that farther back came the tide of foot soldiers.

Even if the sun wouldn't have been in her eyes, Nicci didn't think that she could have spotted anyone in the city. That was as it should be. She wanted people, for the most part, to stay hidden. Even so, it was not reassuring to feel all alone with an angry hornets' nest chasing her.

She had told Victor and Ishaq the route she would try to take when returning so that they could concentrate their defenses to the best advantage. She hoped they were ready. There hadn't been a great deal of time to prepare. They would get no more, though; time was up.

With the city looming closer, Nicci at last spared the effort to snake her right arm through the sleeve of her dress, then reached back and threaded her left arm through the other sleeve. Holding the reins in one hand, leaning forward over the galloping horse's withers, she at last managed to blindly button her dress back up. She smiled at the small victory.

The first small buildings flashed by. Although there had been a cutoff from the main road that would have more quickly gotten her into the confines of the city, Nicci had kept to the main road down out of the hills. Entering Altur'Rang, the road turned into a broad boulevard, the main east-west thoroughfare. As the buildings grew closer together, they also rose up higher. In places along the road trees lined the way. She could see fastened on the bark of those trees the split-open, empty skins of cicadas that had molted. It gave Nicci a fleeting memory of lying in the shelter, in the warmth of Richard's arm.

Sa'din was sweating into a lather and she knew that he had to be tiring, but he didn't show any sign of wanting to slow. She had to urge him to ease up just a little anyway so that the cavalry would get closer to her. She wanted them to believe they were catching her. Once a predator chasing prey was closing in they tended to lose sight of everything else. The instinct to chase was as strong in soldiers as it was in wolves. Nicci wanted them to throw caution to the winds as they ran her down, so she leaned a little to the side, making it look as if she might be wounded and ready to fall.

Running down the center of the road, trailing a ribbon of dust, she began to recognize groups of buildings. She remembered patterns of windows. She saw a butter-colored clapboard building to the left and red shutters to the right that she recognized. In the shadows down an alleyway just beyond a row of closely packed buildings that she knew were homes because of the laundry hanging on lines between them, she spotted some of the men hiding. They all had bows. She knew she wasn't far.

She suddenly came upon the three story brick building. In the late light she almost didn't recognize it. The spikes lying across the road were covered with a thin layer of dirt to hide them from the soldiers. As she galloped past, she spotted men hiding just around the corner, ready to pull up the spikes once she was by.

"Wait until most are past!" she called out to the waiting men just loud enough for them to hear but not so loud that those following could hear.

She saw one of them nod to her. She hoped they understood. If the spikes were pulled up at the head of the cavalry, bottlenecking them all, then only those in the lead would be taken out and most of those in the rear would escape injury and regroup. If that happened then they would have lost their chance to break up the cavalry. Nicci needed the defenders manning the spikes to allow most to get past.

Nicci looked back over her shoulder to see the big men with their weapons raised thundering past the brick building. Most cleared the rear of the building, but then, there was a sudden howling boom as charging warhorses crashed headlong into the iron spikes. Horses behind weren't able to stop and violently collided with the animals that had been impaled.

Riders cried out as they were crushed. Other men tumbled over the heads of their horses.

From the windows, arrows rained down as soldiers now on foot tried to halt the tail of the cavalry still charging in. Men desperately slowed their mounts. As they did they were hit with arrows. Men and horses were hit with a withering flight of arrows from several directions. Most of the men put an arm up, only to then realize that they had neglected to take the time to get their shields.

As the last of the riders were still crashing into the sudden blockade, Nicci went right at the fork in the wide road. The cavalry was right on her heels and swept down the street after her.

"Wait until half are past!" she yelled at the men hiding around the corner of a tall stone wall as she raced past.

Again came the hard impacts and terrible noise of animals screaming in pain and terror as they were unexpectedly impaled or torn open. Soldiers cried out as they were violently unhorsed. Men carrying spears rushed out from behind the building, running the soldiers through before they had a chance to get to their feet and fight. Axes, swords, and flails belonging to fallen soldiers were swept up by men to be used against the Order.

Some of the cavalry, fooled a second time, didn't intend to be fooled again and at a full gallop peeled off from the main column, some taking another street to the left. Others turned down a narrow road to the right.

The riders following her had gone hardly any distance at all and had not had a chance to fully consider if they should break off the charge, when Nicci cleared the third barrier of iron spikes as men yanked them up and jammed posts in place. The horses just behind her crashed into the spikes. From immediately behind came the most terrible noise of the immense weight of horseflesh thudding into the lead animals already caught up on the iron spikes and stopped cold in their tracks. A great cry lifted from the cavalrymen as they were ensnared in the violent debacle. Almost at the same time the riders who had taken roads to the right and left suddenly found themselves caught up in the same iron traps. The enemy found themselves in a box canyon of brick and iron, rather than rock.

The impact of the horses running at full speed clouting into a tangled pile of broken men and animals blocking the main road was ghastly. Flesh pounded against flesh and bones snapped. Horses screamed in pain. So powerful was the force of the impact that it broke the spike wall and blew a hole through the bottleneck of carcasses. Great warhorses, some with their face armor and some without, spilled through the gap, slipping and sliding on the blood and gore of slain comrades and other animals. In the treacherous footing, some of the horses and riders fell. Others pouring through the gap at a full gallop didn't have anywhere else to go and trampled them.

Men bristling with spears rushed out of alleyways to the sides and into the path of the charging cavalry to close the breach in the line. The horses, already in shock from the carnage and terrible destruction of so many of their kind, now faced rank upon rank of men running in at them, yelling battle cries, thrusting spears into their sides. The animals squealed with horrific, desperate screams as they were mercilessly gored. The fallen animals tripped up those still running in an attempt to escape. The evening air sounded as if it were ripping as archers rained down a hail of arrows on cavalrymen struggling to escape the carnage.

Nicci doubted that these Imperial Order troops would have deliberately attacked into the city, using the cavalry in such a fashion, if they had not been goaded into it. These kind of horses were not meant for this kind of fighting. They simply couldn't maneuver properly in the close quarters and the cavalrymen couldn't effectively cut down their opposition. To make matters more difficult for them, the defenders had too many places to hide for a cavalry charge to be truly effective. The purpose of the cavalry would have been to swiftly crush any organized resistance out in the open hoping to stop the Order before they reached the city, and then to run down anyone who tried to escape the city after the troops were sent in. Had the commanders been properly in control of the situation and their men, Nicci doubted they would have allowed such a crazy cavalry charge into the confines of a city. Nicci, of course, had known all that when she went to whack the hornets' nest.

The folly of a cavalry attack into a city was becoming all too apparent. The killing was as swift as it was brutal. The gruesome sight of so many horses and men torn open seemed somehow unreal. The stench of blood was gagging.

When she saw a column of the enemy turn down an alleyway to make an escape, Nicci cast her Han outward, using a concentrated spike of force to snap the bones of the lead horse. As the animal's legs folded under it the horses following crashed into it at full speed, breaking their legs as the first horse rolled under them before they were able to leap up out of the way. A few of the horses following behind, seeing what was happening and having more time to react, were able to jump clear. Nicci saw the men at the far end of the narrow alleyway close off their escape route.

Nicci cut around the corner to reach the main bottleneck and help prevent any Imperial Order cavalry from escaping the trap. As she rounded the final building, she encountered a knot of cavalry as they broke through the lines of men with spears. Nicci sent a molten ball of flame howling toward the enemy. It cleared the heads of the defenders and hit the street, splashing liquid fire across the horses' flanks. The animals, their hides ablaze, reared up, allowing the flames to roll up onto the men on their backs.

Nicci raced around tightly packed buildings to come up behind the tail end of the center trap that had ensnared a large number of the enemy. The men of the city had already set upon them. For once, the cavalrymen were outnumbered, disorganized, and unable to break free of the onslaught. Men fighting for their freedom had a burning determination that the soldiers had not expected to encounter. Their tactics of intimidation and simple slaughter had fallen apart.

In the fading light of dusk, Nicci spotted Victor swinging a heavy mace at any Imperial Order head he could find. She urged Sa'din through the slaughter.

"Victor!"

The man looked up with a murderous scowl. "What!" he cried out over the din of the battle, blood dripping from the steel blades of his weapon.

Nicci stepped her horse closer. "The soldiers are coming right behind the cavalry. They will be the real test. We don't dare let them change their mind about attacking now. Just in case they are having any second thoughts, I'm going to go give them something irresistible to chase into the city."

Victor flashed her a grim grin. "Good. We will be ready for them."

Once the army poured into Altur'Rang, there was no way they would be able to stay together. They would split up to move down different streets. Once they did that, each of those groups could be further divided by the defenders. As each group fled or charged, they would face hidden archers and groups of men with spears, to say nothing of the numerous traps.

Altur'Rang was huge. As darkness took the city, many of the invaders would become disoriented and lost. Because of the narrow warren of streets they wouldn't be able to stay together to present a coordinated attack. They would not be allowed to go where they wished, as they wished, attacking helpless people; they would be relentlessly pursued and harried. Each group would get smaller all the time, both because they would be whittled down while under constant attack, and because some of their men would try other routes to find a way to safety. Nicci had made sure that there was no place of safety in the city.

"There is blood all down the front of you." Victor called up to her. "Are you all right?"

"I got clumsy and fell off my horse. I'm fine. This must end tonight," she reminded Victor.

"In a hurry to go after Richard?"

She smiled but didn't answer his question. "I'd better go whack the hornets' nest. I will bring them on my heels."

He nodded. "We're ready."

When she spotted three soldiers in the distance trying to make an escape without their horses, Nicci paused to cast a shimmering spell down a narrow twisting street. With three rapid thuds, the lance of power slammed through flesh and bone to drop the three.

"And Victor," she said turning back to the man, "there's one last thing."

"What would that be?"

"No one gets away alive. No one."

With the sounds of battle raging behind him, he appraised her eyes for a moment. "I understand. Ishaq will be waiting for you; try to get the hornet's nest there as quickly as you can."

Nicci, checking the reins to hold Sa'din in place, nodded. "I will bring the soldiers right down—"

She turned to the sudden whoosh of flame. Great gouts of fire flared up to the east. She knew that it could mean only one thing.

Victor cursed and climbed up to stand on the carcass of a dead warhorse as he craned his neck, trying to get a view over the rooftops at the thick smoke billowing up into the darkening sky.

He cast a suspicious scowl at Nicci. "You failed to get Kronos?"

"I got Kronos," she growled through gritted teeth, "and another wizard. It would appear that they have another gifted with them. I guess they came prepared." Nicci laid the reins over, turning Sa'din toward the distant sounds of screams. "But they didn't come prepared for Death's Mistress."

What do you think it could mean?" Berdine asked.

Verna glanced over at the Mord-Sith's blue eyes. "Ann didn't say."

The library was dead quiet but for the soft hiss of oil lamps. What with the row upon row of aisles along with the woodwork and shelves of dark walnut, the lamps and candles did little to illuminate the vast inner sanctuary. Had Verna lit all of the reflector lamps lining the walls and hung on the end caps of shelves, the place could have been made to be considerably brighter but, for their purpose, she didn't think it necessary.

In a way, Verna felt that if they were to light too many lamps, pull out too many ancient volumes, disturb the sanctum to a large degree, it might wake the ghosts of all the Master Rahls who haunted the place.

Heavy beams divided the dark, frame and panel woodwork of deep-set ceiling coves. Gilded carvings of vines and leaves meandered up columns to the side that supported those massive timbers. Strange yet beautiful symbols were painted in rich colors across the faces of the beams. Underfoot were spread luxurious carpets woven with elaborate designs in muted colors.

And everywhere, around the outer walls in cases behind glassed doors and in freestanding shelves marching through the library in orderly row upon row, were books by the thousands. Their leather bindings, mostly in deep colors with at least some gold or silver leaf on the spines, added a rich, mottled texture to the place. Verna had rarely seen libraries so grand. The vaults at the Palace of the Prophets where she had spent a great deal of time in study had also held thousands of books, but the place had been utilitarian, serving only the function of storing books and providing a practical place to read them. This palace revealed a reverence for the books and the knowledge they contained.

Knowledge was power, and throughout the ages each Lord Rahl in turn had such power at his fingertips. Whether or not he used that knowledge wisely was another question. The only problem with such vast amounts of information would be accessing a specific item, or even knowing that it existed in such an immense collection.

Of course, in times long past there would have been scribes who, besides their work of making copies of important works, attended the libraries and were responsible for specific sections. The master could then easily ask a few relevant questions, narrowing the search to the individual dedicated to the particular area of interest, and be pointed in the right direction. Now, without such specialists tending the libraries, the priceless information contained in the countless volumes was considerably more difficult to retrieve. In a way, the magnitude of information became a hinderance to its own purpose, and, like a soldier carrying so many weapons he couldn't move, nearly useless.

The books held in this one library alone represented almost an unimaginable amount of work by countless scholars and a great many prophets. A short stroll through the isles had revealed works here on history, geography, politics, the natural world, and prophecy that Verna had never seen before. A person could spend a lifetime lost in the place, and yet, Berdine had said that the People's Palace had a number of such libraries, from some that a variety of people were allowed to visit, to some that no one but the Lord Rahl, and, Verna assumed, his most trusted confidants, could enter. This library was one of the latter.

Berdine had said that because she knew High D'Haran, Darken Rahl had sometimes brought her into the most private of the libraries to get her opinion on translations of obscure passages in ancient texts. As a result, Berdine was in a unique position to know at least something about the wealth of potentially hazardous knowledge stored in the palace.

Not all prophecy was equally troublesome, though. A lot of it turned out to be incidental and rather harmless. What most people didn't realize was that a lot of prophetic space was taken up with what amounted to little more than the stuff of gossip.

But by no means was all prophecy so congenial or frivolous, and wandering through the titillating trivia of everyday lives tended to lull one into complacency and then when you least expected it, dark things came out of the pages to snatch at your soul.

While there were volumes that were by and large completely harmless, there were others that were, for anyone but the untrained, unsafe from the first words to the last. This particular library held some of the most dangerous books of prophecy Verna knew of, books that at the Palace of the Prophets were considered so volatile that they were not kept in the main vault, but in smaller, heavily shielded vaults restricted to all but a handful of people at the palace. The presence of those books was probably the reason why this particular library was a very private retreat for Master Rahl alone; Verna seriously doubted that the guards would have allowed her in had a Mord-Sith not been escorting her.

Verna could happily spend a great deal of time in such a cozy place, exploring countless books she had never seen before. Unfortunately, she didn't have the luxury of time. She idly wondered if Richard had ever even seen what was now his as the Lord Rahl.

Berdine tapped a finger to the blank page in *The Glendhill Book of Deviation Theory*. "I'm telling you, Prelate, I studied this book with Lord Rahl at the Wizard's Keep in Aydindril."

"So you said."

Verna found it interesting, to say the least, that Richard knew of *The Glendhill Book of Deviation Theory*. She found it even more curious, considering his distaste for prophecy and the fact that this book of prophecies was mostly about him, that he'd studied it.

There seemed no end to the curious little things that from time to time Verna discovered about Richard. Part of his dislike for prophecy, she knew, was his aversion to riddles: He hated them. She also knew, though, that in large measure his animus toward prophecy was due to his belief in free will, his belief that he himself, and not the hand of destiny, made his own life what it was.

While enormously complex and with layers of meaning beyond most people's comprehension, prophecy certainly did revolve around core elements of the preordained in its nature, and yet Richard had more than once fulfilled prophecy while at the same time proving it wrong.

Verna sourly suspected that, in a perverse way, prophecy had foretold of Richard's birth just so that he could come into the world to prove the concept of prophecy invalid.

Richard's actions had never been easy to predict, even, or perhaps especially, for prophecy. In the beginning Verna had been baffled by the things he would do and was perpetually unable to predict how he would react to situations or what he might do next. She had come to learn, though, that what she had thought was his confounding switching in a blink from one matter to something completely unrelated was, simply, at its core, his singular consistency.

Most people were not able to remain riveted to a goal with such dedicated determination. They tended to become distracted by a variety of other urgent matters requiring their attention. Richard, as if in a sword fight with a number of opponents at once, prioritized those ancillary events, holding them in abeyance or dispatching them as need be, while always keeping his goal firmly fixed in his mind. It sometimes gave people the false impression that he was skipping from one unrelated thing to another, when in reality he was, to him, innocently dancing across rocks in the river of events around him as he worked his way steadily toward the opposite bank.

At times he was the most wonderful man Verna had ever met. At other times, the most exasperating. She'd long ago lost track of how often she had wanted to strangle him. Besides being the man born to lead them in the final battle, he had by force of his own will become their leader, the Lord Rahl, the linchpin of everything she had struggled for as a Sister of the Light.

Just as prophecy foretold.

But not at all in the manner it had so carefully laid out.

Perhaps more than anything else he meant to them all, Verna valued Richard as a friend. She ached for him to be happy, the way she had once been happy with Warren. Her time with Warren after they were married and before he had been killed had been the most alive she had ever felt. Since then, she felt like the living dead, alive but not part of life.

Verna hoped that some day, maybe when they finally won the struggle against the Order, that Richard could find someone to love. He loved life so much; he needed someone to share that with.

She smiled inwardly. From the first day she had met him and put the collar around his neck to take him back to the Palace of the Prophets to be trained to use his gift, her life had felt as if it had been caught up in the whirlpool that was Richard. She vividly remembered that snowy day, back at the mud people's village, when she had taken him away. It had been profoundly sad, because it had been against his will, and at the same time it had been a momentous relief after having searched for him for twenty years.

To be sure, he had not gone willingly into such benevolent captivity. In fact, two of the Sisters with Verna had died in the effort to make Richard put on that collar he so hated.

Verna frowned . . . put on the collar.

That was odd. She tried to recall exactly how it was that she had managed to get him to put the collar around his neck, as it had to be done. Richard hated collars—especially after having once been a captive of a Mord-Sith—and yet he had put it on of his own free will. For some peculiar reason, though, she couldn't seem to recall just how she had managed to get him to—

"Verna, this is really strange . . ." The brown leather of Berdine's outfit creaked as she leaned in a little more, peering intently at the last of the text in the ancient volume laid open on the table before her. She carefully turned a page, checking, and then turned it back. She looked up. "I know this book had writing in it before. That writing is now missing."

As Verna watched the candlelight dance in Berdine's blue eyes, she set aside memories from long ago and returned her full attention to the important matters at hand.

"But it wasn't this book, now, was it?" When Berdine frowned, Verna went on to explain. "It may have been the same title, but it wasn't this very book. You were at the Keep; it was a different copy of this book. Yes?"

"Well, sure, I guess you're right that it wasn't this actual book. . . ." Berdine straightened and scratched her head of wavy brown hair. "But if it's the same title, then why do you think that the copy at the Wizard's Keep has all the writing in it while this one has big sections of the writing missing?"

"I didn't say that the copy there still has all the writing in it. I'm only saying that the copy at the Keep, not this one, was the one you studied with Richard. That you recall reading it and not seeing any blank pages doesn't prove anything because it wasn't this very same book. But even more importantly, this book might in fact be identical in that it contains all the same text, but the scribe who made this duplicate might have simply left blank pages among that text for any number of reasons."

Berdine looked skeptical. "What reasons?"

Verna shrugged. "Sometimes books with incomplete prophecy, such as these here, have blank places left in them to provide room for future prophets to finish the prophecy."

Berdine planted her fists on her hips. "Fine, but answer me one question. When I look through this book I recall the things I'm reading. I may not understand most of it, but I remember it in a general sense, remember reading these passages. So why is it that I can't remember a single thing about the sections that are missing from the book?"

"The simple explanation is that you don't recall anything of the blank sections because they are simply that, blank places, as I said, that were left in the book by the person who made the copy."

"No, that's not what I mean. I mean, I recall the general nature of the prophecies—the length of them. As a gifted person you would be more attuned to what you're reading. I wouldn't. Since I never really understood these prophecies, I instead remember more of the way they looked. I remember how long they were. These are no longer complete. I didn't understand them, and I remember how long they seemed and how hard it was to make sense of such long prophecies."

"When something is hard to understand it always seems longer than it really is."

"No." Berdine screwed up her face with conviction. "That's not it." She turned to the last prophecy and tapped the page. "This one here is only a page long followed by a number of blank pages. I can't say that I remember the others so well, but for some reason I paid more attention to the last one. I'm telling you, I remember that this one for sure was a lot longer. I can't swear to how long the others were, or how long this one is supposed to be, but I do know for certain that this last one, at least, was more than a page. It wasn't incomplete, as this one here is, now. No matter how hard I try, I can't seem to remember how long it was, or what it said, but I *know* that it was more than a single page."

That was the confirmation Verna had been waiting for.

"While most of it makes little sense to me," Berdine went on, "I do remember this part, this beginning having to do with all the talk about a forked source and the confusing business about going back to a mantic root, and then the 'splitting the horde that vaunts the Creator's cause'— that part at least sounds like the Imperial Order—but I can't recall the rest of it that's blank after 'a leader's lost trust.'

"I'm not imagining it, Verna, I'm not. I can't say why I'm so sure that the rest of it is missing, but I am. And therein lies what has me so bothered—why is the part that's missing from the book missing from my memory?"

Verna leaned close and lifted an eyebrow. "Now, that, my dear, is the question that I find troubling."

Berdine looked startled. "You mean, you know what I'm talking about? You believe me?"

Verna nodded. "I'm afraid so. I didn't want to plant the seed of suggestion in your mind. I wanted you to confirm my own suspicions."

"Then this is what Ann was concerned about, what she wanted us to check?"

"It is." Verna shuffled through the disorderly jumble of books on the sturdy table, finally pulling out the one she wanted. "Look here at this book. This is the one that is perhaps the most troubling to me. *Collected Origins* is an exceedingly rare prophecy in that it was written entirely in story form. I studied this book before I left the Palace of the Prophets to search for Richard. I practically knew the story by heart." Verna fanned through the pages. "The book is now entirely blank and I can't remember a single thing about it except that it had something to do with Richard— exactly what, I have no idea."

Berdine studied Verna's eyes the way only a Mord-Sith could study someone's eyes. "So this is some kind of trouble, and that trouble is a threat to Lord Rahl."

Verna let out a deep breath. The flames of several of the closer candles fluttered as she did so.

"I'd be lying if I said otherwise, Berdine. While the missing text doesn't all have to do with Richard, it all pertains to a time after his birth. I don't have a clue as to the nature of the problem, but I admit that it has me greatly concerned."

Berdine's demeanor changed. Usually the woman was the most good-natured of any of the Mord-Sith that Verna knew. Berdine had a kind of simple, childlike glee about the world around her. At times she could be heartwarmingly curious. Despite hardships that had others complaining, Berdine usually wore an unaffected smile.

But at the impression of some kind of threat to Richard, she changed in a flash to all business. And now she had turned as suspicious and coldly menacing as any Mord-Sith ever was.

"What could be the cause of this?" Berdine demanded. "What does it mean?"

Verna closed the book full of blank pages. "I don't know, Berdine, I really don't. Ann and Nathan are as puzzled as we are—and Nathan is a prophet."

"What does that part about people losing trust in their leader mean?"

For an ungifted person, Berdine had managed to single out the most crucial part of a very oblique prophecy.

"Well," Verna said, cautiously framing her answer, "it could mean a number of things. It's hard to tell."

"Maybe hard for me, but not hard for you."

Verna cleared her throat. "I'm not an expert in prophecy, you understand, but I think it has something to do with Richard."

"I know that much. Why would this prophecy talk about people losing trust in him?"

"Berdine, prophecy is rarely as straightforward as it seems." Verna wished the woman would stop staring at her. "What it seems to say usually has nothing at all to do with the actual event involved in the body of the prophecy."

"Prelate, this prophecy seems to me to suggest that questions of soundness of mind are going to be the cause of 'a leader's lost trust.' Since this prophecy names the leader as the one opposed to the horde that vaunts the Creator's cause—that would be the Imperial Order—that means it has to be talking about Lord Rahl. It then follows that Lord Rahl is the leader in whom people will lose trust. It comes after the part about the splitting of the horde, which the Order has now done. That makes the threat imminent."

Verna felt sorry for anyone who ever made the unfortunate mistake of underestimating Berdine.

"It is my experience that prophecy sometimes tends to fret over Richard like a doting grandparent."

"This sounds to me like a specific threat."

Verna folded her hands before herself. "Berdine, you are a very smart woman, so I hope you can understand why it would be a grave mistake for me to argue or even discuss this prophecy with you. Prophecy is beyond the mind of the ungifted. It has little to do with how smart a person is. Prophecy is a creation of the gifted and meant only for those who are gifted in the same way. They are not even intended for other types of wizards.

"Even us Sisters, talented sorceresses though we may be, had to train for years before we were allowed to even look at prophecy, much less work with it. It is exceedingly dangerous for the untrained to hazard guesses at the meaning of prophecy. You may recognize the words, but you do not recognize the meaning of those words."

"That's silly. Words are words. They have meaning. That is how we can understand the world around us. Why would prophecy take words that mean something and use them for some other unknown meaning?"

Verna felt as if she were stepping gingerly through a field of bear traps. "That isn't exactly what I meant by what I said. Words can be used to make people understand, to explain, to veil, and to interpret the world, but they can also be used to explain things that are only speculation. If I foretell that dark times will come into your life, those words may be true, but it could mean that you will suffer a loss that will sadden you, or it could mean that you will be murdered. Though the words might be true, their exact meaning is not yet known. It would be a grave injustice to use those words as a reason to start killing everyone around you because the words made you fear you would be murdered.

"Wars have started over such misunderstandings about prophecy. People have died as the result of the untrained hearing what they think are the simple words of prophecy. That is why the books of prophecy were kept in secure vaults below the Palace of the Prophets."

"These books of prophecy are not kept in vaults."

Verna's brow drew down as she leaned toward the Mord-Sith. "Perhaps they should be."

"Are you saying that I'm wrong in what I believe this prophecy says?"

Verna heaved another sigh. "Right or wrong is impossible to discern in this instance. We can't even begin to intelligently dissect this prophecy because it's incomplete. We have here only the beginning of it and then a number of blank pages."

"So?"

"So, it could be just as you say, that it's about Richard and people will question his judgment and lose faith in him, but maybe the missing text says that the issue will be resolved the next day by some other event of consequence and they will think more of him than they ever had before. Not only can prophecy be forked, meaning that it may be an either-or kind of statement, but the same prophecy could mean opposite things."

"I don't see how it can mean opposite things. And how could something happen in the missing text of this prophecy to change people's minds?"

Verna shrugged as she gazed around the vast, dimly lit library, trying to think of an example. "Well, say that they thought his battle plan was crazy. Maybe the army officers think it ill advised. That could be something that would result in this prophecy, in people losing faith in him. Then, say that, despite the advice of officers, Richard insists and so, despite their doubts and lack of faith, the soldiers follow his plan as ordered and achieve a victory that they never thought they could win. Their faith in Richard as their leader would be restored and they would probably have even more respect for his judgment than they ever did before.

"But if the prophecy were to be acted upon without understanding its true meaning, those actions very well could countermand the rest of the event as it would have taken place naturally and give the illusion that the prophecy had been fulfilled, but in fact the real and truly prophesied events had been bypassed by foolishly invoking a misinterpretation of the actual prophecy."

Berdine, watching Verna the whole time, drew her single brown braid through a loose fist. "I guess that could make sense."

"You see, Berdine, why prophecy is so confusing, even for those of us trained in it? But to make matters worse, without the whole prophecy we dare not even begin to try understand them or to assign any significance to them. The complete text is indispensable if one is to even begin to try to understand prophecy. Without all the text it's as if prophecy has gone blind. That's one reason why this is so disturbing."

"One reason?" Berdine looked up again, still running her braid through her fist. "What is the other reason?"

"It's bad enough to be without the text that was previously there, but the cause behind such an unprecedented event—the text of prophecy vanishing—is troubling in the extreme."

"I thought you just said that we shouldn't jump to conclusions when it comes to prophecy."

Verna cleared her throat, feeling as if one of those bear traps just snapped closed on her leg. "Well, that's true, but it's obvious that something is going on."

Berdine folded her arms as she pondered the problem. "What do you think could be happening?"

Verna shook her head. "I can't begin to imagine. Such a thing, to my knowledge, has never happened before. I have no idea why it's happening now."

"But you think it's trouble that involves Lord Rahl."

Verna gave Berdine a sidelong look. "The simple fact that so much of prophecy involves him makes that conclusion impossible to avoid. Richard is born to trouble. He is at the center of it."

Berdine didn't appear to like that one bit. "That is why he needs us."

"I've never argued that he didn't."

Berdine relaxed, if only a notch, and flicked her braid back over her shoulder. "No, you have not."

"Ann is searching for him. Let's hope she can find him, and soon. We need him to lead us in the coming battle."

As Verna spoke, Berdine idly pulled a book from one of the glass cases and began leafing through it. "Lord Rahl is supposed to be magic against magic, not the steel against steel."

"That is a D'Haran proverb. Prophecy says that he must lead us in the final battle."

"I suppose," Berdine mumbled without looking up as she slowly turned pages.

"With part of Jagang's forces headed south around the mountains, we can only hope that Ann will find him in time and bring him to us."

Berdine was puzzling at the book. "What is it that is buried with the bones?"

"What?"

Berdine was still frowning as she tried to work out something in the book. "This book caught my attention before because it says *Fuer Grissa Ost Drauka* on the cover. That's High D'Haran. It means—"

"The bringer of death."

Berdine glanced up. "Yes. How did you know?"

"There was a widely known prophecy that the Sisters back at the Palace of the Prophets used to debate. It had, actually, been hotly debated for centuries. The first day I brought Richard to the palace he declared himself to be the bringer of death and thus named himself to be the one in the prophecy. It caused quite a stir among the Sisters, I can tell you. One day, down in the vaults, Warren showed Richard the prophecy and Richard himself solved the riddle of it, although to Richard it wasn't a riddle. He understood it because he had lived portions of the prophecy."

"This book has a lot of blank pages in it."

"No doubt. It sounds like it's about Richard. There are probably a great number of books here that are about him."

Berdine was reading again. "This is in High D'Haran. Like I said, I know High D'Haran. I would have to work at it to be able to translate it more completely, and it would help if there wasn't so much missing text, but this place is apparently talking about Lord Rahl. It says something like, 'what he seeks is buried with the bones,' or maybe even 'what he seeks is buried bones'—something like that."

Berdine looked up at Verna. "Any idea what that's about? What it could mean?"

"What he seeks is buried bones?" Verna shook her head with regret. "I have no idea. There are probably countless volumes here that have interesting, or puzzling, or frightening things to say about Richard. As I told you, though, with copy missing, what is there is next to useless."

"I suppose," Berdine said in disappointment. "What about 'central sites'?"

"Central sites?"

"Yes. This books mentions places called 'central sites.' " Berdine stared off as she considered something to herself. "Central sites. Kolo mentioned something about central sites."

"Kolo?"

Berdine nodded. "It's a journal written ages ago—during the great war. Lord Rahl found the book at the Wizard's Keep, in the room with the sliph. The man who kept the journal is named Koloblicin. In High D'Haran the name means 'strong advisor.' Lord Rahl and I call him Kolo, for short."

"What did this Kolo have to say about these places, these central sites? What are they?"

Berdine turned through the pages of the book she held. "I don't recall. It was nothing I understood at the time so I didn't devote a lot of effort to it. I'd have to go study it again to refresh my memory." She squinted in recollection. "It seemed like there was something buried at the places called central sites. I can't remember if it said what was buried."

The Mord-Sith stood frozen in her same pose as she studied the little book. "I was hoping this might give me a clue."

Verna let out a heavy sigh as she glanced around at the library.

"Berdine, I would love to stay and spend time researching all these books. I would truly like to know what this library and the others here at the palace contain, but there are more pressing matters at hand. We need to get back to the army and my Sisters."

Verna took a last look around. "Before I go, however, there is one thing here at the People's Palace that I would like to check on. Maybe you can help me."

Berdine reluctantly closed the book and replaced it on the shelf. She carefully closed the glass door.

"All right, Prelate. What is it you want to see?"

Verna paused at hearing the single, long peal of a bell.

"What was that?"

"Devotion," Berdine said, stopping to look back at Verna as the deep toll reverberated through the vast marble and granite halls of the People's Palace.

People, no matter where they seemed to be headed, turned and instead moved toward the broad passageway from where the deep, resonant sound of the bell had come. No one looked to be in a hurry, but they all very deliberately walked toward the slowly dying sound of the bell.

Verna puzzled at Berdine. "What?"

"Devotion. You know what a devotion is."

"You mean a devotion to the Lord Rahl? That devotion?"

Berdine nodded. "The bell announces that it is time for the devotion." Pensively, she gazed off in the direction of the hall where people were headed.

Many of the gathering crowd were dressed in robes of a variety of muted colors. Verna assumed that white robes with gold or silver banding on them were the mark of officials of one sort or another who lived and worked at the palace. They certainly had the manner and bearing of officials. Everyone from those administrators to messengers in tunics trimmed in green and carrying leather satchels with an ornate letter "R" on them, standing for the House of Rahl, continued their casual conversations even as they made their way to the convergence of wide halls. Other people who worked at any of the countless variety of shops were dressed more appropriately for their profession, whether it was working at leather, silver, pottery, cobbling, or tailoring, providing the many foods and services, or doing any of the various palace work from maintenance to cleaning.

There were a number of people dressed in the simple clothes of farmers, tradesmen, and merchants, many with their wives and some with children. Like those Verna had seen in the lower levels within the great plateau atop which sat the People's Palace or at the markets set up outside, they appeared to be visitors come to trade or make purchases. Others, though, were dressed in finery for their sojourn to the palace. From what Verna had learned from Berdine, there were rooms that guests could rent if they wished to stay for an extended period. There were, as well, quarters for the many people who lived and worked at the palace.

Most of the people in robes walked calmy, as if this were just another part of their day. Those dressed in finery tried to look just as calm and not stare at the exquisite architecture of the palace, but Verna saw their wide eyes wandering. The simply dressed visitors, as they fell in with the flow of all the people making their way toward the fork that would take them to the passageway with the bell, openly peered about at everything, at the towering statues of men and women in proud poses carved from variegated stone, at polished two-story fluted columns soaring past balconies, at the spectacular black granite and honey-onyx floors.

Verna knew that such intricate and precise patterns in the stone floors, set with such tight grout joints, could have been created only by the most talented master craftsmen in all of the New World. Serving as Prelate at the Palace of the Prophets for a time, she had had to deal with the matter of the replacement of a section of beautifully patterned floor that had in the dim past been damaged by young wizards in training. The precise events leading to the damage and who, exactly, had been the guilty party remained shrouded in oaths not to tattle, but the result was that the bit of mischievous magic had in an instant torn up a long section of exquisitely laid marble floor. While the debris and loose tiles had long since been removed, the floor sat damaged for decades, filled in with serviceable but unsightly limestone, while life at the Palace of the Prophets moved on. The palace attitude toward the boys had been one of indulgence, in part out of a sense of regret for having to hold such young men against their will.

Verna had always been vexed that the damage had never been fixed—in part because by not fixing it it represented to her an attitude that had indulged such bad behavior. It had always seemed like she was the only one—except maybe until Richard came along—who was bothered by seeing such beauty marred. Richard expected the boys there to take responsibility for their actions. Even though he was held against his will, he never tolerated such senseless destructive behavior.

Warren saw matters the same way as Richard. Perhaps that was part of the reason they had become such fast friends. Warren had always been serious and dedicated about everything. After Richard had left the palace, Warren had reminded Verna that as the new prelate she no longer needed to complain about either the behavior or the floor; he encouraged her to act on her convictions. So, as Prelate, she both set new rules and set about seeing to the completion of the repairs to the floor.

That was when she had come to learn a thing or two about such floors and that while there were any number of men who boldly professed to be master craftsmen, very few actually were. Those who were let their work make clear the distinction. The former made the task a nightmare, the latter a joy.

She remembered how proud Warren had been of her for seeing the task through and for not accepting anything less than the best. She missed him so much.

Verna gazed around at the spectacular palace, at the intricate stone work, and yet such beauty now failed to move her. Since Warren had died everything seemed bland, uninteresting, and unimportant to her. Since Warren had died, life itself seemed drudgery.

Everywhere throughout the palace, wary soldiers patrolled, probably not ever realizing, or even considering, the staggering amount of human imagination, skill, and effort that had gone into the creation of such a place as the People's Palace. Now, they were a part of it, a part of what kept it viable, like thousands of men just like them who for centuries had walked these same halls and kept them safe.

Verna noticed that some of the guards moved through the halls in pairs, while others patrolled in larger groups. The muscular young men were dressed in smart uniforms with molded leather shoulder and breast plates and all carried at least a sword. Many of the soldiers also carried pikes with gleaming metal points. Verna noticed special guards who wore black gloves and carried crossbows slung over their shoulders. The quivers at their belts held red-fletched bolts. The soldiers' eyes were always on the move, watching everything.

"I seem to recall Richard mentioning the devotion," Verna said, "but I didn't think that they still did it when the Lord Rahl wasn't at the palace. And especially not since Richard became the Lord Rahl."

Verna hadn't exactly meant it to be condescending, although she realized after she'd said it that it must have sounded that way. It was just that Richard was . . . well, Richard.

Berdine glanced at Verna askance. "He is still the Lord Rahl. We are no less bonded to him because he is away. The devotion is always done at the palace, whether the Lord Rahl is here or not. And regardless of how you may view him, he is the Lord Rahl by every measure. We have never had a Lord Rahl we respected as much as we respect him. That makes the devotion more meaningful, and more important, than it ever was before."

Verna kept her mouth shut, but she cast Berdine a look that came all too easily to her as a Sister of the Light and now as Prelate. Even though she understood the reasons behind it, she was the Prelate of the Sisters of the Light, devoted to seeing the Creator's will done. As a Sister of the Light, living at the Palace of the Prophets under the spell that slowed their aging, she had seen rulers come and go. The Sisters of the Light never bowed down to any of them.

She reminded herself that the Palace of the Prophets was gone. The Imperial Order now controlled many of the Sisters.

Berdine lifted an arm, indicating the palace around them. "The Lord Rahl makes all this possible. He gives us a homeland. He is the magic against magic. His rule keeps us safe. While in the past we have had masters who regarded the devotion as a demonstration of servitude, its origin is actually nothing more than an act of respect."

Verna's aggravation seethed just below the surface. This was not some mythic leader Berdine was talking about, some wise old king; it was Richard. As much as Verna respected and valued him, it was still Richard. Woods guide Richard.

Swiftly on the heels of her flash of indignation come regret for such unkind thoughts.

Richard always fought for what was right. He had valiantly put his life in peril for his noble beliefs.

He was also the one named in prophecy.

He was also the Seeker.

He was also the Lord Rahl, the bringer of death, who had turned the world upside down. Because of Richard, Verna was prelate. She wasn't sure if that was a blessing or a curse.

Richard was also their last hope.

"Well, if he doesn't hurry up and join up with us to lead the D'Haran army in the final battle there will be none of us left to respect him."

Berdine withdrew her reproachful stare and unexpectedly started toward the passageway that turned off to the left—the one where the bell had rung. "We are the steel against steel. Lord Rahl is the magic against magic. If he doesn't come to fight with the army it is only because of his duty to protect us all from the dark forces of magic."

"Simpleminded gibberish," Verna muttered to herself as she hurried to catch up with the Mord-Sith. "Where are you going?" she called after the woman.

"To devotion. At the palace everyone goes to devotion."

"Berdine," Verna growled as she caught Berdine's arm, "we don't have time for this."

"It is devotion. It is part of our bond to Lord Rahl. You would be wise to go to devotion and then maybe you will remember that."

Verna stood frozen in the vast hall, stunned, watching the Mord-Sith stalk off. Verna had a vivid memory of the time that the bond to Richard had been severed. It hadn't been for long, but in Richard's absence from the world of life the protection of the bond to the Lord Rahl had ceased to exist.

In that brief window in time, when Richard and the bond were gone from them all, Jagang had stolen into Verna's dreams to capture her mind. He had captured Warren as well. It had been beyond horror to have the dream walker in control of her consciousness, but it had been all the worse to know that Warren was just as helpless. Jagang's brutal presence had dominated every aspect of their existence, from what they could think, to what they had to do. They no longer had control of their own will; Jagang's will was all that mattered. Just the memory of the searing pain that had been sent through that link into her—and into Warren—unexpectedly brought the sting of tears to Verna's eyes.

She quickly swiped away the tears and hurried after Berdine. Verna had important things to do, but she would lose untold time trying to find her way all alone in the vast interior of the People's Palace. She needed the Mord-Sith to show her the way. If Verna had control of her gift it might help her find what she sought, but in the palace her Han was virtually useless. She would just have to go along with Berdine and hope that they could then get back to business without the loss of too much time.

The passageway to the left led under an interior bridge with a rail and balusters made of gray marble struck through with white veins. At a convergence of four passageways, the hall expanded into a square open to the sky. In the center of the square was a square pond with a short, polished, speckled gray granite seat all the way around that held the water within it. A large pitted rock sat in the water a little off center. Atop the rock sat the bell—apparently the one that had rung calling people to the devotion.

Gentle rain had begun to fall in through the open roof. The surface of the pond danced with the drops. Verna saw that the floor all around the square was gently sloped toward drains in order to handle any rain. The clay tiles helped reinforce the realization that the square was really out-of-doors.

All around the people were going to their knees, bowing down on the clay tile floor, facing the pond that held the now silent bronze bell.

Berdine's dark discontent evaporated at seeing that Verna was coming with her. She smiled back happily and then did the strangest thing. She reached out and took Verna's hand.

"Come on, let me take you up by the pond. It has fish."

"Fish?"

Berdine's grin widened. "Yes. I love the squares with fish."

Sure enough, after they wove their way through all the people kneeling down on the floor and reached the front of the crowd close to the pond, Verna saw that there were schools of orange fish meandering through the water. There was hardly enough room for them to stand among all the people bowed down on the floor around them.

"Aren't they pretty?" Berdine asked. She had that little-girl air about her again.

Verna glared at the young woman. "They're fish."

Berdine seemed unfazed and knelt in a spot that opened up as people moved aside for them. Verna could see by the sidelong glances that everyone had at least a healthy respect for the Mord-Sith, if not open fear. While none of them appeared frightened enough to leave, they clearly didn't want to be where Berdine wanted to be when she wanted to be there. They also seemed more than a little worried about who the Mord-Sith was dragging to the devotion, as if it might be a repentant sinner and the lesson might involve bloodshed.

Berdine glanced over her shoulder at Verna before leaning forward and placing her hands on the tile floor. The brief look had been an admonition for Verna to do the same. Verna saw that the guards were watching her. This was crazy; she was the Prelate of the Sisters of the Light, an advisor to Richard and one of his close friends.

But the guards didn't know that.

Verna knew all too well that her power was diminished to next to nothing in the palace. This was the ancestral home of the House of Rahl. The entire palace had been built in the shape of a spell-form designed to enhance their power and deny others theirs.

Verna let out a sigh and finally went to her knees, bowing forward on her hands like everyone else. They were close to the pond, but the opening in the roof was only about the size of the pond itself, so the rain was confined mostly to the pond and whatever stray rain the gentle breeze carried beyond. The few sprinkles that reached her actually felt rather refreshing, considering her heated mood.

"I'm too old for this," Verna complained in a whisper to her devotion partner.

"Prelate, you are a young, healthy woman," Berdine chided.

Verna let out a sigh. It was no use arguing the foolishness of kneeling on the floor and saying a devotion to a man she was already devoted to in more ways than one. But it was more than foolish. It was silly. And a waste of time besides.

"Master Rahl guide us," the crowd all began together, if not all quite in harmony, as they bowed down and put their foreheads against the floor.

"Master Rahl teach us," they all said, coming more into unison.

Berdine, her forehead against the tile, still managed to cast a fiery look Verna's way. Verna rolled her eyes and bent forward, placing her forehead against the tile.

"Master Rahl protect us," she muttered, finally joining in with the devotion she knew and had already once given to Richard himself. "In your light we thrive. In your mercy we are sheltered. In your wisdom we are humbled. We live only to serve. Our lives are yours."

Verna sourly considered how, if Richard didn't wisely hurry up and get his hide to the D'Haran army, he wasn't going to be able to protect anyone.

Together, the assembled throng softly chanted the devotion again.

"Master Rahl guide us. Master Rahl teach us. Master Rahl protect us. In your light we thrive. In your mercy we are sheltered. In your wisdom we are humbled. We live only to serve. Our lives are yours."

Verna leaned a little toward Berdine and whispered. "How many times are we going to have to say the devotion?"

Berdine, looking very much the Mord-Sith, shot Verna a stern glare. She didn't say anything. She didn't have to. Verna recognized the look. She herself had countless times used the same look as she peered down her nose at novices who were misbehaving or young wizards-in-training who were being mulish. Verna turned her eyes back to the tile under her, feeling very much like a novice again as she softly spoke the chant along with the rest of the people.

"Master Rahl guide us. Master Rahl teach us. Master Rahl protect us. In your light we thrive. In your mercy we are sheltered. In your wisdom we are humbled. We live only to serve. Our lives are yours."

The murmur of the chanted devotion, in the single joined voice of all the people gathered in the square, echoed through the cavernous halls.

After the look Berdine had given her, Verna thought it best if, for the time being, she kept her objections to herself and said the devotion along with everyone else.

She spoke the words softly, thinking about them, and how many times they had proven true for her, personally. Richard had changed everything about her life. Verna had thought that the most important mission for the Sisters was to put a collar around gifted boys' necks and train them in the use of their ability. Richard had humbled her for that unthinking belief. He had changed everything, made her rethink everything.

If not for Richard, Verna doubted that she would ever have been thrown together with Warren and that their fondness for each other would have blossomed into love. In that, Richard had given her the greatest thing she had ever had in her life.

"Master Rahl guide us. Master Rahl teach us. Master Rahl protect us. In your light we thrive. In your mercy we are sheltered. In your wisdom we are humbled. We live only to serve. Our lives are yours."

The cadence of the murmured words of all the voices of the gathered people joined into a reverent sound that swelled until it filled the great hall.

Verna felt so all alone, even among the gathered crowd of so many people. She ached with how much she missed Warren. She had built a wall around her feelings and had shut herself away from such thoughts, as well as those around her, hoping to be spared the pain that always seemed to lurk just below the surface. Now she was suddenly overwhelmed by the raw misery of how much she missed Warren, how much she loved him. He was the best thing that had ever happened in her entire life—and now he was gone. Tears from her hopeless heartache welled up. She felt so alone.

"Master Rahl guide us. Master Rahl teach us. Master Rahl protect us. In your light we thrive. In your mercy we are sheltered. In your wisdom we are humbled. We live only to serve. Our lives are yours."

Verna sucked back a sob as she remembered kissing Warren for the last time as he lay dying. That had been the most dreadful moment in her entire life. Despite the time that had passed, it seemed as if it had happened yesterday. She missed him so much that it made her bones ache.

"Master Rahl guide us. Master Rahl teach us. Master Rahl protect us. In your light we thrive. In your mercy we are sheltered. In your wisdom we are humbled. We live only to serve. Our lives are yours."

Verna spoke the words of the devotion along with everyone else, pouring her feelings into them, over and over, yet without haste. The murmured chant filled her mind. She wept as she remembered the time she'd had with Warren.

She remembered his last words to her: *Give me a kiss,* Warren had whispered, *while I still live. And don't mourn what ends, but what a good life we've had. Kiss me, my love.*

Pain and longing twisted her insides. Her world was ashes. Nothing seemed worthwhile. She didn't want to live anymore.

"Master Rahl guide us. Master Rahl teach us. Master Rahl protect us. In your light we thrive. In your mercy we are sheltered. In your wisdom we are humbled. We live only to serve. Our lives are yours."

Verna choked back her sobs as she chanted the devotion. It never even occurred to her to wonder if anyone noticed her.

It had all been so senseless, a young man of no ability for anything worthwhile, with no interest in any values, of no use to anyone, including himself, murdering Warren just to prove his loyalty to the cause of the Imperial Order, which was, in essence, that people like Warren had no right to live his own life but instead should sacrifice themselves for the likes of his murderer.

Richard fought to end such madness. Richard fought with everything he had against those who brought such senseless brutality to the world. Richard had given himself over to ending it so that others would not have to lose those they loved as Verna had lost Warren. Richard truly understood her pain.

Verna sank into the rhythm of the chant, allowing it to wash through her. Richard stood for everything she had fought for her whole life—solidity, meaning, purpose. A devotion to such a man, rather than being blasphemy, seemed altogether right. In a way, because of who Richard was and what he stood for, it was actually a devotion to life itself rather than some otherworldly goal.

Richard had been Warren's good friend, his first real friend. Richard had brought Warren up out of the vaults and into the sunlight, into the world. Warren loved Richard.

The soft chant had become a calming refuge.

Verna felt a warm shaft of sunlight settling on her as it broke through the clouds. She was bathed in the gentle, golden glow of light. It embraced her with its warmth that seemed to seep down and touch her very soul.

Warren would want her to embrace all the precious beauty of life while she had it.

In the loving touch of glowing light she felt peace for the first time in ages.

"Master Rahl guide us. Master Rahl teach us. Master Rahl protect us. In your light we thrive. In your mercy we are sheltered. In your wisdom we are humbled. We live only to serve. Our lives are yours."

The soft flow of the words of the devotion, as she knelt in the warm shaft of sunlight, filled her with a profound calm, a serene sense of belonging unlike she ever had before. She whispered the words, letting them lift away the shards of pain. As she knelt, her head to the tiles, putting her heart and soul into saying the words, she felt free of any and every worry; she was suffused with the simple joy of life, and with reverence for it. As she chanted along with everyone else, she basked in the tender glow of the sunlight. It felt so warm, so protective. So loving.

It almost felt like Warren's loving embrace.

As she chanted along with everyone else, over and over, without pause but for breath, time slipped by, incidental, inconspicuous, unimportant within the core of calm she felt.

The bell rang out twice, a low, mellow, comforting affirmation that the devotion had ended, but at the same time would always be there with her.

Verna looked up when she felt a hand on her shoulder. It was Berdine smiling down at her. Verna looked around and saw that most of the people were already gone. She alone still bowed forward on her hands and knees on the floor before the pool. Berdine was kneeling beside her.

"Verna, are you all right?"

She straightened up on her knees. "Yes . . . it's just that it felt so good in the sunlight."

Berdine's brow twitched. She glanced over at the drops of rain dancing in the water of the pond.

"Verna, it has been raining the whole time."

Verna peered around as she stood. "But . . . I felt it. I saw the glow of the shaft of light all around me."

Berdine seemed to catch on, then, and put a comforting hand on the small of Verna's back. "I understand."

"You do?"

Berdine nodded with a compassionate smile. "Going to devotion in a way gives you a chance to consider your life and along with that it brings comfort in many forms. Maybe one who loves you came to comfort you."

Verna stared at the soft smile on the Mord-Sith's face. "Has that ever happened to you?"

Berdine swallowed as she nodded. Her eyes brimming with tears said that it had.

They followed what seemed like a meandering, wandering, convoluted course through the People's Palace, not because they were lost or because they were taking their time and picking random routes as they came upon intersections of hallways, but because there was no straight route.

The complex, confusing passage through the labyrinth was necessary because the place had not been built to accommodate ease of travel through the palace, but, rather, it had been constructed in the explicit shape of a power spell that had been drawn on the face of the ground. Verna found it astonishing to consider that this was not only a spell-form similar to spells she herself had drawn, but that she was actually inside the elements that made up the spell. It was an entirely new perspective on conjuring and one on an imposing scale. Since the power spell for the House of Rahl was still active, she knew that the configuration of the foundation would probably have had to have been first drawn in blood . . . Rahl blood.

As the two of them walked down vast halls, Verna could not get over her astonishment at the utter beauty of the place, to say nothing of its size. She had seen grand places in the past, but the sheer magnitude of the People's Palace was staggering. It was less a palace and more of a city in the desolate Azrith Plains.

The palace atop the immense plateau was only a part of the vast complex. The interior of the plateau was honeycombed with thousands of rooms and passageways, and there were innumerable stairs taking different routes up through the chambers inside. A great number of people sold goods and services in the lower reaches of the plateau. It was a long and tiring climb up endless flights of stairs to reach the elaborate palace at the top, so many of the visitors who came to trade or make purchases did their business in those lower reaches, never taking the time to make it up all the way to the palace proper at the top. Even more people did business at open-air markets around the base of the plateau.

There was a single winding road, interrupted by a drawbridge, along the outside of the plateau. Even if it weren't heavily defended it would still be virtually impossible to attack the palace by that road. The interior of the plateau offered many more ways up—there were even ramps used by horsemen—but there were thousands of troops guarding the inside passages, and, if need be, there were colossal doors that could be closed, sealing off the plateau and the palace within.

Black stone statues standing to either side of a wide, white marble hallway watched Verna and Berdine as they made their way down the long hall. Torchlight glimmered off the polished black marble of the towering sentinels, making them almost seem alive. The contrasting color of stone, the black statuary in a white marble hall, added a sense of foreboding to the passage.

Most of the stairwells they ascended were quite large, some with polished marble balustrades more than an arm's length across. Verna found the variety of stone within the palace amazing. It seemed like each vast room, each passageway, each stairwell had its own unique combination of colors. A few of the more utilitarian or service areas that Berdine took them through were done in bland, beige limestone, while the more important public areas were composed of startlingly vivid colors in contrasting patterns that lent an uplifting sense of life and excitement to the space. Some of the private corridors that served as shortcuts for officials were paneled in highly polished woods illuminated by silver reflector lamps that added warm light.

While some of those private corridors were relatively small, the main passageways stood several stories high. Some of the largest—main branches of the spell-form—were lit from above by windows in the roof that let the light stream in. Rows of soaring columns to each side rose to the roof, far above. Balconies, between those fluted pillars, looked down on the people passing below. In several places there were walkways that crossed over Verna's head. In one spot, she saw two levels of walkways, one above the other.

At times they had to go up to some of these higher levels, cross bridges over the passageways and then descend again into a different branch of hallways, only to once more have to go back up in another place. Despite the up and down of the serpentine route, they steadily worked their way higher into the center of the palace.

"Through here," Berdine said as she reached a pair of mahogany doors.

The doors were twice as tall as Verna. Carved in the face of the thick mahogany were a pair of snakes, one on each door, their tails coiled around branches higher up with their bodies hanging down so that the heads were at eye level. Fangs jutted out from gaping jaws, as if the pair were about to strike. The door handles, not much lower than the snakes' heads, were bronze mellowed with a patina that spoke of its age. The handles were life-sized grinning skulls.

"Lovely," Verna muttered.

"They are a warning," Berdine said. "This is meant to command people to stay out."

"Couldn't they just paint 'keep out' on the door?"

"Not everyone can read." Berdine lifted an eyebrow. "Not everyone who can read will admit to it when caught opening the door. This gives them no excuse to cross the threshold innocently and lets them know that they will have no excuse when confronted by guards."

From the chill that the sight of the doors gave her, Verna could imagine that most anyone would give them a wide berth. Berdine threw her weight into the effort of pulling open the heavy door on the right.

Inside a cozy, carpeted room paneled in the same mahogany as the tall doors, but without any more of the carved snakes, four big soldiers stood guard. They looked more fearsome than the bronze skulls.

The closest soldier casually stepped into their path. "This area is restricted."

Berdine, wearing a dark frown, skirted the man. "Good. See to it that it stays that way."

Remembering all too well that her power was next to useless in the palace, Verna stayed close on Berdine's heels. The soldier, apparently not eager to grab the Mord-Sith, instead blew a whistle that let out a thin, shrill sound, no doubt used because such a sound would carry up the stairs to other guards on patrol. The two farthest soldiers, however, stepped together to block the pathway through the room.

One of the two held up a hand, if politely, commanding them to halt. "I'm sorry, Mistress, but as he said and as you should well know, this is a restricted area."

Berdine put one hand on a cocked hip. Her Agiel spun into her other fist. She gestured with it as she spoke.

"Since we both serve the same cause, I will not kill you where you stand. Be thankful that I'm not wearing red leather today, or I might take the time to teach you some manners. As *you* should be well aware, Mord-Sith are personal bodyguards to the Lord Rahl himself and we are not restricted from anywhere we choose to go."

The man nodded. "I'm well aware of that. But I've not seen you around the palace for quite some time—"

"I've been with Lord Rahl."

He cleared his throat. "Be that as it may, since you've been gone the commander general has tightened security in this area."

"Good. As a matter of fact, I am here to see Commander General Trimack about that very subject."

The man bowed his head. "Very well, Mistress. Top of the stairs. Someone will be able to see to your wishes."

When the two guards stepped apart, Berdine flashed an insincere smile and swept between them, Verna in tow.

Crossing thick carpets of golds and blues, they came to a stairwell made of a rich, flushed, tawny marble webbed with rust-color veins. Verna had never seen stone quite like it. It was strikingly beautiful, with polished vase-shaped balusters and a wide handrail that was smooth and cool under her fingers.

Changing direction at a broad landing, she spotted at the top of the stairs not just patrolling soldiers, but what appeared to be an entire army waiting for them. These were not going to be men Berdine would be able to so easily get past.

"What do you think all the soldiers are doing here?" Verna asked.

"Up there and then down a hallway," Berdine answered in a low voice, "is the Garden of Life. We've had trouble there in the past."

That was the very reason Verna wanted to check on things. She could hear orders being passed and the sound of metal jangling as men came running.

They were met at the top of the stairs by dozens of the guards, many with weapons drawn. Verna noticed that there were a lot more of the men wearing black gloves and carrying crossbows. This time, though, the crossbows were cocked and loaded with the red-fletched arrows.

"Who's in charge, here?" Berdine demanded of all the young faces staring at her.

"I am," a more mature man called out as he pushed his way through the tight ring of soldiers. He had piercing blue eyes, but it was the pale scars on his cheek and jaw that caught Verna's attention.

Berdine's face brightened at seeing the man. "General Trimack!"

Men made way for him as he stepped to the fore. He deliberately took in Verna before turning his attention to Berdine. Verna thought she detected the slightest smile.

"Welcome back, Mistress Berdine. I haven't seen you for quite a while."

"Seems like forever. It's good to be home." She lifted an introductory hand to Verna. "This is Verna Sauventreen, the Prelate of the Sisters of the Light. She is a personal friend of Lord Rahl and in charge of the gifted with the D'Haran forces."

The man bowed his head but kept his cautious gaze on her. "Prelate."

"Verna, this is Commander General Trimack of the First File of the People's Palace in D'Hara."

"First File?"

"When he is at his palace, we are the ring of steel around Lord Rahl himself, Prelate. We fall to a man before harm gets a glance at him." His eyes shifted between the two of them. "Because of the great distance, we can only sense that Lord Rahl is somewhere far off to the west. Would you happen to know where Lord Rahl is, exactly? Any idea when he will be back with us?"

"There are a number of people wanting to know the answer to that question, General Trimack," Verna said. "I'm afraid that you will have step to the rear of a very long line."

The man looked genuinely disappointed. "What of the war? Do you have any news?"

Verna nodded. "The Imperial Order has split their forces."

The soldiers glanced knowingly at one another. Trimack's face hardened with worry as he waited for her to elaborate.

"The Order left a sizable part of their force on the other side of the mountains, up near Aydindril in the Midlands. We had to leave men and some of the gifted on this side of the mountains to guard the passes so the enemy can't come over and get into D'Hara. A large contingent of the Order's best troops are presently heading back down through the Midlands. We believe that their plan is to take their main force down around the far side of the mountains and then eventually swing around and up to attack D'Hara from the south. We are taking our main army south to meet the enemy."

None of the men said a word. They stood mute, showing no reaction to probably the most fateful news they had ever faced in their young lives. These were indeed men of steel.

The general wiped a hand across his face, as if all their concern was distilled into him alone. "So our army coming south is close to the palace, then."

"No. They are still some distance to the north. Armies don't move rapidly unless necessary. Since we don't have nearly as much distance to cover as the Order, and Jagang moves his troops at a slow pace, we felt it would be better to keep our men healthy and strong, rather than exhaust them on a long race south. Berdine and I rode on ahead because it was urgent that I examine some of the books here . . . on matters to do with magic. As long as I'm here, I thought I should check on things in the Garden of Life to make certain that everything is safe."

The man took a breath as he drummed his fingers on his weapons belt. "I'd like to help you, Prelate, but I have orders from three wizards to keep everyone out of there. They were quite specific: no one, not even the gardening staff, is to be allowed to go in there."

Verna's brow tightened. "What three wizards?"

"First Wizard Zorander, then Lord Rahl himself, and lastly wizard Nathan Rahl."

Nathan. She might have known he would be trying to make himself look important at the palace, no doubt dramatically playing up the part of being a gifted Rahl, an ancestor to Richard. Verna wondered what other trouble the man had been mucking about in while he was at the People's Palace.

"Commander General, I am a Sister, and Prelate of the Sisters of the Light. I'm fighting on the same side as you."

"Sister," he said with an accusatorial, squint-eyed glare that only an army officer could conjure up. "We had a Sister visit us before. Couple years back. Remember, lads?" He glanced around at the grim faces before turning back to Verna. "Wavy, shoulder-length brown hair, about your size, Prelate. She was missing the little finger on her right hand. Maybe you remember her? One of your Sisters, I believe."

"Odette," Verna confirmed with a nod. "Lord Rahl told me about the trouble you had with her. She was a fallen Sister, you might say."

"I don't really care what side of the Creator's grace she was on the day she visited us. I only know that she killed almost three hundred men getting into the Garden of Life. Three hundred! She killed nearly a hundred more getting back out. We were helpless against her." As his face reddened, his scars stood out all the more. "Do you know what it's like to see men dying and not be able to do a bloody thing about it? Do you know what it's like not only to be responsible for their lives but to know that your duty is to keep her out of there . . . and not be able to do anything to stop the threat?"

Verna's gaze fell away from the man's intent blue eyes. "I'm sorry, General. But she was fighting against Lord Rahl. I am not. I'm on your side. I'm fighting to stop those like her."

"That may be true enough, but my orders from both Zedd and Lord Rahl himself—after he killed that vile woman—are that no one else is to be allowed in there. No one. If you were my own mother I'd not be able to let you go in there."

Something didn't make sense to her.

Verna cocked her head. "If Sister Odette was able to get in there, and you and your men couldn't stop her"—she lifted an eyebrow—"then what makes you think you can stop me?"

"I'd not like it to come to that, but, if need be, this time we have the means at hand to carry out our orders. We are no longer helpless."

Verna frowned. "What are you talking about?"

Commander General Trimack plucked a black glove from his belt and pulled it on, flexing his fingers to draw the snug glove all the way onto his hand. With a thumb and first finger of his gloved hand, he carefully lifted a red-fletched arrow from the rack of six in a quiver at the belt of a soldier beside him. The soldier already had one of the bolts nocked in his crossbow, leaving four in the special quiver rack.

Holding the bolt by the nock end, General Trimack lifted the razor-sharp steel point before Verna's face so that she could see it up close. "This is tipped with more than steel. It's tipped with the power to take down those with magic."

"I still don't know what are you talking about."

"It's tipped with magic that is said to be able to penetrate any shield the gifted can erect."

Verna reached out and with a finger carefully touched the rear of the shaft. Pain shot up her hand and wrist before she was able to jerk her arm back. Despite her gift being diminished in the palace, she had no trouble being able to detect the powerful aura given off by the web of magic that had been spun around the deadly point. This was indeed a potent weapon. Even with their full powers, the gifted would indeed be in trouble if they encountered one of these arrows coming toward them.

"If you have these arrows, then why weren't you able to stop Sister Odette?"

"We didn't have them back then."

Verna's frown darkened. "Then where did you get them?"

The general smiled with the satisfaction of a man who knew he would not again be defenseless against a gifted enemy. "When Wizard Rahl was here he asked me about our defenses. I told him about the attack by the sorceress and how we were helpless against her power. He searched the palace and found these weapons. Apparently they were in some safe place where only a wizard could retrieve them. He is the one who supplied my men with the arrows and the crossbows to fire them."

"How good of Wizard Rahl."

"Yes, it was."

The general carefully replaced the bolt in the special quiver rack that kept the arrows separated. She understood, now, why that was necessary. There was no telling how ancient these weapons really were, but Verna suspected that they were relics from the great war.

"Wizard Rahl instructed us on how to handle such dangerous weapons." He held up his hand and wiggled his gloved fingers. "Told us that we must always wear these special gloves to handle the arrows."

He removed the glove and tucked it behind his belt with its mate. Verna clasped her hands before herself, taking a deep breath and with it care in how she framed her words.

"General, I have known Nathan Rahl since long before your grand-mother was born. He is not always candid about the dangers involved in the things he does. Were I you, I would handle those weapons with the ut-most care, and treat anything he told you about them, even casually, as a matter of life and death."

"Are you suggesting he's reckless?"

"No, not deliberately, but he often tends to downplay matters that he finds . . . inconvenient. Besides that, he is very old and very talented, so sometimes it's easy for him to forget just how much more he knows about some very arcane subjects than most other people, or that he can do things with his gift that they aren't able to do, much less comprehend. You might say he's like an old man who forgets to tell visitors that his dog bites."

Men up and down the hall exchanged looks. Some of them lifted an elbow or a hand away from the quivers at their belts.

General Trimack hooked a thumb around the hilt of the short sword in its sheath at his left hip. "While I take seriously your warning, Prelate, I hope that you will understand that I also take seriously the lives of the hundreds of my men who died the last time a Sister showed up and we were defenseless against her magic. I take seriously the lives of these men here. I don't want any such thing to happen again."

Verna wet her lips and reminded herself that the man was only doing his job. With the way the palace drained away her Han, she had an uncomfortable empathy with his feeling about being powerless.

"I understand, General Trimack." She smoothed back a wave of hair. "I, too, know the heavy weight of responsibility for the lives of others. Of course the lives of your men are valuable and anything that will prevent the enemy from taking those lives is worthwhile. It is in that vein that I'm advising you to be careful with weapons that are wrought with magic. Such things are not typically intended for the unsupervised use of the ungifted."

The man nodded once. "We take your warning seriously."

"Good, then you should also know that what is in that room is dangerous in the extreme. It's a danger to all of us. It would be in all our interest if, while I'm here, I just make sure it's safe."

"Prelate, I understand your concern, but you must understand that my orders gave me no discretion for exceptions. I simply can't allow you to go in there on your word that you are who you say you are, or that your intent is only to help us. What if you were a spy? A traitor? The Keeper himself in the flesh? A sincere looking woman though you may be, I didn't get to the rank of commander general by letting attractive women talk me into things."

Verna was momentarily startled by being called an "attractive woman" in front of all these people.

"But I can personally assure you that no one—no one at all—has been in there since Lord Rahl himself was in there last. Not even Nathan Rahl went in there. Everything in the Garden of Life remains untouched."

"I understand, General." It would be a long time before she ever made it back to the palace. There was no telling where Richard was or when he would return. She rubbed her fingers on her forehead as she considered the quandary. "Tell you what, how about if I don't go in and instead I just stand in the doorway—outside the Garden of Life—and look in to make sure the three boxes being held in there are safe. You can even have a dozen of your men point those deadly arrows at my back."

He chewed his lip as he considered. "Men in front of you, men to the sides, and men to the back will have you under the points of their arrows and their fingers will be on the release levers. You can look past my men, through the doorway, and into the Garden of Life, but you may not cross the threshold under penalty of death."

Verna didn't actually need to get close enough to touch the boxes. Truth be told, she didn't really even want to get close to them. All she really wanted to do was to make sure that they were untouched by anyone else. At the same time, she wasn't exactly comfortable with the idea of all those men being only a finger twitch away from releasing one of those deadly arrows at her. After all, the notion to check on the boxes of Orden had only been an afterthought, being as she was already at the palace. It wasn't why she had come to the palace. Still, she was so close.

"Bargain struck, General. I only need to see that they are safe so that we all can sleep a little easier."

"I'm all for sleeping easier."

Berdine and Verna, with a knot of soldiers surrounding them, were led by Commander General Trimack down a broad passageway of polished granite. Columns spaced against the wall framed great slabs of stone as if they were artwork. To Verna, they were visual evidence of the Creator's hand, artwork from the garden he had cultivated that was the world of life. The sound of all the men moving along with them echoed up and down the great hallway as they passed a series of intersections that were arms of the spell-form all pulling back into the center that was the Garden of Life. They at last came to a pair of doors covered in carvings of rolling hills and forests and sheathed in gold.

"Beyond is the Garden of Life," the general told her in a sober tone.

As soldiers surrounded her, raising their crossbows, the general began drawing one of the great gold doors open. Some of the men to the side and rear pointed their arrows at her head. The four men who moved in front of her leveled their crossbow bolts at her heart. She was at least relieved not to have the ones in front of her pointed at her face. She thought the whole thing was silly, but she knew that these men were dead serious, so she treated it as such.

As the gold-clad door was swung wide, Verna, in lockstep with her cadre of personal assassins, shuffled closer to the opening so that she could see. She had to crane her neck and finally swish a hand to gently urge one of the men to move a little to the side so that she could have a clear view into the great room.

From the rather dimly lit hallway, Verna peered inside and saw that overcast skies lit the place in all its glory through leaded windows high overhead. She was astonished to see that all the way up in the center of the People's Palace, the Garden of Life looked just like . . . a lush garden.

From what she could see, around the outside of the room walkways wound their way through flower beds. The ground was littered with petals, a few still-colorful reds and yellows but most long since dried and shriveled. Beyond the flowers grew small trees and then beyond them were short, stone, vine-covered walls. Contained within the walls was a variety of shrubs and ornamental plants, although they were in sorry shape from lack of care. Many were gangly with long, new shoots and in need of a trimming. Others were infested with invasive vines. It looked as if General Trimack had been telling the truth that no one, not even the gardeners, had been allowed into the place.

At the Palace of the Prophets they had had an indoor garden, although on a much smaller scale. There had been a system of pipes coming from collection barrels on the roof that kept the garden watered. Recognizing similar pipes in a corner, Verna realized that rainwater collected on the roof provided a constant supply of water in this place as well or everything in the garden, lit by such wonderful light, would be dried up and dead.

In the center of the expansive room was an area of shaggy lawn that swept around almost into a circle, the grass ring interrupted by a wedge of white stone. On that stone sat two short, fluted pedestals that held a slab of smooth granite.

Atop the granite altar sat three boxes, their surfaces such an inky black that it almost surprised her that they didn't suck the light entirely out of the room and pull the whole world with it into the eternal darkness of the underworld. Just the sight of such sinister things made her heart feel as if it were coming up in her throat.

Verna knew the three boxes as the gateway, and they were exactly what the name implied. In this case, they were together a kind of gateway between the world of the living and the world of the dead. The gateway was constructed of the magic of both worlds. If that passage between worlds were ever to be undone, the veil would be breached and the seal would be off the Nameless One . . . the Keeper of the Dead.

Because the information had been in highly restricted books, only a few people at the Palace of the Prophets were even aware of the gateway by its ancient name, the boxes of Orden. The three boxes worked together, and together they constituted the gateway. As far as anyone at the Palace of the Prophets knew, the gateway had been lost for over three thousand years. Everyone thought that it was gone, vanished, disappeared for good. There had even been speculation for centuries as to whether or not such a gateway had ever really existed. If such a gateway could even exist had been the source of much heated theological debate.

The gateway—the boxes of Orden—did exist, and Verna was having trouble taking her eyes off it.

It made her heart race to see such vile things. Cold sweat dampened her dress.

It was small wonder that three wizards had ordered the general to allow no one into the room. Verna reconsidered her opinion of Nathan for equipping the First File with such dangerous weapons.

The jeweled covering had been removed, leaving the sinister black of the boxes themselves, because Darken Rahl had put the boxes in play and had planned to use the power of Orden to claim mastery over the world of the living. Fortunately, Richard had stopped him.

Stealing the boxes now, though, wouldn't do a thief any good. Extensive information was required to understand how the magic of Orden worked and how the gateway functioned. Part of that information was contained in a book that no longer existed except in Richard's mind. That, in fact, had been part of how he had defeated Darken Rahl.

In addition to vast knowledge and information, any thief would also would need to have both Additive and Subtractive Magic in order to use the gateway or to claim the power of Orden for himself.

The real danger would probably be to any person foolish enough to handle such treacherous things.

Verna sighed with relief at seeing the three boxes untouched, right where Richard had said he'd left them. For now, there was no safer place to keep such dangerous magic. Someday, maybe Verna could help find a way to destroy the gateway—if such a thing were even possible—but for now it was safe.

"Thank you, General Trimack. I'm relieved to see that everything is as it should be."

"And it will stay that way," he said as he put his weight against the door. It soundlessly moved closed. "No one is getting in there except Lord Rahl."

Verna smiled at the man. "Good." She glanced around at the magnificent palace around her, the illusion of permanence, peace, and security it exuded. If only it were so. "Well, I'm afraid that we need to be on our way. I have to get back to our forces. I will tell General Meiffert that things here at the palace are well in hand. Let us hope that Lord Rahl will be joining us soon and we can stop the Imperial Order before they ever reach this place. Prophecy says that if he joins us for the final battle, we have a chance to crush the Imperial Order, if not drive them back to the Old World."

The general gave her a grim nod. "May the good spirits be with you, Prelate."

With Berdine at her side, Verna made her way back out of the restricted area and away from the Garden of Life. As they once again descended the stairs, she was relieved to be on her way back to the army, even if she was worried over their mission. She realized that since coming to the palace she felt more of a sense of commitment, and more of a sense of connection to what had became the D'Haran empire under Richard. Even more than that, she seemed to care more about life.

But if they didn't find Richard and get him to lead their forces in the battle they would face when they finally met the Imperial Order, then the mission to stop Jagang's army was suicide.

"Prelate?" Berdine said as she pushed closed the door with a snake carved on it.

Verna paused and waited as the woman tapped the palm of her hand on the top of the bronze skull door handle.

"What is it, Berdine?"

"I think I should stay here."

"Stay?" Verna met the Mord-Sith's gaze. "But why?"

"If Ann finds Lord Rahl and takes him to the army, he will have you and a number of other Mord-Sith who are there to protect him—and he will be where you say he needs to be. But maybe she won't find him."

"She must. Richard is also aware of the weight of prophecy and he knows that he must be there at the final battle. Even if Ann doesn't find him, I have faith that he will come to join us."

Berdine shrugged with the difficulty of trying to find the right words. "Maybe. But maybe not. Verna, I've spent a lot of time with him. He doesn't think like that. Prophecy doesn't mean as much to him as it does to you."

Verna heaved a sigh. "You said a mouthful, Berdine."

"This is Lord Rahl's home, even if he never really lived here except as a captive. Even so, he has come to care about us as his people, and his friends. I've spent time with him; I know how much he cares about us and I know that he is aware of how much we all care about him. Maybe he will feel a need to come home.

"If he does, I think I should be here for him. He depends on me to help him with books, with translations—at least, I like to believe he does. He makes me feel important to him, anyway. I don't know, I just think I should remain at the palace in case he comes here. If he does, he will need to know that you are desperately trying to find him. He will need to know of the impending final battle."

"Does your bond tell you where he is?"

Berdine gestured west. "Somewhere in that direction, but very distant."

"The general said the same thing. That can only mean that Richard is at least in the New World again." Verna found reason to smile. "At long last. That much is good to know."

"The closer those with the bond are to him, the better able they will be to help you find him."

Verna considered it a moment. "Well, I will miss your company, Berdine, but I guess you must do as you see fit and I have to admit that what you say does make some sense. The more places we watch for him to show up, the better our chances of finding him in time."

"I really think it's right for me to stay here. Besides, I want to study some of the books and try to match up some of what Kolo says. There are a few things bothering me. Maybe if I work it out, I can even help Lord Rahl to win that final battle."

Verna nodded with a sad smile. "See me out?"

"Of course."

Both turned to the sound of footsteps. It was another Mord-Sith, in red leather. She was blond, and taller than Berdine. Her piercing blue eyes took Verna in with the kind of measured calculation that betrayed utter, fearless confidence.

"Nyda!" Berdine called.

The woman smiled with one side of her mouth as she came to a halt. She placed a hand on Berdine's shoulder, a gesture that Verna recognized as being as close to wild jubilation as it got among Mord-Sith, except perhaps for Berdine.

Nyda gazed down at Berdine, her eyes drinking her in. "Sister Berdine, it has been a while. D'Hara has been lonely without you. Welcome home."

"It's good to be home and see your face again."

Nyda's gaze slid to Verna. Berdine seemed to remember herself.

"Sister Nyda, this is Verna, the Prelate of the Sisters of the Light. She is a friend and advisor to Lord Rahl."

"He is on his way here?"

"No, unfortunately," Berdine said.

"Are you two sisters, then?" Verna asked.

"No," Berdine said, waving a hand at the notion. "It's more like you calling the other women of your kind 'Sister.' Nyda is an old friend."

Nyda glanced around. "Where is Raina?"

Berdine's face went white at the unexpected encounter with the name. Her voice fell to a whisper. "Raina died."

Nyda's face was unreadable. "I didn't know, Berdine. Did she die well, with her Agiel in her hand?"

Berdine swallowed as she stared at the floor. "She died of the plague. She fought it until her final breath . . . but in the end it took her. She died in Lord Rahl's arms."

Verna thought that she could detect that Nyda's blue eyes were just a little more liquid as she gazed at her sister Mord-Sith.

"I'm so sorry, Berdine."

Berdine looked up. "Lord Rahl wept as she died."

By the silent but astonished look on Nyda's face, Verna could see that it was unheard of for the Lord Rahl to care if a Mord-Sith lived or died. By the look of wonder that surfaced, such reverence for one of them was homage of profound proportions.

"I have heard such tales about this Lord Rahl. They are really true, then?"

Berdine smiled radiantly. "They are true."

What are you reading that's so absorbing?" Rikka asked as she used a shoulder to push the thick door closed.

Zedd grunted with displeasure before glancing up from the book lying open before him. "Blank pages."

Through the round window to his left, he could see the roofs of the city of Aydindril spread out far below. In the golden light of the setting sun the city looked beautiful, but that appearance was but an illusion. With all the people gone, fleeing for their lives before the hordes of invaders, the city was no more than an empty, lifeless husk, like the shed skin of the cicadas that had recently emerged.

Rikka leaned toward him over the magnificent, polished desk and tilted her head to see better as she peered down at the book. "It's not all blank," she announced. "You can't read something that is blank. You therefore must be reading the writing, not the blank places. You should try to be more accurate in what you say, if not more honest."

Zedd's frown darkened as his gaze rose to meet hers. "Sometimes what isn't said is more meaningful than what is said. Did you ever think about that?"

"Are you asking me to keep quiet?" She set down a large wooden bowl containing his dinner. The steam drifting up carried the aroma of onions, garlic, vegetables and succulent meat. It smelled distractingly delicious.

"No. Demanding it."

Through the round window to his right, Zedd could see the dark walls of the Keep soaring high up overhead. Built into the side of the mountain that overlooked Aydindril, the Wizard's Keep was nearly a mountain itself. Like the city, it too was empty—with the exception of Rikka, Chase, Rachel, and himself. It wouldn't be long, though, before there would be more people in the Keep. At last the Keep would once again have a family living in it. The empty halls would again ring with laughter and love as they once had when countless people called the Keep home.

Rikka contented herself with gazing around at the shelves in the round turret room. They were filled with jars and jugs in a variety of shapes, and delicately colored glass vessels, some filled with ingredients for spells, and, in one case, polish for the desk, the ornately carved straight-backed oak chair, the low chest beside his chair, and the bookcases. Books in a variety of languages filled most of the space on the shelves. The corner cases with glassed doors held more of the tomes.

Rikka folded her arms as she leaned close and studied some of the gilded spines. "Have you actually read all these books?"

"Of course," Zedd muttered. "Many times."

"It must be boring being a wizard," she said. "You have to do too much reading and thinking. It's easier to get answers by making people bleed."

Zedd harrumphed. "When a person is in agony they may be eager to talk, but they tend to tell you what they think you want to hear, whether it's true or not."

She pulled out a volume and thumbed through it before replacing it on the shelf. "That is why we are trained to question people by using the proper methods. We show them how very much more painful it is for them when they lie to us. If they understand the profoundly terrible consequences of lying, people will tell the truth."

Zedd wasn't really listening to her. He was concentrating on trying to figure out what the fragment of prophecy could mean. Every single possibility he came up with only served to further ruin his appetite. The steaming bowl sat waiting. He realized that she was probably hanging around, waiting for him to comment on dinner. Maybe she was waiting for a compliment.

"So, what's to eat?"

"Stew."

Zedd stretched his neck a bit to glance in the wooden bowl. "Where's the biscuits?"

"No biscuits. Stew."

"I know, stew. I can see that it's stew. What I mean is where are the biscuits to go with the stew?"

Rikka shrugged. "I can get you some fresh bread if you'd like."

"It's stew," he exclaimed with a scowl. "Stew calls for real biscuits, not bread."

"If I had known you wanted biscuits for dinner I could have made you biscuits rather than the stew. You should have said something earlier."

"I don't want biscuits *instead* of stew," Zedd growled.

"You change your mind a lot when you're grumpy, don't you?"

Zedd squinted at her with one eye. "You really are talented at torture."

She smiled, turned on a heel, and strode regally out of the small room. Zedd thought that Mord-Sith must strut even when they were alone.

He went back to the book, trying to come at the problem from a different angle. He had only had time to read the passage again a couple of times when the latch on the door lifted and Rachel shuffled into the room carrying something in both hands. She used her foot to push the door closed

"Zedd, you should put your book away, now, and have some supper."

Zedd smiled at the child. She always made him smile. She was infectious that way.

"What have you got there, Rachel?"

She reached up and set the tin bowl on the desk, then stretched her arm out as she pushed it across the desk toward him.

"Biscuits."

Flabbergasted, Zedd rose up a little from his chair to lean over and look in the tin bowl.

"What are you doing with biscuits?"

Rachel's big eyes blinked at him as if it were the strangest question she had ever heard. "They're for your supper. Rikka asked me to carry them for her. She had her hands full with a bowl of stew for you and one for Chase."

"You shouldn't help that woman," Zedd said with a menacing scowl as he sat back down. "She's evil."

Rachel giggled. "You're silly, Zedd. Rikka tells me stories about the stars. She makes pictures out of them and then tells a story about each picture."

"Is that so. Well, sounds like a nice thing for her to do."

With the light fading, it was getting hard to read. Zedd cast out a hand, sending a spark of his gift into the dozens of candles in the elaborate iron candelabrum. The warm light brightened the cozy little room, lighting the finely fit stone of the walls and the heavy oak beams across the ceiling.

Rachel grinned, her eyes glistening with both reflected points of candlelight and with wonder. She liked seeing him light candles. "You have the bestest magic, Zedd."

Zedd sighed. "I wish you weren't leaving me, little one. Rikka doesn't appreciate my candle-lighting trick."

"You will miss me?"

"No, not really. I just don't want to be left alone with Rikka," he said as he read the last bit again.

They will at first contest him before they plot to heal him. What could that mean?

"Maybe you could get Rikka to tell you some stories about the stars." Rachel began looking sad as she came around the desk. "I'll miss you something awful, Zedd."

Zedd looked up from the book. Rachel held her arms out, wanting a hug. A smile overcame him as he scooped her into his arms. There were few things in life that felt as good as a hug from Rachel. She was a devotee of the hug, never putting less than her full enthusiasm into it.

"You have good hugs, Zedd. Richard has good hugs, too."

"Yes he does."

Zedd remembered being in that very room, so long ago, when his own daughter was about the same age as Rachel. She, too, would come to see him and want a hug. Now, all that he had left was Richard. Zedd missed him terribly.

"I will miss you, little one, but before you know it you will be back here with the rest of your family and then you will have brothers and sisters to play with instead of just an old man." Zedd sat her on his knee. "It will be good to have all of you at the Wizard's Keep with me. The Keep will be a joyful place, what with life in it again."

"Rikka said that she will never have to cook again once my mother comes here."

Zedd took a sip of lukewarm tea from a pewter mug on the chest beside him. "Did she now."

Rachel nodded. "And she said that my mother would probably make you brush your hair." She held out her hands, wanting to share a drink from his mug. He let her gulp tea.

Zedd cocked his head. "Brush my hair?"

Rachel nodded with a serious look. "It sticks all out. But I like it."

"Rachel," Chase said as he ducked in through the round-topped doorway, "are you bothering Zedd, again?"

Rachel shook her head. "I brought him biscuits. Rikka said he likes biscuits with his stew and I should bring him a whole bowl full."

Chase planted his fists on his hips. "And how is he supposed to eat his biscuits with ugly children sitting on his lap? You could scare his appetite right out of him."

Rachel giggled as she hopped down.

Zedd glanced at the book again. "Are you all packed up?"

"Yes," the big man said. "I want to get an early start. We'll leave first thing in the morning, if that's still all right with you."

Zedd dismissed the concern with a wave of his hand as he studied the prophecy. "Yes, yes. The sooner you get your family back here, the better. We'll all feel better having them here where we know they will be safe and you will all be together."

Chase's heavy brow drew lower over his intent brown eyes. "Zedd, what's the matter? What's wrong?"

Zedd looked up with a frown. "Wrong? Nothing. Nothing is wrong."

"He's just busy reading," Rachel assured Chase as she hugged his leg and put her head against his hip.

"Zedd," Chase said in a demanding drawl that said he didn't believe a word of it.

"What makes you think something is wrong?"

"You haven't eaten a thing." Chase rested one hand on the wooden handle of a long knife at his belt and with the other caressed Rachel's head of long, golden blond hair. The man probably had a dozen knives of various sizes strapped around his waist and to his legs. When he left in the morning he would add swords and axes to the knives. "That can only mean something is wrong."

Zedd popped a biscuit in his mouth. "There," he mumbled around the mouthful. "Satisfied?"

While Zedd chewed the warm biscuit, Chase leaned down and lifted the girl's chin. "Rachel, go to your room and finish getting your things packed up. And I expect your knives to be cleaned and sharp as well."

She nodded earnestly. "They will be, Chase."

Rachel had had a hard life for one so young. For reasons that had always made Zedd suspicious, she'd been at the center of a variety of consequential situations. When Chase had taken the orphaned girl in to raise as his own daughter, Zedd himself had admonished the man to teach her to protect herself, to teach her to be like him so that she could defend herself and stay safe. Rachel adored Chase and eagerly learned all the lessons he taught her. With one of the smaller knives she carried, she could pin a fly to a fence post at ten paces.

"And I want you in bed early so that you will be rested," Chase told her. "I'm not carrying you if you're tired."

Rachel gave him a puzzled look. "You carry me when I tell you I'm not tired."

Chase cast Zedd a pained look before giving her a clearly feigned scowl. "Well, tomorrow you're just going to have to keep up on your own."

Rachel nodded seriously, unruffled by the man towering over her. "I will." She looked at Zedd. "Will you come and kiss me good night?"

"Of course," Zedd said with a smile of his own. "I'll be in after a bit to tuck you in."

He wondered if Rikka would stop by her room to tell her a story. It was heartwarming to think of the Mord-Sith telling a child stories about pictures made by the stars in the sky. Rachel seemed to have that effect on everyone.

Chase watched through the doorway as his daughter raced off down the broad rampart. Zedd had been gratified at the way she had taken to the Wizard's Keep. In short order she had made it hers and was happily skipping through halls that were thousands of years old. She minded well and never strayed from the areas Zedd had warned her about. She was a child who understood danger. Out on the rampart, she looked completely at ease as she paused momentarily to gaze through a crenellation down at the city below before racing off again. It seemed to Zedd a wonder that such spindly legs could carry the child so swiftly.

After Chase was sure that she was safely on her way, he closed the heavy oak door and stepped closer to the desk. His size made the cozy room, a room that Zedd had always thought quite comfortable, seem rather cramped.

"Now, what's the problem?"

The man wasn't going to be satisfied until he knew more. Zedd sighed and used a finger to spin the book around for the boundary warden to read.

"Take a look. You tell me."

Chase glanced at the ancient book. He lifted a page to each side and briefly took a look before setting each page back down.

"Like I said, what's the problem? It doesn't look like there is much here to worry about."

Zedd arched an eyebrow. "That's the problem."

"What do you mean?"

"It's a book of prophecy. It's supposed to have writing in it—prophecy. You can't have a book with no writing and have it still be a proper book, now can you? The writing is gone."

"Gone?" Chase scratched a graying temple. "That doesn't make any sense. How can writing be gone? It's not like someone could steal the words right off the page."

That was an interesting way to look at it—that someone had stolen the words right off the page. Having been a boundary warden most of his life—until the boundary came down a few years back—Chase was the kind of man who would suspect theft before anything else. Zedd hadn't considered that possibility. His mind was already rushing down the unexplored dark alley of deliberation.

"I don't know how the words could be gone," he confided as he took a sip of tea.

"What is the prophecy about?" Chase asked.

"This happens to be a book of prophecy mostly about Richard."

Chase looked completely calm, which of course meant that he was anything but. "Are you certain it used to have writing in it?" he asked. "If it's old, maybe you just forgot that it had blank pages. After all, when you read a book you tend to recall the writing, not the blank pages."

"True enough." He set the pewter mug aside. "I can't swear for certain that I remember it having writing in it, but I just don't believe it was ever mostly blank. Now it is."

Chase's expression didn't betray his feelings as he considered the mystery. "Well, I admit that it does sound strange . . . but is it really a problem? Richard never was one for prophecy; he wouldn't have heeded them anyway."

Zedd rose up and stabbed a finger at the book, tapping insistently. "Chase, this book has been here in the Keep for thousands of years. For thousands of years it's had writing—prophecy—in it. I'm sure of it. Now it's suddenly blank. Does that sound trivial to you?"

Chase shrugged as he hooked his thumbs in his back pockets. "I don't know, Zedd. I'm no expert in such things. I think the day that you have to come to me for answers about books of prophecy is the day you're in big trouble. You're the wizard, you tell me."

Zedd put his weight on his hands as he leaned toward the man.

"I can't recall anything that used to be in this book. I can't recall anything about the blank places in all the other books of prophecy that have missing text."

Chase's expression turned grim. "There are others with blank places?"

Zedd nodded as he smoothed back his hair. He gazed in the darkening window, trying to see himself reflected, but he couldn't, yet—it was still too light outside.

"Does my hair need to be brushed?" He looked back at Chase. "Does it stick out too much?"

Chase cocked his head. "What?"

"Never mind," Zedd muttered with a dismissive wave of his hand. "The point is, I've discovered blank places in a number of books of prophecy and I'm baffled by it."

Chase shifted his weight and folded his arms. His brow bunched. He was beginning to look seriously concerned, which on Chase meant that he looked like he thought he might need to slaughter large numbers of people.

"Maybe I'd better stay for now. We don't have to leave tomorrow. We can wait until you find out if there is some sort of trouble at hand."

Zedd sighed, beginning to wish that he wouldn't have mentioned anything. This wasn't really a problem for Chase. Zedd shouldn't have gotten the man all worked up over something he wouldn't understand or could do anything about. It was just that it was so blasted odd.

"That isn't necessary. This kind of trouble isn't likely to need to have you strangle it into submission. It's an entirely different kind of problem. This is book trouble. I don't want to burden you with worry. It's my area and I'm sure I'll figure it out sooner or later. I only wondered what you might think of such a thing. Sometimes it helps to have a fresh view."

Chase waggled a finger over the book. "Well, what does that last part mean? That *first contest him before they plot to heal him* part? You said it was prophecy about Richard. That sounds like trouble—like someone is going to plot against him."

"No, not necessarily." Zedd wiped a hand across his mouth as he tried to think of a way to explain it. "The word *plot* in prophecy often means nothing more sinister than to 'lay out a plan.' Like plotting a course of action, you might say. In this case, the passage was talking about those who are his closest advisors, his allies, so when it talks about plotting to heal him, it most likely means that they must first convince him that he needs their help and then once they are able to convince him, these allies—that would most likely be some of us—are going to set about planning a way to heal him."

"Heal him from what?"

"It doesn't say."

"So then it isn't serious."

Zedd gave the boundary warden a meaningful look. "I believe that may be the part that is blank."

"Then it is serious. Richard is in trouble. He needs help. Maybe he's hurt."

Zedd shook his head unhappily. "In my experience prophecy is rarely so overt."

"But that could be the case."

Zedd appraised the man for a moment. "We're a long way from needing to dream up things to worry about. In addition, the chronology of prophecy is always troublesome. For all I know, the part we're discussing could have already happened. It could, for instance, be talking about a time Richard had a fever as a child and I had to find the proper herbs to heal him."

"Then it just as well could be past history."

Zedd turned up his palms in frustration. "It could be. Without the missing text—or knowing a lot more about prophecy than I do—it's probably impossible to put this in the context of his life."

Chase nodded but then stepped out of the way as the door opened and Rikka swept into the room. She reached out to take the bowls, but paused when she saw they were still full.

"What's the matter? Why haven't you eaten?" When Zedd waved a hand as if trying to swish the issue away, she looked over her shoulder at

Chase. "Is he sick? I thought he would have scraped the bowl clean by now and licked the smell off the ceiling. Maybe we had better think of a way to make him eat."

"See what I mean about plotting?" Zedd said to Chase. "It could be no more serious than that."

Rikka surveyed Zedd's face for a moment, as if checking for any overt signs of insanity, then turned her attention to Chase. "What is he jabbering about?"

"Something about books," Chase told her.

She turned a growing glare on Zedd. "Well, after all the trouble I went to fixing you this meal, you are going to sit right down and eat it. If you don't, then I'll feed it to the worms in the midden heap, instead. Then, when you get hungry later and come to me complaining, you will only have yourself to blame. You'll get no sympathy from me."

Startled, Zedd blinked at her. "What? What did you say?"

"I'm going to feed it to the worms if you don't—"

"Bags!" Zedd snapped his fingers. "That's it!" He held his arms out to her. "Rikka, you're a genius. I could hug you."

Rikka straightened defiantly. "I prefer to accept your adoration from afar."

Zedd wasn't listening to her. He rubbed his hands together as he tried to remember exactly where it was that he'd seen the reference. It had been ages ago. But how long ago, exactly? And where?

"What is it?" Chase asked. "Have you solved the puzzle?"

Zedd's mouth twisted with the effort of thought. "I recall reading a reference to such an event. I remember seeing some kind of exegesis."

"A what?"

"An explanation. An analysis of this issue."

"So then it is some . . . book thing."

Zedd nodded. "Yes, exactly. I just need to remember where it was that I saw the passage. It was about worms."

Chase cast a sidelong glance at Rikka before he scratched his head of thick, graying brown hair. "Worms?"

Zedd dry-washed his hands as vague recollections ghosted through his mind. Those shadowy memories were real, he was sure of it, but despite his frantic effort to grasp them and pull them into the light of consciousness, they remained just out of reach.

"Zedd, what are you talking about?" Rikka asked. "What did you say? Worms?"

"What? Oh, yes, that's right. Worms. Prophetic worms. It was some kind of evaluation, I think, examining if such a thing might be able to erode prophecy."

Chase and Rikka stared at him as if he were crazy but said nothing.

Zedd paced from the table to the corner bookcase and back. He pushed the heavy oak chair aside with a foot as he walked back and forth, thinking. He ran through a list of places that might have a book that would contain such a reference. There were libraries all over the Keep. There were thousands of books in those libraries—maybe tens of thousands. If he had even seen the reference at the Wizard's Keep. He had visited any number of libraries in other places. There were a number of archives in the Confessors' Palace, down in Aydindril. There were palaces on Kings Row, also in Aydindril, that contained extensive collections of books. There were any number of cities that Zedd had visited with repositories and archives. There were so many books, how was he to remember one he hadn't seen for ages—perhaps since he was young?

"What, exactly, are you talking about?" Rikka asked when she tired of watching him pace. "What explanation are you talking about?"

"I'm not sure, yet. It was a long time ago. Had to be. Had to be when I was young. I will remember, I'm sure of it. I just have to give it some thought. Even if it takes all night, I will remember where I saw the passage. I wish I had my reason chair," he muttered as he turned away.

Rikka frowned at Chase as she kept an eye on Zedd as he paced. "His what?"

"Back in Westland," Chase said in a low voice, "he had a chair on his porch where he would sit and think—where he would reason out problems. That was back when everything started, when Darken Rahl came and tried to capture him and Richard. They fled just in time. They came to me and I led them through a gap to the boundary."

"Seems to me that there are chairs enough around here. He's practically tripping over that one, there." Rikka's mouth twisted with exasperation. "Besides, a person doesn't need a chair to make their brain work. At least, if they do, they have bigger problems."

"I suppose." Together with Rikka, Chase watched Zedd pace for a while. Finally, not being one to stand around, he caught the sleeve of Zedd's robes. "I guess I'd better go see to Rachel while you work out your solution. I want to make sure she gets her things together and gets to bed."

Zedd swished a hand, urging the man on his way. "Yes, you're right. Go ahead. Tell her I will come to kiss her good night after a while. I just need to think on this a bit."

Once he was gone, Rikka leaned a leather-covered hip against the heavy desk and folded her arms under her breasts. "Are you saying that the words of prophecy vanishing was caused by some kind of worm, like a bookworm that eats the paste or the paper?"

"No, it eats the words, not the paper."

"Then it's . . . what? Some kind of tiny little worm that eats ink?"

Annoyed at the interruption, Zedd halted his pacing to stare at her. "Eats . . . ? No, no, not in that way. This is something of magic. A tricky little twist of something clever. If I recall correctly it was referred to as a prophetic worm because it could eat away at the branches of prophecy, much like wood bore worms eat away at a tree. It starts with related prophecy, either in subject or in chronology, like wood bores might infest a particular branch. Once established this kind of worm begins eating away the tree of prophecy. In this case, the branch is the one having to do with the time since Richard was born."

Rikka looked genuinely fascinated and at the same time distraught. She straightened and tilted her head toward him. "Really? Magic can do such a thing?"

Zedd, holding his elbow in one hand and his chin in the fingertips of the other, made a low sound deep in his throat. "I think so. Maybe. I'm not sure." He heaved an impatient, irritable sigh. "I'm trying to remember. I only saw the reference once. I can't recall if it was a theory I read or if it was the spell itself, or if it was only a suggestion in a book of records, or if it . . . Wait—"

He stared up at the beamed ceiling as he squinted with the effort of recollection. "It was before Richard was born, I'm sure of that much. I remember that I was a young man. That would mean that it had to be when I was here. That much makes sense. And if I was here . . ."

Zedd's head came back down. "Dear spirits."

Rikka leaned in. "What? Dear spirits what?"

"I remember," Zedd whispered, his eyes going wide. "I remember where I saw it."

"Where?"

Shoving his sleeves higher up his bony arms, Zedd headed for the door. "Never mind. I will see to it. You just go about your patrolling, or something. I'll be back later."

With the sun going down, the air was beginning to cool as Zedd raced down the broad rampart. The huge stones of the crenellated wall radiated heat they had stored from the hot sun beating down on them all day. The city far below the mountainside was melting into a sea of gloom, while pink rays of the departing sun caressed the tops of some of the tallest towers of the Keep high overhead. The dying light of dusk had brought a still quiet touched only by the distant whisper of the cicadas.

At an intersection of ramparts, Zedd ran around the corner to the right. Unlike the rampart at the edge of the Keep, which overlooked a drop-off of thousands of feet down the sheer face of the mountain, the narrower interior bastion wall had precipitous drop-offs to both sides, yet within the massive complex that gave a clear view of nearly windowless walls descending down into the darkness. Courtyards far below provided the refreshment of open air directly off some of the lower floors within the Keep. Zedd imagined that people who in the past had worked in the lower reaches of the Keep must have appreciated being able to step outside from time to time.

As he ran down the narrow bastion path, bridges to various towers crossed overhead. Soaring up before him at the end of the pathway was an immense, imposing wall with vertical rows of projecting keystones for interior floors. There was a grand, double entrance door at the base of that looming wall with designs above reliefs of columns carved in the wall beneath the arched stone lintel, but Zedd instead took to an opening in the side rail to take the steps down. The seemingly eternal flight of stairs descended down a long, sloping lip built into the side of the clifflike bastion wall.

He needed to go down into the lower reaches of the Keep, deep within the mountain, to places where no one ever went.

To places no one but he even knew existed.

The stone banister on the open, exposed side of the stairs wasn't very high and as a consequence the descent down the straight run of hundreds of feet of stairs, with no landings, was a harrowing experience. To his left rose the carefully fit stone blocks of the imposing bastion wall, to his right was a drop-off that would make any self-respecting cliff proud. Going down that monumental run of stairs always made Zedd feel tiny. He could see little more at the bottom than the jagged formation of dark rock at the base of one of the round towers rising up from the small courtyard.

Partway down, Zedd realized that he heard footsteps racing to catch him. He stopped and turned. It was Rikka.

"What do you think you're doing?" He called up to her.

The wind rising up the narrow canyon formed by the stone walls all around lifted his hair and his robes. It almost felt as if his bony frame might lift right off the stairs and be carried away like a dried leaf on an updraft.

Rikka came to a panting halt a few steps above him. "What does it look like I'm doing?"

"It looks like you're not doing what I told you to do."

"Let's go," she said, swishing her hand to urge him on. "I'm coming with you."

"I told you that I would see to this. I told you to go patrol or something."

"This is trouble that concerns Lord Rahl."

"It's just some information in old books that I need to check into."

"Chase and Rachel are leaving early in the morning. You would be in with Rachel, telling her a story and tucking her in, unless there was something going on that has you really worried. This is about Lord Rahl. If it has you worried, then it has me worried. I'm going with you."

Zedd didn't want to stand out on the open steps arguing with her, so he didn't. He turned and raced downward, holding up his robes in both fists so that he wouldn't trip and fall. Besides going on seemingly forever, the steps were frighteningly steep. A fall so high up on the steps could easily be fatal.

Finally reaching the bottom, Zedd stopped on the first stepping stone and turned back. "Stay on the stones."

Rikka glanced around at the expanse of viny groundcover. Beyond were walls on two sides that rose up for hundreds of feet without interruption. Behind was the stairs and bastion wall. To the right was a jutting mass of bedrock from which the tower rose.

"Why?" She asked as she followed Zedd across the stepping stones.

"Because I said so."

He didn't feel like spending time explaining traps of magic. Were she to step off the stones, the shields would not just warn her, but prevent her from going where she shouldn't be. Still, for those not possessing the proper power, it was always best to stay completely away from shields whenever possible.

If the shields failed to stop intruders from crossing this secluded courtyard, the vines would snare them. While the victim struggled to escape, these particular vines would tangle around the ankles. Stimulated by struggling, the vines rapidly sprouted wicked thorns that penetrated into bone where they then anchored themselves. Freeing anyone trapped in the vines was a painful, bloody affair and, more often than not, fatal. Defenses at the Wizard's Keep were not hesitant in their purpose.

"Those vines are moving." Rikka snatched his sleeve. "Those vines are moving like a nest of snakes."

Zedd scowled back over his shoulder. "Why do you think I told you to stay on the stepping stones?"

He lifted a lever and pulled open the second round-topped door he came to and ducked inside. He could feel Rikka practically breathing down his neck. Reaching blindly in the darkness his bony fingers found a smooth sphere in the bracket to the right. As he passed his hand over the glossy surface it began to glow with a greenish light. The entry room was small, made of simple, undecorated stone block walls. Overhead was a beam and plank ceiling. Against the wall to the right was a single, short slab of slate built in to provide a bench in case the stairs had left any visitor in need of a brief rest. In both of the other two walls were two dark passageways going off in separate directions.

Along the wall above the slab bench were dozens of brackets, over half of them holding spheres that glowed faintly with the same color of greenish light as the one he had first touched. Zedd lifted one of the spheres from a bracket. It was heavy, made from solid glass, but there were other elements fused into this glass and those elements responded to the stimulus of the gift. In his hand the greenish cast changed to a warmer yellow glow. He let a spark of his gift lift through the sphere and it brightened, throwing harsh shadows down the two halls ahead of them.

With a sharp jab of a bony finger, he sat Rikka on the bench. "This is as far as you go."

Grim determination was etched on her face as her blue eyes watched him. "Something strange is happening with the books of prophecy. You've been fretting over those books for days, now. You haven't eaten or slept. But worse by far is that the prophecies that are vanishing are about Lord Rahl."

It was an observation, not a question. He'd thought that his turmoil had been all internal. She had been quietly paying more attention than he'd given her credit for. Or maybe he had just been too distracted to notice her paying attention. In either case, it was not a good sign that he had been so preoccupied that he hadn't even been aware of her marking how absorbed and unsettled he'd been.

"Near as I can tell, you are right in that a great many of those vanished prophecies are about Richard, but I don't think they all are. From what I have been able to determine, however, they all have to do with prophecy pertaining to a time after he was born. That doesn't mean that they are all about him, though. The blank places in the books are extensive. Since I can't remember what those blank places said, there obviously is no way to tell what they were about, making it impossible to know the subject individual of the missing prophecies."

"But from what you can piece together they mostly have something to do with Lord Rahl."

This, too, had not been a question, but a statement of observation, or, at least, reasoned speculation. This was a Mord-Sith asking questions that revolved around the issue of the safety of her Lord Rahl. Zedd could see that she was in no mood for any evasive explanations.

"I would have to agree that Richard, if not central, is at least deeply connected with the trouble in the books of prophecy."

Rikka rose up from the bench. "Then this is no time for you to go all secretive on me. This is important. Lord Rahl is vital to all of us. This is not only about the safety of your grandson, but about the future of all of our lives."

"And I'm seeing to—"

"It is not only important to you; he is important to all of us. If you alone discover something significant and anything happens to you, then we could all be left at a dead end. This is more important than you keeping your secrets."

Zedd put his hands on his hips and turned away for a moment, considering. He finally turned back to her.

"Rikka, there are things down there that no one knows about. There are good reasons for that."

"I'm not going to steal any treasure and if you fear me seeing some 'secret of the ages,' then I will be willing to swear on my life to keep it secret unless it is necessary for me to reveal it to Lord Rahl."

"It's more than that. Many of the things in the lower reaches of the Keep are incredibly dangerous to anyone who goes near them."

"There are things of incredible danger outside the Keep as well. We no longer have the luxury of secrets."

Zedd watched her eyes. She had a point. If anything happened to him, the information, too, was as good as dead. He had always planned on someday letting Richard know about this, but there had never been any time and, until the problem with the books of prophecy had cropped up, it hadn't seemed critical. Still, this was not Richard who would see these things.

"What do you think, wizard? That I will go to town and gossip about what I've seen? Who is left to tell? The Order has overrun most of the New World and everyone has fled Aydindril for D'Hara. D'Hara hangs by a thread. Our future hangs by a thread."

"There are reasons that some knowledge is kept hidden."

"There are also reasons that wise men sometimes must share what they know. Life is what matters. If knowledge will help preserve and advance life, then that knowledge should not be hidden—especially when it may be lost right when it could be that it's needed most."

Zedd pressed his lips tight as he considered her words. He had discovered this secret when he had been a boy. His whole life he'd never told another person about it. No one had instructed him to keep it a secret—nor could they, no one but he knew about it. Still, he knew that there had to be a reason that this was not something that was meant to be widely known. This had been kept secret for a reason.

He just didn't know what that reason was.

"Zedd, for Lord Rahl's sake, for the sake of our cause, let me come with you."

He appraised her determination for a moment. "You can never reveal this to anyone."

"Except for Lord Rahl, I will never reveal it to another. Mord-Sith often go to their graves without revealing the things they know."

Zedd nodded. "All right. It goes to your grave with you, unless something happens to me. If so, then you must tell Richard what I show you this night. You must swear to me that you will never tell anyone else about this, though, not even your sister Mord-Sith."

Without hesitation Rikka held her hand out to him. "I swear."

Zedd clasped her hand and in so doing struck the agreement, accepting her word.

When he had been First Wizard during the war with D'Hara, before he had put up the boundaries and killed Panis Rahl, Darken Rahl's father, if anyone had told him that he would someday make such an agreement with a Mord-Sith over something so important, he would have thought they were crazy. He was grateful that such things had changed for the better.

It's a complex route," Zedd told her.

Rikka arched an eyebrow. "Have you ever had to come find me because I got lost patrolling the Keep?"

Zedd realized that he hadn't. He knew very well how easy it was to become lost in the Keep. In fact, that was one of its defenses.

In several places when trying to travel through the Keep one came upon interconnected rooms numbering in the thousands. In those places there were no hallways except for the stairs going up or down. Passage through those three-dimensional mazes was necessary to get into several well-protected areas. It was deceptively easy to become forever lost in the morass of those interconnected rooms. Even people who had grown up in the Keep could easily become lost in there.

An invader, unfamiliar with the place and if they went too deep into the labyrinth, faced a formidable challenge just to find their way back out, much less to make a passage all the way through, and then to escape. Once you had been through a few rooms, through a few doorways, it was amazing how similar everything looked. There were no windows to help and direction soon became meaningless. There was virtually no way to tell if you recalled seeing a room or a doorway before. One looked much like the last dozen you'd seen. There had been spies and such in the past who had become lost in the maze of rooms. In ages past it had not been entirely unusual to find a body in there.

Of course, not all those who intended harm were strangers. In the past some had been traitors.

"No, I guess you never have become lost," Zedd finally agreed. "Not yet, anyway. You've not been here long enough to begin to explore the majority of the place. There are dangers of every sort. Getting lost in the labyrinth that is the Keep is only one of the perils. Where we're going is like that. It's even easier to get lost down there. You will have to do your best to remember your way. I'll help you where I can."

Rikka nodded, seemingly unconcerned. "I'm good at remembering things like a series of turns. I memorize them when I patrol."

"Don't get overly confident. This is more complex than a series of turns. I myself have become lost in the Keep, and I grew up here. There is not only one right way to get where we're going. Sometimes the route you took the last time won't work this time because down in the lower reaches of the Keep the shields sometimes shift by themselves to different passageways. It's part of their design to make it more difficult to get through—for instance if a spy were to draw a map for their cohorts."

Unimpressed, Rikka shrugged. "I understand. The People's Palace is like that in some of the sections where the public isn't allowed—complex, with the open passages one can get through changing from time to time. Additionally, there is no direct route to anywhere, even if all the passages happen to be open, which they never are."

"I remember; I was there before, although I was in the public sections, but that was confusing enough." It had been after Darken Rahl had captured Richard. "I had the advantage, though, in that the People's Palace is made in the form of a spell drawn on the face of the ground and I know how that particular spell is constructed, so I know where the primary arms and the connecting links are located."

"Well," Rikka said, "we had to be able to find different passages through the place so that we could get from area to area if it was ever invaded. Or, if we are chasing someone, we had to be able to think of a way to get ahead of them. We have to be able to do more than simply remember a series of turns. We must comprehend the whole of the place we pass through. In my head the turns I take make up parts of a picture of a place. Every turn adds to that picture. With that ever growing image in my mind I can find my way by taking a different way because I can see where the other parts are and how they lock together."

Zedd blinked in astonishment. "That seems quite a remarkable talent."

"I always could understand that kind of thing better than I can understand people."

Zedd grunted a brief laugh. "I think you understand people more than you admit to."

She only smiled.

"All right, now listen to me," he said. "You will not only need to remember a great many turns this night. There is more. The only way to get where we are going is through a number of shields. You are not gifted so the only way for you to pass through those shields is for a gifted person to help get you through. If it ever becomes necessary, Richard can take you through them, like I will take you through tonight. But no matter how well you know the place, or how the shields shift, there is no way to get through without having to pass the shields, so you won't be able to get through alone. That means you won't be able to practice the route by yourself."

He shook a finger before her face to make his point. "Don't even think to try to force your way through the shields. To attempt to do so would be fatal."

Rikka nodded. "I understand. I would have no reason to need to get through without you or Lord Rahl."

Zedd leaned even closer to her. "On your word and your life."

"I have already given you my word and sworn it on my life. That is the way it will be."

Zedd closed the matter with a single nod. "Good. Let's go."

With Rikka close at his heels, Zedd rushed down the narrow stone hall to the left, their way lit by the globe he carried. Glass spheres in brackets in the distance glowed faintly once coming into sight. As they passed them, each brightened at his approach and dimmed as he moved on with the one he had taken. At the first stairway they came to, Zedd took it up, knowing that to descend to his destination he first needed to traverse several impassable areas of the lower Keep by going higher.

They made their way down broad corridors lined with elegant wood paneling and patterned stone floors and then through several rooms that served as study areas outside nearby libraries. The rooms had dozens of thick carpets scattered about at various angles among the comfortable chairs. There was ample table space, and there were a number of lamps to provide adequate light for reading. Zedd knew because he had spent a great deal of time reading books from the libraries.

After passing through a series of plain stone halls that came from various parts of the Keep, they at last reached the main artery hallway in the section they had to pass through. The hall was nearly a hundred feet tall, with the sloping walls getting closer together at the top; it felt like walking through an immense cleft in the Keep. The sun was already down so the high slits in the stone did little to illuminate the hallway. They did, however, allow the bats out. Every night at dusk, thousands of the bats poured

up from hidden, dark, damp places in the Keep and made their way out the
high slits in the main hallway.

At a gilded doorway, Zedd turned to Rikka. "This passage is shielded.
Take my hand and you will be able to pass."

She didn't hesitate. Zedd went through the shield first. The shield produced a gentle tingling sensation against his skin along the plane of the
opening. When he turned back toward her and pulled her hand through
that plane of the shield at the doorway, she flinched.

"It won't hurt you as long as I hold on to you," he assured her. "Shall I
continue?"

She nodded. "It's just so cold. The feel of it surprised me, that's all."

Holding her hand tightly, he drew her the rest of the way through the
doorway. Once through she vigorously rubbed her arms.

"What would have happened had I tried to go through without you?"

"It's hard to say, since different shields do different things, but let's just
say that you wouldn't have made it through. This one has no preliminary
warning field, so it may not be fatal. There are a number of shields we will
have to pass through that would take the flesh right off your bones. Those
kind give ample warning, though."

She didn't look too pleased to hear it, but she made no protest. Mord-
Sith didn't like magic, so he knew she was putting in a great effort to sup-
press her natural resistance.

The gilded doorway led down a hall of white marble all around—the
floors, walls, and ceiling. The white color was designed to prevent certain
gambits of magic that used conjuring involving color to trick the shield at
either end of the hall. At the far end, Zedd helped Rikka through the
shield—this one using heat rather than cold.

Once clear of the hall, they went down several flights of dusty black
marble steps. At the bottom of the steps he led her down the left of three
forks. The sphere he carried provided a bubble of light around them as
they raced through the roughly hewn stone tunnel that took them into simple rooms that were made of simple stone blocks.

Most of the rooms had one or two doorways, but some had three, or
even four openings that led to other rooms. Some were reached by going
up a short flight of stairs to yet more rooms. A number of rooms were either up or down only a step or two. Most of the rooms, though, were level
with one another. The sizes of the rooms varied little and not a single one

had any furniture whatsoever. Some of the rooms were plastered to make the walls smooth and a number of those were painted, although the chipped, peeling paint was so faded that the colors were barely discernible, leaving them all looking a similar dingy color, since dust had been settling in them for centuries. When Zedd had been a boy he had been lost in the maze of rooms for an entire day. The place was so undisturbed that there were still faint footprints evident in the fine dirt coating on the floors.

After going through a seemingly endless series of rooms, they finally emptied into a broad corridor of coarse, gray granite blocks. While the corridor was wide, the ceiling was so low that they had to bend down slightly so as not to bump their heads. It was a place that, while empty and simple looking, had always felt ominous to Zedd. Around a corner, iron brackets holding more of the glass spheres brightened as they passed, and then faded as they continued on. In several places utilitarian stone stairwells emptied into the low corridor. Several other taller halls branched off the main passageway.

At the end of the broad, low hall they finally entered a major passageway that was plastered and painted a sandy color. Reliefs of pillars were spaced down the passage, giving it a grander appearance. When they reached the middle, Zedd finally paused. He pointed up at the ceiling.

"See there, that iron grate overhead that lets the Keep breathe, lets fresh air down here?"

She peered up at the ornate grate. "Is that a book?"

Within the design, crafted from the iron bars, was the outline of an open book. The design, intended as a quick visual reference, denoted a section of the Keep that contained a number of libraries.

"Yes. The grate will help you remember that this is where you must turn. This corridor with that grate above is a main trunk of passageways. There are a number of ways down to this place, and from here you can go by various routes to nearly anywhere in the Keep, but here, under this grate, you must turn down this hall." He gestured toward a small hallway. "It's the only way to get to where we are going."

Zedd watched her as she looked around at her surroundings and once more checked the grate overhead. When she was sure and had nodded, they started down a small side hall.

The hall contained a series of rooms that Zedd believed were once used for maintenance supplies. He knew that one of the rooms still had a number of tools. Beyond, at the end of the hall, were a few roughly constructed rooms made of stone followed by small, square passageways running off in several directions. At the end of the center passageway, they came to a warren of short runs through low service shafts taking them on a winding route that changed levels by a few feet from time to time. They passed empty rooms and rusted iron doors that stood closed. Cobwebs clogged the shafts in places. In other places, sections of hall that were several feet lower held stagnant water. The rotting carcasses of rats floated in the fetid water. Without a word they waded through to reach higher ground beyond.

When they reached a spiral stone staircase beyond the maze they descended into the inky darkness, the silent sphere bringing harsh light and shadows to places that had not been lit for years. The stairs were tiny, only large enough for a single body at a time to slip downward. It felt rather like being swallowed down the gullet of some stone monster.

At the bottom of the spiral stairs, the light cast harsh shadows down roughly cut passageways that were inspection shafts for part of the Keep's foundation. Flecks of quartz in stone foundation blocks the size of small palaces sparkled when the light fell across them. Zedd led Rikka to the narrow stairs that descended down beside the face of that glittering foundation wall. They both peered over the edge of that slit in the ground before starting down.

At the bottom they followed the narrow slit along the base of the foundation blocks. The stone rose up into the darkness, the sparkling quartz above looking like stars. To the right was a roughly cut wall of crumbling rock. If that softer wall were to collapse, they would be buried alive where no one would ever search for them.

The foundation in this part of the Keep was kept clear of the soft surrounding rock so that it could move a little if it had to. The foundation blocks had been set down into the harder bedrock below. The narrow slit also provided an areaway for inspection of the foundations. Zedd had always thought it remarkable that he had never found any block that was failing. There were some that had cracks, but those were said not to be structural problems. When they came to another narrow flight of stairs at the end of the slit, they again went down, deeper into the pitch black cut.

"Is there any end to this?" Rikka asked.

Zedd looked back over his shoulder, the glowing sphere casting her face in harsh yellow light. "We're deep in the mountain and getting closer to one of the side slopes. We still have quite a ways to go."

She simply nodded, resigned to however far it was.

"Do you think you can get this far—providing you have me or Richard to get you through the shields?"

There had been a number of shields, some that she had not liked going through. For one without the protection of the gift it was in places a very uncomfortable experience, even with Zedd helping her.

"I think so," she said.

In the lower inspection channels, they came to round, tile-lined tunnels that when need be also served as drains. Zedd entered the complex of tunnels, taking intersections that he remembered since he was a boy. Dripping water echoed through the passages. It was cold enough to see their breath in the humid air. Water dripped between the tiles in places, making the tunnel slick.

At various places, right in the middle of nowhere in the tunnels, they encountered powerful shields that he helped her pass through. Several were so strong that they gave off preliminary warnings long in advance. Zedd had to wrap his arms around her in order to protect her enough to get her safely through.

"There's a lot of rats down here," Rikka said.

Zedd could hear them squeaking by the hundreds all through the honeycombed passageways. The little beasts seemed to scatter before the light could fully illuminate them, so they were in evidence by sound, not by sight, except the dead ones.

"Yes. Are you afraid of rats?"

She halted and scowled at him. "No one likes rats."

"Can't argue with you about that."

At each intersection Zedd pointed out to her the way they had to go. He couldn't imagine how she was ever going to remember the way. He hoped it never became necessary. He hoped to be the one to show Richard. As a boy Zedd had used tracers of magic to learn his way through. Rikka paid close attention and watched each of the dark intersections they came to. He was sure that it was more than she had bargained for and that she would not be able to remember her way. He thought that perhaps he would take her through several more times in order to help her get it all mapped out in her head. After that, he would test her and let her lead the way down.

After what seemed like an endless journey working their way ever lower, they finally entered a colossal room, an immense, cavelike chamber, that was hollowed out from the interior of the mountain. The granite quarried out of the mountain down in this place had provided some of the stone for the foundation. The quarry, abandoned after the construction was completed, had left behind the huge room.

In some places around the sides, the builders of the Keep had left fat pillars of stone in place to hold up what they apparently had found to be weaker areas of the ceiling. In spots around the room there were broad veins of obsidian, a black, glassy rock that was unsuitable for building material. Zedd had seen it used in a few places in the palace, mostly for decoration. In the glow of the light from the sphere, the surface of the obsidian showed the shiny curved arcs left by being chipped away with chisels, leaving it looking like dazzling fish scales.

The center of the gigantic room, where the rock was the hardest, was vaulted to a height of over two hundred and fifty feet. From the stone evidence, it appeared that the workers had started at the top, taking out huge blocks of stone right under what was the present ceiling. They then began quarrying the next lower level of rock until they eventually had hollowed out the cavelike room. The different levels of galleries around the side were just tall enough, and just wide enough between the large square columns, for the foundation blocks to be hauled though. Beyond the room were ramps where the blocks had been eased down to the lower parts of the foundation.

"See there, across the room?" Zedd asked, pointing at an enormous, dark corridor to which he knew the surrounding ramps led. "That was constructed first. It's the main channel where the foundation blocks were transported from this room to the foundation all along that section of the Keep. Look at how the floor is worn by the work."

The floor leading into the yawning dark chasm was worn so smooth that it almost looked as if it had been polished.

"Why didn't we come that way—it would have been a much shorter route."

He was impressed that she realized that the primary passageway ran in the direction from which they had come. The stone blocks for the foundation would not have taken the circuitous route they had.

"You're right, it would have been shorter, but there are shields there that I can't pass. Since I can't get in there, because of those shields, I don't know what is in there, but I suspect that the builders probably created rooms in there that contain things that must be protected. I can't really think of any other reason for those shields."

"Why can't you pass them? You are First Wizard."

"The wizards of that time had both sides of the gift. Richard is the first in thousands of years to be born with the Subtractive side as well as the Additive. Shields with Subtractive Magic are deadly and are typically reserved for the most dangerous places, or the places that have exceptionally important items they were most concerned about protecting."

Zedd led Rikka across the vast room by a route that kept them close to the outer wall. He rarely came down to this room and so he had to watch the stone wall carefully as they made their way around. When they reached the place he was looking for, he snatched Rikka's arm and pulled her to a stop.

"This is it."

Rikka blinked as she looked around. To the inexperienced eye, it looked the same as the rest of the room. "This is what?"

"The secret place."

It looked like the rest of the huge room. Everywhere the walls were scarred with the gouges left by tools used by workers thousands of years before.

Zedd held up the glass sphere so she could see where he pointed. "Here. See that gouge up high? The one going at this angle, following the fissure, and a little fatter in the middle? Slip your left hand into it. There's a cleft in the back of the gouge, deeper into the fissure."

Rikka frowned at him but then stood on her tiptoes and slid her hand into the grove up to her knuckles.

"There's a lip in the rock down here," he said. "I used it when I was smaller. If you can't reach, step up on the edge."

"No, I got it," she said. "Now what?"

"You're only halfway in. Put your hand in deeper."

She wiggled her fingers and worked her hand in farther until it was in up to her wrist. "That's as far as it will go. It's solid where my fingertips are."

"Move your longest finger up and down until you find a hole."

She made a face as she worked her fingers. "Got it."

Zedd took her right hand and guided it into a similar gouge in another part of the same fissure down at waist level. "Find a hole in the back of this one as well. When you do, push a finger firmly into both holes."

She made a little sound deep in her throat with the effort. "Found it! I've got them both. I'm pushing."

"All right, now, as you push with both fingers, put your right foot up here, on the wall right on the other side of this chink, and give it a good shove."

She frowned at him, but did as he said. Nothing happened.

"Can't you push any harder than that? Don't tell me that you aren't as strong as a skinny old man."

She shot him a scowl and then used her grip in the handholds for leverage as she grunted with effort and gave the wall a good shove with her boot. Suddenly, the face of the rock began moving away. Zedd urged Rikka to step back. They both watched as a section of the wall silently slid back as if it were a massive door, which was exactly what it was. Despite its monumental weight, it was so perfectly balanced that once the two finger latches were released, it pivoted with nothing more than a stout shove.

"Dear spirits," Rikka whispered as she leaned toward the opening and peered into the dark maw. "How did you ever find such a place?"

"I found it as a child. Actually, I found the other end. Once I came through into here, I knew where this spot was and I took careful note so that I was able to find it again. The first few times I couldn't find it, so I had to come through again."

"Well, what is it?"

"When I was a boy, it was my salvation. It was the way I was able to sneak back into the Keep without having to come across the bridge and in the front, like everyone else."

She suspiciously arched an eyebrow. "You must have been a troublesome child."

Zedd smiled. "I have to admit that there were those who would agree with that. This place served me well. I was also able to get in here when the Sisters of the Dark had taken the Keep. They only knew to guard the front entrance. They, like everyone else alive, didn't know this place existed."

"So this is what you wanted to show me? A secret way into the Keep?"

"No, that's by far the least important or remarkable thing about this place. Come on and I'll show you."

Her suspicion flared again. "Just what kind of place is it?"

Zedd held up the sphere of light as he leaned toward her and whispered. "Beyond is eternal night: the passage of the dead."

The distant howl of a wolf woke Richard from a dead sleep. The forlorn cry echoed through the mountains, but went unanswered. Richard lay on his side, in the surreal light of false dawn, idly listening, waiting, for a return cry that never came.

Try as he might, he couldn't seem to open his eyes for longer than the span of a single, slow heartbeat, much less gather the energy to lift his head. Shadowy tree limbs appeared to move about in the murky darkness.

Richard gasped as he fully awoke. He awoke angry.

He was lying on his back. His sword lay across his chest, one hand clutching the scabbard, the other gripping the hilt so hard that the letters of the word TRUTH were pressed painfully into his palm on one side and his fingertips on the other. The Sword of Truth was pulled partway out of its scabbard. Its anger, too, had partly slipped its bounds.

The first, faint traces of dawn were just beginning to silently steal through the forested mountainside. The thick woods were quiet and still.

Richard slid the blade back into its scabbard and sat up, laying the sword down beside him on his bedroll.

He drew his legs up and put his elbows on his knees as he ran his fingers back through his hair. His heart still raced from the sword's rage. It had stolen into him without his conscious awareness or direction, but he wasn't surprised or alarmed. It was hardly the first time he had begun to draw the sword as he'd remembered that fateful morning while slipping the bonds of sleep. Sometimes he woke to find that he'd pulled the blade completely free.

Why did he keep having that memory as he awoke?

He knew all too well the reason. That was the morning he had awakened to find Kahlan missing. It was the terrible memory of the morning she'd disappeared. It was a waking nightmare about the nightmare that had become his life, and yet, he knew that there was something about it that kept making it go through his mind. He had been over it a thousand times but he couldn't figure out what was so meaningful about that particular memory. The wolf waking him had been a bit odd, but that didn't seem so strange that it would keep haunting him.

Richard looked around in the deep gloom but he didn't see Cara. Off through the thick stands of trees he could just make out the faint stain of red streaking the rim of the eastern sky. The slash of color almost looked like blood seeping through a gash in the slate black sky beyond the perfectly still trees.

He was bone-weary from the relentless pace of their wild ride up from deep in the Old World. They had been stopped a number of times by patrolling soldiers scattered throughout the Midlands, and by occupying troops. It was by no means the main force of the Imperial Order, but they had been trouble enough. Once they'd let Cara and Richard, posing as a stone carver and his wife, go on their way to a job Richard had invented for the glory of the Order. The rest of the times the two of them had had to fight their way out of the situation. Those encounters had been bloody.

He needed more sleep—they had gotten very little on their journey— but as long as Kahlan was missing they couldn't afford to sleep any more than was absolutely necessary. He didn't know how much time he had to find her, but he didn't intend to waste any of it. He refused to believe that his time had long since run out.

One of the horses had died of exhaustion not long ago; he couldn't remember exactly when. Another had come up lame a while back and they'd had to abandon it. Richard would worry about finding more horses later. There were more important concerns at hand. They were close to Agaden Reach, Shota's home. For the last two days they had been climbing steadily into the formidable mountains that ringed the Reach.

As he stretched his aching, tired muscles, he again tried to think of how he would convince Shota to help him. She had helped him before, but that was no guarantee she would help him this time. Shota could be difficult, to say the least. There were people who were so terrified of the witch woman that they wouldn't even say her name aloud.

Zedd had told him once that Shota never told you anything you wanted to know without also telling you something that you didn't want to know. Richard couldn't really imagine what he didn't want to know, but he understood quite clearly what it was he did want to know and he intended

Shota to tell him anything she knew about Kahlan's disappearance or where she might be. If Shota refused, there was going to be trouble.

As his anger heated he realized that he felt the cool, tingling touch of mist on his face.

It was then that he also noticed something moving in the trees.

He squinted in an effort to see in the darkness. It couldn't be the breeze moving the leaves; there was no wind in the silent predawn woods.

Shadowy tree limbs appeared to move about in the murky darkness.

There had been no wind at all that morning, either.

Richard's sense of alarm rose to match his heart rate. He stood in his bedroll.

Something was slipping through the trees.

It wasn't disturbing the branches or brush the way a person or an animal would. It was higher up, maybe at eye level. There simply wasn't enough light for him to see what it was. As dark and still as the morning was, though, he couldn't be certain that there really was something there. It might have been his imagination; being this close to Shota certainly was enough to make him uneasy. While she might have helped him in the past, she had also caused him no end of trouble.

But if nothing was there in the trees, then why was his skin tingling with dread? And what was the almost imperceptible sound he heard, like a soft hiss?

Without taking his eyes off the dark woods, Richard reached out and put his fingertips against a nearby spruce for balance as he carefully squatted down enough to pick up his sword from where it lay on the bedroll. As he quietly slipped the baldric over his head, he tried to focus his eyes in the darkness out ahead of him to see what, if anything, was moving. Whatever was moving, it couldn't be much, yet he was more and more convinced by the moment that it really was something.

The most disconcerting aspect of it was the way it moved. It didn't move in short bursts, like a bird flitting from branch to branch, or in rapid start-and-stop spirts like a squirrel. It didn't even move with the stealth of a snake that glided, then paused, then glided some more.

This moved not only fluidly and quietly, but continuously.

The horses, off through the trees in a corral Richard had constructed by using saplings to fence off the end of a narrow chasm, snorted and stamped their hooves. A flock of birds in the distance suddenly burst from their roost and took to wing.

For the first time, Richard realized that the cicadas were silent.

Richard detected the faint scent of something out of place in the forest. Carefully, quietly, he sniffed the air, trying to place the scent. He thought it might be a whiff of something burning. The odor wasn't anywhere near as strong as a fire would be. It almost smelled like a campfire, but they had no campfire; Richard hadn't wanted to take the time or to chance attracting attention. Cara had a lantern with a light shield around it, but it didn't smell like the lantern flame.

He scanned the woods all around, checking for Cara. She was on watch so she was probably nearby, but Richard didn't see her anywhere. Surely she wouldn't have gone far, especially not after the attack the morning Kahlan had disappeared. She was all too worried about his safety and knew that this time, if he was shot with an arrow, there would be no Nicci to save his life. No, Cara would be close.

His instinct was to call out for her, but he suppressed the urge. He first wanted to find out what was happening, to find out what was wrong, before he called out an alarm; an alarm would also alert any adversary that he was already aware of them. It was better to let an opponent, especially an opponent sneaking up on you, believe that they had not been detected.

As he studied the surrounding area, Richard thought that there was something not right about the woods. He couldn't put his finger on it, but they looked wrong. He supposed that he had that impression in part because of the curious burning smell. It was still too dark to be able to see anything clearly, but from what he was able to see, the branches didn't seem to look right. There was something odd about the pine boughs, the leaves. They didn't seem to be hanging naturally.

He remembered all too well coming to Agaden Reach the first time. Farther back down the mountains he had been attacked by some strange creature. As he had been frantically fighting it off, Shota had snatched Kahlan and taken her down into the Reach. That attack had been in the guise of a stranger trying to lead him to an ambush. The creature had finally been frightened off. And, this time there was no such stranger. Still, that didn't mean that such a creature, having failed before, might not this time try a different approach. He remembered, too, that his sword had been all that had kept the monstrous thing at bay.

As quietly as possible, Richard slowly drew his sword from its sheath. In an attempt to keep it from making any noise, he pinched the sides of the blade right at the throat of the scabbard, letting the steel slide between his finger and thumb as it slipped out of the scabbard. Even so, the blade hissed ever so softly as it came free. The sword's rage, too, slipped its bounds.

As he steadily drew his sword, he began cautiously moving toward the spot where he thought he saw movement. Whenever he was looking elsewhere, he thought that out of the corner of his eye he could see a faint shape of something ahead of him, but when he then looked directly at the place, he couldn't see anything. He didn't know if it was a trick of his sight, or if there was nothing to see.

He was well aware that in dark conditions the center of the eyes' vision was not nearly as good as the peripheral vision. Being a guide and having spent a great deal of time outdoors at night, he had often used the technique of not looking directly at what it was that he needed to see, but instead gazing at least fifteen degrees away from it. At night, the peripheral vision worked better than direct vision. Since leaving his woods where he had been a guide, he had learned that the knack of focusing his awareness to specific places in his peripheral vision while not turning his eyes there was invaluable in sword fighting.

Before he had gone three steps, his pant leg came up against something that shouldn't have been there. It was a light contact, almost like a low branch. He halted immediately, before putting any pressure on it. He smelled something again, only stronger. It smelled like scorched cloth.

He then felt the intense heat against his shin. Quickly, and without making a sound, he drew back.

For the life of him, Richard could not figure out what it was he had touched. It was not anything natural that he could think of. He might have suspected that it was a tripwire of some sort to warn anyone hidden in the trees nearby if he moved, but a tripwire wouldn't burn him the way this thing had.

Whatever it was, it pulled at his pants, like it was sticky, when he drew away. When he backed free of it, the sleek movement in the trees abruptly halted, as if it had detected the contact against his pant leg being broken. The dead silence ringing in his ears was almost painful.

The mist was too fine to make any sound hitting the leaves and the moisture that the pine needles combed from the damp air was not enough to collect and drip very much. Besides, the sound he had heard had been something different than rainwater. Richard focused his concentration into the dark shadows, trying to make out what it was that had stopped moving.

Then, it started in again, only more rapidly, as if with more purpose. The soft, silky sound whispering among the limbs of the trees in a way that reminded him of the blade of an ice skate gliding across smooth ice.

As Richard backed away, something caught his other pant leg. It was sticky, just like the thing that he'd snagged before. It too, felt hot.

As he turned to see what it was that was against his pant leg, something brushed his arm, just above his elbow. He didn't have on a shirt, and the instant the sticky thing touched him it burned into his flesh. He jerked his arm back and then stepped away from the thing touching his pant leg. With the hand holding the sword, he silently comforted the searing pain on his left arm. Warm blood ran down over his fingers. His anger, and the anger flooding into him from the sword, together threatened to overpower his sense of caution.

He turned around, trying to see in the darkness what was there that should not be there. The razor-thin red slash of light at the horizon glinted off his blade as he turned, making the polished metal look like it was coated in blood to match the very real blood covering his hand on the hilt.

The shadows around him were beginning to pull inward toward him. Whatever it was, as it moved closer it caught limbs and boughs all around him, gently pushing leaves and brush aside as it advanced. Richard suspected that the soft hissing sound he heard was actually the sound of vegetation being scorched when it was touched. The smell of burning leaves he had first detected began to make sense to him; he just didn't have any idea what could be causing it, or how. He would doubt his judgment, doubt that such a thing could be real, were it not for the fierce burning pain of its touch. He certainly wasn't imagining the blood running down his arm.

Instinctively, Richard knew that he was running out of time.

Richard swiftly, but silently, raised the sword before himself in preparation for an attack—what kind of attack he wasn't sure, but he fully intended to be ready. He touched the cold steel of the blade to his sweat-slick forehead.

He spoke the words "Blade be true this day" in a softly inaudible whisper, fully committing himself and his sword to whatever was necessary.

A few fat drops of rain splashed against his bare chest. At first sporadic, the fitful rain gradually began to increase a bit. The soft whispering sound of raindrops against the thick canopy of leaves began to spread through the quiet of the woods. Richard blinked drops of water from his eyelashes.

At the sound of the limbs moving, he then heard the sudden rush of footsteps starting to run toward him. He recognized Cara's unique gait. Apparently, she had been patrolling around the perimeter of their campsite and had heard the same sounds as he had. Knowing Cara, he wasn't in the least surprised that she had been paying close attention.

But under the cover of the sound of the rain, all around him, Richard could hear branches and limbs slowly pulling past one another. Here and there a few small twigs snapped as something drew in closer all around him. Something touched his left arm. He flinched backed a step, pulling his arm away from the gummy contact. The burn throbbed painfully. Warm blood now trickled down his arm in two places. He felt something catch the back of his pant leg. He tugged his leg away from the sticky contact.

Cara crashed through the trees not far away. Subtle, she was not. She threw open a small door on the shield around the lantern she carried, letting a weak beam of light fall across the campsite.

Richard was able to see what he thought looked like a strange, dark web of something crisscrossed all around him, woven through trees, shrubs, limbs, and brush. It looked like thick cords of some sort, but organic and gummy. He couldn't imagine what it was or exactly how it had gotten itself everywhere around him.

"Lord Rahl! Are you all right?"

"Yes. Stay where you are."

"What's going on?"

"I'm not sure, yet."

The sound came closer as the still, dark strands all around him again began to draw tighter. One of them pressed against his back. He flinched away, spun, and slashed with the sword.

As soon as he cut it, the whole of the tangle all around him tensed and contracted in toward him.

Cara threw open the entire shield around the lantern, hoping to see better. Richard could suddenly see that the glistening threads were nearly cocooning him. He even saw lines of the stuff crisscrossing overhead. As close in as it all was, he was running out of clear space to maneuver.

With a flash of comprehension, he understood the silken sound he had heard at first. The fluid, continuous movement was something spinning the filaments around him as if he were a meal for a spider. These filaments, though, were as thick as his wrist. What exactly they were, he had no idea. What he did know was that when they had touched him, sticking to his pant leg, his left arm, and his back, they delivered painful burns.

He could see Cara and her lantern as she dodged this way and that, looking for a way to get through to him.

"Cara, stay back! It will burn you if you touch it."

"Burn?"

"Yes, like acid, I think. And, it's sticky. Keep away from it or you're liable to get caught in it."

"Then how are you to get out of the middle of it?"

"I'll just have to cut my way out. You stay there and let me come to you."

When the strands pulled in tighter to the left side, he finally swung the sword and struck out at them. The blade flashed in the light of Cara's lantern, slashing through the enveloping tangle of sticky fibers. As they were parted by the blade, they whipped around as if they'd been under tension. Some stuck to trees or limbs, hanging down like murky moss. In the light of the lantern, he could see the leaves shrivel up, evidently from being burned when they were touched by the strands.

Whatever was creating the webs of the stuff, Richard didn't see it.

The rain began to come down a little harder as Cara darted from side to side, trying to find a way in. "I think I can—"

"No!" he yelled at her. "I told you—keep away from it!"

Richard swung the sword at the thick, dark ropes wherever they drew in toward him, trying to check their constriction and weaken their integrity, but he was forced not to do so unless he had no choice because the sticky strands were beginning to cling to the blade.

"I need to help you stop this thing!" she called back, impatient to see him free.

"You'll just get caught up in it. If you do that, then you can be of no help to me. Stay back. I told you, let me cut my way out and come to you."

That, at least, looked to have finally dissuaded her from any immediate attempt to try to fight her way through. She stood half crouched, lips pressed tight in frustrated fury, Agiel in her fist, not knowing what to do— not wanting to go against what he told her and realizing the sense of what he'd said—but at the same time not wanting him to have to fight his way out all by himself.

It was a strange, confounding, nonviolent kind of battle. There looked to be no rush. The gashes he inflicted didn't seem to cause the thing any pain. The slow, inexorable approach of the surrounding tangle seemed to be trying to lull him into holding back, inasmuch as there appeared to be plenty of time to analyze the situation.

Despite that quiet appearance, that deceptive calm, Richard found the implacable advance of the surrounding trap alarming in the extreme. Not wanting to give in to that appeal to inaction, Richard swung the sword again, driving into the walls of the tangled web.

He could see more of the strands appearing in the woods all around him even as he tried to fight his way through it. It was reinforcing itself, adding a backdrop even as he slashed the part closest to him. For every dozen strands he cut, two dozen more enfolded him. He kept scanning the forest, trying to see what was creating the growing entanglement so that he could attack the cause and not the result. Try as he might, he couldn't see a lead end or what was spinning the morass, but the viscous ropes of it were moving swiftly through the trees and brush, the strands lengthening and multiplying all the time, endlessly adding to and forming more of themselves all around him.

Even though it seemed like he had ample time to figure a way out, he knew that such a notion was a fool's empty hope. He was well aware that his time was swiftly running out. His level of alarm rose steadily. His burned flesh throbbed in pain, reminding him of what fate awaited him if he didn't get out. There would come a point, he knew, when action would no longer be possible. He knew that once the intricate trap contracted enough, he would die, but he doubted that it would be a quick death.

As the net reinforced itself around him and moved inward, Richard attacked, slashing furiously, making a mad effort to hack his way through the tightening entrapment. Every time he swung the sword, though, the blade was further ensnared in the tacky substance that made up the strands. The more of it he cut, the more of it stuck to what was already clinging tenaciously to his sword. The unwieldy mass was getting heavy and making it ever more difficult to cut through the wall.

As he tried to hack and slash his way through, a knot of the filaments not only continued to tangle together in a clotted mass around his blade, but began to adhere to the wall of the trap, making it a formidable task just to move the sword. He felt like a fly caught in a spiderweb. It took a mighty effort to pull the sword away from the wall of the strands. They, in turn, sticking to the sword, stretched and pulled away in gummy strings.

This was the first time that Richard had ever encountered an adversary of any sort that gave the sword such difficulty. He had cut through armor and iron bars with it, but this sticky substance, even though it yielded to being cut, simply fell away and stuck to everything.

He remembered Adie once asking him which he thought was stronger, teeth or tongue. She had made the point that the tongue was stronger, even though it was much softer, and would endure long after the teeth gave out. Although it was in a different context, it had a frightening significance in this instance as well.

Some of the gooey strings stretched out and stuck to his pant legs. As he pulled his sword back, a string fell across his right arm. He cried out in pain and dropped to his knees.

"Lord Rahl!"

"Stay there!" he called before Cara had a chance to try again to reach him. "I'm all right. Just stay where you are."

Snatching up a handful of leaves, bark, and dirt, he used the debris to protect his hand as he pulled the dark, clinging substance from his arm.

The searing pain caused him to nearly forget everything else except getting it off.

As the surrounding fibrous structure drew tighter, the thick strands pulled small saplings over. Branches snapped. Limbs were torn from trees. The woods were filled with a pungent, burning smell.

Even with the fury of the sword storming up through him, pulling his anger forth, Richard realized that he was losing the battle. Wherever he cut it, a great many of those cut strands fell back to stick together with others and close the gap. Despite his cutting through the snarled mass of the webs, the net only tangled together and stuck to itself, creating an ever more tightly woven web.

His calm frustration began to give way to the panicked realization that he was trapped. That fear powered his muscles as he put all his effort into swinging his sword. He could imagine the strange, dark mass miring him, burning his flesh, congealing as it enfolded itself around him, eventually to suffocate him if it didn't first kill him by scorching the flesh off his bones.

With all his might Richard brought the sword down over and over, slashing through a wall of the stuff. More strands beyond those he cut caught up the ones he had severed as they whipped around and fell back. The ones he cut only served to cross over strands beyond and reinforce them. He was not simply failing, but in so doing helping to strengthen his executioner.

"Lord Rahl—I need to get to you."

Cara clearly understood the deadly nature of the threat he was under and wanted to find a way to help get him out of the trouble. And, like him, she didn't really have any idea what to do.

"Cara, listen to me. If you get tangled in it, you'll die. Stay away from it—and whatever you do, don't touch it with your Agiel. I'll figure something out."

"Then hurry up and do it before it's too late."

As if he wasn't trying. "Just give me a minute to think."

Panting, trying to catch his breath, he put his back against the protection of a large spruce tree close to his bedroll as he tried to figure out what to do to escape. There was not much room left around the tree, and not much time before that space, too, would be gone. Blood ran down his arms from the wounds where the dark substance had touched him. Those wounds burned and throbbed, making it difficult to think. He needed a way to get across the sticky tangle, to get out of the middle of it, before it finally captured him for good.

And then it came to him.

Use the sword for what the sword could do best.

Without wasting another moment, Richard stepped away from the tree, spun around, drew back, and with all his might swung the sword as hard as he could. Knowing that his life depended on it, he put every bit of fury and energy behind the blade, driving it with all his power. The tip whistled as it came around with lightning speed.

The blade crashed through the tree with a loud boom that sounded like a lightning strike and did just as much damage. The tree's trunk shattered. Jagged splinters flew everywhere. Long fragments spiraled through the air. Smaller chips and a shower of bark were netted by the sticky tangle beyond.

The mighty spruce groaned as the towering crown pulled itself through the tangled canopy above as the tree began to topple. With gathering speed, it plunged through the tight stand of trees, ripping thick branches from other trees as the great weight of the spruce dropped through the crowded forest.

As the tree fell, it ripped the strands where the trunk rose through the tangled web above him, pulling gummy ropes along with it, and then it crashed down atop the entanglement of sticky strands, whipping them down against the ground, burying them under the trunk and the thick thatch of limbs.

Before the web had time to re-form or heal itself and close the yawning gap, Richard leaped up onto the trunk even as it was still rebounding from hitting the ground. He held his arms out and crouched for balance. The rain was picking up and the trunk of the tree was slippery. As the great trunk bounced and settled to the ground, and limbs, bark, branches, needles, and leaves still rained down on him, Richard used the opportunity to race across the length of the spruce, using it like a bridge to cross the sticky net.

Panting, he reached Cara, free at last of the trap. Cara, having seen him coming, had climbed up on a stout limb to be ready to help him across. She seized his arm to keep him from falling on the wet bark as he ran through the snarl of branches.

"What in the world is going on?" Cara asked through the roar of the downpour as she helped him down to the ground.

Richard was still trying to catch his breath. "I have no idea."

"Look," she said, pointing at his sword.

The gummy substance still stuck to his sword had begun melting away in the rain.

The mass of strands tangled all through the woods were also beginning to soften and sag. As strands came apart, the rain beat the net down, pulling yet more of the long, thick fibers from the trees. It dropped to the ground in dark masses, where it hissed in the rain and melted like the first snow of the season failing to survive as the storm turned back to rain.

In the gray dawn Richard could see the extent of the mass that had woven its way around him. It was an immense snarl. When the tree ripped the weave of the mesh open at the top it seemed to have undone the integrity of the whole thing, causing its weight to tear itself apart and collapse.

With the cold rain coming down harder all the time, the dark strands were washed from the branches and brush. They lay on the ground looking like nothing so much as the dark viscera of some great dead monster.

Richard wiped his sword on wet bushes and grasses until the sticky substance was all off.

The mass on the ground melted away with increasing speed, evaporating into a gathering gray fog. Back in the shadows of the trees, like steam rising from the entrails of a fresh corpse on a winter day, that dark fog slowly lifted from the ground. Carried on a faint breeze that had come up, murky patches drifted away beyond the thick veil of trees.

Back in the cover of trees, that dark fog shifted abruptly in some vague manner that Richard couldn't quite follow, solidifying into an inky black shadow. In a flash, before he could make sense of it, that sinister apparition disintegrated into a thousand fluttering shapes that darted off in every direction, as if a dark phantom were decomposing into the rainy shadows and mist. In an instant they were gone.

A chill ran up Richard's spine.

Cara stared in astonishment. "Did you see that?"

Richard nodded. "It looked something like what the thing back in Altur'Rang did after it came though the walls after me. It disappeared in much the same way just before it would have had me."

"Then it has to be the same beast."

In the early morning downpour, Richard surveyed the shadows among the trees all around them. "That would be my guess."

Cara, too, watched the woods all around for any sign of threat. "Lucky for us the rain came when it did."

"I don't think it was the rain that did it."

She wiped water from her eyes. "Then what did?"

"I don't know for sure, but maybe just the fact that I escaped its trap."

"I can't imagine a beast with that kind of power being so easily discouraged—the last time or this time."

"I don't have any other ideas. I know someone who might, though." He took Cara by the arm. "Come on. Let's get our things together and get out of here."

She gestured off through the woods. "You go get the horses. Let me pack up our bedrolls. We can dry them out later."

"No, I want us out of this place right now." He quickly pulled a shirt out of his pack, along with a cloak to try to keep relatively dry. "We'll leave the horses. With them fenced into a place where they have grass and water they'll be fine where they are for a while."

"But the horses would get us away from here faster."

Richard kept an eye on the surrounding woods as he stuffed his arms through the sleeves of his shirt. "We can't take them over the mountain pass—it's too narrow in places—and we can't take horses down into Agaden Reach where Shota lives. They can get a needed rest while we go see the witch woman. Then, when we find out what Shota knows about where Kahlan is, we can come back and get the horses. Maybe Shota will even know how we can get rid of this beast that's following me."

Cara nodded. "Makes sense, except I'd rather get out of here as quickly as we can and horses would help in that."

Richard squatted down and started rolling up his sodden bedroll. "I agree with the sentiment, but the pass is close and the horses can't make it over, so let's just get moving. Like I said, the horses need a rest anyway or they're not going to be any good to us."

Cara stuffed the few things she had out back into her pack. She, too, pulled out a cloak. She lifted the pack by a strap and threw it up onto a shoulder. "We'll need to get things out of our saddlebags, back with the horses."

"Leave them. I don't want to have to carry any more than we must; it would just slow us down."

Cara gazed off through the veil of rain. "But someone might steal our supplies."

"Thieves won't come near Shota."

She frowned up at him. "Why not?"

"Shota and her companion walk these woods. She's a rather intolerant woman."

"Oh great," Cara muttered.

Richard swung his pack around onto his back and started out. "Come on. Hurry."

She scurried after him. "Have you ever considered that maybe the witch woman is more dangerous than the beast?"

Richard glanced back over his shoulder. "You're a regular little miss sunshine this morning, aren't you?"

The rain had turned to snow after they'd climbed out of the dense forest and made it into the crooked wood at the transition out of the tree line. Because of the harsh conditions common at that elevation, the stunted trees, mantled in meager vegetation, grew in bizarre, windblown shapes. Walking through the crooked wood was like passing among the petrified forms of desiccated souls whose limbs were frozen for all time in tormented stances, as if they had emerged from their graves only to find their feet forever anchored in hallowed ground, preventing them from ever escaping the temporal world.

While there were those who would not enter the surreal world of the crooked wood without some form of mystical protection, Richard wasn't superstitious about the place. In fact, he considered all such beliefs to be the refuge of the willfully ignorant. Richard saw through the trappings to what lay beneath all superstition—nothing less than the call to surrender to the view of man as helpless in accomplishing his own ends and dealing with the reality of the world around him in order to further his own survival, instead embracing the notion that he existed only at the whim of vague and unknowable forces that can only be persuaded to stay their cruel and merciless impulses if man falls to his knees in supplication, or, if they have to enter a spiritual place, by carrying the proper fetish.

While Richard had always found it eerie being in a crooked wood, he knew what it was and why it had grown to be that way, even if it still felt rather haunting to be in such a place. He was aware that there were basically two ways to deal with that primordial emotion. The superstitious solution was to carry sacred talismans and amulets to ward off spiteful demons and incomprehensible dark forces thought to inhabit such places, hoping that the fates would be persuaded to kindly stay their fickle hand. Even though people proclaimed with complete confidence that such mysterious forces were fundamentally unknowable to mere mortals, they nonetheless passionately believed, without evidence, that they could be certain that the power of charms would soothe the savage temper of those menacing forces, insisting that faith was all that was necessary—as if faith were a mystical plaster with the power to patch over all the yawning holes in their convictions.

Believing in free will, Richard instead chose the second way of dealing with such fear, which was to be watchful, alert, and ready to take responsibility for his own survival and life. At its core, that battle of belief between the cruel fates and free will was his essential disagreement with prophecy and why he discounted it. To choose to believe in fate was at once an admission of free will and at the same time an abdication of one's responsibility to it.

As he and Cara passed through the crooked wood, Richard kept a watchful eye out but he saw no legendary beasts or vengeful ghosts. Only the wind-borne snow wandered the wood.

Having traveled at a breakneck pace for so long in the oppressive heat and humidity of summer, they found that the encounter with bitter cold high up in the mountain pass made the effort of the climb all the more difficult, especially after being drenched by the miserable rain. Despite being fatigued from the altitude, Richard knew that, as wet as they were, they had to keep moving at a brisk pace to keep warm or the cold could easily overcome them. He was well aware that the seductive song of the cold could entice people to stop and lie down for a rest, luring them to surrender to sleep and the death that waited under its inviting cloak. As Zedd had once told him, dead was dead. Richard knew that he would be no less dead from the cold than he would be from an arrow.

More than that, though, he and Cara were both eager to put distance between them and the trap that had nearly captured him back at their camp. His burns from the brief contact with his would-be death trap had blistered. He shuddered to think of what had nearly happened.

At the same time, he was leery about going to see Shota in her lair at Agaden Reach. The last time he had been in the Reach she had told him that if he ever came back there she would kill him. Richard didn't doubt her word or her ability to carry out the threat. Even so, he believed Shota would be his best chance of getting the kind of help necessary to find Kahlan.

He was desperate to find someone who could tell him something useful, and after going through a list of things he might do, people he might go to, and in the end he couldn't come up with anyone else who could be as potentially informative as Shota. Nicci hadn't been able to offer any solutions. Zedd, he knew, might be able to help him in some ways, and maybe there were others with the capacity to be able to add some piece to the puzzle, but to Richard's mind, when all was said and done, none of them were as likely as Shota to be able to point him in the right direction. That alone made the choice simple.

When he glanced up, Richard briefly saw the snowcap through gaps in the driving snow. Some distance off, over the open, broken ground of the steep slope, the trail over the pass would skirt the lower reaches of the mountain's year-round icy mantle. The clouds, laden with moisture, clung to the soaring gray rock. The low trailers of mist and fog dragging past left visibility limited in most places and nearly nonexistent in others. It was just as well; the precipitous drop-offs in spots along the infrequently used and increasingly slippery trail offered frightening glimpses down the towering mountainside.

When a fresh flight of icy gusts carried curtains of wet snow into their faces, Richard pulled his cloak tight against the buffeting onslaught. Out of the cover of the trees, making their way across the loose scree, they had to lean not only into the steep incline, but into the wind. Richard hunched a shoulder, trying to keep the icy wet sting off his face. Wind-driven snow built a brittle crust on one side of his cloak.

With wind howling through the mountain pass, talking was difficult at best. The altitude and the exertion left them both winded and in no condition to be able to easily carry on a conversation. Just getting the air they needed was effort enough and he could tell by the look on Cara's face that she felt just as nauseated by the altitude as he did.

Richard wasn't in the mood to talk, anyway. He'd been talking to Cara for days and it never got him anywhere. Cara, for her part, seemed just as frustrated by his questions as he was by her answers. He knew that she thought his questions were absurd; he thought her answers were. The inconsistencies and gaps in Cara's recollection were at first disappointing and confounding but eventually they became maddening. Several times he'd had to bite his tongue and remind himself that she was not doing it to be malicious. He knew that if Cara could have honestly said what he wanted to hear she would have eagerly done so. He knew, too, that if she lied it would be of no help in getting Kahlan back. He needed the truth; that, after all, was why he was going to see Shota.

Richard had systematically gone through a long list of times when Cara had been with him and Kahlan. Cara, though, remembered events that should have been momentous to her in ways that were not consistent with what had really happened. In a number of cases, such as the time he had gone to the Temple of the Winds, Cara simply didn't recall key parts of the circumstances in which Kahlan had been involved. In other instances, Cara remembered events very differently from how they had actually happened.

Happened, at least, as Richard remembered them. There were depressing moments when he sank into a despondent fear that it was he who was for some reason the one with the problem. Cara thought that it was he who was remembering things that had never taken place. Although she didn't try to put too fine an edge to her convictions, the more things he brought up the more she thought his delusions about a fantasy wife were cropping up everywhere in his memory like weeds after a rain.

But Richard's clear memory of events and the way those events were knit tightly together always brought him back to the solid conviction that Kahlan was real.

Cara's memory about certain incidents was very clear and very different from his, while in regard to other things her memory was agonizingly fuzzy. That his story of situations was so different from her memory of those same situations only served, in Cara's mind, to further convince her that he was even more delusional than she had previously realized or feared. While that obviously saddened her, he'd continued to press her.

At his and Kahlan's wedding, Cara had been the only Mord-Sith in attendance. Richard knew that such an event had been significant to her in more ways than one, yet Cara remembered only that she'd gone with him to the Mud People's village. And why did they go there if not for the wedding? Cara said that she didn't know for certain why he'd gone there, but she was sure that he had his reasons; her duty was to go where he went and protect him, not to question his motive every time he turned around. Richard wanted to pull his hair out.

Cara didn't remember that she, Kahlan, and Richard had traveled together to the wedding site in the sliph. At the time Cara had been apprehensive about climbing down into the sliph's well and breathing in what appeared to be living quicksilver. Yet now she had no awareness that Kahlan had helped her overcome her anxiety about traveling within such a creature of magic. Cara remembered Zedd being there at the Mud People's village, and Shota making a brief appearance, but instead of the witch woman coming to offer Kahlan the necklace as a wedding gift and truce, Cara only recalled Shota being there to congratulate Richard on stopping the plague by going to the Temple of the Winds.

When Richard questioned Cara about Wizard Marlin, the assassin Jagang had sent, she clearly remembered him coming to kill Richard, but not any of the parts where Kahlan had been involved. When he asked how in the world she thought he could have even gotten to the Temple of the Winds in the first place, or how he had been cured of the plague, were it not for Kahlan's help, Cara only shrugged and said "Lord Rahl, you're a wizard, you know about such things—I don't. I'm sorry, but I can't tell you how you managed to accomplish astonishing things with your gift. I don't know how magic works. I only know that you did it. I only remember you doing what you had to do in order to make things work out—and they did, so I must be right. I could no more easily tell you how you healed me; I only know that you used your gift and you did it. You were the magic against magic, as is your duty to us. I simply don't recall this woman being any part of it. For your sake I wish I did, but I don't."

For every single instance where Kahlan had been present, Cara remembered it either differently or not at all. For every one of those events, she had an answer to explain it away with an alternate version or, when that would have been impossible, simply didn't recall what he was talking about. To Richard, there were a thousand little inconsistencies in her version that just didn't add up or make sense; to Cara's mind, it seemed not only simple and clear, but straightforward.

To say that it was exasperating trying to convince Cara of the reality of Kahlan's existence would not begin to touch the depth of his frustration.

Because it was pointless to continue to remember significant events in an effort to try to help her remember, when it never did any good, Richard had lost interest in trying to bring Cara around to reality. She simply didn't recall Kahlan. It seemed that her mind had healed over missing chunks of what had really happened.

Richard realized that there had to be an actual, rational cause, possibly some kind of spell or something, that was altering her memory—altering everyone's memory. He was coming to accept the fact that if that was the case, and it had to be, then there simply was no single event, or body of events, that he was going to be able to question her about that would bring back Cara's memory.

What was worse, he was realizing, was that such attempts to make her—or anyone else—remember were actually a dangerous distraction from the effort of finding Kahlan.

Richard glanced back to make sure that Cara was staying close to him on the steep mountainside. One didn't have to go far up in the jagged mountains ringing Agaden Reach to find a cliff to fall off of. With loose scree lurking beneath the coating of fresh snow it would be easy to lose their footing and tumble down the slope.

He didn't want to chance losing contact with Cara in the poor visibility. With the howl of the wind it would be hard to hear voices calling out if they became separated, and their tracks would be covered over in mere moments by the blowing, drifting snow. When he saw that Cara was within an arm's length, he pushed on ahead into the teeth of the wind.

As he went over it all in his mind, it occurred to him that by constantly trying to think of some incident that Cara, or those closest to him, would surely have to remember, he was falling into the trap of devoting his thoughts and efforts to the problem rather than the solution. Ever since he had been young, Zedd had cautioned him to keep his sights on the goal—to think of the solution—and not the problem.

Richard vowed to himself that he would keep his focus exclusively on the problem and disregard the distractions created by Kahlan's disappearance. Cara, Nicci, and Victor all had answers to explain away the inconsistencies. None of them remembered the things that Richard knew had happened. By dwelling on the specifics of what he had done with Kahlan, and going round and round with people over how it was impossible for them to have forgotten such important events, he was only letting the solution slip farther and farther away from him—letting Kahlan's life slip farther and farther away from him.

He needed to get a grip on his feelings, stop agonizing over the problem, and concentrate exclusively on the solution.

But setting his feelings aside was so difficult. It was almost like telling himself to forget Kahlan even as he looked for her. Memory had played a central part in his life with her. Going to see Shota only served to bring much of it back to him. He had met Shota for the first time when Kahlan had taken him to see the witch woman in order to ask for her help in finding the last missing box of Orden after Darken Rahl had put them in play.

Kahlan was inextricably tied to his life in so many ways. He had, in a manner of speaking, known her as a Confessor ever since he had been a boy, long before he met the woman herself that day in the Hartland woods.

When he had been a boy, George Cypher, the man who had raised him and who Richard had at the time thought was his father, had told him that he had rescued a secret book from great peril by bringing it to Westland. His father had told him that there was grave danger to everyone as long as the book existed, but he couldn't bring himself to destroy the knowledge in it. The only way to eliminate the danger of the book falling into the wrong hands and yet save the knowledge was to commit the book to memory and then burn the book itself. He chose Richard for the prodigious task of memorizing the entire book.

Richard's father took him to a secret place deep in the woods and, day after day, week after week, watched Richard sit reading the book over countless times as he worked to memorize it. His father never once looked in the book; that was Richard's responsibility.

After a long period of reading and memorizing, Richard began to write down what he'd memorized. He would then check it against the book. At first he made a lot of mistakes, but he continually improved. Each time, his father burned the papers. Richard repeated the task untold times. His father often apologized for the burden he was placing on Richard, but Richard never resented it; he considered it an honor to be entrusted by his father with such a great responsibility. Even though he was young and didn't understand all of what he read, he was able to grasp what a profoundly important work it was. He also realized that the book involved complex procedures having to do with magic. Real magic.

In time, Richard eventually wrote the book out from beginning to end a hundred times without error before he was satisfied that he could never forget a single word. He knew not only by the text of the book, but by its idiosyncratic syntax, that any word left out would spell disaster to the knowledge itself.

When he assured his father that the entirety of the work was committed to memory, they put the book back in the hiding place in the rocks and left it for three years. After that time, when Richard was beyond his middle teens, they returned one fall day and uncovered the ancient book. His father said that if Richard could write the whole book, without a single mistake, they could both be satisfied that it had been learned perfectly and they would together burn the book. Richard wrote without hesitation from the beginning to the final word. When he checked his work against the book, it confirmed what he already knew: He had not made a single mistake.

Together he and his father built a fire, stacking on more than enough wood, until the heat drove them back. His father handed him the book and told him that, if he was sure, he should throw the book into the fire. Richard held *The Book of Counted Shadows* in the crook of his arm, running his fingers over the thick leather cover. He held in his arms not just his father's trust, but the trust of everyone. Feeling the full weight of that responsibility, Richard cast the book into the fire. In that moment, he was no longer a child.

When the book burned it gave off not only heat but cold, and it released streamers of colored light and phantom forms. Richard knew that for the first time he had actually seen magic—not sleight of hand or the stuff of mysticism, but real magic that existed, real magic with its own laws of how it functioned just like everything else that existed. And some of those laws had been in the book he had memorized.

But in the beginning, that day in the woods, when he had been a boy and for the first time lifted open the cover, Richard had, in a way, met Kahlan. *The Book of Counted Shadows* began with the words *Verification of the truth of the words of The Book of Counted Shadows, if spoken by another, rather than read by the one who commands the boxes, can only be insured by the use of a Confessor. . . .*

Kahlan was the last Confessor.

The day he met her, Richard had been looking for clues to his father's murder. Darken Rahl had put the boxes of Orden in play and in order to open them he needed the information in *The Book of Counted Shadows.* He didn't know that by that time the information existed only in Richard's mind, and that to verify it he would need a Confessor: Kahlan.

In a way, Richard and Kahlan had been bound together by that book, and the events surrounding it, from the time Richard had first opened the cover and encountered the strange word "Confessor."

When he met Kahlan in the woods that day, it seemed to him that he had always known her. In a way, he had. In a way, she had played a part in his life, been a part of his thoughts, ever since he had been a boy.

The day he first saw her standing on a path in the Hartland woods, his life suddenly became whole, even though at the time he had not known that she was the last living Confessor. His choice to help her that day had been an act of free will carried out before prophecy had a chance to have its say.

Kahlan was so much a part of him, so much a part of what was the world to him, what was life to him, that he could not imagine going on without her. He had to find her. The time had come to go beyond the problem and seek the solution.

A gust of icy wind made him squint and brought him out of his memories.

"There," he said, pointing.

Cara paused behind him and peered over his shoulder into the swirling snow until she was able to make out the narrow pathway along the edge of the mountainside. When he glanced back she nodded, letting him know that she saw the path skirting the lower fringe of the snowcap.

With the blowing snow starting to pile up, the path had begun to drift over. Richard was eager to get through it and to lower ground. As they went farther, conditions deteriorated and the only way he could make out the path was by the lay of the land. The snow had a gentle curve to it as the mountainside rose up from below on the left. It leveled out with a slight dip where the path was, and then to the right humped up where the year-round snow rose higher up.

As they trudged through the ankle-deep snow, Richard glanced back over his shoulder. "This is the highest point. It will start going downhill soon and then it will get warmer."

"You mean we'll be back in the rain before we even have a chance to get down to lower altitudes and get warm," she grumbled. "That's what you're telling me."

Richard understood all too well her discomfort, but could offer no prospect of relief anytime soon.

"I guess so," he said.

Suddenly, something small and dark skittered down out of the white curtains of snow. Just as he saw it, and before he had a chance to react, it knocked Richard's feet right out from under him.

Richard saw the ground flash past his face as his legs flipped up in the air, then all he could see was white. For an instant he couldn't tell up from down or where he was in relation to anything else.

And then his full weight came crashing to the ground, the momentum pitching him down the slope. The snow offered little cushion. His breath was driven from his lungs. Rolling over and over he saw only brief glimpses of the ground. The world spun crazily. He couldn't control or stop what he quickly realized was his tumbling descent down an increasingly steep slope.

It had all happened so unexpectedly and so fast that Richard hadn't had much time to brace for the fall. At that moment, inattention seemed a poor excuse and no comfort. He bounced over a knob of hard ground and landed on his chest. With the wind knocked out of him, he tried to gasp a breath as he slid face-first down the mountain, but instead of air he got only a mouthful of icy snow.

With the force of the fall and the precipitous angle of the incline, there was nothing at hand to help stop him as he skidded with increasing speed down the steep incline. Heading downward face-first made it all the more difficult to take effective action. In a frantic attempt to stop or at least slow his fall, Richard spread his arms. He fought to dig his hands and feet into the snow and scree to slow his out of control plunge down the side of the mountain, but the snow and the scree only began to slide along with him.

He saw a shadow flash by. Over the sound of the wind he could hear wild screams of rage. Something solid slammed into the back of his ribs. He dug his fingers and boots deeper into the scree beneath the snow, trying to slow his frightening slide. With the snow billowing up around him as he slid, he couldn't seen anything but white.

The dark shape again came flying out of the the swirling snow. Again something hammered into him, only this time it was much harder and it was a direct blow to his kidneys meant to help accelerate his plunging fall.

Richard cried out with the shock of pain. As he twisted in distress onto his right side, he heard the unique ring of steel as the Sword of Truth was yanked from its scabbard.

As he slid down the slope, Richard twisted and reached for the sword as it was torn away from him. He knew that if he were to grab the razor-sharp blade itself it could easily slice his hand in two, so he tried instead to seize the hilt or at least snag the crossguard, but he was too late. The assailant dug in his heels to stop himself as Richard sailed out of sight.

Twisting awkwardly as he reached for his sword left Richard even more off balance. As he bounced over the uneven ground he was thrown into a headfirst roll.

In the middle of pitching over, just as he started spreading his arms and legs to stop the tumbling, if nothing else, his back slammed into a jut of rock under the snow. Again the wind was violently driven from him, only this time more painfully.

The force of the impact flipped him over the obstruction.

Tingling dread surged through him as he found himself in midair. With frantic effort, Richard reached out and snatched the rock outcropping he had hit. He held fast as his legs whipped out and over a drop-off.

Richard clutched the rock with frantic strength. For a moment, he clung to the rock, collecting his wits and gulping air. He had at least stopped falling. Snow and small flakes of scree still sliding down the steep slope bounced off the rock he was holding as well as his arms and head.

Carefully, he swung his legs all around, trying to catch them up onto something, trying to find some support for his weight. There was nothing. He swung helplessly, a living pendulum clutching a knob of icy rock.

He glanced over his shoulder and saw blowing snow and dark clouds scudding by underneath him. Through a brief gap, he spotted bits of scree in the midst of a long fall through the air toward trees and rock far below.

Above him, feet spread, stood a short, dark form with long arms, a pallid head, and gray skin. Bulging yellow eyes, like twin lanterns glowing out from the murky bluish light of the snowstorm, glared down at him. Bloodless lips curled back in a grin to expose sharp teeth.

It was Shota's companion, Samuel.

He was gripping Richard's sword in one hand and looked more than content with himself. Samuel wore a dark brown cloak that flapped like a flag of victory in the wind. He backed away a few paces, waiting to see Richard fall from the mountain.

Richard's fingers were slipping. He tried to get his arms around the rocks to climb up, or at least get a better hold. He wasn't successful. He knew, though, that if he did manage to get a better hold, Samuel stood ready to use the sword to insure that Richard fell.

With his feet dangling over a drop of at least a thousand feet, Richard was in a very precarious and vulnerable position. He could hardly believe that Samuel had gotten the better of him in such a way—and that he had managed to snatch Richard's sword. He surveyed the gloomy gray trailers of fog carried along with the blowing snow but he didn't see Cara.

"Samuel!" Richard screamed into the wind. "Give me back my sword!"

Even to himself, it seemed a pretty ridiculous demand.

"My sword," Samuel hissed.

"And what do you think Shota would say?"

The bloodless lips widened with his smile. "Mistress not here."

Like a wraith materializing out of the substance of the shadows themselves, a dark shape appeared behind Samuel. It was Cara, her dark cloak billowing in the wind, giving her the aspect of a vengeful spirit. Richard realized that she had probably followed his rolling trail down through the snow. What with the blustery wind in his ears and, more importantly, his gaze riveted on Richard's predicament, Samuel didn't notice Cara looming behind him.

In a single glance she took in the ominous sight of Samuel gripping Richard's sword, standing above Richard as he clung to the edge of the cliff. Richard had learned in the past that Samuel's attention and actions were pretty firmly ruled by his rampant emotions; his feet just followed. With the gleeful distraction of having the object of his rabid hatred at the point of a sword he'd once carried and to this day coveted, Samuel was too busy gloating to watch for the Mord-Sith showing up behind him.

Without a word, Cara unceremoniously rammed her Agiel into the base of Samuel's neck at the back of his skull. With the slippery conditions, she couldn't maintain the contact.

Samuel shrieked in pain and sudden, confused terror as he dropped the sword and toppled back into the snow. Writhing in agony, not understanding what had happened, he pawed frantically at the back of his neck where Cara had pressed her Agiel. He squealed as he flopped in the snow like a fish in sand. Richard knew that the horrifying shock of pain from an Agiel when applied in that spot felt like a lightning strike.

Richard recognized the look on Cara's face as she started to lean over the squirming figure. She intended to used her Agiel to finish Samuel.

Richard wouldn't really care if she killed the treacherous companion to the witch woman, but he had far more urgent problems right then.

"Cara! I'm hanging on the edge of a cliff. I can't hold on. I'm slipping."

She immediately snatched up the sword from beside a thrashing Samuel so that he couldn't get at it as she ran to help Richard. Stabbing the blade in the ground beside herself, she dropped down, braced her boots against the rocks, and seized his arms. She had not been an instant too soon.

With her help, Richard was able to get a better grip on the rocks. With both of them struggling in the difficult conditions, he at last managed to hook his arm over the outcropping. Once he had a firm hold with an arm he was finally able to swing a leg up and hook it over the rocks. Cara grabbed his belt and helped haul him up. Straining with effort, he dragged himself up and over the slippery outcropping.

Richard sagged over onto his side, gasping, trying to get enough of the thin air. "Thanks," he managed.

Cara glanced back over her shoulder, keeping an eye on Samuel. Richard quickly gathered his strength and staggered back to his feet. As soon as he had his footing at the brink of the cliff, he pulled up his sword from where Cara had stuck it in the ground.

He could hardly believe that Samuel had managed to catch him off guard that way. Ever since Richard and Cara had left their camp that morning, he'd been watching for Samuel to show up unexpectedly. He knew, though, that despite expecting such an attack, it was impossible to forestall it every moment—much as it had been impossible to stop every arrow that morning that Kahlan had disappeared.

Richard brushed some of the snow off his face. The tumbling fall, the sudden plunge, and hanging by his fingers over a cliff had left him shaken but, more than anything, angry.

Samuel, still lying crumpled in the snow, wriggling and squirming, puled to himself, mumbling something Richard couldn't hear over the sound of the wind.

When Samuel saw Richard stalking toward him, he scrambled awkwardly to his feet, still suffering from the lingering pain. Despite that pain, though, he saw what he wanted.

"Mine! Gimme! Gimme my sword!"

Richard lifted the point toward the disgusting little fellow.

Seeing the point of the blade approaching, Samuel lost his courage and scuttled a few steps backward up the slope. "Please," he whined, holding his hands out to ward Richard's wrath, "no kill me?"

"What are you doing here?"

"Mistress sends me."

"Shota sent you to kill me, did she?" Richard mocked. He wanted Samuel to admit the truth.

Samuel vigorously shook his head. "No, not to kill you."

"So then that was all your idea."

Samuel didn't answer.

"Why, then?" Richard pressed. "Why did Shota send you?"

Samuel eyed Cara as she moved to the side, halfway hemming him in. Samuel hissed at her, showing his teeth. Cara, unimpressed, showed him her Agiel. His eyes grew big with fear.

"Samuel!" Richard yelled.

Samuel's yellow eyes turned back to Richard and they again turned hateful.

"Why did Shota send you?"

"Mistress . . ." he whimpered as his anger flagged. He stared off longingly in the direction of Agaden Reach. "She sends companion."

"Why!"

Samuel flinched when Richard yelled and took an aggressive stride forward.

Samuel, trying to keep watch on both of them, pointed a long finger at Cara. "Mistress say for you to bring pretty lady."

This was a surprise—for two reasons. "Pretty lady" was what Samuel had always called Kahlan.

Secondly, Richard would never have expected that Shota would want Cara to come down into Agaden Reach with him. He found that somehow troubling.

"Why does she want the pretty lady to come with me?"

"Don't know." Samuel's bloodless lips pulled back in a grin. "Maybe to kill her."

Cara waggled her Agiel for him to see. "If she tries, maybe she will get a lot more than you got. Maybe I'll kill her, instead."

Samuel squealed in horror, his bulging eyes going wide. "No! No kill mistress!"

"We didn't come to harm Shota," Richard told him. "But we will defend ourselves."

Samuel pressed his knuckles to the ground as he leaned toward Richard. "We will see," he growled with contempt, "what mistress does with you, Seeker."

Before Richard could answer, Samuel suddenly darted off into the swirling snow. It was surprising how fast he could move.

Cara started after him, but Richard caught her arm to stop her.

"I'm in no mood to go running after him," he said. "Besides, it's unlikely we'll catch him. He knows the trail and we aren't familiar with it. We can't follow his tracks as fast as he can make them. Besides, he will be heading back to Shota and that's where we're going anyway. No use to waste our energy when we'll catch up with him in the end."

"You should have let me kill him."

Richard started up the slope toward the trail. "I would have, but I can't fly."

"I suppose," she conceded with a sigh. "Are you all right?"

Richard nodded as he slid the sword home into its scabbard, putting away, too, the flush of hot anger. "Thanks to you."

Cara flashed him a self-satisfied smile. "I keep telling you, you couldn't get along without me." She glanced around in the gray-blue murk. "What if he tries that again?"

"Samuel is basically a coward and an opportunist. He only attacks when he thinks you're helpless. He is without any redeeming qualities as far as I can tell."

"Why would a witch woman keep him around?"

"I don't know. Maybe he's just a sycophant and she enjoys the groveling. Maybe she lets him stay around to run errands for her. Maybe Samuel is the only one who would willingly be her companion. Most people are terrified of Shota and from what I hear no one will come near this place.

Although, from what Kahlan told me, witch women can't help bewitching people—it's just the way they are. Even if they didn't, Shota is certainly seductive in her own right so I imagine that if she really wanted a worthwhile companion, she could have her pick.

"Now that we've driven him off, I really doubt that Samuel would have the courage to attack again. He's delivered Shota's message. Now that we've scared him, and hurt him, he will probably want to run back to Shota's protection. Besides, he probably thinks she may kill us and he'd be just as happy to have her do it."

Cara stared off into the swirling snow for a moment before following Richard up the steep slope. "Why do you think Shota would send a messenger to make sure that I come with you down into Agaden Reach?"

Richard found the trail and started down it. He saw Samuel's footprints but they were already filling in with the blowing snow.

"I don't know. That part has me puzzled."

"And why does Samuel think that your sword belongs to him?"

Richard slowly let out a deep breath. "Samuel carried the sword before me. He was the last Seeker before me—although not a legitimately named Seeker. I don't know how he acquired the Sword of Truth. Zedd came into Agaden Reach and took it back. Samuel believes that the sword still belongs to him."

Cara looked incredulous. "*He* was the last Seeker?"

Richard cast her a meaningful look. "He didn't have the magic, the temperament, or the character required by the sword to be the true Seeker of Truth. Because he wasn't able to be the master of the sword's power, that power changed him into what you see today."

With one finger, Richard swiped the sweat and drizzle from his brow. Little light penetrated the gloom at the lower stories of the swamp, but even without the sun beating down on them the steamy heat was oppressive. After coming down from the storm raging up in the mountain pass, Richard didn't mind the heat so much as he otherwise might have. Cara wasn't complaining, either, but then she rarely did about her own discomfort. As long as she was near him she was satisfied, although whenever he did anything she considered risky, it did tend to make her ill-tempered, which explained her irritable disposition about going to see Shota.

Here and there in the mud and soft ground of the forest floor, Richard saw fresh footprints left by Samuel. It was clear to Richard that Shota's companion had been eager to get back to her protection and had hurried along the trail at a constant lope. Cara, too, saw the tracks. Richard had been impressed when she had pointed them out when she'd first spotted them. She had been more observant of tracks ever since the day Kahlan had disappeared and Richard had shown her, Nicci, and Victor some of the kinds of things that tracks revealed.

Even though Samuel's tracks made it clear that he had been rushing and it didn't look like he intended to try to jump them again, Richard and Cara still kept careful watch in case he, or anything else, were to be lurking in the shadows. The swamp was, after all, a place meant to keep intruders away. Richard wasn't sure just what waited back under cover of leaf and shadow, but people in the Midlands, including wizards, didn't fear to come into Shota's sanctuary without sound reason.

It was no longer raining, but as foggy and humid as it was it might as well have been. The forest canopy collected the mist and drizzle, releasing it as sporadic, fat drops. Broad leaves on long arching stalks sprouting up from the tangled growth at the forest floor and vines twisting through the branches of trees all around bobbed under the assault of those heavy drops, giving the whole forest a constant, nodding movement in the still air.

The trees in the swamp grew in gnarled, twisted shapes, as if tormented by the load of vines and curtains of moss that hung limp and heavy from their branches in the mist. Crusty lichen and in places black slime grew on the bark. Here and there, in the distance, Richard spotted birds perched on the branches, watching.

Vapor hovered just above the surface of stagnant expanses of murky water runoff collected in the lap of the mountains. At the water's edge tangles of roots snaked down into the depths. Things moved through the dark pools, lifting the film of duckweed on the slow rolling waves. From the shadows back across the water, eyes watched.

All around the cacophonous calls of birds rang though the damp air while Richard and Cara had to swish at the bugs buzzing around them. Other animals back in the mist let out whoops and whistles. At the same time, the thick, still vegetation and the oppressive, muggy, weight of the air lent the place a kind of uneasy stillness. Richard saw Cara wrinkle her nose at the pervasive, rotting stench.

The path through the dense growth almost seemed more like a living, growing tunnel. Richard was glad they didn't have to venture off the trail and back into the surrounding quagmire. He could imagine all too well claws and fangs waiting patiently for dinner to happen by.

When they reached the brink of the gloomy swamp, Richard paused in the deep shadows. Peering out of the dark tangle of branches, hanging moss, and clinging green growth was like looking out from a cave at a glorious new day beyond. Despite the drizzle and mist up in the swamp, the late-day sun had broken through the cloud cover in places to cast golden shafts of sunlight on the distant valley, as if were a jewel on display.

Around the verdant valley the rocky gray walls of the surrounding mountains ascended almost straight up into a dark rim of clouds. As far as Richard knew, there was no way into Shota's home but through the swamp. The valley floor below was spread with a rolling carpet of grasses dotted with wildflowers. Stands of oak, maple, and beech mottled some of the hills and congregated in low places along the stream, their leaves shimmering in the late light.

In the dark forest where Richard and Cara stood, it felt like standing in night, looking out on day. Not far off through the vines and brush, water tumbled off the craggy rock at the edge of the swamp to disappear into vertical columns of mist on its way down to the clear pools and streams far below where it made a distant roar that, at their height, sounded like little more than a hiss. That spray and mist wet their faces as they gazed off the edge of the cliff.

Richard led Cara through a narrow path off the main trail that simply ended at the cliff. The small side track would be nearly impossible to find had he not known where to look for it from his previous visit. It passed through a maze of boulders nearly hidden beneath a layer of pale green ferns. Vines, moss, and brush also helped conceal the obscure route.

At the edge they finally began the descent. The trail down into the valley in large part was made up of steps, thousands of them, cut from the stone of the cliff wall itself. Those steps twisted and tunneled and turned ever downward, following the natural shape of the tiers of rock, sometimes following around soaring natural stone columns, only to spiral back on themselves to pass underneath the pathway bridging above.

The view on the way down the side of the cliff was spectacular. The streams carrying mountain runoff meandering through gentle hills were as beautiful as any Richard had ever seen. The trees, in places gathered into bands and in other spots standing alone as a single monarch atop a hill, were as calm and inviting a sight as he could hope for.

In the distant center of the valley, set among a carpet of grand trees, was a beautiful palace of breathtaking grace and splendor. Delicate spires stretched into the air, wispy bridges spanned the high gaps between towers, and stairs spiraled around turrets. Colorful flags and streamers flew atop every point. If a majestic palace could be said to look feminine, this one did. It seemed a fitting place for a woman like Shota.

Other than his home of Hartland and the mountains to the west of there, where he had taken Kahlan to recover over the span of a magical summer, Richard had never seen another place to compare to this valley. That alone had given him pause in his judgment about Shota before he'd met her for the first time. Passing through the swamp back then, he had thought it a fitting place for a witch to live. When he had been told that the valley was actually her home, he had thought that, surely, someone who could call such a peaceful, beautiful place home had to have some good qualities. Later, when he had seen the beauty of the People's Palace, Darken Rahl's home, he came to discount such indulgent notions.

At the bottom of the cliff beside the waterfall a road led off through grassy fields to wind its way among the small hills. Before they took to the road, though, Cara asked if they could take the opportunity for a quick dip to get clean.

Richard thought it sounded like a good idea, so he stopped and took off his pack. Most importantly, he wanted to wash the painful burns so they would have a better chance to heal. He was drenched in sweat and filth and imagined that he must look like a beggar.

Kahlan had told him once that it was important to convey the proper impression to people. She had wanted him to come up with something better than his woods-guide attire. At the time, she had been trying to tell him that if he expected people to believe in him and follow him, if he was to be the Lord Rahl and command the D'Haran Empire, he had to look the part.

Appearance, after all, was a reflection of what a person thought of themselves and therefore, by extension, of others. A person crippled by self-loathing or self-doubt reflected those feelings in their appearance. Such visual clues did not inspire confidence in others because, and while not always completely accurate, for the most part they did reflect the inner person—whether or not that person realized it.

No self-respecting bird in good health would allow its feathers to look ruffled. No confident cougar would let its fur long remain matted and dirty. A statue meant to represent the nobility of man did not convey that concept by portraying him disheveled and dirty.

Richard had understood Kahlan's point, and, in fact, had already begun to see to it before she mentioned it. He had found most of an outfit from a former war wizard up in the Wizard's Keep. He used the important elements of that outfit and had some other things made. He didn't know how it impressed other people, but he remembered quite clearly how it had impressed Kahlan.

Richard went around the rocks at the bottom of the waterfall to find a private place for a quick wash while Cara picked another spot for herself. She promised that she wouldn't be long.

The water felt soothing, but Richard didn't want to waste any time. He had a lot more important matters on his mind. Once rinsed clean of sweat and grime and after cleaning the burns, he put on his war wizard's outfit, which he had pulled from his pack. He thought that today, of all days, would be the proper day to appear to Shota as a leader come to speak with her, rather than a helpless beggar.

Over black trousers and a black, sleeveless shirt, he put on his black, open-sided tunic, decorated with symbols snaking along a wide gold band running all the way around its squared edges. A wide, multilayered leather belt bearing a number of silver emblems in ancient designs held a gold-worked pouch to each side and cinched the tunic at his waist. Pins on the leather lashing around the tops of his black boots also carried those symbols. He carefully placed the ancient, tooled-leather baldric holding the polished gold- and silver-wrought scabbard over his right shoulder and attached the Sword of Truth at his left hip.

While to most people the Sword of Truth was an awesome weapon, and it certainly was that, it was much more to Richard. His grandfather, Zedd, in his capacity as First Wizard, had given the sword to Richard, naming him Seeker. In many ways that trust was much the same as his father's trust had been in asking him to memorize the book. It had taken Richard a long time to come to fully understand all that the trust and responsibility of carrying the Sword of Truth meant.

As a formidable weapon, the sword had saved his life countless times. But it had not saved his life because it came with redoubtable power, or because it was capable of remarkable feats. It had saved his life because it had helped him learn things not just about himself, but about life.

To be sure, the Sword of Truth had taught him about fighting, about the dance with death, and how to prevail against seemingly impossible odds. And while it had helped him when he had to carry out that most terrible of all acts—killing—it had also helped him learn when forgiveness was justified. In those ways it had helped him come to understand what values were important in helping to advance the cause of life itself. And it had helped him learn the importance and necessity of judging those values, and of how to put each in context.

In some ways, like the way that learning *The Book of Counted Shadows* had taught him that he was no longer a child, the sword had helped him learn to be a part of the wider world, and his place in it.

It had, in a way, also brought him Kahlan.

And Kahlan was why he needed to see Shota.

Richard closed the flap on his pack. There was a cape, looking like it had been spun from gold, that he'd found with the rest of the war wizard's outfit up in the Keep, but, since it was such a warm day, he left that in the pack. Finally, on each wrist he put on a wide, leather-padded silver band bearing linked rings encompassing more of the ancient symbols. Among other things, those ancient bands were used to call the sliph from her sleep.

When Cara called out that she was ready, Richard lifted his pack and made his way around the rocks. He saw, then, why she had wanted to stop. She had done more than simply take a quick bath.

She had put on her red leather outfit.

Richard cast a meaningful glance at the Mord-Sith's bloodred uniform. "Shota may be sorry she invited you to the party."

Cara's smile said that if there was any trouble, she would see to it.

As they started down the road, Richard said, "I don't know exactly what powers Shota has, but I think that maybe you should try something today that you have never tried before."

Cara frowned. "What would that be?"

"Caution."

Richard scanned the surrounding hills, watching for any sign of danger, as he and Cara entered a place where the magnificent beech and maple trees had grown clustered together at the top of a rise. The straight, tall trunks forked ever wider in gentle, ascending arcs, giving Richard the sense of massive columns holding up the vaulted ceiling of a great, green cathedral. The fragrance of wildflowers drifted in on a gentle breeze. Through the canopy of rustling leaves he could get tantalizing glimpses of the soaring spires of Shota's palace.

Streamers of golden sunlight flickered through the leaves and cavorted around on the low grass. Water from a spring burbled up through an opening in a low boulder and ran down its smooth sides into a shallow, meandering stream. Spread through the stream were rocks covered with a coat of fuzzy green moss.

A woman with a thick mane of blond hair and wearing a long black dress sat in the dappled sunlight on a rock beside the stream, leaning on one graceful arm as she ran her fingers through the clear water. She seemed to glow. The very air around her seemed to glow.

Even with her back to him, she looked all too familiar.

Cara leaned toward Richard and spoke in a confidential tone. "Is that Nicci?"

"In a way I wish it were, but it isn't."

"Are you sure?"

Richard nodded. "I've seen Shota do this before. The first time I ever saw her, in that exact same place, she appeared to me as my deceased mother."

Cara glanced over at him. "That's a rather cruel deception."

"She said that it was a gift, a kindness, meant only to briefly bring a cherished memory to life."

Cara huffed skeptically. "So why would she be trying to make you remember Nicci?"

Richard looked over at Cara, but didn't have an answer for her.

When they finally reached the rock, the woman gracefully rose and turned to him. Blue eyes he knew met his gaze.

"Richard," the woman who looked like Nicci said. Her voice had the exact same silken quality as Nicci's. The low neckline of the laced bodice seemed to Richard to be cut even lower than he recalled. "I'm so pleased to see you again." She rested her wrists on his shoulders, casually locking her fingers together behind his head. The air around her seemed filmy, giving her a soft, blurred, surreal appearance. "So very pleased," she added with breathless affection.

She could not have looked or sounded any more like Nicci if it had been Nicci herself. The illusion was so convincing that Cara stood with her jaw hanging. Richard almost felt a sense of relief at seeing Nicci again.

Almost.

"Shota, I've come to talk with you."

"Talk is for lovers," she said, a coy smile seeping through her exquisite features.

She slipped her fingers into the hair at the back of his head as her soft smile warmed affectionately. Her eyes, joining in her smile, reflected her delight at seeing him. She seemed at that moment more pleased, more quietly satisfied, more at peace than he had ever seen Nicci look. She also looked so much like Nicci that he was having trouble convincing himself to keep in mind that it was Shota. If nothing else, she acted far more in character with Shota than with Nicci. Nicci would never be so forward. It had to be Shota.

She gently pulled him closer. At that moment, Richard had trouble trying to think of a reason to resist. None came presently to mind. He couldn't stop gazing into her alluring eyes. He felt himself being swept away with the simple pleasure of gazing at Nicci's entrancing face.

"And if that is your offer, Richard, then I accept."

She had drifted so close to him that he could feel the sweet breath of her words on his face. Her eyes closed. Her soft lips met his in a slow, luxurious kiss that he did not return. Nonetheless, he didn't force her away, either.

As her arms drew him tighter into the embrace, into the kiss, it seemed to scramble his thinking and completely immobilize him. Even more than the kiss, that embrace awakened a terrible longing for the comfort of steadfast support, sheltering devotion, and tender acceptance. More than anything, the promise of that long-absent solace was what disarmed him.

He could feel every inch, every curve, every rise and fall of her firm body pressing against his. He knew that he was trying to think of something other than that kiss, that embrace, that body, but he couldn't for the life of him remember what it was. In fact, he was having a great deal of difficulty making himself think at all.

It was because of that kiss. It was a kiss that made him forget who he was, or why he was there, even though, oddly enough, it didn't seem to be a kiss that necessarily promised love, or even lust. He wasn't sure what it promised. It almost seemed to be conditional.

One thing he did know was that it was very different from the kiss Nicci had given him back in the stable in Altur'Rang just before he'd left. That kiss had carried the extraordinary pleasure and serenity of magic, if not other things. The real Nicci had been behind that kiss. Despite the visual illusion, this was not Nicci. This was a kiss that seemed irresistible, as a great weight might be irresistible, but not really all that . . . erotic. Even so, it threatened to tangle him up in its cautious questions and silent promises.

"Nicci—or Shota—or whoever you are," Cara growled through clenched teeth, fists at her sides, "just what do you think you're doing?"

She pulled away, turning her head slightly, her cheek resting against Richard's, to gaze curiously at Cara. Delicate fingers idly twined their way through the hair at the back of his head. Richard's mind was reeling.

Cara backed away a bit as Shota-in-Nicci's-skin, with her other hand, tenderly cupped the Mord-Sith's chin.

"Why, nothing more than what you want."

Cara backed another step so that her face would be out of range of the comforting hand. "What?"

"This is what you want, isn't it? I would think that you would be grateful that I'm helping you with your grand plan."

Cara planted her fists on her hips. "I don't know what in the world you're talking about."

"Why so angry?" The smile turned sly. "I didn't come up with this. You did. This is your plan—the one you hatched all by yourself. I'm simply helping you bring it to life."

"What makes you think . . . ?" Cara seemed to run out of words.

The blue-eyed gaze that looked so much like Nicci's slid to Richard. The smile returned as she studied his features from only inches away.

"This young woman is such a dear friend and loyal protector. Has your dear friend and loyal protector told you what she has all planned out for you, Richard?" She touched his nose. "Such plans, they are, too. She has the rest of your life all thought out and arranged for you. You really should ask her sometime what she is plotting for you."

Cara's face suddenly went slack with understanding and then it went crimson.

Richard grasped Shota by the shoulders and eased her back, forcing her hand to slip off his shoulder. At the same time he renewed his efforts to regain control of himself.

"You've already said it—Cara is my friend. I do not fear what she may want for my life. You see, despite what friends and loved ones want for me, or hope I will achieve, it's my life and I decide what I will try to make of it. People can plan or hope all they want for those they care about, but in the end it is each individual who must take responsibility for their own life and make the choice for themselves."

Her wide smile showed her teeth. "How deliciously innocent you are to think such things." Her fingers combed back his hair. "I would strongly advise you to ask her what she is plotting to do with your heart."

Richard glanced to Cara. She looked at the same time on the verge of both exploding in rage and fleeing in panic. Instead of either she stood her ground and kept quiet. Richard didn't know what Shota was talking about, but he did know that this was not the time or place to find out. He couldn't allow Shota to lead him away from his purpose.

He also noticed that Cara had a white-knuckled fist around her Agiel.

"Shota, enough of this charade. Cara's wishes and intentions are my concern, not yours."

Nicci smiled sadly. "So you think, Richard. So you think."

The hazy air around the woman shimmered and Nicci was no longer Nicci, but Shota. She was no longer a dreamy phantasm, but a clear vision. Her hair, instead of blond, was just as thick but a wavy auburn. Her black dress had changed into a wispy, variegated gray, layered affair, cut just as low, with loose points that lifted ever so slightly in the breeze. She was every bit as beautiful as the valley around her.

As Shota turned her attention to Cara, her expression tightened danger-ously. "You hurt Samuel."

"I'm sorry." Cara said with a shrug. "I didn't mean to hurt him."

Shota arched an eyebrow over her threatening glare, as if to say she didn't believe a word of it.

"I meant to kill him," Cara said.

Shota's anger melted away. An incandescent smile accompanied a gen-uine, if brief, laugh. She regarded Richard with a sidelong glance, the smile still on her lips.

"I like her. You can keep her."

Richard recalled that Cara had once made that very same pronounce-ment to him about Kahlan.

"Shota, I told you, I have to talk to you."

Her bright, clear almond eyes took him in with a sense of wonder. "So you have come offering to be my lover?"

Richard noticed Samuel off through the trees, watching, his yellow eyes glowing with hatred.

"You know I haven't."

"Ah." Her smile returned. "What you mean to say, then, is that you have come because you want something from me." She caught one of the float-ing points of her dress. "Isn't that right, Richard?"

Richard had to remind himself to stop staring into her ageless eyes. But it was so hard to make himself glance away. It was as if Shota controlled where his gaze rested and he was having trouble keeping it resting in proper places.

Kahlan had told him once that Shota had been bewitching him. Kahlan said that Shota couldn't help it, it was just what witch women did. It came naturally to them.

Kahlan.

That thought of her again jolted his mind.

"Kahlan is missing."

Shota's brow wrinkled ever so slightly. "Who?"

Richard sighed. "Look, something terrible is going on. Kahlan, my wife—"

"Wife! Since when did you take a wife?"

Her expression curdled into a heated glare. By the sudden anger power-ing her features and the way her cleavage heaved at the brink of the low-cut dress, Richard knew that she was not feigning surprise. She truly didn't remember Kahlan.

Richard ran his own fingers back through his hair as he gathered his thoughts and started again.

"Shota, you've met Kahlan several times. You know her quite well. Something has happened to erase everyone's memory of her. No one remembers her, you included, and—"

"Except you?" she said with incredulity. "You alone remember her?"

"It's a long story."

"Length won't make it true."

"It is true," Richard insisted. He gestured heatedly. "You were at our wedding."

She folded her arms. "I don't think so."

"The first time I came here, you had captured Kahlan and had covered her in snakes—"

"Snakes." Shota smiled. "You're saying I liked this woman and are suggesting that I treated her indulgently?"

"Not exactly. You wanted her dead."

The smile widened. She returned her wrists to his shoulders. "Now, Richard, that's awfully harsh, don't you think?"

Richard grasped her by the waist and gently moved her back. He knew that if he didn't stop her she would soon hamper his ability to think.

"I certainly thought so," he said. "Among other things, you didn't want us to wed."

Shota ran a red lacquered nail down his chest. She looked up at him from under her brow.

"Well, maybe I had my reasons."

"Yes—you didn't want us to bring a child into the world. You said we would be creating a monster because from me it would have the gift and from Kahlan it would be a Confessor."

"Confessor!" Shota took a step back as if he had turned poisonous. "A Confessor? Are you out of your mind?"

"Shota—"

"There aren't any more Confessors. They're all dead."

"That's not quite accurate. All of them are dead except Kahlan."

She turned to Cara. "Has he had a fever or something?"

"Well . . . he was shot with an arrow. He nearly died. Nicci healed him but he was still unconscious for days."

Shota suspiciously held up a finger as if she had uncovered a devious plot. "Don't tell me—she used Subtractive Magic."

"Yes, she did," Richard answered in Cara's place. "And because she did she was able to save my life."

Shota took back the step she had put between them when she had retreated. "Used Subtractive Magic . . ." Shota muttered to herself. She looked up at him again. "How did she use it—for what purpose?"

"She used it to eliminate the barbed arrow embedded in me."

Shota rolled a hand, wanting him to continue. "She must have done something more."

"She used Subtractive Magic to purge all the blood pooling in my chest. She said that there was no other way to get either the arrow or the blood out of me and either would kill me if left in."

Shota turned her back to them and, one hand on a hip, walked off a few paces as she considered the brief account.

"That explains a great many things," she said unhappily under her breath.

"You gave Kahlan a necklace," Richard said.

Shota frowned back over her shoulder. "A necklace? What sort of necklace would I give her? And why, my dear boy, do you imagine I would ever do such a thing for your . . . lover?"

"Wife," Richard corrected. "You and Kahlan had spent time together— by yourselves—and had come to an understanding of sorts. You gave the necklace to Kahlan as a gift so that she and I could . . . well, be together. It had some kind of power so that we wouldn't conceive children. While I don't agree with your view of future events, right now, what with the war and all, we decided to accept your gift and the truce that went with it."

"I can't imagine how you could possibly imagine that I would do any of those things." Shota looked to Cara again. "Did he have a bad fever on top of the injury?"

Richard might have thought that Shota was being sarcastic, but he could see by the look on her face that she was asking a serious question.

"Not exactly a bad fever," Cara said, hesitantly. "It was a slight fever. Nicci said, though, that his problem was partly with how close he came to death but mostly had to do with the extended time that he was unconscious." Cara sounded rather reluctant to speak about it to a person she considered a potential threat, but she at last finished her answer. "She said that he was suffering from delirium."

Shota folded her arms as she heaved a sigh while taking him in with her almond eyes. "What am I to do with you," she murmured half to herself.

"The last time I was here," Richard said, "you told me that if I ever came back into Agaden Reach you would kill me."

She showed no reaction. "Did I, now. And why would I say such a thing?"

"I guess you were rather angry with me for refusing to kill Kahlan and for refusing to allow you to do it." He pointed with his chin back up toward the mountain pass. "I thought you might have meant to keep your word and so you sent Samuel to fulfill your threat."

Shota glanced to her companion off through the trees. He looked suddenly alarmed.

"What are you talking about?" She asked with a frown as she looked back at Richard.

"Are you now claiming you didn't know?"

"Know what?"

Richard briefly considered the angry yellow eyes glaring at him.

"Samuel hid up in the pass and jumped me from out of the storm. He snatched my sword and kicked me over a cliff. I just managed to catch the edge. If Cara wouldn't have been there, Samuel would have used the sword to see to it that I fell from the cliff. He very nearly killed me. That he didn't wasn't because he didn't intend to or try his best."

Shota's glare glided to the dark figure crouched off in the trees. "Is that true?"

Samuel could not bear her scrutiny. Puling with self-pity, his gaze sank to the ground. That was answer enough.

"We will discuss this later," she told him in a low voice that carried unequivocally through the trees and gave Richard goose bumps.

"That was not my intention, Richard, nor my orders, I can assure you. I told Samuel only to invite your devious little guardian to come along."

"You know what, Shota? I'm getting pretty tired of Samuel trying to kill me and you then claiming that you never gave him any such instructions. Once might have been credible, but it's growing too routine. Your innocent surprise every time it happens is beginning to strike me as rather convenient. It appears to me that you find deniability quite useful and so you stick to it."

"That isn't true, Richard," Shota said in a measured tone. She unfolded her arms and clasped her hands as she looked at the ground at her feet. "You carry his sword. Samuel is a little touchy about that. Since it was taken from him, not given freely, that means it still belongs to him."

Richard nearly objected, but then reminded himself that he wasn't there to argue the point.

Shota's gaze rose to meet his. It came up angry.

"And how dare you complain to me about what Samuel does without my knowledge when you knowingly bring a deadly menace into the peace of my home?"

Richard was taken aback. "What are you talking about?"

"Don't play stupid, Richard, it doesn't fit you. You are hunted by a wildly dangerous threat. How many people have already died because they were unfortunate enough to be near you when the beast came looking for you. What if it decides to come here to kill you? You come here and in so doing cavalierly risk my life, without my permission, simply because you happen to want something?

"Do you think it's right that I'm put at risk of death because of your wants? Does the fact that you think I have something you need put my life at your disposal and therefore at great risk?"

"Of course not." Richard swallowed. "I never looked at it that way."

Shota threw her hands up. "Ah, so your excuse is that I am to be put in peril because you didn't think."

"I need your help."

"You mean you have come as a helpless beggar, begging for help, without regard to the danger it puts me in, simply because you want something."

Richard rubbed a fingertips across his forehead. "Look, I don't have all the answers, but I can tell you that I have good reason to believe that I'm right, that Kahlan exists and she has disappeared."

"Like I said, you want something and you don't bother to consider the risk to anyone else."

Richard took a step closer to her. "That isn't true. Don't you see? You don't remember Kahlan. No one but me does. Think, Shota, think of what it means if I'm right."

Her brow twitched as she puzzled at him. "What are you talking about?"

"If I'm right, then there is something gravely wrong in the world that's making everyone—including you—forget her. She has been wiped from your mind. But it's more serious than that. It's not just Kahlan that is missing from everyone's mind. Everything that you or anyone else ever did with her is also missing. Some of those missing bits may be trivial, but other parts of it very well could be vital.

"You don't remember that you said you would kill me if I ever came back here. That means that when you said that, in your mind that threat had to be somehow connected to Kahlan. She contributed to your choice to make that threat. Now, since you don't remember Kahlan, you also don't recall saying that to me.

"What if there's something vastly important that you've likewise forgotten. Because you've forgotten Kahlan, you've lost part of what you've done in your own life—lost some of the decisions you've made. How many ways do you have a connection with Kahlan that you are completely unaware of that are now wiped away? How important are those missing bits? How much of your life has been altered because you now don't recall the changes in your thinking that you made because of her influence?

"Shota, don't you see the magnitude of the problem? Can't you fathom how this has the potential to change everyone's perception? If everyone forgets how Kahlan changed their individual lives, they will act without the benefit of the shifts they made in their thinking."

Richard paced, one hand on a hip, gesturing with the other. "Think of someone you know." He turned back to her, meeting her gaze. "Think of your mother. Now, just try to imagine all that you would lose if you lost every memory of her and everything she taught you, every one of your decisions in which she had an influence, both directly and indirectly.

"Now, imagine everyone forgetting someone important like your mother was to you—but imagine them being central to events important to everyone. Imagine for a moment how your life—your thinking—would be altered if you forgot that I exist and you no longer recalled the things you've done with me, the things you've done because of me. Can you begin to see the significance?

"You gave Kahlan that necklace as a wedding gift to both of us to prevent her from conceiving—at least for now. It was a gift that was more than that, though. It was a truce. It was peace between you and me as much as between you and Kahlan. What other truces, alliances, and oaths have been made because of Kahlan that, like the necklace, are now forgotten? How many important missions will be abandoned?

"Don't you see? This holds the potential to throw the world into turmoil. I have no idea of the possible effects of such a wide-ranging event, but for all I know it could alter the complexion of the fight for freedom. It could usher in the dawn of the Imperial Order. For all I know, it could usher in the end of life itself."

Shota looked astonished. "Life itself?"

"Something this significant does not happen randomly. It's not an unfortunate accident or some casual mistake. There has to be a cause, and anything that could cause a universal event of this enormity carries sinister implications."

For a time, Shota regarded him with an unreadable expression. She finally caught a floating corner of the layered material that made up her dress and turned away as she thought about his words. Finally she turned back.

"And what if you are simply suffering from a delusion? Since that is the simplest explanation, that makes it most likely the true answer."

"While the simplest explanation is usually the true answer, it is not infallibly so."

"This is no ordinary choice as you paint it, Richard. What you describe is extravagantly complicated. I'm having trouble even beginning to envision the complexities and consequences that would be involved in such an event. It would have to cause so many things to come undone, with such compounding disorder, that it would soon become all too obvious to everyone that something was terribly wrong in the world—even if they didn't know what. That just isn't happening."

Shota swept her arm out in grand fashion. "Meanwhile, what damage to the world will you cause because of this mad mission you have undertaken to find a woman who does not exist?

"You came to me the first time to get help in stopping Darken Rahl. I helped you, and in so doing I helped you become the Lord Rahl.

"The war rages on, the D'Haran Empire fights desperately on, and now you are not there to be a part of it, as is your place as the Lord Rahl. You have been effectively removed from your position of authority by your own delusions and unthinking actions. A void is left where there should be leadership. All the help you would be able to provide is no longer available to those who fight for the cause you have championed."

"I believe that I'm right," Richard said. "If I am, then that means there is a grave danger that no one but me is even aware of. Therefore, no one but me can fight it. Only I stand opposed to some unknown but impending ruin. I can't in good conscience ignore what I believe to be the truth of a hidden threat more monstrous than anyone realizes."

"That makes a convenient excuse, Richard."

"It's not an excuse."

Shota nodded mockingly. "And if the newly founded free empire of D'Hara falls in the meantime? If the savages of the Imperial Order raise their bloody swords over the corpses of all those brave men who will perish defending the cause of freedom while their leader is off chasing phantoms? Will all those brave men be any less dead because you alone see some inscrutable danger? Will their cause—will your cause—be any less ended? Will the world then be able to slide merrily into a long dark age where millions upon millions will be born into miserable lives of oppression, starvation, suffering, and death?

"Will chasing off after the enigma in your mind alone make liberty's grave acceptable to you, Richard? A mere consequence of what you stubbornly think is right in the face of overwhelming evidence to the contrary?"

Richard had no answer. In fact, he feared to even attempt to give her one. After the way she'd put it, anything he said would sound hollow and selfish. He felt sure that he had sound reasons to stick to his convictions, but he also knew that to everyone else the proof had to seem pretty thin, so he thought that maybe it was best to just keep quiet.

More than that, though, lurking beneath the surface was the terrible shadow of fear that she could be right, that it was all some dreadful delusion in his mind alone and not some problem with everyone else.

What made him right and everyone else wrong? How could he alone be right? How could such a thing even be possible? How could he know himself that he was right? What proof, other than his own memory, did he have? There was not one concrete shred of evidence that he could hold, that he could point to.

The crack in his confidence terrified him. If that crack widened, if it ruptured, the weight of the world would crash in and crush him. He couldn't bear that weight if she didn't exist.

His word alone stood between Kahlan and oblivion.

He couldn't go on without her. He didn't want to go on in a world without her. She was everything to him. Until that moment, he had been pushing her personal, private, intimate loving memory aside and instead dealing with details in order to endure the pain of missing her for yet another day even as he worked toward finding her. But that pain was now tightening around his heart, threatening to take him to his knees.

With the pain of missing her came a flood of guilt. He was Kahlan's only hope. He alone kept the flame of her alive above the torrent trying to drown out her existence. He alone worked to find her and bring her back. But he had not yet accomplished anything useful toward that end. The days marched past, but so far he hadn't gained anything that would get him any closer to her.

To make matters all the worse, Richard knew that Shota was also right in one very important way. While he worked toward helping Kahlan, he was failing everyone else. He had been the one who, to a large extent, had made people believe in the idea, the very real possibility, of a free D'Hara, of a place where it was possible for people to live and work toward their own goals in their own lives.

He was only too aware that he was also largely responsible for the great barrier coming down, allowing Emperor Jagang to lead the Imperial Order into the New World to threaten the newfound freedom in the New World.

How many people would be at risk, or lose their lives, while he pursued this one person that he loved? What would Kahlan want him to do? He knew how much she cared for the people of the Midlands, the people she had once ruled. She would want him to forget her and to try to save them. She would say that there was too much at stake to come after her.

But if it was he who was missing, she would not abandon him for anything or anyone.

Despite what Kahlan might say, it was her life that was important to him, her life that meant the world to him.

He wondered if perhaps Shota was right, that he was merely using the concept of the danger Kahlan's disappearance represented for the rest of the world, as an excuse.

He decided that the best thing to do for the moment, until he could think of a better way to get the help he needed, and to buy himself time to gather his courage, to harden his resolve, was to change the subject.

"What about this thing," Richard asked, gesturing vaguely, "this beast, that's chasing me." The passion was gone from his voice. He realized how tired he was from the long trek over the pass, to say nothing of the blur of days riding up from the Old World. "Is there anything you can tell me about it?"

He felt on safer ground with this question because the beast could interfere not only with his search for Kahlan, but with the mission Shota was urging him to return to.

She watched him for a moment, her voice finally coming much softer, as had his, as if without realizing it they had reached a wordless truce to lower the level of antagonism. "The beast that hunts you is no longer the beast it once was, the beast it was as it was created. Events have caused it to mutate."

"Mutate?" Cara asked, looking alarmed. "What do you mean? What has it become?"

Shota appraised them both, as if to make sure they were paying attention.

"It has become a blood beast."

A blood beast?" Richard asked.

Cara moved close to his side. "What's a blood beast?"

Shota took a breath before explaining. "It is no longer simply a beast linked to the underworld, as it was when it was created. It was inadvertently given a taste of your blood, Richard. What's worse, it was given that taste through Subtractive Magic—magic also linked to the underworld. That event changed it into a blood beast."

"So . . . what does that mean?" Cara asked.

Shota leaned closer, her voice dropping to little more than a whisper. "That means that it is now oh so much more dangerous." She straightened after she was sure she had made the intended impression. "I'm not an expert on ancient weapons created in the great war, but I believe that once such a beast as this one has tasted the blood of its mark in such a way, there is no turning it back, ever."

"All right, so it won't give up." Richard rested his palm on the hilt of his sword. "What can you tell me to help me kill it, then? Or at least stop it, or send it back to the underworld. What does it do, precisely, how does it know that—"

"No, no." Shota waved a dismissive hand. "You are trying to think of this in terms of some ordinary threat hunting you. You're trying to put a nature to it, trying to give it a defining behavior. It has none. That is the peculiarity of this thing—the absence of a defining description, of a makeup. At least one that is of any use, since its nature is precisely that it has none. Because of that it therefore cannot be predicted."

"That makes no sense." Richard folded his arms, wondering if Shota really knew as much about this beast as she said she did. "It has to function by some fundamental nature. It has to behave in certain ways that we can at least come to understand and therefore begin to anticipate. We just need to figure it out. It can't possibly have no nature."

"Don't you see, Richard? Right from the beginning, here you are trying to figure it out. Don't you suppose that Jagang would know that you will try to figure it out so that you can defeat it? Haven't you done that sort of thing with him in the past? He has figured out your nature, and to counter you he has created a weapon that, for that very reason, has no nature.

"You are the Seeker. You seek answers to the nature of people, or things, or situations. To a greater or lesser extent, all people do. Had the blood beast a specific nature, its actions could then be learned and understood. If something can be understood enough to predict its behavior, then precautions can be taken, a plan to counter it can be made. Decoding its nature is essential to effective action being taken. That's why this thing has no nature—so that you can't do those things to stop it."

Richard ran his fingers back though his hair. "That doesn't make any sense."

"It's not supposed to. That, too, is part of its trait—to have no trait. To make no sense in order to foil you."

"I agree with Lord Rahl," Cara said. "It still has to have some kind of makeup, some way of acting and reacting. Even people who think they are being clever by trying to be unpredictable still fall into patterns even though they may not realize it. This beast can't just run around hither and thither hoping to come across Lord Rahl napping."

"In order to prevent it from being understood and stopped, this beast was intentionally created as a creature of chaos. It was conjured to attack and kill you, but beyond that mission, it functions toward that end through disordered means." Shota gathered up another floating point of her dress as she spoke. "Today it attacks with claws. Tomorrow it spits poison. The next day it burns with fire, or crushes with a blow, or sinks fangs into you. It attacks by random action. It does not choose a course of action based on analysis, previous experience, or even the situation at hand."

Richard pinched the bridge of his nose as he thought about her explanation. So far, it seemed like Shota was right in that there had been no pattern to the attacks. They had come in completely different ways—so different, in fact, that they had questioned whether or not it was really the same beast Nicci had warned was after him.

"But Lord Rahl has evaded this beast several times now. He has proven that it can be bested."

Shota smiled at the very idea, as if a child had come up with the assertion. She strolled off a ways and then returned as she considered the problem. The twitch of her brow told Richard that she had come up with a better way to explain it.

"Think of the blood beast as if it were rain," she said. "Imagine that you want to stay out of the rain, like you would want to avoid being caught by the beast. Imagine that your goal is to stay dry. Today you may be inside when the rain comes, so you remain dry. Another day the rain may come on the other side of the valley and you again stay dry. Another day you leave an area just before the rain begins. Another day, you may decide not to travel, and there the rain visits. Maybe on another day as you walk down a road the rain moves in and falls in the field to your right, but on the road and to your left it remains dry. Each time the random rain event missed you, and you stayed dry—sometimes because you took preventative measures, such as staying inside, and sometimes by sheer chance.

"But, as often as it rains, you realize that it will sooner or later get you wet.

"So, you may decide that the best approach in the long run is to gain an understanding of exactly what you are up against. Therefore, in an effort to understand your adversary, you watch the sky and try to learn to predict the rain. Some patterns begin to reveal themselves as relatively reliable, so you use them as a means of prediction and as a result there will be times when you are correct and accurately anticipate the approaching rain. By this means you are able to stay inside when the rain comes and thus you stay dry. You have succeeded, it would seem, by applying what you've learned about how to anticipate and predict the rain."

Shota's intent, ageless eyes took in Cara and then fixed on Richard with such power that it almost halted his breathing. "But sooner or later," she said in a voice than ran a shiver up his spine, "the rain will catch you. You may be taken by complete surprise. Or, you may have forecast that it was coming, but believed that you would have time to be able to take to shelter first, and then it suddenly sweeps in faster than you ever thought possible. Or, on a day when you are far from shelter because you thought that on that day there was no chance of rain at all and so you ventured far from your shelter, it unexpectedly catches you. The result of all these different events is the same. If it is the beast, rather than the rain, you are not wet, you are dead.

"Confidence in your ability to predict the rain will eventually be your downfall because, while you may be able to accurately predict it on a number of occasions, it is not in reality reliably predictable based on the amount of knowledge actually available to you or possibly your ability to understand all the information you do have. The more times you escape, though, the stronger your false sense of confidence will become, making you all that much more vulnerable to a surprise event. Your best efforts to know the nature of rain will eventually fail you because even if you are right with a number of your forecasts, the things that brought about successful predictions are not always relevant, yet you have no way of knowing that. As a result, the rain will sneak up and envelope you when you are not expecting it."

Richard glanced at the worried look on Cara's face, but didn't say anything.

"The blood beast is like that," Shota said with finality. "It has no nature precisely so that you cannot predict its behavior by any patterns to its conduct."

Richard took a patient breath. He couldn't keep quiet any longer. "But all things that exist have to have a nature to them, laws of their existence, even if we don't understand them—otherwise what you are proposing is that they could contradict themselves and they can't.

"Lack of understanding on your part does not mean that you can pick an explanation of your choice. You can't say that since you don't know the nature of it, it therefore has none. You can say only that you don't yet know the nature of this thing, that you haven't yet been able to understand it."

With a slight smile, Shota gestured toward the sky. "Like the rain? You may be theoretically correct, Richard, but some things, for all practical purposes, are so far beyond our understanding that they appear to be driven by happenstance—like the rain. For all I know, weather may very well have laws that drive it, but they are so complex and so far-reaching that we cannot realistically hope to comprehend or know them. The rain may not truly, in the end, be an event caused by chance, but it is still outside our ability to predict so to us the result is the same as if it were entirely random and without order or nature.

"A blood beast is like this. If there are in fact laws to its nature, as you believe, it would make no difference to you. All I can tell you is that from what I know, it's a beast created specifically to act without order and the creation of it was successful to the degree that it functions consistently with having no discernible nature—at least none that is of any use in understanding or stopping it.

"I grant the possibility that you may be right. I suppose it's possible that there is some complex nature behind the beast's seeming disorder, but if that is the case, I can tell you that it is so far beyond our ability to understand that for our purposes it functions by chaos."

"I'm not sure I understand you," Richard said. "Give me an example."

"For instance, the beast will not learn from what it does. It may try the same failed tactic three times in a row, or it may try something even weaker the next time that obviously has no chance of success. What it does appears random. But if it is driven by some grand, complex equation, it is not revealed through its actions; we see only chaotic results.

"What's more, it has no consciousness, as we would think of it, anyway. It has no soul. While it has a goal, it doesn't care if it succeeds. It doesn't get angry if it fails. It's devoid of mercy, empathy, curiosity, enthusiasm, or worry. It was given a mission—kill Richard Rahl—and it randomly uses its myriad abilities to achieve that goal, but it has no emotional or intellectual interest in seeing its purpose accomplished.

"Living things have self-interest in seeing themselves succeed at their goals, whether it's a bird flying to a berry bush, or a snake following a mouse down a hole. They act to further their life. The blood beast does not.

"It's just a mindless thing advancing toward the completion of its built-in conjured objective. You might say it's like the rain, given the mission of 'get Richard wet.' The rain tries and tries, a downpour, a drizzle, a quick shower, and all fail. The rain doesn't care that it failed to get you wet. It may idle itself with a drought. It doesn't get eager or angry. It doesn't redouble its efforts. It will just go on raining in different ways until eventually it drenches you. When it does, it will feel no joy.

"The beast is irrational in that sense—but make no mistake, it is vicious, fierce, and mindlessly cruel in its actions."

Richard wearily wiped a hand across his face. "Shota, that still makes no sense to me. How could it be like that? If it's a beast, it has to be driven by purpose of some sort. Something has to drive it."

"Oh, it is driven by something: the need to kill you. It was created to be a creature that acts with pure disorder so that you may not counter it. In a way, you have proven yourself to be an opponent so difficult to defeat that

Jagang had to come up with something that would work by avoiding your striking abilities, rather than overpowering them."

"But if it was created to kill me, then it has purpose."

Shota shrugged. "True enough, but that one bit of information is of no use to you in predicting how, when, or where it will try to kill you. As you should know by now, its actions toward that goal are random. You should clearly see the profound danger in that tactic. If you know the enemy will attack with spears, you can carry a shield. If you know that one assassin with a bow is hunting you, you can have an army search for a man with a bow. If you know a wolf is hunting you, you can set a trap, or stay indoors.

"The blood beast has no preferred method of killing or hunting, so from the standpoint of defending yourself from it, it's profoundly difficult to protect against. One day it may attack and easily kill a thousand soldiers who are protecting you. The next time it may timidly withdraw after mauling a single child who toddles in front of you. What it does one time can tell you nothing about what it will do the next time. That, too, is part of the terror engendered by such a beast—the terror of not knowing how the attack will come.

"Its strength, its lethality, is that it isn't anything in particular. It isn't strong, or weak, or fast, or slow. It's constantly changing yet it sometimes stays the same or reverts to a previous state, even an unsuccessful one.

"The only thing that mattered after it was created was the first time you used your gift. That's when it locked on to you. After that, you can never know what it will do next or when it will do it. You know only that it's coming for you and no matter how many times you escape its clutches, it will continue to come—maybe several times in the same day, maybe not again for a month, or a year, but you can be sure it will eventually come after you again. It will never quit."

Richard wondered how much of what Shota was telling him she knew to be fact and how much she was filling in with what she thought, or maybe even imagined.

"But you're a witch woman," Cara said. "Surely, you can tell him something that will help counter it."

"Part of my ability is the capacity to see how events flow in the river of time, to see where they're going, you might say. Since the blood beast cannot be predicted, it, by that practical definition of its character, exists outside my ability to predict. My ability is linked in a way to prophecy.

Richard is a man who in a way also exists outside prophecy, a man others often find frustratingly unpredictable—as the Mord-Sith have no doubt discovered. With this beast I can offer him no advice about what might happen or what he must avoid."

"So then, books of prophecy would be of no use?" Richard asked.

"Just as I am blind to it, so is all prophecy. Prophecy cannot see a blood beast any more than it can see any chaotic, chance event. Prophecy may be able to say that a person will be shot with an arrow in the morning of a day that it will rain, but prophecy cannot name every day it will rain, or which of those days that it does rain the arrow will precede it. You might say that the most prophecy can predict is that sooner or later it will rain and you will get wet."

With his left hand resting on his sword, Richard nodded reluctantly. "I have to admit, that's close to my own views on prophecy—that it might be able to tell you that the sun will rise tomorrow but not what you will choose to do with your day."

He frowned at her. "So, you can tell me nothing about what this blood beast will do, because your ability is with the flow of time." When she nodded, he asked, "So then how do you seem to know so much about it?"

"The flow of events through the river of time is not my only ability," she said, rather cryptically.

Richard sighed, not wanting to argue with her. "So that's all you can tell me, then."

Shota nodded. "That's all I am able to tell you about the blood beast and what such a thing holds for you. If it continues to exist, sooner or later it will likely get you. But, because it's not predictable, even that outcome is not able to be predicted. When, where, or how soon it will get you is impossible to know. It may be today, or, for all I know, it may be that before it is able to find you and kill you, you will first die of old age."

"Well, there is that possibility, then," Richard muttered.

"Not much to lay your hopes on," she said in a sympathetic tone. "As long as you live, Richard, as long as blood pumps in your veins, the blood beast will hunt you."

"Are you suggesting that it finds me by my blood? The way a heart hound is said to be able to find a person by the sound of their beating heart?"

Shota lifted a hand as if to forestall the notion. "Only in a manner of speaking. It has tasted your blood, in a sense. But your blood, as you are thinking of it, is not what it is meaningful to this beast. What is material is what it sensed from that taste: your ancestry.

"It already knew that you live. It was already hunting you. Your use of your gift the first time was enough to bind it to you for all eternity. It is the gift carried in your blood that it sensed and that caused it to change."

Richard had so many questions he didn't know what to ask first. He started with what he thought might be the easiest to understand. "Why is it linked to the underworld? Is there a purpose for that?"

"A couple that I'm aware of. The underworld is eternal. Time has no meaning in eternity. Therefore, time means nothing to the beast. It will feel no urgency to kill you. Urgency would make it act with a kind of conscious intent that would give it a nature. It feels no pressure with every setting sun to finish the job. One day is the same as the next. The days are never-ending.

"Because it has no sense of time, it needs no nature. Time helps give dimension to every living thing. It allows you to put off chores that you know can be done later. It makes you rush to set up camp before it gets dark. It makes a general act to get his defenses in place before the enemy arrives. It makes a woman want to have children while she still has time. Time is one element that helps shape the nature of everything. Even a moth that emerges from its cocoon to live a life with wings for only a single day must mate in that day and lay eggs or there will be no more of its kind.

"The beast is untouched by time. A constituent element of its makeup is the eternity of the underworld, which is antithetical to the very notion of Creation, since the underworld is the undoing of Creation. That mix, that internal conflict, is part of the driving mechanism which churns its actions and makes it chaotic. When Nicci used Subtractive Magic to eliminate your spent blood, the beast, from its roots in the underworld, got its taste of you, or, more accurately, a measure of your magic.

"Your blood carries both Additive and Subtractive Magic. The beast was created to be able to know you by your essence, magic, thereby allowing it to transcend typical worldly limits. The beast needed you to use magic the first time so that it could link to you. Through that link, it could hunt you. But when it received that taste of your blood, it became able to know you in a whole different way.

"The unique element of magic carried in your blood, inherited from

Zedd's side and from Darken Rahl's side, is what the beast tasted. That taste is what mutated it from the beast that Jagang's minions created.

"It's not your blood itself that it senses, but rather it detects those elements of magic inherent in it. That's why any use of magic will draw the beast—that's how it became more dangerous. It now recognizes any use of your magic anywhere in the world. Each person's magic is unique. The beast now knows yours. That's why you must not use your gift.

"For this very reason, the Sisters who brought the beast into existence for Jagang would have loved to have been able to use your blood in the beginning, but they had no way of getting any. They could link the beast to your gift, but without your blood, it was a weak link that didn't really know the full measure of your magic.

"Nicci gave the beast what it really needed, right after it had been awakened by your first use of the gift. She may have done it to save your life, and she may have had no choice, but she did it. Now, any use of magic can much more easily bring the blood beast to you. It would seem that Nicci has, in a way, fulfilled her oath as a Sister of the Dark."

The hair at the back of Richard's neck had lifted. He wanted to think of a way to prove Shota wrong, to find a chink in the armor of the monster she had given shape to in his mind.

"But the beast has attacked when I wasn't using magic. Just this morning it attacked at our camp. I wasn't using magic."

Shota gave him one of those looks that had the power to make him feel hopelessly ignorant. "You were using magic this morning."

"I wasn't," he insisted. "I was asleep at the time. How could I be using . . ."

Richard's words trailed off. His gaze wandered to the distant hills of the valley and the mountains beyond. He remembered waking up and having that terrible memory of the morning Kahlan had disappeared and then realizing that he was holding the hilt of his sword, its blade drawn halfway from its scabbard. He remembered feeling the sword's stealthy magic coursing through him.

"But that was the sword's magic," he said. "I was holding the sword. It wasn't my magic."

"It was your magic," Shota insisted. "Using the Sword of Truth calls its power, which joins with your gift—your magic—which is recognized by the blood beast. The sword's magic is part of you, now. Using it will chance calling the beast."

Richard felt like everything was pressing in on him, closing off every option, shutting off his ability to do anything to stop what was coming for him. He felt the way he had earlier, when he woke up to find himself in a ever-tightening trap.

"But the sword will help me fight it. I don't know how to use my gift. The sword is the one thing I can count on."

"It's possible that in some instances it may save you. But because the blood beast has no nature, and because it is now a part of the underworld, there will be times when you think your sword will protect you and it will not. Thinking you can predict the ability of your sword to work against the beast will beguile you into having false confidence. As I told you, the beast can't be predicted, so there will be times when your sword can't protect you. You must guard not only against false reliance on your sword, but on it unwittingly calling the beast.

"It's always hunting you, and could attack at any time, but when you use your gift it vastly increases the ability, and therefore the likelihood, of the beast initiating an attack. Magic baits it."

Richard realized that he was gripping the hilt of the sword so hard in his fist that he could feel the raised letters of the word TRUTH pressing into his palm. He could also feel the sword's anger urgently trying to steal into him to protect him against the threat. He took his hand off the hilt as if it were burning him. He wondered if that magic had ignited his own, if he had just called the blood beast without even realizing what he was doing.

Shota clasped her hands. "There is something else."

Richard's attention returned to the witch woman. "Great, what next?"

"Richard, I'm not the one who created this beast. I'm not responsible for its danger to you." She looked away. "If you wish to hate me for telling you the truth, and want me to stop, then say so and I will stop."

Richard waved an apology. "No, I'm sorry. I know it's not your fault. I guess I'm just feeling a bit overwhelmed. Go on. What were you going to say?"

"If you use magic—any magic—the blood beast will know it. Because it acts in a random manner, it very well may not use that magic link to come after you right then. It may inexplicably not respond. But the next time, it may pounce. So you dare not gain confidence in that manner."

"You already told me that."

"Yes, but as of yet you have not realized the full implications of what I'm telling you. You must understand that any use of magic will give the beast the scent of your blood, so to speak."

"Like I said, you told me that."

"That means *any* use of your gift." When he stared at her with a blank look, she impatiently tapped a finger to his forehead. "Think."

When he still didn't understand, she said "That includes prophecy."

"Prophecy? What do you mean?"

"Prophecy is given by wizards who have the gift for prophecy. An ordinary person who reads prophecy will see only words. Even the Sisters of the Light, guardians of prophecy though they thought they were, do not see prophecy in its true state. You are a war wizard. Being a war wizard merely means that your gift carries a variety of latent abilities. Part of that is that you are able to use prophecy—to understand it as it was intended.

"Do you see? Do you see how easy it is to inadvertently use your gift?

"It doesn't matter how you use your gift—if you use your sword, or heal with your gift, or call down lightning—it doesn't matter; it will call the beast. To the blood beast, any use of your gift is the same—a means of recognition. It will not distinguish between a small use, or a spectacular use. To the beast, the gift is the gift."

Richard was incredulous. "Do you mean to say that if I simply heal someone, or draw my sword, it will alert the beast to me?"

"Yes. And likely in short order while it knows precisely where you are. Being that it's elementally Subtractive, it exists only partially in this world, so, while the beast is not hampered by things such as distance or obstacles, it also doesn't function in this world with ease. It can't fully conceive of the laws of this world, such as time. Still, it doesn't get tired, it doesn't get lazy, or angry, or eager.

"By all this I do not mean to suggest that because you use your gift the beast will therefore act. As I've said, its actions can't be predicted, so, like everything else, the use of magic cannot be used as a predictive factor. It only means that it increases its ease in being able to find you. Whether or not it will do so is not knowable."

"Great," Richard muttered as he went back to pacing.

"How can he kill it?" Cara asked.

"It isn't alive," Shota said. "You can no more kill the blood beast than you can kill a boulder that is about to fall on you, or kill the rain before it has a chance to get you wet."

Cara looked as frustrated as Richard felt. "Well, there has to be something that it's afraid of."

"Fear is a function of living things."

"Maybe, then, something it doesn't like."

Shota frowned. "Doesn't like?"

"You know, fire, or water, or light. Something it doesn't like and so avoids."

"Today it might choose to avoid water. Tomorrow it might slither up from a bog, snatch his leg, and drag him under the water to drown him. It moves through this world as it would through an alien landscape that has little effect on it."

"Where in the world could someone learn how to create such a beast?" Richard asked.

"I believe that the core of the knowledge was discovered by Jagang in ancient books on weapons that originated during the great war. He is a student of ancient subjects having to do with warfare; he collects such knowledge from all over. I have a suspicion, though, that he took what he found and added specifications he wanted in order to defeat you. We do know that he then used the gifted Sisters to spawn the beast.

"Since they used Subtractive Magic along with their stolen wizardry, they were able to make use of other gifted people as constituent parts of the beast, ripping their souls from them, ripping away all but what was needed in order to conjure, combine and create the beast. It is a weapon beyond anything we have ever encountered before. Jagang is the one who caused the beast to be created. He has to be stopped before he creates anything else."

"I couldn't agree more," Richard muttered.

"You can't stop him if you are off chasing phantoms," Shota said.

Richard halted his pacing and stared at her. "Shota, you can't just tell me all this without at least telling me something that will help."

"You are the one who came to me asking questions. I did not go looking for you. Besides, I have helped you. I told you what I know. Maybe by using the information you now have, you can live another day."

Richard had heard enough. The blood beast had no nature, but not to have a nature, in a way, was its nature, so it had one as far as he was concerned. It may be true, as Shota had said, that there was no accurate way to predict what it would do next, but lack of understanding or knowledge did not constitute a lack of a nature. It was, however, a point that was not worth arguing. He thought that it might be an important distinction sooner or later, but right then it didn't matter much. Everything Shota had said largely confirmed what Nicci had already reported. While she had added facets and details that Nicci hadn't known about, Shota hadn't provided any solutions.

In fact, it seemed to him that she had gone to a great deal of trouble to make sure she had painted a hopeless picture.

Richard almost rested his hand on his sword. He stopped and ran his fingers through his hair, instead. He was at his wits' end. He turned and stared off at the trees spread across the valley, their leaves shimmering in the late-day sun.

"So, there is nothing I can do to protect myself from the blood beast."

"I didn't say that."

Richard spun back around. "What? You mean there is a way?"

Without emotion, Shota studied his eyes. "I believe that there is one way to keep you alive."

"What way?"

She clasped her hands, twining her fingers together. She looked down at the ground a moment, as if considering, and then met his gaze with steady resolution.

"You could stay here."

He saw Samuel come to his feet. Richard returned his attention to Shota's waiting gaze. "What do you mean, I could stay here?"

She shrugged, as if it were a trivial offer. "Stay here and I will protect you."

Cara straightened, her arms coming unfolded. "You can do that?"

"I believe I can."

"Then come with us," Cara suggested. "That would solve the problem."

Richard already didn't like Cara's idea.

"I can't," Shota said. "I can only protect him if he stays here, in this valley, in my home."

"I can't stay," Richard said, trying to make it sound casual.

Shota reached out and gently grasped his arm, not allowing him to so easily dismiss the issue. "You can, Richard. Would it be so bad, staying with me?"

"I didn't mean it that way. . . ."

"Then stay here with me."

"For how long?"

Her fingers tightened ever so slightly, as if she feared to say it, feared his reaction, but at the same time was steadfast in her course.

"Forever."

Richard swallowed. He felt like he'd walked out onto thin ice without realizing it, and now he found that it was a long, long way back to safety. He knew that if he said the wrong thing he would be in over his head. His flesh tingled as he realized how dangerous the late day air had suddenly become.

At that moment, he wasn't sure that he wouldn't rather face the beast than Shota's scrutiny.

Richard spread his arms, as if to ask her understanding. "Shota, how can I stay here? You know that there are people counting on me—people who need me. You said so yourself."

"You are not the slave to others, chained to them by their need. It's your life, Richard. Stay, and have a life."

Cara, looking more than suspicious, tapped a thumb to her own chest. "And what about me?"

Without looking over at Cara, without taking her gaze from Richard's, Shota said, "One woman in this place is enough."

Cara glanced between Richard and Shota as they stared into each other's eyes, but she then did what Richard had earlier advised: she turned cautious and said nothing.

"Stay," Shota whispered intimately.

Richard could see a terrible kind of vulnerability laid bare in Shota's eyes, in her hungering expression—an open look he had never seen on her before. From the corner of his eye, he could also see Samuel glaring at him.

Richard tipped his head, indicating her companion. "And what about him?"

She did not shy from the question—in fact she seemed to have expected it.

"One Seeker in this place is enough."

"Shota—"

"Stay, Richard?" she pressed, cutting him off before he could turn her down, before he crossed a line he hadn't known was there until right then.

It was both an offer and an ultimatum.

"But what about the blood beast? You said yourself that you can't know its nature. How can you know that we would be safe here if I stayed? A lot of men near me were killed when the beast attacked the first time."

Shota lifted her chin. "I know myself, know my abilities, my limits. I believe that I can keep you safe, here, in this valley. I can't be completely certain, but I sincerely believe it to be true. I do know that if you leave here you will have no protection. This is your only chance."

He knew that the last part had more than one meaning.

"Stay, Richard. . . . Please? Stay here with me?"

"Forever."

Her eyes brimmed with tears.

"Yes, forever. Please? Stay? I will take care of you, forever. I will make sure you never regret it, or ever miss the rest of the world. Please?"

This was not Shota, the witch woman. This was simply the woman, Shota, desperately laying herself open to him in a way she never had, offering her unprotected heart, taking a chance. The naked loneliness he saw there was terrifying. He knew, because he felt the same anguish of being so alone that it hurt.

Richard swallowed and took the step out onto the ice.

"Shota, that's probably the kindest thing you've ever said to me. To know that you respect me enough to ask such a thing means more to me than you will ever understand. I have more respect for you than you know—that's why when I needed answers I thought of no one but you.

"I sincerely appreciate all you are offering . . . but I'm afraid I can't accept. I have to go."

The look that came to her face made Richard go as cold as if he'd been plunged into icy water.

Without another word, Shota turned and started away.

CHAPTER 42

Richard caught Shota's arm, stopping her before she could leave. He couldn't allow it to end in this way—for more than one reason.

"Shota, I'm sorry. . . . But you said it yourself; it's my life to live. If you consider me—even a little—to be a friend, someone you really do care about, then you would want me to live my life as I think I must, not as you might wish I could."

Her chest heaved. "Fine. You have made your choice, Richard. Leave. Go and live what is left of your life."

"I came to you because I need your help."

She turned around fully toward him and cast him as forbidding a look as he had ever seen on anyone. It was the unmistakable mask of a witch woman. He could almost see the air around her sizzling.

"I have given you help—gained through an effort on my part that I seriously doubt you can begin to imagine. Use that help as you wish. Now, leave my home."

As much as he wanted right then to do as she asked, as much as he wanted not to press her, he had come for a reason and she had not yet addressed it. He wasn't leaving until she did.

"I need your help to find Kahlan."

Her look turned even colder. "If you are wise, you will use the knowledge I have given you to stay alive as long as you can to help to defeat Jagang, or to go chasing after phantoms—I don't care which anymore. Just go, before you find out why wizards fear to come into my home."

"You said that your ability helps you see events in the flow of time. What does your ability see about me in the future?"

Shota was silent for a moment before she finally glanced away from his steady gaze. "For some reason, the river of time has become obscured to me. It happens." Her gaze returned, more determined than ever. "You see? I can be of no further help. Now, go."

He was determined not to allow her to dodge the issue. "You know that

I came here for information, for something that could help me find out the truth about what's going on. This is important. It's important to more people than just you or me. Don't close yourself off from me like this Shota, please. I need your help."

She arched an eyebrow. "Since when have you ever followed anything I've ever told you?"

"Look, I admit that in the past I haven't always agreed with everything you've had to say, but I wouldn't be here if I didn't think you were an astute woman. While some of the things you've told me in the past were true, if I would have done things strictly your way without using my own judgment as the situation developed I would have failed and we would all be either under the rule of Darken Rahl or in the merciless embrace of the Keeper of the underworld."

"So you say."

Richard lost his indulgent tone as he leaned toward her. "You do remember the time you came to see me at the Mud People's village, don't you? The time you begged me to close the veil so that the Keeper wouldn't have us all? You do remember telling me how much the Keeper wanted those with the gift, wanted you, a witch woman, to suffer unimaginably for all eternity?"

He jabbed her with a finger, punctuating his points. "You did not suffer all the frightful things necessary to stop what was happening—I did. You did not have to fight the Keeper's terrors to close the veil—I did. You did not save your own hide from the Keeper—I did."

She was watching him from under her lowered brow. "I remember."

"I succeeded. I saved you from that fate."

"You saved yourself from that fate. That it saved me as well was not your purpose, merely a side consequence."

He let out a breath, trying to be patient. "Shota, I know that you must know something about this—something about what's happened to Kahlan."

"I told you, I don't remember any woman named Kahlan."

"Yes, and the reason is that something is terribly wrong and I realize that because of that you don't recall her, but you must know something that will help me in my search for the truth—some bit of information that will help me find out the truth about what's really going on."

"And you expect that you can just walk uninvited into my home, put my life at risk, do your little dance, and get whatever part of my life, my ability, that you want for yourself."

Richard stared at her. She had not denied that she knew something that might help him. He realized that he had indeed been right about her.

"Shota, stop posturing and stop acting like I'm unfairly making demands of you. I've never lied to you and you know it. I'm telling you that this is important to you, too, whether or not you yet realize it. For all I know, it could yet be something the Keeper has initiated in order to get us all. I need whatever information you can give me to prevent the success of whatever it is that's going wrong. I'm not playing games. I will have what you know!"

"And you think that such a demand entitles you to it?" Her eyes narrowed. "You think that just because I have something, your perceived need means that I must surrender whatever I have? That you are entitled to any part of my life you feel you need? You think that my life is not mine, but I am merely meant to serve you? You think my life means nothing but to be at your disposal when you deign to have use of me? You think you can come in here and make demands, but when I dare ask for something, you get indignant?"

"I wasn't indignant," he said, trying to restrain his tone. "I appreciated the sincerity of your offer. I understand very well the empty feeling of being alone. But if you're the woman I believe you are, you wouldn't want me even though my heart wasn't in it. You deserve to have someone who can love you. I'm sorry, Shota, but I can't lie and tell you that I can be that one for you or I would only in the end be hurting you worse. I can't lie to you; I'm already in love with someone.

"And even if you already realized that, would you really want someone who was so casually unfaithful as to just take up such an offer on the spot? I think what you really want is your equal, a true partner in your life, someone with whom to share the wonders of life. I don't think you really want the empty reward of a lapdog. I think you already know that a lapdog can bring you no real joy.

"If you care about me, if you made such an offer because you really care, if you were sincere, then help me."

She didn't look like she intended to answer, so he pressed on. "Shota, I need to know any information you can give me. It's important. As important as it was to you when you came to ask me to seal the breach in the veil. I don't know enough to solve this problem. If I fail, I fear we all will lose. I don't have time for games. I need the information you have."

"How dare you make such an arrogant demand of me. I've already told you, already given you my answer. It's my ability, my life. You have no right to it."

Richard pressed his thumb and middle finger to opposite temples as he took a calming breath. He grudgingly realized that maybe she had a point.

He turned his back to her and walked off a few paces as he considered what he might do. One thing he knew for certain, he wasn't leaving without every bit of help available.

"You're saying, then, that you know something that would help me in my search for the truth."

"I know a lot of things about a lot of different areas of the truth."

"But you know something that I need in order to find the truth about what brought me here to see you."

"Yes."

He knew it. With his back still to her, he said, "Name your price."

"You would not be willing to pay the price."

He considered the price he expected her to revisit.

Richard turned to her. She was watching him in that way that made him feel transparent. He was not leaving without the information and that was all there was to it. This was Kahlan's life.

Whatever he had to do to save her life, including giving up his, he would do.

"Name your price."

"The Sword of Truth."

The world seemed to stop. "What?"

"You asked the price for what I can tell you. The price is the Sword of Truth."

Richard stood paralyzed. "You can't be serious."

The corners of her lips curled ever so slightly. "Oh, but I am."

Off through the trees, Richard saw Samuel stand up, suddenly very attentive.

"What do you want with the sword?"

"You asked the price, I named it. What I want with the payment after it has been made is not your concern."

Richard felt sweat trickle down between his shoulder blades.

TERRY GOODKIND

"Shota . . ."

He couldn't seem to make himself move, or speak. This was not at all what he had expected.

Shota turned her back and started for the road. "Good-bye, Richard. It's been nice knowing you. Don't come back."

"Wait!"

Shota paused to look back over her shoulder, waves of her auburn hair glistening in a streamer of golden sunlight. "Yes or no, Richard. I have given you enough of myself for nothing in return. I will give you no more. If you want this, you will pay for it. I will not offer you the chance again."

She watched him a moment and then started to turn away again. Richard gritted his teeth.

"All right."

She paused. "You agree, then?"

"Yes."

She turned fully around to face him, waiting.

Richard immediately reached up to pull the baldric off over his head. Cara jumped in front of him and seized his wrist in both her hands.

"What do you think you're doing?" she growled. Her red leather glowed in the low sunlight, as if to match the fire in her eyes.

"Shota knows something about this whole mess," he told her. "I need to know what she can tell me. I don't know what else to do. I don't have any choice."

Cara let go of his wrist with one hand to press her fingers to her forehead as she tried to gather her senses, tried to calm her sudden rapid breathing.

"Lord Rahl, you can't do this. You can't. You're not thinking clearly. You're swept up in the passion of the moment, the passion of wanting something you think she has. You've got it in your head that you have to have it no matter what. You don't even know what she's offering. As angry as she is at you, it's most likely that she has nothing of any real value."

"I have to know something that will help me find the truth."

"And there is no assurance that this will. Lord Rahl, listen to me. You're not thinking clearly. I'm telling you, the price is too high."

"There is no price too high for Kahlan's life—especially if the price is merely an object."

"This isn't her life you would be buying. It's just a witch woman's word that she can tell you something useful—a witch woman who wants to hurt you for rejecting her. You said yourself that nothing she's ever told you before ever turned out to be the way she said. This will be no different. You will lose your sword and it will be for nothing of value."

"Cara, I have to do this."

"Lord Rahl, this is crazy."

"And what if it's me that's crazy?"

"What are you talking about?"

"What if all of you are right and there really isn't any Kahlan? What if I'm crazy? Even you think I am. I need to know what Shota can tell me. If I'm wrong about everything I believe, then what good is a sword going to do a crazy man? If all of you are right that I'm delusional, then what good can I do anyone else? What good am I to anyone if I'm crazy? What good am I at all?"

Her eyes looked liquid. "You're not crazy."

"No? Then you believe there really is a woman named Kahlan and I'm married to her?" When she didn't answer, he pulled her other hand off his wrist. "I didn't think so."

Cara turned angrily to Shota, pointing with her Agiel. "You can't take his sword! It isn't fair and you know it! You're taking advantage of his condition. You can't take his sword!"

"The price I asked is but a trifling. . . . The sword isn't even his. It never was."

Shota beckoned with a finger. Samuel, watching from the shadows, scurried toward them through the trees.

Cara stepped between Richard and Shota. "It was given to Lord Rahl by the First Wizard. Lord Rahl was named to the post of Seeker and given the Sword of Truth. It's his!"

"And where do you suppose the First Wizard got the sword in the first place?" Shota pointed a finger tipped with a long red-lacquered nail downward at the ground. "He got it here. He came here, into my home, and stole it. That's where Zedd got the sword.

"Richard doesn't carry it by right, but by theft. Giving it back to its rightful owner is a small penance to pay for what he wants to know."

Cara had a dangerous look in her eyes as she lifted her Agiel. Richard gently grasped her wrist and lowered her arm before she started something that he knew could quickly turn ugly. He wasn't sure of the results of such a confrontation, but he dared not risk losing what Shota could tell him . . . or risk losing Cara.

"I'm doing as I must," he told Cara in a calm voice. "Don't make this any more difficult than it already is."

Richard had seen Cara in every sort of mood imaginable. He'd seen her happy, sad, disheartened, resolved, determined, and enraged, but until that moment he had never seen her anger focused so intently, deliberately, so directly at him.

And then he had a sudden vision of her taken by cruel anger once before, a long time ago.

He couldn't afford to suffer the distraction of any such memory right then and shoved it out of his mind. This was about Kahlan, and about the future, not about the past.

Richard pulled the baldric off over his head and gathered it together with the scabbard. Samuel, not far behind his mistress's skirts, stood quietly watching, his greedy eyes riveted on the wire-wound hilt.

Holding the gleaming gold and silver scabbard in both hands, bundled together with the ancient, tooled leather baldric, Richard lifted it out to Shota.

She made a move to take it. "The sword belongs to Samuel, my loyal companion." She smiled triumphantly. "Give it to him."

Richard stood frozen. He couldn't let Samuel have the Sword of Truth. He just couldn't.

He wondered then just what he thought Shota would want with the sword if not to give it to Samuel. He guessed that he had been trying not to think of what it really meant to hand it over to Shota.

"But the sword made him like that. Zedd told me that the sword's magic did that to him, turned him into what he is now."

"And when he has back what belongs to him, he will be who he once was, before it was stolen from him by your grandfather."

Richard knew Samuel's character. As far as Richard was concerned, Samuel was capable of anything, including murder. Richard could hardly give something so dangerous as the Sword of Truth to someone like that.

Too many people like Samuel had carried the sword, had fought over it, stolen it from one another, sold it to the highest bidder, who then became a Seeker whose services were for sale to any loathsome cause that could pay the price. In the shadows it passed from hand to hand, used for vile and violent purposes. By the time Zedd had finally gotten the Sword of Truth back and eventually given it to Richard, the Seeker had become an object of scorn and contempt, seen as nothing more than a criminal, and a dangerous one at that.

If he gave the sword to Samuel, it would be that way again. It would start all over again.

But if he didn't, then Richard had no chance of ever stopping the far greater threat very likely loose in the world, or of ever seeing Kahlan again. While Kahlan was of paramount importance to him, personally, he was convinced that her disappearance augured an ominous menace far more sinister, with potential harm on a scale he feared to contemplate.

His responsibility as the Seeker of Truth was to the truth, not to the Sword of Truth.

Samuel inched closer, his eyes on the sword, his arms reaching, his palms held up, waiting.

"Mine, gimme," Samuel growled impatiently, his hateful eyes glaring.

Richard lifted his head to look at Shota. She folded her arms, as if to say that this was his last chance. This was the last chance Richard had of ever finding the truth.

If he had known of any other way to find a solution, no matter how remote that chance might be, he would have taken the sword back and taken that chance instead. But he couldn't lose this chance, lose what information Shota had. There was nothing else to do.

With trembling hands, Richard lifted the sword out.

Samuel, unwilling to wait the final seconds until it reached him, lunged and snatched the sword away, finally clutching the coveted object to his breast.

The instant he had it, a strange look came over his face. He glanced up into Richard's eyes, his own wide with wonder, his mouth hanging agape. Richard couldn't imagine what Samuel was seeing as a result of having his hands on the Sword of Truth. Richard thought that perhaps he was simply awestruck to realize that he actually did have it again.

He suddenly skittered away, swiftly disappearing into the trees. The Sword of Truth was once again among the shadows.

Richard felt naked, and stunned. He stared off in the direction Samuel had gone. He wished now that he had killed Shota's companion the first time Samuel had attacked him. Samuel had attacked Richard more than once. Richard had let those chances slip away.

He turned a harsh glare on Shota. "If he harms anyone, it will be on your head."

"I am not the one who gave him the sword. You did so of your own free will. I did not twist your arm or use my powers to force you. Do not try to shed responsibility for your own choices and actions."

"And I am not responsible for his actions. If he harms anyone, I will see to it that this time he pays for his crimes."

Shota glanced off among the trees dotting the sweep of grass. "There is no one here for him to harm. He has his sword. He is happy, now."

Richard seriously doubted that.

With quiet fury, he turned his attention to the matter at hand. He didn't want to hear any of her excuses so he came right to the point.

"You have your payment."

She stared at him a long time, her face unreadable. Finally, in a quiet voice, she spoke a single word.

"Chainfire."

She turned and started toward the road.

Richard seized her arm and turned her back. "What?"

"You wanted what I know that can help you find the truth. I have given it to you: Chainfire."

Richard was incredulous. "Chainfire? What does that mean?"

Shota shrugged. "I have no idea. I only know that it is what you need to know to find the truth of all this."

"What do you mean, you have no idea? You can't just tell me some word I never heard of and then leave. That's not a fair trade for what I've given you."

"Nonetheless, that is the agreement you made, and I have upheld my end of the bargain."

"You have to tell me what it means."

"I don't know what it means, but I do know that it is worth the price you paid."

Richard couldn't believe that he had agreed to a deal in which he got nothing of value in return. He was no closer to finding Kahlan than he had been before he'd come to see Shota. He felt like sitting down right there on the ground and giving up.

"Our business is concluded. Good-bye, Richard. Please leave. It will be dark, soon. I can assure you, you would not like to be here when it gets dark."

Shota started down the road toward her palace in the distance. As he watched her go, Richard reprimanded himself for embracing failure without even trying for success. He now knew something linked to the mystery. It was a piece of the puzzle, a piece of the solution, so valuable that it had previously been known only to a witch woman. It confirmed for him that Kahlan was real. He told himself that he was a step closer. He had to believe that.

"Shota," Richard called.

She paused and turned back, waiting to hear what he might say, looking like she expected a tirade.

"Thank you," he said in a sincere voice. "I don't know what good knowing the word *Chainfire* will do me, but thank you. You have at least given me a reason to go on. When I came here, I had none; now I do. Thank you."

She stared at him. He could not imagine what she could be thinking.

Finally, she took a slow step back toward him. She clasped her hands before herself, looking down a moment before she stared off at the trees, apparently considering something.

At last, she spoke. "What you seek is long buried."

"Long buried?" he cautiously asked.

"Like the word *Chainfire*, I can't tell you what that means. Things come to me in regard to issues, problems, questions. I am the carrier of the information, the channel you might say. I am not the source. I can't tell you the meaning, but I can tell you that what you seek is long buried."

"Chainfire, and seek something long buried." Richard repeated as he nodded. "Got it. I'll not forget."

Her brow twitched, as if something else had just came to her. "You must find the place of the bones in the Deep Nothing."

Richard felt goose bumps racing up his legs. He had no idea what the "Deep Nothing" was, but he didn't like the sound of it, or the sound of looking for bones. He refused to consider the dire implications.

Shota turned again to the road and started making her way toward her palace. She had not gone more than a dozen paces when she stopped and turned back. Her ageless eyes met his gaze.

"Beware the viper with four heads."

Richard cocked his head expectantly. "I don't know what that means—the viper with four heads."

"Whether or not you realize it right now, I have given you a fair trade. I have given you the answers you needed. You are the Seeker—or at least, you were; you will have to seek the meaning to be found in those answers."

With that, she turned for the final time and walked off through the golden light down the long road.

"Let's go," he said to Cara. "I'd not like to find out why we don't want to be here when it gets dark."

Cara cast him an icy glare. "I would imagine it has something to do with a murderous maniac wielding a deadly sword coming at you out of the darkness."

Richard gloomily supposed that she might be right. Samuel would probably not be content to simply have the sword. He would probably want to eliminate the rightful owner and thereby any chance that Richard might lay claim to it or somehow get it back.

Despite what Shota had said, the real thief had been Samuel. The Sword of Truth was the responsibility of the First Wizard. He was the one who named Seekers and gave them the sword. It did not belong to whoever might possess it by any means, it belonged to the true, wizard-named Seeker, and that was Richard.

With sickening dread, he realized that he had betrayed the trust his grandfather had placed in him when he had given Richard the sword.

But what value would the sword be to him if keeping it meant that Kahlan would lose her life?

There was no higher value to him than life.

Richard was so deep in thought that he wasn't fully aware of the arduous climb up the steep face of the cliff and out of Agaden Reach. In the golden light of the valley below them the long shadows of trees lengthened across the green fields, yet the quiet beauty of the place as the sun sank behind the enfolding mountains was lost on him; he wanted to be far away from the valley and out of the swamp before darkness took hold for good. He tried to devote his efforts to that task, that mission, of putting one foot before the other, of moving, advancing.

By the time they reached the top of the cliff and the vast swamp guarding the approach to Shota's home, it was an early dusk in the deep niche of the towering mountains that ringed the place. Because the walls of rock cut the sunlight off early, it left the sky overhead a deep blue, but that light was unable to effectively penetrate the forest canopy, so that in the late day the vast green bog seemed mired in a perpetual gloom of half-night. The deep shadows were very different than those in Shota's valley. The shadows in the swamp concealed palpable but for the most part ordinary threats; the shadows around Shota concealed dangers that were not so easily appreciated, but that Richard suspected were far more pernicious.

The sounds of the dank swamp all around him, the chirps, the whistles, the hooting calls, the clicks, the distant cries, hardly registered in Richard's consciousness. He was deep in his own world of despair and purpose tangled together in a titanic struggle.

While Shota had told him a great deal about the blood beast that was hunting him, Nicci had already told him that he was being hunted by a beast conjured at Jagang's behest. The visit to Shota had not been worth the minutiae he learned about the beast. It was the precious few things that Shota had said at the end that really mattered to him. It was those things for which he had traveled to this place. It was for those things he had paid a price so dear that he was only now beginning to fully grasp its significance. His fingers itched to touch the hilt of his sword for reassurance, but that familiar and faithful weapon was no longer there.

He tried not to think about it, and yet he could think of little else. He felt relief that he had gained what he felt sure would be crucial information, but at the same time he felt a crushing sense of personal failure.

He paid only enough attention to where he was walking to keep from stepping on a yellow-and-black-banded snake he spotted coiled in the lap of a root, or letting the fuzzy spiders clinging to the underside of leaves silently slide down silken lines to alight on him. He skirted brush when something within hissed at him.

Richard followed the darkening trail as fast as safely possible while in his mind he went over Shota's every word, concentrating on the treasure for which he had paid such a terrible price. Cara followed close on his heels, swinging and swatting at the cloud of bugs hovering around their faces. Occasionally a bat fluttered in out of the dark shadows to snatch up some of those bugs.

As he made his way through the tangle of growth, Richard pushed aside vines and branches and stepped carefully around snarls of roots—some of which writhed like a nest of snakes when they got too close. On his first visit Samuel had shown him how those roots could grab an ankle if you got too close. Richard was so totally absorbed in trying to figure out what "Chainfire" could possibly mean, or what it could be, that he nearly stepped into a stretch of black water that was hard to see in the murky light. Cara's hand snatching his arm halted him just in time. He glanced around and spotted the log they had crossed on before and took to that route.

He racked his brain trying to think if he had ever heard the word *Chainfire* before, but his hopes grew as dim as the failing light. It was a strange enough word, it seemed, that he would have remembered it if he had ever heard it before. He wished that Shota would have known its source or meaning, but he believed that she was telling the truth about these kinds of answers coming to her without explanation or insight.

On the other hand, he feared that he knew all too well what Shota meant when she'd said, "What you seek is long buried."

That warning made his chest ache. He dreaded that it very well might mean that Kahlan was already dead and long ago buried.

He'd felt lost ever since that morning he awoke to find her missing. Without Kahlan, everything else in the world seemed meaningless.

He couldn't allow himself to envision her death as being true. Instead, he thought about her beautiful, intelligent green eyes, her special smile, her singular manner as being very real and very alive.

Shota's words, though, kept returning to him. He had to figure out what meaning they could hold if he was to find Kahlan.

The last part, that he should "Beware the viper with four heads," had made no sense to him at first, but the more he mulled it over, the more it began to feel to him like he should understand it, as if it was something that should make sense to him or something he should be able to figure out if he just thought about it hard enough. The implication that seemed obvious was that this four-headed viper—whatever it was—was somehow responsible for Kahlan's disappearance.

He wondered if he only suspected that because it sounded sinister. He didn't want to allow himself to start down the wrong roads on groundless impulses. That would only waste valuable time. He feared that he had already used too much time.

"Where are we going?" Cara asked, lifting him out of his snare of thoughts.

He realized that it was the first thing she had said since leaving Shota. "To get the horses."

"You intend to try to make it over the pass tonight?"

Richard nodded. "Yes, if we can. If the storm has blown away, the moon will provide enough light."

The first time he had come to see Shota, the witch woman had taken Kahlan back to her valley. Richard had followed their tracks over the pass at night. It wasn't easy, but he knew it could be done. He knew how tired he was from the hard day of crossing the pass, and he knew that Cara had to be just as tired, but he didn't intend to stop so long as he could still put one foot in front of the other.

It was obvious by the set of Cara's jaw that she didn't like the idea of making such a journey at night, but, instead of objecting, she asked something else.

"And when we get the horses? Then where?"

"To try to get answers to what I've found out so far."

All around, the mist had slowly drifted in among the gnarled trees, hanging vines, and expanses of still water, as if it were coming closer to listen in on their conversation. There was no wind to move the trailers of moss, so they hung limp from crooked branches. Shadows moved in the dark places beneath vines and brush. Unseen things distantly splashed in the black stretches of stagnant water.

Richard didn't really want to discuss the long and difficult ride ahead of them, so before Cara could say anything, he asked, "Have you ever heard the word *Chainfire*?"

Cara let out a sigh. "No."

"Any guesses at all about what it could mean?"

She shook her head.

"What about the place of the bones in the Deep Nothing? Does that mean anything to you?"

Cara didn't answer for a moment. "It seems like 'the Deep Nothing' might be vaguely familiar, like I might have heard it once before."

Richard thought that that sounded encouraging. "Can you recall where, or anything about it?"

"No, I'm afraid not." She reached out and casually plucked a heart-shaped leaf from a vine as she walked beside him. "The only thing I can think is that maybe I heard it as a child. I've tried and tried, but I just can't recall if that's really true—that I might have heard it—or it's just that 'deep' and 'nothing' are common enough words and so that's the reason it seems like I must know them."

Richard let out a disappointed sigh. That was what he wondered, too— if they were simply common words and that was what was making the Deep Nothing sound like maybe he should know it.

"What about a viper with four heads?" he asked.

Cara shook her head again as she dropped back a step to fall in behind him in order to skirt a tree limb hanging over into the trail. A small leaf-green snake was curled on the branch, watching them pass close by, licking the air for the scent of them.

"It makes no sense to me," she said as she twirled the leaf by its stem. "I've never heard of such a beast—or whatever it is. Maybe the four-headed viper lives in a place called the Deep Nothing."

Richard had considered that possibility himself, but because of the way Shota mentioned them separately he doubted it. They had seemed to come to her as individual, distinctly different pieces of information. He supposed that since they were connected to his question about something that could help him discover the truth, they could be associated as Cara had suggested.

At the place in the trail where the trees opened up to the dark mass of the mountains rising up before them, Cara paused.

"Maybe Nicci will catch up with us soon. She knows a lot about magic and all sorts of things. She might know what Chainfire means, or even some of the rest of it. Nicci would be happy to do anything to help you."

Richard hooked a thumb behind his belt. "Do you want to tell me what you and Nicci have cooked up?"

It seemed rather obvious to him, but he wanted to hear her admit the extent of it. He watched her eyes as he waited.

"Nicci had nothing to do with it. It was my idea."

"What, exactly, was your idea?"

Cara turned away from his direct gaze and stared off up the pass. The sky was mostly clear, with stars beginning to appear. Ragged clouds scudded past on the silent wind higher up. It wouldn't be long before the moon rose.

"When you healed me, I felt some of the terrible loneliness haunting you. I think that you may have thought up this woman, Kahlan, in order to fill that void. I don't want you to have to suffer the terrible anguish I sensed in you. Someone who does not exist can't ever fill such a void."

When she didn't say anything else, he did.

"And so you want that void to be filled by Nicci?"

She looked back to his eyes, frustration overtaking her features. "Lord Rahl, I only wanted to help you. I think you need someone to be with you—to share your life—like Shota wanted someone. Like she wanted you. But Shota is the wrong person—for both of you. I think Nicci would be good for you, that's all."

"So you thought that in my place you could give my heart away to someone?"

"Well . . . it sounds wrong the way you put it."

"It is wrong."

"No it's not," she insisted as her hands fisted at her sides. "You need someone. I know that right now you feel lost. I think you're getting worse. Dear spirits, you just gave up your sword.

"You need someone, I know you do. You seem somehow incomplete. In all the time I've known you, you have never seemed that way to me before. My whole life I've never before thought of the Lord Rahl as being with just one woman, much less being married, but with you, it just seems that you need a soul mate.

"Nicci is a better fit than anyone else. She's smart—Nicci is smart enough that you two can really talk. You share things about magic and such. I've seen the way you two talk, the way you both smile. You just look natural together. You're both smart—and both gifted. And, she's beautiful. You should have someone beautiful and Nicci is that."

"And what part did Nicci play in your little plot?"

"Nicci had much the same objections you have—which in a way only proves that I'm right about you two being such a good fit."

"So she didn't like you planning her life, either?"

Cara shrugged one shoulder. "No, that's not what I mean. She had the same objections for you—she spoke up on your behalf, not hers. She only cared about what you wanted. She seemed to know that you would take a dim view of such an idea."

"Well, you're right about one thing, she is smart."

"I was only trying to get her to think about it. I wasn't telling her to throw herself at you. I thought that maybe you two could complete each other, fill the void you both feel. I thought that maybe if I encouraged her to consider it, that nature could take its course, that's all."

Richard wanted to strangle her, but he kept his voice calm because Cara's actions, while wrong, were so touchingly human, so caring, that at the same time he wanted to hug her. Who would ever have thought that a Mord-Sith could ever care about love and companionship. He guessed that he had. But still . . .

"Cara, what you're trying to do is the same thing Shota was trying to do—decide for me what I should feel, how I should live."

"No, it's not the same."

Richard's brow drew down. "And how is it not the same?"

Cara pressed her lips together. He waited. She finally answered in a whisper.

"She doesn't really love you. I do. But not that way," she was quick to add.

Richard wasn't in the mood to argue, or to yell. He knew that Cara's intent was well-meaning, if misguided. More than anything, he could hardly believe what he had just heard her admit out loud. Were it not for every-thing else going on, he would have been overjoyed.

"Cara, I'm married to the woman I love."

She sadly shook her head. "Lord Rahl, I'm sorry, but Kahlan just doesn't exist."

"If she doesn't exist, then why was Shota able to give me clues that will help me prove the truth?"

Cara looked away again. "Because the truth is that there is no Kahlan. The things she told you will only help you discover that sad truth. Did you ever think of that?"

"Only in my nightmares," he said as he started for the mountain pass.

Jillian turned and gazed up into the sky when she heard the raven croak.
The great bird's wide-spread wings rocked as it rode the invisible currents
in the perfectly clear blue sky. As she watched, it croaked again, a harsh,
grating sound that echoed through the deep silence of chasms and carried
out across the parched, rolling landscape baking in the afternoon sun.

Jillian snatched up the small, dead lizard lying on the crumbling wall
beside her and then scrambled up the dusty lane. The raven wheeled ma-
jestically overhead as he watched her running up the rise. She knew that
he had probably seen her ages ago, long before she knew he had been
there.

Holding the lizard by its tail as she rose up on the balls of her feet, Jillian lifted her arm as high as she could toward the sky and wiggled the offering. She laughed when she saw the inky black bird look almost as if it
stumbled in midair when it spotted the ringed lizard dangling from her
fingers. The bird rolled into a steep dive with its wings pulled partly in to
enable it to gather speed as it plummeted.

Jillian hopped up and sat on the dilapidated stone wall beside some of
the exposed paving stones that had once been part of a road. Over eons,
much of that road had been buried beneath layers of dirt. Atop those layers of wind- and rain-borne soil, wild grasses and scraggly trees now
grew. Her grandfather had told her that this was part of a special place and
very old.

Jillian had trouble imagining how old it could be. When she'd been
younger and had asked Grandfather if it was older than him, he had
laughed and said that while he admitted to being old, he was nowhere near
that old and that the ground did not in a single lifetime so swiftly cover
over the accomplishments of man. He said that such slow work required
not only time, but neglect. There had been plenty of time, and with virtually no people left, neglect had worked its ways.

Grandfather had told her how this empty, ancient city had once been inhabited by their ancestors. Jillian loved to hear his stories about the mysterious people who had once lived in this place and had built the incredible city up on the headland beyond the stone spires.

Her grandfather was a teller, and, since she was always so eager to hear his tellings of the old lore, he said that if she was willing to put in the effort he would make her the teller who would one day take his place. Jillian was excited at the prospect of learning to be a teller and mastering all the things there was to learn, someone respected for their knowledge of the ancient times and their heritage, but at the same time she didn't like the implication that such an eventual advancement among her people would mark her grandfather's passing.

Lokey alighted next to her and folded in his glossy black wings, bringing her out of her consideration of weighty subjects, of ancient people and the cities they built, of wars and great deeds. The curious raven waddled closer.

Jillian set down the freshly dead lizard and, holding the tip of its tail, wiggled it temptingly.

Lokey cocked his head, watching. Instead of taking the offering, he blinked his black eyes. He waddled closer to her, leading with his right foot in the cautious sideways manner he always used when approaching carrion. Rather than flapping his wings and hopping back several times in the guarded practice he employed when coming upon what he hoped would be a meal but could potentially turn into a threat, he stepped boldly forward and snatched her buckskin sleeve in his heavy bill.

"Lokey, what are you doing?"

Lokey tugged insistently. The curious bird usually plucked at the beads down the sleeve or the leather thongs at the end, but now he pulled the sleeve itself.

"What?" she asked. "What do you want?"

He let go of her sleeve and cocked his head as he peered at her with one gleaming eye. Ravens were intelligent creatures, but she was never quite sure just how intelligent. Sometimes she thought that Lokey was smarter than some people she knew.

Lokey's throat feathers and ears lifted out aggressively.

He suddenly let out a piercing caw that sounded very much like angry frustration at not being able to talk so that he could tell her something. *Kraaah.* He fluffed out his feathers again and cawed again. *Kraaah.*

Jillian stroked his head and then his back, scratching gently but firmly under his raised black plumage—something he loved to have done—before smoothing down his ruffled feathers. Instead of clicking contentedly and blinking lazily, as he usually did when she gave him a such a scratch, he hopped back a step out of her reach and let out three piercing caws that made her ears hurt. *Kraaah. Kraaah. Kraaah.*

She covered her ears. "What's gotten into you today?"

Lokey hopped up and down, flapping his wings. *Kraaah.* He ran across the top of the old cobble road, flapping and croaking. At the other side he fluttered up into the air, alighted, and then lifted off the ground again. *Kraaah.*

Jillian stood. "You want me to come with you?"

Lokey cawed noisily as if to confirm that she had at long last guessed correctly. Jillian laughed. She was sure that the crazy bird could understand every word she said and sometimes read her thoughts besides. She loved having him around. Sometimes when she talked to him he would quietly stand nearby and listen.

Her grandfather had told her not to let Lokey sleep in her room or he would know her dreams. Jillian mostly had wonderful dreams, so she didn't mind if Lokey knew them. She suspected that maybe her friend did know her dreams and that was why she often awoke to find him perched on the nearby windowsill, sleeping contentedly.

But she was always very careful not to send him any nightmares.

"Did you find yourself a nice dead antelope? Or maybe a rabbit? Is that why you're not hungry?" She shook her finger at him. "Lokey," she scolded, "did you steal another raven's cache?"

Lokey was always hungry. Her ravenous raven, she often called him. He would share her dinner with her if she would let him and steal it if she wouldn't. Even if he was too full to eat the lizard, she was surprised that he didn't at least take it away and hide it for later. Ravens hid whatever they couldn't manage to eat—and they could eat a lot. She couldn't understand how it was that the bird didn't get fat.

Jillian stood and brushed the dust from the seat of her dress and her knobby knees. Lokey was already airborne, circling, cawing, urging her to hurry.

"All right, all right," she complained as she held her arms out for balance while scurrying along the top of the fat wall along an enclosure strewn with rubble.

At the crest of the small hill she stood with one hand on the sash of cloth wrapped around her hip while with her other hand she shielded her eyes as she peered up into the bright sky to watch her friend pitching and rolling in a bid to keep her attention. Lokey was a shameless show-off. If he couldn't do aerial stunts to impress other ravens, he would happily do them for her.

"Yes," she yelled into the sky, "you're a clever bird, Lokey."

Lokey cawed once and then swiftly beat his wings. Jillian's gaze followed him, her hand shielding her eyes from the sunlight, as he flew south out over the vast expanse before her. Random ribbons of green summer grasses, up closer to the foot of the headland and mountains behind her, cut through the barren landscape. To the sides, hazy violet fingers of distant mountains, each farther one a shade softer and lighter, extended down into the desolate plain that seemed to go south forever. She knew it didn't, though. Grandfather said that to the south was a great barrier and beyond a long forbidden place called the Old World.

In the distance, down among the green patches on the plain that lay close up against the foothills, she could see the place where her people lived in the summers. Wooden fences filled the broken gaps in ancient stone walls that held their goats, pigs, and chickens. Some of their cattle grazed out on the summer grasses. There was water in this place, and some trees, their leaves shimmering in the bright sunlight. Gardens stretched out beside the simple brick houses that had withstood the harsh winter winds and baking summer sun for untold centuries.

And then, when she glanced up again at Lokey, Jillian saw at the horizon toward the west a faint cloud of dust rising up.

It was so far away that it seemed tiny. The smudge of dust against the deep blue of the sky where it met the horizon seemed to hang in the air, motionless, but she knew that it was just a trick of the distance that made it look tiny and still. Even from this far, she was able to tell that it was spread across a broad swath. It was still so far away that it was hard to see much of its cause. Had it not been for Lokey, Jillian likely wouldn't have spotted it for some time.

Even though she couldn't yet see what was causing the dust, she knew that she had never before seen such a sight.

Her first thought was that it had to be a whirlwind or a dust storm. But as she watched it she realized that it was too broad to be a whirlwind and a dust storm didn't stream up into the sky the way this did. A dust storm, even if it did extend high up, still had at the base what looked like huge, billowing, brown clouds running along the ground that was actually where the gusty winds were churning up the dust.

This wasn't at all like that. This was dust rising up from something coming—from people coming on horses.

Strangers.

More strangers than she could fathom. Strangers in such numbers that it was like something in her grandfather's stories.

Jillian's knees began to tremble. Fear welled up through her, coming to lodge in her throat where screams were born.

This was them. The strangers her grandfather always said would come. They were coming now.

People never doubted her grandfather—to his face, anyway—but she didn't think they really worried about the things in his tellings. After all, their lives were peaceful; no one ever came to disturb them or their homeland.

Jillian, though, had always believed her grandfather and so she'd always known that the strangers would eventually come, but, like other people, she'd always thought it would be sometime in the dim future, maybe when she was old, or, maybe even, if they were lucky, generations in the future.

It was only in her infrequent nightmares that the strangers arrived in the present, rather than the far future.

Seeing those columns of dust rising, she knew without a doubt that this was them and they were coming now.

In her whole life she had never seen strangers. No one but Jillian's people ever wandered the inhospitable barrens of the vast and forbidding place known as the Deep Nothing.

She stood trembling in terror, staring at the smudge of dust at the horizon. She was about to see a great many outsiders . . . the ones from the stories.

But it was too soon. She hadn't had a life yet, hadn't had a chance to live and love and have children. Tears brimmed in her eyes, giving everything a watery appearance. She looked over her shoulder and up into the ruins. Was this what they had faced, like in Grandfather's tellings?

Tears began to run down through the dust on her cheeks. She knew, she knew without a hint of doubt, that her life was about to change, and that her dreams would no longer be happy.

Jillian scrambled down off the top of the rubble she had been standing on and ran down the hill, past the wall, the crumbled empty squares of brick buildings, the pits where once buildings had risen up. Her racing feet raised their own cloud of dust as she ran through the ruins of what once had been outposts of an ancient city. She ran down roads that no longer had life around them, no longer were lined with standing buildings.

She had often tried to imagine what it would have been like when people had lived in the houses, when people had walked the streets, cooked in the homes, hung the wash outside their brick houses, traded goods in the squares. No more. They were all long dead. The whole city was long dead, except for the few of Jillian's people who sometimes stayed in the most remote of the old buildings.

As she got closer to those ancient buildings of the outposts that they used when they lived in this area for the summer, Jillian saw people hurrying about, yelling to one another. She saw that they were gathering up their things and collecting the animals. It appeared they were going to move on, maybe back into the shelter of the mountains, or out onto the barrens. She had seen her people do such a thing only a few times before. The threat had always turned out to be imaginary. Jillian knew that this time it was real.

She wasn't sure, though, if they would have enough time to flee the approaching strangers and hide. But her people were strong and swift. They were used to moving around on the empty land. Grandfather said that no one else but her people could survive so well in this forsaken place. They knew the mountain passes and places of water, as well as the hidden passages through what seemed like impassable canyons. They could vanish into the inhospitable land in short order and survive.

Most of them could, anyway. Some, like her grandfather, were no longer swift.

With that renewed fear, her feet ran all the faster, padding with a steady beat over the dusty ground. As she got closer, Jillian saw men packing their travel goods on the mules. Women collected cooking utensils, filled water containers, and carried clothes and tents out from their summer homes and storage buildings. It looked to Jillian that they had been aware of the approaching strangers for some time as they were already well advanced in their preparations to depart.

"Ma!" Jillian called out when she saw her mother packing her pot atop a mule already piled high with their belongings. "Ma!"

Her mother flashed a quick smile and held out a sheltering arm. Even though she was getting past the age for such things, Jillian nuzzled under that arm like a chick burrowing under a mother hen's wing.

"Jillian, get your things." Her mother shooed her with a hand. "Hurry."

Jillian knew better than to question at a time like this. She wiped away her tears and ran to the small, square, ancient building they used as their home when they summered on the plains near the headland. The men sometimes had to replace the roofs when the worst of the weather tore them off, but, other than that, the rest of the stout, squat buildings were the very same buildings constructed by their ancestors who had once built and lived in the deserted city of Caska, up on the headland.

Grandfather, looking drawn and pale as she imagined a ghost might look, waited in the shadows just inside the door. He was not hurrying. Terror swelled in Jillian's chest. She realized that he couldn't come with them. He was old and frail. Like some of the other older people, he wouldn't be swift enough to keep up with the rest of them if they were to escape. She could see in his eyes that he had no intention of trying.

She sank into her grandfather's tender embrace and started wailing even as he comforted her.

"There, there, child," he said, his hand stroking her short-cropped hair. "No time for this."

Grandfather grasped her arms and eased her away as she tried her best to bring her sobbing under control. She knew that she was old enough that she shouldn't be crying in such a way, but she just couldn't help it. He squatted down, his leathery face wrinkling as he smiled at her and brushed away a tear.

Jillian swiped away the rest of her tears, trying to be strong and act her age. "Grandfather, Lokey showed me the strangers who are coming."

He was nodding. "I know. I sent him."

"Oh" was all she could think to say. Her world was turning upside down and it was hard to think, but somewhere in the back of her mind she realized that he had never before done such a thing. She'd never known he could, but, knowing her grandfather, it didn't really surprise her.

"Jillian, listen to me. These men who are coming are the ones I always told you would come. Those who can are going away for a while to hide."

"For how long?"

"For as long as necessary. These men who ride this way are only a small number of those who will eventually come."

Her eyes grew wide. "You mean there are more? But there are so many. They raise more dust than I have ever seen before. There can be more strangers than these?"

His smile was brief and bitter. "These are only a survey party, I expect—the first advance scouts of many more to come. This vast and desolate land is unknown to them. I expect they are looking for routes through it, testing to see if there will be any opposition. I'm afraid that according to the tellings, the men they scout for are more in number than even I can grasp. I believe that these other men, with their uncountable numbers, are yet some time in coming, but even this advance party will be dangerous, ruthless men. Those of our people who are able must flee and hide for now.

"Jillian, you cannot go with them."

Her jaw dropped. "What . . . ?"

"Listen to me. The times I have told you about are upon us."

"But, Ma and Pa won't allow—"

"They will allow what I tell them they must, just as our people must," he said in a stern voice. "This is about far greater matters, matters that have never before involved our people—at least not since our ancestors filled the city. Now these things concern us as well."

Jillian nodded solemnly. "Yes, Grandfather." She was terror stricken, but at the same time she felt an awakening sense of duty to her grandfather's call. If he intended to trust her with such things, then she could not fail him.

"What is it am I to do, then?"

"You are to be the priestess of the bones, the carrier of dreams."

Jillian's mouth again fell open. "Me?"

"Yes, you."

"But I'm still too young. I've not been trained in such things."

"There is no more time, child." He leaned toward her in admonition. "You are the one to do this, Jillian. I have already taught you much of the tellings. You may think you are unprepared, or that you are not old enough, and all that may have some truth to it, but you know more than you may realize. What's more, there is no other. It is upon you to do this."

Jillian couldn't seem to make herself blink. She felt completely inadequate, and at the same time faintly excited and guardedly inspired. Her people were depending on her. More importantly, her grandfather was depending on her and he believed she could do it.

"Yes, Grandfather."

"I will prepare you to be among the dead, and then you must hide among them and wait."

Fear began to wrap its arms around her again. She had never stayed all alone among the dead.

Jillian swallowed. "Grandfather, are you sure that I'm ready for such a thing? To be there, alone, among the dead? Waiting for one of them?"

The light coming in from the open door cast his face with a forbidding look. "You are as ready as I can make you. I had hoped there would be time left to teach you many more things, but at least I have taught you some of what you must know."

Outside, people rushed around in the sunlight, tending to the preparations. They were careful not to look into the shadows, to Grandfather, after he had pulled her away from the rest of them, telling her what she must face.

"To tell you the truth," he said, "this has taken me unprepared as well. The tellings have been carried down from our people for thousands of years, but they never said when it would happen. I never really believed that it would come during my life. I remember my own grandfather telling me the things I have told you and not really believing it would ever happen except maybe in some far future time that didn't really mean anything to my life. But the time is now upon us and we must do our best to honor our ancestors. We must be ready—you must—as we have been taught through the tellings."

"How long will I have to wait?"

"There is no way I can tell you that. You must hide among the spirits.

As the tellers have done down through the centuries, you and I have stashed food, as Lokey does, for just such an eventuality. You will have food to keep your belly full. You can fish and hunt for game when it is safe to be out."

"Yes, Grandfather. But couldn't you hide with me?"

"I will take you up there, help prepare you, and tell you all I can. But I must then return here to help make these strangers think we are out in the open and welcoming to them while the others of our people escape—and so that you will be able to hide. I could not be as swift as you, nor as small to slip through the narrow places so that these men cannot follow you. I will have to return here and do my part."

"What if the strangers hurt you?"

Grandfather took a breath and let it out with weary resolve. "It may be that they do so. These men who come will be capable of such brutality— that is why this is so important. Their cruel ways are why we must be strong and why we must not give in to them. Even if I die"—he shook a finger at her—"and you can be sure that I will do my best not to, I will be buying the rest of you the time you need."

Jillian chewed on her lip. "Aren't you afraid to die?"

He nodded as he smiled. "Very. But I have lived a long life and because I love you so, I would choose that you have a chance to do the same."

"Grandfather," she said through choking tears, "I want you to be with me for my life."

He took her hand. "Me too, child. I wish to see you grow into a woman and have your own children. But I don't want you to worry too much for me; I am not so helpless nor a fool. I will sit in the shade with the others and present no threat to these men. We will confess to the strangers that the younger of our people ran away in terror, but we could not. The strangers will likely have more important things to do than waste their energy harming us. We will be fine. I want you to think about what you must do, and not worry about me."

Jillian felt a little better about his safety. "Yes, Grandfather."

"Besides," he told her, "Lokey will be with you, and he will carry my spirit with him, so it will be almost like I am watching over you." When she smiled at that, he said, "Come, now. We must go and make preparations."

Jillian's mother and father were allowed a brief farewell after Grandfather told them in a stern voice that he was taking her to be with their spirit ancestors and see to the safety of their people.

Her mother and father either understood the importance of allowing their daughter to go, or were too afraid of Grandfather to refuse. In either case they hugged her and bid her strength until they could be together again.

Without speaking more of it, Grandfather led her away as eyes followed them. He took her up the ancient roads and through gorges, past the deserted outposts and mysterious buildings, and up the great rise of the land. As they climbed, the sun lowered in the western sky behind the golden tail of dust that slowly but steadily came ever closer. She knew that before the sun set, most of her people would be gone.

The lowering sun allowed the murky shadows to begin to haunt the defiles. The smooth stone, layered with twisting bands of rock, invited them ever onward to see what might be around each curving bend. Along the bottom the gravel was littered here and there with bones of small animals. Most, she knew, were the leavings of the coyotes and the wolves. She tried very hard to banish the mental image of her own bleached bones lying scattered in the gravel.

Overhead, Lokey lazily circled in the deepening blue of the sky as he watched her making her way with Grandfather up toward the headland. When they reached the stone spires, the bird silently glided among the columns' pinnacles, as if it were a game. He had followed them up to the ancient city enough times that he must have thought nothing of it. To Jillian, even though Grandfather had taken her up through the maze of ravines, gullies, and deep canyons a great many times, this time it all seemed new to her.

This time she was going as the priestess of the bones, the carrier of dreams.

At a place where a quiet stream followed a twisting route through the graveled bottom of a very deep canyon, Grandfather led her to a small boulder in the cool shade and sat her down. All around, the smooth, undulating sides of the canyon rose nearly straight up, leaving no way to climb out if a sudden rain brought a flood. It was a dangerous place—for more than the reason of the threat of flash floods. It was a tangle of side gullies and canyons that in places took complicated routes around huge standing columns so that it was possible to go around in circles and never find your way out. Jillian, though, knew her way through this labyrinth, as well as others.

As she sat quietly, waiting, Grandfather opened a pouch he always carried tied to his belt. He pulled out a folded piece of oilcloth from among the things he carried in the pouch, and opened it in one palm. He dipped his first finger in the oily black substance inside.

Grandfather lifted her chin. "Hold still, now, while I paint your face."

Jillian had never been painted before. She knew of the formality from Grandfather's stories, but she just never thought about it being her who would be the priestess of the bones, the one to be painted. She sat as still as she could while he worked, feeling that everything was happening too fast—before she had even had time to really think about it. Earlier that day the most she had on her mind was catching a lizard for Lokey. Now it felt as if the weight of the world was on her shoulders.

"There," Grandfather said. "Come see."

Jillian knelt beside a still pool and bent forward. She gasped. What she saw was frightening. The face staring back had a painted black band across it, like a blindfold, but one she could see through. Her copper-colored eyes stared back at her from the dark midst of that smoky black mask.

"Now the evil spirits will not be able to see you," he told her as he stood. "You can safely be among our ancestors."

Jillian stood as well, feeling very strange indeed. She felt transformed. The face she'd seen had been the face of the priestess. She'd heard about it in Grandfather's tellings, but she'd never seen such a face in real life, much less expected it to ever be her own.

She leaned over and stole a cautious peek into the still pool. "This will truly hide me?"

"It will keep you safe," he said as he nodded.

She wondered if Lokey would know her, if he would be afraid of her. The face staring back from the still water certainly scared her.

"Come," Grandfather said, "we must get you up there and then I must get back so the men will find me there with those of our people who remain behind."

When at long last they climbed out of the spires and stone canyons, they were finally up near the city, just outside the great main wall but within some of the outer rings of smaller walls.

They had emerged near the graveyard.

Grandfather gestured. "You lead the way, Jillian. This is your place now."

Jillian nodded and started out toward the city glowing in the golden, late-day sunlight. It was a beautiful sight, as it always was, but this day it also seemed haunting to her. It seemed she was seeing it through new eyes. She felt a very real connection with her ancestors now.

The grand buildings looked as if people might still occupy them, as if she might spot some of them through the empty window openings as they went about their daily lives. Some of the structures were immense, with soaring pillars holding up projecting sections of slate roofs. Other buildings had rows of arched windows on each level. Grandfather had taken her into some of those buildings. It was amazing to see places that were stacked inside with layers of rooms so that one had to climb stairs—stairs actually built right inside the buildings—to get to rooms above. The ancient builders seemed almost magical in the things they had accomplished. From a distance, glowing in the golden light, it truly was a majestic sight.

Now, she would walk the streets alone, accompanied only by the spirits of those who had once lived here. She felt safe, though, knowing that Grandfather had painted upon her the mask of the priestess of the bones.

She would be the one who would cast the dreams at the strangers.

If she did her job well, the strangers would be so frightened that they would flee and her people would be safe.

She tried not to think about how the people who once had lived here had done the same thing and yet had failed.

"Do you think there will be too many?" she asked, suddenly frightened by the tellings of the ancient debacle.

"Too many?" he puzzled at her as they walked beside a wall that had long ago been encased by living nets of vines that now held the crumbling stones in place.

"Too many for the dreams. I'm only one person—and I'm not experienced, or older, or anything. It's just me."

His big hand gave her an assuring pat between her shoulder blades. "Numbers do not matter. He will help give you the strength you need." Grandfather lifted a cautionary finger. "And don't forget, Jillian, the tellings say that you must be devoted to this one. He is to be your master."

Jillian nodded as they entered the vast graveyard. In the lower reaches there were simple stone markers. As they climbed higher, past row upon row of graves, they eventually came to larger and more ornate monuments to the dead. Some of them had grand statues of people in proud poses atop them. Some had carvings of the flame of life that represented the Creator's light. Some had ancient inscriptions of lasting love. A few had only an ancient symbol on them that her grandfather told her was called a Grace. Some of the great monuments had only a name.

Deep in the place of the dead, near the highest spot, where the weathered trees grew large and twisted, they came at last to a grand grave marked with a huge, ornately crafted stone monument. Atop it sat a speckled gray granite urn that held olives, pears, and other fruits, with grapes spilling out over one side, all carved from the same piece of stone. Grandfather, who had taken her to see this monument many times as he gave her tellings, said that the urn was meant to represent the bounty of life that man created through his creative efforts and hard work.

He watched her as she paused and then stepped closer to a huge gravestone for someone long dead, carved from one piece of stone back in the time that the ancient city had been alive. She wondered what he had been like. She wondered if he had been kind, or cruel, or young, or old.

Lokey alighted atop the carved stone grapes and ruffled his glossy black feathers before settling himself. She was glad that Lokey would keep her company in such a lonely place.

Jillian reached out and traced a finger through the letters that spelled out the name carved in the gray granite.

"Do you think the tellings are true, Grandfather? I mean, really true?"

"I was taught that they are."

"Then he really will come back to us from the world of the dead? Really, truly come back to life from the dead?"

She looked back over her shoulder. Her grandfather, standing close behind her, reached out and reverently touched the stone monument. He nodded solemnly.

"He will."

"Then I will wait for him," she said. "The priestess of the bones will be here to welcome him and serve him when he returns to life."

Jillian briefly glanced at the dust rising at the horizon and then turned back to the tomb. "Please hurry," she implored of the dead man.

As her grandfather watched, she gently ran her small fingers through the bold letters on the tomb.

"I can't cast the dreams without you," Jillian said softly to the name carved in the stone. "Please hurry, Richard Rahl, and return to the living."

As Nicci's horse, Sa'din, stepped through the empty city, the clop of his hooves on the stone cobbles echoed among the canyons of deserted buildings like a forlorn call that went unanswered. Colorful shutters stood open on some of the windows, closed on others. On the second floor of many of the buildings, tiny balconies overlooking the empty streets had wrought-iron railings standing in front of doors with drapes pulled tightly closed. There was no breeze to move the legs of a pair of pants Nicci saw hanging on a line strung between the second floors on opposite sides of an empty alleyway. The owner of the pants had long ago walked off without them.

The quiet was so imposing that it bordered on ominous. It was an eerie feeling being within a city without its people, the mere shell that had once held life and vitality, now with form but no purpose. It was somewhat reminiscent of viewing a corpse, the way that it seemed so nearly alive and yet so still that there could be no doubt as to the terrible truth. If left this way, if not brought back from the cold brink with life, it would eventually crumble into forgotten ruins.

Through narrow gaps between buildings, Nicci caught glimpses of the Wizard's Keep embedded in a rocky slope high up on the monstrous mountain. The vast, dark complex perched like a menacing vulture ready to pick over the remains of the silent city. Spires, towers, and high bridges rising up from the Keep snagged clouds slowly drifting past the sheer, fractured face of the rock. The immense edifice was as sinister a sight as she had ever seen. Still, she knew that in reality it wasn't a sinister place, and she was relieved to at last have arrived.

It had been a long and difficult journey from the Old World up to Aydindril. There had been times when she had feared she would never be able to escape the snares of troops strung out along the way. There had been times when she had for a time lost herself in killing them. There were so many, though, that she knew she had no realistic hope of making any meaningful reduction in their numbers. It had enraged her that she could be little more than a pest to them. Still, her real purpose had been to reach Richard. The Order troops were merely an obstacle in her way.

Through the conjured connection she had forged with Richard, Nicci knew that she was at long last near to him. She hadn't found him yet, but she knew she soon would.

For a time, before she had even started on her way, she had come to think that she would never again have a chance to see him.

The fighting for control of Altur'Rang had been brutal. The troops who had attacked, having been surprised and bloodied in the beginning as evening had fallen, being as experienced and battle-hardened as they were, had quickly gathered their wits and their numbers and, by the light of fires they'd set, made a concentrated effort to turn the tide of battle.

Even with as much as Nicci knew about the manner in which Jagang would deal with the insurrection in Altur'Rang, even she didn't expect all that he had thrown an them. For a time, with the help of an unexpected third wizard, it had seemed that the Order troops would overpower the inexperienced defenders. It was a darkly hopeless moment when it appeared that the efforts of the people of Altur'Rang to defend themselves were to be for naught. The specter of failure, and the ensuing slaughter everyone knew such a failure would bring, came to seem not only inevitable, but all too real. For a time, Nicci and those with her believed they would not survive the night.

Despite her wounds and exhaustion, and even more than her sincere desire to help the people she knew in Altur'Rang and all the innocent and helpless souls who would be slaughtered if they lost, the thought of never seeing Richard again had galvanized Nicci and given her the extra strength of will to push on. She used her fear of never seeing Richard again to ignite a fierce rage that could only be quenched with the blood of the enemy who stood in her way.

At the crucial point in the battle, in the harsh, flickering light of the roaring blazes from buildings burning all around, as the enemy wizard stood on the platform of a public well in an open square casting death and ghastly suffering as he urged his men onward, Nicci appeared like an avenging spirit in the midst of their ranks and bounded up onto the platform. It was an event so unexpected that it caught the attention of everyone. In that brief fraction of time when they all stared in stunned surprise, in full view of the Order troops, she abruptly cleaved the chest of their astonished wizard and with her bare hands ripped out his still beating heart. With a cry of primal anger, Nicci held the bloody trophy up for his soldiers to see and promised them the same.

At that moment, Victor Cascella charged with his men into the center of the invaders. He was gripped by rage of his own, not just that the marauding thugs would murder and pillage the people of Altur'Rang, but that they would steal his hard-won liberty. Had he the gift, his fierce glare alone might have cut down the enemy. As it was, his bold attack was as unexpected as it was ferocious. That combination of events broke the courage of the attackers. None of them wanted to face the wrath of the blacksmith and fall under the fury of his mace any more than they wanted a mad sorceress who seemed like the avenging spirit of death itself to rip out their hearts.

The elite Order troops turned and tried to escape from the city, from the middle of an enraged populous. Rather than let the people of the city be satisfied with victory, Nicci had insisted that the enemy be pursued and killed to a man.

She alone fully understood how important it was that none of the soldiers escaped to tell the tale of their loss. Emperor Jagang would be awaiting word that his home city had been brought back under his command, that the insurrectionists had been tortured to death, and that the people of the city had been driven to their knees, that there was such slaughter that it would for all time serve as a warning for others.

Even though he expected success, Nicci knew that Jagang would have taken word of the defeat in stride. He had lost battles before. It did not deter him. From losses he learned the measure of the opposition. He would have simply sent more troops the next time, enough to accomplish the task, and to do so as viciously as possible not only to insure victory, but to insure an extra measure of punishment for resisting his authority.

Nicci knew the man. He did not care about the lives of his soldiers—or the lives of anyone, for that matter. If men fought for the Order and died, then glory in the afterlife would be their reward. They could expect only sacrifice in this life.

But if no word of the battle for Altur'Rang ever arrived, that was something altogether different.

Nicci knew that Jagang was nettled by lack of knowledge more than any enemy. He did not like the unknown. She knew that sending off crack troops—along with three rare and valuable wizards—and then never again hearing another word from any of them, would gall him no end. He would work the mystery over and over in his mind the way a nervous man worked a worry stone in his fingers.

In the end, not having any testimony whatsoever as to the outcome of the battle for Altur'Rang would spook him more than a simple defeat. He did not fear losing men—life meant little to him—so a defeat he could handle, but he didn't at all like the unknown. Perhaps worse, his army, composed of men prone to superstition, would take such an event as a bad omen.

As Nicci followed the twisting turns of the narrow cobblestone street, she came around a curve and looked up to see, between the buildings lining each side, a sight that nearly took her breath away. On a hill in the distance, lit by the sun, set on a sweep of beautiful grounds of emerald green, stood a magnificent palace of white stone. It was as elegant as anything she had ever seen. It was a structure that stood proud, strong, and pleasingly possessed of a distinctly feminine grace. This, she knew, could be nothing other than the Confessors' Palace.

The sight of it, exquisite, authoritative, pure, stood in stark contrast to the towering mountain behind it upon which rose the dark, soaring walls of the Keep. It seemed clear to Nicci that the Confessors' Palace was meant to be majesty backed by dark threat.

This had been, after all, the place that for millennia had ruled the Midlands. The larger lands of the Midlands had palaces in the city for their ambassadors and members of the Central Council, which had ruled the collective lands of the Midlands. The Mother Confessor reigned over not only the Confessors, but the Central Council as well. Kings and queens answered to her, as did every ruler of every land of the Midlands. From the narrow street she was on, Nicci didn't see the palaces representing the various lands, but she knew that not a one of them would be as grand as the Confessors' Palace—especially not with the imposing Keep as a backdrop.

Through a gap in the buildings to the side, movement caught Nicci's attention. When she saw that it was dust rising into the still air, she laid the reins over and swung Sa'din around, directing him down a side street. Squeezing her lower legs, she urged him into a canter. Without pause he charged off down the narrow dirt street. In flashes between buildings, she could see the dust rising in the distance. Someone was riding at speed up a road toward the mountain where the Keep stood. Through her link with him, she knew who it had to be.

Nicci had helped end the threat to Altur'Rang as swiftly as possible primarily so that she could be off after Richard. It wasn't that she didn't care about those people, or eliminating the animals sent to massacre them, it was just that she cared more about getting to Richard. At first, she had it in her mind to ride as fast as she could and catch up with him and Cara. It had quickly became apparent, however, that there was no chance of that. He was simply traveling too swiftly. When Richard was focused on a goal and determined to get to it, he was relentless.

Nicci realized that her only hope of ever catching up with him again was, instead of chasing him, to head toward where he would go next and intercept him. She knew that the witch woman couldn't help him find a woman who didn't exist, so Nicci reasoned that Richard would next head north to try to get help from the only wizard he knew, his grandfather, Zedd, at the Wizard's Keep in Aydindril. Since she'd still been a long way back to the southeast, Nicci had decided to take the shortest route to Aydindril, thereby needing to cover much less distance than he would and thus be able to intercept him there.

As she broke out of the narrow confines of the buildings of the city, Nicci's heart quickened when she saw that she was right, when she finally saw Richard.

He and Cara were charging up a road, pulling a long ribbon of dust behind them. Nicci recalled that they'd left Altur'Rang with six horses; they now had only three. By the way they were riding, Nicci strongly suspected that she knew why. When Richard had his mind set on something he was unstoppable. He had probably ridden the other horses to death.

As Nicci galloped out of the city to cut them off, Richard immediately spotted her and slowed his pace. Sa'din carried her swiftly over the small rises, past paddocks, stables, workshops, deserted market stands, a black-smith's shop, and fenced pastures with buildings for animals that were no longer there. Stands of pine trees flashed past and she raced under the broad crowns of white oaks crowded close to the road in places.

Nicci couldn't wait to see Richard again. Her life suddenly had purpose again. She wondered if anything had happened with the witch woman to finally convince him that there was no woman from his dreams that he re-membered as real. Nicci even held out some hope that he had recovered from his delusions and was now back to his old self. Her relief at seeing him sitting tall atop his horse overcame her concern as to why he would be racing for the Keep.

Since she had been separated from him, Nicci had gone over every-thing that had happened, trying to pinpoint the source of his delusion, and she had come to a frightening theory. Going over it a thousand times in her mind, trying to remember every detail, Nicci had come to fear that she had actually been the cause of his problem.

She had been working at a rapid pace as she tried to save his life. There were other people around creating a distraction. She was worried that en-emy soldiers would attack at any moment and so she dared not slow what she was doing. Even worse, she was attempting things she had never done before—things she'd never even heard of before. After all, Subtractive Magic was used to rain ruin, not to heal. She was doing things she wasn't sure would work. She also knew that there was no other hope and so she had no choice.

But she feared that in that dangerous mix, she was the one who had ac-cidentally induced the problem with Richard's memory, with his mind. If that was true, she would never forgive herself.

If she had made a mistake with Subtractive Magic, and had eliminated some element of his mind, some vital part that made him able to interact effectively with reality, there would be no way to restore such a loss. Elim-inating something with Subtractive Magic was as irreversible as death. If she had damaged his mind, he would never again be the same, dwelling forever in a twilight world of his own imagination, never again able to rec-ognize the truth of the world around him . . . and it would all be her fault.

That thought had taken her to the edge of despair.

Richard and Cara halted beside the road as they waited for Nicci to reach them. Fields of tall summer grass grew at the base of wooded hills beyond. Their horses took the opportunity to crop at that long grass where it came close to the side of the road.

The sight of Richard swelled Nicci's heart with joy. His hair was a little longer, and he looked dusty from the ride, but he looked as taut, as tall, as powerful, as handsome, as masterful, as incisive, as focused, as driven as he always looked, like nothing in the world around him escaped his notice. Despite his simple and dusty travel clothes, he looked every inch the Lord Rahl himself.

Still, it seemed there was something not right about him.

"Richard!" Nicci called out as she raced up to him and Cara, even though they saw her. Nicci reined in Sa'din as she reached them. Once she was stopped, the dust she had outpaced began to catch up and drift past. Richard and Cara waited. With the way Nicci had shouted they looked like they expected her to say something urgent, when it had been nothing more than her excitement at seeing him.

"I'm relieved to see that you're both well," Nicci said.

Richard visibly relaxed and draped both hands over the pommel of his saddle. His horse shivered flies off its rump. Cara sat up straight in her saddle, her horse close and behind Richard's, tossing its head a little at how tightly she had him reined in after the gallop.

"I'm glad to see you looking well, too," Richard said. His warm smile said that he meant it. Nicci could have bubbled over into joyous laughter at seeing that smile, but she restrained herself and simply returned it. "How did it go in Altur'Rang?" he asked. "Is the city safe?"

"They destroyed the invaders." Nicci tightened the reins to settle down an excited Sa'din. She gave his neck a reassuring pat to help calm him down. "The city is safe for now. Victor and Ishaq said to tell you that they are free and will stay that way."

Richard nodded with quiet satisfaction. "You're all right, then? I was worried about you."

"Fine," she said, unable to restrain her grin at the very idea that he had been worried for her and not the least bit interested in telling him about injuries that were now healed. None of that mattered anymore. She was with Richard again.

He looked weary, as if he and Cara had not gotten much sleep on their journey north. By the distance they had covered in such a short time, they could not have rested much.

Nicci then realized what it was that was wrong with him.

He didn't have his sword.

"Richard, where's—"

Cara, behind him, flashed Nicci a forbidding look and at the same time quickly drew a finger across her throat, warning Nicci to cut off what she had been about to ask.

"Where are the other horses?" Nicci quickly asked, altering the course of her question to cover over the ominous silence that had oozed up in the brief pause.

Richard sighed, apparently not realizing the truth of what she had been about to ask. "I'm afraid I've been pushing them pretty hard. A few of them came up lame and the rest died. We've had to get new horses along the way. These we stole from an Imperial Order encampment near Galea. They have troops billeted all over the Midlands. We helped ourselves to their horses and supplies along the way."

Cara smiled with sly satisfaction, but remained silent.

Nicci wondered how he had managed such things without his sword. She then realized how foolish such a thought was; the sword didn't make Richard the man he was.

"And the beast?" Nicci asked.

Richard glanced over his shoulder at Cara. "We've had a few encounters."

For some reason, Nicci sensed something disquieting in his voice, if not his words.

"A few encounters?" she asked. "What sort of encounters? What's the matter? What's wrong?"

"We managed, that's all. We'll talk about it later when we have time." She could see by the irritable look in his eyes that he was understating it and was in no mood to have to relive it right then. He pulled the reins over, taking his horse's attention away from the grass. "Right now I need to get up to the Keep."

"And what of the witch woman?" Nicci asked as she walked her horse alongside his. "What did you find out? What did she say?"

"That what I seek is long buried," he muttered dejectedly to himself. Richard wiped a weary hand across his face and then came out of his private thoughts to fix her in his penetrating gaze. "Does the word *Chainfire* mean anything to you?" When Nicci shook her head, he asked, "What about the Deep Nothing?"

"Deep Nothing?" Nicci thought it over briefly. "No, what is it?"

"I have no idea, but I need to find out. I'm hoping Zedd will be able to shed some light on it. Come on, let's get moving."

With that, he galloped away. Nicci immediately urged Sa'din into a gallop to keep up.

The road up to the Keep offered magnificent views of the city of Aydin-dril spread out below, even though clouds had slipped in over the mountains to mute the late-afternoon light and leave the still air muggy. Were it not for her concerns, Nicci might have found the views from the road up to the Keep to be one of the most beautiful vistas she had ever seen—and an appreciation of such beauty was something relatively new to her, something that Richard had awakened in her.

As it was, though, she brooded over his continuing fixation on finding the woman Kahlan that he was so sure he remembered. He hadn't said anything about her, yet, probably because from their previous disagreements he had become frustrated by the futility of trying to convince her that he had to find a woman Nicci knew did not exist. Despite not mentioning her, it was clear to Nicci that he was no less determined to find Kahlan now than he had been the last time Nicci had been with him. Her hopes that he would be better by the time she finally caught up with him had faded. Her pleasure over the view dimmed.

There was something, though—a look in his eyes—that seemed to Nicci somehow different. She couldn't put her finger on what it was, or what it could mean. He'd always had a penetrating gaze, a cutting, raptor-like appraisal, but now, the way he met her gaze, it was even more acute, as if he were laying her open and searching her soul. Nicci had nothing to hide, though, especially from Richard. She had nothing but his best interest at heart. She wanted nothing more than for him to be happy. She would do anything to help him to be happy.

She supposed that was why her mood had sunk; even though he was still determined, she knew that he was growing ever more dispirited. The light of life in his eyes was something Nicci treasured. She would not want to see it go out.

Trying to keep up with him left Nicci no opportunity to ask him about what had gone on with the witch woman. From Cara's silence, Nicci knew that, whatever had happened, it had not gone as well as Richard had expected. That was no surprise to Nicci. How could a witch woman, even if she wanted to help, be of any use in finding a woman who existed only in Richard's mind?

Whatever Chainfire could be, Nicci had no idea, but she could sense in his voice, as well as his tense expression, how eager Richard was to discover its meaning. After having lived with him for so long, Nicci knew his feelings without him having to say a word. It was obvious he'd placed a lot of significance on the meaning behind Chainfire.

More than that, though, Nicci was worried as to what could have happened to his sword. She couldn't imagine why he didn't have it with him. Her concern had been heightened all the more by the way Cara had immediately cut off the question, to say nothing of the way Richard had not mentioned it. The Sword of Truth was not something Richard would have lightly forgotten all about.

Higher up on the mountain, as they rode up the switchbacks, the road emerged from a thick growth of towering spruce trees before a stone bridge spanning a chasm of immense depth. It looked to Nicci as if the mountain were split open to its core, with the closer side pulled away from the rest of the mountain. As they rode single-file across the bridge spanning the yawning abyss, she glanced over the edge and could see sheer rock walls to each side dropping down through cottony clouds drifting by below them. It was a dizzying sight that made her stomach feel queasy.

Nicci could tell by Sa'din's gait how tired he was. His ears lazily swiveled toward the drop to each side as they crossed the bridge. Richard and Cara's horses, though, were lathered and blowing hard. Nicci knew how well Richard treated animals, and yet he was showing these no mercy. He obviously thought there were higher values involved than the lives of animals. She knew what that value was: human life. One in particular.

The walls of the Keep, composed of intricately joined blocks of dark granite, rose up like a cliff before them. Coming off the bridge, riding between Richard in front and Cara at the rear, Nicci stared up at the Keep's complex maze of ramparts, bastions, towers, connecting passageways, and bridges. The place looked somehow alive, as if it were watching them approach the gaping entrance of arched stone where the road tunneled under the base of the outer wall.

Without hesitation, Richard trotted his horse in under the raised, massive portcullis. Given a choice, Nicci would have been a bit more cautious in her approach to such a place. Her skin crawled with the power emanating from within. She had never before felt such a strong sense of the force of magic from within a place. It was like standing alone on a plain as a vast, massive thunderstorm was about to envelope her.

The sensation gave her some measure of the shields that guarded the Keep. From what she had to conclude by what she could sense, the shields at the Palace of the Prophets had been child's play by comparison. Too, those were predominantly Additive and the palace had been built for an entirely different purpose. Here, Subtractive shields were employed in equal service. The lethality of their dominion was not concealed, but manifest to those whose business it was to know of such things.

Almost unnoticed, hazy clouds had closed in overhead, leaving the late-afternoon sky a flat, steel gray. The gloom that replaced the sunlight made the stone of the Keep look all the darker, all the more forbidding, almost as if the Keep itself had drawn a shroud of clouds tightly around itself as it watched the approach of a sorceress and a wizard able to command powers that yet haunted this place.

After coming out from under the arched opening in the thick outer wall, they emerged on a road that continued through the deep interior canyon of the Keep. Beyond, the road tunneled through another dark wall that provided a second barrier, should one ever be necessary. Without pause, Richard rode on into that long, dark passageway. The sounds of the horses' hooves echoed off the damp stone under the murky, arched passage.

Beyond the tunnel, they emerged beside an expansive paddock growing thick with lush grass. The gravel road ran along the side of a wall to the right with several doors. The first doors they'd encountered just inside the portcullis would have been where visitors entered. Nicci surmised that this, beyond the second wall, was probably the working entrance to the Keep. A fence along the other side of the road enclosed the paddock. Beyond, to the left, the back side of the paddock was walled off by the Keep itself. At the far end stood the stables.

Without a word, Richard dismounted and opened the gate to the paddock, letting his horse go in but leaving it saddled. Perplexed, Cara and Nicci nonetheless followed his example before following him across the grounds toward an entrance with a dozen wide granite steps worn smooth and swaybacked over time. They led up into a recessed entryway where simple but heavy double doors into the Keep proper began to creak open.

An old man, wavy white hair in disarray, peered out like a homeowner surprised by visitors. He gulped air, apparently winded from having run through the Keep when he'd realized that someone was coming. He had no doubt been alerted by webs of magic that announced anyone taking the road up to the Keep. In ancient times there would have been people closer at hand to see to anyone newly arrived. Now there was only the old man. By the way he was breathing he must have been clear across the Keep when the alarms had warned him.

Even through the look of astonishment on his thin, wrinkled face, Nicci recognized elements of the features. She knew that he could be none other than Richard's grandfather Zedd. He was tall, but as thin as a sapling. His hazel eyes were wide with wonder and a kind of childlike excitement, if not innocence. His plain, unadorned robes marked him as a great wizard. He wore his age well. It was a pleasing preview of how, in part, time might treat Richard.

The old man threw his arms up over his head. "Richard!" A joyous grin swept across his face. "Bags, is that really you, my boy?"

Zedd emerged from the doorway and started down the worn steps into the dreary light.

Richard ran to his grandfather and lifted him off the steps, hugging him fiercely enough to drive the wind from the already winded old man. They both laughed, a pleasing sound with obvious kinship.

"Zedd! You can't imagine how glad I am to see you!"

"And you, my boy," Zedd said in a voice turning teary. "It's been too long. Far too long."

He reached a sticklike hand past Richard and gripped Cara's shoulder. "How are you, my dear? You appear to be near to spent. Are you all right?"

"I am Mord-Sith," she said, looking a bit indignant. "Of course I'm all right. Why would you think I look anything but perfectly fine?"

Zedd chuckled as he pushed back from Richard. "No reason, I suppose. You both look like you could use some rest and a meal or two is all. But you do look fine and I'm mighty happy to see you again."

Cara smiled at that. "I've missed you, Zedd."

Zedd waggled a finger. "Not very Mord-Sith of you to miss an old man. Rikka will be astonished to hear such a thing."

"Rikka?" Cara asked in surprise. "Rikka is here?"

Zedd waggled a hand back in the direction of the partly opened door. "She's back in there, somewhere . . . patrolling, I imagine. She seems to have two preoccupations in life, patrolling and harassing me. I'm telling you, I have no peace of mind with the woman. Worse, she's too clever for her own good. At least she's a talented cook."

Cara's brows lifted. "Rikka can cook?"

Zedd winced, pulling a breath through his teeth. "Don't tell her I said that or I'll never hear the end of it. The woman—"

"Zedd," Richard interrupted, "I have trouble and I need help."

"Are you well? You aren't ill, are you? You don't look entirely yourself, my boy." Zedd pressed a hand to Richard's forehead. "Summer fevers are the worst, you know. Heat on top of heat. Bad combination."

"Yes—no—I mean, it's not that. I need to talk to you."

"So talk. It has been a long time. Far too long of a time. What's it been? Two years this past spring, if I'm not mistaken." Zedd drew back a bit and squeezed Richard's arms as he looked him up and down. "Richard, where's your sword?"

"Look, we'll talk about that later," Richard said, irritably disengaging himself from Zedd's grip in order to wave away the question.

"You said you wanted to talk. So talk and tell me where your sword is." Zedd redirected his broad grin at Nicci. "And who is this lovely sorceress you've brought along?"

Richard blinked at Zedd's smile and then glanced at Nicci. "Oh, sorry. Zedd, this is Nicci. Nicci, this—"

"Nicci!" Zedd roared as he danced back up two of the steps as if he'd spotted a viper. "The Sister of the Dark who took you away to the Old World? That Nicci? What are you doing with this vile creature? Why would you dare to bring such a woman—"

"Zedd," Richard said, forcefully cutting his grandfather off. "Nicci is a friend."

"A friend! Are you out of your mind, Richard? How in the world do you expect—"

"Zedd, she's on our side now." He gestured heatedly. "Much the same as Cara, or Rikka. Things change. Before, either of them would have . . ."

His voice trailed off as his grandfather stared at him. "You know what I mean. I trust Cara with my life, now, and she has proven worthy of my trust. I trust Nicci the same. I trust them both with my life."

Zedd finally gripped Richard's shoulder and gave it an affectionate joggle. "I guess I do know what you mean. Since I gave you the Sword of Truth you've changed a great many things for the better. Why, I would never in my life have imagined that one day I'd happily be eating meals cooked by a Mord-Sith. And delicious meals they are, too." He caught himself and pointed at Cara. "If you tell her I said that I'll skin you alive. The woman is already incorrigible."

Cara only smiled.

Zedd redirected his gaze to Nicci. He didn't have that raptorlike Rahl quality, but in its own way it was just as disarming and looked to have the potential to be just as disturbing.

"Welcome, sorceress. If Richard says you are a friend, then you are. Sorry to get so huffy."

Nicci smiled. "Perfectly understandable. I didn't like myself back then either. I was under the influence of dark delusions. I was called Death's Mistress for good reason." Nicci gazed into Richard's gray eyes. "Your grandson brought me to see the beauty of life."

Zedd smiled proudly. "Yes, that's it exactly. The beauty of life."

Richard pounced on the opening. "And life is what this is about. Zedd, listen, I need—"

"Yes, yes," Zedd said, waving off Richard's impatience. "You always need something. Haven't been back long enough to get in the door and already you want to know something. If I recall correctly, the first word you ever spoke was 'why.'

"Come on, then, come inside. I want to know why you don't have the Sword of Truth with you. I know you wouldn't let anything happen to it, but I want to hear the whole story. Don't leave out a thing. Come along, then."

Motioning them all to follow, Richard's grandfather climbed the stairs toward the doorway.

"Zedd! I need—"

"Yes, yes, my boy. You need something. I heard you the first time. I think it looks like rain. No use getting started when we're about to get wet. Come inside and I will hear what you have to say." Zedd's voice began echoing as he disappeared into the darkness. "You look like you could use a meal. Is anyone else hungry? Reunions always give me an appetite."

Richard's arms dropped, his hands flopping against his thighs in frustration. He sighed and then hurried up the steps after his grandfather. Nicci knew that had it been anyone else, Richard would have handled it quite differently. People who loved you, and had raised you since you were little, and had comforted you when you cried at a thunderstorm or the howl of a wolf tended to be disarming to deal with. She could see that it was no different with Richard. His love of his grandfather tied his hands with unbreakable ropes of respect.

It was a view of Richard Nicci had never seen before, and one she found quite endearing. Here was the Lord Rahl, the leader of the D'Haran Empire, the Seeker of Truth, a man who could make just about anyone tremble with a look, brought to flustered silence by a kindly if bewildering lecture. Had the matters involved not been so serious, Nicci would have been unable to keep herself from grinning at Richard's utter helplessness before such a frail-looking old man.

The sound of water reverberated inside the dark anteroom. Zedd cast a hand casually to the side and a lamp on the wall lit. At the ignition of the flame Nicci recognized the reiteration of a spark of power that marked it as a key lamp. With a succession of whooshing sounds, starting on both sides of the entrance, hundreds of lamps around the vast room lit in pairs. Each *whoosh* as a pair of lamps caught flame was followed almost simultaneously by another as the lamps around the huge room each took to flame from the engendering magic initiated by the key lamp, the effect being a ring of fire seeming to dance its way around the room. Nicci knew that it would have worked the same had someone lit that particular lamp with a flame rather than magic. The light in the room swelled, and in a span of seconds the anteroom was nearly as bright as day.

A clover-leaf-shaped fountain stood centered in the tiled floor. Water spouted high into the air above the top bowl, from where it cascaded down each successive tier of ever wider, scalloped bowls, finally running from points around the bottom bowl in perfectly matched arcs into the surrounding pool contained by an outer wall of variegated white marble made wide enough to act as a bench.

All the way around the oval-shaped room, highly polished, deep red marble columns stood below arches supporting a continuous balcony. A hundred feet overhead a section of glassed roof let in some of the somber, late-day light to balance the glow of the lamps down in the heart of the room. At night, the glassed roof would probably also let in the soft cold light of the moon to give the darkened room a spectral feel, but with it being the new moon, to say nothing of the gathering clouds, there would be no moonlight this night. By the look of the sky through the glassed roof section, Nicci thought that Zedd was right; it did look like it might rain.

Belying first impressions of the Keep, the room was a beautiful, warm entrance to what seemed such a cold and austere exterior. It hinted at the life the place once held. Like the forsaken city down in the valley, Nicci was rather saddened by the emptiness.

"Welcome to the Wizard's Keep. Perhaps we all should—"

"Zedd," Richard growled, cutting his grandfather short, "I need to talk to you. Right now. It's important."

Beloved grandfather or not, Nicci could see that Richard was at the end of his patience. Tight, white knuckles stood out in stark contrast against his tanned skin and the prominent veins on the backs of his fists. Judging by the way he looked, he hadn't gotten much sleep in recent days or had much to eat. She didn't think that she had ever seen him looking this exhausted or this near his wits' end. Cara, as well, looked well past the limits of her endurance, although she did a good job of covering it; Mord-Sith were trained to ignore physical discomfort. Despite being overjoyed at seeing his grandfather, Richard's preoccupation with finding the woman from his imagination had cut the pleasantries of the reunion short.

The mad rush that had become life, since that day he had been shot with the arrow and had nearly died, seemed to have come down to this moment.

Zedd blinked in innocent surprise. "Well of course, Richard, of course." He spread his arms as he spoke in a gentle voice. "You know that you can always talk to me. Whatever is on your mind, you know that—"

"What's Chainfire?"

That was nearly the first thing he had asked of Nicci, too.

Zedd stood unmoving, a blank look on his face. "Chainfire," he repeated in a flat tone.

"Yes, Chainfire."

A serious expression weighing on his face, Zedd considered the ques-

tion with care, turning toward the fountain as he thought it over. The waiting was almost painful. The fountain burbled and splashed and echoed in
the otherwise silent room.

"Chainfire," Zedd drawled to himself as he ran a sticklike finger along
his smooth jawbone while staring into the tumbling, dancing water cas-
cading down each successive tier of the fountain. Nicci stole a glance at
Cara, but the Mord-Sith was unreadable. Her drawn face looked as tired
and ill-fed as Richard's, but, being Cara, she stood tall and straight, not allowing her exhaustion to get the better of her.

"That's right. Chainfire," Richard said impatiently through gritted
teeth. "Do you know what it means?"

Zedd turned back to his grandson, lifting open his hands. He looked not
only puzzled but apologetic.

"I'm sorry, Richard, but I've never heard the word *Chainfire* before."

The fury leaving him, Richard looked like he might fall down. The disappointment was only too evident in his eyes. His shoulders slumped as
he let out a breath. Cara carefully, but quietly, slipped a step closer, ready
to help him if he collapsed. To Nicci, that looked like a real possibility.

"Richard," Zedd said, his voice taking on an edge, "where is your
sword?"

Richard erupted. "It's just a piece of steel!"

"Just a piece—"

Richard's face went crimson. "It's just a stupid chunk of metal! Don't
you think that there might be more important things to worry about?"

Zedd cocked his head. "More important things? What are you talking
about?"

"I want my life back!"

Zedd stared at him, but remained silent, and in doing so thereby almost
commanded his grandson to say something more to fill in some of the
blanks.

Richard paced from the fountain to a broad band of triple steps that led
up between two of the red marble pillars. A long red and gold carpet bordered with simple, black geometric designs ran between the pillars off under a balcony and into the darkness.

Richard raked the fingers of both hands back through his hair. "What difference does it make? No one believes me. No one will help me find her."

Nicci felt a deep sense of sorrow for him. At that moment she regretted every harsh thing she had ever said trying to convince him that he had only dreamed up Kahlan. He needed to be helped over his delusions, but, at that moment, she would have been happy to let him hold on to them if it would have brought the light of life back into his eyes.

She longed to hold him and tell him that it would be all right, but she couldn't, for more reasons than one.

Cara, arms hanging straight at her sides, looked just as saddened to see Richard agonizing so. There seemed no end in sight. Nicci suspected that the Mord-Sith would have agreed with Nicci to let Richard have his beautiful dream of the woman he loved. But a lie would not soothe such real pain.

"Richard, I don't know what you're talking about, but what does it have to do with the Sword of Truth?" Zedd asked, the edge returning to his voice.

Richard closed his eyes a moment against the torment of saying aloud what he had said so many times, so many times when no one ever believed him.

"I have to find Kahlan."

Nicci could see him draw tighter, bracing for the usual disconcerting questions as to who he was talking about and where he could ever have gotten such a notion. Nicci could see that it was almost too much for him to bear another person telling him he was imagining things, questioning his sanity. She could see him dreading it even more coming from his grandfather.

Zedd tilted his head a little. "Kahlan?"

"Yes," Richard said with a sigh and without looking up, "Kahlan. But you wouldn't know who I'm talking about."

Ordinarily, Richard would have launched into a ready explanation, but now he looked too dejected to want to bother to explain yet again, to be greeted with incredulity and disbelieving questions.

"Kahlan." Zedd's brow drew down in cautious query. "Kahlan Amnell? Is that the Kahlan you're talking about?"

Nicci froze.

Richard looked up, his eyes wide. "What did you say?" he whispered.

"Kahlan Amnell? That Kahlan?"

Nicci's heart skipped a beat. Cara's jaw had dropped.

In a blink, Richard had the front of Zedd's robes in his fists and had lifted the old man clear of the floor. Richard's sweat-slicked muscles glistened in the lamplight.

"You said her whole name, Kahlan Amnell. I didn't tell you her whole name. You said it on your own."

Zedd was looking more confused by the moment. "But, that's because the only Kahlan I know of is Kahlan Amnell."

"You know Kahlan—you know who I'm talking about?"

"The Mother Confessor?"

"Yes, the Mother Confessor!"

"Well, of course. Most people know her, I expect. Richard, what's gotten into you? Let me down."

Nicci felt dizzy. She couldn't believe her own ears. How was such a thing possible? It wasn't. It was so overwhelmingly, inconceivably impossible that she thought she might faint.

His hands trembling, Richard set his grandfather down. "What do you mean, everyone knows her?"

Zedd pulled on each sleeve in turn, pulling them back down his skinny arms. He rearranged his disheveled robes at his hips, all the time watching his grandson. He looked truly bewildered by Richard's behavior.

"Richard, what's the matter with you? How could they not know her? She's the Mother Confessor, for crying out loud."

Richard swallowed. "Where is she?"

Zedd shot a brief, confused glance at Cara and then Nicci before looking back at Richard.

"Why, down at the Confessors' Palace."

Richard let out a cry of joy and threw his arms around his grandfather.

Gripping his grandfather's skinny shoulders, Richard shook the old man. "She's here? Kahlan is at the Confessors' Palace?"

Worry spreading across Zedd's wrinkled face, he cautiously nodded.

With the back of his hand, Richard wiped away the tears running down his cheek. "She's here," he said, turning to Cara. He gripped her shoulders and gave her a firm shake. "She's in Aydindril. Did you hear? I wasn't imagining it. Zedd remembers her. He knows the truth."

Cara looked as if she were doing her best to come to grips with her astonishment without letting it be mistaken for unhappiness at the startling news.

"Lord Rahl . . . I'm . . . happy for you—really I am—but I don't see how . . ."

Richard, not seeming to notice the Mord-Sith's halting uncertainty, turned back to the wizard. "What's she doing down there?" he asked, his voice bubbling over with excitement.

Zedd, looking gravely troubled, again glanced to both Cara and Nicci before tenderly laying a hand on Richard's shoulder.

"Richard, that's where she's buried."

The world seemed to stop.

In a flash of understanding, Nicci realized the truth.

Suddenly, it all became clear. Zedd's behavior now made sense. The woman Zedd was talking about was not the Kahlan, the Mother Confessor, from Richard's imagination, the woman he imagined loved him and had married him.

It was the real Mother Confessor.

Nicci had warned Richard that in his dream he had done a dangerous thing by imagining a woman as his bride who was not simply some anonymous imaginary woman, but, instead, was a woman he had heard of before—a woman who, it so happened, was well known in the Midlands. This was the real Kahlan Amnell, the real Mother Confessor, who was buried down at the Confessors' Palace, not the one Richard had dreamed up to be his love. It had been this very reality that Nicci had feared would eventually come to shatter Richard's world.

She had warned him that this was bound to happen. She had warned him that he would one day come face-to-face with the truth. This was the moment, this was the very thing she had been trying to prevent.

Still, Nicci felt no joy at all in being right. She felt only crushing sadness at what Richard must be feeling. She couldn't even begin to imagine how confusing, how disorienting, it had to be for him. For someone as firmly grounded in reality as Richard always had been, this entire ordeal had to be devastating.

Richard could only stare.

"Richard," Zedd finally said, giving him a gentle squeeze on his arms, "are you all right? What's going on?"

Richard slowly blinked. He looked in a state of shock.

"What do you mean she's buried down at the Confessors' Palace?" he asked in a shaky voice. "When did it happen?"

Zedd guardedly licked his lips. "I don't know when she died. When I was down there—when Jagang's army was marching on Aydindril—I saw the grave marker. I didn't know her. I just saw her grave, that's all. It's a pretty big marker. It would be hard to miss. The Confessors were all killed by the quads that Darken Rahl sent. She must have died back then.

"Richard, you couldn't possibly have known the woman; she had to have been dead and buried before we ever left our home in Westland—back before the boundary came down. Back when you were still a woods guide in the Hartland forest."

Richard pressed his palms to his forehead. "No, no, you don't understand. You're having the same problem as everyone else. It's not her. You know Kahlan."

Zedd lifted a sympathetic hand toward his grandson. "Richard, that's not possible. The quads killed the Confessors."

"Yes, the other Confessors were killed by those assassins, but not her, not Kahlan." Richard waved a hand as he dismissed the argument. "Zedd, she's the one who came to ask you to appoint the Seeker—that's why we left Westland. You know Kahlan."

Zedd frowned. "What in the world are you talking about? We had to leave when Darken Rahl came hunting us. We had to run for our lives."

"In part, but Kahlan came looking for you first. She's the one who told us that Darken Rahl had put the boxes of Orden in play. He was on the other side of the boundary; if not for Kahlan coming, how would we have even known?"

Zedd peered at Richard as if he suspected he might be quite ill. "Richard, when the boxes of Orden are put into play, the snake vine grows. It even says so in *The Book of Counted Shadows*. You, of all people, know that. You were in the Upper Ven and were bitten by a snake vine. It caused a fever and you came to me for help. That's how we knew the boxes of Orden were in play. Darken Rahl then came to Westland and attacked us."

"Well, yes, that's all true, in a way, but Kahlan told us what was happening in the Midlands—she confirmed it." Richard growled in frustration. "It's more than that, more than her coming to ask you to appoint a Seeker. You know her."

"I'm afraid that I don't, Richard."

"Dear spirits, Zedd, you spent last winter with her and the D'Haran army. When Nicci took me down to the Old World, Kahlan was there with Cara and you." He pointed insistently at Cara, as if it would somehow prove the point and end the nightmare. "She and Cara fought with you all winter."

Zedd glanced up at Cara. Cara, behind Richard's back, turned her palms up and shrugged at Zedd to let him know that she didn't know any more about it than Zedd did.

"As long as you brought up the business about you being the Seeker, where is your—"

Richard snapped his fingers, his face suddenly lighting up.

"That's not Kahlan's grave."

"Of course it is. There's no mistaking this grave. It's prominent and I clearly recall that it has her name carved right in the stone."

"Yes, it's her name, but not her grave. I realize what you're talking about, now." Richard chuckled with relief. "I'm telling you, it's not her grave."

Zedd didn't think it was funny. "Richard, I've seen her name on the stone. It's her, the Mother Confessor, Kahlan Amnell."

Richard shook his head insistently. "No, that's not her. That was a trick—"

"A trick?" Zedd cocked his head, frowning. "What are you talking about? What sort of trick?"

"They were hunting her—the Order was after Kahlan when they occupied Aydindril. They had taken over the council, condemned her to death, and they were hunting her. To keep them from chasing her, you put a death spell on her—"

"What! A death spell! Richard, do you have any idea of the magnitude of what you're suggesting?"

"Of course I do. But it's true. You needed to feign her death so that the Order would think they had succeeded and wouldn't come after her—so that she could get away. Don't you remember? You made that headstone, or at least you had it made. I came here to find her—it was a few years back. Your spell even fooled me. I thought she was dead. But she wasn't."

His confusion had receded and now Zedd was looking seriously worried. "Richard, I can't imagine what is wrong with you, but this is simply—"

"You two escaped to safety but you left me a message on her headstone," Richard said, jabbing a finger at Zedd's chest, "so that I would know that she was really still alive. So that I wouldn't despair. So that I wouldn't give up. I almost did, but then I figured it out."

Zedd was nearly boiling over with frustration, impatience, and concern. Nicci knew the feeling.

"Bags, my boy, what message are you talking about?"

"The words on the headstone. The inscription. It was a message to me."

Zedd planted his fists on his hips. "What are you talking about? What message? What was this message?"

Richard started pacing, pressing his fingertips to his temples as he mumbled to himself, apparently trying to recall the exact wording.

Or, Nicci thought, trying to dream it up the way he always dreamed up answers to talk his way out of facing the truth. She knew that this time he was making a mistake that would catch him up. Reality was closing in around him, even if he didn't yet recognize it. He soon would.

Nicci dreaded that unequivocal juncture of delusion and truth. Despite wanting Richard to get better, to get over the false memories he had been suffering, she dreaded the pain she knew it would bring him when he eventually came face-to-face with the unambiguous truth. Even more, she dreaded what would happen to him if he couldn't see the truth, or refused to see it, if he sank forever deeper into a world of illusion.

"Not here," he muttered. "Something about not being here. And something about my heart."

Zedd pushed his cheek out with his tongue, apparently in an effort to keep still while he watched his grandson pacing back and forth and at the same time probably tried to imagine what could be happening to him.

"No," Richard said abruptly as he halted. "No, not my heart. That's not what it said. It's a big monument. I remember now. It said, 'Kahlan Amnell. Mother Confessor. She is not here, but in the hearts of those who love her.'

"It was a message for me not to give up hope because she wasn't really dead—she wasn't really there, in that grave."

"Richard," Zedd said in soft consolation, "it's a common enough thing to say on a grave marker, that someone isn't dead but rather lives on in the hearts of those who love her. Gravediggers probably have stacks of grave markers made up with that sentiment, carved with those very words."

"But she wasn't buried there! She wasn't! It says that—'she is not here'—for a reason."

"Then who is buried in her grave?" Zedd asked.

Richard went still for a moment.

"No one," he finally said, his gaze wandering off as he thought. "Mistress Sanderholt—the cook at the palace—she was fooled by your death spell like everyone else. When I finally got here she told me that you stood there on the platform while Kahlan was beheaded—she was in mourning over it and terribly upset—but I realized that you wouldn't do such a thing and so it had to be one of your tricks. You told me that—remember? Sometimes the best magic is just a trick."

Zedd nodded. "That part is true enough."

"Mistress Sanderholt told me that Kahlan's body had been burned in a funeral pyre, the whole thing supervised by the First Wizard himself. She said that Kahlan's ashes were then buried before that immense stone marker. Mistress Sanderholt even took me out to the secluded courtyard beside the palace where Confessors are buried. She showed me the grave. I was horrified. I thought it was her, that she was dead, until I figured out the message carved in the stone—the message the two of you left for me to find."

Richard gripped his grandfather's shoulders again. "Do you see? It was just a trick to throw our enemies off her trail. She wasn't really dead. She wasn't really buried there. Nothing is buried there, except maybe some ashes."

Nicci thought that it was rather convenient that Richard imagined her being cremated in his story of the death-spell bluff so that all that remained were ashes that couldn't be identified. He always came up with something that to his mind logically explained the lack of evidence. Nicci didn't know if Confessors really were cremated, but if they were, that would only provide him with another useful pretext to prop up his story so that he could continue to deny that it was her. They would again have no way to prove otherwise.

Unless, of course, he was dreaming up the funeral pyre part of his story and Confessors weren't ordinarily cremated.

"And so you say that you went there?" Zedd asked. "Down to where the gravestone stands?"

"Yes, and then Denna came—"

"Denna was dead," Cara said, interrupting for the first time. "You killed her in order to escape from her at the People's Palace. She couldn't have been there . . . unless of course she appeared as a spirit."

"Yes, that's right," Richard said, turning to Cara. "She did. She came as a spirit and took me to a place between worlds so that I could be with Kahlan there."

Cara's eyes briefly turned to the wizard. Her incredulity was impossible for her to mask so she looked away from Richard and occupied herself with scratching the back of her neck.

Nicci wanted to scream. His story grew more insanely convoluted by the moment. She remembered the Prelate once teaching Nicci as a novice how the seed of lies, once planted, only grew more tangled and out of control over time.

Zedd came up from behind and gently grasped Richard's shoulders.

"Come on, my boy. I think you need to get some rest and then afterwards we can—"

"No!" Richard cried out as he twisted away. "I'm not imagining it! I'm not making it up!"

Nicci knew he was doing just that. In a certain sense, it was remarkable the way he was able, on the spot, to weave new events, based on his original delusion, to continually manage to escape the trap of the truth.

But he could not escape it forever. There was the matter of the true Mother Confessor buried in the grave and that was all too real—unless it turned out that the Midlands actually did cremate their Confessors, in which case Richard would be able to continue to hobble along, clinging to his dream for a little while longer, until the next problem cropped up. Sooner or later, though, something was going to shatter those dreams.

Zedd tried again. "Richard, you're tired. You look like you've been living on a horse for—"

"I can prove it," Richard said in calm defiance.

Everyone went quiet.

"You don't believe me, I know. None of you do—but I can prove it."

"What do you mean?" Zedd asked.

"Come on. Come with me down to the gravestone."

"Richard, I told you, the gravestone very well could say what you said you remember, but that proves nothing. It's a common enough sentiment to express on a gravestone."

"Do they typically burn the bodies of the Mother Confessor on a funeral pyre? Or was that just part of your trick so that you wouldn't have to produce her body at the funeral when she was supposedly buried."

Zedd was beginning to look more than just a little indignant. "When I used to live here the bodies of Confessors were never desecrated. The Mother Confessor was placed in a silver-clad coffin in her white dress and the people were allowed to view her one last time, to say their farewells, before she was buried."

Richard glared at his grandfather, at Cara, and finally at Nicci. "Good. If I have to dig up the grave and prove to all of you that there is nothing buried under the gravestone, then that's what I will do. We need to get this settled so that we can move on to the solution to what's happening. In order to do that, I need you all to believe me."

Zedd spread his hands. "Richard, that isn't necessary."

"Yes it is! It is necessary! I want my life back!"

No one offered an argument.

"Zedd, have I ever told you a malicious lie?"

"No, my boy, you never have."

"I'm not lying now."

"Richard," Nicci said, "no one is saying that you're lying, only that you're suffering the unfortunate effects of delirium induced by an injury. It's not your fault. We all know you aren't doing this deliberately."

He turned to his grandfather. "Zedd, don't you see? Think about it. Something is going wrong in the world. Something is terribly wrong. For some reason that I haven't been able to figure out, I'm the only one who is aware of it. I'm the only one who remembers Kahlan. There has to be something behind this. Something wicked. Maybe Jagang is responsible."

"Jagang had the beast created to come after you," Nicci said. "He put everything into that effort. He wouldn't need to do anything else. Besides, with the beast already stalking you, what purpose would it serve?"

"I don't know. I don't have all the answers, but I know the truth of part of it."

"And how can it be that you alone know the truth and everyone else is wrong, that everyone's memory but yours has failed them?" Zedd asked.

"I don't know the answer to that, either, but I can prove what I'm telling you. I can show you the grave. Come on."

"I told you, Richard, the marker says common words."

Richard's expression turned dangerous. "Then we will dig up the grave so that you can all see that it's empty and that I'm not crazy."

Zedd lifted a hand toward the still open door. "But it will be dark soon. What's more, it's going to rain."

Richard turned back from the doorway. "We have an extra horse. We can still make it down there while we have daylight. If we need to, we can use lanterns. If I must, I will dig in the dark. This is more important than worrying about a little rain or the lack of light. I need to get this over— now—so that we can get on to solving the very real problem and so that I can find Kahlan before it's too late. Let's go."

Zedd gestured heatedly. "Richard, this is—"

"Let him do as he asks," Nicci said, interrupting, drawing all eyes. "We've all heard enough. This is important to him. We must allow him to do as he thinks he must. It's the only chance we have to finally settle the matter."

Before Zedd could answer her, a Mord-Sith appeared from between two red pillars at the opposite side of the room. Her blond hair was pulled back into a single braid like Cara's. She wasn't quite as tall as Cara, and not as lean, but she looked just as formidable in the way she carried herself, as if she feared nothing and lived for an excuse to prove it.

"What's going on? I heard—" She stared in sudden astonishment. "Cara? Is that you?"

"Rikka," Cara said with a smile and a nod, "it's good to see your face again."

Rikka bowed her head to Cara more deeply than Cara had before staring at Richard. She stepped forward into the room.

Her eyes widened. "Lord Rahl, I haven't seen you since . . ."

Richard nodded. "Since the People's Palace, in D'Hara. When I came to close the gateway to the underworld you were one of the Mord-Sith who helped get me up to the Garden of Life. You were the one who held my shirt at my left shoulder as all of you guided me safely through the palace. One of your sister Mord-Sith gave her life that night that I might complete my mission."

Rikka smiled in astonishment. "You remember. We were all in our red leather. I can't believe you have that good a memory that you could remember me, much less that I was the one at your left shoulder." She bowed her head. "And you honor us all to remember one who fell in battle."

"I do have a good memory." Richard cast a dark glare at Nicci and then Zedd. "That was just before I came back to Aydindril and the gravestone with Kahlan's name on it." He turned back to Rikka. "Watch over the Keep, will you, Rikka? We all have to go down to the city for a while."

"Of course, Lord Rahl," Rikka said, bowing her head again, looking almost giddy to be in Richard's presence, and to be remembered.

Richard again swept his raptorlike glare across the rest of them. "Let's go."

Richard vanished out the doorway. Zedd caught Nicci's sleeve on her way by.

"He was hurt, wasn't he?" When she hesitated, he went on. "You said he was suffering delusions from being injured."

Nicci nodded. "He was shot with an arrow. He almost died."

"Nicci healed him." Cara leaned in as she spoke in a low voice. "She saved Lord Rahl's life."

Zedd lifted an eyebrow. "A friend indeed."

"I healed him," Nicci confirmed, "but it was difficult beyond anything

I've ever attempted before. I may have saved his life, but I now worry that I didn't do a good enough job of it."

"What do you mean?" Zedd asked.

"I fear that I may have somehow done something to cause his delusions."

"That isn't true," Cara said.

"I wonder if it is," Nicci said, "if I might have done more, or done things differently."

She swallowed past the lump growing in her throat. She feared that it was true, that Richard's problem was her fault, that she hadn't acted quickly enough, or that she might have done something dreadfully wrong. She constantly fretted over her decision that terrible morning to get Richard to a safe place before working on him. She had feared an attack that would have fatally interrupted her efforts to heal him, but maybe if she would have simply started right then and there on the battlefield he might not now be chasing phantoms.

After all, an attack never had come, so she'd made the wrong judgment about needing to get him to the deserted farmhouse. She didn't know at the time that no attack was imminent, but maybe if she would have taken the time to have Victor's men scout the area she could have started healing Richard much sooner. She hadn't done that because she feared that if they scouted, and she was right about more of the enemy being nearby, then they would have had to move Richard anyway, and by then his time would have run out.

Even so, she was the one who had made the decisions and Richard was the one now suffering delusions. Something had gone wrong that terrible night.

There was no one in the world who mattered to her more than Richard. She feared that she was the one who had caused him the harm that was ruining his life.

"What exactly was wrong with him?" Zedd asked. "Where was he shot with the arrow?"

"In the left side of his chest—with a barbed bolt from a crossbow. That barbed head lodged in his chest without penetrating all the way through his back. He was able to partially deflect it, so it just missed his heart, but his lung and chest were rapidly filling with blood."

Zedd lifted an eyebrow in astonishment. "And you were able to get the arrow out and heal him?"

"That's right," Cara confirmed with forceful passion. "She saved Lord Rahl's life."

"I don't know . . ." Nicci had difficulty putting it all into words. "I've been separated from him as I made my way here. Now that I see him again, see how he has latched so strongly onto his delusion and can't come to see the truth, I'm not so sure I did him any good. How can he live if he can't see the truth of the world around him? While his body may be healed, he's suffering a dreadful kind of slow death as his mind fails him."

Zedd gave her shoulder a fatherly pat. Nicci recognized the light of life in his eyes. It was the same spark that Richard had. At least the same spark he used to have.

"We'll just have to help him see the truth."

"And if it destroys his heart?" she asked.

Zedd smiled. It reminded her of Richard's smile, the smile she missed so much.

"Then we'll just have to heal his heart, now won't we?"

Nicci was unable to bring forth more than a whisper that bordered on tears. "And how are we to do that?"

Zedd smiled again and gave her shoulder a firm squeeze. "We'll have to see. First we have to let him see the truth, then we can worry about healing the wound it will bring his heart."

Nicci could only nod. She dreaded seeing Richard hurt.

"And what is this beast you mentioned? The one Jagang created?"

"A weapon created with the use of Sisters of the Dark," Nicci said. "Something from the time of the great war."

Zedd cursed under his breath at the news. Cara looked like she had something to say about the beast, but she thought better of it and instead started for the door. "Come on. I don't want Lord Rahl to get too far ahead of us."

Zedd grumbled his agreement. "Looks like we're going to get wet."

"At least if it rains," the Mord-Sith said, "it will wash some of the horse off of me."

The drizzle started before they were out of the paddock. Richard was already gone. There was no telling how far ahead of them he had gotten. Cara wanted to hurry and catch up with him, but Zedd told her that they knew where he was going and there was no point in risking breaking the leg of one of the tired horses because, if that happened, then they would only end up having to walk down the mountain after Richard and then, after visiting the graveyard of the Confessors, walk all the way back up.

"Besides," Zedd told her, "you'll never be able to catch him."

"Well, you might be right about that," Cara said as she spurred her horse into a canter, "but I don't want him alone any longer than necessary. I'm his protection."

"Especially since he's without his sword," Zedd muttered sourly.

They had little choice but to hurry after Cara.

By the time they'd raced down the mountain and reached the city, the daylight was fading and the drizzle strengthening. Nicci knew they were going to be soaked before it was over, but there was no helping it. Fortunately, it was warm enough that at least they wouldn't be freezing in the wet weather.

Knowing where Richard would be, they made their way to the grounds of the Confessors' Palace where they quickly found his horse, tied to one of the rings holding chains strung between decorative granite stanchions. Since there was no opening in the chains, they were apparently meant to indicate a private area of the grounds. After the three of them tied their horses alongside Richard's, Cara and Nicci followed Zedd as he stepped over the chain.

This was clearly not a place where outsiders were welcome. The secluded courtyard was screened from public view by a row of tall elms and a dense wall of evergreen junipers. Through the thick branches of the grand trees Nicci saw glimpses of the white walls of the Confessors' Palace looming close by, enfolding and sheltering the wooded graveyard.

Because of the way it was hidden away, Nicci had expected it to be small, but the place where Confessors were buried was actually quite extensive. Trees were placed so as to cut the openness and give each section of the graveyard an intimate feel. By the manner in which it was laid out, with a path and a small vine-covered colonnade ushering people approaching from the palace, it was apparently intended to be accessed solely from the palace through elegant, double glassed doors. In the muted gray light the quiet place beneath the canopy of trees had a hallowed feel to it.

They found Richard up a slight rise in what would be the shady courtyard were it sunny, standing in the drizzle before a polished stone monument, running his fingers through the letters carved in the granite, through the letters of the name KAHLAN.

Somewhere on the grounds to the Confessors' Palace Richard had managed to find shovels and picks. They lay at the ready nearby. Scanning the area, Nicci saw that there were storage buildings for grounds keepers set back among hedges partly hidden around a corner of the palace and reasoned that Richard had found them there.

As she quietly approached him, Nicci knew that Richard was on the brink of something potentially very dangerous . . . to him. She stood behind him, hands folded, waiting, as he tenderly touched Kahlan's name in stone.

"Richard," Nicci finally said in a soft voice, feeling the need for a reverent tone in such a place, "I hope that you will think about everything I've told you, and if things don't turn out the way at this moment you believe they will, know that we will all help you in any way we can."

He turned away from her name in stone. "Don't be worried about me, Nicci. There is nothing under this ground. She isn't here. I'm going to show that to all of you and then you will have to believe me. I'm going to get my life back. When I do, then you're all going to understand that something is very wrong. Then we're going to have to work to find out what's going on and we're going to find Kahlan."

After holding her gaze for a moment, waiting to see if she would dare to challenge him, Richard, without another word, snatched up a shovel and with a forceful push of his foot, sank the blade into the slightly mounded grassy ground in front of the stone marker to the dead Mother Confessor.

Zedd stood nearby, silent, unmoving, as he watched. He'd brought two lanterns with him. They sat on a stone bench nearby, giving off a weak but steady glow in the still dampness. The drizzle was giving rise to ground fog. Although the sky was completely covered over with iron gray clouds, by the failing light Nicci thought that it must be just after sunset. With it being the darkest night of the new moon, and with thick clouds to hide even the stars, it was going to be a blackest of nights.

Even without the drizzle and approaching darkness, it was a miserable time to be digging up dead people.

As Richard worked with a kind of controlled but focused anger, Cara finally picked up another shovel. "The sooner we get this over with, the better."

She plunged her shovel into the damp ground and started helping Richard dig. Zedd stood nearby, silent and grim as he watched. Nicci would have helped get it over with, but she doubted that more than two people would have room to dig without getting in the way of each other. She might have used magic to accomplish the deed of opening the ground, but she had a strong sense that Zedd would not have approved, that he wanted this to be Richard's effort, his muscle, his sweat. His doing.

As the light gradually dimmed, Richard and Cara worked themselves ever deeper into the ground. They had to resort to the pick to get through thick roots crisscrossing the gravesite. Such good-sized roots told Nicci that the grave had to be older than Richard believed. If he realized as much, he didn't mention it as he worked. Nicci supposed that he could somehow be right that this was no real grave, which would explain why the roots had grown as thick as they were. If Richard was right, only a small hole would have had to have been dug among them, just big enough for a ceremonial vessel containing ashes to have been buried, but she didn't for a moment believe it. Shovelful by shovelful, the pile of black dirt to the side of the hole grew ever larger.

Although Zedd said nothing as he watched, Nicci could read in the deep lines of his face that, moment by moment, he was becoming ever more incensed at exhuming the Mother Confessor, even if it would settle the matter. He looked like he had a thousand things to say, all bottled up inside him. Nicci thought that he would wait until after Richard found the buried truth, but by the grim set of the wizard's jaw, she didn't think that when he finally had his say that it was going to be at all pleasant or understanding. This was behavior that crossed a line with him.

When Richard's and Cara's heads, dripping sweat and rainwater, were even with the surface of the ground, Richard's shovel abruptly thunked against something that sounded solid.

He and Cara paused. Richard looked stunned and confused; according to his story, there ought not to be anything in the grave, except maybe a small container holding ashes, and it was hard to believe that such a container would be buried this deep.

"It has to be a container for the ashes," he finally said as he looked up at Zedd. "That has to be it. You wouldn't have simply dumped ashes in the hole in ground. At the funeral they would have used a receptacle of some kind for the ashes you tricked them into thinking were Kahlan's."

Zedd said nothing.

Cara watched Richard for a moment and then plunged her shovel in the ground. It also made a resounding thunk. With the back of her wrist she swiped a strand of blond hair off her face as she looked up at Nicci.

"Well it would appear you've found something." Zedd's ominous voice seemed to carry through the low fog that had gathered along the ground in the private graveyard. "I guess we ought to see what it is."

Richard stared up at his grandfather a moment, and then went back to digging. It wasn't long before he and Cara had exposed a flat surface. It was too dark to see it clearly, but Nicci knew what it was.

It was the truth about to be uncovered.

It was the end of Richard's delusion.

"I don't understand," Richard murmured, confused by the size of what they were uncovering.

"Dig the top clear," Zedd ordered with barely restrained displeasure.

Richard and Cara worked to carefully but quickly clean the wet dirt away from what was becoming all too clear was a coffin. When they had it fully exposed, Zedd ordered them out of the hole they'd dug.

The old wizard held his hands over the open grave and turned his palms up. As Richard, Cara, and Nicci watched, the heavy coffin began to rise. Dirt fell away as the long object rose up out of the dark void. Stepping back away from the open breach in the sacred ground, Zedd gently used his gift to set the coffin on the grass beside the open grave.

The exterior was elaborately carved with designs of enfolding fern fronds overlaid with silver. It was reverently, sorrowfully beautiful. Richard could only stare in terror at what the coffin might contain.

"Open it," Zedd commanded.

Richard looked up at him for a moment.

"Open it," Zedd repeated.

Richard finally knelt close to the silver-clad coffin and used the tip of his shovel to carefully pry the top loose. Cara retrieved the two lanterns, handing one to Zedd. She held the other lantern up over Richard's shoulder to help him see.

When the it finally came loose, Richard lifted the heavy lid enough to slide the top portion aside.

The glow from Cara's lamp fell across a decomposed corpse, now almost entirely skeletal. The careful workmanship of the coffin appeared to have so far kept the body dry on its long journey toward dust. The bones were mottled with stains from long burial and the inescapable process of deterioration. A fall of long hair, most still attached to the skull, draped over the shoulders. Little tissue was left, mostly connective tissue, especially that holding the bones of the fingers together. Even this long after death, those fingers still clutched a long-ago-crumbled bouquet of flowers.

The body of the Mother Confessor was wearing an exquisite, simply styled, satiny white dress, cut square at the neckline, that now revealed bare ribs.

The bouquet clutched in her hands had been enfolded in a wrapping of pearled lace with a broad golden ribbon attached to it. On the gold ribbon, in stitched letters of silver thread, it said, "Beloved Mother Confessor, Kahlan Amnell. She will always be in our hearts."

There could hardly be any doubt anymore as to the true fate of the Mother Confessor, or to the reality that what Richard had so strongly believed was his memories was nothing more than sweet delusions now turned to dust.

Richard, his chest heaving, his breath catching, could only stare into the open coffin at the skeletal remains, at the white dress, at the golden ribbon around the black fragments of what had once been a beautiful bouquet of flowers.

Nicci felt sick.

"Are you satisfied now?" Zedd asked in a measured tone of smoldering anger.

"I don't understand," Richard whispered, unable to take his eyes from the ghastly sight.

"You don't? I think it seems pretty clear," Zedd told him.

"But I know she isn't buried here. I can't explain this. I don't understand the contradiction to what I know is true."

Zedd clasped his hand. "There is no contradiction to understand. Contradictions don't exist."

"Yes, but I know—"

"Wizard's Ninth Rule: A contradiction cannot exist in reality. Not in part, nor in whole. To believe in a contradiction is to abdicate your belief in the existence of the world around you and the nature of the things in it, to instead embrace any random impulse that strikes your fancy—to imagine something is real simply because you wish it were.

"A thing is what it is, it is itself. There can be no contradictions."

"But Zedd, I have to believe—"

"Ah, you believe. You mean that the reality of this coffin and the Mother Confessor's long buried body has shown you something you did not expect and don't want to accept and so you wish to instead take refuge in the blind fog of faith. Is that what you mean to say?"

"Well, in this case . . ."

"Faith is a device of self-delusion, a sleight of hand done with words and emotions founded on any irrational notion that can be dreamed up. Faith is the attempt to coerce truth to surrender to whim. In simple terms, it is trying to breathe life into a lie by trying to outshine reality with the beauty of wishes. Faith is the refuge of fools, the ignorant, and the deluded, not of thinking, rational men.

"In reality, contradictions cannot exist. To believe in them you must abandon the most important thing you possess: your rational mind. The wager for such a bargain is your life. In such an exchange, you always lose what you have at stake."

Richard ran his fingers back into his wet hair. "But Zedd, something is wrong here. I don't know what, but I know it is. You have to help me."

"I just did. I've allowed you to show us the proof that you yourself named. Here it is, in this coffin. I admit that it isn't as desirable as what you wish were true, but the reality of it can't be evaded. This is what you seek. This is Kahlan Amnell, the Mother Confessor, just as it says on the gravestone."

Zedd arched an eyebrow as he leaned a little toward his grandson. "Unless you can show that this is some kind of trickery, that someone for some reason buried this here as part of an elaborate hoax just to make it look like you're wrong and everyone else is right. That would seem a pretty thin contention, if you ask me. I am afraid that from the clear evidence right here this is the reality—the proof you sought—and there is no contradiction."

Richard stared down at the long dead body before him.

"Something is wrong. This can't be true. It just can't be."

The muscles in Zedd's jaw flexed. "Richard, I've allowed you this gruesome indulgence when by all rights I shouldn't have, now tell me why you don't have the sword. Where is the Sword of Truth?"

Rain patted softly on the canopy of leaves above as Richard's grandfather waited. Richard stared into the coffin.

"I gave the sword to Shota in exchange for information I needed."

Zedd's eyes went wide. "You did what!"

"I had to," Richard said without looking up at his grandfather.

"You had to? You had to!"

"Yes," Richard answered in a meek voice.

"In exchange for what information?"

Richard put his elbows on the edge of the coffin as his face sank into his hands. "In exchange for what might help me find the truth of what's going on. I need answers. I need to know how to find Kahlan."

In fury Zedd thrust his finger toward the coffin. "There is Kahlan Amnell! Right where the gravestone has always said she is buried. And what oh-so-valuable bit of information did Shota give you after she tricked you out of the sword?"

Richard made no effort to contend the characterization of being tricked out of the sword.

"Chainfire," he said. "She told me the word *Chainfire*, but she didn't know what it meant. She told me that I must find the place of the bones in the Deep Nothing."

"The Deep Nothing," Zedd mocked. He gazed up at the black sky as he took a breath. "I don't suppose Shota was able to tell you what this Deep Nothing is."

Richard shook his head but didn't look up. "She also said to beware the viper with four heads."

Zedd let out another angry breath. "Don't tell me, neither she nor you have any idea what that means, either."

Again, Richard shook his head without looking up at his grandfather.

"Is that it? That's the great prize of valuable information you got in exchange for the Sword of Truth?"

Richard hesitated. "There was one other thing." He spoke so softly that he could hardly be heard over the gentle whisper of rain. "Shota said that what I seek . . . is long buried."

Zedd's smoldering rage threatened to explode. "There," he said, thrusting out a finger to point, "there is what you seek: Kahlan Amnell, the Mother Confessor, long buried."

Richard, head down, said nothing.

"For this you traded the Sword of Truth. A weapon of incalculable value. A weapon that can bring down not only the wicked but the good as well. A weapon handed down from the wizards of the ancient times, meant to be entrusted to only a select few. A weapon I entrusted to you.

"And you gave it to a witch woman.

"Do you have any idea at all what I had to go through to recover the Sword of Truth from Shota the last time she got her hands on it?"

Richard shook his head as he stared at the ground beside the coffin, looking like he dared not test his voice.

Nicci knew that Richard had a number of things to say in his own defense, had a number of things having to do with his reasoning behind his beliefs and actions, but he said none of them even when offered the chance. As his grandfather raged at him, he knelt in silence, hanging his head, beside the open coffin holding the end of his fantasy.

"I trusted you with something of great value. I thought such a dangerous object was safe in your hands. Richard, you've let me down—you have let everyone down—so that you could chase a dream. Well, here it is, bones long buried. I hope you think the trade fair, but I certainly don't."

Cara stood nearby, holding the lantern, her hair plastered to her head by the slow but steady rain. She looked like she wanted to defend Richard, but couldn't think of anything to say. Nicci, likewise, feared to say anything. She knew that at that moment anything they said would only make matters worse. Only the soft hiss of the rain against the leaves filled the otherwise silent, foggy night.

"Zedd," Richard said haltingly, "I'm sorry."

"Sorry won't get it back from Shota's clutches. Sorry won't save those people who Samuel will have beneath that sword. I love you like a son, Richard, and I always will, but I've never before been this disappointed in you. I would never have believed that you would do anything this unthinking and reckless."

Richard nodded, unwilling to justify his actions.

Nicci's heart was breaking for him.

"I will leave you to bury the Mother Confessor while I go try to think of a way to get the sword away from a witch woman who was a lot smarter than my grandson. You should realize that you may very well be responsible for what comes of this."

Richard nodded.

"Good. I'm glad you can at least understand that much of it." He turned to Cara and Nicci, the look in his eyes every bit as intimidating as the look of a Rahl. "I want you two to come back to the Keep with me. I want to know all about this beast business. Everything about it."

"I must stay and watch over Lord Rahl," Cara said.

"No," Zedd told her, "you will come with me and tell me in detail everything that happened with the witch woman. I want to know every word out of Shota's mouth."

Cara looked torn. "Zedd, I can't—"

"Go with him, Cara," Richard told her in quiet command. "Do as he asks. Please."

Nicci recognized how helpless Richard felt at defending his actions in the presence of his grandfather, regardless of how certain he might have been that he did what he thought was necessary. She understood because she had always been just as helpless in the presence of her mother when her mother told her, as she often did, that she had acted wrongly. Nicci had never been able to defend herself against what her mother thought she should have done. Her mother was always able to effortlessly make

Nicci's choices seem petty and selfish. No matter how old she was, she was still a child before those who raised her. Even when she had been at the Palace of the Prophets for years, her mother could still make her feel ten years old and foolish.

Because Richard loved and respected his grandfather, that actually made it all that much more difficult for him than it had been for Nicci. Despite everything Richard had accomplished, his strength, his knowledge, his ability, his mastery, he could not argue or reason his way out of the reality of having disappointed his grandfather, and, because he loved and respected him, it hurt all the more.

"Go on," Nicci told Cara as she gently put her hand on the small of the woman's back. "Do as he says for now. I think Richard could use some time alone to think this through and get his bearings."

Cara, her gaze going back and forth between Nicci and Richard, looked like she thought this was something Nicci might be better able to handle and so nodded her agreement.

"You, too," Zedd told Nicci. "The Mother Confessor needs to be laid to rest; let Richard see to it. I need to know your part in this, every bit of it, so that I can try to figure out how to reverse all the trouble born not just of this, but of what Jagang has done."

"All right," Nicci said. "Get the horses and I'll be right there."

Zedd cast a brief last look at Richard still huddled on his knees beside the coffin before agreeing with a nod to Nicci.

After he'd vanished with Cara through the junipers and into the fog, Nicci crouched down beside Richard and laid a hand on his back between his slumped shoulders.

"It will be all right, Richard."

"I wonder if anything will ever be all right again."

"It may not seem that way right now, but it will. Zedd will get over his anger of the moment and come to understand that you were doing your best to act responsibly. I know that he loves you and that he didn't intend what he said to hurt you so."

Richard nodded without looking up as he knelt in the mud beside the open coffin holding the corpse of the long dead Kahlan Amnell, the woman he had imagined had been his love.

"Nicci," he finally asked so softly she could hardly hear him over the soft sound of the gentle rain, "will you do something for me?"

"Anything, Richard."

"One last time . . . be Death's Mistress for me."

She rubbed his back and then stood, tears mixing with the rain on her face. By sheer force of will, past the sob struggling to escape, she made her voice steady.

"I can't Richard. You've taught me to embrace life."

The heavy paneled door opened partway. Rikka stuck her head into the silent room. "Someone is coming."

Nicci pushed her padded chair away from the polished library table. "Coming?"

"Up toward the Keep."

"Do you know who?" she asked as she stood.

Rikka shook her head. "Zedd just told me that the shields warned him that someone was on their way up the road. He thought you ought to know. I tell you, all the magic flying around in this place makes my skin crawl."

"I'll go find Richard."

Rikka nodded before vanishing out of the doorway. Nicci quickly returned the book she had been studying to its slot in the vast expanse of mahogany shelves that filled the quiet library. The book was a tedious report on activities in the Keep during the great war. Nicci found it rather strange, reading about all the people who had once lived in the Wizard's Keep thousands of years ago. It seemed a disconnected history except when she intermittently reminded herself that they were talking about the very place where she was. She considered how, in contrast, the Palace of the Prophets had been so full of life and activity for so long. Nicci couldn't imagine the Palace of the Prophets empty of all but a few souls, and the Keep was vastly larger. Of course, now the palace was no more while the Keep still stood.

Nicci hadn't really been interested in the book she'd been reading. It was boring but she didn't really care. It was merely something to occupy her time. She couldn't force herself to concentrate on anything that would be absorbing or that would require her to put any great effort into thinking. She was too distracted.

The new moon at the time they had dug up the grave of the Mother Confessor had grown to a full moon and was now approaching its last quarter again, and yet nothing much had changed. A few days after dig-

ging up the body, Zedd had told Richard that he loved him and was sorry
to have been so hard on him when maybe he should have found out a little
more before saying the things he'd said. Zedd promised that they would
figure out a way to get Richard's sword back and everything would be all
right.

It might have been sincere, and it might have been true, but for Richard
the hurt of such a personal failure was hard to put back into the bottle. He
had not just disappointed and angered his grandfather; he had failed to
prove his dream was in fact the truth. He had put everything he had into
the effort. He had been certain and in the end he had only proved himself
wrong.

Richard had only nodded to Zedd's words. Nicci didn't think it mattered much to him either way if Zedd had softened his viewpoint. He had
reached the end of his ideas, his hopes, and his efforts. Nothing had
helped him. After that night, the life had gone out of him.

Zedd had interrogated Cara and Nicci for hours that first night. Nicci
had been stunned to hear from Cara what Shota had said about the beast
becoming a blood beast because Nicci had inadvertently given it the measure of Richard's ancestral blood. She was horrified to learn that she had
been responsible for intensifying the danger to Richard.

While astonished at how Nicci had accomplished saving Richard's life,
Zedd had quietly assured her that had she not acted, Richard would most
certainly have died right then and there. He said that she had given
Richard a chance at life, and now they could work to solve the problem of
the beast Jagang's Sisters had created, as well as Richard's strange delusions and the matter of recovering his sword. From what Shota had revealed about the beast, on top of what Nicci already knew, it didn't look to
Nicci that they had much of a chance of success. She had no idea at all of
how to even begin to destroy such a beast spawned of dark powers.

She had also been embarrassed to hear Cara telling about how Shota
had revealed to Richard Cara's plan for Nicci to interest Richard romanti-
cally. Zedd, thankfully, had withheld any comments on that part of Cara's
story.

That, among other things, had left Nicci feeling rather hopeless—and
helpless. The Imperial Order was rampaging unchecked through the New
World, the beast was stalking Richard, and he was not himself, to say the
least.

In some ways, it reminded her of her dead attitude toward life, back before Richard. She had been taught that she had been born lucky in every way, and because she had ability it was her duty to devote herself to those in need. No matter how hard she worked, the needs always outpaced her ability to meet them, leaving her perpetually in debt to the ever worsening lives of others while her own life was not her own. Her feeling about what was happening now with the beast and Richard's delusions were different in almost every way, except they were the same in that they gave her that familiar feeling of hollow hopelessness.

Richard had spent the long days, since opening the grave and discovering the truth, off by himself—with the exception that Cara, after answering all of Zedd's tedious questions about everything she knew about what had happened with Shota, refused to leave Richard's side for any reason. Since Richard was in no mood to talk to anyone, Cara had become his silent shadow.

It was strange seeing the two of them together, totally at ease with each other even at such a time. It didn't seem to Nicci like the two of them even needed to speak, yet they managed, with a look, a slight shrug, or a nothing at all, to all the time understand each other.

Nicci felt like an unwelcome outsider to his misery and so she let him be. She remained as close as she could, so that she would be at hand should the beast attack, but she stayed out of his sight and left him to his solitude.

The first four or five days after arriving at the Keep Richard had spent in the Confessors' Palace—wandering the magnificent rooms and vast network of halls. Nicci stayed in a guest room in the palace, out of sight, while Richard roamed aimlessly about the empty place. After that, he'd gone out and wandered the city of Aydindril for a half-dozen days, walking the streets and alleys as if reliving the life that had once been there. It was a lot more difficult for Nicci to stay close to him when he walked all day long through the city. After that he had spent yet more days wandering the forests of the mountains around Aydindril, sometimes not even returning at night. Richard was at home in the woods, so Nicci had decided not to follow him, knowing how difficult it would have been for her to keep Richard from knowing she was there. She was comforted somewhat by her connection of magic with him that allowed her always to be aware of what direction he was and roughly how far way. When he didn't come back at night, though, Nicci paced, unable to sleep.

Zedd finally asked Richard to please remain at the Keep so that in case the beast were to attack, Zedd and Nicci could help stop it. Richard had done as he'd been asked without comment or objection. He'd spent recent days, instead of wandering the palace, or the city, or the woods, wandering the outer ramparts of the Keep, staring off into the distance.

Nicci desperately wanted to do something to help him, but Zedd had insisted that there was nothing to do but wait and see if time would begin to bring him around to the reality that he had only dreamed up his relationship with Kahlan during the time he had been unconscious. In this, Nicci didn't really think time would solve anything. She'd been with Richard long enough to realize that this was something bigger. She believed that he needed some kind of help, but she didn't know what that help could possibly be.

Nicci hurried down the wood-paneled hall outside the library, her feet swishing across thick carpets. She rushed up through the maze of stairwells and passageways, using her sense of her gifted connection with Richard to guide her, letting that thread of magic take her where it may, rather than trying to deliberately remember and find her way through the Keep.

As she made her way ever closer to him, she reminisced about the kiss she had given him to link them so that she could find him. She felt rather guilty about that kiss, even if it had been achingly wonderful to do it. It had been far more than she needed to do. She could have simply touched a finger to the back of his hand, or a shoulder, and established a link without him feeling a thing.

But Cara had just been telling her how maybe she needed to make him more aware of her and filled her mind with heady thoughts of the possibilities. That kiss would certainly have planted her firmly in his thoughts. In a way, though, she felt it was too forward, considering his mental state; he was in love with someone else, even if it was a dream, and Nicci hadn't respected that. She regretted, in a way, giving him that kiss. In another way, she wished she had planted it on his lips instead of his cheek.

As Shota had done.

It burned her to hear Cara telling them how Shota had kissed him and tried to get him to stay with her. Nicci knew how the witch woman felt— but that didn't make her any happier about it.

Nicci would give anything to be able to hold him, now, to comfort him, to tell him that it would be all right for no other reason than simply to try to make him feel just a little better, to reassure him that there were others around who cared about him.

But she knew that this was not the time or circumstances for such things.

At the same time, she knew that this could not continue. He simply could not go on like this. His life could not stay in this static state, drifting without his conscious direction. He had to come to his senses.

Nicci hurried onward, quickening her pace, down the endless maze of halls and through empty but grand rooms, suddenly feeling, for some reason, the urgent need to be with him.

Richard stood at the brink of the wall, an arm resting on a massive merlon to each side, as he stared out through the crenellation. It felt like standing at the edge of the world. Gray patches of shade drifted slowly over the hills and fields far below as their mothering clouds shepherded them along.

He seemed to have lost all track of time. Every day had become the same monotonous, pointless, empty existence. He didn't even know how long he had been standing at the gap in the wall, staring out at nothing in particular.

With Kahlan dead and gone, nothing mattered anymore. He had trouble imagining why it ever had. He couldn't even imagine for sure, now, that she had ever been real.

But whether or not she had been, it was over.

Cara was close. She was always close. In a way it was comforting, knowing that he could depend on her for anything. In some ways, though, it was wearing to have her always there, so that he was never able to have a moment's privacy.

He wondered if she believed she was close enough to snatch him if he jumped.

He knew that she wasn't.

He gazed at the tiny little roofs crowded together in the city of Aydindril far below. In a way, he felt an affinity for the city. It was empty. He was empty. Life was gone from both of them.

Since digging up the grave—he couldn't bring himself to call it Kahlan's grave, even in his own mind, much less out loud—he didn't think there was anything worth being alive for, anymore. If a person could die by sheer will alone, he would already be dead, but death, when invited, had suddenly grown shy. The days dragged endlessly on.

He had been so stunned by that grave that it seemed his mind had been scrambled on the spot. It felt like he had lost his ability to think. Nothing he knew made sense to him. The things he'd thought were true somehow no longer were. His whole world had been turned upside down. How could he function if he couldn't tell what was real and what wasn't?

He didn't know what else to do. For the first time in his life, he was baffled and defeated by the way things were. He always seemed to have a variety of options that he knew he could try. Now, he didn't. He had tried everything he could think of. None of it worked. He was at the end of his rope, and there was none left.

And all the time, in his mind, he kept seeing her body in the coffin.

He saw, he heard, he felt, but he could not think, could not put anything together in a meaningful way. It was a walking, living, imitation of death—a poor one, he believed. What good was living if it felt this way? He longed only for that dark, forever embrace of nothingness to take him.

He was so far beyond hurt, beyond sadness, beyond grief, that there was only an unthinking, empty, blind, confused agony that never for a second would release him enough to get a breath. He wanted desperately to escape the truth, to refuse to allow it to be real, but he couldn't and it was suffocating him.

The wind coming up the mountain ruffled his hair as he stared out over a precipitous drop of thousands of feet.

What good was he to anyone? He'd let Zedd down. He'd given Shota the Sword of Truth for nothing of value. Nicci thought he was out of his mind, that he was delusional. Not even Cara believed him, really believed him. He was the only one who believed him, and he had proved himself wrong by digging up her grave.

He guessed he must be crazy, that Nicci had to be right. Everyone was right. He could only be imagining things. He could see it in all their eyes the way they looked at him, that he had lost his mind.

Richard gazed down the sheer drop of the dark stones of the massive outer Keep wall. They fell away below him for thousands of feet toward the rock and forest below. Gusts of wind coming up the face of the wall buffeted him. It was a dizzying sight. A dizzying drop.

What good was he to anyone, most of all to himself?

He stole a sidelong glance at Cara. She was close, but not nearly close enough.

Richard didn't see any reason to continue the agony. He didn't have his mind, and his mind was life.

He didn't have Kahlan. She was his life.

From what everyone told him, from what he saw in the coffin that terrible night, he never had her. It was all just a mad delusion. A wish. A whim.

He glanced down again at the forever drop off the towering wall on the side of the keep, at the rocks and trees spread out below. It was a very, very long way down.

He recalled people saying that just before you died you relived your life.

If he were to relive his life, he would relive every precious moment he'd had with Kahlan.

Or thought he'd had.

It was a long way down.

A long time to relive such wonderful, romantic, loving times. A long time to relive every precious moment he'd spent with her.

Nicci opened an iron-strapped oak door to bright daylight. Puffy white clouds skimmed by just overhead in a sparkling azure sky that on any other day would have lifted her spirits. A fresh breeze carried her hair across her face. She pulled it away as she gazed down the narrow bridge to a rampart in the distance. Richard stood beyond the end of the bridge, at the far wall of the rampart, in the gap of the crenellation, looking down the mountain. Cara, nearby, turned when she heard the door.

Nicci hurried across the bridge above courtyards far below. She could see several stone benches down among the rose garden at the bottom of a tower and juncture of several walls. When she finally reached Richard's side he glanced over, giving her a brief, small smile. It warmed her to see it even though she knew the smile was little more than a polite formality.

"Rikka came and told me that someone approaches the Keep. I thought I should come and get you."

Cara, standing only three strides away, stepped a little closer. "Does Rikka know who it is?"

Nicci shook her head. "I'm afraid not, and I'm more than a little worried."

Without moving or taking his eyes from the distant countryside, Richard said "It's Ann and Nathan."

Nicci's eyebrows lifted in surprise. She looked over the edge. Richard pointed them out far below on the road that wound its way up the mountain toward the Keep.

"There are three riders," Nicci said.

Richard nodded. "It looks like it might be Tom with them."

Nicci leaned out a little farther past Richard and peered down the face of the stone wall. It was a frightening drop. The feeling came over her that she didn't at all like where he was standing.

With a hand on his shoulder to steady herself, Nicci looked out again at the three horses plodding their way up the sunlit road. They briefly disappeared under trees only to emerge a moment later as they continued steadily up toward the Keep.

A gust of wind suddenly threatened to unbalance her from her footing in the slot in the immense stone wall. Before it could, Richard's arm around her waist steadied her. She instinctively drew back from the edge. Once she was on safe footing, his protective arm released her.

"You can tell for sure, from here, that it's Ann and Nathan?" she asked.

"Yes."

Nicci wasn't especially enthusiastic about seeing the Prelate again. As a Sister of the Light and having lived at the Palace of the Prophets for most of her life, Nicci had had just about all she wanted of the Sisters and their leader. In many ways the Prelate was a mother figure to her, as she had been to all the Sisters, someone who was there to remind them whenever they were a disappointment and lecture them that they had to redouble their efforts to help others in need.

When she had been young, should self-interest ever rear its ugly head, Nicci's mother had always been at the ready to bitterly slap it down. Later in Nicci's life the Prelate served in that same capacity, if with a kindly smile. Slap or smile, it was the same thing: servitude, even if under a nicer name.

Nathan Rahl was another matter. She didn't really know the prophet. There were Sisters, and novices especially, who trembled at the mere mention of his name. From what everyone always said, though, he was not simply dangerous but possibly deranged, which, if true, had disturbing implications for Richard's present condition.

The prophet had been held in secure quarters almost his entire life, the Sisters seeing not only to his needs but seeing to it that he never escaped. People in the city of Tanimura, where the palace had been, were both titillated and terrified of the prophet, of what he might tell them of the future. Whispers were, among the people of the city, that he was most surely wicked, since he could tell them things about their future. Ability tended to arouse the ire of a great many people, especially when that ability was not one that could easily be made to serve their wants.

Nicci wasn't much worried about what people said about Nathan, though. She'd had experience with truly dangerous people—with Jagang only the most recent to grace the top of her list of the wicked.

"We'd better get down there," Nicci told Richard and Cara.

Richard stared out over the countryside. "You go on, if you want."

He sounded like he couldn't have cared less that someone was coming, or who it was. It was obvious that his mind was elsewhere and he only wanted her to go away.

Nicci pulled a flag of hair back off her face. "Don't you think you ought to see what they want? After all, they must have traveled a long way to get here. I'm sure they didn't come bringing milk and cakes."

Richard shrugged one shoulder, showing no reaction to her attempt at humor. "Zedd can see to it."

Nicci so missed the light in Richard's eyes. She was at the end of her endurance of the situation.

She glanced over at the Mord-Sith and spoke in quiet but unmistakable command. "Cara, why don't you go for a little walk? Please?"

Cara, surprised by such an unusual but clear directive coming from Nicci, took in Richard standing at the opening in the wall, staring off into the distance, and then gave Nicci a conspiratorial nod. Nicci watched Cara walk off down the rampart before finally addressing Richard again, but this time in a boldly forthright manner.

"Richard, you have to stop this."

As he gazed out at the vast scene below, he didn't answer.

Nicci knew that she couldn't allow herself to fail in what she had to say, what she had to accomplish. She would do almost anything to have Richard care about having her in his life, but she didn't want to win him this way. She didn't want to be second best to a corpse, or a substitute to a dream he couldn't make real. If she was ever to have him, she would only have him because he chose her, not because he was left with nothing else. There had been a time when she would have accepted on those grounds, but no more. She respected herself more than that, now, and all because of Richard.

But even more than that, this was not the Richard she knew and loved. Even if she could never have him, she still wouldn't allow him to sink to the terribly dark place he was in. If she could give him a needed push back up toward life, and that was all she could ever do for him, then she would.

Even if she had to play the role of antagonist to get him out of his downward spiral, and she could be no more than that to him, then she would.

She laid a hand on the stone merlon, making herself impossible to avoid, and took an even more confrontational tone.

"Aren't you going to fight for what you believe in?"

"They can fight if they want." His voice didn't sound despondent; it sounded dead.

"That's not what I mean." Nicci grasped his arm and gently but firmly pulled him around, turning him from the drop-off, forcing him to face her. "Aren't you going to fight for yourself?"

He met her gaze but didn't answer.

"This is because Zedd told you that he was disappointed in you."

"I think the grave I dug up might have had a bit to do with it."

"You may think so but I don't. Why should it? You have been devastated and sent reeling by things before. I captured you and took you away to the Old World, and what did you do? You stood up for yourself and acted like yourself and on your beliefs, within the limits of what I would allow you to do. By being who you are you exerted your love of life and that changed my life. You showed me the truth of the joy of life and all it means.

"This time you woke up from nearly dying to me and Cara and everyone else not believing in your memory of Kahlan, but that never stopped you. You kept arguing your convictions despite everything we said."

"What was in that coffin is different, and I'd say a little more than a simple argument when someone doesn't believe you."

"Is it? I don't think so. It was a skeleton. So what?"

"So what?" Annoyance crept into his features. "Are you out of your mind? What do you mean, so what?"

"Far be it from me to argue your case when I don't believe in it, but I don't seek to win you to what I believe is the truth by default. I would want to win you over with the true facts, not with this flimsy evidence."

"What do you mean?"

"Well, was it Kahlan's face you saw to prove to you that it really was her? No, it couldn't be—there was no face left. Just a skull—no face, no eyes, no features. The skeleton was wearing the dress of the Mother Confessor. So what? I was in the Confessors' Palace and there were other dresses there like that.

"So was a name stitched on a gold ribbon enough to prove it to you? Enough to bring you to an end of your search, your beliefs? After all the things that Cara and I have said to you, have argued to you, have reasoned to you, you all of a sudden feel that this flimsy evidence proves you delusional? A skeleton in a coffin holding a ribbon with her name stitched on it is enough to suddenly convince you that you dreamed her up, just as we've been telling you all along and you've refused to believe? Don't you think that the ribbon is just a little too convenient?"

Richard frowned at her. "What are you getting at?"

"I don't believe that's what is really going on with you. I think you're wrong about your memories but I don't believe that the Richard I know could be convinced by the dubious evidence in that grave. This isn't even because Zedd doesn't believe your memories any more than Cara and I do."

"Then what's it about?"

"This is all because you believed a corpse in a coffin was her because you were afraid it was true after your grandfather said that he was disappointed in you and that you let him down."

Richard started to turn away, but Nicci seized his shirt and pulled him back, forcing him to face her.

"That's what I think this is about," she said with fierce resolve. "You're sulking because your grandfather said you were wrong, said that you disappointed him."

"Maybe because I did."

"So what?"

Richard's face screwed up in confusion. "What do you mean, 'so what'?"

"I mean, so what if he's disappointed in you. So what if he thinks you did a stupid thing. You're your own man. You did what you reasoned you had to do. You acted because you thought you had to act and do the things you did."

"But I . . ."

"You what? You disappointed him? You made him angry at what you decided to do? He thought more of you and you let him down? You came up short in his eyes?"

Richard swallowed, not wanting to admit it aloud.

Nicci lifted his chin and made him look into her eyes.

"Richard, you have no responsibility to live up to anyone else's expectations."

He blinked at her, looking speechless.

"It's your life," she insisted. "You're the one who taught me that. You did what you thought you must. Did you turn down Shota's offer because Cara disagreed with you? No. Would you have turned down Shota's offer if you knew I thought you were wrong to give her your sword? Or would you have turned her down if both of us told you that you'd be a fool to accept? No, I don't think so.

"And why not? Because you were doing what you thought you must do and as much as you would hope we would agree with you, in the end it didn't matter what we thought. Your conviction was what you had to act upon. You didn't quail at the decision, you acted. You did what you felt you had to do. You were making the decision based on what you believed, for reasons only you can truly know, and that it was the right thing to do. Isn't that correct?"

"Well . . . yes."

"Then what difference should it make if your grandfather thinks you're wrong. Was he there? Does he know everything you knew at the time? It would be nice if he believed in what you did, if he supported you and said 'good for you, Richard,' but he didn't. Does that suddenly make your decision wrong? Does it?"

"No."

"Then you can't let it take over your mind. Sometimes the people who love us the most have the highest expectations for us, and sometimes those expectations are idealized. You did what you had to do, given what you believed and what you know, to find the answers you needed to solve the problem. If everyone else in the world thinks you're wrong, but you believe you're right, you have to act on what you have sound reason to believe. Numbers of those against you don't change the facts and you must act to find the facts, not satisfy the crowd or any particular individual.

"You have no responsibility to live up to anyone else's expectations. You have only to live up to your own expectations."

Some of the light, the fire was back in his intent gray eyes. "Does this mean that you believe me, Nicci?"

She sadly shook her head. "No, Richard. I think your belief in Kahlan is a result of your injury. I think you dreamed her up."

"And the grave?"

"The truth?" When he nodded, Nicci took a deep breath. "I think that is the real Mother Confessor, Kahlan Amnell."

"I see."

Nicci seized his jaw again and made him look back at her. "But that doesn't mean that I'm right. I'm basing my belief on other things—things I know. But I don't think that anything I saw in that coffin, as much as I believe it's her, really proves it. I've been wrong in my life before. You've thought I'm wrong all along in this. Are you going to do as someone says who you think is wrong? Why would you do that?"

"But it's so hard when no one believes me."

"Sure it is, but so what? That doesn't make them right and you wrong."

"But when everyone says you're wrong it starts to make you have doubts."

"Yes, sometimes life is really hard. In the past doubts have always made you dig all the harder for the truth, to be sure you were right because knowing the truth can give you the strength to fight on. This time, your shock at seeing a body in the Mother Confessor's grave when you hadn't anticipated even the possibility of one being there, coupled with your grandfather's unexpectedly harsh comments right in that moment of horror, overwhelmed you.

"I can understand how it was the last straw and you couldn't fight it anymore. Everyone can sometimes reach the limits of their endurance and give up—even you, Richard Rahl. You are mortal and you have your limits just like everyone else does. But you have to deal with that and move on. You've had time to temporarily give up, but now you have to take control of your own life again."

She could see him thinking, considering. It was a thrilling sight to see Richard's mind back and working. She could still see, though, his hesitation. She didn't want him to come this far and slip back now.

"People must have not believed you before, in other things," she said. "Weren't there ever times when this Kahlan of yours didn't believe you? A real person would have sometimes disagreed with you, doubted you, argued with you. And when that happened, you must have done as you thought you had to, even though she thought you were wrong, maybe even a little crazy. I mean, come on, Richard, this isn't the first time I've thought you were crazy."

Richard smiled briefly before before thinking it over. Then, a broad grin spread on his face.

"Yes, there certainly were times like that with Kahlan, when she didn't believe me."

"And you still did as you believed you had to, didn't you?"

Richard, still smiling, nodded.

"Then don't let this incident with your grandfather ruin your life."

He lifted an arm and let it flop back down. "But it's just that—"

"You gave up because of what Zedd told you without even using what you got from Shota."

He looked up sharply, his attention suddenly riveted on her. "What do you mean?"

"In exchange for the Sword of Truth, Shota gave you information to help you find the truth. One of the things she told you was 'What you seek is long buried.'

"But that's not all. Cara told Zedd and me everything Shota said. Apparently the most vital thing she gave you, because it was the first and almost all she thought she had to tell you, was the word *Chainfire*. Right?"

Richard nodded as he listened.

"She then told you that you must find the place of the bones in the Deep Nothing. Shota also told you to beware the viper with four heads.

"What is Chainfire? What is the Deep Nothing? What is the viper with four heads? You paid a dear price for that information, Richard. What have you done with it? You came here and asked Zedd if he knew and he said no, then he told you that he was disappointed in you.

"So what? Are you going to throw away everything you've gained in your search just because of that? Because an old man who has no idea what Kahlan means to you or what you've been through the last couple of years thinks that you acted foolishly? Do you want to move in here and be his lapdog? Do you want to stop thinking and just depend on him to do your thinking for you?"

"Of course not."

"At the grave Zedd was angry. He went through things we probably can't imagine to get the Sword of Truth away from Shota. What would you expect him to say? 'Oh, yes, that's a good idea, Richard, just give it back to her; that's fine.' He had a lot invested in getting that sword back from her and he thought you made a foolish trade. So what? That's his view. Maybe he's even right.

"But you thought it was important enough to sacrifice something he had entrusted to you alone, something very precious to you, in order to gain a higher value. You believed that it was a fair trade. Cara said that at first you even thought Shota might be cheating you, but then you came to believe that she had given you fair value. Did Cara tell it true?"

Richard nodded.

"What did Shota tell you about your bargain?"

Richard gazed up at the soaring towers behind Nicci as he recalled the words. "Shota said, 'You wanted what I know that can help you find the truth. I have given it to you: Chainfire. Whether or not you realize it right now, I have given you a fair trade. I have given you the answers you needed. You are the Seeker—or at least, you were. You will have to seek the meaning to be found in those answers.'"

"And do you believe her?"

Richard considered a moment, his gazed dropping away. "I do." When he looked back up into her eyes, the spark of life was again blazing there. "I do believe her."

"Then you should tell me and Cara and your grandfather that if none of us are going to help you, then we ought to get out of your way and let you do as you must."

He smiled, if somewhat sadly. "You're a pretty remarkable woman, Nicci, to convince me to keep fighting even when you don't believe in what I'm fighting for." He leaned in and kissed her on the cheek.

"I truly wish I could, Richard . . . for your sake."

"I know. Thank you, my friend—and I say friend because only a true friend would be more concerned with helping me face reality than what it means for her." He reached out and, with his hand cupped to her face, used a thumb to wipe a tear from her cheek. "You have done more for me than you know, Nicci. Thank you."

Nicci felt giddy joy mixed with sinking frustration that they were right back to where they had started.

Still, she wanted to throw her arms around him, but instead she simply cupped both her hands over his on the side of her face.

"Now," he said, "I think we had better go see about Ann and Nathan, and then I need to find out what part Chainfire plays in all this. Will you help me?"

Nicci smiled as she nodded, too choked up to speak, and then, unable to stop herself, at last threw her arms around him and clutched him tightly to her.

The look on Ann's face as she stepped in the big door and saw Nicci entering the anteroom from between two red pillars was priceless. Nicci would have laughed aloud had her talk with Richard not so emotionally drained her.

The prophet, Nicci knew, was very old, but he was by no means feeble looking. He was tall and broad-shouldered, with distinguished white hair that hung to his shoulders. He looked like a man who could bend iron, and he wouldn't even need his gift to do so. It was the raptor gaze of his dark azure eyes, though, that made him at once intimidating and alluring. They were the eyes of a Rahl.

Ann stared, her own eyes wide. "Sister Nicci . . ."

The Prelate didn't say "So good to see you again," or anything cordial. She seemed momentarily unable to think of what to say. Nicci found it just a little remarkable that this squat woman beside the towering prophet had for so long seemed so big in her eyes. Novices and Sisters often went for long periods without even seeing the Prelate around the Palace of the Prophets. Absence, Nicci guessed, added to her mythic stature.

"Prelate. I'm glad to see you well, especially after your unfortunate death and funeral." Nicci glanced over at Richard as she finished the thought. "I hear that everyone believed you were dead. Amazing how a burial can be so convincing, and yet here you are, alive and well, it would appear."

Richard's twitch of a smile told her that he caught her meaning. Zedd, to the side, at the brink of the three steps leading down into the center of the room with the fountain, gave Nicci a curious frown. The meaning hadn't been lost on him, either.

"Yes, well, that was unfortunately necessary, child." Ann's expression darkened. "What with the Sisters of the Dark having infested the ranks of our Sisters of the Light." She glanced briefly at Richard, Cara, and Zedd,

the edge to her countenance softening. "It appears by the company you
keep, Sister Nicci, that you have come back into the fold. I can't tell you
how much it pleases me, personally. I can only think that the Creator Himself must have had a hand in saving your soul."

Nicci clasped her hands behind her back. "The Creator had nothing to
do with it, actually. I guess that while I was forced to spend my life serving
everyone who decided they wanted the blood and sweat of my abilities, the
Creator was busy. I guess he couldn't be bothered while I was being used
by pious men telling me how it was my duty to serve and to submit and to
grovel to them and to kill those who opposed the Creator's ways.

"I guess that all the times those champions of the Creator were raping
me, the Creator didn't catch on to the irony.

"No more. Richard helped show me the value of my life to myself.
And it is no longer 'Sister' Nicci—either of the Light or the Dark. Nor is
it Death's Mistress, or the Slave Queen. It is just Nicci, now, if you
please . . . and even if you don't."

Ann's expression flashed between incredulity and indignation as her
face went red. "But once you are a Sister you are always a Sister. You have
done a wonderful thing and renounced the Keeper, so you are again a Sister of the Light. You can't simply decide on your own to forsake your duty
to the Creator's—"

"If He has any objections, then let Him speak up right now!" As the
echo of Nicci's heated words faded away, the room fell silent but for the
splash of water in the fountain. She made a show of looking around, as if
if she thought that maybe the Creator might be hiding behind a pillar
ready to pop out and make His wishes known.

"No?" She again clasped her hands. She put back on the defiant smile.
"Well then, since He has no objections, Nicci it is, I guess."

"I'll not have—"

"Ann, enough," Nathan said in a deep, commanding voice. "We have
important business and this isn't it. We didn't travel all this way simply
for a dead prelate to lecture a reformed Sister of the Dark."

Nicci was somewhat surprised to hear the voice of reason coming from
the prophet. She allowed that perhaps she had put too much stock into idle
gossip.

Ann's mouth twisted in resignation as she fingered a stray lock of hair
into the loose bun at the back of her head. "I suppose you're right. I'm

afraid that I'm a little out of sorts, my dear, what with all the trouble going on. Please forgive my rash presumption, will you, Nicci?"

Nicci bowed her head. "Happily, Prelate."

Ann smiled, more genuinely, Nicci thought. "And it's just Ann, now. Verna is Prelate, now. I'm dead, remember?"

Nicci smiled. "So you are, Ann. Wise choice, Verna. Sister Cecilia always said that there was no hope of converting that one to the Keeper."

"Someday when we have the luxury of time, I would appreciate hearing more about Sister Cecilia in addition to Richard's former teachers." She sighed at the thought. "I never knew for sure that you and all five of the others were Sisters of the Dark."

Nicci nodded. "I'd be happy to tell you what I know about them—the ones still alive, anyway. Liliana and Merissa are dead."

"Tom, how is my sister?" Richard asked as soon as there was a brief break in the conversation. Nicci recognized that he had listened long enough and was signaling that he wanted to move on to more important matters.

"She is well, Lord Rahl," the big blond-headed man near the door said.

"Good. Nathan, what's going on?" Richard anxiously asked, getting right to the point. "What trouble are you here about?"

"Well . . . among other things, prophecy trouble."

Richard visibly relaxed. "Oh. Well, that's not something I can help you with."

"I wouldn't be so sure," Nathan said, cryptically.

Zedd stepped off the gold and red carpet and down into the room. "Let me guess. You're here about the blank places in the books of prophecy."

Nicci had to run Zedd's words through her mind a second time before she was sure she'd heard him right.

Nathan nodded. "You've just sat down in the middle of the muck."

"What do you mean you're here about blank places in the books of prophecy?" Richard looked suddenly suspicious. "What blank places?"

"Extensive sections of prophecy—that is, prophecy written down in the books of prophecy—have simply vanished off the pages of a number of the books we've so far inspected." Nathan's brow bunched in an expression of apprehension. "We've checked with Verna and she confirmed that the books of prophecy at the People's Palace in D'Hara are suffering the same inexplicable problem. Therein lies the heart of our worry. We came, in part, to see if the works of prophecy here at the Keep are still intact."

"I'm afraid not," Zedd said. "The books here have been similarly corrupted."

Nathan swiped a hand across his tired face. "Dear spirits," he murmured. "We had been holding out hope that whatever is causing such havoc among the prophecies had not affected the books here as well."

"You mean that entire sections of prophecy are missing?" Richard asked, stepping down into the heart of the room.

"That's right," Nathan confirmed.

"Would there happen to be a pattern to the missing prophecy?" Richard asked, suddenly focusing on a line of reasoning that Nicci knew would end up being somehow related to his own search. Ordinarily she would have been frustrated or even annoyed that he could think of nothing else but his fixation with the missing woman, but this time she was heartened to see that the familiar Richard was back.

"Why yes, there is a pattern. They are all prophecies having to do with events beginning roughly around the time of your birth."

Richard stared, dumbfounded. "What are the missing prophecies about—specifically? I mean, are they related to specific events, or are they nonspecific and instead share only a time period?"

Nathan stroked his chin as he considered the question. "That's the thing that makes this so strange. Many of the prophecies that are missing we know we should be able to recall, but they are suddenly and completely just as blank in our minds as they are on the page. We can't remember a single word of them. We don't recall what they were about, and since they're gone from the books as well I can't tell you if they were event related or time related—or something else. We realize that they are missing, but that's about all."

Richard's eyes turned to Nicci, as if to ask if she caught the correlation. She thought he could see that she did. His voice remained casual, but Nicci knew how intent was the interest behind his words.

"Pretty odd that something you've known all your lives can just vanish right out of your memory, wouldn't you say?"

"I certainly would," Nathan said. "Any thoughts on the subject, Zedd?"

Zedd, who had been silently and intently watching Richard, nodded. "Well, I know what's causing it, if that will help you out."

He smiled innocently. Nicci noticed that Rikka, standing in the shadows back behind the red pillars, smiled as well. Nathan, at first stunned, became animated with curiosity.

Richard gently tugged Zedd's robes at his shoulder. "You know?"

"You do?" Nathan asked, urging Richard back out of the way as he stepped closer. Ann rushed forward with him. "What is it? What's happening? Tell us."

"A prophecy worm, I'm afraid."

Nathan and Ann blinked, their faces blank of any comprehension.

"A what?" Nathan finally ventured, somewhat cautiously, if not suspiciously.

"The text vanishing is caused by a prophecy worm. Once a fork of prophecy is infected with this scourge, it worms its way entirely through that branch, consuming it as it goes. Since it consumes the actual prophecy itself, that means that over time all manifestations of it, such as the written prophecy or any memory of it, are destroyed. It's quite virulent." Zedd regarded their rapt stares with another polite smile. "If you want, I can show you the reference work."

"I should say so," Nathan said.

"Zedd this is important," Richard said. "Why haven't you said something?"

Zedd gave him a familiar clap on the shoulder as he started away. "Well, my boy, when you arrived you weren't much in the mood to listen to anything but what you were here about. Remember? You were rather insistent that you had trouble and you needed to talk to me about it. Since then you haven't exactly been willing to talk. You've been rather . . . distracted."

"I guess I was." Richard caught his grandfather's arm, halting him before he could get far. "Zedd, look, I need to tell you something about all of that, and about that night."

"Like what, my boy?"

"I know that a contradiction cannot exist."

"I never really thought you did, Richard."

"But there was more to it that night. The rule most involved down there at the grave site was not the one you quoted. It may have seemed that way to you at the moment, but the rule I made a mistake about was another— the one that says in part that people can be made to believe a lie because they fear that it's true. That's what I was doing. I wasn't believing a contradiction, I was believing a lie because I was so afraid it was true. The rule of noncontradiction is one of the ways I should have checked my assumptions. I didn't, and in that I made a mistake.

"I understand what it must have looked like to you since you weren't aware of everything that's been happening, but that doesn't mean I should have stopped looking for the truth out of a misplaced wish to make you happy, or out of fear of what you would think of me."

He met Nicci's gaze for a brief moment. "Nicci helped me see what I was doing wrong."

He looked back at his grandfather. "I think you meant to show me that the rule you quoted is more, though. It also means you can't hold contradictory values or goals. You can't say, for instance, that honesty is a meaningful value, and at the same time lie to people. You can't say that justice is your goal but refuse to hold the guilty responsible for their actions.

"At the heart of our struggle, the fact that contradictions can't exist is why the Imperial Order's regime is so ruinous. They hold up altruism as their highest purpose. Yet, out of their proclaimed selfless concern for one individual, they sacrifice another, soothing over the bloodletting by proclaiming that such a sacrifice is the moral duty of the sacrificial victim. It's really nothing more than organized looting, a passion for the happiness of thieves and murderers without any concern for their victim. Attempts at goals that depend on such contradiction can only lead to widespread suffering and death. It's the fraudulent advocacy of the right to life by embracing death as a means to achieve it.

"The rule you quoted means I can't, like Jagang's followers, say I want the truth and then, without checking my assumption, willingly believe a lie in its stead, even if out of fear. That's the way I violated the rule you quoted. I should have sorted out what looked like contradictions and found the truth staring me in the face. That's where I let myself down."

"Are you saying that you now don't believe that was Kahlan Amnell?" Zedd asked.

"Who says that corpse has to be the woman you think it is? There were no facts there to contradict my belief that it wasn't her. I only believed there were out of fear that it was true. It wasn't."

Zedd took a deep breath, letting it out slowly. "You're stretching things mighty thin, Richard."

"Am I? You wouldn't be too pleased with my rationale if I said that there is no such thing as prophecy and held up the blank books as proof that your belief in the existence of prophecy is wrong. For you to believe that prophecy exists in the face of the fact that the supposed books of prophecy are blank is not a contradiction. It is a perplexing situation with insufficient information to as of yet explain the facts. You have no obligation to reach a conclusion or hold an opinion you don't accept for other reasons without adequate information or before you have finished investigating.

"What kind of Seeker would I be if I did that? After all, it's the mind of the man that makes him the Seeker, not the sword. The sword is merely a tool—you're the one who told me that.

"In the case of Kahlan, there are still too many unanswered questions for me to be convinced that what we saw that rainy night is really the truth. Until it's proved one way or another, I'm going to continue to look for the answers—for the truth—because I believe that what is going on is far more dangerous than anyone but me realizes, to say nothing of needing to find a person I love who needs my help."

Zedd smiled in a grandfatherly way. "Fair enough, Richard, fair enough. But I expect you to prove it to me. I won't take your word for it."

Richard gave his grandfather a firm nod. "For starters, I think you have to admit it's rather suspicious that prophecies revolving around Kahlan's and my lives are missing. The memory of her is gone. Now the prophecies are gone that would have to contain reference to her. In both cases everyone's memory of both real entities—the person and the prophecies referring to that real person—have been wiped away.

"Do you see what I'm getting at?"

Nicci was immeasurably relieved to see that Richard was thinking rationally again. She was also concerned that in a strange way, what he said actually did make some sense.

"Yes, my boy, I do see your point, but do you see that there is a problem with your theory?"

"What's that?"

"We all remember you, now don't we? And the prophecies about you are missing. As it turns out, in this case the problem with prophecy doesn't have anything at all to do with what you are hoping will explain or prove the existence of Kahlan Amnell."

"Why not?" Richard asked.

Zedd started up the steps. "It has to do with the nature of what I found out when I did my own investigation of the problem with the books of prophecy. I'm not without my own sense of curiosity, you know."

"I know that, Zedd. But it could be connected," Richard insisted as he walked along beside his grandfather.

Nicci hurried after him. Everyone else was forced to fall in behind.

"It might seem that way to you, my boy, but your speculation is flawed because all the facts just don't fit your conclusion. You're trying to wear boots that look good but are too small." Zedd clapped Richard on the shoulder. "When we get to the library I'll show you what I mean."

"Who's Kahlan?" Nathan asked.

"Someone who vanished and I haven't found yet," Richard said over his shoulder. "But I will."

Richard paused and turned back to Ann and Nathan. "Do either of you know what Chainfire is?" They both shook their heads. "How about a viper with four heads, or the Deep Nothing?"

"I'm afraid not, Richard," Ann said. "But as long as we're on the subject of important matters, we do have other things we need to speak with you about."

"After we see Zedd's reference about prophecy," Nathan said.

"Well, come on, then," Zedd told them as he started off with a flourish of his simple robes.

In the plush library, Richard stood behind Zedd, watching over his grandfather's bony shoulder as he flipped open a thick book bound in tattered, tan leather. The room was rather dimly lit by a number of silver reflector lamps on all four sides of five thick mahogany posts standing in a line down the center of the room. They held up the leading edge of a balcony running the length of the room. Heavy, dark wooden tables with polished tops lined the center of the room down the line of posts. Wooden chairs were spaced around the outside of the tables. Opulent carpets with elaborately woven patterns felt soft and quiet underfoot. Perpendicular to the long walls on each side were aisles of shelves packed with books. Above, the balcony held closely spaced shelves filled with yet more volumes.

A gray-blue shaft of sunlight slanting in from the single window up high at the very end of the room lit the dust floating in the stuffy air. The freshly lit lamps added an oily smell. The room had a vaultlike quiet about it.

Cara and Rikka stood off by themselves in the darker area beneath the window at the end of the room, arms folded, heads together, talking in low voices. Nicci stood beside Zedd along one edge of a table lit in a glowing rectangle of sunlight while Ann and Nathan stood impatiently on the opposite side, waiting for Zedd's explanation of how prophecy had vanished. Standing there, in the island of light, the rest of the room faded away into gloomy shadows around them.

"This book was compiled, I believe, sometime not long after the great war had ended," Zedd told them as he tapped the open cover near the title: *Continuum Ratios and Viability Predictions*. "The gifted back then had discovered that, for whatever reason, fewer and fewer wizards were being born and the ones who were being born were not being born with both sides of the gift, as had almost always been the case before. What's more, the ones who were being born with the gift were all being born with only the Additive side. Subtractive Magic was vanishing."

Ann looked up from under her brow. "It is hardly a novice and a boy wizard standing before you, old man. We know all this. We have spent our lives devoted to this very problem. Get on with it."

Zedd cleared his throat. "Yes, well, as you may know, this also meant that there were fewer and fewer prophets being born."

"How remarkably fascinating," Ann mocked. "I, for one, would never have guessed such a thing."

Nathan irritably hushed her. "Go on, Zedd."

Zedd pushed back his sleeves, briefly casting a scowl Ann's way. "They realized that, with ever fewer wizards born to prophecy, the body of work of prophecy was of course going to cease to grow. In order to understand what the consequences of this might mean, they decided that they needed to do an intensive investigation of the entire subject of prophecy while they still could, while they still had prophets and other wizards with both sides of the gift.

"They approached the problem with the gravest of concern, realizing that with them, this might very well be mankind's last opportunity to comprehend the future of prophecy itself, and to offer future generations an insight to understanding what these wizards were increasingly coming to believe would one day be seriously corrupted or even lost."

Zedd glanced up to see if Ann looked like she intended to offer anymore disparaging comments. She did not. This was apparently something she hadn't known.

"Now," he said, "to their work."

Richard moved up to the table beside Nicci and with a finger turned over pages as he listened to Zedd. He quickly noticed that the book was written in such strange technical jargon having to do with the intricacies of not only magic but prophecy as well that it was nearly incomprehensible to him. It might as well have been a different language.

One of the surprises was that the book contained a series of complex mathematical formulas. These were interrupted by diagrams of the moon and stars marked with angles of declination. Richard had never before seen a book about magic that contained such equations, celestial observations, and measurements—not that he had actually seen that many books about magic. Although, he recalled, *The Book of Counted Shadows* that he had memorized as a boy did have a number of sun and star angles that were necessary to know in order to open the boxes of Orden.

Yet more formulas were scratched in the margins, but by different hands, as if someone had come along and done the sums to check the work in the book, or perhaps approached it with updated information. In one instance, several of the numbers in an elaborate table were crossed out, with arrows pointing from new numbers scribbled in the margins to the stricken numbers in the tables. Zedd occasionally stopped Richard from turning pages in order to point out an equation and explain the symbols involved in the calculation.

Like a dog watching a bone, Nathan's dark azure eyes tracked the pages as Richard slowly turned each over, idly looking for anything that made sense to him as Zedd droned on about overlapping transpositional forks and triple duplexes bound to conjugated roots compromised by precession and sequential, proportional, binary inversions shrouding flawed bifurcations that the formulas revealed which could only be detected through Subtractive levorotatory.

Nathan and Ann stared without blinking. Once, Nathan even gasped. Ann incrementally went ashen. Even Nicci seemed to be listening with uncharacteristic attention.

The unfathomable concepts made Richard's head spin. He hated that feeling of drowning in incomprehensible information, of trying to keep his head above the dark waters of complete confusion. It made him feel dumb.

Intermittently, Zedd referred to numbers and equations from the book. Nathan and Ann acted like they thought Zedd was on the verge of revealing not only how the world was going to end but the precise hour.

"Zedd," Richard finally asked, interrupting his grandfather in the middle of a sentence that showed no signs of ever coming to an end, "is there any way you can boil this stew down to some meat that I can chew?"

Mouth agape, Zedd regarded Richard for a moment before pushing the book across the table to Nathan. "I'll let you read it for yourself."

Nathan cautiously picked up the book as if the Keeper himself might pop out at him.

Zedd turned back to Richard. "Basically, to put it in terms you might better grasp, and at great risk of oversimplifying it, imagine that prophecy is like a tree, with roots and branches. Like a tree, prophecy was continually growing. What these wizards were basically saying was that the tree of prophecy behaved as if there were a kind of life to it. They weren't saying that it was alive, mind you, only that in a number of ways it mimicked—not duplicated—some attributes of a living organism. It was this property that allowed them to come up with their theory and from that run their calculations—in much the way there are parameters by which you can judge the age and health of a tree and from that extrapolate about its future.

"During a previous time when there had been a great many prophets and wizards around, the works of prophecy and its many branches grew quite rapidly. With all the prophets who had contributed, it had solid, fertile ground in which to grow, and deep roots. With new prophets constantly bringing new vision to the collected works, new forks of prophecy sprouted continuously and those new branches, over time as other prophets added to them, grew thick and strong. As it grew, prophets continually examined, observed, and interpreted events, enabling them to tend the living stock and prune the deadwood.

"But then, the birthrate of prophets began to plummet and with each passing year there were fewer and fewer of them to attend to such duties. Because of this, the growth of the tree of prophecy began to slow.

"In essence, to explain it in simple terms you can understand, the tree of prophecy had in a way matured. Like an old monarch oak in a forest, these wizards knew that the vast tree of prophecy had many years of life ahead of it as a mature entity, but they also knew what the future eventually held in store.

"Like all things, the existence of prophecy could not be eternal. As time passed, prophetic events came to pass, becoming outdated. These no longer served any use. In this fashion, if nothing else, the passage of time would eventually supersede all the predictions dealt with in the work. In other words, without new prophecy, all the existing prophecy, whether or not they turned out to be true forks, nonetheless would eventually reach their chance in the chronological flux. As they did, their time passed— they would be used up.

"Thus, the commission studying the problem came to realize that the tree of prophecy, without the growth and life that it drew from prophets, from the constant stream of prophecy feeding the many branches, would eventually die. Their task, and the purpose of this book, *Continuum Ratios and Viability Predictions*, was to try to predict how and when this would happen.

"The best minds in prophecy studied the problem, took a measure of the health of the tree of prophecy. Through known formulas and predictions based on not only observed patterns in the decline of growth in prophecy, but a decline in prophets to sustain it, they determined how this particular tree of knowledge would become heavy with the deadwood of false and expired prophecy as prophetic forks were reached and chronology moved on down the sections of branches still viable. As this happened—as the tree of prophecy grew thick with age and deadwood that could no longer be culled by true prophets—they predicted how it would become susceptible to, to, well, a kind of malady, a decay, much like an old tree in the forest will eventually become susceptible to disease.

"That decline in viability, they found, would, over time, leave prophecy vulnerable to any number of ever growing problems. The infirmity that they concluded would be the most likely to strike first would come in a form they described as wormlike. They thought that it would begin to infest and destroy the living portions of the tree of prophecy itself, meaning the branches that are contemporary at the time of this wormlike infestation. In fact, they called it just that—a prophecy worm."

The air felt heavy in the thick silence.

Hands in his back pockets, Richard shrugged. "So what's the cure?"

Astonished by the question, Zedd stared at Richard as if he'd just asked how to heal a thunderstorm. "Cure? Richard, these experts who wrote this book predicted that there wasn't any cure, as such. They concluded, in the end, that without the vitality provided by new prophets, the tree of prophecy would eventually rot and die.

"They said that prophecy would only come back strong and healthy when new prophets returned to the world—in effect, when a seed of new prophecy sprouted and flourished. Old trees die and make room for the new shoots. It was determined by these learned wizards that the fate of prophecy as we know it is also doomed to aging, infirmity, and eventual death."

Richard had had to deal with any number of problems caused by prophecy, but the gloomy expressions around the table were infectious. It almost felt like a healer had come out of a back room to announce that an aging relative was near to passing on.

He thought about all the gifted prophets, devoted to their calling, who had worked all of their lives to contribute to this great body of work that was now withering and dying. He thought about the statue he himself had worked so hard to create and how it made him feel when it was destroyed.

He thought, too, that it might simply be the concept of death itself, in any form, that was so dismal because it reminded him of his own mortality . . . and of Kahlan's mortality.

He also thought that it might be the best thing that could happen. After all, if people no longer believed that prophecy had foreordained what would become of them, then maybe they would realize that they had to think for themselves and decide what was in their own best interest. Maybe, if unchained from a deterministic mindset, people would realize that it was they themselves who actually controlled their own destiny. If people comprehended what was really at stake, maybe they would come to realize the value of reason in the choices they made, instead of mindlessly just waiting for what was to happen, to happen.

"From what Ann and I have discovered," Nathan said into the still, stale air of the library, "the branch of prophecy that is vanishing is that which refers to times roughly since Richard was born. That, of course, makes the most sense because temporal souls nourish the active, living tissue of prophecy upon which this prophecy worm would feed. But I was able to determine that it hasn't all simply vanished, yet."

Zedd nodded. "It's dying back, but from the root, so some of it is still alive. I've found pockets of it alive and well."

"That's right—especially the portions from the present on into the future. As you suggest, it seems that the scourge has attacked the core of these branches, which began two or three decades back and so far have not extensively eaten their way into future events.

"That leaves sections of this prophetic branch—the branch involving you—that are still alive," the prophet said as he leaned on his hands toward Richard, "but once it dies, we will then lose even those prophecies, along with the memory of how profoundly important they are."

Richard glanced from Nathan's grim expression to Ann's equally serious face. He knew they had arrived at last at the heart of their purpose.

"That is why we've come looking for you, Richard Rahl," Ann said with grave intonation, "before it's too late. We have come about prophecy that so far is still alive and has warned us of the most serious crisis to face us since the great war."

Richard frowned, already unhappy that prophecy once again seemed about to cause him trouble. "What prophecy?"

Nathan pulled a small book out of a pocket and flipped it open. As he held it in both hands, he fixed Richard with a steady gaze to make sure he looked like he was going to listen carefully.

When Nathan was at last sure he had everyone's attention, he began. " 'In the year of the cicadas, when the champion of sacrifice and suffering, under the banner of both mankind and the Light' "—he glanced up from under his bushy eyebrows—"that would be Emperor Jagang— 'finally splits his swarm, thus shall be the sign that prophecy has been awakened and the final and deciding battle is upon us. Be cautioned, for all true forks and their derivatives are tangled in this mantic root. Only one trunk branches from this conjoined primal origin. If *fuer grissa ost drauka* does not lead this final battle, then the world, already standing at the brink of darkness, will fall under that terrible shadow."

"Dear spirits," Zedd whispered. "*Fuer grissa ost drauka* is a cardinal link to a prophecy founding a principal fork. Conjoining it with this prophecy establishes a conjugate bifurcation."

Nathan arched an eyebrow. "Exactly."

Richard didn't fully understand what Zedd had said, but he caught the drift. And he didn't need them to tell him who *fuer grissa ost drauka*, the bringer of death, was; it was him.

"Jagang has split his forces," Ann said with quiet power as she fixed Richard in her steady gaze. "He brought his army up near to Aydindril, hoping to finish it, but the D'Haran forces, along with the people of the city, made use of winter to escape over the passes to D'Hara and out of Jagang's clutches."

"I know," Richard said. "That escape over the passes in winter was by Kahlan's orders. She's the one who told me about it."

Cara looked up in surprise, apparently intending to dispute his account, but after a glance at Nicci she decided to remain silent . . . at least for the moment.

"At any rate," Ann said, sounding annoyed by the interruption, "Jagang, unable to effectively use his vastly superior numbers to break through those heavily defended, very narrow passes, has finally decided to split his forces. Leaving an army to watch the passes, the emperor himself took the main element of his army south, headed all the way back down through the Midlands to skirt around the barrier of mountains and then hook around and make his way up into D'Hara.

"Our forces are headed south, down through D'Hara, to meet them. That was why when we were able to get a message from Verna about the condition of the books of prophecy at the People's Palace in D'Hara; she was able to ride south ahead of our army and go look them over herself."

"This is the year that the cicadas are returning," Nicci said, sounding alarmed. "I've seen them."

"That's right," Nathan said, still leaning forward on both hands. "That means the chronology is now fixed. The prophecies have all made their connections and have tumbled into place. Events are marked." In turn, he met the gaze of everyone in the room. "The end is upon us."

Zedd let out a low whistle.

"More importantly," Ann said in an authoritative tone, "it means that it is time for Lord Rahl to join the D'Haran forces and lead them in the final battle. Without you there, Richard, prophecy is quite clear; all will be lost. We have come to escort you to your forces, to help insure that you make it. We dare not risk delay; we must leave at once."

For the first time since they started talking about prophecy, Richard's knees felt weak.

"But I can't," he said. "I have to find Kahlan."

It sounded to him like a plea into a gale.

Ann took a deep breath, as if to bite her tongue while she searched for some urgently needed patience, or maybe words that would persuade him and finally settle the matter once and for all. The two Mord-Sith shared a look. Zedd pressed his thin lips tight while he considered. In frustration Nathan tossed the book he was holding on the table and wiped his hand across his face as he planted his left fist on a hip.

Richard didn't know what he could say to them all that would have any chance of making them understand that something profoundly serious was wrong in the world and Kahlan was only a piece of the puzzle—by far the most important piece, but still a part of something much larger. Ever since the morning when she had disappeared, he had argued himself sick about the urgent need to find her and it never seemed to do any good at convincing anyone that he knew what he was talking about. He had no interest in yet again wasting his energy on the same fruitless explanations.

"You what?" Ann said, her displeasure bubbling up to the surface like dross in a cauldron. At that moment, she was very much again the Prelate, a squat woman who somehow managed to seem towering.

"I have to find Kahlan," Richard repeated.

"I don't know what you're talking about. We simply don't have time for any of this nonsense." Ann had dismissed his wants, interests, and needs out of hand, to say nothing of what he believed were his rational and important reasons. "We have come to see to it that you get to the D'Haran army immediately. Everyone is waiting on you. Everyone is depending on you. The time has come when you must lead our forces in the final battle that is now rapidly descending upon us."

"I can't," Richard said in a quiet but firm voice.

"Prophecy demands it!" Ann shouted.

Richard realized that Ann had changed. Everyone had changed in little ways since Kahlan had disappeared, but Ann had changed in more overt ways. The last time she had come, with the very same purpose, to demand that Richard go with her to lead the war, Kahlan had thrown Ann's journey book in a fire, telling the former Prelate that prophecy was not driving events, but rather Ann was by trying to make people follow prophecy in an effort to make it come true, that she was acting as prophecy's enforcer. Kahlan had shown Ann how she herself, as the Prelate, by being prophecy's handmaiden, might very well have actually been the one who'd brought the world to the brink of cataclysm. Because of Kahlan's words, Ann had done some deep soul-searching that had eventually helped make her more rational, and more understanding of how Richard was the one who had to choose to do what was right.

Now, with the memory of Kahlan gone, everything that had happened with Kahlan was also wiped away. Ann, like everyone else, had reverted to the disposition she'd shown before Kahlan's influence. It made Richard's head hurt, sometimes, just trying to recall exactly what Kahlan had done with everyone that they wouldn't now remember so that he could take that into account when he dealt with them. With some people, like Shota, it had actually in some ways helped him. Shota, for instance, because of losing her memory of Kahlan, hadn't recalled that she told Richard that if he ever returned to Agaden Reach she would kill him. With other people, like Ann, it was proving to make matters much more difficult.

"Kahlan threw your journey book in a fire," he told her. "She was fed up with you trying to control my life, as am I."

Ann frowned. "I accidentally dropped my journey book in the fire myself."

Richard sighed. "I see." He didn't want to argue because he knew it would do no good. No one in the room believed him. Cara would do whatever he wanted her to do, but she didn't believe him. Nicci didn't believe him, but wanted him to act as he believed he must. Nicci was the one who had actually given him the most encouragement he had gotten since Kahlan had disappeared.

"Richard," Nathan said in a gentler, more benevolent voice, "this is not some simple little thing. You have been born to prophecy. The world stands at the brink of a great dark age. You hold the key to preventing a slide into that long, terrible night. You are the one prophecy says can save our cause—the cause you yourself believe in. You must do your duty. You can't let us down."

Richard was sick and tired of being driven by events. He was at his wits end with not understanding what was going on, with always feeling like he was one step behind the rest of the world and two steps behind whatever had happened to Kahlan. He was getting angry that everyone was telling him what to do and no one was interested in what was of paramount importance to him. They didn't even want to let him decide his own fate. They thought prophecy had already decided for him.

It had not.

He needed to find out the truth of what had happened to Kahlan. He needed to find Kahlan, period. He was fed up with wasting time on what prophecy, along with any number of people, thought he ought to be doing. Anyone who was not helping him was, in reality, holding him back from something vitally important.

"I have no responsibility to live up to what anyone else expects of me," he said to Ann as he picked up the small book Nathan had brought with him.

Ann and Nathan stared in surprise.

He felt Nicci's reassuring hand on the small of his back. She may not believe in his memory of Kahlan, but at least she had helped him see that he had to be true to his principles. She wouldn't allow him to lose by default. She had been a valued friend when he needed one the most.

The only other person he knew who would stand by him in that way, stand up to him in that way, was Kahlan.

He thumbed past all the blank pages in the book Nathan had brought. Richard was curious to see if there was more that might change the picture, if they were only telling him what they wanted him to believe. He also would like to find something—anything—that would help him understand what was going on.

And something was going on. Zedd's explanation of the prophecy worm sounded airtight, but something about it bothered Richard. It explained the missing text in the books of prophecy in a way that suited what these people wanted to believe. It was too convenient and, worse, it was too much of a coincidence.

Coincidence always made Richard suspicious.

Nicci had a good point as well; it seemed just a little too convenient that the body buried down at the Confessors' Palace would have a ribbon with Kahlan's name embroidered on it. . . . Just in case there was any doubt, should someone dig up the body?

After blank page upon blank page, Richard found the writing. It was exactly as Nathan had read it.

In the year of the cicadas, when the champion of sacrifice and suffering, under the banner of both mankind and the Light finally splits his swarm, thus shall be the sign that prophecy has been awakened and the final and deciding battle is upon us. Be cautioned, for all true forks and their derivatives are tangled in this mantic root. Only one trunk branches from this conjoined primal origin. If fuer grissa ost drauka *does not lead this final battle, then the world, already standing at the brink of darkness, will fall under that terrible shadow.*

There were several things about the passage that puzzled Richard. For one thing, the reference to cicadas. It seemed a lowly creature to be worthy of prophetic mention, to say nothing of such a central role in the— purportedly—most important prophecy in three thousand years. He supposed that it could make sense that it was a key that helped set the chronology, but, from what others had told him, prophecy never went out of its way to set chronology, making it one of prophecy's most difficult issues.

It also troubled him that this prophecy, so distant in so many ways from the other he had read at the Palace of the Prophets, would also refer to him in High D'Haran as *fuer grissa ost drauka*. He supposed that it could be, as Zedd had suggested, that such a linkage meant it was important.

But the link to the prophecy Richard had seen at the Palace of the Prophets with the reference to *fuer grissa ost drauka* was strongly connected to something else: the boxes of Orden.

In the old prophecy that named Richard the bringer of death, the word *death* meant three different things, depending on how it was used: the bringer of the underworld, the world of the dead; the bringer of spirits, spirits of the dead; and the bringer of death, meaning to kill. Each meaning was different, but all three were intended.

The second meaning had to do with how he used the Sword of Truth, and the third simply that he'd had to kill people. But the first meaning involved the boxes of Orden.

He supposed that in the context of the prophecy at hand, the third meaning seemed the obvious, that he had to lead the army and kill the enemy, so calling him *fuer grissa ost drauka* did make sense. Yet again, things seemed awfully convenient.

All the convenient explanations and coincidences were making Richard more than just a little suspicious. With Kahlan's disappearance involved, he felt that there had to be more to what was going on.

He turned to the page ahead of the passage, and then the one preceding it, checking. They were blank.

"I have a problem with this," he said, looking up at all the eyes watching him.

"And what would that be?" Ann asked as she folded her arms. She used the same tone of voice she would have if she'd been talking to an inexperienced, untrained, ignorant boy freshly brought to the Palace of the Prophets to be trained in the use of his gift.

"Well, there's nothing around it," he said. "It's all blank."

Nathan covered his face with a hand while Ann threw her arms in the air in a gesture of baffled outrage. "Of course not! They've vanished, along with a great deal more. That's what we've just been talking about. That's why this one is so important!"

"But without knowing the context, you can't really say that this one is important, now, can you? To understand any information one must know the context."

Contrary to Ann and Nathan's agitation, Zedd smiled to himself at lessons taught long ago and remembered.

Nathan looked up. "What does that have to do with this prophecy?"

"Well, for all we know, there might have been mitigating text right before this, or something right after that went on to dismiss this. With the copy missing how are we to know? This prophecy could have been superseded by just about anything."

Zedd smiled. "The boy has a point."

"He's not a boy," Ann growled. "He's a man, and the Lord Rahl, the head of the D'Haran Empire that he himself pulled together to fight the Imperial Order, and he's supposed to lead those forces. All of our lives depend on him doing so."

As Richard flipped back through the book, he saw writing that he hadn't seen the first time. He paged back to it.

"Here's something else that didn't vanish," he said.

"What?" Nathan asked with incredulity as he twisted around to look. "There was nothing else. I'm sure of it."

"Right here," Richard said, tapping a finger on the words. "It says, 'Here we come.' What could that mean? And why did it not vanish?"

" 'Here we come'?" Nathan's face distorted in a look of confusion. "I never saw that before."

Richard turned back more pages. "Look. Here it is again. Same thing. 'Here we come.' "

"I could have missed it once, perhaps," Nathan said, "but there is no way I could have missed a second one. You must be wrong."

"No, look," Richard said, turning the book to show the prophet. He went backward through the book, turning blank pages until he came to writing. "Here it is again. A whole page of the same thing written over and over."

Nathan's jaw hung in speechless astonishment. Nicci peered over Richard's shoulder. Zedd rushed around next to him to see the writing in the book. Even the two Mord-Sith came to have a look.

Richard turned a page forward, to what a moment before had been blank. There, down the page, was the same sentence written over and over and over.

Here we come.

"I watched you turning it back." Nicci's silken voice carried a clear undertone of disquiet. "I know that page was blank an instant ago."

Goose bumps prickled up Richard's arms. The hair at the nape of his neck lifted.

He looked up and saw something dark coalescing out of the deep shadows beneath the beam of sunlight coming from the high window at the end of the room.

Too late, he remembered Shota's warning not to read prophecy, that if he did the blood beast would be able to find him.

He reached for his sword.

His sword wasn't there.

With a wail that sounded like the condemned souls of a thousand sinners, tumbling angles and swirls and streaks of darkness materialized out of the darkness itself, like shadows coming to life.

As the tables at the far end of the room were violently upended, the dark tangle exploded through them. Splinters of wood of every size flew through the air.

Tables shattered in succession as the beast born of a clutch of shadows came raging across the room toward Richard.

The sound of popping and splintering wood boomed through the dusty air of the library.

Cara and Rikka both sprang in front of Richard, each with her Agiel in her fist. He knew all too well what would happen should they encounter the beast. The thought of Cara being hurt like that again ignited his rage. Before they could charge toward the dark mass smashing through the heavy library tables, he snatched them both by their long blond braids and with a roar of anger tossed them back.

"Don't get in its way!" he yelled at both Mord-Sith.

Ann and Nathan both cast their arms toward the thing, unleashing magic that made the room shimmer as if seen through the waves of heat over a roaring fire. Richard knew that they were compressing the very air itself in an attempt to drive back the attack. Their efforts had no effect on the knot of shadows that rolled and twisted through solid wood as it came across the room. They all backed away, trying to keep distance between them and the threat.

Richard ducked as a long board—the entire edge of one of the shattered tables—whipped past his head and smashed against a post. One of the lamps broke open, sending flaming oil splashing across the ancient carpets, setting them ablaze. Gray smoke billowed up behind them as they faced the beast charging for Richard.

Zedd unleashed a fiery bolt of lightning that passed right through the center of the dark mass of disorder as if it were not even there, only to hit the bookshelves against the far wall. Books and flaming paper flew up into the air. Great clouds of dust and smoke boiled up as the room filled with the sound of the cacophonous blast.

Terrible wails and keening, like the howls of the doomed through an open doorway down into the depths of the underworld, came from the beast as it came ever onward, crashing through the thick mahogany posts. Lamps spun through the air as they were flung aside, their silver reflectors casting flickering light around the room and creating shadows that gathered into the beast as it grew more dense, and darker yet.

Magic being hastily conjured by Ann and Nathan wasn't visible to Richard, but it seemed to pass right through the beast, as if it were made of nothing more than it appeared, shadows all jumbled together, and yet the knot of darkness crashed through solid wooden tables and posts, splintering them as the thing advanced across the room. Twisting beams squealed and boards shrieked under the stress as another post snapped. The edge of the balcony sagged, then dropped several feet before hanging drunkenly. Another post exploded as it was pushed past its capacity to bend by the onward rush of the dark menace. The edge of the balcony dropped several more feet. Bookshelves teetered on the tilting floor and then toppled, sending an avalanche of books plunging down into the main room.

Amidst all the confusion, destruction, and noise, as he backed across the room, watching the approaching menace, trying to think of how to counter it, Richard found his shirt grabbed at the shoulder. With surprising strength, Nicci rammed him through the open doorway. Tom, standing guard in the hallway, snatched Richard's other arm and helped pull him out of the library as Cara and Rikka followed, guarding his retreat.

In the room, the beast continued onward, smashing anything in its way as it turned toward the doorway, toward Richard.

Ann, Nathan, and Zedd all summoned forces Richard couldn't even see, but he could sense them by the hum in the air and the radiating waves of a queazy feelings it gave him in the pit of his stomach. He could feel the air being buffeted as magic was conjured and cast.

None of it did any good. They might as well have been attacking shadows.

Nicci turned back to the room from the doorway and lifted a fist toward the snarl of shadows tumbling toward her. The sudden explosion made everyone wince and duck as she unleased a bolt of power that was both blindingly bright and icy dark laced together into one terrible blast. The discharge of thundering power rocked the Keep, shaking the floor and rising dust from every crack and corner. The twisting rope of destruction exploded through the beast, spraying apart. Showers of sparks rained down as bookshelves flew asunder. Wood, debris, and hundreds of books along with sheafs of paper were blasted into the air, leaving fluttering pages to drift through the pandemonium. It looked like a blizzard of paper had been turned loose in the room.

The deafening discharge of power from Nicci that rocked the Keep also sliced right through the stone walls like flaming pitch through paper. Through the jagged slashes cut in solid stone, ribbons of dusty bluish sunlight suddenly penetrated into the room. The contrast of harsh light against the otherwise dark room made it all the harder to see the murky collection of shade and shadow as it moved through the confusion of destruction.

Everyone covered their ears as the terrible wail that sounded like lost souls increased to a terrifying pitch, as if the power Nicci had set upon it had reached down into the underworld to sear them in their dark sanctuary.

While it didn't look to have done much to stop the shadowy beast, it did seem to get its attention. Nothing else had.

Nicci ran out through the door and shoved Richard, starting him moving down the hallway. He was reluctant to leave Zedd to such a threat, but Richard knew that the thing was after him and not his grandfather. Zedd would be safer if Richard ran. He didn't think, though, that running was necessarily the solution to his safety.

"Stay out of its way," Richard told Tom. "It will rip you to shreds. That goes for you two as well," he said to Cara and Rikka as they shepherded him down the hall.

"We understand, Lord Rahl," Cara said.

"How do we kill it?" Tom asked as they ran sideways down the hall, keeping a wary eye toward the library.

"You can't," Nicci answered. "It's already dead."

"Oh great," he muttered as he turned back to help Nicci, Cara, and Rikka make sure that Richard kept moving. Richard didn't really think that he needed any physical encouragement. The wails of the dead were enough to urge him to run.

Flashes of light along with angry shrieks came from the doorway as those in the room still fought to destroy, or at least contain, what looked like nothing so much as living shadows. Richard knew that they were wasting their time. It was made in part with Subtractive Magic and they had no weapon against that. The thing had already proven that much to them, but they were probably trying to distract it so as to give Richard time to get away. So far, it hadn't proven itself susceptible to such tactics. Shota had told him as much.

At an intersection, Richard took the paneled hall to the right. The rest of them followed. At intervals they passed open areas with chairs and couches and dark lamps. Such spots must have once hosted warm conversation and companionship.

As they turned and ran down a wider corridor with tan, troweled plaster walls and golden oak floors, a wall ahead exploded. Dust and debris billowed toward them. Richard slid to a stop on the polished wood floor and reversed direction as the jumble of shadows emerged from the white cloud of dust. Everyone else had previously pushed him on ahead, so that now, having had to turn around, he was at the rear as the beast rapidly closed the distance.

The dark snarl looked like it had collected yet more random shadows along the way—small angled shadows, broad leafy shade, inky dark corners, dark haze of dusk—and crumbled them all together like wadding up paper. The way the shadows folded back on themselves made swirling black shapes that constantly eddied over and under and through one another. It was dizzying to watch, even for the brief glimpses he took as he ran.

And yet, it was so insubstantial that when he glanced over his shoulder he could see light from windows far off down the hall right through the thing. Even so, as they raced around corners, the beast would sometimes go wide and graze the walls, and when it did, it ripped apart the wood, or plaster, or stone as easily as a bull going through bramble.

Richard had no idea how to fight a cluster of crumbled shadows that could tear through solid stone without even slowing.

He recalled Victor's men in the woods, so violently ripped to shreds in mere moments. He wondered if this was the thing that had slashed through them, if this was the fate they faced that terrible morning when the blood beast came looking for Richard.

Two wizards and two sorceresses had now tried to stop Jagang's conjured beast without any practical effect. And Nicci was more than a mere sorceress. She had been taught the sinister art of how to use Subtractive Magic in exchange for dark oaths that Richard feared to think about. Even that hadn't stopped the beast, although it did seem to get a reaction.

Nicci stopped and turned to the dusky collection of shadows careening down the paneled oak halls behind them. She looked like she intended to make a stand. As he caught up with her, Richard, without slowing, planted his shoulder into her middle, knocking the wind from her as he lifted her clear of the floor, carrying her over his shoulder like a sack of grain as he ran.

The halls all around lit in a blinding flash of white light as Nicci—having quickly recovered her breath—cast magic behind even as she was being carted down the hall. The floor shook, nearly knocking Richard from his feet as he ran. Blackness, like the flash of light, caught them and swept past for an instant as Nicci unleashed terrible power at the thing chasing them. By the haunting keening that echoed through the halls, Richard thought that Nicci's effort must have done something.

She seized his shirt in both fists as she squirmed. "Let me down, Richard! Let me run myself! I'm only slowing you down and it's catching up with us! Hurry!"

Richard immediately spun her around in his right arm so that she would be facing the right way. As he dropped her to the ground he kept his arm around her waist until he was sure she had her balance and was up to speed with the rest of them.

With Nicci beside him and Tom, Cara, and Rikka right in front of him, they all raced down halls without knowing where they were going. They switched randomly from right turns to left, going past some intersections while taking others. He could hear the beast crashing after them. Sometimes it followed down the halls and corridors, sometimes, when they went around a corner, it clipped though the walls, trying to close the distance, trying to get to him. Stone, mortar, and wood seemed to make no difference to the thing as it broke through each with equal ease. He knew that a thing conjured by Sisters of the Dark and tied to the underworld would have abilities that no ordinary creature would possess, so he had no idea what the limits of it might be.

As he ran, he yelled to the two Mord-Sith and Tom. "You three go straight! Try to get the thing to follow you!"

They looked back as they ran and nodded to his orders.

"That thing isn't going to follow them," Nicci said in a low voice as she leaned toward him as best she could at a full run.

"I know. I have an idea. Stay with me—I'm going to take those stairs up ahead."

At a stairwell, as the three in front shot past it, Richard hooked a hand on the black stone sphere atop the granite newel post, spinning himself around it and to the right. Nicci did the same and they both shot down the stairs at full speed. The beast cut the corner, crashing through the post, sending granite fragments riccocheting off the walls and the sphere bouncing down the hall. Cara, Rikka, and Tom, having already passed the stairs, slid to a stop on the polished marble floor. They were trapped above the beast. They immediately followed it down the stairs.

Richard and Nicci bounded down the steps three or four at a time. He could hear the otherworldly howl of the thing right behind him. It felt as if it were touching the hair at the back of his neck—it was that close.

At the bottom of the stairs, Richard cut to the right, following a stone passageway. The beast went wide, crashing into a tan, polished marble wall. The stone slab shattered with a loud bang but the beast rushed onward. At the first stairwell Richard came to he raced down it, then took the second and third flight down as well to the bottom.

The broad hallway running straight off from the stairs had carpets at regular intervals, making it more difficult to keep their footing. The walls had beaded wainscoting beneath smooth plaster. Brackets spaced down the passageway, centered above each carpet held what looked like glass globes that brightened as Richard raced toward each one in turn. He ran as fast as he could, Nicci at his side, the shadows tumbling onward like death itself right on their heels.

At spiral iron stairs, Richard jumped sidesaddle onto the railing and slid at breakneck speed in a corkscrew course down into the darkness. Right with him, Nicci threw one arm around his neck for balance and did the same. Together they plummeted downward, gaining some precious distance on their pursuer.

At the bottom the railing spilled them out onto a cold, tiled floor. They both tumbled across the smooth green tiles and slid to a sprawling stop. Richard scrambled to his feet and snatched one of the glowing spheres from a bracket.

"Come on, hurry," he said as Nicci did the same.

They raced through endless rooms and passageways, taking as wild a route as he could in an effort to shake their hunter. Occasionally they gained a precious few paces. At other times, especially in the halls, the thing regained the distance and inched ever closer. Some of the rooms were cozy paneled suites. The beast seemed to suck the shadows right out of the cold, dark fireplaces as it passed them. The globes they carried cast a warm glow across intricately woven carpets and richly upholstered chairs. Bookcases held leather volumes. Richard accidentally knocked over a bookstand, but kept his balance and kept running.

After charging down yet more flights of stairs, some broad with landings and others nothing more than narrow shafts that seemed bottomless, the rooms began to become less grand. Some of the halls were tiled on all sides with odd patterns. One of the chambers was immense and empty, with fat round stone pillars spaced evenly throughout. The lights they carried were not enough to penetrate the farthest reaches. Occasionally, the passages were little more than shafts chiseled through solid rock.

Other rooms and halls were protected with shields that Richard deliberately charged through. He didn't want Cara, Rikka, and Tom coming near the thing chasing him. He didn't want them meeting the same fate as Victor's men. He knew that Cara would be furious at him when she found herself blocked by shields. He hoped he lived to hear her lecture.

They emerged from what appeared as they'd run through it to be a storage room for construction material, with burlap bags and stone stacked to each side. Richard recognized the material from his time in Altur'Rang at forced labor working on Emperor Jagang's palace. Now Jagang's beast was hunting him down.

They emerged on the far side of the storage room into a long, corridor with a slate floor. The smooth, stone block walls rose uninterrupted to a lofty ceiling that had to be at least a hundred and fifty feet overhead, creating a narrow, towering vertical slash through the interior of the Keep. Down at the bottom of that soaring passageway, Richard felt like an ant.

He immediately cut to the right down the immense corridor. The booming drumbeat of their boots echoed all around him as he ran with all his strength. He soon had to slow a bit for Nicci. They were both near the end of their endurance. The wail of a thousand dead souls tumbled ever onward, never seeming to tire.

As he ran, Richard couldn't even see the end of the tall passageway disappearing into the distance. That this was just one corridor of many gave him a profound sense of the enormity of the Keep.

Arriving at an intersecting passage to the left, Richard turned and ran down it a short distance to where they encountered an iron stairwell. Trying to catch his breath, he glanced back and saw the knot of shadows round the corner. Pushing Nicci ahead of him, they bounded down the stairs together.

At the bottom they found themselves in a small, square room that was little more than an intersection of stone passageways going off in three directions. Richard held the glowing sphere out, taking a quick glance in each passageway. He could see nothing down two of them. In the one to the right he thought he saw something glimmering. He'd been down in the Keep before and had encountered strange places and one of those places was what he needed now.

Together he and Nicci raced down the passageway. As he'd thought, it wasn't very long, just long enough to take them under the colossal corridor and then a little farther to where it opened into a kind of entry area with walls covered in small fragments of colored glass meticulously arranged into elaborate geometric designs. The light from the two glowing spheres glinted off the small glass pieces to send thousands of colored reflections sparkling and shimmering around the room. There was only one other opening, off against a far wall.

Richard staggered to a halt. The strange glittering room made his skin crawl with a sensation much like spiderwebs brushing against him. Nicci turned her head away, swiping at her face as if to get something off her. He knew that such a sensation was a part of a broader warning to stay away.

Small pillars made of polished, gold-flecked stone stood to each side of the distant opening holding up an entablature. The passageway beyond the pillars, not much taller than Richard, appeared to be roughly square and made of simple stone blocks that disappeared off into darkness. It seemed an elaborate and impressive entry for such a plain hallway down in the bowels of the place.

Richard hoped he was right about the reason.

As they crossed the entry room and approached the opening, the area before the pillars began to give off a faint reddish glow. The air itself began to hum in a very troubling way.

Nicci, her hair lifting out from her head as if she were about to be struck by lightning, seized his arm, pulling him back. "That's a shield."

"I know," Richard said as he dragged her by her grip on his arm.

"Richard, you can't. It's not just an ordinary shield—not just Additive. It's laced with Subtractive Magic. Such shields are deadly, this one especially so."

He looked back the way they'd come and saw the shadowy beast tumbling down the passageway toward them. "I know, I've been through places like this before."

He hoped he was right that this particular shield was like the ones he'd been through. He needed the kind that he'd encountered before, the kind that guarded the most restricted areas. If it was anything less, or one that was actually more powerful or more restrictive than the ones he'd seen before, then they were going to be in a great deal of trouble.

The only way out of the room they were in was back through the passage with the beast that was coming for them, or onward through the shield.

"Let's go. hurry."

Nicci's chest heaved as she struggled to catch her breath. "Richard, we can't go through there. That shield will take the flesh right off our bones."

"I'm telling you, I've done it before. You can command Subtractive Magic, so you can make it through as well." He started running toward the passage. "Besides, if we don't, we're dead anyway. It's our only chance."

With a growl of surrender, she ran along with him through the shower of glittering reflections from the glass mosaics that covered the walls of the room. "You'd better be right about this."

He grabbed her hand and held it tight, just in case being born with the Subtractive side was necessary. Nicci had not been born with it, but had acquired the use of it. He didn't know a great deal about magic, but from what he'd learned, there was a great gulf between being born with it and simply being able to use it. He had helped others, without the gift, through shields before, so between her abilities, and his hold of her, he figured he could get her through—if, that was, he could make it through himself.

The air all around them turned as red as a crimson fog. Without pause, Richard charged right though the doorway, pulling Nicci along with him.

The sudden avalanche of pressure felt like it would crush them. Nicci gasped.

Richard had to force himself against that pressure in order to advance. At the razor edge of the plane along the opening surrounded by polished stone pillars, heat seared across his flesh. It was so intense that for an instant he thought he'd made a huge mistake, that Nicci had been right, and that the shield would burn the flesh right off his bones.

Even as he flinched in reaction to the unexpected burning sensation, his momentum carried him through the doorway. He was somewhat surprised not only to find himself alive and well and not at all harmed, but that the passageway was not at all what it appeared from the other side. When he'd looked through the opening before, it looked like a simple stone block passage. Once past the pillars, it was polished stone that seemed to shimmer with a rippling silver surface that made it appear three-dimensional.

A glance back showed the snarl of shadows streaking for the entrance to the opening. Still holding Nicci's hand, Richard backed them farther into the sparkling passageway.

He was too exhausted to run anymore.

"Here we live or die," he told her as he labored to catch his breath.

The shadow hit the opening with such a resounding thud that Richard thought the passageway they were in would certainly be blown apart. What had been a somewhat cohesive, dark shape exploded apart like glass on granite, shattering into thousands of dark shards. Piercing wails of frightful anguish echoed through the passageway in terrible, heartbreaking finality as light ignited in a blinding crimson flash. At the shielded opening, black fragments of shadows tumbled back through the room that was filled with shimmering, sparkling reflections off the glass mosaics. With what looked like a year's worth of meteor showers all compressed into a single instant, the shadowy fragments burst into bright flares that flew in every direction as they glimmered into nothingness.

It was suddenly quiet but for Richard and Nicci's labored breathing.

The beast was gone. At least it was gone for the moment.

Richard let go of Nicci's hand and they both flopped down heavily on the floor and slumped back against the iridescent silver wall as they panted in exhaustion.

"You were looking for one of those shields, weren't you?" Nicci asked as she worked at recovering enough breath to talk.

Richard nodded. "Nothing Zedd or Nathan or Ann conjured did anything to stop the beast. What you did at least seemed to have had an effect, even if a small one. That made me think that there must be something that would be able to counter it, maybe not in totality, but at least in the form it presented this time.

"I knew that the wizards from the time back when this place was built needed to stop anything that didn't belong in here—and the beast, after all, was something from back in those times, something that Jagang had found described in old books. So I figured that those who made the shields here must have had to take such eventualities into account.

"Since they're made to stop such threats, it takes, at the least, an element of Subtractive Magic to get through the shields. But because the enemy would have had Subtractive powers as well, I think the shields must also somehow read the nature of who is trying to pass through them, perhaps thereby interpreting the potential level of threat. It could even be that as we were chased through the Keep and kept going through shields, they somehow gathered information on the nature not only of us, but of the beast as well so that when we reached these higher threshold shields, they had finally judged it a threat and stopped it."

Nicci considered what he'd said as she pulled sweaty strands of blond hair back off her face. "No one really knows a great deal about the gifted back then, but it makes sense that such an ancient threat would be vincible to ancient defenses." She frowned as if an idea had come to her. "Maybe such shields would even be a way to protect you if it reappears."

"Sure," he said, "if I want to live down here like a mole."

She looked around. "Any idea where we are?"

"No," he said, letting out an exhausted sigh, "but I guess we'd better try to find out."

They struggled to their feet and made their way the rest of the distance down the short passageway. At the end they emerged into a simple room constructed of stone blocks once covered in plaster that was now crumbling. The room was no more than fifteen paces long and not nearly as wide, with books on shelves along most of the length of the wall to the left.

While it did have some books, it was not a library like so many others he had seen in the keep. For one thing, it was far too small. For another, it was not at all elegant, or even nice, but rather stark. At best, it could be called utilitarian. Besides the shelves, the room was only wide enough for a table at the far end beside a passageway leading out the other side. There was a fat candle on the table and a wooden stool under it. The far passageway looked very much like the one they had come in through.

When Richard took a look, he saw that it had the same shimmering silver stone walls and another shield that looked just like the one they had come in through at the other end of the room, so that, unlike a number of places in the Keep that had shields, there was no way to go around and get into the room by way of another route without such powerful shields. It was through one of the two shields or not at all.

"With all the dust in here," Nicci said, "it doesn't look like anyone has cleaned in here for thousands of years."

She was right. The room was devoid of color other than the dirty gray color of the dust that coated everything. The hair at the nape of Richard's neck stood on end as he fully realized why.

"That's because no one has been in here for thousands of years."

"Really?"

He gestured to the far passage he'd just inspected. "The only two ways into here are protected with shields that require Subtractive Magic to cross. Not even Zedd, the First Wizard himself, has ever been in here. He can't pass Subtractive shields."

Nicci brushed her hands together. "Especially these shields. I've dealt with shields most of my life. From what I felt of these, they're deadly. I suspect that without your help even I might have had some difficulty getting through them the first time."

Richard tilted his head to be able to better read the titles as he perused the books along the shelves. Some had no titles on the spines. Some were in languages he couldn't read. Some looked like they might be journals. Several, though, looked curious. One small book, *Gegendrauss*, in High D'Haran meant *Countermeasures*. He pulled out another beside it of a similar small size titled *Ordenic Theory*. As he blew off a thick coating of dust, he realized then that it must have caught his attention because *Ordenic* reminded him of Orden, as in the boxes of Orden. He wondered if there was any connection.

"Richard, look at this," Nicci called to him from the far passage.

Richard tossed the book on the table as he made his way into the passageway, toward the shield. "What is it?"

"I don't know." Her voice echoed, and then he saw the crimson glow brighten and finally fade.

He realized that she must have gone beyond the shield. Alarmed at first, Richard was hugely relieved that there had been no horrific results. Nicci was an experienced sorceress. He suspected that after having gone through the last shield, she must have known what dangers to look for to tell her if she could pass this one as well. He reasoned that perhaps the first shield, when he had helped her through it, had keyed to her, allowing her to cross shields like it.

Pushing on through the plane of pressure and briefly searing heat, he entered a small room beyond with glass mosaics, like the one at the other end of the little reading room. Both rooms had to be a kind of entryway before the shield to provide warning to anyone coming near, or maybe they were somehow an aid to the shields themselves. Nicci was standing just beyond, at an open iron door, her back to him, her thick fall of blond hair down around her shoulders.

At the railing on the platform beside her, Richard looked out into a round tower room at least a hundred feet across. Stairs spiraled up around the inside of the curving outer wall. The tower rose above them for over two hundred feet. At irregular intervals, small landings like the one where they stood interrupted the steps wherever there was a doorway. In the gloomy expanse above, shafts of light pierced the darkness.

The place smelled of rot. At the bottom of the tower, not too far below the landing were they stood, he saw a walkway with an iron railing that ringed the inside of the tower wall. Rain that could come in the openings above, along with seepage from the mountain itself, collected down in the center of the tower. Insects swarmed above the stagnant, inky water. Others skittered on its surface.

"I know this place," Richard said as he peered around, getting his bearings.

"You do?"

He started down the steps. "Yes, come on."

At the bottom, he followed the iron railing around to a wide platform in the walkway before a spot where a door had once been. The doorway had been blasted apart and the opening was now perhaps twice its previous size. The jagged edges of the broken stone were blackened in places. In other places the stone itself had been melted as if it were no more than candle wax. Twisting streaks on the surface of the stone wall ran off in every direction away from the blasted hole, marking where a kind of lightning had flailed against the wall and burned it.

Nicci stared in amazement. "What in the world happened here?"

"This room was once sealed away, along with the Old World. When I destroyed the barrier to the Old World, it blew this seal open."

"Why? What's in here?"

"The sliph's well."

"The thing you told me about that those in ancient times used to travel great distances? The thing you've traveled in?"

"That's right," he said as he stepped through the jagged opening that once had been a doorway.

The room inside was round, perhaps sixty feet across, its walls were also scorched in ragged lines as if lightning had gone wild in the place. A circular stone wall about waist-high, forming what looked like a huge well, occupied the center of the room.

The domed ceiling was nearly as high as the room was wide. There were no windows or other doors. To the far side of the sliph's well was a table and a few shelves. That was where Richard had found the remains of the wizard who had in ancient times been sealed in the room when the barriers that had ended the great war had been brought to life. Thus trapped, the man had died in the sealed room. He had left behind a journal that the Mord-Sith Berdine now had. That journal had in the past, as Richard and Berdine had translated it, revealed valuable information.

Because of the importance of the information they'd gotten from the journal, they had called the man who wrote it *Koloblicin*, a High D'Haran word meaning "strong advisor." Berdine and Richard had eventually taken to simply referring to the mysterious wizard as Kolo.

Nicci held her glowing globe over the side and peered down the well. The smooth walls fell away seemingly forever, the light illuminating the stone for hundreds of feet down before fading away into blackness.

"And you say that you put the sliph to sleep?"

"Yes, with these." Richard tapped the insides of the leather padded silver wrist bands he wore against one another. "She told me that when she 'sleeps,' as she put it, she goes to be with her soul. She says it's rapture for her to sleep."

"And you can call her back the same way? By using those bands?"

"Well, yes, but, just like putting her to sleep, I would need to use my gift to do it. Not something I'd be at all eager to do again. I especially wouldn't like to be inside this room, with only one door, calling the sliph, when the blood beast was also called by my gift."

Nicci nodded as she saw his point. "Do you think the beast could follow you through the sliph?"

Richard thought it over for a moment. "I can't say for sure, but I imagine it's possible. But even if it couldn't it still manages to appear wherever I am, so I'm not sure it would even need to bother with using the sliph. From what I've learned of its nature from you and Shota, as well as from experience, I suspect that the beast is able to travel the underworld."

"And other people?" Nicci asked. "Can any of them use this?"

"To travel in the sliph you need to have at least some element of both sides of the gift. That made it a problem in the great war and that's why they had a wizard always standing guard in this room and in the end why they had to seal it off—so the enemy couldn't come through right into the heart of the Keep.

"Now, because of the requirement for an element of both sides of magic, there are few who can use the sliph. Cara has captured gifted people who have Additive Magic, and she captured a man who Kahlan said wasn't entirely human and who happened to have an element of Subtractive Magic. It was enough so that Cara is able to travel in the sliph. A Confessor's power is ancient and has an element of Subtractive to it, so Kahlan can travel in the Sliph. Those are the only ones I know who could travel in the sliph—other than Sisters of the Dark. One of my former teachers, Merissa, went through the sliph after me. You could travel in the sliph as well. That's about it.

"Still, it remains a danger if awakened because Jagang could theoretically send any of his Sisters of the Dark through it."

"What happens if you don't have at least some element of both sides?" Nicci asked. "If, for example, someone like Zedd, a gifted person had only Additive Magic, tried to travel?"

Richard reached over to rest his hand on the pommel of his sword, but his sword wasn't there. It made him sick to expect it and then realize he'd given it to Shota—to Samuel, actually. He put the constant, haunting worry of it from his mind.

"Well, traveling takes you great distances, but it still takes some time—it isn't an instant procedure. I think the time varies according to distance, but I know that it takes a number of hours, at least. The sliph looks something like living quicksilver. To remain alive within her while she takes you to the place you wish to travel, you must breathe her in, breathe in that silvery liquid. You breathe the sliph, that liquid, and it somehow keeps you alive. If you don't have an element of both sides, it doesn't work and you die. Simple as that."

For a fleeting moment, Richard gave thought to waking the sliph to ask if she remembered Kahlan, but the ancient wizards, men of prodigious ability, had created the sliph out of a very exclusive and high-priced whore. She had become caught up in political intrigue that had eventually cost her her life. The nature of that woman was still partly evident in the sliph; she never revealed the identity of one of her "customers."

"We'd better get back up there and let Zedd know we're all right." Richard's thoughts returned to the immediate problems. "Cara is probably fit to be tied by now."

"Richard," Nicci said in a soft voice as he started to leave.

He turned back to see her watching him. "Yes?"

"What are you going to do about Ann and Nathan?"

He shrugged. "Nothing. What do you mean?"

"I mean, what are you going to do about the things they had to say? What are you going to do about the war? The time has come, and I think you know it. You can't go on chasing after your dream while the rest of the world faces the end of everything good—the end of all their hopes and dreams."

He stared at her a moment. She didn't shy away from his gaze.

"Like you said, that body down there didn't prove anything."

"No, but it certainly does prove one thing: that you were wrong about what we would find there. Digging up the grave failed to prove what you thought it would—at the very least. That begs the question of why? Why was it different than you said it would be? The only possible answer I can think of is that someone put it there with the idea that you would find it. But why?

"It's been a while since that night down at the grave. Since then you've accomplished nothing. Maybe it's time you thought about the bigger picture. And in the bigger picture, that prophecy makes the stakes pretty clear. I understand the value of one life you love—even if she were real— but to some extent don't you think you have to balance that one life against the lives of everyone else?"

Richard slowly paced off a ways, trailing his fingers along the top of the stone wall around the sliph. The last time he had traveled in the sliph he had taken Kahlan to the mud people so they could be married.

"I have to find her." He looked back at Nicci. "I am not the tool of prophecy."

"Where will you go? What can you do next? You've been to Shota, and you came here to Zedd. No one knows anything about Kahlan, or Chainfire, or the rest of it. You've exhausted all your ideas, all your options. If not now, then when is the time to finally face reality?"

Richard rubbed his fingertips across his brow. As much as he didn't want to admit it, he feared that Nicci was right. What was he going to do?

He could think of nowhere else to go, nothing else to do. At least, nothing specific, not at the moment, anyway. He couldn't imagine what good it would do him to wander around without a plan, without any idea where to look for Kahlan.

The room was dead quiet. The sliph's well was empty, the sliph off somewhere with her soul. He wondered if Kahlan was still alive. He swallowed as he experienced one of those brief but terrifying moments when he wondered if she ever had been. He was so tired of the ever growing doubts, not just about Kahlan, but about himself.

At the same time, he was being crushed under the weight of guilt for not answering the call to lead the D'Haran people against the terrible threat to their freedom. He thought often of all the countless good people he didn't even know who also had loved ones under mortal threat from the coming storm of the Imperial Order. Could he just desert all of them in order to chase around, forever looking for Kahlan?

Nicci moved closer.

"Richard," she said in a soft, silken, sympathetic voice, "I know it's hard to say it's over . . . to say it's over, and realize that you have to move on."

Richard broke the gaze first. "I can't do that, Nicci. I realize that I can't explain it to anyone's satisfaction, but I just can't do that. I mean, if she got sick and died, then I would be devastated, yet eventually I know I would have to deal with the business of life. But this is different. It's almost as if I know she's in some dark river somewhere, calling for help, and I'm the only one who can hear her, who knows she in terrible danger of drowning."

"Richard—"

"Do you really think I don't care about all the innocent people under the threat of the horde coming to slaughter and enslave them? I do care. I can't sleep with worry, and not only worry for Kahlan. Can you even begin to imagine how torn I feel?

"How would you feel if you were torn between someone you loved and doing what everyone else said was the right thing to do?

"I wake in a cold sweat in the dead of night not only seeing Kahlan's face, but the faces of people who will never have a chance at life if Jagang isn't stopped. When people tell me how all those people are depending on me, it breaks my heart—both because I want to help them, and because they think they need me, because they think that I, one man, can be the difference in a war involving millions of people. How dare they put that much responsibility on me?"

She came closer yet and gently put a hand to the side of his arm, rubbing up and down in a reassuring gesture. "Richard, you know that I wouldn't want you to do anything that you thought was wrong. Not even when it was to let you believe she was dead based on what I knew wasn't good evidence, even though I believe that evidence, if for other reasons."

"I know."

"But since that night when you dug up the grave, while you've been wandering around thinking about what you can do, I, too, have been doing a lot of thinking."

Richard flicked small stone fragments from the top of the well, not wanting to have to look up at her. "And what have you come up with?"

"Among other things, as I watched you walk the ramparts, a troublesome idea came to me. I haven't said anything about it yet partly because I don't know for sure if it could be the answer to what is happening to you, and partly because if it is, then it would be even more trouble than any mere delusion caused by your injury. I don't know if it's really the answer, but I fear that it very well might be. Mostly, though, I haven't said anything because the evidence is gone, so I have no way of proving it, but I think the time has arrived to broach the subject."

"Evidence?" Richard asked. "You said that the evidence is gone?"

Nicci nodded. "The arrow you were shot with. I fear that this may have all been caused by that arrow, but in a different and far more disturbing way than we've realized."

Richard was taken aback by her grave expression. "What do you mean?"

"Did you see who shot the arrow that hit you? Who held the crossbow?"

Richard took a deep breath while staring off as he sifted through the dim snatches of mental images of the morning of the fight. He'd only just awakened after hearing the howl of a wolf. Shadowy tree limbs had appeared to move about in the darkness. Then there had been soldiers all around him. He'd had to fight off men from all sides rushing in at him. He remembered quite vividly the feeling of holding the Sword of Truth, of feeling the wire wound hilt in his hand, of its power surging through him.

He recalled seeing men back in the trees shooting arrows at him. Most had bows, but there had been some with crossbows. That would have been rather typical for such a patrol of Imperial Order troops.

"No . . . I can't say as I recall seeing who shot the bolt that hit me. Why? What is it that you've come up with?"

Nicci appraised his eyes for what seemed an eternity. Her ageless eyes sometimes reminded him of others with magic; Ann, the old Prelate; Verna, the new Prelate; Adie; Shota; and . . . Kahlan.

"The barbs on that arrow made it impossible to get it out of you in any ordinary way in time to save your life. I was in a desperate hurry. I never gave any thought to checking the arrow before I used Subtractive Magic to take it out of existence."

Richard didn't like the direction toward which her worry seemed to be drifting. "Check it for what?"

"A spell. A diabolically simple spell that would be profoundly destructive."

Richard was now sure he didn't like her idea even though he hadn't heard it, yet.

"What kind of spell?"

"A glamour spell."

"Glamour?" Richard frowned. "How would that work?"

"Well, think of it as a love potion."

Richard stared at her in surprise. "A love potion?"

"Yes, after a fashion." She lightly tapped the fingers of opposite hands together as she reflected on how best to explain it. "A glamour spell would cause you to have a mental vision of a woman, a real woman would be the normal object of the spell, but as I thought about it I realized that it would work just as well for an imaginary woman. Either way, it would make you fall in love with her. But even that is a rather weak way of describing such a powerful spell. Under a glamour spell the woman would become an obsession. Such an obsession would be to the exclusion of almost everything else.

"A glamour spell is a kind of dark secret among sorceresses, usually taught by a gifted mother. Such a spell would be used to make a specific person fixate on the subject of the spell, usually a real individual—the sorceress herself, in most cases. Like I said, it's a kind of love spell.

"Some gifted women could not resist the lure of using a glamour on men. The spell is so effective that at the Palace of the Prophets it was a very serious matter for one of the Sisters to even be suspected of using a glamour. To be caught using a glamour was a grave crime, the moral equivalent to rape. The punishment was severe. The sorceress was at the least banished, but she could just as well be hanged. There have been sisters convicted of such a crime.

"As I recall, the last one caught at the palace was over fifty years ago. She was a novice, Valdora. The tribunal was split between hanging or banishment. The Prelate broke the tie and had the young novice banished.

"I would expect that Jagang's Sisters know how to invoke a glamour spell. It wouldn't have been all that hard for one of them to tag a glamour to that arrow, or a number of the arrows that morning. If the arrow didn't kill you, it would spell you."

"This is no spell," Richard said, his tone turning darker.

Nicci ignored not just his tone, but his denial as well. "It would explain a great deal. A glamour spell seems absolutely real to the victim. It bends their mind, their thinking, around the subject of the obsession."

Richard again raked his fingers back through his hair, trying not to get angry with Nicci. "What would be the purpose of doing such a thing? Jagang wants to kill me. You're the one who came and told me that he created a beast to accomplish that task. The spell you're talking about doesn't make any sense."

"Oh, but it makes all the sense in the world. It would accomplish far more than merely killing you, Richard. Don't you see? It would destroy your credibility. It would leave you alive to destroy your cause yourself."

"Myself? What do you mean?"

"It would make you obsessed with the subject of the glamour to the exclusion of anything else. It would make people think there was something wrong with you, think you were crazy.

"It would make people begin to doubt you, and therefore your cause.

"This spell would condemn you to a living death. It would destroy everything that means anything to you. It would give you a mad obsession that you totally believe is something real, but that you can never satisfy. There is good reason why using a glamour spell was a serous crime.

"In this case, at the same time as you go about trying to find the object of your manufactured memory, you see your cause begin to crumble because those you inspired and who believed in you now start to think that if you're crazy, then maybe the things you've said were crazy as well."

Richard imagined that a victim of such a web would not be able to recognize the glamour spell within himself. And it was certainly true that nearly everyone was coming to think he was crazy.

"Truth does not depend on the person who says it. The truth is still the truth even if stated by someone you don't respect."

"That may be true, Richard, but others don't necessarily act with such clear insight."

He sighed. "I guess not.

"As far as the beast, Jagang does not necessarily count on just one thing to do the job and he has no reluctance to do more than is necessary to crush his opponents. He might have figured that two plagues will be more certain to end the threat of Richard Rahl than one alone."

Richard certainly didn't doubt what she said about Jagang. Still, he didn't believe it. "Jagang didn't even know where I was. Those troops just happened across me as they were sweeping the woods, checking for threat, for their supply convoy."

"He knows you started the revolt down in Altur'Rang. He might have ordered that his troops in the area carry arrows that were spelled by his Sisters just in case they ran across you."

Richard could see that she had indeed been doing a lot of thinking. She had an answer for everything.

He opened his arms out to the side and lifted his chin. "Then lay your hands on me, sorceress. Grab the spell and pull its wicked tentacles out of me. Restore my sanity. If you really believe that a glamour spell is the cause of all of this, then use your gift to seek it out and put an end to it."

Nicci turned her gaze away and stared out the broken doorway at the gloom within the base of the huge tower.

"To do that, I would need the arrow. It no longer exists. I'm sorry, Richard. I never thought to check the arrow for a spell before I eliminated it. I was frantic to get it out of you in order to save your life. Still, I should have checked."

He laid a hand on the back of her shoulder. "You didn't do anything wrong, my friend. You saved my life."

"Did I?" She turned to him. "Or did I condemn you to a living death?"

He shook his head. "I don't think so. Like you said, you wouldn't let me believe something if you thought the evidence was insufficient. That body buried down there wasn't sufficient proof. Yet, at the same time, it shouldn't have been there, so I'm convinced that it proves that something really is going on. I just haven't figured out what."

"Or it proves that maybe your story is nothing more than part of a fabrication spawned by the mad obsession of a glamour spell."

"No one remembers what happened and that Kahlan isn't buried there, but I do. It's something solid that shows me, at least, that I'm not imagining all this."

"Or it is simply part of the delusion—whatever its cause. Richard, this just can't go on forever. It has to come to a close at some point. You're at a dead end. Have you come up with anything else to try?"

He put his hands on the stone wall of the sliph's well. "Look, Nicci, I admit that I'm running out of ideas, but I'm not ready to give up on her, to give up on her life. She means too much to me to do that."

"And how long do you think you can wander around not giving up on her, all the while the Imperial Order marches ever closer to our forces? I don't like Ann's meddling in my life any more than you like her meddling in yours, but she isn't doing it because she is trying to be malicious. She's trying to preserve freedom. She's trying to save innocent people from being slaughtered by brutes."

Richard swallowed back the lump in his throat.

"I need to think about things, to gather my thoughts. I found some books in that room back there. I want to study them for a while, just a while, and try to think things through, try to see if I can figure out what's happening and why. If I can't think of something . . . I just need to think of what to do next."

"And if you can't think of what to do next?"

Richard leaned on both hands as he stared off into the dark well, doing his best to stifle his tears.

"Please . . ."

If he only knew who to fight, if only he could strike out at an enemy. He didn't know how to fight shadows in his mind.

Nicci laid a hand gently on his shoulder. "All right, Richard. All right."

Nicci knocked on the round-top oak door and waited. Rikka, standing at her back, waited with her.

"Come in," came a muffled voice.

Nicci thought that it sounded like Nathan's deep, powerful voice, rather than Zedd's. Inside the small, round room that Richard's grandfather was fond of using, she saw the prophet along with Ann, her hands pushed into opposite sleeves of her simple, dark gray dress as she stood patiently waiting for their invited guest. Nathan, in dark brown trousers and high boots, with a ruffled white shirt under a sweeping cloak, looked more like an adventurer than a prophet.

Zedd, in his simple robes, stood quietly at a round leaded window between book cabinets with glassed doors, his hands clasped behind his back. He appeared to be lost in thought as he gazed out at the city of Aydindril far below at the base of the mountain. It was a beautiful view; Nicci could understand why he favored the cozy room. Rikka started pushing the thick oak door closed.

"Rikka, dear," Ann said with a Prelate's practiced smile, drawing the Mord-Sith's attention, "my throat is still terribly dry from all that smoke yesterday when that dreadful creature set the library ablaze. Would you mind making me some tea, maybe with a spot of honey?"

Rikka, holding the half-closed door, shrugged. "Not at all."

"Any of your biscuits left?" Nathan asked with a wide smile. "Your biscuits were wonderful, especially when they're warm."

Rikka gazed briefly at everyone in the small room. "I will bring biscuits and tea along with some honey."

"Thank you so much, my dear," Ann said, the smile never breaking, as Rikka vanished out the door.

Zedd, still watching out the window, hadn't said anything.

Nicci, ignoring Ann and Nathan, instead turned and addressed Zedd. "Rikka said that you wanted to see me."

"That's right," Ann said in his place. "Where is Richard?"

"Down in that place I told you about, the place he found between the shields where he will be safe. He is reading, looking for information, doing what a Seeker does, I suppose." With exaggerated care, Nicci folded her fingers together. "So, the three of you want to talk to me about Richard."

Nathan huffed a short laugh that transformed itself into a throat-clearing cough when Ann glanced his way. Zedd, standing with his back to the rest of them, stared out the window without saying anything.

"You always were a bright one," Ann said.

"It wasn't exactly a guess that required great intellect," Nicci said, not wanting to allow Ann to get away with such empty flattery. "If you please, withhold your praise until I do something to deserve it."

Both Nathan and Ann smiled. Nathan's even looked genuine.

Flattery had been a plague that had followed Nicci her whole life. "Nicci, you're such a bright child, so you must give more of yourself." "Nicci, you're so beautiful, the most beautiful creature I've ever seen. I must hold you." "Nicci, my dear, I simply must be allowed to sample your exquisite charms or I will surely die an impoverished man." To Nicci, vacuous flattery was the sound of a prybar, a tool used by a thief as he tried to get at what she had.

"What is it I can do for you," Nicci asked in a businesslike voice.

Ann, hands still pushed up opposite sleeves, shrugged. "We need to talk to you about Richard's unfortunate condition. It was quite shocking to discover him suffering from delirium."

"I can't say I disagree with that," Nicci said.

"Do you have any ideas?" the Prelate asked.

Nicci glided her fingers back and forth across the polished top of the magnificent desk. "Ideas? What do you mean, ideas?"

"Don't play coy," Ann said, her indulgent humor evaporating from her voice. "You know very well what we mean."

Zedd finally turned around, apparently not liking Ann's tack. "Nicci, we're very worried about him. Yes, we're worried because of the prophecy and that it says he must be the one to lead our forces and all the rest of it, but . . ." He lifted a hand and let it drop in frustration. "But we're worried for Richard himself. There is something very wrong with him. I've known him from the day he was born. I've spent years with him, alone with him, with him around others. I've been so proud of that boy that I can't begin to tell you. He always has been one to occasionally do puzzling things, things that frustrate and confuse me, but I've never seen him act like this. I've never seen him believe such crazy stories. You can't imagine what it does to me to see him like this."

Nicci scratched an eyebrow, using it as an excuse to look away from the pain in his hazel eyes. His white hair looked in even more disarray than usual. He looked more thin than usual; he looked gaunt. He looked like a man who had not gotten much sleep for weeks.

"I think I can understand your feelings," she assured him. She took a deep thoughtful breath as she slowly shook her head. "I don't know, Zedd. I've been trying to figure it out since I found him that morning gasping for breath and almost in the Keeper's clutches."

"You said he lost a lot of blood," Nathan said. "And that he was unconscious for days."

Nicci nodded. "It's possible that such a condition, such desperate fear of not having enough breath and thinking he was going to die that way, caused him to dream up someone who loved him—a kind of trick to try to calm himself. I used to sometimes do something similar when I was afraid; I would put my mind in another else, a pleasant place, where I was safe. With Richard, with the heavy loss of blood and the abnormally long sleep after being healed, while he was regaining some of his strength— enough strength to try to survive the ordeal—well, I think that the whole time the dream could have grown and grown in his mind."

"And have taken over his thoughts," Ann finished.

Nicci met her gaze. "That was my thought."

"And now?" Zedd asked.

Nicci turned her eyes up to gaze at the heavy oak beams across the ceiling as she searched for words. "I don't know anymore. I'm no expert in such things. I've not exactly spent my life as a healer. I would think that the three of you would know a great deal more about such maladies than I do."

"Well, yes, as a matter of fact," Ann said, making a face like she was glad to hear Nicci admit as much, "we would tend to agree with that assessment."

Nicci eyed all three of them suspiciously. "So, what do all of you think is his problem?"

"Well," Zedd began, "we're still not ready to rule out a number of things that—"

"Have you considered a glamour spell?" Ann asked, fixing Nicci in her steady stare the way she used to do to make novices tremble and confess to shirking their chores.

Nicci was no novice and no longer susceptible to such intimidation from on high. After having Jagang, in a blind rage, hold her with one meaty fist around her throat and pound her face with the other, a stare was hardly something to make Nicci tremble. In fact, had the subject not been one so serious, one that sincerely did concern her so, she might have laughed at the very effort of such a stern look to elicit an incautious report.

"It crossed my mind," she said, seeing no purpose in denying it. "But I had to eliminate the arrow with Subtractive Magic if I was to save his life. I'm afraid that, at the time, I never gave any thought to such an idea. I was frantically tying to keep him from dying. Perhaps I should have thought about the arrow being spelled, but I didn't. With the arrow now gone there is no way to tell if that really was the case and, without the arrow, there's no way to do anything about it if true."

Zedd rubbed his clean-shaven jaw as he looked away. "That certainly makes things more difficult."

"Difficult?" Nicci said. "Such a spell isn't at all easy to reverse even if you have the object that in this manner infected the victim with a glamour. Without that object, only the sorceress who cast the glamour can eliminate it. You must have the web that carried the infection if you are to heal it.

"And that's if you know for certain that it was a glamour spell. It could be something else. Whatever it is, spell of some sort, or delirium, you have to know the cause if you're to heal it."

"Not necessarily," Ann said as she again stared at Nicci. "At this point the cause is no longer much of an issue."

Nicci's brow twitched. "No longer an issue—what in the world are you talking about?"

"If a person has a broken arm you set it and splint it. You don't waste your time running around asking questions, trying to figure out exactly how they managed to break their arm. You need to take action to correct the ailment; talk won't correct it."

"We think he needs our help," Zedd offered in a more conciliatory tone. "We all know that the things he is saying are flat impossible. At first, when he said that he gave the Sword of Truth to Shota, I thought he had done something profoundly foolish, but I've come to see that his actions weren't willful nor were the dimensions of them so simply grasped. I reacted with an angry reprimand when I should have seen how ill he really is and dealt with it in that context.

"There are times when you can see how someone might come to believe something odd, but Richard's behavior is far beyond anything that could remotely be described as odd. It's become clear that he is delusional and we all now realize as much." He opened his hands in a beseeching gesture. "Is there anything at all you can say in his behalf that makes any sense and that demonstrates how we may be wrong in our analysis?"

Zedd looked truly under great distress. It was obvious how genuinely concerned he was for his grandson.

Nicci turned her eyes downward, unable to look into the hurt in his eyes. "I'm sorry, Zedd, but I know of nothing that makes any sense. Unfortunately, I don't think that the body he dug up proves anything conclusively or we might have a chance to force him to accept the reality of the evidence. On the other hand, I think the body he dug up really was the Mother Confessor, Kahlan Amnell, the woman that he dreamed he had a relationship with while in his confused state of pain when he was injured.

"He probably heard the name somewhere when he first traveled to the Midlands and it just stuck in his mind. It was probably a nice fantasy. For someone who grew up to be a woods guide, I think it would be a natural enough daydream, like imagining that he might one day go off to a strange land and marry a queen, but then it turned into a dream while he was hurt, and then into an obsession."

Nicci had to make herself stop. It hurt to the bone to say such things to other people about Richard, even if those other people also loved and cared about him and wanted to help him. Even Ann, as much as Nicci often thought the woman had ulterior motives, really did care a great deal about Richard. He was a man Ann believed was necessary to fulfil prophecy, but she still felt warmly toward him as an individual.

Nicci knew she was doing the right thing in what she said about Richard, but it still made her feel like she was betraying him. She could see his face in her mind, watching, silently hurt that she would be so coldly unbelieving.

"We think that, whatever the cause of his false belief," Ann said, "Richard needs to be brought back to reality."

Nicci didn't say anything. While she thought they were right, she didn't know that there was anything that could be done, other than letting him, as time went on, arrive at the truth on his own.

Nathan took a step forward and smiled down at Nicci. In the small room he seemed even more imposing. But it was his dark azure eyes that were so riveting. He spread his hands in a gesture of open appeal.

"Sometimes it hurts a person to help them, but later they see how it was the only way, and then, when they are finally well, they're happy that you did as had to be done."

"Like setting a broken arm," Ann offered, nodding to Nathan's words. "No one wants to go through the pain of having that done, but sometimes such things are necessary if they are to be well and have their life back."

"So," Nicci asked with a frown, "you want to heal him?"

"That's right," Zedd told her. He smiled, then. "I found a prophecy about Richard that says *They will at first contest him before they plot to heal him.* I never thought it would come to pass so soon or in quite this manner, but I think we all agree that we love Richard and want him well and back with us as himself."

Nicci thought that there must be more to this than what any of them were saying. She began to wonder why they had sent Rikka off for tea— why, exactly, they would not want the Lord Rahl's bodyguard around.

"I told you, I'm not exactly a healer."

"You did quite a good job of healing him when he was shot with that arrow," Zedd said. "Even I could not have accomplished such a feat. None of us in this room, other than you, Nicci, could have accomplished such a thing. You may not think you are much of a healer, but you were able to do what would have been impossible for any of us."

"Well, I was only successful because I used Subtractive Magic."

No one said anything. They all just stared at her.

"Wait a minute," Nicci said, looking from one person to the next, "are you suggesting that I again somehow use Subtractive Magic on Richard?"

"That's exactly what we're suggesting," Zedd told her.

Ann flicked a hand out toward Zedd and Nathan. "If one of us could do it, we would, but we can't. We need you to do it."

Nicci folded her arms. "Do what, exactly? I don't understand what it is you expect me to do."

Ann laid the hand on Nicci's arm. "Nicci, listen to us. We don't know what is causing Richard's malady. We have no way of trying to cure something when we don't know what it is. Even if we knew for sure that it was a glamour spell that had tainted that arrow, short the one who cast such a web, or absent the arrow, none of the three of us could eliminate the spell.

"But we can't be certain it was such a spell, or an entirely different kind of spell, or if it's simply delirium brought on by the injury. We don't know the cause. We may never know.

"What must be done, now," she said in a serious manner that no longer tried to be anything but straightforward and honest, "is is to eliminate the obsession—whatever its origin. It doesn't matter if it was brought about by a spell, a dream, or by some sudden onset of insanity. The memory of this woman, Kahlan, is a false memory that is distorting his thinking and therefore must be eliminated from his mind."

Nicci was stupefied by what she was hearing. She looked from the former prelate to Zedd. "Are you seriously suggesting that I use Subtractive Magic on your grandson's mind? You want me to eliminate a part of his consciousness? A part of who he is?"

"No, not part of who he is—never. I would never want that." Zedd licked his thin lips. His voice came out sounding helpless and despairing. "I want you to heal him. I want Richard back, the Richard I know, the Richard we all know—the real Richard, not the Richard with these foreign notions taking over his mind and destroying him."

Nicci shook her head. "I can't do that to the man I—" She closed her mouth before she finished the sentence.

"I would have back the Richard I love," Zedd said in soft supplication. "The Richard we all love."

Nicci backed away a step, shaking her head, unable to think of what to say to such desperation. There had to be another way to bring Richard to his senses.

"Show her," Nathan said to Ann, his voice suddenly sounding very much like the towering prophet he was, the Rahl he was.

Ann nodded in resignation and pulled something from her pocket. She held it out to Nicci. "Read this."

When Ann dropped it into Nicci's hand, she saw that it was a journey book. She looked up at Nathan, Ann, and finally Zedd.

"Go on," the prophet said. "Read the message Ann received from Verna."

Journey books were incredibly rare. In fact, Nicci had thought they had all been destroyed at the Palace of the Prophets. She knew that what was written in one of the matched pair of twinned books would appear in the other. The stylus kept in the spine that was used to write in the book was also used to wipe away old messages. In that way the journey books never wore out or became obsolete. Nicci opened the invaluable product of ancient magic and turned to the writing.

Ann, it began in a clear hand, *I fear to report that things are not going well with our forces. Where is Richard? Have you found him yet? I apologize for pressing you yet again for I know you are traveling with all due haste, but the problems with the army grow more serious every day. Men have deserted—not a great many, mind you—but we are in D'Hara now, and the whispers are growing that Lord Rahl will not lead them in a battle that they all believe will be suicide. Richard's continuing absence only confirms this fear for them. Day by day they grow to feel they have been abandoned by their Lord Rahl. None of the men believe that they have a chance against the enemy if Richard is not with his own troops to lead them.*

General Meiffert and I grow more desperate by the day as to what to tell disheartened men. Even if there was a good reason, it is still difficult enough for men knowing they face death not to have word from the first leader in their lives whom they truly believed in.

Please, Ann, as soon as you reach Richard, tell him how much all these brave young men, who have borne the brunt of defending our cause for so long and have suffered so much, need him. Please find out how soon he will join us. Ask him to please hurry.

Urgently awaiting word,
Yours in the Light,
Verna.

The book lowered in Nicci's hands. Tears stung her eyes.

Ann lifted the journey book from Nicci's trembling fingers. "What would you have me tell Verna? What would you have her say to the troops?" Ann asked in a quiet, even gentle, tone.

Nicci blinked at the tears. "You want me to take away his mind? You want me to betray him?"

"No, not at all," Zedd assured her, gripping her shoulder in his powerful fingers. "We want you to help him . . . to heal him."

"We fear to even approach Richard in his present condition," Ann said.

"We fear he may suspect something. I'm afraid I'm partly responsible for that because of my harsh reaction to his delusions. The Creator forgive me, but I have spent my life ruling people's lives and expecting compliance. Old ways die hard. Now, he thinks I intend to inflexibly force him to follow prophecy. He grows increasingly distrustful of us . . . but not of you."

"He would trust you," Zedd told her. "You could lay a hand on him and he would not suspect anything."

Nicci stared. "Lay a hand on him . . . ?"

Zedd nodded. "You would have control of him before he ever knew what had happened. He won't feel a thing. When he wakes up, the memory of Kahlan Amnell will be wiped away and he will be our Richard again."

Nicci bit her lower lip, unable to trust her voice.

Zedd's hazel eyes brimmed with tears. "I love my grandson dearly. I would do anything for him. I would do this myself, if I could do as good a job of it as you. I want him to be well. We all need him well."

He squeezed her shoulder again. "Nicci, if you love him, too, please, do this. Please do what only you can do and heal him one more time."

"*Master Rahl guide us. Master Rahl teach us. Master Rahl protect us,*"
Kahlan murmured yet again.

"*In your light we thrive. In your mercy we are sheltered. In your wisdom
we are humbled. We live only to serve. Our lives are yours.*"

Her shoulders ached from kneeling on the floor with her forehead
against the tiles, saying the devotion over and over. Despite the aching fatigue, she didn't really mind it.

"*Master Rahl guide us,*" Kahlan said as she started in again in harmony
with the joined voices that echoed softly through the marble halls.

"*Master Rahl teach us. Master Rahl protect us. In your light we thrive.
In your mercy we are sheltered. In your wisdom we are humbled. We live
only to serve. Our lives are yours.*"

In fact, she found it rather pleasant saying the same words over and
over. They filled her mind, helping numb the terrible void. The words
made her feel not so alone.

So lost.

"*Master Rahl guide us. Master Rahl teach us. Master Rahl protect us.
In your light we thrive. In your mercy we are sheltered. In your wisdom we
are humbled. We live only to serve. Our lives are yours.*"

Some of those concepts struck a cord with her and she found them comforting: safe, thriving lives where knowledge and wisdom prevailed. She
liked the image of that. Such ideas seemed quite the marvelous dream.

The others with her had been in a hurry, but when they'd seen the soldiers look their way, they had decided that they'd better go with the rest of
the people collecting in a square that was open to the overcast sky. Under
that cloudy sky lay white sand raked in concentric lines around a dark, pitted rock. On the top of the rock sat a bell in a stout frame. This was the
bell that had rung and called all the people together.

Pillars supported arches on all four sides of the opening in the roof of
the square. On the tile floor among the columns, all around Kahlan, peo-

ple were on their knees, bent forward, with their foreheads touching the tile. In unison, everyone chanted the devotion to the Lord Rahl.

Right near the end of the next repetition, the bell atop the dark, pitted rock rang twice. The voices all around Kahlan trailed off as they all finished together with *"Our lives are yours."*

In the sudden quiet, people rose up on their knees, many of them stretching and yawning before getting to their feet. Conversation welled up again as the people began moving off, going back to their business, to whatever they had been doing before the bell had called them to devotion.

When the others with her gestured, Kahlan followed the orders and moved off down the passageway, away from the open square. They passed statues and an intersection before they angled their way over to one side of the broad hall. The other three stopped. Kahlan stood silently as she waited and watched people going past.

The long climb up endless stairs, down miles of corridors, and up random flights of yet more stairs, all after the journey to get there in the first place, had left her dead on her feet. She would have liked to have sat down, but she knew better than to ask. The Sisters didn't care if she was exhausted. Worse, though, she could tell how tense and edgy they were, especially after the unexpected interruption for the chanting. They would not react sympathetically or kindly to a request to sit down.

With the mood they were in, if Kahlan even asked, she knew they would not have the slightest compunctions about beating her. She didn't think that they would do it right there, not with all the people around, but they certainly would later. She stood quietly, trying to be invisible and not draw their ire.

She guessed that the kneeling would have to be rest enough; it was all she was going to get.

Soldiers in handsome uniforms, carrying a variety of polished weapons at the ready, patrolled the halls, watching everyone. Each time guards passed, whether in pairs or larger groups, their gazes took careful note of the three women standing with Kahlan. When that happened, the three Sisters pretended to be looking at statues, or some of the rich tapestries of country scenes. One time, to avoid the attention of passing soldiers, they huddled close, pretending to be oblivious of the soldiers as they pointed out a grand statue of a woman holding a sheaf of wheat as she leaned on a spear. They smiled as they spoke softly among themselves as if enjoying a pleasant discussion of the artistic merits of the work until the soldiers had gone on past.

"Would you two sit down on that bench," Sister Ulicia growled. "You look like cats being sniffed by a pack of hounds."

Sisters Tovi and Cecilia, both older, glanced around and saw the bench a few steps behind them, up against the white marble wall. They scooped their dress under their legs as they sat beside each other. Tovi, as heavy as she was, appeared especially weary. Her wrinkled face was red as a beet from kneeling with her face to the floor. Cecilia, always tidy, used the opportunity provided by sitting on the bench to fuss with her gray hair.

Kahlan started for the bench, relieved at last have a chance to sit.

"Not you," Sister Ulicia snapped. "No one is going to notice you. Just stand there beside them so I will be better able to keep an eye on you."

Sister Ulicia lifted an eyebrow in warning.

"Yes, Sister Ulicia," Kahlan said.

Sister Ulicia expected an answer when she spoke.

Kahlan had learned that lesson the hard way, and would have answered sooner had she not stopped really listening after she'd been told that the offer to sit didn't include her. She reminded herself that even if she was tired she had better pay more attention or she would earn a slap for now and a lot worse later.

Sister Ulicia did not look away, or allow Kahlan to, but instead placed the tip of her stout, oak rod under Kahlan's chin and used it to forcefully tilt her head up.

"The day is not over, yet. You still have your part to do. You had better not even think of letting me down in any way. Do you understand?"

"Yes, Sister Ulicia."

"Good. We're all just as tired as you, you know."

Kahlan wanted to say that they may be tired, but they had ridden horses. Kahlan always had to walk and keep up with their horses. Sometimes she had to trot or even run to keep from falling behind. Sister Ulicia was never pleased if she had to turn her horse and go back to collect her lagging slave.

Kahlan glanced around the passageway at all the wondrous things displayed. Her curiosity overcame her caution.

"Sister Ulicia, what is this place?"

The Sister tapped her rod against her thigh as she briefly took in her surroundings. "The People's Palace. Quite the beautiful place." She looked back at Kahlan. "This is the home of the Lord Rahl."

She waited, apparently to see if Kahlan would say anything. Kahlan had nothing to say. "Lord Rahl?"

"You know, the man we've been praying to? Richard Rahl, to be precise. He is the Lord Rahl now." Sister Ulicia's eyes narrowed. "Have you ever heard of him, my dear?"

Kahlan thought about it. Lord Rahl. Lord Richard Rahl. Her mind seemed empty. She wanted to think things, to remember, but she couldn't. She guessed that there was simply nothing for her to remember.

"No, Sister. I don't believe I have ever heard of the Lord Rahl."

"Well," Sister Ulicia said with that sly smile she brought out from time to time, "I don't suppose you would. After all, who are you? Just a nobody. A nothing. A slave."

Kahlan swallowed back her urge to protest. How could she? What would she say?

Sister Ulicia's smile widened. It seemed her eyes could look right down into Kahlan's soul. "Isn't that right, my dear? You are a worthless slave who is fortunate for the charity of a meal."

Kahlan wanted to object, to say that she was more, to say that her life had value and was worthwhile, but she knew that such things were only a dream. She was tired to the bone. Now, her heart felt heavy, too.

"Yes, Sister Ulicia."

Whenever she tried to think about herself, there was only an empty void. Her life seemed so barren. She didn't think it was supposed to be, but it was.

Sister Ulicia turned when she noticed Kahlan's gaze going to the returning Sister Armina, a mature woman with a straightforward personality. Sister Armina's dark blue dress swished as she hurried down the wide corridor in a weaving course to make her way among the people strolling through the palace engaged in conversation and not watching where they were going.

"Well?" Sister Ulicia asked when Sister Armina reached them.

"I got caught up in a mass chanting to our Lord Rahl."

Sister Ulicia sighed. "Us, too. What did you find?"

"This is the place—just behind me at the next intersection, then down the hall to the right. We need to be careful, though."

"Why?" Sister Ulicia asked as Sisters Tovi and Cecilia hurried close to listen.

The four Sisters put their heads closer.

"The doors are right there at the side of the hallway. There isn't any way to go in there without being seen. At least for us. It's pretty clear that no one is supposed to even think of going in there."

Sister Ulicia glanced up and down the hall to make sure no one was paying them any heed. "What do you mean, it's pretty clear?"

"The doors are made specifically to warn people away. They have snakes carved on them."

Kahlan shrank back. She hated snakes.

Sister Ulicia slapped her rod against her leg as she pressed her lips together. Fuming, she finally turned her sour visage on Kahlan.

"You remember your instructions?"

"Yes, Sister," Kahlan answered immediately.

She wanted to get it over with. The sooner the Sisters were happy the better. It was getting late in the day. The long climb up through the inside of the plateau and then the chanting had taken more time than the Sisters had expected. They had thought they would be finished and on their way by now.

Kahlan was hoping that when she was done they could make camp and get some sleep. They never let her get enough sleep. Setting up camp meant more work for her, but at least there was sleeping to look forward to—as long as she didn't earn the Sisters' displeasure and a beating.

"All right, this actually makes little practical difference. We will just have to stand off a little farther than we planned, that's all." Sister Ulicia scratched her cheek as an excuse to take a careful look, checking for guards, before leaning in again. "Cecilia, you stay here and watch this end of the hall for any sign of trouble. Armina, you go back past the entrance and watch the other side. Start now so that it doesn't look like we're together as we near the doors, in case they're being watched."

Sister Armina flashed a crafty grin. "I will saunter down the halls and look like an awed visitor until she's done."

Without further word, she hurried off.

"Tovi," Sister Ulicia said, "you come with me. We'll be two friends, walking and chatting while visiting the Lord Rahl's grand palace. Meanwhile, Kahlan will be seeing to her tasks."

Sister Ulicia snatched Kahlan's upper arm and spun her around. "Come on."

With a shove, Kahlan was pushed on ahead of them. She hiked her pack up as she was hurried along. Together, the two Sisters followed her down the hall. As they reached the intersection where they had to turn right, two big soldiers came around toward them. They gave Sister Tovi only a passing glance, but they smiled at Sister Ulicia's smile. Sister Ulicia could appear innocently enchanting when she wanted to, and she was attractive enough that men paid her notice.

No one noticed Kahlan.

"Here," Sister Ulicia said. "Stop here."

Kahlan halted, staring across the hall at the thick mahogany doors. The snakes carved in the doors stared back at her. Their tails coiled around branches carved into the tops of the doors. The snakes' bodies hung down so that the heads were at eye level. Fangs jutted out from gaping jaws, as if the pair were about to strike. Kahlan couldn't imagine why anyone would carve such hideous creatures in doors. Everything else in the palace was beautiful, but these doors were not.

Sister Ulicia leaned close. "You remember all of your instructions?"

Kahlan nodded. "Yes, Sister."

"If you have any questions, ask them now."

"No, Sister. I remember everything you told me."

Kahlan wondered why it was that she could remember some things so well, but so many other things seemed lost in a fog.

"And don't dawdle," Tovi said.

"No, Sister Tovi, I won't."

"We need what you're being sent to recover for us, and we need it without any foolishness." Malevolence gleamed in Tovi's eyes. "Do you understand, girl?"

Kahlan swallowed. "Yes, Sister Tovi."

"You'd better," Tovi said, "Or you'll answer to me and you would not want that, believe me."

"I understand, Sister Tovi."

Kahlan knew that Tovi was deadly serious. The woman was usually relatively even tempered, but when provoked she could turn vicious in a flash. Worse, once she started in, she enjoyed seeing others helpless and in agony.

"Go on then," Sister Ulicia said. "And don't forget, don't talk to anyone. If the men up there say anything, just ignore them. They will leave you be."

The look in Sister Ulicia's eyes gave Kahlan pause. She nodded before hurrying off across the hall. Her exhaustion forgotten, she knew what she had to do, and she knew that if she didn't there would be trouble.

At the doors she grasped one of the handles that looked like a grinning skull, only made of bronze. She deliberately didn't look at the snakes as she put her muscle into pulling open the heavy door.

Inside, she paused, letting her eyes adjust to the dim light of lamps. The thick carpets of golds and blues quieted the room and prevented any of the echoes like there were in so many of the halls. The intimate room, paneled in the same mahogany as the tall doors, seemed a quiet refuge from the sometimes noisy palace.

With the door closed behind her, she realized that she was finally, totally away from the four Sisters. She couldn't remember a time when she had ever been alone from them. At least one of the Sisters was always watching her, watching their slave. She didn't know why they watched her so closely, after all, Kahlan had never actually tried to escape. She had often used to seriously consider it, but she had never actually gotten to the point of trying it.

Just the thought of trying to escape from the Sisters brought on such terrible pain that it made her feel like blood would run from her ears and nose and that her eyes would surely burst. When she thought of leaving the Sisters and the pain closed in to bear down on her, she couldn't get the thought out of her head fast enough, and even then the pain lingered. Such an episode usually left her so sick to her stomach that it was hours before she could even stand, much less walk.

The Sisters always knew when it happened, probably because they found her in a heap on the ground. When the pain in her head finally faded, they beat her. The worst was Sister Ulicia because she used the stout stick she always carried. It left welts that were slow to heal. Some still had not healed.

This time, though, they had ordered Kahlan to leave them and go in alone. They had told her that it would not bring on the pain so long as she kept to her instructions. It felt so good to be away from those four terrible women that Kahlan thought she might cry with joy.

Inside the room, though, were four big guards to replace the four Sisters. She paused, unsure what to do.

Serpents on one side of a door with serpents carved on it, and serpents on the other. She seemed never to be able to find any peace.

Kahlan stood frozen for a moment, afraid to try to go past the guards, afraid of what they might do to her for being in a place that she so obviously did not belong.

They were staring at her in a most curious way.

Kahlan gathered her courage, hooked some of her long hair behind an ear, and started for the stairwell she saw across the room.

Two guards stepped together to block her way. "Where do you think you're going?" one of them asked her.

Kahlan kept her head down and kept moving. She turned a little sideways to be able to slip between them.

As she went past, the second guard said to the first "What did you say?"

The first man, who had asked Kahlan where she thought she was going, stared at him.

"What? I didn't say anything."

As Kahlan made it to the stairs, the other two guards strolled over to the ones who had tried to block Kahlan's path.

"What are you two babbling about?" one of them asked.

The first waved a hand. "Nothing. It's nothing."

Kahlan hurried up the steps as fast as her tired legs would carry her. She paused on the broad landing to catch her breath, but she knew she dared not rest for long. She grabbed the polished stone handrail and hurried on up the rest of the way.

A soldier at the top immediately turned to the sound of her footsteps. He stared at her as she climbed up into the hallway. She rushed past him. He paused only briefly before turning and ambling off to continue his patrol.

There were other men in the hall—soldiers. Soldiers everywhere. Lord Rahl had a lot of soldiers, all of them huge, intent looking men.

Kahlan swallowed in wide-eyed fright at seeing so many soldiers in the way of what she had been told to do. If they slowed her, Sister Ulicia would not be understanding nor forgiving. Some of the soldiers saw

Kahlan and started her way, but when they reached her they lost their intent gazes and walked right by. As Kahlan hurried along the hall, other guards turned urgently to officers, but then, when questioned, said that it was nothing, and to forget it. Other men lifted an arm to point, only to then let the arm drop before continuing on their way.

As the men saw her and at the same time forgot her, Kahlan steadily made her way down the hall toward where she had been told she had to go. It concerned her, though, that so many of the men were carrying crossbows. The men with the crossbows wore black gloves. Their cocked weapons were loaded with deadly-looking red-fletched arrows.

Sister Ulicia had told Kahlan that as part of the magic that brought on the pain to prevent her from escaping, she was shrouded by webs of magic that kept people from noticing her. Kahlan tried to think of why the Sister would do such a thing, but her thoughts simply would not connect, would not link together into understanding. It was the most ghastly thing, not being able to make herself think about specific things when she wanted to. She would start out with the question, then the answer would begin to form, but simply run out as if there was nothing more there.

Despite the conjured shroud around her, though, Kahlan knew that if one of the soldiers pointed his crossbow at her and pulled the bolt release before he forgot her, she would be dead.

She wouldn't mind being dead because it would at least mean being freed of the anguish that was her life, but Sister Ulicia had warned her that the Sisters had great influence with the Keeper of the dead. Sister Ulicia said that if Kahlan ever thought to slip away from her duties to them by slipping the bounds of the world of the living and taking the long journey into the world of the dead, she would find that it was no refuge and in fact would prove to be a far worse place. It was then that Sister Ulicia had told Kahlan that they were Sisters of the Dark, as if to drive home the veracity of the warning.

Kahlan hadn't really needed the assurance; she had always been sure that any of the four Sisters could chase her down any hole and get her, even if that hole was a grave like the one they'd opened one dark night for reasons Kahlan couldn't even imagine and didn't want to know.

Looking into the Sister's terrible eyes, Kahlan had known that she was hearing the truth. After that, while death invited her with release, it also terrified her with dark promises.

She didn't know if this had always been her life, the life of chattel belonging to others. No matter how hard she tried, though, she could remember no other.

As she slipped by men patrolling, she made her way through a series of intersections that Sister Ulicia had drawn in the dirt for her at various camps as they traveled. The Sister had used her oak rod to diagram the halls so that Kahlan would know where she had to go.

As she moved through those halls she had memorized, no one ever tried to stop her. In a way, it was depressing that the men paid her no heed.

It was the same everywhere, though, no one ever noticed her, or if they did, they immediately disregarded her and went back to their own business. She was a slave, without her own life. She belonged to others. It made her feel invisible, insignificant, unimportant. A nobody.

Sometimes, like when making the long underground climb up into the palace, Kahlan would see men and women together, smiling, an arm around each other, touching one another. She tried to imagine what that would feel like—to have someone care about her, cherish her . . . to cherish them.

Kahlan swiped a tear off her cheek. She knew she would never have that. Slaves did not have a life of their own, they were used for their master's purposes; Sister Ulicia had made that very clear. One day, when Sister Ulicia had gotten that vicious look in her eyes that she sometimes got, she said that she was thinking of having Kahlan bred so that she could produce them an offspring.

But how did it come to be this way? Where had she come from? Surely, everyone's past didn't evaporate out of their minds the way Kahlan's had.

In the fog of her thoughts, she couldn't make her mind work the problem through. She asked the questions, but the concepts seemed to be soaked up into a dim haze of nothingness. She hated the way she couldn't think. Why could other people think while she could not? Even that question quickly faded away into irrelevance among the mire of twisting shadows, just the way she faded away when people saw her.

Kahlan stopped when she arrived at a pair of huge doors covered in gold. The doors looked like Sister Ulicia had said they would—a scene of rolling hills and forests all sheathed in gold. Kahlan looked both ways, then put all her weight into the task of pulling one of the massive doors open enough to slip inside. She took a last look, but none of the guards were watching her. She pulled the door closed behind herself.

It was much brighter inside than the hallway had been. Even though it was an overcast day the skylights let in a flood of light that lit a most astonishing garden. Sister Ulicia had told her about the garden, in general terms, but for Kahlan to see it, up here in the palace, was beyond anything she had imagined. The place was wondrous.

Richard Rahl was a lucky man to have such a garden that he could visit any time he wanted. She wondered if he would come and visit while she was in there, and see her . . . and then forget her.

Remembering her task, Kahlan admonished herself to keep her mind on what she had been sent to do. She hurried down one of the paths through a sprawl of flower beds. The ground was littered with fallen red and yellow petals. She wondered if Richard Rahl picked flowers here for his lady love.

She liked the sound of his name. It had a comforting ring to it. Richard Rahl. Richard. She wondered what he was like, if he was as pleasant as his name was to her ear.

As she made her way along the path, Kahlan gazed up at the small trees growing all about her. She loved the trees. They reminded her of . . . of something. She growled in frustration. She hated it when she couldn't remember things that she was sure were important. Even if they weren't important, she hated forgetting things. It was like forgetting parts of who she was.

She hurried past shrubs and vine-covered stone walls until she reached the grassy place that Sister Ulicia said would be there in the center of the garden. Across the way the grassy ring was broken by a wedge of stone atop which sat a slab of granite, looking much like a table.

Atop the granite slab were supposed to be the things Kahlan had been sent to retrieve. Seeing them suddenly, she quailed. The three objects were as black as death itself. They looked as if they were sucking in the light from the room, from the skylights, from the very sky, and trying to swallow it all.

Her heart hammering with dread, Kahlan rushed across the grass to the granite table. Being that close to such sinister looking objects made her nervous. She slipped the shoulder straps off and set the pack down beside the black boxes she had been sent to recover. Her bedroll, lashed underneath, made the pack not want to sit up, so she had to lean it a little to the side.

She laid her hand on the bedroll for a moment, feeling the soft contour of what was rolled up inside. It was her most precious possession.

She remembered, then, that she had better get back to business. She immediately realized, though, that she was going to have a problem. The boxes were bigger than Sister Ulicia had said she thought they would be. They each were nearly as big as a loaf of bread. There was no way they would all fit in her pack.

But those had been her explicit instructions. The wishes of the Sisters conflicted with the reality that the boxes weren't going to fit. There was no way to satisfy the contradiction.

Memories of previous punishments flashed through her mind, bringing a sheen of sweat to her brow. She wiped the sweat from her eyes as the visions of torture came back to her. This, of all things, she cursed silently, she had to remember.

Kahlan decided that there was nothing else she could do; she would have to try.

At the same time, she also fretted about stealing things out of Lord Rahl's garden. After all, they didn't belong to the Sisters, and Lord Rahl would not have that many men posted all around the garden unless the boxes were important to him.

She was no thief. But was it worth the kind of punishment she would receive should she refuse? Was her blood worth Lord Rahl's treasure? Was Lord Rahl the kind of man who would want her to refuse to steal and as a result suffer the Sisters' torture?

She didn't know why, and maybe she was only coddling her doubts, but she told herself that Richard Rahl would say to take the boxes rather than sacrifice her life.

She flipped open the top of her pack and attempted to shove things down in tighter, but there was very little give. They were already packed as tightly as they were ever going to pack.

With rising worry that she was taking too much time, she pulled on clothes, trying to get something to wrap the first black box in.

Out came part of her satiny white dress.

Kahlan stared at the silken, nearly white material in her fingers. It was the most beautiful dress she had ever seen. But why would she have it? She was a nobody. A slave. What would a slave be doing with such a beautiful dress? She couldn't make her mind work to answer such a question.

The thoughts simply would not come together into answers.

Kahlan snatched up one of the boxes and rolled it up in the skirt of the dress and stuffed it all into the pack. She leaned on the box, trying to shove it down deeper, then closed the flap to test the fit. The flap hardly covered the top of the box and she only had one of them inside. She had to cinch the flap down with the strap just to get it to stay. There was no way in the world that the other boxes were going to fit in her pack.

Sister Ulicia had been very explicit that Kahlan had to hide the boxes in her pack or the soldiers would see them. They would forget Kahlan, but Sister Ulicia had said that the soldiers would recognize the boxes Kahlan was taking out of the garden room and then they would send up alarms. Kahlan had been told in no uncertain terms that she had to hide the boxes. But she could see that there was no way all three would fit.

Around the camp fire a few nights before, Sister Ulicia had put her face right up close to Kahlan's and whispered exactly what she would do to Kahlan should she fail to do as instructed.

Kahlan started trembling at the memory of what Sister Ulicia had told her that terrible night. She thought of Sister Tovi and trembled all the more.

What was she going to do?

Kahlan pushed open one of the doors with the snakes on the other side of it. Sisters Ulicia and Tovi immediately spotted her and with furtive gestures motioned for her to come to where they waited down the hall. They didn't want to be seen near the doors with the snakes and the skulls.

Kahlan crossed the hallway, watching the patterns in the marble floor, not wanting to look up into Sister Ulicia's eyes.

As soon as she had walked down the corridor and was close enough, Sister Ulicia snatched Kahlan's shirt at her shoulder and pulled her over to a niche in the far wall. Both Sisters Ulicia and Tovi caged her in.

"Did anyone try to stop you?" Sister Tovi asked.

Kahlan shook her head.

Sister Ulicia let out a sigh. "Good. Let's see them."

Kahlan drew the pack off one shoulder and pulled it around enough in front so that the sisters could open the flap. Both of them pawed at the strap cinching it down. They finally got it loose and flipped it back.

Both Sisters huddled close together, shoulder to shoulder, so that people in the hall couldn't see what they were doing, see what terrible thing they were about to bring out into the light of day. Sister Ulicia carefully pulled off the satiny white fabric of Kahlan's dress still stuffed partly down into the pack to see the black box nestled within.

Both stood in silent awe, staring.

Sister Ulicia, her fingers trembling with excitement, stuck her arm down in and started pawing around, searching for the others. When she didn't find them she stepped back, a dark look coming over her face.

"Where are the other two?"

Kahlan swallowed. "I could only fit one into the pack, Sister. The others wouldn't fit. You told me that I had to conceal them inside, but they were too big. I will—"

Before Kahlan could say another word, before she explained that she planned to make two more trips to recover the other boxes, Sister Ulicia, in a rage, whipped her stout rod around so hard that it whistled through the air.

Kahlan heard a deafening crack as it hit the side of her head with full force.

The world seemed to go silent and black.

Kahlan realized that she was on the floor in a heap, crumpled on her knees. She cupped a hand over her left ear, gasping in paralyzing pain. She saw blood splattered all over the floor. She took her hand away and saw that it looked like she was wearing a warm, bloody glove.

She could only stare at her hand and pant in little gasps. So crushing was the pain that her voice wouldn't work. She couldn't even cry out in agony. It seemed as if she were looking through a long, fuzzy, black tunnel. Her stomach felt queasy.

Suddenly, Sister Ulicia seized Kahlan's shirt and hoisted her up from the floor only to slam her against the wall. Kahlan's head smacked the stone, but compared to the pain radiating from the side of her head, her jaw, and her ear, it seemed inconsequential.

"You stupid bitch!" Sister Ulicia railed as she pulled Kahlan away and again slammed her against the wall. "You stupid, incompetent, worthless bitch!"

Tovi looked like she, too, wanted to get her hands on Kahlan. She saw that down the corridor half of Sister Ulicia's broken rod lay against the wall. Kahlan struggled to find her voice, knowing it was her only salvation.

"Sister Ulicia, I couldn't fit all three inside." Kahlan could taste salty tears along with blood. "You told me to hide them in my pack. They wouldn't fit. I planned to go back and get them, that's all. Please—I'll go back for the others. I swear, I will get them for you."

Sister Ulicia backed away, the smoldering anger in her eyes was frightening. Even though the woman backed away, she pointed at the center of Kahlan's chest with one finger and Kahlan was slammed hard against the marble and pinned to the wall with a force that felt as massive as a bull leaning against her. It was a struggle to draw each breath against the crushing pressure. It was a struggle to see through the blood running into her eyes.

"You should have rolled the other two boxes in your bedroll, then you would have them all right now. Isn't that right?"

Kahlan hadn't considered doing that because it wasn't an option.

"But Sister, I have something else rolled in the bedroll."

Sister Ulicia leaned in again. Kahlan feared that she was now going to be made to wish she was dead, or fear that she was about to be. She wasn't at all sure which fate would be worse. She felt the pain come on within her head to match the pain on the outside from the blow. Pinned against the wall, Kahlan couldn't fall to the ground, cover her ears, and scream, or she would have.

"I don't care what trifle you have rolled up in your bedroll. You should have left it out. The boxes are more important."

Kahlan could only stare, unable to move because of the force keeping her flattened to the wall, and unable to talk because of the force of pain crushing her mind. It felt like ice picks were being slowly shoved and twisted into her ears. Her ankles and wrists twitched involuntarily. She gasped with each throbbing wave of agony wrenching through her head, trying, but unable to squirm away from the piercing pain.

"Now," Sister Ulicia said in a low, menacing voice that carried deadly threat, "do you think you can do that? Do you think you can go back up there and roll the other two boxes in your bedroll and bring them back to me like you should have done in the first place?"

Kahlan tried to talk, but couldn't. She nodded instead, desperate to agree, desperate for the pain to stop. She could feel the blood running from her ear and the side of her head soaking the collar of her shirt. She was on her tiptoes, pressed back, wishing she could melt through the wall in order to get away from Sister Ulicia. The pain wouldn't let up enough for her to catch a breath.

"Do you remember seeing some of the hundreds and hundreds of big, lonely soldiers quartered down in the lower reaches of this place as we were coming up?" Sister Ulicia asked.

Kahlan nodded again.

"Well, if you fail me again, then, when I'm done breaking every bone in your body and making you suffer the agony of a thousand deaths, I'm then going to heal you enough so that I can sell you to those soldiers down there to be their barracks whore. That will be where you spend the rest of your life, being passed from one stranger to another with no one to care what happens to you."

Kahlan knew that Sister Ulicia never made empty threats. The Sister was absolutely ruthless. Kahlan averted her eyes as she sucked back a sob, unable to stand the Sister's scrutiny any longer.

Sister Ulicia seized Kahlan's jaw and turned her face back. "Are you certain that you understand the price should you fail me again?"

Kahlan, her chin held firm, managed to nod.

She felt the pressure pinning her to the wall suddenly release. She collapsed to her knees, gasping with the waves of searing pain all along the left side of her face. She didn't know if any bones were broken, but it certainly felt like it.

"What's going on here?" A soldier asked.

Sisters Ulicia and Tovi turned and smiled at the man. He glanced down at Kahlan, frowning. She stared up pleadingly at him, hoping to be rescued from these monsters. The man looked up, his mouth open, about to say something to the Sisters, but then he never did. He looked from Sister Ulicia's smile to Tovi's, and smiled himself.

"Is everything all right, ladies?"

"Oh, yes," Sister Tovi said with a jovial chuckle. "We were just about to have a rest on the bench, here. I was complaining about my backache, that's all. We were both saying what a nuisance it is to get older."

"I guess it is." He bowed his head. "Good day, then, ladies."

He walked off without ever acknowledging Kahlan's existence. If he saw her, he forgot about her before he could say anything. Kahlan realized that it was the way she, too, seemed to forget things about herself.

"Get up," the voice over her growled.

Kahlan struggled to her feet. Sister Ulicia jerked Kahlan's pack around in front again. She flipped back the flap and dragged out the sinister black box wrapped in Kahlan's satiny white dress.

She handed the bundle to Sister Tovi. "We've already been here too long. We're starting to draw attention. Take this and get going."

"But that's mine!" Kahlan cried out as she grabbed for the dress.

Sister Ulicia backhanded her hard enough to make her teeth slam together. The blow knocked her sprawling. Lying on her side on the floor, Kahlan drew her legs up as she cradled her head in agony. Blood was smeared all over the marble. She shook as the pain bore down and would not let up.

"You want me to leave without you?" Sister Tovi asked as she tucked the box wrapped in the white dress under her arm.

"I think it would be best. It will be safest if we get this box on its way while this worthless bitch goes back to get the others. If it takes as long as the first one, I'd just as soon not have us both standing around here in the hall waiting for soldiers to decide to have a look. We don't need a battle; we need to slip away without a trace."

"If we were questioned it wouldn't do to have them find we had one of the boxes of Orden," Sister Tovi agreed. "I should just start out, then, and wait for you somewhere? Or keep going until I reach our destination?"

"You'd best not stop for now." Sister Ulicia motioned Kahlan to her feet as she spoke to Sister Tovi. "Sisters Cecilia, Armina, and I will meet back up with you once we get to where we're going."

Sister Tovi leaned a little toward Kahlan as Kahlan staggered to her feet. "I guess that gives you a few days to think about what I'm going to do to you when the rest of you join up with me again, doesn't it?"

Kahlan could manage only a whisper. "Yes, Sister."

"Swift journey," Sister Ulicia said.

After Sister Tovi had rushed off down the wall, taking Kahlan's beautiful dress with her, Sister Ulicia seized a fistful of Kahlan's hair and twisted her head close. The Sister's fingers groped along the side of Kahlan's face, making her cry out.

"You have broken bones," she announced after her examination of Kahlan's injuries. "Complete your mission and I will heal you. Fail, and it will only be the beginning.

"The other Sister and I have a number of other things we must do before our goals are accomplished. So do you. If you complete your task today you will be healed. We would like you to be healthy for those future duties"—Sister Ulicia patted Kahlan's cheek in a patronizing manner— "but I can always make other arrangements should you fail in this one. Now, hurry up and get me the other two boxes."

She had no choice, of course. As much pain as she was in, she knew that if she didn't comply, and soon, then it was only going to be worse for her. Sister Ulicia had shown her that there was always more pain just waiting to be applied. Kahlan knew, too, that there was no escape from the Sisters.

Kahlan wished she could forget the pain like she seemed to have forgotten the rest of her life. It seemed that only the bad parts of her existence remained in the dark vaults of her memory.

With her breath catching on the ragged edge of tears from the throbbing hurt, she pulled her pack back around, slipped her arm through the strap, and hiked the whole thing up on her back.

"And you had better do as I said and bring them both," Sister Ulicia growled.

Kahlan nodded and rushed off across the broad corridor. Everyone ignored her. It was as if she were invisible. The few people who did look her way only seemed to see her for a fleeting moment, before they, too, forgot that they had ever noticed her.

Kahlan grabbed the bronze skull in both hands and pulled open one of the snake doors. She raced across the plush carpets and was past the guards before they could think to wonder what they had seen. She dashed up the stairs, ignoring soldiers patrolling the halls, some of whom briefly turned her way, as if trying to hold the image of her in their memories, before losing their mental grip of her and going on about their duties. Kahlan felt like a ghost among the living; there, but not.

She grunted with the effort of pulling open one of the gold-clad doors enough to slip inside the garden. She was in so much pain that she could not rush fast enough. She just wanted to get back and have the Sister make the hurt stop. As before, the garden was as quiet as a sanctuary should be. She had no time to notice or enjoy the flowers and trees. She paused on the grass, staring at the two black boxes sitting on the stone slab, momentarily immobilized by the sight of them, and by the thought of what she had been told to do.

More slowly, she closed the rest of the distance, not wanting to ever get there, not wanting to ever have to do what she knew she must. But the agony of the twisting, throbbing pain all along the side of her head drove her on.

Standing before the slab, she finally slipped off her pack and set it down beside the boxes on its back, rather than its bottom. She wiped her runny nose on the back of her sleeve. Gently, she caressed the side of her face, fearing to touch it and make it hurt worse, but at the same time aching to comfort the throbbing pain. She almost fainted when she felt something jagged sticking out. She didn't know if it was a splinter from Sister Ulicia's broken oak rod, or if it was a splinter of bone. Either way, she felt light-headed and thought she might vomit.

Knowing she had little time, she crossed one arm across her stomach and with the other hand began untying the leather thongs holding her bedroll to the bottom of her pack. Her fingers were slick with blood, making the task of untying the knots more difficult. She finally had to resort to using both hands.

When she at last had them undone, she carefully unfurled her bedroll and took out what lay inside, setting it on the stone slab so as to make room for the loathsome black boxes. She sucked in a sob, trying not to think of what she was leaving behind.

Kahlan forced herself to set to work wrapping the two remaining boxes in her bedroll. When she was finished, she laced up the thongs, securely fastening them to insure that the boxes would not fall out. At last finished, she swung the pack onto her back again and reluctantly started across the open area of bare ground in the center of the immense indoor garden.

As she crossed the ring of grass, she paused and turned, looking back through her watery vision at what she was leaving on the stone slab in place of the boxes.

It was the most precious thing she had.

And now she was leaving it behind.

Overwhelmed and unable to go on, feeling more hopeless and helpless than she could ever remember feeling, Kahlan sank to her knees in the grass.

She crumpled forward as she broke down sobbing. She hated her life. She hated living. The thing she loved most was being left behind because of those evil women.

Kahlan wept uncontrollably, gripping the shaggy grass in her fists. She didn't want to leave it. But if she didn't, Sister Ulicia would never let her get away with violating such a direct order. Kahlan sobbed at how sorry she felt for herself, for her helpless situation.

No one but the Sisters knew her, or even knew that she existed.

If only just one person would remember her.

If only the Lord Rahl would come to his garden and save her.

If only, if only, if only. What good was wishing?

She pushed herself up then and, sitting back on her heels, stared off through the tears at the granite slab, at what she had left standing there.

No one was going to save her.

She didn't used to be this way. She didn't know how she knew that, but she knew. Somewhere in her dim, vanished past, it seemed like she used to be able to depend on herself, on her own strength, to survive. She didn't used to waste her time lamenting "If only."

Staring across the garden, Lord Rahl's beautiful, peaceful garden, she drew strength from what she saw standing there now, and, at the same time, from somewhere deep inside herself. She had to do that now—be resolute, as she was sure she used to be. She had to somehow be strong for herself, for her own sake.

Kahlan somehow had to save herself.

What stood there now was no longer hers. It would be her gift to Richard Rahl in exchange for the nobility of life—her life—that she had remembered in his garden.

"Master Rahl guide us," she quoted from the devotion. "Thank you, Master Rahl, for guiding me this day, for guiding me back to what I mean to myself."

She swiped the backs of her wrists across her eyes, wiping away the tears and blood. She had to be strong or the Sisters would defeat her. They would take everything from her. Then they would win.

Kahlan couldn't let them do that.

She remembered then, and touched the necklace she wore. She turned the small stone between a finger and thumb. This, at least, was still hers. She still had the necklace.

Kahlan struggled to her feet and straightened under the weight of the pack. She first had to get back so that Sister Ulicia would at least heal the injury she had inflicted. Kahlan would willingly take that help because she would then be able to go on and find a way to succeed.

With a last look back, she finally turned and headed for the door.

She knew now that she couldn't surrender her will to them, to their belief that they had a right to her life. They might defeat her, but it couldn't be because she allowed it.

But even if she lost her life in the end, she knew now that they would not defeat her spirit.

Richard slowly paced the small room, deep in thought, going over the memory of the morning Kahlan had disappeared. He had to figure it out, and soon—for more reasons than one. The most important of those reasons, of course, was to help Kahlan. He had to believe that he still could help her, that she was still alive and there was still time.

He was the only one who knew her, who believed in her existence. There was no one but him to help her.

There were also the implications of the wider concerns that her disappearance engendered. There was no telling how far-reaching those problems could turn out to be. In that, too, he was the only one opposing what hidden designs lurked behind events.

Since it seemed Kahlan had so far not been able to escape her captors, that meant she couldn't and was going to need help. With the beast seemingly able to strike again at any time, Richard was painfully aware of how easily he could die at any moment, and if he did, then the one person who was her connection to the world would be gone.

He had to use every minute of what time he had available to work toward helping her. He couldn't even bother wasting time reprimanding himself for all the days he had already let slip through his fingers.

It had all started that morning, not long before he'd been shot with the arrow, so he had decided to concentrate on that single event and to start anew. He had pushed the enormity of the problem from his mind in order to narrow his focus on the solution. He would never come to understand who had Kahlan by pulling out his hair and agonizing over the fact that someone had her, or by trying to convince others that she existed. None of that had accomplished anything, nor would it.

He had even set aside the books, *Gegendrauss* and *Ordenic Theory*, that he'd discovered in the little room. The first was in High D'Haran. It had been a long time since he had worked with the ancient language, so he knew he couldn't afford to spend time on it. A brief examination had told him that the book might hold remarkable information, although he hadn't spotted any that was material. Besides, he was out of practice translating High D'Haran. He didn't have time to work on it until he first resolved other issues.

The second book was difficult to follow, especially with his mind elsewhere, but he had read just enough of the beginning to realize that the book was indeed about the boxes of Orden. Other than *The Book of Counted Shadows*, which he had memorized as as child, he didn't recall ever seeing another book about the boxes of Orden. That alone, to say nothing of the profound danger of the boxes themselves, told him that the book was of immeasurable valuable. But the boxes were not his problem at the moment. Kahlan was the problem. He'd set that book aside as well.

There were also other books in the small, shielded room, but he had not had the time or inclination to search through them. He had decided that devoting himself to the books before he had a true understanding of what was going on would only waste yet more time. He had to approach the problem in a logical manner, not in random, frantic attempts to somehow pluck an answer out of thin air.

Whatever the cause of Kahlan's disappearance, it had all started that morning just before the fight when he'd been shot with the arrow. When Richard had climbed into his bedroll the night before the battle, Kahlan had been with him. He knew she had. He remembered holding her in his arms. He remembered her kiss, her smile in the dark. He was not imagining it.

No one would believe him, but he was not dreaming up Kahlan.

He put that part of the problem aside as well. He couldn't concern himself anymore with trying to convince others. Doing so was only diverting his attention from the real nature of the problem.

Nor could he afford to give in to fear that others might be right that he was only imagining her; that, too, was a dangerous distraction. He reminded himself of the very real evidence: the issue of her tracks.

Even if he couldn't make others understand the lifetime of learning that went into understanding the meaning of what he saw when he looked at tracks, he knew for certain what the evidence on the ground had revealed to him. There was a language to tracks. Others may not understand that language, but Richard did. Kahlan's tracks had been swept away, undoubtedly with magic, leaving behind a forest floor too artificially perfect and, more importantly, the rock that he'd discovered kicked out of place. That rock told him he was right. Told him that he was not imagining things.

He had to reason out what had happened to Kahlan—and that meant how had she been taken. Whoever had done it had magic, that much he knew. He at least knew that much because of the way their tracks had been altered. Knowing that narrowed the possibilities of who could be responsible. It had to be someone with magic sent by Jagang.

Richard remembered waking from a dead sleep that morning and laying there on his side. He remembered not being able to open his eyes for more than a brief moment at a time and not being able to lift his head. Why? He didn't think it was because he was groggy from still being half asleep; it had been more overwhelming than that. It had felt like sleepiness, yet stronger.

But the part of the memory that had him at the tantalizing, frustrating brink of near understanding was what he remembered seeing in the murky darkness of false dawn as he had laid there trying to fully wake. That part of the memory was where he now put all his attention, all his mental effort, all his concentration.

He remembered shadowy tree limbs that appeared to move about, as if carried to and fro in the wind.

But there had been no wind that morning. Everyone had been sure about that point. Richard himself remembered how dead still it had been. But the dark shapes of the tree limbs had been moving.

It seemed a contradiction.

But, as Zedd had pointed out with the Wizard's Ninth Rule, contradictions can't exist. Reality is what it is. If something contradicted itself then it wouldn't be what it is. It was a fundamental law of existence. Contradictions can't exist in reality.

Tree limbs could not wave around by themselves and there had been no wind to move them.

That meant he was looking at the problem all wrong. He was always stumped by how the tree limbs could move about in the wind when there was no wind. The simple fact was that they couldn't. Maybe someone had been moving them.

Pacing across the little room, Richard halted.

Or maybe it wasn't the tree limbs that had been moving.

He'd seen the shadowy movement and had assumed it was the tree limbs. Maybe it wasn't.

With that single insight, Richard gasped with sudden realization.

He understood.

He stood frozen, eyes wide, unable to move, as the sequence of events and scraps of information from that morning tumbled together in his mind, forming a framework of comprehension of what had happened. They had been taking Kahlan, probably using a spell of some sort on her, as they did to keep Richard asleep, then collected her things and tidied up the camp to erase evidence of her having been there. That was the movement he remembered. It hadn't been tree limbs moving back and forth in the near darkness, it had been people. Gifted people.

Richard saw a red glow. When he looked up, Nicci was coming into the small room.

"Richard, I need to talk to you."

He stared at her. "I understand. I know what the viper with four heads means."

Nicci's gaze turned away, as if she couldn't bear to look into his eyes. He knew that she thought he was merely adding another layer to his delusion.

"Richard, listen to me. This is important."

He frowned at her. "Have you been crying?"

Her eyes were red and puffy. Nicci was not the sort of woman given to tears. He had seen her cry, but only for very good reason.

"Never mind that," she said. "You have to listen to me."

"Nicci, I'm telling you, I've figured out—"

"Listen to me!" Fists at her sides, she looked as if she might again burst into tears. He realized that he had never seen her looking quite this distraught.

He didn't want to waste any more time, but he decided that it might hurry things along if he let her have her say.

"All right, I'm listening."

Nicci stepped close and gripped him by both shoulders. With an intent expression, she peered into his eyes. Her brow wrinkled with conviction.

"Richard, you have to get out of here."

"What?"

"I've already told Cara to collect your things. She's bringing them now.

She said she knows her way down here, down into the tower, anyway, without having to go through shields."

"I know, I taught her before." Richard's sense of alarm began to rise. "What's going on? Is the Keep under attack? Is Zedd all right?"

Nicci cupped one hand to the side of his face. "Richard, they are determined to heal you of your delusion."

"Kahlan is no delusion. I just now figured out what happened."

She seemed not to notice what he said, or maybe she was ignoring what she thought was no more than yet another in a long series of attempts to prove the impossible. This time, though, he wasn't really interested in proving it to her.

"Richard, I'm telling you, you have to get out of here. They wanted me to use Subtractive Magic to eliminate your memory of Kahlan."

Richard blinked in surprise. "You mean Ann and Nathan want to do that. Zedd never would."

"Zedd too. They convinced him that you're sick and the only way to heal you is to excise what they consider to be the diseased portion of your thoughts responsible for your false memories. They convinced Zedd that time is running out and this is the only way to save you. Zedd is so heartbroken to see you like this that he has snatched at what he thinks may be the only chance to make you well again."

"And you agreed to this?"

She indignantly smacked the side of his shoulder. "Are you crazy? Do you really think I would do that to you? Even if I thought they were right, do you seriously think I would ever consider taking away part of who you are? After what you've shown me about life? After what you have done to bring me back to embracing life? Do you really think that I would do that to you, Richard?"

"No, I guess you wouldn't do such a thing. But why would Zedd? He loves me."

"He is also terrified for you, terrified that you are being taken over by this delusion, or bewitchment, or whatever is causing this sickness that is leaving you alive but not really yourself, turning you into a stranger they don't know.

"Zedd feels that this might be their only chance to ever have you whole again, to ever have you be Richard, the real Richard, again.

"I don't think that any of them—Ann, Nathan, or Zedd—really wants to do this, but Ann truly believes that you alone are the salvation for our cause. She has faith that prophecy has revealed this as the only chance we have and she is desperate to make you well lest we all be lost.

"Zedd was reluctant, but then they showed him a message in the journey book and talked him into it."

"What message?"

"Verna is with the D'Haran troops. She sent word that our soldiers are becoming disheartened that you haven't joined them. Verna fears that unless you are there to lead them they may choose not to go on. She sent a desperate message wanting to know if Ann had found you yet, trying to find out when you could be expected to join your men in the coming battle with the Imperial Order."

Richard was stunned. "I suppose I can understand why the three of them are so worried, but to ask you to use Subtractive Magic . . ."

"I know. I think it's a solution born of desperation, not clear thinking. But worse, I fear that once they discover that I don't intend to do as they wanted, they will then decide that they can't let this opportunity slip away from them and so their only alternative will be to try to somehow use their gift to cure you themselves. That kind of blind tampering with consciousness would be unpredictable, to say the least.

"They're desperate because they fear we all are running out of time before Jagang ends our chances forever. They believe this is the only solution. They are no longer listening to reason.

"You have to get out of here, now, Richard. I only agreed to their plan so that I could warn you first and give you time to get away. You must leave immediately if you are to escape."

Richard's head was spinning at the very notion of what they wanted to do. "That presents a problem. I don't know how to cover my trail with magic, the way Zedd can. If they are as committed as you say they are, then they will come after me. If they follow me and take me by surprise, what am I going to do, then? Fight them?"

She lifted her arms in frustration. "I don't know, Richard. But I do know their state of resolve. Nothing you say is going to talk them out of this because they think you are suffering under a condition where you aren't rational, so they feel that for your own good they must take control.

They may be doing it for loving reasons, but they're wrong to do it this way. Dear spirits, I, too, think you're suffering from some problem, but I just couldn't allow them to do this."

Richard squeezed her shoulder in a gesture of appreciation before he turned away as he tried to take it all in. It was near to impossible for him to imagine that Zedd would agree to such a thing. It just wasn't like him.

Wasn't like him.

Of course. It also wasn't like Ann to be so certain of how Richard must be made to play out his role in prophecy. Kahlan had changed everyone who knew her. She had made Ann come to see how Richard wasn't meant to follow the literal reading of prophecy as if it were a book of instruction.

Since Kahlan had vanished, everyone had changed. Zedd was different, too, and not in ways that were at all helpful. Even Cara had changed. She was just as protective, but now she was protective in a somehow more . . . feminine way. Nicci had changed as well, although in her case Richard thought the results were more positive—from his standpoint, anyway. She had forgotten everything having to do with Kahlan, and as a result she had become more sheltering of him despite her own views and interests, more willing to champion him despite everything he said and did. She was more devoted to him and thus more dedicated to safeguarding him.

But Zedd had changed in ways that were more troubling, much as Ann had become more overbearing and willing to directly interfere with Richard's decisions and impose her views of what she believed Richard had to do.

Richard had been telling people all along that the implications of Kahlan's disappearance were far broader and more complex than anyone but he was seeing. This change in everyone's behavior, some subtle and some overt, was further manifestation of those far-reaching effects. And yet, even Richard hadn't realized the full extent of the hidden corollaries and consequences.

Things had changed. Richard could no longer allow past characteristics to confuse the reality of how matters were in the present. It was vital that he recognize the truth of the way things were, now, and not be influenced by how they had once been. Nicci had become even more of an ally. Cara was just as protective as ever, if in a subtly different way. But Zedd and Ann, and possibly Nathan, had become less than dependable in ways that mattered most.

He had to take the way people had changed into account and act accordingly. He had to keep his objectives in mind and act to accomplish those goals even if it meant no longer fully trusting people he once had, people he cared about.

With Kahlan's disappearance, everything was being altered. The rules had changed.

He turned back to Nicci.

"This couldn't have happened at a worse time. I just figured it out. The viper with four heads are the Sisters of the Dark."

"Jagang's Sisters?"

"No—my former teachers, Sisters Tovi, Cecilia, Armina, and their leader, Sister Ulicia. Sister Ulicia was the one who assigned all of my teachers, including you."

"Richard, that's just crazy. I don't—"

"No, it's not. That morning when I thought I saw the tree limbs moving when there was no wind, it wasn't the tree limbs. It was those Sisters I saw move about in the near darkness."

"But Jagang has all the Sisters of the Dark."

"No, he doesn't."

"He's a dream walker, Richard. With the bond to you the Sisters of the Light who are free are out of his grasp, but he captured those Sisters—I was there, with them, when Jagang first got his clutches on us. They are Sisters of the Dark; without the bond they're helpless against the dream walker. My . . . feelings are what bonded me to you and allowed me to escape his control. But they couldn't escape; they're not loyal to you nor could they be."

"Oh, but they are. They swore a bond to me."

"What! That's impossible."

Richard shook his head. "You weren't with them the day it happened. It was when Jagang's troops were trying to take the Palace of the Prophets. Sister Ulicia and my former teachers—except you were gone and Liliana was dead—knew where Kahlan was being held. They wanted free of Jagang's domination and so they made me an offer. They traded the whereabouts of Kahlan in exchange for being allowed to swear loyalty to me so they could escape the dream walker's domination."

Nicci was in near apoplexy with bottled objections. She looked as if the idea was so bizarre that she had trouble even deciding where to start. She heaved a breath to gain control of her galloping objections.

"Richard, you simply have to stop coming up with such flights of fancy. None of this even works in your story. The viper, as you think you figured out, would really then have to have five heads. You forgot Merissa."

"No, Merissa is dead. She was trying to kill me—she came after me. She said she intended to bathe in my blood."

Nicci pulled a strand of hair through her finger and thumb. "Well, I admit, I often heard her make that vow."

"She tried to make good on the vow. She had followed Kahlan and me in the sliph. The Sword of Truth is incompatible with life in the sliph. When I got here I retrieved the sword and plunged it into the sliph before Merissa was able to get out. She died in there.

"Of those Sisters of the dark who swore loyalty to me, only four are still alive. Those Sisters are the viper with four heads. They're the ones who came that morning and took Kahlan. They used magic to spell me so that I wouldn't awake easily. The spell they used must have been something simple, like magnifying my sleepiness so that I wouldn't realize that magic had been used on me. The single wolf that called wasn't a wolf, but a signal given by the approaching troops. Because of the spell I didn't recognize it for what it was—the spell made me so sleepy I couldn't think, but still, I knew there was something strange about it. The Sisters then used magic to cover their trail. They took Kahlan."

Nicci seized fists full of blond hair as she growled in agitation. "But they're Sisters of the Dark! They can't be bonded to you and the Keeper both. That whole concept is crazy."

"I thought so too. Sister Ulicia convinced me that I was only looking at it from my perspective. She wanted to swear loyalty and in return I got to ask where Kahlan was. They had to answer truthfully to honor their bond. They then were to leave. If I asked any more than that it would break our agreement and we would all be back where we started—them subjects of Jagang and Kahlan a captive. Sister Ulicia said that after swearing their bond to me and my asking one question, they would then leave. They got the bond, I got Kahlan."

"But they're Sisters of the Dark!"

"Sister Ulicia said that if they didn't actively try to kill me thereafter they considered that to definitely be to my benefit so that was in their view conforming to the requirements of their bond, since not killing me was what I wanted, therefore keeping their bond to me intact."

Nicci turned away, one hand on a hip. "In an odd sort of way, that actually makes sense. Sister Ulicia is more than devious. That's the way she thinks."

Nicci turned back. "What am I saying? Now you're starting to suck me into your delusions. Richard, stop this. Look, you have to get out of here, and you have to do it now. Come on. Cara will be right behind me with your things."

Richard knew that Nicci was right. He couldn't find Kahlan if he had to worry about warding off three people with the gift who knew quite well how to use it and wanted to alter his very thoughts. They weren't likely to give him any chance to explain anything. He had already tried explanations and that hadn't worked.

They would most likely do what they thought they had to do. Richard didn't believe that they would give him any warning. Before he knew what had hit him it would be over.

He hated to admit it to himself, but he knew that Zedd was capable of such a thing. After giving Richard the Sword of Truth, when they were on their way to try to recover the boxes of Orden that Darken Rahl had put into play, Zedd had once said that so many lives were at stake that he would not hesitate to kill even Richard, if necessary, to save all those innocent people. He had told Richard how, to be the Seeker and carry the Sword of Truth, he had to be ready to be just as committed to their cause, that he had to understand the larger picture.

It was hardly out of the question to imagine Zedd now being willing to use magic to try to erase Richard's memory of Kahlan—a memory that Zedd thought was a sickness that was harming him and their cause and thereby endangering the lives of millions.

"I think you're right," Richard admitted in a dejected voice. "They will try to stop me." He picked up the two small books lying on the table and slipped them into a back pocket. "I think we had better get out of here before they can do that."

"We? You want me to go with you?"

Richard paused and shrugged self-consciously. "Nicci, you and Cara are the only true friends I have right now. You've been there to help me when I needed it most. I can't afford to leave valued friends behind just when I'm beginning to figure out what's going on. Once I do have it figured out I may need your help with it, but even if I don't I'd like you there with me just for the advice and support you give me.

"I mean, if you're willing to come. I'd not force you, of course, but I'd like you to come."

Nicci smiled that rare smile she had, the smile that revealed the nobility of the woman Nicci really was, the smile he had only seen since she had come to love life.

Cara stood impatiently waiting on the other side of the shield. Rikka, standing guard near the iron door, was watching out into the tower room. Both turned when they saw the red glow and heard Richard coming. He saw packs and other gear collected into a neat pile just inside the door. He pulled his pack out from among the others and stuffed the two books inside.

"We're leaving, then?" Cara asked.

Richard put his arms through the straps and hiked the pack up onto his back. "Yes, and I think we best not waste any time."

As he picked up his bow and quiver, everyone else started gathering their own things.

It appeared that Cara, wanting Nicci to be near Richard so that she would be handy to help protect him, had brought the sorceress's things along as well. Richard wondered how much of wanting Nicci along had to do with what Shota had said.

He saw that Rikka, too, had a pack. He almost asked her what she thought she was doing, but realized then that she was Mord-Sith and she would say that her place was with him. He had spent so much time with only Cara protecting him that he thought it would feel a bit odd having more than one Mord-Sith around again.

"Everyone ready?" he asked as he saw them all tightening straps and buckles.

After each woman nodded, Richard led the grim-faced group out the doorway. He knew that Cara might have followed him without question, but she wouldn't blindly follow Nicci or anyone else's orders without good reason, so he suspected that Cara had probably asked a lot of pointed questions—something Mord-Sith were wont to do—and found out why they had to leave.

At the base of the tower, Richard ran his hand along the iron railing as he started around the walkway, but then a sudden realization brought him to a halt. Everyone waited, watching him, wondering why he had stopped.

Richard looked at Nicci's puzzled blue eyes. "They're not going to trust you in this."

"What do you mean?" Nicci asked.

"It's too important. They aren't going to leave it to you to do as they instructed. They will be concerned that you'll lose your courage, or that you might fail and allow me to slip away."

Cara stepped closer. "You mean you think they will come looking for you?"

"No, not looking for me," Richard said, "but I bet that somewhere between here and the way out of the Keep they will be lying in wait, just in case I get past Nicci and try to leave. If we come upon them unexpectedly then it will be too late."

"Lord Rahl," Rikka said, "Mistress Cara and I would not allow anyone to harm you."

Richard lifted an eyebrow. "I'd just as soon not have it come to that. Those three think they need to help me. They aren't intent on harming me—at least not intentionally. I don't want you two to hurt them."

"But if they surprise us with the intent of using their magic on you, you can't expect us to let them do it," Cara said.

Richard met her gaze for a moment. "Like I said, I don't want it to come to that."

"Lord Rahl," Cara said in a low voice, "I simply can't allow anyone to attack you in such a way, even if they think it's to help you. You can't equivocate in a situation like that. If they attack you, it must be stopped— period. If they were allowed to succeed, then you would never be the same again. You would no longer be the Lord Rahl we know, the Lord Rahl you are."

Cara leaned even closer and fixed him with that look that Mord-Sith had that always made him sweat. "If they do attack you and are allowed to succeed because you fear to harm them, then when they are finished you will no longer remember this woman, Kahlan. Is that what you want?"

Richard clenched his jaw as he let out a deep breath. "No, it's not. Let's try to avoid having it come to such things. But if it does, then I guess you're right. They can't be allowed to do as they intend. But if we must stop them, let's not use any more force than necessary."

"Hesitation is a mistake that invites defeat," Cara said. "I would not be Mord-Sith had I not hesitated when I was young."

Richard knew she was right. The Sword of Truth had taught him that much, at least. The dance with death allowed no compromise between life and death.

He laid a hand on Cara's shoulder. "I understand."

Nicci gazed up the tower, her blue eyes taking in the doors all around it. "Where do you think they will wait?"

"I don't know," Richard said as he hooked his thumbs under the shoulder straps of his pack. "The Wizard's Keep is immense, but in the end there's only one way out. Since there are so many routes we could take, I'd guess it will be when we get nearer the courtyard out to the portcullis."

"Lord Rahl," Rikka spoke up, looking a little uneasy once he met her gaze, "there is another way out."

Richard frowned at her. "What are you talking about?"

"There is another way out besides the main entrance. It is only accessible through passages deep in the Keep."

"How do you know such a thing?"

"Your grandfather showed it to me."

Richard didn't have time to wonder at such a thing. "Do you think you can find it again?"

Rikka considered a moment. "I believe so," she finally said. "I sure wouldn't want to get us lost down in the Keep, but I believe I can find the way. Starting out from here we're already part of the way, so it won't be quite so hard."

Richard went to rest his hand on the hilt of his sword as he considered. The sword wasn't there. He rubbed his palms together, instead.

"Maybe it would be better if we went that way."

Rikka turned, her blond braid whipping around as she did so, and started away. "Follow me, then."

Richard let Nicci go ahead of him, then followed, letting Cara bring up the rear. He hadn't gone a dozen steps when he stopped. He turned and looked back.

Everyone glanced to where he was looking and then watched him, puzzled by what he could be thinking.

"We can't go that way, either." He turned back to Rikka. "Zedd showed you that way out of the keep. He knows Mord-Sith. he knows that despite how well you two got along, if presented with a choice, your loyalties will fall to me.

"Zedd is fond of using tricks. He will let Ann and Nathan guard the routes to the main entrance to the Keep. He will lie in wait on the route he showed you, Rikka."

"Well, if there are only two ways out," Nicci said, "that means they will have to split up to make sure both are blocked. That's if Zedd goes through the thought process as you've laid it out. He might forget that he told Rikka about the other way out, or he might not think that she would tell you. That way still might be clear."

Richard slowly shook his head as he stared off at something else—the wide platform partway back around the walkway around the stagnant water in the bottom of the gloomy interior of the tower.

"While what you say is possible, counting on Zedd to make such a strategic mistake would be foolish."

Nicci was looking a bit worried. "Well, you can't use your power without chancing calling the beast, but I certainly can use mine. And I have more power at my command than Zedd does. If they split up as you suggest, then we will not have all three to contend with at once."

"No, but I'd not like to have that kind of a test, especially not in the Keep. It's possible that there are defenses here that he has initiated to protect the First Wizard should he be attacked. You might simply try to catch him up in a conjured tangle to slow him down while we escape and it might be all it takes to trigger something lethal. Besides, even if you do manage to succeed at such a thing, he could still come after us.

Nicci folded her arms. "Then what, exactly, do you suggest we do?"

He turned back and once again met her blue eyes. "I suggest that we take a way out that they can't follow."

Her nose wrinkled up. "What?"

"The sliph."

Everyone looked back down the walkway as if the sliph might be standing there waiting for them to come and travel with her.

"Of course," Cara said. "We could escape without them ever knowing where we've gone. There will be no tracks. More than that, though, it can put us a tremendous distance away from the danger. They will have no hope of ever following us."

"Exactly." Richard clapped her on the back of the shoulder. "Let's go."

They all followed him as he rushed down the walkway and through the blasted open doorway. Inside the sliph's room, Nicci cast magic, igniting the torches in brackets on the walls as they all gathered around the well. Everyone peered down together.

"There's only one problem," Richard said out loud as the thought came to him while gazing down into the black abyss. He looked up at Nicci. "I have to use magic to call the sliph."

Nicci took a deep breath and let it out with a discouraged look. "That is a problem."

"Not necessarily," Cara said. "Shota told us that using your magic had the potential to call the blood beast. But it acts randomly. When you use magic, it would be logical that it would thus find you, but the beast doesn't act through logic. It might come when you use magic, Shota said, or it might not. There's no way to tell or predict."

"And we're pretty certain that we're not going to be able to walk out of this place without having to confront the others," Nicci pointed out.

"Trying to run will present two problems," Richard said, "getting past them and then keeping out of their grasp to prevent them from trying to 'heal me.' This makes more sense. The sliph would be a certain way to escape without Zedd, Ann, and Nathan having any way to either follow or know where I went—and it would also avoid confronting them, something I'd not like to have to do. I love my grandfather; I don't want to have to defend myself against him."

"I almost hate to say it," Cara said, "but this makes more sense to me, too."

"I agree," Rikka said.

"Call the sliph." Nicci held a handful of her hair back as she looked down to peer into the well again. "And hurry, before they come looking to see what's taking me so long."

Richard didn't hesitate. He stretched his fists out over the well. He needed to call his own gift in order to call the sliph and calling his own ability was not something he was good at. He resolved that he had done it before; he would have to do it again.

He let his tension go. He knew that he had to do this or he very well might lose his chance to ever find the one woman he loved more than life itself. For a moment, the pain of how much he hurt every day without her nearly made him pull inward with the aching misery of it.

With his sincere and burning need to do whatever he must in order to help Kahlan, his need ignited deep within him. He felt it roaring up from the core of his being, taking his breath. He tightened his abdominal muscles against the power of the feeling within him.

Light ignited between his outstretched fists. He recognized the sensation from having done it before. He pressed the padded silver-leather wristbands he wore together. He had not had these the first time, but they were what the sliph had told him he should use to call her again. They brightened to such intensity that through his flesh and bone Richard could see the other side of the heavy silver bands.

He focused his intent. He wanted nothing else but for the sliph to come to him so that he could help Kahlan. He hungered for it. He demanded it be done.

Come to me!

The glow of light wailed as it ignited in a line down the center of the well, like a lightning bolt, but instead of the sound of thunder, the air crackled with the ripping roar of fire and light racing away at incredible speed into the depths of blackness.

Those around the stone wall gazed anxiously down inside the well lit by the flash of light. Nicci also glanced around, keeping an eye on the room around them, apparently worried about the appearance of the beast. The echo of the power Richard had sent down into the well was a long time in fading away, but at last all fell silent.

In the stillness of the Keep, in the quiet of the mountain of dead stone towering around and above them, came a distant, deep rumbling.

A rumbling of something coming to life.

The floor began to quake with growing force, until it began lifting dust from the joints and cracks. Small pebbles danced on the trembling stone floor.

Far down in the distant depths the well began filling with something rushing up the shaft at impossible speed, roaring with a howling shriek of velocity as it came. The howl grew as the sliph rushed upward to meet the call.

Nicci, Cara, and Rikka backed away from the well as shimmering silver shot upward, coming to an instantaneous stop that somehow seemed graceful.

Within the undulating silver pool, a lustrous metallic hump mounded up, rising above the edge of the stone wall surrounding the well. It drew up into a bulk, rising of its own accord, gathering into a recognizable shape. Its glossy surface, like a liquid mirror, reflected everything around the room, distorting the images reflected off its surface as it grew and transformed.

It looked like living quicksilver.

The rising shape continued to contort, bending into edges and planes, folds and curves, until it warped into a woman's face.

A silver smile widened in what seemed to be recognition. "Master, you called me?"

The sliph's eerie, feminine voice echoed around the room, but her lips hadn't moved.

Richard stepped closer, ignoring Nicci and Rikka's wide-eyed astonishment. "Yes. Sliph, thank you for coming. I need you."

A silver smile was pleased. "You wish to travel, Master?"

"Yes, I wish to travel. We all do. We all need to travel."

The smile widened. "Come, then. We will travel."

Richard herded everyone close to the wall. Liquid metal formed into a hand that reached out to touch each of the three women in turn.

"You have traveled before," the sliph said to Cara after only brief contact with her forehead. "You may travel."

The glistening hand gently brushed a palm across Nicci's brow, lingering for a bit longer. "You have what is required. You may travel."

Rikka lifted her chin, ignoring her distaste for magic, and stood her ground as the sliph touched her forehead.

"You may not travel," the sliph said.

Rikka looked indignant. "But, but, if Cara can—why can't I?"

"You do not have both sides required," said the voice.

Rikka folded her arms defiantly. "I must go with them. I'm going, too. That's all there is to it."

"It is your choice, but if you try to travel in me, you will die, and then you will not be with them either."

Richard laid a hand on Rikka's arm before she could say anything else. "Cara captured the power of someone who had an element of the required magic; that's why she can travel. There is nothing to be done about it. You have to stay here."

Rikka didn't look at all happy, but she nodded. "The rest of you had better get going, then."

"Come," the sliph said to Richard, "and we will travel. To which place do you wish to travel?"

Richard almost said it aloud, but then stopped himself. He turned to Rikka.

"You can't come with us. I think you had better leave now, so that you don't even hear where I'm going. I don't want to take the chance that if you know, then the others might somehow find out. My grandfather can be clever when he wants to be and pull tricks to get his way."

"You don't need to tell me." Rikka sighed in resignation. "You're probably right, Lord Rahl." She smiled at Cara. "Protect him."

Cara nodded. "I always do. He's pretty helpless without me."

Richard ignored Cara's boast. "Rikka, I need you to tell Zedd something for me. I need you to give him a message."

Rikka frowned as she listened intently.

"Tell him that four Sisters of the Dark have captured Kahlan, the real Mother Confessor, not the body buried down in Aydindril. Tell him that I intend to come back as soon as I can and I will bring him the proof. I ask that when I return, before he tries to cure me, he allow me to show him the evidence I will bring. And tell him that I love him and understand his concern for me, but that I'm doing as the Seeker must do, as he himself charged me to do when he gave me the Sword of Truth."

When Rikka had gone, Cara asked, "What evidence?"

"I don't know. I haven't found it yet." Richard turned to Nicci. "Don't forget what I told you before. You have to breathe in the sliph once we go under. At first you'll want to hold your breath, but that just isn't possible. Once we arrive and come up out of the sliph, you must let her out of your lungs and again breathe in the air."

Nicci was looking more than a little nervous. Richard took her hand. "I'll be with you, as will Cara. We've both done this before. I won't let go of you. It's hard to make yourself breathe in the sliph for the first time, but once you do, you will see that it's quite a remarkable experience. It's rapture to breathe the sliph."

"Rapture," Nicci repeated with more than just a little incredulity.

"Lord Rahl is right," Cara said. "You'll see."

"Just remember," Richard added, "when it ends you will not want to let go of the sliph and breathe air again—but you must. If you don't, you'll die. Do you understand?"

"Of course," Nicci said with a nod.

"Come on then." Richard started to climb up on the wall, pulling Nicci up with him.

"Where will we travel, Master?"

"I think we should go to the People's Palace, in D'Hara. Do you know the place?"

"Of course. The People's Palace is a central site."

"A central site?"

If living quicksilver could be said to look puzzled by a question, the sliph looked puzzled. "Yes, a central site. Like this place here is a central site."

Richard didn't understand, but didn't think it was relevant and so didn't press the issue. "I see."

"Why the People's Palace," Nicci asked.

Richard shrugged. "We have to go somewhere. We'll be safe at the Palace. But more importantly, they have libraries there with rare ancient books. I'm hoping that maybe we can find something about Chainfire. Since the Sisters have Kahlan, I'm thinking that Chainfire might have something to do with some kind of magic.

"From what we've heard, the D'Haran army is somewhere in the vicinity on their way south. What's more, the last time I saw Berdine, another Mord-Sith, was when I left her here in Aydindril, so she will probably be either close to our troops or the palace. I need her to help me translate some of the material from the books I'm bringing along. Besides that, she has Kolo's journal and she may already know something helpful."

He glanced at Cara. "Maybe we can see General Meiffert and see how things are going with the troops."

Cara's face lit with surprise and a broad grin.

Nicci nodded thoughtfully. "I guess all that makes sense, and I guess it's as good a place as any. It gets you out of immediate danger and that's what matters most right now."

"All right, sliph," Richard said, "we wish to travel to the People's Palace in D'Hara."

A liquid silver arm came up and slipped around all three of them. Richard felt the warm, undulating grip compressing to get a firm grasp on him. Nicci had his hand in a death grip.

TERRY GOODKIND

"Lord Rahl?" Cara asked.

Richard held up the hand that wasn't holding Nicci's to halt the sliph before she could lift them into the well. "What?"

Cara bit her lip before finally speaking. "You're holding Nicci's hand. Will you hold my hand, too? I mean, I wouldn't want the three of us to get separated."

Richard tried not to smile at the worry on her face. Cara feared magic, even if she had already done this before.

"Sure," Richard said as he took her hand. "I wouldn't want us to get separated."

A sudden thought struck him.

"Wait!" he said, stopping the sliph before she could start.

"Yes, Master?"

"Do you know a person named Kahlan? Kahlan Amnell, the Mother Confessor?"

"This name means nothing to me."

Richard sighed in disappointment. He hadn't really expected the sliph to know Kahlan. No one else did, either.

"Would you happen to know a place called the Deep Nothing?"

"I know several places in the Deep Nothing. Some have been destroyed, but some still exist. I can travel to them if you wish."

Richard's heart quickened in surprise. "Are any of these places in the Deep Nothing also a central site?"

"Yes, one of them," the sliph said. "Caska, in the Deep Nothing, is a central site. Would you like to travel there?"

Richard glanced to both Nicci and Cara. "Do either of you know this place, Caska?"

Nicci shook her head.

Cara was frowning. "I think I remember hearing something about it when I was little. I'm sorry Lord Rahl, but I don't remember exactly what—just that the name sounds familiar from old legends."

"What do you mean, legends?"

Cara shrugged. "Old D'Haran legends . . . something about dream casters. Stories people told. Something about the history of D'Hara. It seems like Caska is a name from olden times."

Olden times. Dream casters. Richard remembered that when he'd skimmed through some of the book *Gegendrauss* that he'd found back in the shielded room, he had seen something about casting dreams, but he hadn't translated the passage. Even though Richard was the leader of the D'Haran Empire, he knew very little about the mysterious D'Hara.

Even if Cara didn't know more, Richard still felt as if he had just taken a step closer to finding Kahlan.

"We wish to travel," he said to the sliph. "We wish to travel to Caska, in the Deep Nothing."

It had been a long time since Richard had traveled in the sliph and he felt a bit apprehensive. But his excitement that he was finally making connections to find the answers that had for so long eluded him swept away any concern.

"We travel to Caska, then," the sliph said, her voice echoing around the stone room where once Kolo had died standing guard over her as the great war had come to an end. At least, everyone thought it had come to an end, but those ancient conflicts had not ended so easily and now they had again flared to life.

The arm lifted all three of them off the wall and plunged them down into the silver froth. Nicci's grip on his hand tightened and she gasped in a breath before going under.

With an arrow's speed, Richard flew through the silken silence of the sliph, yet at the same time he glided with the slow grace of a raven riding the stilled currents above towering trees on a moonlit night. There was no heat, no cold. In the silence, sweet sounds filled his mind. His eyes beheld light and dark together in a single, spectral vision, while his lungs swelled with the sweet presence of the sliph as he breathed her into his soul.

It was rapture.

Abruptly, it ended.

Grainy darkness exploded in his sudden vision. There seemed to be blocky shapes all around as he broke the surface. Nicci's hand gripped his in terror.

Breathe, the sliph told him.

Richard let out the sweet breath, emptying his lungs of the rapture. With a needful gasp, he sucked in the alien air. Cara, too, gasped in the hot, dusty air.

Nicci floated face down, rocking gently in the silver fluid.

Richard threw an arm over the stone wall at the side of the sliph, pulling Nicci with him. He took his bow off his back to get it out of his way and quickly set it against the outside of the wall. With the sliph's help, he hopped up on the wall, and then with the sliph lifting her, pulled the dead weight of Nicci up enough to get her shoulders and head up into the warm, dark air.

Richard slapped her on the back. "Breathe, Nicci. Breathe. Come on, you have to let go of the sliph and breathe. Do it for me."

At last she did. She gasped in the air, her arms flailing in terror at being confused and lost in such strange surroundings. Richard pulled her close as he helped her get her arms over the side and, panting, climb up on the wall.

Brackets on the walls nearby held glass spheres, like back at the Keep, that glowed brighter as he climbed out of the well.

"What do you think this place is?" Cara asked as she peered around in the dim light.

"That was . . . rapture," Nicci said, still under the sway of the experience.

"I told you," Richard said as he helped her climb out.

"It looks like we're in a stone room of some kind," Cara said as she walked around the perimeter of the room.

Richard made his way toward the darkness at one end and two larger spheres in tall iron brackets brightened with an eerie green glow. He saw that they flanked steps. The steps, though, marched up to the ceiling.

"That's pretty strange," Cara said as she stood on the second step, inspecting the dark ceiling.

"Here," Nicci said. She was leaning over to the side of the steps. "There's a metal plate."

It was the kind of metal plate Richard had seen in other places. They were trigger plates for shields. Nicci tapped her palm against it but nothing happened.

Richard pressed his hand to the icy cold plate and stone started grating as it moved. Dust came down in streamers.

The three of them ducked back as they all peered around in the gloomy light, trying to figure out what, exactly, was moving. The ground trembled. It felt like the whole room might be shifting and somehow changing shape. Richard then realized that it was actually the ceiling that was pulling aside.

A growing patch of moonlight fell across the steps.

Richard had no idea where they were, other than down in a stone room that appeared to be buried. He didn't know where Caska was, other than the sliph said that it was in the Deep Nothing, and he didn't know where that was, so he didn't really know what to expect. He felt decidedly uneasy.

He reached for his sword.

The sword wasn't there. For what felt like the thousandth time, he felt the sinking regret of realizing why and where it now was.

He drew his long knife instead as he started up the steps in a crouch, ducking low not only so as not to hit his head on the ceiling before it had moved out of the way, but out of caution for who might be outside and have heard stone sliding aside. Cara, seeing him draw his knife, spun her Agiel up into her fist. She tried to get out ahead of him, but he held his arm out, keeping her behind to the left. Nicci was close behind to his right.

As he came up out of the ground, he saw the shadowed shapes of three people standing not far ahead. He knew that from being in the sliph, until he fully recovered, his vision was more acute than ordinary. He could probably see them better than they could see him.

With that sharp vision, Richard saw that the big man in the middle was holding a slender girl back against him. He had one hand over her mouth. He could see the girl squirming. Moonlight gleamed off the blade he held to her throat.

"Drop your weapons," the man holding the girl growled, "and surrender to the Imperial Order, or you will die."

Richard flipped the knife into the air, let it make a half turn, and caught it by the tip. An inky shape suddenly swooped atop the man's head. The bird let out a piercing caw. The man flinched. Richard didn't take the time to wonder at such an unexpected assault. He heaved the knife.

On broad wings, the bird lifted into the air. The blade hit the man in the center of his face with a solid thunk. Richard knew that the blade was long enough to have penetrated all the way through the man's brain and that the tip would have pierced the back of the skull. The man dropped straight down behind the trembling girl—dead before he could think to do her harm.

Before the men to either side of the girl could take a half a step, Nicci unleashed a scything whisper of power that took the heads off the other two men. The only noise it made was the sound of the heads hitting the ground with twin, dull thuds. The bodies toppled to either side of the girl.

The night was still but for the drone of cicadas.

The girl hesitantly stepped closer and dropped to her knees. She bent forward before the steps until her forehead touched the stone at his feet.

"Lord Rahl, I am your humble servant. Thank you for coming and protecting me. I live only to serve. My life is yours. Command me as you will."

Even as the girl was still speaking in a quavering voice, Cara and Nicci were spreading out to the sides, searching for other threats. Richard crossed his lips with a finger to let them know to be quiet about it so as not to alert any other troops that might be near. Both saw his signal and nodded.

Richard waited, listening for any threat. Since the girl was on the ground, he let her stay there, out of harm's way. He heard the whisper of feathers against air as the raven landed on a nearby limb and then the soft rustle as it folded in its wings.

"It's clear," Nicci announced in a quiet voice as she returned from the shadows. "My Han tells me there are no others in the immediate vicinity."

Relieved, Richard let the tension go out of his muscles. When he heard the girl weeping in quiet terror, he sat down on the top step right near her. He suspected her terror was fear that she might be killed just as the three men had been. Richard wanted to assure her that she was not going to die.

"It's all right," he told her as he gently grasped her shoulders and urged her up. "I'm not going to hurt you. You're safe, now."

As she came up he gathered the frightened girl into his arms, embracing her protectively, holding her head to his shoulder when she glanced to the three dead men as if they still might jump up and snatch her away. She was a slender lithesome creature, the kind of girl on the brink of being a woman, yet looking as frail as a bird about to leave the nest. Her slender arms came gratefully around Richard as she wept with relief.

"The bird a friend of yours?" he asked.

"Lokey," she confirmed with a nod. "He watches over me."

"Well, he did a good job tonight."

"I thought you weren't going to come, Master Rahl. I thought it was my fault, that I wasn't a good enough priestess for you."

Richard ran a hand down the back of her head. "How did you know I was coming here?"

"The tellings say it is so. But I already waited so long that I thought they might be wrong. I was near to despairing that you would find us not worthy, and then I feared it was my failing"

He surmised that the "tellings" must mean prophecy of some sort. "You are a priestess, you say?"

She nodded as she pulled back to look up at his smile. Richard saw then that her big copper-colored eyes peered out from a dark mask painted in a band around her face. It was a disturbing visage.

"I am the priestess of the bones. You have returned to help me. I am your servant. I am the one meant to cast the dreams."

"Returned?"

"To life. You have come back from the dead."

Richard could only stare.

Nicci squatted down beside the girl. "What do you mean, he returned from the dead?"

The girl pointed behind them, at the structure from where they had emerged. "From the world of the dead . . . back to we the living. It says his name there, on his tomb."

Richard turned and indeed did see his name carved in the monument. The thing that came immediately to mind was seeing Kahlan's name carved in stone, too. Both of them were alive, despite their graves.

The girl glanced at Cara and then at Nicci. "The tellings say that you will come back to life, Lord Rahl, but they did not say that you would bring your spirit familiars."

"I haven't come back from the dead," Richard told her. "I came through the sliph—down there, in that well."

She nodded. "The well of the dead. The tellings mention such mysterious things, but I never knew their meaning."

"Do I call you 'priestess,' or by your name?"

"You are Master Rahl; you can call me as it pleases you. My name is Jillian, though. I have had that name my whole life. I'm afraid I have not been a priestess a long time, and so I'm not very good at it, I don't think. My grandfather said that when it is time, it matters not how old I am, but that it is time."

"How about if I call you Jillian, then?" he asked with a smile.

She appeared still too frightened to return the smile. "I would like that, Master Rahl."

"My name is Richard. I'd like it if you called me Richard."

She nodded, still with that look of awe filling her round eyes. Richard didn't know if her awe was at the Master Rahl, or a dead man returned to life and walking up out of his grave.

"Now look, Jillian, I don't know anything about your tellings, yet, but you need to understand that I haven't returned from the dead. I traveled here because I have trouble and I'm looking for answers."

"You have found the trouble, then. You killed three of them. The answer is for you to help me cast the dreams so that we might drive these evil men away. They have driven most of my people into hiding. The older ones are down there." She pointed down the dark slope. "They tremble in fear that these men will kill them if they do not find what they seek."

"What are they looking for?" Richard asked.

"I'm not sure. I have been hiding among the spirits of our ancestors. The men must have made someone down there tell them of me because they knew my name when they finally chased me down, today. I have been staying out of their grasp for a long time. Today they were hiding where I had cached some food. The men grabbed me and wanted me to show them where the books are."

"These aren't the regular Imperial Order troops," Nicci explained to the frowning look on his face. "They're advance scouts."

Richard glanced at the bodies. "How do you know?"

"Because regular Imperial Order troops would never ask you to put down your weapons and surrender. Only the scouts, searching routes through strange lands and hunting for any information they can uncover would take prisoners. They question people. Those who won't talk are sent back to be tortured. These scouts are the men who first find stashes of books that are then collected for the emperor to see. Scouts like this find not only the best routes for the troops, but they are meant to find something even more important for the emperor: knowledge, especially that in books."

Richard knew the truth of that. Jagang seemed to be an expert on history and what had been done in ancient times. He used that information to great advantage. It seemed like Richard was always trying to catch up with what Jagang already knew.

"Have these men found any of the books, yet?" Richard asked Jillian.

Her copper-colored eyes blinked. "My grandfather has told me about books, but I know of none that are here. The city has been abandoned since ancient times. If there were books, they have long ago been looted along with anything else of value."

That was not what Richard had hoped to hear. He had been hoping that maybe there would be something here that would help answer the questions he had. After all, Shota had told him that he must find the place of the bones in the Deep Nothing. The graveyard all around him certainly was a place of bones.

"This place is called the Deep Nothing?" he asked her.

Jillian nodded. "It is a vast land where little lives. None but my people can scrape a life from this forbidding place. People have always feared to come here. The bleached bones of those who do venture here are out there, in this place and to the south, before the great barrier. The land is called the Deep Nothing."

Richard realized that it must be a place much like the wilds in the Midlands.

"The great barrier?" Cara asked, suspiciously.

Jillian looked up at the Mord-Sith. "The great barrier that protects us from the Old World."

"This has to be southern D'Hara," Cara told him. "That's why I heard stories about Caska when I was a child—because it's in D'Hara."

Jillian pointed. "This is the place of my ancestors. They were destroyed by those from the Old World back in ancient times. They, too, were ones who cast dreams." She looked off into the darkness to the south. "But they failed and were destroyed."

Richard didn't have time to try to figure it all out. He had enough problems.

"Have you ever heard of Chainfire?"

Jillian frowned. "No. What is Chainfire?"

"I don't know." He tapped a finger against his bottom lip as he thought about what to do next.

"Richard," Jillian said, "you must help me cast the dreams that will drive these men away so that my people will be safe again."

Richard glanced up at Nicci. "Any ideas how I can do such a thing?"

"No," she said. "But I can tell you that the rest of the men will sooner or later come looking for these three dead men. These aren't your average Imperial Order soldiers. They may be brutes, but they are the smartest of them. I imagine that casting dreams is something that involves your gift . . . not an advisable thing to be doing," she added.

Richard stood up and put one hand on a hip as he stared off at the dark city on the headland.

"Seek what is long buried . . ." he whispered to himself. He turned back to Jillian. "You said that you were a priestess of the bones. I need you to show me everything you know about the bones."

Jillian shook her head. "First you must help me cast the dreams so that I can chase the strangers away and my grandfather and the rest of our people will be safe."

Richard sighed in frustration. "Look, Jillian, I don't know how to help you cast dreams and I don't have time to figure it out. But I would imagine, as Nicci said, that it involves magic, and I can't use magic or it very well could call a beast that could kill all of your people. This beast has already killed a lot of my friends who were with me. I need you to show me what you know about what is long buried."

Jillian wiped at her tears. "Those men have my grandfather and others down there. They will kill him. You must save my grandfather first. Besides, he is a teller. He knows more than me."

Richard put a reassuring hand on her shoulder. He could not imagine how he would feel if someone whom he thought was powerful refused to help save his grandfather.

"I have an idea," Nicci said. "I'm a sorceress, Jillian. I know all about these men and how they work. I know how to handle them. You help Richard, and while you do that I'll go down there and see to getting rid of these men. When I'm done they will no longer be a danger to you or your people."

"If I help Richard, you will help my grandfather?"

Nicci smiled. "I promise."

Jillian looked up at Richard.

"Nicci keeps her word," he told her.

"All right. I will show Richard everything I know about this place while you make those men leave us be."

"Cara," Richard said, "go with Nicci and watch her back."

"And who will watch yours?"

Richard put a boot on the head of the man he had killed and yanked his knife free. He pointed with the weapon. "Lokey will watch our backs."

Cara did not look amused. "A raven is going to watch your back."

He wiped the blade clean on the man's shirt, then returned the knife to its sheath at his belt. "The priestess of the bones will watch over me. After all, she's been here waiting all this time for me to come here. Nicci is the one who will be in danger. I'd appreciate it if you protected her."

Cara glanced at Nicci as if grasping some greater meaning. "I will protect her for you, Lord Rahl."

As Nicci and Cara started down toward where Jillian said the rest of the Imperial Order soldiers were, Richard went back into his tomb and recovered the smallest of the glass spheres. He slipped it into his pack so that it wouldn't interfere with his night vision, but would be handy if they had to go into any of the buildings of the city. Searching ancient decaying buildings in the dark was not a prospect he relished.

Jillian was like a cat that knew every nook and cranny of the ancient city on the headland. They went through streets that had nearly disappeared under rubble and wreckage of walls long since fallen. Some of the debris had collected weather-borne dust and dirt that had eventually filled it in, making small hills where trees now grew among the buildings. There were a number of buildings Richard didn't want to enter because he could see that they were ready to collapse if the wind blew the wrong way. Others were still in relatively good condition.

One of the larger buildings Jillian took him to had arches all along the front that at one time had probably held windows, or maybe had even been open to what seemed an inner courtyard. As Richard walked across the floor, small bits of crumbled mortar crunched underfoot. A mosaic made of tiny square colored tiles covered the entire floor. The colors were long since faded, but Richard could still make them out well enough to see that the swirling lines of tiles made up a sprawling picture of trees dotting a landscape surrounded by a wall, with paths through places where there were graves.

"This building is the entrance to a section of the graveyard," Jillian told him.

Richard frowned as he leaned down a little, studying the picture. There was something odd about it. Moonlight fell across figures in the mosaic that were carrying platters with breads and what looked like meats into the graveyard, while other figures were coming back with empty platters.

Richard straightened when he heard a horrifying cry drift up to them from the far distance, both he and Jillian stood up stock still, listening. More of the distant, faint wails and laments drifted in on the cool night air.

"What was that?" Jillian asked in a whisper, her copper-colored eyes wide.

"I think Nicci is getting rid of the invaders. Your people will be safe once she is finished."

"You mean she is hurting them?"

Richard could see that such concepts were alien to the girl. "These are men who would do terrible things to your people—including your grandfather. If they are left to come back another day, they will kill your people."

She turned and looked back out through the arches. "That wouldn't be good. But the dreams would have driven them away."

"Did casting dreams save your ancestors? Save the people of this city?"

She looked back to his eyes. "I guess not."

"What matters most is that people who value life, like you, your grandfather, and your people are safe to live their lives. Sometimes that means it's necessary to eliminate those who would do you harm."

She swallowed. "Yes, Lord Rahl."

He put a hand on her shoulder and smiled. "Richard. I am a Lord Rahl who wants people to be safe to live as they wish."

At last she smiled.

Richard looked back to the mosaic, studying the picture. "Do you know what this means? This picture?"

Finally pulling herself away from the distant, ghastly screams of pain that drifted in from the darkness, she looked down at the picture. "See this wall here?" she asked as she pointed. "The tellings say that these walls held the graves of the people of the city. This place, here, is where we are, now. This place is the passage to the dead.

"The tellings say that there were always dead, but only this place to put them within the city walls. The people didn't want their loved ones to be far from them, far from what they considered the sacred place for their ancestors, so they made passages where they could find resting places for them."

Shota's words echoed around in his memory.

You must find the place of the bones in the Deep Nothing.

What you seek is long buried.

"Show me this place," he told Jillian. "Take me back there."

It was more difficult to reach than he had expected it would be. There was a labyrinth of passages and rooms back through the building. Some of it went between walls that were open to the stars, only to reenter the dark depths of the building.

"This is the way of the dead," Jillian explained. "The deceased were brought in through here. It is said that it was made this way in the hopes that the souls of the dead would be confused by the passages and these new spirits would not be able to wander back out. Instead, confined in this place and unable to come back among the living, they would then go on to be where they belonged in the spirit world."

They at last came back out into the night. The crescent moon was rising above the ancient city of Caska. Lokey circled above and called down to his friend. She waved back. The graveyard spread out before him was good sized, but seemed inadequate for a city.

Richard walked with Jillian on the path through the crowded graves. Gnarled trees stood in places. In the moonlight it was a peaceful place, with wild flowers spread across the rising and falling contour of the land.

"Where are the passages you spoke of?" he asked her.

"I'm sorry, Richard, but I don't know. The tellings speak of them, but do not say how to find them."

Richard searched the graveyard, Jillian at his side, as the moon rose higher in the sky, and he could not find any evidence of passages. It all looked like any graveyard he had ever seen. Some of the ground was mounded with a number of markers. The stones for each grave were crowded close. Some yet stood, while others had long since fallen to lie flat on the ground, or be grown over.

Richard was running out of time. He couldn't stay down in Caska, forever listening to the cicadas sing. This was getting him nowhere. He needed to look for answers where he was apt to find them. This ancient place did not appear to be the place.

At the People's Palace in D'Hara there would be valuable books that Jagang had not yet been able to loot. It was more likely that he would find useful information there than in an empty graveyard.

He sat down on the side of a small hillock beneath an olive tree to consider what he might do.

"Do you know of any other place where there would be these passages that were mentioned in the tellings?"

Jillian's mouth twisted as she considered. "I'm sorry, but no. When it is safe, we can go down and talk to my grandfather. He knows many things—much more than me."

Richard didn't know how much time he had to devote to listening to her grandfather's stories, either. Lokey fluttered down to the ground nearby to feast on the newly emerging cicadas. After the seventeen years they'd lived underground, more of them were emerging—only to be pecked up by the raven.

Richard recalled the prophecy Nathan had read to him. It had mentioned the cicadas. He wondered why. It had said something about when the cicadas awakened, the final and deciding battle was upon them. The world, it said, was at the brink of darkness.

Brink of darkness. Richard glanced down at the cicadas as they emerged. He watched them coming up out of the ground.

As he watched, he realized that they were all coming up through a space in a gravestone laying facedown against the rise of ground. Lokey had noticed, too, and stood eating them.

"That's odd," he said to himself.

"What's odd?"

"Well, look there. The cicadas aren't coming up through the dirt, they're coming up from under that stone."

Richard knelt down and pushed his fingers down into the space. It seemed hollow underneath. Lokey cocked his head as he watched. Richard lifted, grunting with the effort. The stone began to lift. As it came up, he realized that it was hinged on the left. It finally gave way and opened.

Richard stared down into the darkness. It wasn't a grave marker. It had been a stone cap to a passageway. He immediately pulled the glass sphere out of his pack. As it began to glow, he held it down in the dark maw.

Jillian gasped. "It's a stairway!"

"Come on, but be careful."

The stairs were stone, irregular, and narrow. The leading edge of each was swaybacked and rounded from countless feet making the journey. The passage was lined with blocks of stone, making a clear path down deep into the ground. The steps came to a landing and turned right. After another long run, they turned left and went deeper.

When they finally reached the bottom, the passage opened into wider corridors that were carved from the solid but soft rock of the ground itself.

Richard held the glowing globe out in one hand and Jillian's hand in his other as he bent a little to clear the low ceiling as he led them deeper. It wasn't long before they encountered an intersection.

"Do your tellings say anything about finding our way down here?" She shook her head. "How about all those mazes you learned. Do you think they will do you any good down here?"

"I don't know. I never knew this place existed."

Richard let out a breath as he looked down each of the two passages. "All right, I'll just start going in deeper. If you think you recognize anything, or any of the routes, let me know."

After she agreed, they started down the left fork. To each side of the narrow passageway they began finding niches that had been carved into the walls. Inside each lay the remains of a body. In places the niches were stacked three or five high. Some had two bodies, probably a husband and wife.

Around some of the recesses, ancient painting still remained. The artwork was vines in some places, people with food in others, and in some places simple designs. From the different styles and the varying quality of the art, Richard guessed that it must have been done by loved ones for a member of their family who had died.

The narrow passageway opened up into a chamber with ten openings tunneling off in various directions. Richard picked one and started down it. It, too, opened into broader spaces, with a warren of branches. The elevation changed, from time to time going down deeper, and occasionally going up a bit.

They soon began encountering the bones.

There were rooms with stacks of similar bones in niches. Skulls had been carefully fit into one niche, leg bones all stacked end out in another, arm bones in another yet. Great stone bins carved in the side walls held smaller bones all laid in neatly. As Richard and Jillian moved through vault after vault, they saw walls of skulls that had to number in the tens of thousands. Knowing that he was seeing only one random passageway, Richard could not imagine how many people had to be interred in the catacombs. Even as startling, and even horrifying, as it was to see so many of the dead, each of their bones looked to have been placed reverently. None were simply cast into a hole or a corner. Each had been carefully placed as if each had been a valued life.

For what had to be well over an hour, they made their way through the maze of tunnels. Each section was different. Some were wide, some narrow, some with rooms to each side. After a time, Richard realized that each spot must have been carved out of the soft rock to make space for a family; that was why the niches seemed to fill every available space in such a haphazard fashion.

And then they came to a section of the passage that had partially collapsed. A huge section of stone had toppled and rubble had fallen in around it.

Richard stopped and looked at the tangle of stone. "I guess this is as far as we go."

Jillian squatted down, peering under the stone block lying at an angle across the passageway. "I can see a way under here." She turned to Richard. Her copper-colored eyes looked frightening staring out from the black mask painted across her face. "I'm smaller. Do you want me to go have a quick look?"

Richard held the glowing sphere down in the opening to light it for her. "All right. But I don't want you to keep going if you think it looks dangerous. There are thousands of tunnels down here, so there are plenty others to look in."

"But this is the one the Lord Rahl found. It must be important."

"I'm just a man, Jillian. I'm not some wise spirit returned from the world of the dead."

"If you say so, Richard."

At least she smiled when she said it.

Jillian disappeared into the angular hole like a bird going through a thornbush.

"Lord Rahl!" came her echoing voice. "There are books in here."

"Books?" he called into the hole.

"Yes. A lot of books. It's dark, but it looks like a big room with books."

"I'm coming in," he said.

He had to take his pack off and push it out ahead as he crawled in. It turned out not to be as worrisome as he had feared, and he was soon through. When he stood on the other side, he realized that the huge stone block lying at an angle across the passage had once been a door. It looked like it had been designed to slide out of a slot cut into the side of the wall, but at some point the massive door had broken along a fault in the stone, and it had toppled over. As Richard inspected the mess, he brushed the dust away and saw one of the metal plates that activated a shield.

The idea that these books had been behind a shield made his heart race faster.

He turned back to the room. The warm light from the glowing sphere did indeed show a chamber full of books. The room ran at odd angles, seemingly without reason. Richard and Jillian walked along the passageway, looking at all the books. Most of the shelves were carved into the solid rock, the way the resting places for the dead had been cut out to make room.

Richard held the sphere up as he started scanning the shelves.

"Listen," he said to Jillian, "I'm looking for something specific: Chainfire. It might be a book. You start on one side, and I'll take the other. Make sure you look at each book's title."

Jillian nodded. "If it's in here, we will find it."

The ancient library was discouragingly huge. As they inched along and rounded a corner, they encountered a chamber lined with aisles of shelves. The search was slow going. They had to work in the same area so that they could both see.

For several hours, they painstakingly made their way through the room. Partway through, they encountered side chambers, smaller than the main room, but still full of books. From time to time they each had to blow dust off some of the spines.

Richard was tired and frustrated by the time they came to a spot where he saw another of the metal plates. He pressed the flat of his hand against it and the stone wall in front of them began to move. The door wasn't big, and it quickly pivoted open into blackness. He hoped that the shields keyed off what they recognized of his gift, and didn't actually work by making his power answer some silent, unfelt call. He'd not like to be down in the catacombs and have the beast materialize.

Richard stuck the light into the darkness and saw a small room with books. There was also a table that had long ago collapsed because some of the ceiling had come down on top of it.

Jillian, deep in concentration, ran a finger along the spines of the books as she read each while Richard took five strides across the room to the far wall. He saw another metal plate there and pressed his hand to it.

Slowly, another narrow door in the stone began pivoting away from him into the darkness. Richard crouched lower as he stepped into the doorway and held the light partway in.

"Master, you wish to travel?" a voice echoed.

He was staring at light reflecting back off the sliph's silver face. It was the well room, where they had come in. The doorway was on the opposite side of the steps from where they had found the first metal plate that had opened the ceiling.

They had just spent most of the night going around in a circle, ending up right where they had started.

"Richard," Jillian said, "look at this."

Richard turned back around and came face-to-face with the red leather cover of a book she was holding up.

It said *Chainfire*.

Richard was so stunned that he couldn't talk.

Jillian, grinning with discovery, came into the sliph's room with him as he backed in, taking the book from her hands.

He felt as if he were somewhere else, watching himself hold the book named *Chainfire*.

Richard?" It was Nicci's voice.

Still startled to actually have found *Chainfire*, he walked to the steps and looked up. Both Nicci and Cara, silhouetted by dawn light, were peering down at him.

"I found it. I mean, Jillian found it."

"How did you get down there?" Nicci asked as Richard and Jillian started up the steps. "We just looked in there and you weren't there."

"Jillian?" It was a man's voice.

"Grandfather!" Jillian raced the rest of the way up the steps and flew into an old man's arms.

Richard climbed the steps after her. Nicci was sitting on the top step. "What's going on?"

"This is Jillian's grandfather," Nicci said, lifting out a hand in introduction. "He is the teller of these people, the keeper of the old knowledge."

"Glad to meet you," Richard said, embracing the old gentleman's hand. "You have a wonderful granddaughter. She just helped me out immensely."

"You would have found it if I hadn't seen it first," Jillian said, grinning. Richard smiled back.

He turned to Nicci. "What happened to Jagang's men?"

Nicci shrugged. "Night fog."

As Jillian went with her grandfather to greet Lokey on a nearby wall, Richard spoke confidentially to Nicci and Cara.

"Fog?"

"Yes." Nicci interlaced her fingers around a knee. "Some kind of strange smoky fog drifted past them and made them go blind."

"Not just blind," Cara said with obvious delight, "but burst their eyes right in their sockets. It was a bloody mess. I quite enjoyed it."

Richard frowned at Nicci, wanting an explanation.

"They're scouts," she said. "I know these men and they know me. I didn't want them seeing me. More than that, though, I wanted them to be useless to Jagang—the ones who live, anyway. From what Jillian's grand-father tells me, he doubts that many of them will make it back to Jagang's forces, but I made sure they were near enough to their horses so that their animals will carry them back. I want the ones who live through the ordeal to be able to report only the horror of the fog coming down from the hills—that they were blinded in a strange, forbidding, and haunted land. Such news will send a fright through his men.

"Raping, pillaging, and slaughtering the helpless is all perfectly enter-taining for Jagang's army, but they rather don't like things like this. Dying for the Creator in a grand battle and going to their reward in the afterlife is one thing, being taken by something they can't see coming out of the darkness and ending up helpless in this way is quite another matter.

"I expect that Jagang will decide to skirt this land rather than allow some unknown out here to give his men a fright that could change their minds about fighting for the glory of the Creator and the Imperial Order. That means they will have to continue on south for a good distance. It will add time to their journey before they can finally swing around and come up into D'Hara."

Richard nodded thoughtfully. "Very good, Nicci. Very good."

She beamed. "What do you have there?"

"*Chainfire.*" He moved up on the steps to sit between Nicci and Cara. "It's a book." He hesitated in opening the cover. "In case this is some kind of prophecy or something, I'd just as soon you looked at it first."

Concern settled in her exquisite features. "Of course Richard. Give it here."

Richard handed her the book and stood. He didn't want to risk glancing at it and too late discovering that he shouldn't have, only to discover the beast about to tear into them. Especially not now, not when he was so close to getting answers.

Nicci was already scanning the book, Cara looking over her shoulder.

"It makes no sense," Cara announced as she read from *Chainfire.*

Richard didn't think that Nicci shared that opinion. Her face was drain-ing of color. "Dear spirits . . ." she whispered to herself.

As she kept reading, not saying anything to them, Richard sat on a rise of ground to the side, under an olive tree. There was a vine growing around the trunk. He reached out to idly pluck a leaf from the vine.

He stopped, his hand inches from the dusky, variegated leaves.

Icy gooseflesh prickled up his arms.

He knew what that vine was.

From *The Book of Counted Shadows*, the book that his father had him commit to memory before they destroyed it, the words flooded into his mind: *And when the three boxes of Orden are put into play, the snake vine shall grow.*

"What's the matter?" Jillian whispered to him as she leaned close. "You look like you've seen a spirit."

"Have you ever seen this plant growing here, where your people live?"

"No, I don't believe I have."

"She's right," Jillian's grandfather said in a puzzled voice. "I've lived in these parts all my life. I don't recall seeing that vine before, except for a spell almost three years back, I believe it was. That's right, three years this coming autumn. Then it died away. Haven't seen it since."

Richard didn't see any pods on the newly sprouted vine. He reached out and carefully plucked a sprig.

"Richard, this is an incredibly dangerous book," Nicci said in a gravely troubled voice. She was preoccupied, still reading, and not paying any attention to the rest of them talking. "This is beyond dangerous." She was reading as she spoke. "I'm only in the beginning, but this is . . . I don't even know how to begin . . ."

Richard rose to his feet, holding the sprig of the vine out, staring at it.

"We have to go," he said. "Right now."

Something in the tone of his voice made Cara and even Nicci look up.

"Lord Rahl, what is it?" Cara asked.

"You look like you just saw the ghost of your father," Nicci said.

"No, this is worse," Richard told her, finally looking up. "I understand. I know what's going on."

He ran to the steps down into his tomb. "Sliph! We need to travel!"

"But Richard, you have come to help me cast the dreams so that the evil people will not come here."

"Look, I have to leave. Right now."

"Lord Rahl has already helped us as much as he can for now," her grandfather said as he put an arm around her slender shoulders. "If he can, he will return to us."

"That's right," Richard said, "if I can I'll return. Thank you, Jillian, for helping me. You can't begin to imagine what you have done this day. Tell your people to stay away from that vine."

"Richard," Nicci said, "what's gotten into you?"

He seized Nicci's dress at her shoulder, and Cara's arm.

"We have to get to the People's Palace. Now."

"Why? What's happening? What did you find?"

Richard showed her the sprig of vine before stuffing it in a pocket and grabbing her arm again and forcing her down the steps.

"This is a snake vine. It only grows when the boxes of Orden have been put in play."

"But the boxes of Orden are safe in the palace," Cara protested.

"They're not safe any longer. Those Sisters have put the magic of Orden in play. Sliph! We need to travel to the People's Palace."

"Come, we will travel."

Nicci was still fighting him as he pulled her along. "Richard, I don't see what this has to do with your dream of this woman."

Richard slapped the metal plate, starting the ceiling of the tomb closing. "Good bye, Jillian. Thank you. I will return someday."

As she waved, he snatched up his bow and quiver.

He turned to Nicci. "They need Kahlan. She's the last living Confessor. They put the boxes of Orden in play. They need the book I have memorized. The first thing it says is '*Verification of the truth of the words of the Book of Counted Shadows, if spoken by another, rather than read by the one who commands the boxes, can only be insured by the use of a Confessor. . . .*'"

The ceiling finished closing. In the distance, Richard could hear Jillian call, "Good-bye, Richard. Safe journey."

"Richard, this is crazy. It's just—"

"Now is not the time to argue with me."

She knew by his tone of voice that he meant it.

He climbed up on the wall and hoisted both women up.

"Here, wait," Nicci said as she opened the pack. "You had better keep this safe." She stuffed *Chainfire* down inside and tied the flap down tight.

"Any idea what *Chainfire* is about?" he asked.

Her blue eyes gazed into his. "From what I was able to tell from the tiny bit I saw in the beginning, it's a theoretical formula for conjuring things that have the potential to unravel existence."

"Unravel existence?" Cara asked. "What does that mean?"

"I'm not exactly sure. But it seems to be a discussion of a theory of a specific magic that if ever initiated could potentially destroy the world of life."

"Why in the world would they need that?" Richard asked. "They have the magic of Orden, now."

Nicci didn't answer. She didn't believe his theory; it involved Kahlan.

"Sliph, now, please. Take us to the People's Palace."

The silver arm swept them up. "Come, we will travel."

Just before they plunged into the silvery froth, Nicci and Cara each seized one of his hands.

Nicci had hardly gotten her bearings, hardly recognized that they were in a marble room, hardly let the sliph out of her lungs and pulled in a desperate gasp of air, when Richard was already pulling her up over the wall by the hand.

Despite everything, she was still able, in some dim part of her mind, to thrill at holding his hand, for whatever reason.

She had thought that while in the sliph traveling to the People's Palace, that she would be able to give thought to Richard's strange new twist of finding a bit of a vine and leaping to the conclusion that the boxes of Orden were in play—all in an attempt to prove that Kahlan was real.

The room they were in was shielded. Richard pulled her and Cara through the powerful shield. They ran up a marble hall and out a double silver door with a lake embossed into the metal.

"I know this place," Cara said. "I know where we are."

"Good," Richard said, "then you lead the way. And hurry."

There were times when Nicci almost wished that she had gone along with Zedd, Ann, and Nathan's plan to purge him of his memory of Kahlan.

Except for one thing. She had tried the theory on one of Jagang's men back in Caska. She had tried to use Subtractive Magic to eliminate the man's memory of the emperor. It sounded simple enough. She had done just as the three had wanted Nicci to do to Richard.

There had only been one problem.

It had killed the man. Killed him in a most horrifying fashion.

When she thought about how she had almost done that to Richard, how for a time she had let them talk her into it and had been committed to doing it, she had gotten so weak and dizzy that she had to sit down on the ground next to the dead soldier. Cara had thought Nicci had been about to pass out. The idea of what she had almost done left her shaking for an hour.

"Here," Cara said as she led them up stairs that emptied into a broad corridor with parts of the roof glassed.

The light flooding in was reddish, so it was either almost sunset or just after dawn, Nicci didn't know which. It was a disorienting feeling not to know if it was day or night.

The halls were filled with people. Many of them stopped to stare at the three people running along the corridor. Guards also noticed and came running, hands to weapons, until they saw Cara in her red leather outfit. Many of the people recognized Richard and dropped to a knee, bowing as he ran past. He didn't slow to acknowledge them.

They went up a dizzying array of passages, over bridges, along balconies, between columns, and through rooms. Intermittently they ran up stairs. Occasionally Cara took them through service halls, undoubtedly as shortcuts.

Nicci took note of how magnificent the palace was, how remarkably beautiful. The patterned stone floors were laid with rare precision. There were grand statues—none as remarkable as the statue Richard had carved, but grand nonetheless. She saw a tapestry that was larger than any she had seen in her life. It depicted a sprawling battle and must have had several hundred horses in it.

"This way," Cara said, pointing down a hall as she rushed toward it.

As they came around the corner, Cara crossed over to the other side of the passageway as she ran down it. Nicci, pulled along by her hand, would have liked to have discussed a number of things, to have asked some important and pointed questions, but it was all she could do to get her breath as she ran. Running was not something she really ever did until she met Richard.

Cara slid to slow down as she came to a pair of carved mahogany doors. Nicci was revolted to see the snakes carved into them. Without pause, Richard seized one of the door handles, a bronze skull, and yanked the door open.

Inside the quiet, carpeted room, four guards immediately sprang to block Richard's path. They saw Cara, and looked at Richard again, uncertain.

"Lord Rahl?" One asked.

"That's right," Cara snapped. "Now, get out of the way."

The men immediately pulled back, each putting a fist to their hearts.

"Has anything happened recently?" Richard asked as he caught his breath.

"Happened?"

"Intruders? Has anyone slipped in this way?"

The man snorted a laugh. "Hardly, Lord Rahl. We'd know if that happened and we'd not allow it."

Richard nodded his thanks and raced to the marble stairs, nearly pulling Nicci's arm out of the socket in the process. As they ran up the steps, Nicci thought that her legs might simply quit. Her muscles were so exhausted from the long run up through the palace that she could hardly make them go on, but she had to, for Richard.

At the top of the stairs, soldiers were running toward them, crossbows loaded with red-fletched arrows at the ready. They didn't know it was the Lord Rahl. They thought someone was trying to get into the restricted area. Nicci hoped that someone got hold of their senses before one of the men got careless.

But by their reactions, Nicci realized that these men were highly trained and not prone to shooting arrows before they were sure of their target. Lucky for them, because she would have been faster.

"Commander General Trimack?" Richard asked an officer pushing his way through the ring of steel that had surrounded them.

The man stiffened and clapped a fist to his heart. "Lord Rahl!" He spotted the Mord-Sith. "Cara?"

Cara nodded in greeting.

Richard clasped arms with the man. "General, someone has gotten in here. They've taken the boxes in the Garden of Life."

The general was momentarily struck speechless. "What? Lord Rahl, that's not possible. You have to be mistaken. No one could get past us without our knowing it. It's been peaceful as can be up here for ages. Why, we've only had one visitor."

"Visitor? Who?"

"The Prelate. Verna. It was a while back. She was in the palace checking on something about books of magic, she said. She said that as long as she was here, she wanted to have a look to make sure the boxes were safe."

"So you let her go in there?"

The general looked a bit indignant. A long scar stood out white when his face went red.

"No, Lord Rahl. I wouldn't let her go in there. What we ended up doing was opening the doors so she could look in to see that everything was safe."

"Look in?"

"That's right. We surrounded her with men, all pointing these special arrows at her—arrows Nathan Rahl found for us that will stop even the gifted. We had her ringed in steel. The poor woman looked like a pincushion about to happen."

Men all around nodded at the general's words.

"She looked in the garden and said she was relieved to see that everything was fine. I took a look myself and saw the three black boxes sitting on the stone slab across the room. But I never let the woman set foot beyond the doors, I swear."

Richard heaved a sigh. "And that's it? No one else has opened those doors?"

"No, Lord Rahl. No one else has even been up here but my men. No one. We don't let anyone even use these halls around the Garden of Life. As you may recall, you were rather insistent about it the last time you were here."

Richard nodded, thinking. He looked up. "Well, let's go have a look."

The men, all jangling with weapons and armor, followed the the surprise visitors down the polished granite hall until they reached two huge, gold covered doors.

Without waiting for someone else to do it, Richard pulled one of the heavy doors open and started into the room. The soldiers paused at the doors. This was apparently sacred ground, a sanctuary for the master of the palace alone, and unless invited by the Lord Rahl, none of them would enter. Richard didn't invite them as he rushed off on his own.

Despite how tired she was, Nicci hurried after him as he made his way down a path among beds of flowers. Overhead, through a glassed roof, she could see that the sky had turned to a darker purple, so she knew it was night, rather than dawn.

Just like Richard, Nicci paid little attention to the vine covered walls, or the trees, or all the other things growing all around. The garden was a magnificent place, to be sure, but her gaze was riveted on the stone altar she saw in the distance. She didn't see any of the three boxes that were supposed to be there. There was something else standing on the slab of granite, but she couldn't tell what it was.

By the way Richard's chest was heaving, he did know what was standing there.

They crossed a ring of grass, and the open dirt. In the dirt, Richard stopped cold in mid-stride and stared down at the ground.

"Lord Rahl," Cara asked, "what is it?"

"Her tracks," he whispered. "I recognize them. These aren't covered by magic. She was here alone." He gestured to the dirt. "Two sets. She was in here twice." He looked back at the grass, following what he could see that they couldn't. "She was on her knees there, in the grass."

He took off and ran the rest of the way to the stone altar. Nicci and Cara sprang into a run to keep up with him.

When they reached the slab of granite, Nicci knew at last what it was that stood there all alone.

It was the statue of the woman that had been carved in marble in Liberty Square in Altur'Rang. The original statue Richard had told them he had carved. The statue he said belonged to Kahlan. Nicci could see that there were bloody handprints all over it.

Richard picked up the carved wooden figure in trembling hands and drew it to his breast, gasping back a sob. Nicci thought that he might fall to the ground, but he didn't.

When he had held it for a moment, he turned to them, tears running down his face. He held out to Cara and Nicci the statue of the proud figure, her head thrown back, her hands fisted at her sides.

"This is the statue I carved for Kahlan. This is *Spirit*. This is the statue I told you could not be in Altur'Rang because she had it with her. If they copied this statue in stone down in Altur'Rang in the Old World, then how did it get here?"

Nicci stared at it, her eyes wide, trying to reconcile what she was seeing. She couldn't comprehend the contradiction. She remembered Richard trying to understand what he had seen at the grave site where the Mother Confessor was buried. Now she knew how he had felt.

"Richard, I don't understand how that could have gotten here."

"Kahlan left it here! She left it here for me to find! She took the boxes of Orden for the Sisters! Don't you get it? Don't you at last see the truth standing before you?"

Unable to say more, he pulled the statue back to his chest as if it were the most precious treasure in the world.

In that moment, seeing the pain trembling through him, Nicci wondered what it would be like to have him love her that much.

At the same time, despite her confusion, despite sadness for what she was seeing, for the pain he was so obviously in, she felt joy, joy that Richard had someone who meant that much to him, someone who could make him feel that way . . . even if she was imaginary. Nicci was not yet convinced that she wasn't.

"Do you understand now?" he asked. "Do you two get it, now?"

Cara, looking as stunned as Nicci felt, shook her head. "No, Lord Rahl, I don't understand."

He lifted the small statue. "No one remembers her. She probably walked right past those men and they forgot her, just like you forgot all the thousands of times you've seen her. She's all alone, in the hands of those four Sisters, and they made her come in here and get the boxes. Do you see the blood all over it? Her blood? You should understand that. Can you imagine how she feels, all alone, forgotten by everyone? She left this, probably hoping someone would see it and know she exists."

He thrust it at Cara, then at Nicci. "Look at it! It's covered in blood! There's blood on the altar. There's blood on the floor. There are her footprints. How do you think the boxes are gone and this is here? She was here."

The indoor garden was dead silent. Nicci was so confused she didn't know what to believe. She knew what she was seeing, but it didn't seem possible.

"Do you believe me, now?" Richard asked them both.

Cara swallowed. "Lord Rahl, I believe what you are saying, but I still don't remember her."

When his raptor gaze slid to Nicci, she, too, swallowed at the power of that look.

"Richard, I don't know what is going on. What you say is certainly powerful evidence, but, like Cara says, I still don't remember her. I'm sorry, but I can't lie to you and tell you what you want to hear just to make you happy. I'm telling you the truth. I still don't know what you're talking about."

"I know you don't," he said with sudden, quiet, remarkable sympathy. "It's what I've been telling you. Something terrible is happening. No one remembers her. Anything that could cause such an event is undoubtedly powerful and extremely dangerous conjuring, able to be engendered only by the most powerful people who have command of both sides of the gift. Magic so dangerous that it would be hidden in a book buried in a cata- comb behind shields where the wizards who put it there hoped no one would ever find it."

"*Chainfire*," Nicci breathed. "But from the brief bit I saw of it, this somehow has the power to undo the world of life."

"What do the Sisters care?" Richard asked in a bitter voice. "They've already put the boxes of Orden in play. It is their intent to end life on be- half of the Keeper of the dead. You should understand that better than anyone."

Nicci put a hand to her forehead. "Dear spirits, I think you may be right." She couldn't feel her fingertips. She was tingling all over with dread. "From the little bit I read, *Chainfire* sounds like it might be some- thing along the lines of what Zedd, Ann, and Nathan wanted me to do to you—use Subtractive Magic to make you forget Kahlan. If what you say is true, then in a way, that might be what the Sisters did—they made every- one else forget her."

Nicci looked up into his gray eyes, eyes she could lose herself in. She felt tears of fright run down her cheeks.

"Richard, I tried that."

"What are you talking about?"

"I tried what they wanted me to do to you. I tried it on one of Jagang's men, back at Caska. Tried to make him forget Jagang. It was fatal. What if that's what Chainfire does to everyone?"

Richard heaved an angry breath. "Come on."

He marched out of the garden to a general and his guards waiting out in the polished granite hallway, huddled around the entrance to the Garden of Life.

"Lord Rahl," the general said, "I don't see the boxes any more."

"They've been stolen."

Jaws of men standing all around dropped in stunned astonishment. General Trimack's eyes went wide. "Stolen . . . but, who could have stolen them?"

Richard held up the statue and waggled it in front of the man. "My wife."

General Trimack looked like he didn't know whether to scream in fury or commit suicide on the spot. He instead rubbed a hand back and forth on his mouth as he thought through everything he'd heard and apparently tried to put it together with any other information he had. He looked up at Richard with the kind of intent look that few men other than generals could muster.

"I get reports all the time, Lord Rahl. I insist that I see all reports—you never can tell what bit of information you might learn that could turn out to be helpful. General Meiffert sends me reports as well. Since he's now close by, I get them within hours. Soon he and the troops will be moving south and it will take longer, but for now, I get them fresh."

"I'm listening."

"Well, I don't know if it means anything, but the latest report I got early this morning said that they came across a woman, an old woman, who had been stabbed by a sword. She's in bad shape, according to the report. I don't know why he sent me a report on such a thing, but General Meiffert is a pretty smart fellow, and I have to think that there was just something bloody odd about it for him to want me to know."

"How close is he?" Richard asked. "The army, I mean. How close?"

The general shrugged. "By horse? Ride half way hard and they're not more than an hour or two away."

"Then get me some horses. Immediately."

General Trimack clapped a fist over his heart at the same time as he signaled a couple men forward. "Run on ahead and get some horses ready for the Lord Rahl." He looked at Richard, then glanced at Cara and Nicci. "Three horses?"

"Yes, three," Richard confirmed.

"And an escort of the First File to show him the way and provide protection."

The two men nodded and took off at a dead run for the stairs.

"Lord Rahl, I don't know what to say. I will of course resign—"

"Don't be silly. This isn't something you could have done anything about; it was deception by magic. It's my fault for letting this happen. I'm the Lord Rahl. I'm supposed to be the magic against magic."

Nicci could only think that he had been trying to be, but no one would believe him.

Without sparing any time to rest, Richard, Cara, and Nicci, escorted by a company of the palace guards, rushed through the grand, wide corridors of Richard's ancestral home. People along their route scattered out of the way of the wedge of guards coming down the halls. Behind the guards, Cara marched out in front of Richard. Nicci rushed along at his side.

As they made their way down a smaller corridor, with fewer people, Richard slowed and then stopped. The guards stopped far enough away to be handy, but to give him his privacy. As everyone waited, Richard gazed down a side passageway. Cara looked uncomfortable.

"Quarters for Mord-Sith," Cara explained to Nicci in answer to the unspoken question in her eyes.

"Denna's room was down that hall." Richard gestured the other way. "Your room was down there, Cara."

Cara blinked. "How do you know that?"

He looked at her for a moment, his expression unreadable. "Cara, I remember being there."

Cara turned as red as her leather outfit. "You remember?" Richard nodded. "You know?" she whispered, panic coming into her eyes.

"Cara," he said gently, "of course I know."

Her eyes brimmed with tears. "How did you know?"

He gestured to her right wrist. "When I've touched your Agiel, it hurts. An Agiel only hurts when a person touches it if it was used to train them, or if the Mord-Sith intends it to hurt."

She closed her eyes. "Lord Rahl . . . I'm sorry."

"It was a long time ago, when you were a different person, and I was the enemy of your Lord Rahl. Things change, Cara."

"Are you sure I've changed enough?"

"Others made you into who you were. You made yourself into what you have become." He smiled. "Remember when the beast hurt you, and I healed you?"

"How could I ever forget it?"

"Then you know how I feel."

She smiled at that.

Richard's brow drew together. "Touch . . ." His eyes lit up with sudden recognition.

"The sword."

"What?" Nicci asked.

"The Sword of Truth. That morning, when I was asleep, I think the Sisters cast a spell to make me sleep more soundly so they could take Kahlan. But I put my hand on the sword. I was touching the Sword of Truth when they took her and made everyone forget Kahlan. The sword protected me from that magic. That's why I remember her. The Sword of Truth was a countermeasure to what they did."

Richard started out again. "Come on, we need to get to the encampment and see who that injured woman is."

Baffled, Nicci followed after him.

Nicci was surprised by the encampment. She was so used to being among Jagang's army that she hadn't really given any thought to how different these men might be. It made sense, of course, but she had just never given it any thought.

Even in the dark, there was still the light of all the fires and she expected to be the center of morbid attention, with men calling out the filthiest things they could think of in an attempt to shock her, or humiliate her, or frighten her. Men in the Order encampment always hooted and hollered at her, made obscene gestures, and laughed uproariously as she passed among them.

These men, to be sure, looked her way. Nicci expected that it was a rare experience to see a woman like her riding into their camp. But they only looked. A glance, an admiring gaze, a smile here and there with a bow of the head in greeting was the most she got. It could be that she was riding in beside the Lord Rahl and a Mord-Sith in red leather, but Nicci didn't think so. These men were different. They were expected to conduct themselves with respect.

Everywhere when men saw Richard, they were eager to clap a fist to their hearts in salute as they stood in pride, or trotted alone beside his horse for a time. They looked overjoyed to see him riding into their camp, to see their Lord Rahl among them again.

The camp was also more orderly as well. That it was dry was a help; there were few things worse than an army camp in the wet. In this camp the animals were confined to areas where they wouldn't accidentally create trouble. Wagons were out of the main route through the camp. There actually were deliberate routes through the camp.

The men looked weary from the long march, but their tents were set up in a rather systematic manner, not the haphazard, every-man-for-himself method the Imperial Order employed. The fires were small and were only what was needed, not the drunken revelry of men dancing, singing, and brawling around the bonfires.

The other big difference was that there were not any torture tents set up. The Order always had an active area set aside for torture. A steady stream of people flowed in for questioning, and an equal number of corpses flowed out. The constant screams from victims made for a noisy camp.

That was the other thing. It was rather quiet. Men were finishing with meals and bedding down for the night. It was a quiet time. In the Order's encampment, there wasn't any time that was quiet.

"There," one of the men escorting them said as he lifted an arm to point out the command tents in the darkness.

A big blond-headed officer came out of one of the tents when he heard horses nearby. He had undoubtedly already been alerted that the Lord Rahl was on his way.

Richard swung down off the saddle and stopped the man from going to his knees to do a devotion.

"General Meiffert, it's good to see you again, but we don't have time for that."

He bowed his head. "As you wish, Lord Rahl."

Nicci watched the general's blue eyes glance to Cara as she came up beside Richard.

He smoothed back his blond hair. "Mistress Cara."

"General."

"Life is too short for you two to pretend you don't care for each other," Richard said, his anger surfacing. "You ought to realize that every moment you have together is precious and there is nothing wrong with holding someone in high regard. That's the kind of freedom we're fighting for. Well, isn't it?"

"Yes, Lord Rahl," General Meiffert said, somewhat taken aback.

"We're here because of a report you sent about a woman who was stabbed. Is she still alive?"

The young general nodded. "I haven't checked in the last hour or so, but she was, earlier. My field surgeons attended to her, but there are wounds well beyond their ability. This is one of those. She was stabbed in the gut. It's a slow and painful way to die. She's lived longer than I expected."

"Do you know her name?" Nicci asked.

"She wouldn't tell us when she was wide awake, but when she was in a fevered state, we asked again and she said her name was Tovi."

Richard glanced at Nicci before asking, "What does she look like?"

"Heavy set, older woman."

"Sounds like her," Richard said as he wiped a hand across his face. "We need to see her. Right away."

The general nodded. "Follow me, then."

"Wait," Nicci said.

Richard turned back to her. "What is it?"

"If you go in to see her, she won't tell you anything. Tovi hasn't seen me for ages. The last she knew, I was still a slave to Jagang and she had escaped. I might be able to talk to her in a way that will get the truth out of her."

Nicci could see how impatient Richard was to get his hands on one of the women that he believed was responsible for taking the woman he loved.

Nicci still didn't know what she believed. She wondered if she still believed that he was only dreaming up this other woman simply because of her own feelings.

"Richard," she said as she stepped close to him so that she could talk confidentially, "let me do this. If you go in there it will spoil what I can do. I think I can get her to talk, but if she sees you, the game will be over."

"And how do you plan to accomplish getting her to talk?"

"Look, do you want to know what happened to Kahlan, or do you want to argue about how I'm going to get that information?"

He pressed his lips tight for a moment. "I don't care if you pull her intestines out an inch at a time, just get her to talk."

Nicci briefly put a hand on his shoulder on her way by as she followed after the general. Once they were away, she moved up and walked beside him as they marched through the nearly dark camp. She could see why Cara found the man attractive. He had one of those handsome faces that just didn't look like it could wear a lie well at all.

"By the way," he said, glancing over at her, "I'm General Meiffert."

Nicci nodded. "Benjamin."

He paused in the dark pathway through the camp. "How do you know that?"

Nicci smiled. "Cara told me about you." Still, he stared at her. She took his arm and started him moving again. "And for a Mord-Sith to speak so highly of a man is quite unusual."

"Cara spoke highly of me?"

"Of course. She likes you. But you know that."

He clasped his hands behind his back as they walked. "I guess, then, that you must know that I think a lot of her."

"Of course."

"And who are you, anyway, might I ask? I'm sorry, but Lord Rahl didn't introduce us."

Nicci gave him a sidelong glance. "You may have heard of me as Death's Mistress."

General Meiffert stumbled to a stop, choking on spit from gasping. He coughed until his face was red.

"Death's Mistress?" he finally managed. "People are more afraid of you than Jagang himself."

"For good reason."

"You're the one who captured Lord Rahl, and took him to the Old World."

"That's right," she said as she started out again.

He walked along beside her, thinking it over. "Well, I'd guess that you must have changed your ways, or Lord Rahl wouldn't have you with him."

She simply smiled at him, a smooth, sly smile. It made him uneasy. He gestured to the right.

"Down here. The tent where we put her is over here."

Nicci grasped his forearm to hold him in place. She didn't want Tovi hearing her, yet.

"This is going to take a goodly amount of time. Why don't you tell Richard that I said he should get some rest. I think Cara ought to get some rest, too. Why don't you see to that, as well?"

"Ah, I guess I could do that."

"And General, if my friend Cara doesn't leave here in the morning with a giddy grin, I'll gut you alive."

His eyes widened. Nicci couldn't help but to smile.

"Figure of speech, Benjamin." She arched an eyebrow. "You have the night with her. Don't waste it."

He smiled at last. "Thank you . . ."

"Nicci."

"Thank you, Nicci. I think about her all the time. You don't know how much I've missed her—how much I've worried about her."

"I think I do. But you should tell her that, not me. Now, where is Tovi?"

He lifted an arm and pointed. "Down there, on the right. The last tent in the line."

Nicci nodded. "Do me a favor. See to it that no one disturbs us. Including the surgeons. I need to be alone with her."

"I'll see to it." He turned back and scratched his head. "Ah, it's none of my business, but are you"—he gestured between her and back the way they'd come—"you and Lord Rahl, well, you know."

Nicci couldn't seem to make herself come up with an answer that she wished to voice.

"Time is short. Don't keep Cara waiting."

"Yes, I see what you mean. Thank you Nicci. I hope to see you in the morning."

She watched him rush off into the darkness, then turned to her task. She hadn't really wanted to unnerve the general with talk of Death's Mistress, but she needed to slip back into that part of herself, needed to think that way again, needed to find the icy attitude that was numb to everything.

She pulled the tent flap aside and slipped inside. There was a single candle lit on a holder made of wrought iron that was stuck in the ground beside a cot. The tent was stuffy and warm. It smelled of stale sweat and dried blood.

Tovi's bulk lay on her back in the cot, laboring to breathe.

Nicci sat lightly on a field stool beside the woman. Tovi hardly noticed someone sitting down. Nicci laid a hand on Tovi's wrist and began to trickle in a thread of power to help the woman's suffering.

Tovi recognized such gifted help and immediately looked over. Her eyes went wide and her breathing quickened. She then gasped in pain and clutched at her abdomen. Nicci increased the flow of power until Tovi sagged back with a moan of relief.

"Nicci, where have you come from? What in the world are you doing here?"

"Well, since when do you care? Sister Ulicia and the rest of you left me in Jagang's clutches, his personal slave, left me a captive of that pig."

"But you got away."

"Got away? Sister Tovi, are you out of your mind? No one got away from dream walker—except you five."

"Four. Sister Merissa is no longer living."

"What happened?"

"Stupid bitch tried to play her own game with Richard Rahl. You remember how she hated him—wanted to bathe in his blood."

"I remember."

"Sister Nicci, what are you doing here?"

"The rest of you left me to Jagang." Nicci leaned in so that Tovi could see her glare. "You have no idea of the things I've had to endure. Since then, I've been on a long mission for His Excellency. He needs information and he knows I can get it."

Tovi smiled. "Makes you whore for him, to find out what he wants to know."

Nicci didn't answer the question, instead letting it answer itself. "I just happened to hear about some fool woman who in the process of getting herself robbed or something also managed to get herself stabbed. Something about the description made me decide to come and check myself to see if it could possibly be you."

Tovi nodded. "I'm afraid it's not good."

"I hope it hurts. I came to make sure you're a long time dying. I want you to suffer for what you did to me—leaving me in the clutches of Jagang while the rest of you escaped without bothering to even tell me how it could be done."

"We couldn't help it. We had a chance and we had to take it, that's all." A cunning grin came to her. "But you can get free of Jagang, too."

Nicci pressed forward. "How—how can I get free?"

"Heal me and I'll tell you."

"You mean, heal you so you can betray me like before. No good, Tovi. You're going to tell it all, or I'm going to sit right here and watch you suffer your way into the Keeper's eternal embrace. I may trickle in just enough to keep you alive a little longer." She leaned in. "So you can continue to feel the pain twisting in your guts a little longer."

Tovi seized a fistful of Nicci's dress. "Please, Sister, help me. It hurts so much."

"Talk, 'Sister.' "

She released her grip on Nicci's dress and let her face roll to face away. "It's the bond to Lord Rahl. We swore a bond."

"Sister Tovi, if you think I'm that stupid, I'm going to make you suffer just to make you regret the thought until you die."

She turned back to look at Nicci. "No, it's true."

"How can you swear a bond to someone you want to eliminate?"

Tovi grinned. "Sister Ulicia figured it out. We swore a bond to him, but made him let us go before he could hold us to a list of his commands."

"This story just gets more preposterous all the time."

Nicci withdrew her hand from Tovi's arm, and with it the trickle of relief. As Nicci stood, Tovi groaned in agony.

"Please, Sister Nicci, it's true." She grasped Nicci's hand. "In exchange for letting us go, we traded for something he wanted."

"What could Lord Rahl possibly want that would convince him to let a clutch of Sisters of the Dark loose? That's the craziest thing I've ever heard."

"A woman."

"What?"

"He wanted a woman."

"As the Lord Rahl, he can have any woman he wants. He has but to pick her and have her sent to his bed, unless she would choose the executioner's block instead, and none do. He hardly needs the Sisters of the Dark to cart women to his bed."

"No, no, not that kind of woman. A woman he loved."

"Right." Nicci huffed a sigh. "Good-bye, Sister Tovi. Be sure to give the Keeper of the dead my regards when you get there. Sorry, but I'm afraid that meeting won't be for a while. I think you look like you may linger for a number of days, yet. Pity."

"Please!" Her arm rotated around, searching for the contact of the one person who could save her. "Sister Nicci, please. Please listen, and I will tell you everything."

Nicci sat down and gripped Tovi's arm again. "All right, Sister, but just remember, the power can go both ways."

Tovi's back arched as she cried out in agony. "No! Please!"

Nicci had no compunction about what she was doing. She knew that there was no moral equivalence between her inflicting torture and the Imperial Order doing what might on the surface seem like the same thing. But her purpose in using it was solely to save innocent lives. The Imperial Order used torture as a means of subjugation and conquest, as a tool to strike fear into their enemies. And, at times, as something they relished because it made them feel powerful to hold sway over not just agony but life itself.

The Imperial Order used torture because they had no regard at all for human life. Nicci was using it because she did. While at one time she would have seen no difference, since coming to embrace life she saw all the difference in the world.

Nicci reversed the suffering she was trickling into the old woman and Tovi sank back in grateful, weeping relief.

Tovi was covered in a sheen of sweat. "Please, Sister, give me some comfort instead and I will tell you everything."

"Start with who stabbed you."

"The Seeker."

"Richard Rahl is the Seeker. Do you really think I will believe such a story? Richard Rahl would have taken your head off with one swing."

Tovi's head rolled side to side. "No, no, you don't understand. This man had the Sword of Truth." She pointed at her gut. "I ought to know the Sword of Truth when it runs me through. He caught me by surprise and before I knew who he was or what he wanted, the bastard stabbed me."

Nicci pressed her fingers to her brow in confusion. "I think you better go back to the beginning."

Tovi was already sinking into a stupor. Nicci increased the magic flowing into her, giving her some healing relief without curing her of her injury. Nicci didn't want to cure her, she needed the woman unable to help herself. Tovi looked the kindly grandmother, but she was a viper.

Nicci crossed one leg over the other. It was going to be a long night.

The next time Tovi came around, Nicci sat up straighter. "So you swore a bond to Richard, as the Lord Rahl," Nicci said as if there had been no gap in the conversation, "and that protected all of you from the dream walker."

"That's right."

"And then what?"

"We were able to escape. We kept track of Richard as we went about our work for our master. We needed to find a hook."

Nicci knew very well who their master was.

"What do you mean, a hook?"

"In order to do what we need to do to satisfy the Keeper, we needed a way to make sure Richard Rahl could not interfere. We found it."

"Found what?"

"Something that keeps us bonded to him no matter what we do. It was brilliant."

"So what is it?"

"Life."

Nicci frowned, not knowing if she had heard right. She laid a hand on Tovi's wound and gave some focused comfort.

After Tovi had calmed from the wave of pain, Nicci asked in a quiet voice, "What do you mean?"

"Life," Tovi said at last. "It is his highest value."

"So?"

"Sister, think. In order to stay out of the dream walker's grasp, we must be bonded to Richard Rahl all the time. We dare not waver for a moment. And yet, who is our ultimate master?"

"The Keeper of the dead. We have sworn oaths."

"That's right. And if we were to do something that would harm Richard's life, such as loose the Keeper into the world of life, then we would be going against our bond to Richard. That would mean that before we could free the Keeper from his bounds in the world of the dead, Jagang, in this world, would be able to pounce on us."

"Sister Tovi, you had better start making sense, or I will lose my patience, and I assure you, you would not like that. You would not like it one bit. I want to know what's going on so that I can be let in. I want my place back."

"Of course. Of course. You see, Richard's highest value is life. In fact, he created a statue to it. We were in the Old World. We saw his statue dedicated to life."

"I got that much out of what you said."

Her head rolled back so she could again look at Nicci. "Well, my dear, what is it we are pledged to do in the Oaths we have given?"

"Free the Keeper."

"And what is our reward for performing our task?"

Nicci stared at the woman's cold eyes. "Immortality."

Tovi grinned. "Exactly."

"Richard's highest value is life. You are saying that you plan to grant him immortality?"

"We are. We are working toward his most noble ideal: life."

"But he may not want immortality."

Tovi managed a shrug. "Maybe. But we don't intend to ask him. Don't you see the brilliance of Sister Ulicia's plan? We know that his highest value is life. No matter what else we may do against his wishes, those things do not rise to the level of his most important value. Thus, we are honoring our bond to the Lord Rahl in the most grand way possible, while maintaining the bond—keeping the dream walker out of our minds—and at the same time working to bring the Keeper into the world. See how it goes round and round. Each element locks the others in tighter."

"But it is the Keeper who promises you immortality. You cannot grant it."

"No, not if we seek it through the Keeper."

"Then how can you possibly grant immortality? You don't have any such power."

"Oh, but we will, we will."

"How?"

Tovi fell to coughing and Nicci had to do some swift work on the wound just to keep the woman alive. It was nearly two hours before she again had her conscious and calm.

"Sister Tovi," she said once the woman had opened her eyes and looked like she was seeing again. "I've had to repair some of your injury. Now, before I can repair the rest of your wound and fully heal you— so that you can have your reward of life—I need to know the rest of it. How can you think that you can grant immortality? You don't have that power."

"We stole the boxes of Orden. We intend to use them to destroy all life . . . except that which we wish to have around, of course. With the power of Orden, we will hold sway over life and death. We will have the power to grant Richard Rahl immortality. See? Bond fulfilled."

Nicci's head was spinning. "Tovi, your story is too impossible. It's more complicated than you make it."

"Well, there are other parts to the plan. We found catacombs under the Palace of the Prophets."

Nicci had had no idea that such catacombs existed, but she wanted the woman to go on with her story, so she just let her talk.

"That's when it all started. When we got the idea. You see, we had been wandering the lands, looking for ways to satisfy the Keeper—" She clutched Nicci's arm so hard it hurt. "He comes in our dreams. You know that. He comes to you as well. He comes and torments us, forcing us to do his bidding, to work to free him."

Nicci pulled the clawlike hand off her arm. "Catacombs?"

"Yes. The catacombs. We discovered ancient catacombs and in them books. We found a book called *Chainfire*"

Goose bumps ran up Nicci's arms. "Chainfire, what does that mean? Is it a spell?"

"Oh, it is much more than anything so simple as a spell. It was from ancient times. The wizards of the time had come up with a new theory of how to alter memory—in other words, real events altered with Subtractive power, with all the disconnected parts spontaneously reconstructed independently of one another. Namely, how to make an individual disappear to everyone else by making people forget this person, even as soon as they've just seen them.

"But the wizards who came up with this theory were timid men, fearful of unleashing such things not only because they realized that such a linked event would cause irreparable damage to the subject, but because there was no way for them to control it once it was initiated, it would be self-actuating and self-sustaining."

"What do you mean? What does it do?"

"It unravels people's memory of the subject, but that ignition starts a cascade event that can't be predicted or controlled. It then burns through links they have with others, and then others those people know, and so on. It eventually unravels connections so that it corrupts everything. For our purposes, though, it doesn't really matter, since our aim is to undo life anyway. For fear that it would be discovered what we were doing, we destroyed the book, and the catacombs."

"But why did you need to destroy the memory of someone?"

"Not just someone, but the memory of the woman who bought us the bond in the first place, Kahlan Amnell, Richard Rahl's love. By creating a Chainfire event, we ended up with a woman no one remembers."

"But what can that possibly gain you?"

"The boxes of Orden. We used her to get the boxes, so that we can free the Keeper. With the boxes, we can grant Richard immortal life at the same time we also free the Keeper.

"The Keeper whispered to us in our dreams that Richard has the secret to opening the boxes, he has a necessary knowledge memorized. It exists nowhere else. Darken Rahl revealed it to the Keeper. Richard knows the way to unlock the secrets of Orden, only this time, we know the trick that defeated Darken Rahl.

"The book he knows says that we need a Confessor to open the boxes. And now we have a Confessor who no one remembers—so no one can bother us about her."

"What about prophecy disappearing? Was that caused by Chainfire?"

"It's part of Chainfire. They called it the Chainfire corollary. Part of the initiation phase of Chainfire requires that prophecy also be ignited with a Chainfire event, much the same as people's memories are cast into the conflagration. The Chainfire event feeds on those memories to sustain the event, therefore prophecy must be involved as well. A blank is found in the proper fork—a place where a prophet left a space, should a future prophet wish to complete the work. We then fill in that void in prophecy with a completing prophecy which has the Chainfire formula invested in it. A Chainfire event thus infects and consumes all the associated prophecy on the branch, starting with related prophecy, either in subject or in chronology—in this case both: Kahlan, the woman we wiped away in life, is thus also wiped away in prophecy by the Chainfire corollary."

"You seem to have it all worked out," Nicci said.

Tovi grinned through the pain. "It gets better."

"Better? How could it possibly get more delicious than this?"

"There is a counter to Chainfire." Tovi giggled with the glee of it.

"A counter? You mean you risk Richard finding a counter to what you have done, a counter that could bring the entire plan crashing down?"

Tovi tried to stifle the giggle, but it bubbled up again. Despite the obvious pain, she was enjoying herself too much to stop. "This is the best part of all. The ancient wizards who came up with the Chainfire theory realized the potential for the total destruction of life. So they created a counter, should a Chainfire event ever somehow come to pass."

Nicci gritted her teeth. "What counter?"

"The boxes of Orden."

Nicci's eyes widened. "The boxes of Orden were created to be the counter to the Chainfire event you've initiated?"

"That's right. Isn't that delicious? What's more, we've put the boxes in play."

Nicci let out a deep breath. "Well, like I said, you seem to have it all figured out."

Tovi winced. "Well . . . almost. There is only one minor issue."

"Like what?"

"Well, you see, the stupid bitch only brought out one box the first time we sent her in. We couldn't allow the boxes to be seen, because, unlike Richard's love, people would remember seeing the boxes of Orden.

"Kahlan said she had no room in her pack. Sister Ulicia was furious. She beat the girl to a bloody mess—you would have loved it, Sister Nicci—and told her to leave something out to make room if she had to, then sent her back in to get the other two boxes."

Tovi winced under a pang of pain. "We feared to wait, though. Sister Ulicia sent me on with the first box and said she would catch up with me later." Tovi groaned under the agony of another stitch of pain. "I had the first box with me. The Seeker, the one with Sword of Truth, anyway, surprised me and ran me though. He snatched the box. Once Kahlan finally retrieved them, Sister Ulicia then had those two and thought that I had the third, so before she left the palace, she put the magic of Orden in play."

Nicci staggered to her feet. She felt dizzy. She could hardly believe it. But she knew, now, that it was all true. Richard had been right all along. With almost nothing to go on, he had basically figured it all out. And all along no one in the world would listen to him . . . no one in a world that was unraveling around them in an uncontrolled Chainfire event.

A scream that made the fine hairs on the back of Richard's neck stand on end split the quiet night. Richard, in a bedroll in a simple tent, shot to his feet as the scream ripped the air with its terror. The unending shriek ran a shiver up through his shoulders and instantly brought a sheen of sweat to his brow.

His heart racing, Richard rushed out of his tent even as the haunting cry echoed through the encampment as if trying to reach every corner of darkness to express its horror.

Outside the tent, which was set apart from the others because it was an extra, Richard saw men standing in the darkness, their eyes wide. Up the row a ways, General Meiffert watched out on the night with the rest of them.

Richard saw that it was false dawn, like the morning Kahlan had vanished. The woman he loved, the woman who everyone else had forgotten and didn't care to remember. If she had screamed, no one had heard her.

And then, as the scream died, the world went blacker than black. It was like being plunged into the inky nothingness of the world of the dead, forlorn and forever lost. Richard shivered as his flesh felt like something alien touched the world of living with intimate promise.

As quickly as the darkness had come, it was gone. Men looked around at one another, none speaking.

The thought occurred to Richard that the viper now had only three heads.

"The Keeper took one of his own," he explained to the questioning faces that had all turned to him. He saw the general watching, listening. "Be glad that one so evil is no longer among the living. May all such people find the death they champion."

Men smiled and whispered agreement with the curse as they began crawling back into their tents to try to snatch what was left of their sleep.

General Meiffert met Richard's gaze as he clapped a fist to his heart before vanishing back into his own tent.

In the dim light of the camp that suddenly seemed to be populated only by tents and wagons, Richard spotted Nicci very deliberately heading straight for him. There was something profoundly disturbing about the way she looked. Perhaps it was that she had just vented a rage that he doubted anyone but he could truly understand or value.

Flags of blond hair flying, she reminded him of a raptor descending in on him from out of the night, all tight muscle and talons. When he saw the tears streaming down her face, her gritted teeth, her fury and hurt, her powerful menace and frail helplessness, her eyes filled with more than he could grasp, he stepped back into his tent, drawing her in out of the view of the camp.

She swept into the tent, right for him, like a storm breaking on a headland. He backed as far as he could, having no idea what was wrong or what she intended.

With a sob of such naked desolation that it nearly made him cry out in kind, she fell to the ground at his feet, throwing her arms around his legs. She was clutching something in one hand. Richard realized that it was Kahlan's white Mother Confessor dress.

"Oh, Richard, I'm so sorry," she wailed between racking gasps. "I'm so sorry for what I've done to you. I'm so sorry. I'm so sorry," she kept mumbling over and over.

He reached down and touched her shoulder. "Nicci, what is it?"

"I'm so sorry," she cried as she clutched at his legs as if she were the condemned begging a king for her life. "Oh, dear spirits, I'm so sorry for what I've done to you."

He sank down, lifting her arms off his legs. "Nicci, what is it?"

Her shoulders heaved with her racking sobs. She looked up at him as he lifted her by her arms. She was as limp as the dead.

"Oh, Richard, I'm so sorry. I never believed you. I'm so sorry that I never believed you. I should have helped you and instead I fought you every step. I'm so sorry."

He had rarely seen anyone in such profound misery. "Nicci—"

"Please," she sobbed. "Please, Richard, end it now."

"What?"

"I don't want to live anymore. It hurts too much. Please, use your knife and end it. Please. I'm so sorry. I've done worse than simply not believe you. I've been the one who stopped you at every turn."

She hung like a rag doll from his hands under her arms. She wept in utter misery and defeat.

"I'm so sorry I didn't believe you. You were right about everything and so much more. I'm so sorry. It's all ended now and it's my fault. I'm so sorry. I should have believed you."

She started to almost melt through his grip. Sitting on the floor in front of her, he gathered her up into his arms, much like he had gathered up Jillian.

"Nicci, you were the only one who made me go on when I was ready to give up. You were the only one who made me fight."

Nicci's arms came up around his neck when he pulled her close. She felt hot from the fever of her anguish.

She sobbed and kept mumbling how sorry she was, how she should have believed in him about the rest of it, how it was all too late now, how she wanted to end the pain and die.

Richard held her head to his shoulder as he whispered to her that it would be all right, whispered his comfort, rocked her gently and quieted her without saying anything of consequence except in its empathy.

He remembered, then, when he had first met Kahlan and they had spent that first night in a wayward pine. She had nearly been pulled back into the underworld and he had drawn her back at the last moment. Kahlan had cried like this, in abject terror and misery, but more than that, with the release of having someone hold her.

Kahlan had never had anyone she valued hold her when she cried.

He knew, now, that Nicci never had either.

As he held her in his arms, giving her the unopposed comfort she so needed, she exhausted herself until, feeling safe as perhaps never before, she drifted into sleep. It was such a profound pleasure to be able to give her that rare refuge that he wept silently as he held her and she slept, safe, in his arms.

He must have fallen asleep for a brief time because when he opened his eyes there was pale light coming through the walls of the summer tent. When he lifted his head, Nicci stirred in his arms, like a child cuddling closer and never wanting to wake.

But she did, rather suddenly when she realized where she was.

She looked up into his eyes, her blue eyes weary. "Richard," she whispered in what he knew would be the beginning of the same thing.

He pressed his fingertips to her lips, halting her words.

"We have a lot of things to deal with. Tell me what you learned so that we can get on with it."

She put the white dress in his hands. "You were right about almost everything, even if you didn't know the mechanism. Sister Ulicia and her small band wanted to remain free from the dream walker, just as you said. They resolved, since you value life, to give you immortality. Anything else they did, no matter how destructive, they viewed as of secondary importance. This gave them the freedom to pursue freeing the Keeper."

Richard's eyes went wider as he listened.

"They found Chainfire and used it to make everyone forget Kahlan so that they could steal the boxes of Orden. Your father, in the underworld, let the Keeper know that you have memorized the book they need. They know that they need a Confessor to obtain the truth. Kahlan accomplishes two tasks, stealing the boxes, and helping to get the truth of the book you know.

"Chainfire, not the prophecy worm, is also responsible for what is happening to prophecy.

"The Sisters have two of the boxes of Orden and they put them in play. They have launched that phase of their plan for two reasons: because they want to use Orden to call the Keeper into the world of life, and because the boxes of Orden were created as a counter to the power that can be engendered with Chainfire"

Richard blinked. "What do you mean, they only have two boxes? I thought they used Kahlan to steal all three. All three were in the Garden of Life."

"Kahlan brought out one box. They gave it to Tovi and had her start out ' while they sent Kahlan back in for the other two—"

"Sent her back?" Richard frowned. "What are you leaving out?"

Nicci licked her lips, but she didn't break his gaze. "The reason for Tovi's scream."

Richard felt his eyes watering. A lump rose in his throat.

Nicci laid a hand over his heart. "We'll get her back, Richard."

He clenched his teeth and nodded. "So then what happened?"

"The new Seeker surprised Tovi, stabbed her, and stole the box of Orden she was spiriting away from the People's Palace."

"We have to start a search. They can't have gone far."

"They are long gone, Richard. Just like they covered their tracks when they took Kahlan, they will have done the same this time. That is not the way to find them."

Richard looked up. "Samuel. The Sword of Truth was a counter. When I gave him the sword, he must have recognized the truth about Kahlan." His gaze roved the inside of the tent as he tried to think. "We need to think this through. Collect all the information we can and get ahead of them, instead of always being behind them."

"I'll help you, Richard. Anything you want, I will do. I will help you get her back. She belongs with you. I know that now."

He nodded, thankful that her iron was back. "I think we had better set some things straight and then get some experienced help."

She smiled a crooked smile. "That's the Seeker I know."

Outside the tent, men had begun to gather, all wanting to see the Lord Rahl.

Out of the crowd came Verna. "Richard! Thank the Creator—our prayers have been answered!" She threw her arms around him. "Richard how are you?"

"Where have you been?"

"I was tending to some injured men. Scouts, who met a few of the enemy. General Meiffert sent word for me to return at once."

"And the men?"

"Fine," she said with a smile. "Now that you are finally with us for the final battle."

He took up her hands. "Verna, you know you have had a hard time with me in the past."

She grinned as she nodded that it was true. When she saw that he wasn't smiling, her smile faded. "This is going to be one of those times," he told her. "You are going to have to believe in me and what I say, or we might as well give up to the Order right now."

Richard let go of her hand and climbed up on a crate to be better heard. He realized that a sea of men surrounded him.

Cara and General Meiffert were right near the front. "Lord Rahl, will you be able to lead us?" he asked.

"No," he called out into the still dawn air.

Worried whispers spread back through the men. Richard held up his arms.

"Listen to me!" They quieted. "I don't have much time. I don't have the time to explain things as I wish I could. That is the way it is. I will give you the facts, and I will let you decide.

"The army of the Imperial Order has been slowed a bit down south." Richard held up his hands to stifle the cheers. "I don't have much time. Listen, now.

"You men are the steel against steel. I am the magic against magic. I now must pick one of those two for the coming battle.

"If I stay here and lead you, fight with you, then we are not going to have much of a chance. The enemy forces are huge. I don't need to tell any of you men that much. If I stay and help you fight them, most of us will die."

"I can tell you right off," General Meiffert said, "that I don't like that choice."

Most of the men agreed that the grim picture he had just painted was not something they relished.

"What's the alternative?" a man nearby called out.

"The alternative is that I let you men do your job and present the steel to keep the Order from choosing instead to run rampant through our lands.

"Meanwhile, I pledge to do my job of being the magic against magic. I will do what only I can and work to find a way to defeat the enemy without any of you men having to lose your life in battle with them. I want to find a way, with my power, to banish or destroy them before we have to fight them.

"I can't guarantee that I will succeed. If I fail, I will die in the attempt and you men will have to face the enemy."

"Do you think you can stop them with magic of some sort?" Another man asked?

Nicci jumped up beside him. "Lord Rahl has already set people in the Old World against Jagang's forces. We have fought battles in their own homeland in the hopes of taking away their support.

"If you insist on keeping Lord Rahl here, with you, then you are wasting his singular talent, and you might die as a result. I ask, as one who fights at his side, that you let him be the Lord Rahl, let him do as he must, while you do as you must."

"I couldn't say it any better," Richard told them. "There it is, then. That is the choice I give you."

Unexpectedly, men began going to their knees. Far and wide dust rose as men shuffled to make space to kneel down.

In one voice, the chant began.

"Master Rahl guide us. Master Rahl teach us. Master Rahl protect us. In your light we thrive. In your mercy we are sheltered. In your wisdom we are humbled. We live only to serve. Our lives are yours."

Richard watched out over the sea of men as the sun broke the horizon. The devotion was repeated a second time, and then a third time, as was customary in the field. Once it was done, men began to return to their feet.

"I guess that's your answer, Lord Rahl," General Meiffert said. "Go get the bastards."

The men cheered their agreement.

Richard hopped down and took Nicci's hand to help her down. She ignored the hand and jumped down of her own accord. Richard turned to Cara.

"Well, I have to go. We're in a hurry. Look, Cara, I want you to know that I would be fine with it if you would like to stay with . . . the army."

A dark frown descended over Cara as she folded her arms. "Are you crazy?" She looked up over her shoulder at the general. "I told you, the man is crazy. See what I have to put up with?"

General Meiffert nodded seriously. "I don't know how you do it, Cara."

"Training," she confided. She trailed her fingertips across his cheek, smiling up at him in a way Richard had never seen her do before. "Take care of yourself, General."

"Yes, ma'am." He smiled at Nicci before bowing his head. "As per your orders, Mistress Nicci."

Richard's mind was already elsewhere. "Come on. Let's get going."

Marching down the frame and panel hall, Rikka leading the way, Cara and Nicci in tow, Richard reached the intersection and turned down a stone passageway with a towering vaulted ceiling that soared up for nearly two hundred feet. Fluted columns to the sides rose up at evenly spaced intervals. Through large windows at the top the massive exterior buttresses that supported the lofty walls could be seen. Streamers of light angled in high overhead and from small round windows down lower. Their boot strikes echoed like hammers through the cold hall.

Richard's cape that looked like it was made from spun gold billowed behind him as if in a gathering storm. The gold symbols around the black tunic fairly glowed in the muted light. Passing each shaft of sunlight, the silver emblems in his boots, on his wide, multilayered leather belt, and on his leather-padded wristbands sent blades of light flashing around them, announcing the arrival of a war wizard.

The fury of any Mord-Sith was enough to cause most people's blood to pause in their veins, but cold anger on Cara's attractive features seemed capable of turning that stilled blood to ice. To his other side the former Death's Mistress in black looked no less formidable. From the first time he'd met her, Richard could almost hear the air around Nicci crackle with her power and it was doing that now.

Richard passed padded chairs and tables set in niches. Carpets at angles stuck partly into the hall in places, inviting people into quiet, cozy nooks. Richard skirted the carpets because the sounds of his boots on polished granite suited him. None of those with him walked across the carpets, either. With the reverberation coming back at them from the long hall, the sound built until it sounded almost like an invading army pouring through the Keep.

Rikka turned to him without slowing. She gestured to the right. "They're in here, Lord Rahl."

Richard cut the corner without slowing, aiming his march through the center of the huge double doors that stood open into the exquisite library. Heavy oak mullions crosshatched in the doors divided them into a dozen glass panes each. There were shelves to the ceiling on the thirty-foot back wall of the library, with ladders that rode on brass rails to provide access. Massive mahogany pillars stood gleaming in the streamers of sunlight coming in from high windows. But down low, the light was more gloomy and had to be cut with lamps.

An enormous mahogany table with turned legs that were each bigger around than Richard sat opposite the doors. To each side pillars rose to support vaults overhead. The ends of the room to the far left and right were left to the shadows.

Ann looked astonished. "Richard! What are you doing here? You are supposed to be with our troops."

Richard ignored her as he grasped the red leather book he had tucked under an arm. He used the book like a broom to sweep aside the sprawl of books laid before them, creating a broad, polished, empty spot before the three gifted people.

Richard tossed the red, leather-bound book on table. It made a smacking sound that echoed almost like a clap of thunder.

The gold lettering, *Chainfire*, gleamed in the gloom.

"What's this?" Zedd asked in dismay.

"Proof," Richard said. "Part of it anyway. I promised to bring back proof."

"It's an ancient book," Nicci told them. "A formula for creating what is called a Chainfire event."

Zedd's hazel eyes turned up. "What is a Chainfire event?"

"The end of the world as we know it," Richard said with grim finality. "What they were doing turned out to inadvertently involve an attempt to create a contradiction, violating the Ninth Rule. They finally realized that if anyone ever actually undertook to initiate a Chainfire event, it would have cataclysmic consequences."

Nathan frowned at Nicci, apparently hoping for a little more wisdom and experience from a former Sister. "What is he talking about?"

"Wizards in ancient times came up with a new theory on how to alter memory with Subtractive power, with all the resulting disconnected parts spontaneously reconstructed independently of one another—the creation of erroneous memory to fill in the voids that had been destroyed. They were studying the theory of how to make an individual disappear to everyone else by making people forget this person, even as soon as they've just seen them. Even as they look at them.

"It unravels people's memory of the subject, but it was discovered that the ignition of such an event starts a cascade that can't be predicted or controlled. Much like a wildfire, it continues to burn through links with others whose memory has not been altered. It eventually unravels the world of life itself."

"And the prophecy worm?" Richard asked. "It may be real, but the cause of the prophecy vanishing this time is Chainfire. As part of the process, the person who initiates the event also fills in a void in prophecy, a place left blank by a prophet for future work. This gap is filled in with a completing prophecy which has the Chainfire formula invested in it. A Chainfire event thus infects and consumes all the associated prophecy on the branch, starting with related prophecy, either in subject or in chronology—in this case both: Kahlan. Thus, she is also wiped out of prophecy by what is called the Chainfire corollary."

Nathan sat down heavily. "Dear spirits."

Ann, hands in her opposite sleeves, did not look pleased or impressed. "All well and good, and we will have to study this book and see if anything you've come up with even begins to make sense.

"But that book is not the immediate problem.

"You should have stayed with our men. You must lead our troops in the final battle. You must return at once. Prophecy is quite clear. Prophecy says that if you fail to do this, the world will fall under the shadow."

Richard ignored Ann and met his grandfather's gaze. "Guess what the counter is to a Chainfire event."

Zedd shrugged, looking puzzled by Richard's line of questioning. "How would I know?"

"There is only one. It was created specifically for this purpose."

"What was?" Zedd asked.

"The boxes of Orden."

Zedd's mouth fell open. "Richard, that just isn't—"

Richard reached into his pocket and pulled out what he had brought. He slammed it down on the table before the three of them.

Zedd's eyes went wide. "Bags, Richard, that's a snake vine."

"You may recall from *The Book of Counted Shadows: And when the three boxes of Orden are put into play, the snake vine shall grow.*"

"But, but," Zedd stammered, "the boxes of Orden are in the Garden of Life, in the People's Palace, under incredibly heavy guard."

"Not only that," Nathan put in, "but I personally equipped the men of the First File with weapons that are deadly even against the gifted. No one could get in there."

"I agree," Zedd insisted. "It's impossible."

Richard turned and carefully took what Cara had been carrying. He gently set the statue of *Spirit* down so that the figure was facing the three on the other side of the table, as if she were holding her head high in opposition to their efforts to make her a delusion.

"This is Kahlan's. She left it there, in the Garden of Life, in place of the boxes, so that someone would know she exists. The Chainfire spell erased her from everyone's memory. Those who see her forget her before she even registers in their minds."

Ann waved a hand over the book, the vine, and the statue. "But this, this, this is all still conjecture, Richard. Who in the world could even have dreamed up such a plot?"

"Sister Ulicia hatched the plan," Nicci said. "She had Sisters Cecilia, Armina, and Tovi with her."

Ann frowned. "How do you know this?"

"Tovi confessed to me."

Ann looked more than astonished. "Confessed . . . Why would she do such a thing? How did you even catch her?"

"She was fleeing with one of the boxes of Orden." Richard said. "She was ambushed by the man I gave the Sword of Truth to. He stabbed her and stole the box of Orden she was carrying."

Zedd slapped his forehead, unable to speak, and thumped down into his chair.

"Tovi also told me," Nicci said. "that they were here, in Aydindril, and planted that corpse in the Mother Confessor's grave to make sure no one believed Richard, should he happen to try digging it up to convince people he was telling the truth. They got the dress out of the Confessors' Palace. They wanted to make sure everyone thought Richard was deluded.

"Regarding that, I think you should also know that we traveled to the ruins of a city called Caska, down in southern D'Hara. Imperial Order scouts were there. I conducted an experiment on one of them. I used the Subtractive spell all of you wanted me to use to 'cure' Richard of his supposed delusions."

Ann cautiously cocked her head. "And?"

"He didn't live more than a few moments."

Zedd, nearly as white now as his unruly hair, put his face in his hands.

"I'm sure that some of this will prove quite . . . useful," Ann said, looking rather confused, "and it's good that you have uncovered it. But as I said, the fact remains that you need to be with our troops, Richard. We revealed to you that vitally important prophecy: 'If *fuer grissa ost drauka* does not lead this final battle, then the world, already standing at the brink of darkness, will fall under that terrible shadow.'

"These other matters you bring up are intriguing, to be sure, but the prophecy remains our most important mission. We simply can't fail or the world will fall under the shadow."

Richard gripped his temples between his thumb and second finger as he looked down, trying to gather patience. He reminded himself that these people were trying to do what was right.

He looked up, meeting their gazes. "Don't you see?" He pointed at the snake vine on the table. "*This* is the final battle. The Sisters of the Dark have put the boxes of Orden in play. They intend to bring the Keeper of the dead into the world of the living. They intend to give life over to death in a bid to gain immortality for themselves. The world stands at the brink of darkness.

"Don't you see? If you three had had your way, bent on enforcing prophecy, and tried to live by words you believed to be foreordained, I would not have survived the attempt to 'cure' me. I would be dead. In attempting to fulfill prophecy, you would have insured the success of the Sisters of the Dark, and the end of all life. The world of life would have ended because of you.

"Only free will—Nicci's free will, my free will—has prevented what you three would have brought upon mankind in following your blind faith in prophecy."

Ann, the last one standing, dropped into her chair.

"Dear spirits, he's right," Zedd whispered to himself. "The Seeker has just saved three old fools from themselves."

"No. None of you are fools," Richard said. "We all can do foolish things from time to time by not thinking. The thing to do then is to recognize a mistake and not repeat it. Learn from it. Don't allow yourself to fail the next time. I'm not here to tell you that you are fools, because I know you're not. I'm here because I need your help. I want you to start using your minds. You are all brilliant in your own way. You each have knowledge that probably no one else alive has.

"The woman I love, the woman I'm married to, has been kidnapped by Sisters of the Dark and had a Chainfire event unleashed on her life. That event is now burning through the lives of everyone who knew her and will eventually consume everyone living."

He gestured to the statue of Spirit. "I carved that of your granddaughter's spirit, Zedd. It was precious to her. She left it there, on that stone altar, covered in her blood. I want her back.

"I need help. Neither Nicci nor Cara remembers Kahlan, but they both know the truth of the fact that they don't remember her because of what's in this book, *Chainfire*, not because she doesn't exist. You all lost something incredibly precious when your memory of Kahlan was taken from you. You lost a value in your lives that you could not begin to replace. You lost one of the best . . ."

Richard had to stop because he couldn't get the words past the constriction in his throat. Tears dripped from his face onto the table.

Nicci came close and put a hand on his shoulder. "It will be all right, Richard. We'll get her back."

Cara laid a hand on his other shoulder. "That's right, Lord Rahl. We'll get her back."

Richard nodded, unable to speak as his chin trembled.

Zedd rose up. "Richard, I hope you don't think we will fail you again. We won't. You have my word as First Wizard."

"I'd rather have your word as my grandfather."

Zedd smiled through his own tears. "That, too, my boy. That, too."

Nathan shot to his feet. "My sword's in play as well, my boy."

Ann scowled at him. "Your sword is in play? What in the world does that mean?"

"Well, you know," Nathan said, swirling his hand in a display of cut and thrust. "It means I will fight the good fight."

"The good fight? How about if you help us find Kahlan."

"Well, bags, woman—"

Ann shot a look at Zedd. "Did you teach him to talk like that? He never cursed like that before he spent time with you."

Zedd shrugged innocently. "My goodness, no. Not me."

Ann scowled at the wizard on each side of her before looking at Richard and smiling.

"I remember when you were first born, Richard. When you were a bundle of life in your mother's arms. She was so proud of you then just for being able to cry. Well, I guess she'd be pretty proud of you now. We all are, Richard."

Zedd wiped his nose on his sleeve. "How true."

"If you can forgive us," Ann said, "we'd like to be a part of stopping this threat. I, for one, am quite keen to take care of those Sisters."

Nicci squeezed Richard's shoulder. "I think you may have a fight on your hands over that. I think we'd all like to be the one to get at them."

Cara leaned past Richard. "Sure, easy for you to say. You got to kill Sister Tovi."

Richard stood at the crenellation in the rampart, one foot resting on the low stone, gazing out across the sunlit scene of Aydindril down below the mountain, watching the puffy white clouds parade their shadows across the valley.

Zedd came up from behind and stood beside Richard, and for a time also watched out in silence.

"I can't remember Kahlan," he finally said. "Try as I might, I just can't."

"I know," Richard answered without looking over.

"But for her to be your wife, she must be a remarkable woman."

Richard couldn't help smiling. "She is that."

Zedd laid a bony hand on Richard's shoulder. "We'll find her, my boy. I'm going to help you. We're going to find her. I promise you that."

Grinning, Richard put his arm around his grandfather's shoulders. "Thanks, Zedd. I could surely use the help."

Zedd held up a finger. "We'll get started right away."

"Right away would suit me," Richard told him. "I'm going to need to get me a sword, too."

"Ah, well, the sword isn't important. The sword is just a tool. The Seeker is the weapon, and I'd say you are still the Seeker."

"About that, Zedd. You know, I've been thinking, and I've come to believe that maybe Shota wasn't acting selfishly by demanding the sword in exchange for what she told me."

"How do you figure that?"

"Well, the Sword of Truth draws from my gift. When I use my gift, such as that day we were down in the library and I read from a book of prophecy, it has the very real potential to call the beast to me."

Zedd rubbed his smooth chin. "Well, I guess that's true. Maybe in a way that did help to protect you." He scowled at Richard. "But she gave it to Samuel! He's a thief!"

"And what did he steal since he got the sword back?"

Zedd peered at Richard with one eye. "Steal? I don't know. What do you mean?"

"He near to killed a Sister of the Dark and took the box of Orden she had, preventing the Sisters from having all three so that they can invoke the magic of Orden."

Zedd's scowl deepened. "And just what do you suppose that little thief is going to do with the box?"

Richard shrugged. "I don't know, but at least he bought us some time. We can go after him, now, and prevent the Sisters from having all three boxes, at least."

Zedd scratched the hollow of his cheek as he gave Richard a sidelong glance. "Kind of reminds a fellow of the last time, doesn't it . . . with Darken Rahl having to get the last box."

Richard frowned over at his grandfather. "What are you saying?"

Zedd shrugged. "Nothing. I'm just saying."

"Saying what?"

"Like I said, kind of reminds one of the last time, that's all." Zedd clapped Richard on the shoulder. "Well, come on. Rikka has dinner ready. We'll all get a good meal before we lay out some ideas for how to proceed."

"That sounds great to me."

"How do you know? I haven't even told you what she's cooking."

"No, I mean . . . Never mind. Let's go."

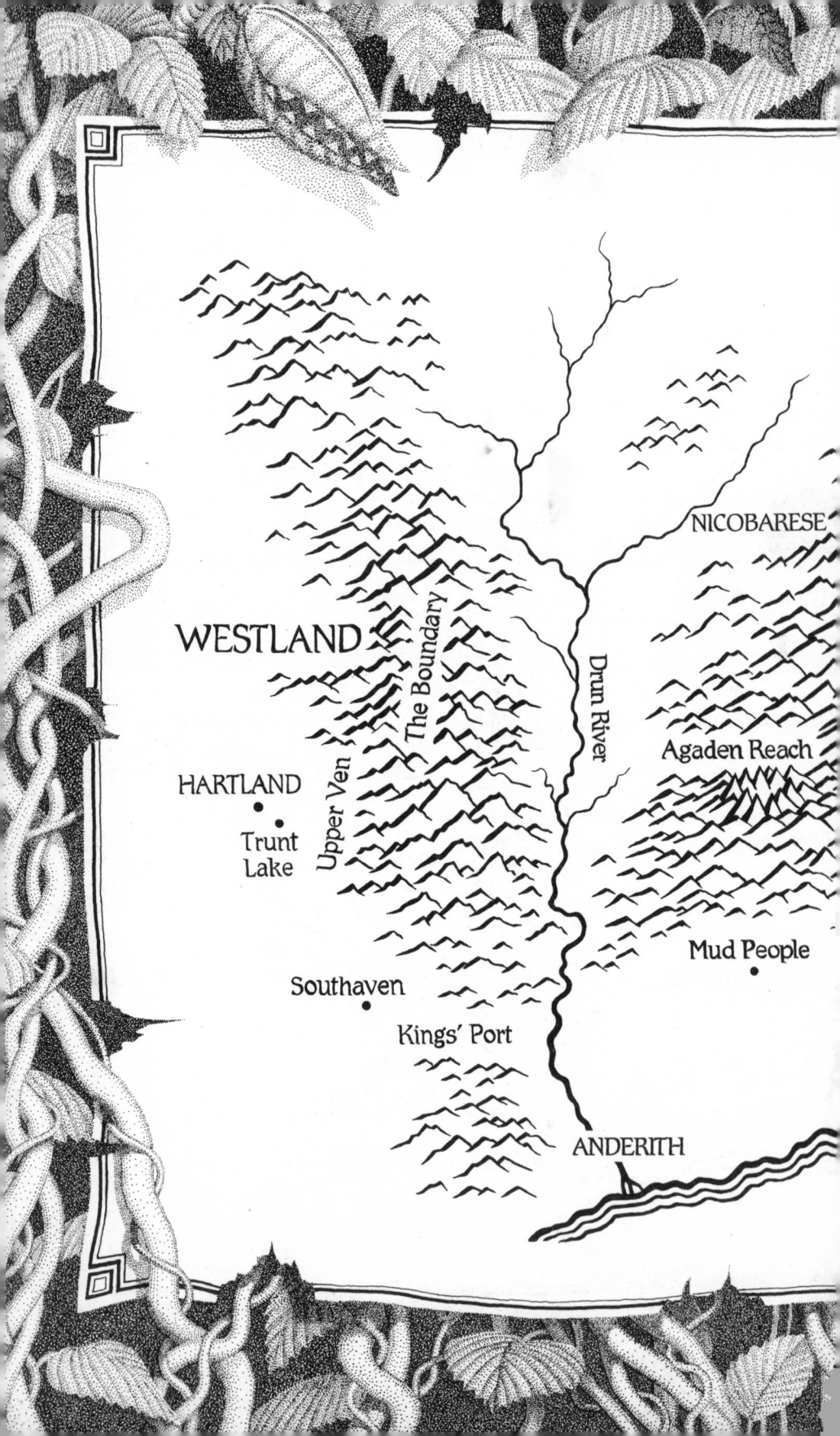

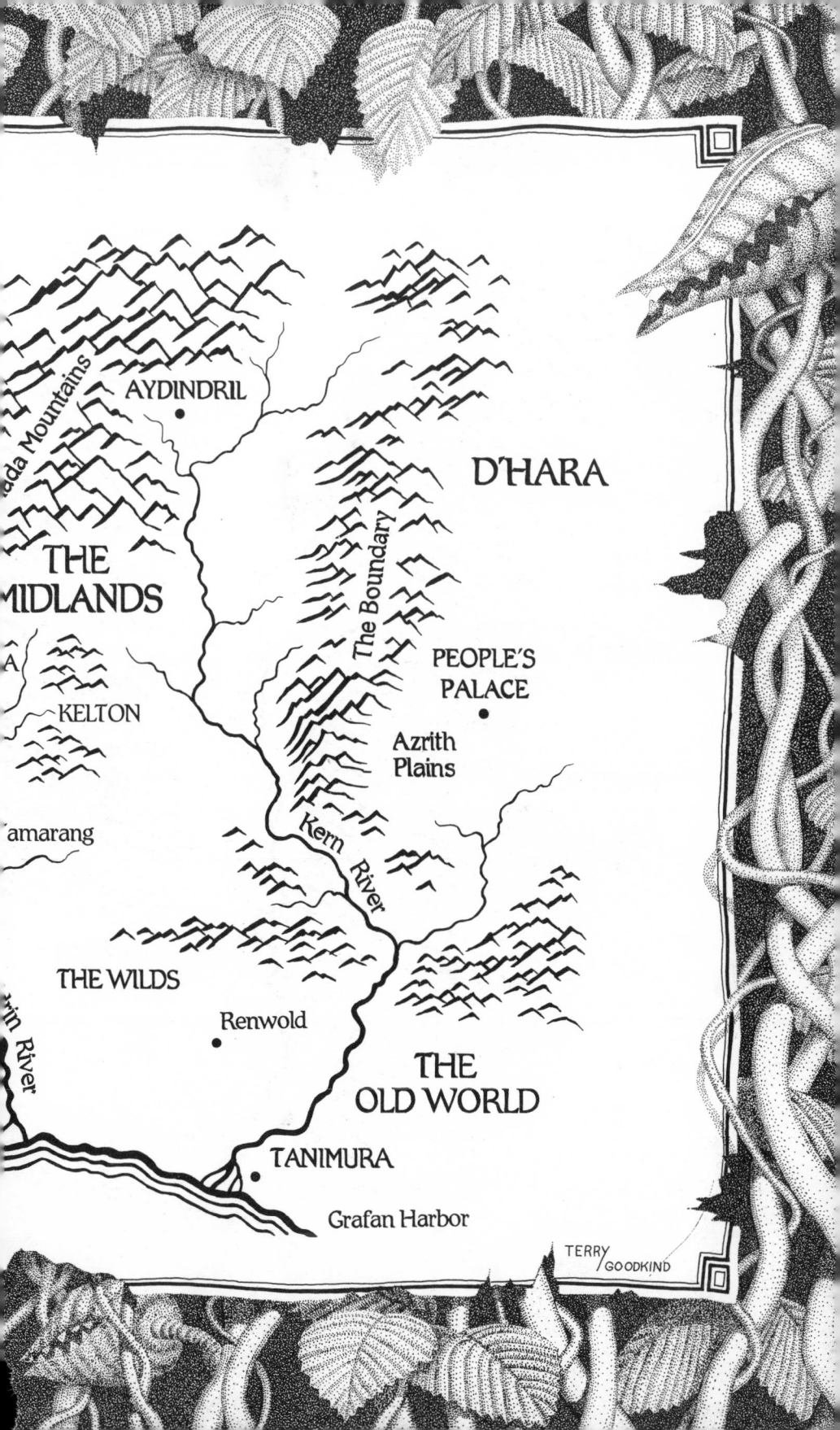